TRUTH WAS THE ONLY LANGUAGE
THAT WOULD BRING THEM TOGETHER.

"Come in," Nick's Welsh voice, firm and unstartled.

Amy pushed the low door open and stepped inside. She stood on the stone-flagged floor and looked at the bare lime-washed walls, and unlit black range and the tiny steep staircase that corkscrewed up to the single room overhead.

Nick was looking steadily at her, one eyebrow raised a fraction. "This is an honor," he said. "So far, so late at night." Amy wasn't certain, but she thought she saw the flicker of a smile. "And alone? Or did you get one of the grooms to bring you over?"

Amy put her basket on the table. The room was so small she only had to stretch her arm out to it from the doorway.

"Please," she said. "Don't let's begin like this again. Can't you see me just as a person? Just as Amy, and nothing to do with my family, wealth, or any of the rest of it?"

There was a small moment of silence. "I'll try," Nick said. "What's in the basket?"

"A peace-offering. My great-grandfather's journals. The history of your orchids."

He reached out and took them. "Why did you really come?"

"I came because I wanted to see you." Amy met his eyes. "I'm afraid of you, but I want to be with you."

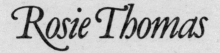

Rosie Thomas

THE WHITE DOVE

BANTAM BOOKS

TORONTO • NEW YORK • LONDON • SYDNEY • AUCKLAND

This low-priced Bantam Book
has been completely reset in a type face
designed for easy reading, and was printed
from new plates. It contains the complete
text of the original hard-cover edition.
NOT ONE WORD HAS BEEN OMITTED.

THE WHITE DOVE

A Bantam Book / published by arrangement with
Viking Penguin Inc.

PRINTING HISTORY
Viking Penguin edition published June 1986
Bantam edition / July 1987

ISBN 0-553-26457-5

Published simultaneously in the United States and Canada

Bantam Books are published by Bantam Books, Inc. Its trademark, consisting of the
words "Bantam Books" and the portrayal of a rooster, is Registered in U.S. Patent and
Trademark Office and in other countries. Marca Registrada. Bantam Books, Inc., 666
Fifth Avenue, New York, New York 10103.

PRINTED IN THE UNITED STATES OF AMERICA

KR   0 9 8 7 6 5 4 3 2 1

FOR CARADOC

The author's thanks are due to:
Mavis King Bamberger, Shirley Sabatino,
Ellen Levine, the Karl Marx Memorial Library,
and in particular to Susan Watt for her
support and encouragement.

Part One

1

The cedar tree was four hundred years old; as old as Chance itself. The shade beneath the cedar was more fragrant, cooler and deeper than the shade of any of the other great trees across the park. From its protective circle the family could look into the dazzle of light over the velvet grass, back to the terrace and the grey walls rearing behind it. The splash of the fountain was a deliciously cool note in the heavy heat of that long afternoon of July 1916.

Amy Lovell sat squarely at the tea-table, her chin barely level with the starched white cloth, wide eyes fixed on the sandwiches as fragile as butterflies, tiny circlets of pastry top-heavy with cream and raspberries, melting fingers of her favourite ginger sponge, and enticing dark wedges of rich fruit cake. A long time had passed since nursery lunch at twelve, and Amy was hungry. But she sat perfectly still, her hands folded in her lap, without even a rustle of her frilled petticoats. Her feet, in highly polished boots with intricate buttons and laces, did not nearly touch the grass, but she held them rigid. Only yesterday Papa had banished her from the tea-table for swinging her legs, and she had not even had a sandwich, let alone a ginger sponge finger. Amy allowed herself one sidelong glance at Isabel, six years old to her own four-and-a-bit, and saw that her sister looked as effortlessly still and composed as always.

A flutter of white cloth to the right of the table heralded the silent arrival of Mr Glass, the butler, with another, subsidiary table. This one was laden with silver tea-things.

'I will pour out myself, Glass, thank you,' said Amy's mother in her special, low voice. When Amy first heard the word 'drawling' it pleased her, because it sounded exactly like Mama.

'Very good, my lady.'

Mr Glass retreated across the grass, flanked by the maids with

9

their apron and cap strings fluttering, and left them alone. Amy sighed with satisfaction. It was the best moment of the day, when she and Isabel had Mama and Papa all to themselves.

Lady Lovell stretched out her hand to the silver teapot. Her dark red hair fell in rich, natural waves, and where it was caught up at the nape of her neck beads of perspiration showed on the white skin. Her afternoon dress of pale rose silk was pleated and gathered, but it failed to disguise the ungainly bulk of the last days of pregnancy. Her hand fluttered back to rest over her stomach, and she sighed in the heat.

'Could you, Gerald? Glass does hover so, and it is so nice to be just ourselves out here.'

'That is his job, Adeline,' Lord Lovell reminded her, but without the irritation he would have felt seven years ago.

He had fallen in love with his first sight of the exquisite eighteen-year-old American steel heiress dancing her way through her first London Season. And Adeline van Pelt from Pittsburgh, her head turned by her aristocratic suitor's ancient title as much as by his formal charm, had agreed to marry him even though he was twice her age.

They had not made an easy beginning of their first months together at Chance. Lord Lovell was a widower, already the father of a twelve-year-old boy. His interests, apart from a well-bred liking for pretty girls, were horses, cards, and his estates. The new Lady Lovell came home with him at the end of the Season with only the barest understanding of what their life together would be like. It had come as an unpleasant shock, after the blaze of parties and admirers, to find herself alone much of the day while Gerald rode, or shot, or saw his farm managers. Yet at night, in her bedroom, he miraculously became everything she could have wanted. It was inexplicable to Adeline that her husband found it necessary to pretend, all day long, to be somebody he clearly wasn't, and only to let the passion, and the laughter, out at night when they were alone.

To his concern, Gerald found that his wife was easily bored, capricious and unpredictable. She was either yawning with ennui, or filling the house with disreputable people and in a whirlwind of enthusiasm for painting the library in pink faux marble. She romped unsuitably in front of the servants, kissed him in public, and had no idea of what was expected of her as Lady Lovell.

And yet the sceptics who smiled behind their hands at the

10

incongruous match and gave it a year to last, found themselves proved wrong. The Lovells grew happy together. Gerald unbent, and Adeline, to please him, learned to obey some of the rules of English upper-class life. Airlie Lovell, the son from his first marriage, remained Gerald's adored heir, but the two little girls, with the look of their beautiful mother, were more important to him than he would have thought girl-children could ever be.

He smiled at Adeline now over their red-brown, ringleted heads.

'Of course I will pour the tea, my darling. Meanwhile Glass can recline in his pantry reading *Sporting Life*, and all will be well with the world.'

'Thank you,' Adeline murmured. Her answering smile was tired. She leaned back in her padded chair and listlessly opened her little ivory fan. Gerald saw that her eyes were shadowed, and even her fan seemed too heavy to hold. Of course her condition wearied her. It would only be a few more days now, please God, and then the baby would be born. Then, soon, he would be welcome in his wife's bedroom again. At the thought of Adeline's long, white legs and the weight of her hair over his face Gerald shifted in his seat and put his finger to his collar.

'Well, little girls,' he said loudly. 'What have you been doing with Miss May this afternoon?'

'Handwriting,' Amy said promptly. 'It's awful. "Press down on the lines, Miss Amy" . . . '

'That will do,' her father said. 'Are these children really allowed cake before bread and butter, Adeline?'

'Of course they are. Didn't you prefer cake at their age?'

Amy, with one ginger sponge securely on her plate and the possibility of at least one more to come, beamed with sticky pleasure.

Then, across the smooth grass, between her mother's rose-pink shoulder and her father's cream-jacketed arm wielding the tea-pot, she saw a man on a bicycle. He was riding along the west drive, which meant he had come through the west gates leading from the village. Against the bright sunlight he looked all black, perched on top of his angular black bicycle, and his spidery black legs were pumping round and round as he spun up the driveway.

He must be bringing something for Cook in the kitchen, Amy thought. The butcher's delivery boy had a bicycle like that, only his had a big basket at the front and a wide, flat tray at the back. All the bicycles from the shops had baskets like that, she remembered, and this one didn't. So it couldn't be a delivery. The man was riding too fast, too. And instead of wheeling away to the side of the house and then to the kitchen courtyard, he rode straight on. He disappeared from sight behind the wing that enclosed the wide, paved court at the front of the house. The man on the bicycle had gone straight to the great main door.

Amy frowned slightly, wondering. She had only ever seen carriages and cars sweeping up to the main door. Then she took another bite of her cake and looked at Isabel. It was usually safe to take a lead from Isabel, but her sister did not seem to have noticed the man on the bicycle. And Mama and Papa had not seen him either, of course, because their backs were turned to the west drive.

It couldn't be anything interesting, then.

Amy had barely given her full attention to her tea once more when something else caught her eye. It was so unexpected that it made her stop short, with her cake halfway to her mouth.

Mr Glass had come out of the tall open doors on to the terrace again. Instead of moving at his usual stately pace, he was almost running. He was down the steps, and covering the width of lawn that separated them from the house. Amy was suddenly aware that the afternoon was almost over, and Glass's shadow was running ahead of him like a long, black finger pointing at them under the shade of the cedar tree. Isabel was looking curiously past her, and she heard the sharp chink as her mother quickly replaced her cup in its saucer.

But her father was frozen, motionless, as he watched Glass coming over the lawn. The butler was carrying an envelope in one hand, and a silver salver in the other. He hadn't even given himself time to put the two together. Then he reached the table under the tree.

'A telegram, my lord,' he said. Yet he still kept hold of it, stiff-fingered, as if he didn't want to hand it over. In his other hand the silver salver dangled uselessly at his side.

'Give it to me,' Gerald Lovell said quietly.

Slowly, as if it hurt him to do it, Glass held out the buff envelope. Lord Lovell took it, tore it open, and read the message it contained.

The little girls looked from one to the other of the adult faces, mystified by the chill that had crept over the golden afternoon.

'Thank you, Glass,' he said quietly. Then, very slowly, he got up and stood with his back to the little group, staring away at the incongruous sun on the grey walls of Chance.

Glass bent his head, and went silently back across the grass.

'Gerald,' Adeline said sharply. 'Please tell me.'

For a long moment, he didn't move. When at last he turned around to face them again, Amy thought for a terrifying second that this wasn't her father at all. The square, straight shoulders had sagged and the familiar, stern face had fallen into bewildered hollows and lines. Even the crisp, greying hair seemed to have whitened. But worst of all was his mouth. It was open, in a horrible square shape that was like a scream, but no sound was coming out of it.

'Oh God,' Amy heard her mother say. 'Dear God. Not Airlie.'

At the sound of his son's name Gerald stumbled forward. His shoulders heaved, and the scream came out of his mouth at last as a low, stricken moan. He dropped to his knees in front of his wife's chair, and the moan went on and on. Amy saw Isabel put her hands up to her ears, as if to shut the sound out. Her sister's face had gone dead white, with her eyes dark holes in the whiteness.

'Hush, my love,' Adeline said. 'Oh, Gerald.'

Lord Lovell rocked forward on his knees and put his head in his wife's lap. The telegram fell on the grass and lay face upwards to the blank sky. Isabel got down from her chair, moving like a stiff-legged little doll. She leant over it, not touching it, and read the words.

> 2nd Lt The Honble Airlie Lovell killed in action July 1.
> Deepest regrets. Lt Col. A. J. S. Warren, O/c 2nd Bn Kings
> Own Rifles.

At last the moaning stopped. 'My son?' Lord Lovell said. His head reared up again and he looked into his wife's face. His tears had left a dark, irregular stain on the rose silk of her skirts.

'My son,' he repeated in bewilderment. Then he put his hands on either side of the mound of Adeline's stomach. 'Give me a son again,' he begged her. 'Give me my son back again.'

Sharply, Isabel turned away. She held out her hand to Amy. 'Come on,' she said, and when Amy didn't respond she whispered urgently, 'Please come.'

Obediently, even though she was puzzled and afraid, Amy slid

13

off her chair and with Isabel pulling her onwards the two little girls ran hand in hand across the grass to the sun-warmed steps, and into the silent house. In the cool dimness of the long drawing-room Isabel hesitated, wondering where to run to next, and in that instant Amy looked back.

The picture she saw was to stay with her for ever. She saw her parents still under the cedar tree, her father almost unrecognizable on his knees with the squareness gone from his shoulders and the line of his straight back bowed and defeated. His face was buried like a child's in the folds of rose silk and her mother's head was bent over his, seeing nothing else.

Amy wanted to run back to them and squeeze herself between them, telling them to make everything all right again, but Isabel's grip on her hand was firm. She mustn't go to them. Isabel seemed to understand something about this sudden cold in the sun that she couldn't.

But now Isabel was saying 'Where can we go?' in a thin voice that suddenly sounded lost. 'It's Nanny's day off, do you remember? And it's after four o'clock, so we can't see Miss May, and Cook doesn't like us to go in the kitchen in the afternoon . . .' Her voice trailed away.

'Up to the nursery,' Amy answered with conviction. 'Everything will be all right there.'

Slowly now but still hand in hand they walked the length of the drawing-room, past the sofa where their mother sat before dinner when they came down to kiss her good night on the evenings when there were no guests, through another salon hung with pictures and past spindly gilt furniture, and out into a great space where a wide staircase curved away above their heads. Isabel and Amy turned their backs on the cathedral-like quiet and slipped through a discreet door hidden in the shadows under the stairway. Beyond the door the corridor was narrow and stone-flagged. From somewhere close at hand came the sound of another door banging, hurrying footsteps and an urgently raised voice. They began to walk faster again, making for the stairs leading up to the sanctuary of the nursery wing.

The day nursery was on the west side of the house, and the blinds were half drawn against the light. Long bars of sunshine struck over the polished floor and the familiar worn rugs.

The last time he had been at home, Airlie had draped himself with them, playing bears on his hands and knees, laughing and

14

puffing and telling the girls that the same rugs had been on the floor when he was a baby. When the game was over he had stood up and brushed the fluff from the new uniform he was so proud of. Amy remembered the smell of wool and leather, and the creak of his highly polished Sam Browne belt.

At first sight the nursery seemed empty, but then there was a rustle and the door of one of the tall cupboards swung to. A girl emerged from behind it, round-faced under a white cap, her arms full of folded linen. She saw their stricken faces and let the linen fall in a heap.

'Miss Isabel, Miss Amy, what's wrong then?'

Bethan Jones was the new nurserymaid. She was sixteen years old and had come to Chance from her home in the Welsh valleys only a month ago, and the little girls barely knew her except as a quick, aproned figure fetching and carrying for Nanny. Her soft Welsh accent sounded strange to them, but they heard the warmth in her voice now. Amy ran to her at once and Bethan's arms wrapped round her.

'There now. Tell Bethan, won't you?'

Bethan pulled her closer, rocking her, and looked across at Isabel, still standing at the door.

'What is it, lamb?'

Isabel was torn between what she believed was the right way to behave, and what she really wanted to do, which was to run like Amy and bury herself in Bethan's arms. She took a deep breath, lifted her chin, and said formally, 'I am afraid that a telegram came. My brother Airlie has been killed in France.'

Amy felt Bethan flinch as if from a blow, but still she didn't fully take in the words.

'The poor boy,' Bethan said simply. 'The poor, poor boy.'

She held out her hand and Isabel stopped trying to behave in the right way and ran to shelter beside her sister.

'What does it mean about Airlie?' Amy asked, and seeing Isabel's wet, crumpled face she began dimly to understand that nothing at Chance would ever be the same again.

'It means that a German soldier shot him with a bullet, and hurt him so much that he's dead, and we won't ever see him again,' Isabel said. 'Never, never, because they will bury him in the ground.' Her voice rose, shrill with horror, and her fingers snatched at the blue cotton of the nurserymaid's uniform skirt.

'Hush, darling,' Bethan soothed her. 'Don't talk about it like that. Amy, it means that your brother was a brave, brave man and you must be proud of him. It's a terrible war, but we should be thankful for all the brave soldiers who are fighting for us and pray for it to be over so that they can come safe home again. Do you understand?'

But how could they? Bethan answered herself.

'Listen,' she said softly, 'your brother wanted to go to war to fight for England, and all the things that he believed are right. All good men do. If I was a man, I'd go. My brothers went as soon as they could, and . . . and my fiancé is in France too. He's a private in the Welsh Division, the 38th, and when he comes home we'll be married. It'll be hard at first, but we'll manage a place of our own and then you can come and see me, wouldn't you like that, to come to Wales and see the valleys? There's nowhere like it, you know. Ah, it's not beautiful country like this, all cornfields and great trees, but it's the best place on earth.' Bethan closed her eyes on the nursery and saw the ranks of tiny grey houses clinging to the steep valley sides, the black slag hills and the skeletal towers of the pit winding-gear, and the sudden moist flashes of green between the laced black fingers of the mine workings. 'He was doing grand, Dai was, before the War came,' Bethan whispered. 'More tonnage out of his pit than ever before, and him with a job at the coal face. There's none to beat Welsh steam coal, you know. None in the world.' And she lowered her head so that her cheek was pressed against the little girls' smooth hair, and cried with them.

When Nanny Macleod came back from her afternoon off she found them still sitting on the nursery floor, and with their three faces identically stained with the runnels of tears.

For three days Chance was as silent as a crypt. Gerald Lovell saw no one. He sat in his library, looking out across the lawns to the trees of the park, his head tilted as if he was listening for a sound that never came. On the third afternoon he went outside, keeping to the shade of the avenues of trees as if he couldn't bear to feel the sun's warmth on his head. He walked painfully to the little church enclosed by the estate, and in the shelter of the thick stone walls he read the memorial tablets of Lovells spanning the centuries. Almost every one of them, lords of the manor and their ladies, old men and matriarchs, children dead in infancy, unmarried daughters and weakly younger sons, had been put finally to rest in the family vault. Even that was denied to Airlie. Bitterness rose like nausea in Gerald Lovell. There could be no burial service here for Airlie as there had been for Gerald's father, as there would be one day for Gerald himself, with the family in heavy mourning in the big, square, screened-off family pew, and the church filled with neighbours, tenants and estate workers paying their dutiful respects. The letter from Airlie's commanding officer following the telegram praised him for his heroism. Airlie had died beneath Thiepval Ridge and was buried with his comrades. 'A soldier's grave for a fine soldier,' the captain had written as he must do in an attempt to comfort the families of every one of the men dead under his command. There was no comfort in it for Gerald. There could be no fittingly solid coffin for Airlie, made from one of Chance's own oaks and heaped with flowers from the scented July borders. Airlie had been hastily huddled into the ground with the mutilated bodies of a hundred, perhaps a thousand others.

Gerald lurched against a pew end, the pain like a living thing inside him. His head arched backwards, and over his head he saw the dim, greenish-black folds of an ancient banner. He reached up with a curse and tore the cloth from its staff, the fibres splitting into tiny, dusty fragments that drifted lazily around him. The gold-thread-embroidered letters were tarnished with age, but still legible.

'*Regis defensor*,' Gerald said loud. 'The King's Defender.' His sudden laugh was shockingly loud in the silent church. 'Is that what he was doing, defending the King? I could have done that just as well. Why wasn't it me? Oh God, Airlie, why not me instead?' He lifted his hands above his head and tore the black banner in two, and then again, letting the shreds of it fall around him until only the gold thread remained, and then twining that around his fingers and pulling it so tight that his fingers went as white as candles. Then, just as suddenly, the fit of rage left him and he dropped the thread, turning away from the debris and walking out of the church as if it didn't exist.

The last time he had held the banner had been the proudest moment of Gerald Lovell's life. As the trumpets sounded he had stepped forward from the ranks of peers and knelt to wait for the procession. When he lifted his head he saw the slow approach of the archbishops and the bishops, and the swaying canopy held

17

over the King's head. And he had stood up, and led the long procession forward to the empty throne, the symbolic jewelled gauntlet clasped across his chest ready to throw down as a challenge to anyone who might threaten the King's safety and happiness. Gerald Lovell's father had undertaken the same proud, slow walk at the Coronation of Edward VII, and his great-grandfather, in the last month of his life, at Victoria's. There had been a Lovell marching as the King's Defender at every coronation since the title had been bestowed on the first Lord by the Black Prince on the battlefield at Crécy. The family had clung proudly to the title ever since, refusing any grander ones.

'That is the end,' Gerald said, as he came out into the sunshine again. 'There won't be any more, after Airlie.' In that stricken moment he had forgotten his wife as completely as if she had never existed. The son he had begged her for while his tears stained the pink silk of her dress was forgotten with her.

Adeline was lying on the day bed in front of her open bedroom window, and she saw her husband walking back from the church like a man at the onset of paralysis. Since the moments under the cedar tree she had barely seen him, and although she had waited patiently and prayed that he would turn to her with his grief, he had never come.

They had been the loneliest days she had spent since the first weeks of her marriage.

Now the awareness of something other than loss was beginning to force itself on her attention. Adeline heaved herself upright on the day bed to ease the pain in her back, and at once felt a corresponding tightening across her belly.

'Not long now,' she whispered into the heavy afternoon heat. She lay back against the satin pillows, pushing the heavy weight of her hair back from her face and looking out into the sunshine. The park was deserted once more. Gerald had shut himself away again, alone.

'It will be a boy,' Adeline promised the sultry air. 'It will be another boy.'

On the fourth day, the outside world intruded itself into the silence that shrouded the house. Early in the morning the local doctor's little car chugged up the west drive from the village, and the doctor and his midwife were discreetly ushered upstairs. Almost immediately afterwards, Amy and Isabel in the schoolroom heard the purr of another car as the chauffeur drove his lordship's big black car down to the station to meet Lady Lovell's fashionable doctor off the fast London train.

The two doctors met at last at opposite sides of the bed, the London man in a morning coat and striped trousers, his wing-collar stiff against his throat, and the overworked local practitioner in the tweed jacket and soft collar that he hadn't had time to change before the urgent summons came. The two men shook hands and turned to the patient. For all the differences in their appearance, they were agreed in their diagnosis. The baby was not presenting properly. Lady Lovell was about to suffer a long and painful labour and a breech delivery.

'There now.' The London doctor straightened up, smiling professionally. 'You'll be perfect. Just try and rest between the pains, won't you?'

'The baby.' Her face was white, with dark patches under the eyes. 'The baby will be all right?'

'Of course,' he soothed her. 'We'll get you your baby just as soon as we can.'

The morning cool under the trees in the park evaporated, and the sun rose in the relentlessly blue sky. The clockwork smoothness of the household arrangements ticked steadily on through the morning, occupying everyone from the august Mr Glass in his pantry to the humblest maid, but everyone was waiting. Mr Rayner the chauffeur, coming into the kitchen for his lunch, reported that neither of the doctors had ordered his car. Up in the nursery Bethan Jones helped Nanny with the children's lunch, and shook her head in the privacy of the kitchen cubbyhole. Her mother was the village midwife back in the valley, and she knew the signs.

Gerald Lovell sat on in the library. He didn't seem to be either waiting or listening, but simply suspended in immobility.

As the afternoon wore on it grew more difficult for the household not to listen. Miss May took the little girls as far from the house as possible for their afternoon walk so that they might not hear their mother screaming. Up in Lady Lovell's room the two doctors had discarded their distinguishing jackets. They worked side by side in their shirtsleeves.

By the evening the screaming had stopped. Lady Lovell seemed

19

barely conscious except when her head rolled to the side and the pain wrung out an almost inaudible gasp. The midwife and a nurse bathed her face and held her arms. Her eyes were sunk deep into their sockets.

The village doctor leant over for the hundredth time to listen to the baby's heartbeat.

'Still strong,' he said. 'It'll make it. If she does.'

'She'll make it,' said the other doctor grimly.

Then, at a few moments before midnight, they told her that it was time. 'Push now,' the midwife whispered to her. 'It's almost over. Push now, and the baby will be here.'

And Lady Lovell struggled back into the black, pain-filled world and pushed with the last of her strength.

At two minutes to midnight the baby was born, feet first. It was a healthy boy.

They held him up for her to see, and she looked at the bright red folded limbs and the mass of wet black hair. Adeline smiled the tremulous smile of utter exhaustion. 'A boy,' she murmured. 'Please. Tell my husband now.'

The nurse rang the bell, and within seconds Mr Glass tapped at the door. The London doctor put his morning coat on again, fumbled to straighten his collar and went out to him.

'Would you be so kind as to take me to his lordship? I am sure that he will want to know he has a fine son.'

The library was lit only by a single green-shaded lamp. Gerald Lovell took his head out of his hands as the doctor was ushered in.

'Congratulations, my lord. A healthy boy.'

Gerald stood up, frowning and trying to concentrate on the seemingly unintelligible words. He had been looking at photographs. A double row of stiffly posed boys with cricket bats resting against their white flannelled knees stared up at him from the desk top. In the middle of them was Airlie in the Eton eleven of 1915.

'A boy. My son?' he asked.

The doctor smiled. 'Yes. Lady Lovell had a difficult time and is very tired, but she will recover with rest. The baby is well.'

Gerald was on his way, past the doctor and out of the room, the stiffness of his movements betraying how long he had been sitting, hunched over his grief, in the silent library. He took the photograph with him.

20

Adeline opened her eyes when he came into her room. Gerald was shocked to see the exhaustion in her face. The hovering nurse backed discreetly away and he sat down at the edge of the bed, putting the photograph down on the fresh sheet with its deep lace edging. He covered her hands with his.

'You're all right,' he said softly, and for a moment Adeline thought that after all, they might recover.

'It's a boy,' she whispered. 'I knew it would be. Look.'

She pointed to the white ribboned cradle at the side of the bed. Gerald leant over it, slowly, and turned back the cover.

This crimson skin and pucker of features, then, was his son? These clenched, helpless hands and unseeing eyes?

No. Oh no. Airlie was his son. He had no memory of Airlie ever being like this, so tiny and so barely human. His head was full of vivid recollections: of Airlie running across the grass to his first pony and flinging himself across its bare back, of Airlie striding down the pavilion steps with his bat under his arm, of Airlie proud in his uniform with the brass buttons shining. But none of a baby.

Now Airlie was gone, and this little creature wasn't him. Nor could he ever be. Adeline couldn't give him his son back. Not Adeline, not anyone.

Gerald smoothed the cover over the baby again and turned back to his wife. Without taking her eyes from his face, Adeline pushed the photograph away from her, further away until it hung at the edge of the bed, and then slid to the floor. Gerald bent at once to retrieve it and she turned her head away from him.

'I'd like to call him Richard,' she said.

'Richard? It's not a family name . . .'

'Does it matter that it's not a family name? I would like it, Gerald.'

'Of course. Call him whatever you like.'

Gerald bent over to kiss her. There were tears on her eyelashes and cheeks.

'Try to rest,' he said heavily. The floor creaked as he crossed it, and then the door closed behind him. As soon as he was gone Adeline tried to call him back, but the effort was too much for her. Her head fell back against the pile of pillows. The nurse was at her side at once.

'Try to sleep, milady. The doctor will give you something to help, and we'll take the baby away now.'

'No.'

The nurse was startled by the insistence.

'Please leave him here with me.'

When at last they went away and left her alone, Adeline turned her head to the white cradle. A tiny clenched fist was just visible under the wrappings.

'Richard . . .' she whispered to him, 'Richard, you're *mine*.'

2

Nantlas, Rhondda Fach, 1924

'You ready then, Mari?'

Mari Powell stepped back from the tiny mirror over the sink in the back kitchen. She had been the first girl in Nantlas to cut her hair, and although everyone had copied her now, even Ellen Lewis who looked a fright whatever she did to herself, she was still proud of the glossy brown cap and the ripple of careful waves over her right temple.

'Don't rush me. Don't you want me to look nice?'

She smiled over her shoulder at Nick Penry waiting impatiently for her on the doorstep, and bobbed up on her toes in an effort to see the reflection of her new blouse. She had made it herself, from a remnant of bright blue cotton from Howell's summer clearance in Cardiff. Although her skirt was old she had shortened it daringly, and judged that the effect was almost as good as a completely new outfit.

'Not a lot of point in looking nice to stay in Nantlas. If you don't come now it's either that or walk to Barry.'

'Oh, all right then. I'm coming.' Mari patted her hair one last time and hurried to the door. For a moment, balanced on the step above Nick, her face was almost level with his. He was smiling back at her, but the look in his eyes disconcerted her, as it had always done. They had known one another for six months now. Nick had come up to the house first on union business, to see her dad, after Dai Powell had moved up from the town of Port Talbot to the Rhondda valley, where the pits clustered thickly together, to work at the Rhondda and Peris-Hughes Associated Collieries Number Two Nantlas Pit.

Nick Penry was deputy miners' agent for the pit, one of the men's elected union representatives, young for it at only twenty-three. Her dad had said to Mari, after Nick had gone,

23

'Well. I'm not saying that he hasn't got the right ideas, because he has. But there's a lad who's got his sights set further than the next yard of coal.'

Mari couldn't have cared less whether or not Nick Penry was fervent enough in his opposition to the hated pit owners, or in his support for the new Prime Minister Ramsay MacDonald and his Labour government. She simply thought that Nick was the handsomest man she had ever seen. He was tall for a Welshman, black-haired, with dark and quick eyes that could flicker with laughter. He had stared straight at her so that Mari knew he was seeing her, but at the same time looking through her to something beyond. He was there, appraising her, amused and friendly, and yet not there at all.

But a week later he had called again, to ask her to go with him to the dance at the Miners' Rest. They had been going together ever since.

Mari wobbled on the doorstep, her cheeks pink and her bobbed brown hair shining. Nick put out his arms to catch her. She fell against him willingly, laughing and smelling his holiday smell of strong soap and ironed flannel.

She put her cheek against her shoulder as he swung her down into the dusty entry behind the row of houses. 'You could give me a kiss if you felt like it.'

'There'll be plenty of time for that later. Why d'you think I'm taking you all the way out to Barry, if it isn't to get you behind a sand-dune?' But he kissed her just the same, in full view of all the back kitchen windows in the row. His mouth was very warm, and Mari felt the curl of it because he was still smiling. She glowed with pride of possession as he drew her arm firmly through his and they turned to walk up the entry. Nick Penry was all she wanted.

'Tara, Mam,' she called up to the little back window. 'We're off now. You'll see us when you see us.'

Out in the steeply cobbled street men in work clothes were straggling home up the hill, still black with pit dirt and with their tin snap boxes under their arms. The shift had changed, and the day men were already at work in Nantlas No. 1 and 2 pits.

Everyone knew Nick. There were friendly waves and greetings as each little group passed them. A big man stopped and grinned at them, lips and tongue and the rims of his eyes very pink in his dust-blackened face.

24

'Where are you two off to then, all done up? Not Sunday, is it?' 'We're going down to Barry. Mari's got a whole day off from up at the Lodge, and it's a holiday for me as well.'

'Lucky for some,' the big man called cheerfully after them. Nick took Mari's hand and began to run, pulling her after him so that her heels clattered on the stones. She was laughing and protesting, and then they heard the ring of heavier boots coming after them, running even faster. Nick looked back over his shoulder and then stopped, frowning.

Flying headlong down the hill was a young man, hardly more than a boy. He was white-faced, with bright, anxious eyes, and his torn shirt showed the hollow chest beneath. Nick caught his arm as the man scrambled by.

'Late is it, Bryn?'

The runner spun round, trying to jerk his shirtsleeve away from Nick's grasp. He was gasping for breath.

'Again. Can't afford it, neither, on the day money, not like you piece men. But I can't sleep at nights, and then in the morning I can't get my eyes open. But mebbe I'll catch them yet, if I run.' He was off, down the hill towards the huddle of buildings at the head of Nantlas No. 1.

'Come and see me after,' Nick shouted. 'I'll see your gang foreman.'

He wasn't smiling any more, and he didn't take Mari's hand again. They began to walk on, soberly now.

'He hasn't a chance,' Nick said. 'They'll have gone down long ago. He might as well have stopped in bed. That's where he should be, anyway.'

Mari glanced sideways. 'The *dicai*, is it?'

'What do you think, looking at him?'

The *dicai* was the word they used, defiantly and almost lightly, for tuberculosis. The miners' curse stalked the pits and the damp, crowded little houses down the hillsides.

'He's got to go down, Nick. There's only him and that doolally sister, and his mam's bad as well now.'

'Do you think I don't know? I'll have to see if I can get something for them from the Fed. He needs to go down the coast, somewhere away from here. Curse it, Mari, and curse *them*.'

The Fed was the South Wales Miners' Federation. Mari knew that *them* could only be the pit owners, and she knew too that there was no point in trying to talk about it now. She slipped her

25

hand back into his and walked quietly beside him, waiting for him to stop glaring ahead at something she couldn't see, and come back to her.

At last Nick shrugged. They had left Nantlas behind them, and their faces were turned away from the rows of houses lined above the pithead clutter of lifting gear and dust-black brick buildings. They were on the Maerdy road, and the high valley sides were suddenly summer green. The sun was already hot. It was a fine day for the seaside. The river splashed beside the road, and if he didn't look at it Nick found that he could forget that the water was clogged with coal waste and the bankside grass was more black than green. Across the river the railway track ran up to the pithead, and rows of empty trucks were waiting to be shunted up for loading. Nick turned away from that too. He squeezed Mari's hand, and then let it go so that he could put his arm around her shoulders. Her skin felt very warm through the crisp blue cotton, and her hair smelt of lilac. He kissed the top of her head and she drew closer under his arm, lengthening her stride comically so that they walked in step with her hip against his thigh.

'It's our holiday,' Nick said softly. 'Come on, let's catch that train.'

He was smiling again. The sun was shining, he had twelve shillings in his pocket, and Mari Powell beside him. He liked Mari. She was cheerful and straightforward, and she was also the prettiest girl in the two valleys. Nick was sure of that, because he had been a committed judge of Rhondda girls from the age of sixteen. No, now wasn't the time to be thinking of the pit, or the South Wales Miners' Federation, or of Bryn Jones's torn chest and the bloody iniquities of the owners who had given it to him.

Mari was pointing down the road with her free hand. 'Look. The train s in. We'll have to run for it, now.'

A frantic dash down to the station brought them out on the platform just as the guard was lifting his whistle to his mouth. Nick tore open the nearest door, swung Mari up so that her skirt billowed and he glimpsed the tops of her white cotton stockings, and leapt in beside her. They collapsed into the dusty seats with Mari tugging at her skirt hem and then putting her hands up to smooth her windblown bob. Nick looked at her pink cheeks and round, shining brown eyes.

'I love you, Mari,' he said, surprising himself.

Mari wasn't surprised. 'I know,' she said simply. 'I love you, too.'

Everyone went down to Barry when they had time and money to spend. In the good days before the War it was always bursting with miners and their wives and children, determined to enjoy themselves in the halls and bars and tea-rooms. On summer afternoons the sands were packed with picknicking families down for the day from the valleys.

It wasn't quite the same in Barry any more, or anywhere across the South Wales coalfields.

Pits were closing because markets were shrinking, and the work wasn't there any longer. The money wasn't there either, even for the lucky ones who were in work, since the terrible days of the 1921 strike and the huge wage cuts that had followed it.

Looking round at the sea front, Nick saw how much it had changed from the times of his childhood outings. Everywhere had seemed freshly painted then, glittering with bright lights and tempting things to buy, or just to look at. Today, even though it was the middle of August, almost every other shopfront seemed to be closed up, some with forbidding boards over the windows. Those that were still open were trying hard, offering jugs of fresh pinky-brown shrimps and mounds of shiny blue-black winkles, green and red and gilt paper hats with 'Barry Island' printed on them, china mugs and brightly patterned souvenirs, sweets and tin spades and buckets and trays of teas for the beach. But the paint was peeling and the awnings were torn and faded, and there were only straggles of people passing in front of them in place of the old, cheerful crowds.

Beyond the pale green railings edging the front the sand was freshly uncovered, hard and brown and glittering in a thousand tiny points under the sun. The air smelt wonderfully clean and salty. That hadn't changed, at least.

Mari ran to the railings and hung over them, calling to him. 'Look at the sea, Nick. Come on, let's run down to the water now.'

'And get sand all over your shoes and those lovely white stockings?' he teased her.

'I'll take them off,' she said, mock-daringly, and then added, 'Or no, later perhaps.'

They walked down to the water's edge where the wavelets turned over themselves and the fringe of foam was swallowed up by the wet sand. There were two or three tiny flawless pink shells amongst the crushed white and grey fragments of larger ones at the tide-line. Nick picked them up and closed them in the palm of Mari's hand, seeing how the skin was rough and reddened from the washing and mending she did for Mrs Peris up at the Lodge.

'Aren't they pretty?' Mari said. 'Like little pink pearls.'

'I'd give you real pearls, if I could,' Nick said. There was something about today that put a rough edge in his voice. It was a happy day, a beautiful day, but it hurt him too.

'That would be nice,' Mari answered. 'But I don't need pearls, do I? I'm happy just as I am. Here, this minute.'

For a long, long moment they looked at each other.

In the end it was Nick who turned away, his back to the glitter of the sun on the sea, to look back at the rows of roofs and windows along the front. It looked better from here. The colours seemed no more than faded and softened by the salt wind, and the blank eyes of windows were less noticeable. In the centre was a red-brick public house, Victorian mock-Gothic with fantastic turrets and spires, topped by a gilded cockerel on a weather vane.

'What would you like to do?' he asked her formally. 'Shall we have a drink at the Cock? Or are you hungry? We can have a fish dinner right away, if you want.'

'Oh, a drink first, please. Then something to eat, and then we can go for a walk afterwards.'

They sat side by side on the hard, shiny red leather seats in the Cock, looking at the other holidaymakers. Nick drank two pints of beer, and Mari had two glasses of dark, sweet sherry. After the second her cheeks went even pinker and she found it doubly difficult to listen to what Nick was saying.

He was talking about the Miners' Federation, and how important it was that every miner should be committed to it and its leaders, so that they could stand together and fight the bosses.

'Nothing like 1921 must ever happen again,' he said. 'No more Black Fridays.'

Mari sighed. It was a part of Nick that she didn't understand. Of course there should be a union, and of course all working men should belong to it. But all his talk of fights, and power bases, and nationalization and public ownership, and radicalization, and the Sankey Commission, she didn't understand that at all.

There always would be bosses, and they never would want to pay the men the proper wage. Nor would they want to put their profits into mechanizing the mines and making them safer to work in, not while there were still plenty of men more than willing to go down them just as they were and for less and less money.

Secretly, Mari didn't believe that all the unions in the world would ever change anything. There always would be men like Mr Peris who owned the third biggest colliery group in South Wales, and his wife who gave her hand-made silk underwear away to her maid after two or three wearings, and there would be men and women like Nick and herself. If the men came out on strike, obedient to Nick and his kind who truly believed in the possibility of change, then the bosses just sent in the police and the troops and the strike-breakers, the miners got angrier and hungrier, and then when they couldn't hold out against the hunger and the cold any longer, they went back down for less money than before. It would be just the same, Mari thought, if she told Mrs Peris's housekeeper up at the Lodge that she rather thought she wouldn't do quite so much of the heavy washing any more, but would like an extra two shillings a week just the same. She would simply find herself replaced by another Nantlas girl who would be glad to do what Mari Powell did, and without making any trouble about it.

Nick had stopped talking now, and he was looking at her with the same queer light in his eyes. Nick had unusual eyes, grey-green and pale against his dark skin and hair.

'You don't understand any of this, do you?' he said.

'Of course I do,' Mari protested rapidly. 'I understand, and I agree with you. So there's no need to lecture me like one of your miners' lodge meetings.' She tried to look indignant, but at the same time she slid closer to him on the hard, slippery seat. 'I don't much want to talk about it, that's all, not today. I'd rather have you to myself, not share you with every collier in Nantlas as well as the South Wales Miners' Federation.'

'I'm sorry,' he said, contrite. 'Let's forget it at once.' But before he put his arm around her shoulders again he said, as if he was warning her, 'It's important, Mari. Not just to me, but to all of us. I just want you to understand that if . . . if you have me, if you *want* me, you have the fight too. Do you?'

'Yes.' She was answering both his questions, thinking only of one.

With surprising gentleness for a big man, Nick touched her cheek with his fingertips. Then he grinned at her. 'Too serious. *Much* too serious. What d'you say, shall we have another drink?'

'Trying to get me drunk, is it?'

'Of course. Then I can have my wicked way with you. A large one, then?'

'No, thanks. You can buy me that fish dinner instead.'

Later, when they came out again, they turned westwards down the front into the sunshine. They dawdled arm in arm past the shopfronts, examining the displays. In the last shop in the line Nick bought a white china mug with *Cymru am Byth* gold-lettered on one side and *Croeso i Barry* on the other over highly coloured views of the resort.

'To remind you of this elegant excursion,' he said gravely.

Mari thanked him, equally gravely.

Then they were walking away from the sea front, down to where the road turned into a sandy track and then wound away around a little headland into an empty space of coarse grass and sunny hollows. For a while they walked in silence, listening to the sea and the grass swishing at their ankles. Although they were barely half a mile from the clamour of Barry, they might have been alone in the world.

Nick stopped at a deep hollow, enclosed on three sides by sun-warmed slopes tufted with seagrass, but open to the sea and the sky at the front. 'Let's stop for a while,' he said.

They sat down with their backs against the sand and at once the steep walls insulated them. The sea was no more than a faint whisper, and the only other sound was the cry of a seagull directly overhead.

Mari thought that it was the first time they had ever been properly alone. Nick was lying back with his eyes closed. Without his penetrating stare and with the quick crackle of his talk silenced, he looked younger, softer-faced.

For once Nick wasn't thinking of anything at all. He was simply relishing the quiet, the clean smell of the salt-scoured air, and the red light of the sun on his eyelids. It was so different from the confined dark, the noise and the often suffocating heat of every day.

When he opened his eyes again it was to look at Mari. She was lying propped up on one elbow, watching the slow trickle of sand grains past her arm. With her rosy cheeks and round brown eyes she looked polished, shiny with health like an apple, and that was an unusual attraction in Nantlas. Nick's appraisal took in the rest of her. She was slim, but not thin, with a neat waist. And although she was short like the other girls in the valley, she had pretty legs and ankles. It amused Nick that she knew he was looking at her, admiring her, and wouldn't meet his eyes.

'Your shoes are full of sand,' he said softly.

At once Mari sat up. 'I said I'd take them off, didn't I?'

She kicked off the shoes and then, deftly and unaffectedly, she unhooked her stockings and rolled them down over her knees and ankles. Her bare skin was very white, and Nick saw that her feet were small and square. Suddenly he was struck by her vulnerability, and his own. He knelt in the sand and kissed the instep of one foot. The skin was smooth and very warm.

He looked up at her and saw that she was smiling.

'How old are you, Mari?'

'Nineteen. I told you before.'

'Do you think that's old enough?'

He liked her better still because she didn't pretend to be shocked, or not to know what he meant.

'Yes. If it's with you.'

The afternoon sun filled their hollow. As he reached to kiss her mouth Nick saw that the light had tipped her brown eyelashes with gold. Then their eyes closed, and for a long moment they didn't see or hear anything else. Nick's hand reached up and fumbled with the buttons of the new blue blouse. They came undone and he slid it off, stroking her shoulders and touching the hollows beside her neck. Then he found the buttons of her skirt and undid those too. Mari sat facing him in her cotton camisole neatly trimmed with cheap lace. Somehow it looked wrong beside the sharp grass and the clean washed sand.

'Please take it off. I don't think I can find the right buttons.'

'*Nick.*' She was genuinely scandalized now, wrapping her arms protectively around herself. 'What if someone sees?'

31

He laughed delightedly. 'So, Mari. It's all right to make love and not be married, and to do it outside in the sunshine, but it's not all right to take your underclothes off? Look, I'm taking mine off.'

Unconcernedly he stripped himself and knelt beside her again. Nick was neither interested in nor ashamed of his own body. For most of the time it was simply an instrument to be worked until it complained, and then in too-rare moments like this it gave him intense pleasure. But Mari was staring in half-abashed fascination, so he waited, trying to be patient with her. She looked at the breadth of his shoulders, and the knots of muscle in his arms. Nick's skin was white too, but with an unhealthy, underground pallor of hard labour in enclosed places. There were bruises too, old ones fading into yellow and new blue ones. Across his upper arm there was a long puckered scar, blueish under the wrinkled skin as if the wound had not been cleaned properly before healing itself.

'What's that?'

'A shovel,' he said indifferently. 'There isn't a lot of room to work in an uncommon seam, and my arm was in the wrong place at the wrong time.'

'Oh.' Mari was looking down to where the sparse dark hair on his chest grew down in a thin line over his belly. Hesitantly, glancing up at him to see if she was doing right, she reached out to touch him.

'That's right.' Nick's voice was quite different now. '*Touch me.*'

There was another long moment of silence before he asked again. 'Please. Take that thing off. If there's anyone anywhere near, they're doing the same as us. Why should they want to spy?'

Mari raised her arms and slipped the thin cotton off over her head. She sat up straight, lifting her head at the novel sensation of the breeze on her bare skin. She had small, firm breasts with pink nipples. Nick's dark head bent forward as he touched one, very gently, with his tongue. Then they lay down in each other's arms, stretching out against each other in the warmth.

'It feels so lovely,' Mari said. It was the oddness of another body next to hers, the same skin and heat as her own, but yet so different, and the sun and air on her flesh, and the prickle of the sand beneath her.

'Here,' Nick said, lifting her up. 'Lie on my shirt.'

'Oh, why? I liked the feel of the sand.'

She felt his deep chuckle in his throat, and suddenly he was the old comical Nick again that she knew quite well from social evenings and dances in the hall of the Miners' Rest, and snatched half-hours alone in her mam's front parlour.

'Because it won't feel nearly as lovely if we're both covered in it, believe me.'

Mari was flooded with the sense of her own ignorance and she buried her face against him. 'Tell me what to do,' she said.

'Like this, my love. Like this.' Nick took her hand, and showed her. Then in his turn he discovered her, a discovery so surprising that it made her forget the sun and the sky, and the sound of the sea, and everything in the world except the two of them. At that moment Mari wouldn't have known or cared if every man, woman and child in Nantlas had been standing at the lip of the hollow watching them.

Then, much later, she fell asleep with her hair fanned out over the scar on his arm, and his shirt spread over her for covering. Nick lay still, holding her close, and watching the light over them change from bright to pale blue, and then to no colour at all except for a rim of palest pink.

At last Mari murmured something inaudible, stretched, and opened her eyes. 'Have I been asleep for very long?'

'Yes, very long. It was nice, watching you.'

She sat up, shaking the sand out of her hair, and his shirt fell away from her shoulders. At once her hands came up to cover herself.

'It's a bit late for that,' he said, smiling at her.

'I know that. It's not you. What if . . .' Gingerly she levered herself to peer over the rim of the hollow. The world stretched away ahead, empty except for the sea birds, and she flopped back in relief.

'Here.' Nick was holding her clothes out to her, shaken free of sand and folded neatly. He helped her to dress, smoothing the blue cotton and fastening the buttons with surprising dexterity. His hands were rough and cracked, but the fingers were slim for a man's, and supple. When they were both dressed, they leaned back against the sand. Nick produced a small, slightly crushed bar of chocolate from his pocket and she bit ravenously into it. From another pocket be brought out a green and yellow Gold

Flake tin and rolled himself a cigarette, and they sat contentedly together.

'Nick?' she asked after a moment. 'What does it mean? What we . . . did, just now?'

Nick thought carefully. He had done it quite often before, with different girls, and he had believed that it meant exactly what it seemed to mean. They did it, and they both enjoyed it. He saw to that, because it was important. And then, after they had enjoyed enough of it, they were both free to move on.

The enjoyment part mattered, that was what made the bargain mutual. His first girl had taught him that. Not that she was a girl, exactly. Forty-year-old Mags Jenkin from Mountain Ash had coolly picked him out from a crowd of his seventeen-year-old mates. She was a widow, and nothing special to look at, but she knew all there was to know. 'I can always tell the ones who'll be natural at it,' she had told him after their first time together. It was the first time that he'd stayed out all night, and the first night of his life that he hadn't slept at all, even though he had to go down the pit just as usual at seven in the morning. 'Listen,' Mags had said. 'The first thing is to make sure that the girl likes it too. It doubles the pleasure of it for you, see? And there's sense in that, isn't there?'

Nick had seen the sense of it so clearly that he had pressed her back against the grey blankets yet again, and had been late down at the shaft head for the first time in his life as well.

In due course, as Mags had assured him he would, he had turned his attentions to a younger, prettier girl. Mags had simply picked out another eager seventeen-year-old, and Nick had gone on from there, grateful for what she had taught him and happy with what seemed a satisfactory arrangement for everyone. But Mari Powell was different. Not all that different, he reflected, but it was enough.

'What would you like it to mean?' he asked her now, watching the averted pink curve of her face.

'I'd like . . .' She hesitated, and then the words came out in a sudden rush. 'I'd like it to mean that we're going to get married.'

I don't want that. Nick heard his own sharp, inner voice. *Do I?*

Yet he had brought Mari down here, knowing that he would

34

make love to her in a hollow by the sea, and knowing that it would be something different from the careful, deliberately casual encounters he had had in the past. He had wanted it to be different.

Nick frowned very slightly, and looked around him as if for another, less obvious avenue to move down.

But there was none. Everyone was married. All the men he worked with, almost all his friends. Rapidly, Nick tried to sum up for himself what being married would mean. Not living in his dad's house any more, but a struggle to find and pay for another, identical house a little way off in one of the terraces. And then there would be Mari, pretty, cheerful Mari to come home to, and warm in bed beside him every night. There would be no other girls, but that would just mean an end to snatched hours in icy front parlours, or out in the cold in some corner of the valley. Mari and he would have their own room, their own bed. A life of their own.

He looked at Mari now, sitting tensely beside him in her blue blouse, apparently intent on the sand trickling out between the fingers of her clenched fist. 'And would you have me?'

Her fists unclenched at once, and Nick saw the full blaze of delighted surprise in her face. 'Nick, you know I would.'

He waited for a second, listening to the sea and the wind, and then he said, 'Will you marry me, Mari?'

'Yes.'

That was it, then, Nick thought. That was how it happened. You loved someone in a way that wasn't quite exactly the same as all the others, for her pink cheeks and her smile and the scent of lilacs, and you found yourself marrying her.

To have and to hold. From this day forth for ever more. It wasn't his voice but a stranger's, mocking him inside his own head. But before Nick could catch himself up short for his own sourness, Mari's delight overpowered him. Her arms were round his neck and her mouth was warm against his.

'I love you, Nick. Oh, I love you.'

Her fervour touched him and made him smile so that he forgot everything else. 'You sure? Me and the Fed? Me and the pit and Nantlas and the owners?'

'Curse the whole bloody lot of them. I only love you.' Her hands reached out to him, touching him and drawing him closer to her. 'Nick, will you do it again? Please?'

35

They lay down once more, and the walls of the sand hollow enclosed them all over again.

It was almost dark when they reached the station, and the train for the valleys was waiting at the platform. Nick helped Mari up into the high carriage again, and was amused to find himself possessively smoothing the hem of her skirt so that no one else might catch a glimpse of the smooth whiteness above her knees. As they sat down, side by side on the gritty seats, he smelt the dust and smoke and knew that their holiday was over. Pushing back the thought, he asked her fiercely, 'Are you mine? Really all mine?'

In the filthy, dimly lit train Mari was beautiful. Her hair was tousled and dark around her face, and her mouth looked fuller, bruised with kissing.

She smiled at him. 'All. Always. We're engaged now, aren't we?'

Their hands were knotted together and Nick rubbed the bare fingers of her left hand with his.

'I'll buy you a ring. We'll go into Cardiff and you can choose one. Does it matter if it isn't a great diamond?'

'Doesn't matter if it's a brass curtain ring, so long as it's yours. I've got my mug, for now. It'll have pride of place, you know, when we're married. In the middle of our parlour mantel. To remind us of today.'

The train jolted savagely and then shuddered forward. Through the smeared window Nick watched the platform lights dropping behind them and the velvety August night wrapping round the train like a glove.

Quietly, he said, 'It isn't going to be easy, my love.'

Mari was too completely happy even to want to listen to his warnings. 'When has it ever been, for our sort?'

'Harder, then. Much harder. Worse than 1921, do you remember that? That was only a rehearsal for what's coming to us.'

Mari remembered 1921. For the four months that the strike had lasted, March to July, neither her dad nor her brothers had worked. She herself had been earning a few pence a week then, doing mending and heavy cleaning for one of the pit managers' wives, and her mother had taken in some washing. The five of them had lived on that, on bread and potatoes and hoarded tea, and had been luckier than many others.

She sighed now. 'Why not be grateful for things as they are? Everyone except you says they're better. They may be bad in other places, but there's work for everyone who really wants it in the Rhondda now. Forty thousand men. You said so yourself.'

Nick turned away from the window, and the lights of towns strung out along the valley sides like so many necklaces, pretty at this distance.

'It won't last. It can't. We can't compete, you see. Not with German reparation coal, not with subsidized exports from everywhere. Nor with oil for shipping, and the hydroelectric. Steam coal's had its day, my love, and so have we. *Unless –*' his dark face was suddenly flooded with vivid colour – 'unless we can change everything. Stop the owners lining their pockets. Nationalize the industry. Invest. Mechanize. Subsidize. And pay a fair wage to the men who do the work.'

Mari stroked his hand, running her fingers over the calluses, soothing him. 'We'll manage somehow, you and me. I know we will. You're strong and willing, and they'll always give you work while there's still work to do.'

'I won't do it,' he interrupted her. 'Not in the old yes-to-me, no-to-him victimizing ways. There has to be work for every man, fair and square. And you're wrong, in any case. I'll be the first out, given what I believe in. And I'll fight for the right for others to believe in too.'

Mari went on stroking his wrist, her voice gentle. It was old ground between them, and she hardly hesitated over it. 'And I work too, don't I? If what you're afraid of does happen, we'll still have something.'

'Mari.' He caught her wrist, almost roughly, stopping the stroking. Then he lifted her hand and rubbed it against his cheek. She felt the prickle of stubble and then his tongue as he kissed her fingers. It brought back the sand hollow and what had happened there, and she blushed. 'Mari, what will happen when the babies come?'

Her face went bright scarlet. Conscious suddenly of the inquisitive faces around them, she whispered, 'Will we have babies? Would you like that?'

For once, his grey-green eyes were neither opaque nor seeing beyond her. She was fully there, in the centre of his gaze, and she thought it was the happiest moment she had ever known.

'Yes,' Nick said. 'Oh yes, I would like that. And I'd like to be able to give them something too. Something more than just enough to eat, and boots for their feet.'

'We'll do it,' she promised him. She rested her head against his shoulder and he kissed the top of it protectively.

'I wish,' he murmured against her hair, 'I wish we were married already. I want to take you home with me now, to my own bed. No sand. Just you and me, under the covers in the dark. Or no, in the light. So I can see you.'

'Nick.' Mari was stifling her laughter. 'Hush, now. People can hear.'

Their arms were still wrapped round each other when they stepped off the train at Maerdy. Because they didn't have eyes for anyone else, they didn't see the shocked and anxious faces on the platform, nor did they hear the buzz of subdued talk that greeted the other passengers.

Nick surrendered their return tickets to the collector at the barrier without a glance, and they began the walk up the valley, still insulated by their happiness. Later, Mari tried to remember what they had talked about, and couldn't remember any of it except Nick's low voice, for no one but herself to hear, his arm around her, and his hand over her breast in the safe cover of darkness.

Then they came to the curve of the road, the point where they had started to run for the train only this morning, and they saw the lights.

All the lights were blazing at the Nantlas No. 1 pithead, even though the night shift should have been safely down long ago. If all was well, the only lights showing would be in the winding house where the night surface team manned the lifting gear, and in the little square window of the shift manager's office. Yet tonight every single window was lit up, and there were other lights too, hand-held because they were bobbing about in the blackness.

In the moment that Nick and Mari stood together at the bend in the valley road, two huge searchlights came on and snuffed out the torches.

Nick had seen those lights before. They were brought to the

pithead and erected on hastily assembled scaffolding to assist the rescue workers. He was already running.

Mari's bewilderment lasted only a split second longer. '*Explosion.*' She caught the word that Nick shouted back at her over his shoulder as no more than an echo of her own shrill scream. She began to run too, slipping and stumbling in the darkness on the rough road.

Nick was way ahead of her, moving much faster, and then she lost sight of him. But when she came gasping up to the silent crowd waiting at the colliery gates she saw him immediately, right up against the gates, his fists clamped on the bars.

He was shouting, and kicking against the solid ironwork. 'Let me in. Let me in. Cruickshank, is that you? Open these bloody gates. Do you hear? Open them, you bastard.'

Mari elbowed and jostled her way through the crowd and reached Nick's side just as Cruickshank, the pit manager, appeared beyond the gates.

'Ah. Nick Penry, is it? Well then, you'd better come in and add your two penn'orth, for all the difference it'll make.'

The gates creaked open and Mari slipped in behind Nick before they clanged shut again. Neither of the men paid any attention to her whatsoever, and she moved quickly into the shadow of a low wall.

'How many?' Nick said.

Cruickshank shrugged awkwardly. 'Thirty, from the night book. Maybe one or two more, unofficial.'

Even Mari knew what 'unofficial' meant. For safety reasons, only an agreed number of men was allowed to work any given seam at any given time. But if extra men were willing to go in, working the awkward places unacknowledged and for less money than their official counterparts, the managers were glad to let them do it and to keep their names off the books. It meant more coal for less money in less time, after all. It was one of the things that Nick was trying to stop, through the Federation, even though his sympathy was with the often desperate men who were forced to do it.

'One or two?' Nick's voice was harsh.

Cruickshank's was level in response. 'Well. Forty-four, we're almost certain, although we haven't got all the names yet.'

'When did it happen?'

'Just before six. Right at the shift end.'

39

'Whose gang?'

'Dicky Goch's.'

In the shelter of her wall, Mari shivered. Dicky Goch, a red-haired giant with a turbulent family of red-haired children, was a popular figure in Nantlas. He had a fine singing voice, in the Rest on Saturday nights and in chapel on Sundays.

Nick was looking away from Cruickshank, back to the silent, waiting crowd at the gates. Mari knew that he was counting up the friends, fathers of families and boys of thirteen or fourteen, who worked with Dicky Goch. Then he turned sharply towards the pit-top.

'Who's gone down for them?' he asked. 'I want to go.'

'*Nick . . .*' Terror clutched at Mari, and her cry came out as a whisper.

Cruickshank said quietly, 'It isn't quite that easy. There's a fire near the friction gear. The men are in number two district, the Penmon seam. The fire's blocking the road to them.'

'In Christ's name, Cruickshank. Why are you standing here? Are the firemen down there?' Nick loomed over the pit manager who stepped back quickly.

'Be careful, Penry. This isn't your pit. We've done everything we can. The shift manager went down right away with some men, but the fire was blocking the road. It's a damp seam, that. There's every chance of another explosion. I've ordered the pit closed.'

'*Closed?*'

Mari shivered again at the cold fury in Nick's face.

'Closed. Do you want to risk more lives, man? There's . . . there's a problem with the reverse intake.'

Mari didn't hear Nick's muttered words, but she saw his fist swing. The manager scuttled backwards to avoid the blow, hands to his mouth. For a moment Nick stood looking at him, his face full of disgust. Then, awkwardly, he rubbed his knuckles although they hadn't so much as grazed Cruickshank's face.

'I'm sorry,' he said in a low voice. 'You're only the manager. What can you do, except what Peris tells you? How does that make you feel, tonight?' Without waiting to hear if Cruickshank had any more to say Nick swung away towards the pit buildings.

Keeping to the protective shadows, Mari followed him. She felt a smothering sense of relief that the pit was closed and Nick would not be allowed to go down and be swallowed up by the fire.

At the power-house door she caught up with him. She pulled at his sleeve and he turned on her, fists clenching again before he saw who it was.

'Mari?' He was frowning, blacker-faced than she had ever seen him. 'What are you doing here?'

'I wanted to be with you. To see you're . . . safe.'

'Don't be a fool. Is there anyone belonging to you down this pit?'

'No.' Like Nick, all Mari's family worked in Nantlas No. 2.

'Well, then. Go home out of the way.' Roughly he pulled her to him and kissed her, and then wrenched her round to face the gates again. Mari wanted to cling to him, dragging him back to her and away from the pit, and her fingers clutched at his Sunday coat.

'Nick,' she said desperately, knowing that it was stupid and unable to stop herself, 'it isn't a bad omen for us, is it, this happening today?'

'*An omen?*' He was crackling with anger now. 'Don't talk such bloody rubbish. More than an omen, isn't it, for Cath Goch? And Dilys Wyn?'

John Wyn was the miners' agent for No. 1. He worked with Dicky Goch too, and his fourteen-year-old twin sons as well.

Mari's arms dropped to her sides. 'I'm sorry,' she whispered. Numbly, she began to walk alone back towards the colliery gates.

Nick pushed open the power-house doors. He blinked in the light. In the high, red-brick interior the great generators were still humming, keeping the searchlights outside uselessly burning. Polished brass winked proudly back at him. At first glance the cavernous space seemed empty, then Nick looked up to the iron gallery that ran round the walls. A group of men was huddled in front of the air gauges. Most of them were still pit-black, and half a dozen wore the cumbersome back-tanks, coiled tubes and orange webbing of rescue breathing apparatus. Through the generator hum, Nick heard their defeated silence.

He ran to the spiral staircase and took the stairs three at a time, his boots clanging on the iron.

'Nick.' The men nodded acknowledgement to him. Among them were their own union representative, Jim Abraham, Nick's own senior agent from No. 2 pit, and John Wyn's No. 1 deputy. The shift manager was there too, his face and clothes grimed from his expedition down the shaft.

41

'Bad?' Nick asked, knowing how bad it must be for there to be this silence, this inactivity. When no one spoke he said roughly, 'What happened, in God's name?'

One of the men wearing breathing apparatus came wearily forward. In a flat voice he began to tell the story. Nick recognized that it was already becoming a set-piece, a tale that would have to be repeated for the Mines Inspector, the manager's meeting, the inquest. Nick served on the Miners' Safety Committee, and he had heard half a dozen similar recitals.

'I went down with Dicky Goch today,' the miner said. 'Unofficial, see? It was a normal shift. I was in the last stall, the one next to Dicky, with Rhys there.' He pointed to one of the other men, also in rescue gear. 'They were all empty, behind us. The rest of the gang was up ahead.' Nick nodded, understanding that the official men would have the best places. 'At ten to six, Dicky came back and told me and Rhys to put up. We were to go back to the main shaft and call through that the rest were coming. We went. We were just passing the junction with two district when we felt the air reversing past us. It was licking the dust up behind us. We knew there was something bad wrong. We ran to the shaft bottom and called through for help. As the cage came down we heard the explosion.'

'Felt it, more like,' the other miner corrected him. 'No noise. Just a shaking and shuddering.'

'I was on my way down in the lift cage,' the shift manager put in quickly. He was anxious to convince the men's representatives that the right things had been done, the right procedures followed. Too eager, too anxious, Nick thought. 'I met the two men here at the shaft bottom and they told me what had happened. I sent up for the breathing apparatus, collected the other men who had come up meanwhile, and we set off again. The air was rushing past us all the time. It's a damp seam, the Penmor . . .' His voice trailed off uncomfortably.

One of the other men took up the story. 'We got within fifty yards of the junction of the main haulage road with the road down to Penmor. The fire had taken proper hold. As we stood there, watching like, a great long tongue of blue flame came licking back up towards us. Then it was sucked back again, and the air behind us with it. There was nothing to do. I've never seen a fire like it. Trying to fight it with what we had would have been like pissing down into hell.'

There was another long, quiet moment. The generators hummed blindly on.

'The district was checked today, was it?' Nick asked softly.

Jim Abraham half-raised his hand to stop him, and then wearily let it fall again. What Nick Penry wanted to know, he found out somehow. And words, whatever they were on either side, could make no difference tonight.

The shift manager, not looking at anyone, said, 'The report book clearly states that the fire-man checked every working stall in the area this morning. There was some gas, but very little. No more than two per cent.'

'And the empty stalls?'

'Ah . . . not today, as it happens. According to the book, that is.'

And so from somewhere, deep in the workings, an outrush of the deadly fire-damp gas had gone undiscovered. It had mixed with the airflow and a tiny spark, perhaps from a cracked safety-lamp or even a piece of overheated machinery, had ignited it. And then it had exploded.

In an even softer, and more dangerous, voice Nick said, 'General Rules, of which even you as shift manager must be aware, state that daily checking for gas escape in every area of the mine is mandatory . . .'

'Save it, Nick,' someone was murmuring. 'This isn't the time.'

Down in the body of the power-house, the door opened again. The pit manager came in. At his shoulder was a bulky, middle-aged man in evening dress.

'Here's Mr Peris, lads,' the manager shouted up to them.

The men crowded forward and leaned over the gallery railings. Nick felt the press of them behind him, solid but defeated. Further behind them, unwatched now, were the rows of air gauges with their nil readings. His hands gripped the cold iron. Beneath him, in Lloyd Peris's upturned face, reddened with food and drink, he read the brazen readiness to bluster out of his responsibilities. Nick felt his throat swell and tighten with the rage inside him.

'Peris? What happened to the air intake reverse?' His shout filled the span of the arched roof and echoed back at him. '*What happened to it, Peris?*'

There was no answer.

Nick pushed through the men and clanged down the iron stairs again. Cruickshank shrank back a little, but the owner stood his ground squarely.

'A little too much of the hothead, Penry,' he said smoothly. 'It won't do you or your men any good. Not shouting at me, nor threatening my manager. Now, as you all know' – he raised his voice so that the men waiting above could hear – 'there has been a sad accident tonight. I have had a full report from Mr Cruickshank here, who has acted very properly. An unavoidable explosion was followed by an outbreak of fire, which cut off the men's egress and prevented a rescue party from reaching them. I understand that a number of brave men, led in an exemplary manner by the shift manager, tried to get down there. Thank you for that.' He smiled, intending a grave, consoling gesture that at the same time took in Nick's clean face and clothes. The smile looked to Nick like the split in a pumpkin.

'The intake?' Nick asked him again, trying to swallow the loathing that was rising inside him as if he was about to vomit.

'An unfortunate aspect of the accident is the failure of the reversing mechanism,' Peris added. 'The trapped men were subject to a negative airflow.'

The redness in front of Nick's eyes swirled and threatened to blot everything out. He would have reached out to Peris and torn his starched shirt front, and tightened the absurd black bow around his neck until the man's eyes popped and his tongue swelled between his lips. But Jim Abraham stepped smartly up behind him and locked his arms behind his back. Nick heard his own roaring voice filling his head, the force of it rasping at his throat.

'They suffocated, man. Why don't you use the proper words? Make your mouth taste nasty, do they? If the explosion didn't get them, they suffocated to death, because your safety mechanism never worked. John Wyn told me himself. He said the installation was never completed. You didn't want to spend the money on it, did you?'

Cut off from the normal air supply by the fire, the trapped men should have been kept alive by a simple switch which would pump in fresh air through the exhaust system. When it had failed, they had been left to die.

Nick twisted to free himself, but Jim Abraham's grip was like iron.

'We all know it, Peris. Every man here. It's your negligence. You murdered forty-four men tonight. *You are a common murderer.*'

Even as he shouted, Nick knew that his words were a pathetically useless weapon against Lloyd Peris. The owner was already at the power-house door.

'You will have a chance to present your unfounded accusations through the proper channels, Penry. Mr Cruickshank has the duty to inform the relatives of the dead men, with my deepest sympathy. He also has my orders to cap the down air supply. The pit will remain closed until the fire is out and we are sure of its safety. Good night.'

'Your sympathy?' Nick was shouting at the closing door, knowing that he sounded like a madman and unable to control himself. 'Your only sympathy is with yourself because this has disturbed your bloody dinner.'

The heavy door was shut.

Jim Abraham released Nick's arms. Briefly the older man hugged him, leaving black marks on Nick's Sunday coat.

'I know, lad,' he said gently. 'We all know. It's like you want to kill them for it, and not even that would be enough. I was at Senghenydd, remember? Four hundred and thirty-nine men, that day.'

'I know how many,' Nick said bitterly. He was suddenly limp, and as defeated with the ebbing of his terrible anger as the ring of men watching him. 'Forty-four or four hundred, it's all the same, isn't it? His fault, and his friends.'

Cruickshank had gone away up the gallery stairs. He had been turning heavy, polished wheels and watching the dials as the pointers flicked and sank back. Now he came to the master switch. He eased it up and the even hum of the generators faltered, dropped in pitch and died away into silence. Outside the searchlights blinked out and the pithead was lit only by the cold, feeble circles of the emergency lights.

Nick had no idea whether it was real or inside his head, but he heard the terrible low cry from the crowd at the gates. There had been no official announcement, but the news would have reached them long ago. They would all know what the sudden dark and quiet meant.

One by one, not looking at each other, the rescue party filed out of the power-house. They would go to the families of the dead men, and try to reassure them that they had done all they could.

Nick found himself standing alone in the shadows with the useless machinery towering around him. Wordlessly, numbed by anger that hadn't yet given way to grief, he made a promise to the men buried in Nantlas No. 1. He promised them that he would fight the greed and callousness and cruelty that had killed them.

Nick shivered. He realized that he had no idea how long he had been standing there. Slowly, moving stiffly, he walked out of the power-house and across to the railings. The coal dust crunched with gritty familiarity under his feet. The crowd that had pressed against the railings was gone, taking its grief with it up to the little houses on the hillside. Nick was on his way up too when he saw that not quite everyone was gone. A little way off someone was standing staring back at the pithead. From the torn shirt showing the white glimmer of skin, Nick recognized Bryn Jones. He remembered that he had promised this morning to have a word with Dicky Goch for him. No one would have any more words for Dicky now.

Coming up beside him, Nick saw that Bryn was crying, silent involuntary tears that ran down his face and dripped on to his hopeless chest.

'All of them, is it?' Bryn asked.

'Yes.' Nick's arm came briefly around his thin shoulders, hugging him as Jim Abraham had hugged Nick himself. 'You didn't get down in time, then? You were lucky today, Bryn.'

'Call it luck, do you?' The bitterness was not against Nick, but against all the things that they both knew.

'Come on,' Nick told him gently. 'Don't stand out in this damp air.'

They turned their backs on the darkened pit and went on up the hill together.

3

Biarritz, August 1924

Two days after the explosion in Nantlas No. 1, Adeline Lovell
was lying on the sun terrace of the Hôtel du Palais, Biarritz.
There was enough of a cooling breeze to stir the flags on the tall
white flagpoles guarding the sea edge of the terrace, and the
strong blue light was softening to dove grey around the curve of
the bay.

A waiter had brought Adeline a cocktail on a silver tray, but
it was untouched on the table beside her white wicker lounge
seat. The frosting on the rim of the glass had melted long ago.
The English papers, neatly folded, lay close at hand but she
didn't pick them up either. Instead she was staring south, to
where the sea and sky melted together over the coast of Spain,
but without seeing any of the beauty of the afternoon.

The terrace had been almost deserted when Adeline wandered
out in search of company, and she had sunk into the wicker chair
with only her own thoughts for entertainment. But now it was
the cheerful hour when tea-cups were replaced with the first
drinks of the evening. Svelte women in tennis dresses, their
bobbed hair held in place with white bandeaux, were flooding
out of the long terrace doors to greet other women in fluttering
tea-dresses and the first sprinkling of evening gowns. The colours
wove patterns in front of Adeline's unfocused eyes, eau-de-nil
and palest peach, cream and rose-pink and gold. Escorting the
women were sun-flushed men in white flannels, blazers or linen
jackets and panama hats. Amongst them those who had already
changed were like sleek, discreet shadows.

Inside the hotel, under the cream and gilt rococo ceilings
of Napoleon and Josephine's summer palace, the plum-coated
barmen were falling into a rhythm with their silver cocktail
shakers. And already, from the vast ballroom, there was music.

Couples were one-stepping to the band. There would be dancing all evening and late into the night, and sometimes Adeline would wake up in the dawn and still hear the jazz playing.

It was what one came to Biarritz for, she reminded herself now, sitting upright against the cushions. To dance and drink cocktails, to lose money at the Casino and to enjoy oneself.

Adeline reached out for her drink and drained it in one gulp, making a wry face at its temperature. She snapped her fingers at a passing waiter. '*Encore, garçon.*' Adeline still had her faint, attractive American drawl and it made her awkward French sound even odder.

To enjoy oneself. That was the aim, and the problem. Of course, they should really have gone to the Riviera. Everyone who mattered went there for the summer nowadays, but Gerald wouldn't hear of it. It was swarming with vulgarians, he said flatly, and he had no desire to mix with them. Biarritz was an awkward compromise. Gerald would have preferred to stay at Chance, or perhaps at the family lodge in Scotland, for the whole of August. France meant Paris and Deauville and no further, to Gerald. Adeline frowned, and drank half of the fresh drink that the waiter had placed discreetly at her elbow.

Gerald belonged to a different generation. He didn't seem to enjoy anything, any more. He was increasingly withdrawn, critical when he spoke at all, and impatient with his children. He didn't want to play tennis or cards with Adeline and her friends, or go for motor rides up into the Pyrenees. He certainly didn't want to dance. He spent most of his time gambling, and losing heavily, at the Casino.

Adeline didn't care about the losses particularly. She was used to seeing money disappear like water into sand, and believed that was how people of her class should treat it. The Lovell fortunes had been at a low ebb when she had married Gerald, and her love for him made her delighted that it was her money repairing the crumbling fabric and restoring the interiors of Chance. Adeline's money had saved the Lovell's town house in Bruton Street from being sold. It was Adeline's money that supported and nurtured their extravagant way of life. They had arrived for their month in Biarritz with thirty-two pieces of luggage, a valet for his lordship and Adeline's maid, a nanny-companion for the two girls, and Richard's tutor. They had taken adjoining suites overlooking the sea. If she had looked up,

Adeline could have seen the heavy, looped curtains and gilt tassels at the window of her private drawing-room directly overhead.

Since the end of the War the output of the great van Pelt steel mills in Pittsburg had quadrupled, and Adeline had inherited a half-share on her father's death in 1920. She was a very rich woman now, and the Lovell fortunes were secure again under the terms of her marriage settlement. No, it wasn't the money Adeline cared about. It was the joylessness of Gerald's losses, as if he couldn't even find it in himself to be excited by the reckless gamble, that she couldn't fathom.

'Excuse me, my lady?'

Adeline looked round to see her daughters' companion. Bethan Jones wasn't quite a nanny any more because the girls didn't need one, and she definitely didn't have it in her to double as a governess. Adeline had quite often thought that Bethan should be replaced by a proper maid, someone with a bit more style who could do the girls' hair properly now that they were growing up. Amy looked a positive hoyden sometimes. But Amy and Isabel were devoted to their plain-faced Bethan, and wouldn't have heard of it.

'Yes? What is it?'

'Parker sent me down, my lady, to ask what time you would like to dress, and whether she should lay out the grey Chéruit satin?'

Lady Lovell's maid, on the other hand, was an autocratic creature of the old school who was glad to have Bethan willingly hurrying to and fro for her.

'Tell her I will be up shortly.' Mechanically, Adeline decided. 'Yes, the grey satin for this evening.'

Around her on the terrace were a score of acquaintances whom Adeline could have joined for drinks, made plans with for dinner, and danced with into the small hours. Yet she felt a shiver of loneliness now.

'Bethan?'

The girl had almost turned away. 'Yes, my lady?'

'Where is everyone?'

'I'm not sure . . . do you mean the other guests?' Bethan was uncomfortable, looking around at the thronged terrace.

'My family,' Adeline said with a touch of asperity. 'My daughters. Mr Richard. I haven't seen anyone all day.'

Bethan relaxed at once, smiling at the mention of the children. 'Oh no, they've all been busy. Mr Richard has been out all day with Mr Hardy. They went straight after breakfast. They took their sketch pads and pencils. They were going to look at some . . . churches, was it now?'

Adeline stared hard ahead. Of course it was right that Richard should know the difference between Gothic and Perpendicular and Romanesque, or whatever the things were that Hardy considered so important to his education. But little Richard seemed happier and far more relaxed in the company of his pale-faced tutor than he did with his own mother and father. Adeline felt a sudden longing to see him and hug him like a baby.

'And Miss Isabel and Miss Amy had their tennis coaching, and then they swam in the sea, and afterwards I took them along the front for an ice at Fendi's. They are in their room now, my lady, if . . .'

And Adeline had spent the afternoon alone on the terrace. She lifted a hand to cut Bethan short. 'Please tell them to be down promptly for dinner. We will all dine together this evening. Mr Richard too.'

'Adeline, *darling* . . .'

A shadow fell over her chair. Blinking, she looked up into it and saw Hugh Herbert. She had met him before, at house parties in England, and she had sat next to him in the car on the way to a picnic in the hills three days ago. She had noticed, from across the dance floor, that he danced like a dream.

'And an empty glass? Let me get you a cocktail at once, immediately. And then perhaps do we have time for one tiny dance?'

His hand was under her elbow. Adeline didn't particularly want to dance, but she did want another drink. And suddenly she wanted some cheerful company very much indeed. She smiled up into Hugh Herbert's blue eyes.

'Only one, Hugh. I've absolutely promised to dine *en famille* tonight.'

Bethan stood respectfully to one side as Adeline and her friend sailed past. Then, looking down automatically to see whether any of her ladyship's belongings needed to be carried up to her suite, she saw the folded English newspaper beside the chair. As she stooped to pick it up a single word in a paragraph at the foot of a page caught her eye.

Nantlas.

The laughter and bustle on the terrace froze into silence. She looked quickly at the elegant people around her. It was unthinkable to stand here and read the paper as if she was one of them. Bethan slipped through the crowd and back into the hotel. Crossing quickly under the great chandeliers in the foyer, she made for a corridor that took a sharp right-angled turn away towards the kitchens. The only people who would penetrate beyond the corner would be servants like herself.

Leaning breathlessly against the wall, Bethan read the brief report. It was headed 'Colliery Disaster'. It said only that forty-four miners had been killed following an explosion at the Rhondda and Peris-Hughes Associated Collieries No. 1 Pit, Nantlas, Rhondda. The owner of the pit, Mr Lloyd Peris, had said that the pit would remain closed until it could be made safe. A full inquiry would be made through the usual channels.

She re-read the paragraph three times, as if it might yield something she had not understood at first. But there was nothing else. Bethan looked up and down the deserted corridor, wanting to run but having no idea where to. Her father and two of her brothers worked in Nantlas No. 1, and she was stranded here, a thousand miles and two whole days separating her from her family and the crowd waiting silently at the pit gates.

Bethan fought against the panic. She clenched her fists and frowned, trying to think. She knew no French. She had used the telephone only a handful of times in her life. Her only contact with home was the weekly letters she exchanged with her mother, and even those took days longer to reach her here. She was quite sure that her mother would have no idea how to reach her in Biarritz if the family needed her. Bethan's mind was blank. She couldn't possibly turn to Lady Lovell for help, even less his lordship. Isabel was the only one who might know what to do. Fixing quickly on the thought that Isabel was fourteen now, and spoke perfect French, Bethan turned and ran towards the stairs, the newspaper clenched in her hand.

Amy was sitting on the window seat in the pretty sitting-room she shared with her sister. Their suite was at the side of the hotel instead of at the front overlooking the great terrace with its flags and flowers, but Amy thought that it was much superior because

51

it looked south along the curve of coast. At odd times when the haze cleared she could see the blue line of Spain. It was so pretty here, from the height of the hotel, with the town spread out in front of her and the figures moving on the beach. When she was down in the midst of it all Amy felt gawky and ignorant amongst the glittery people, and curious and impatient in equal parts with all the dancing and parties and furious enjoyment that made up a summer in Biarritz. But from up here she could imagine that it belonged to her, and that she was the star in its firmament.

Amy wrapped her arms around her drawn-up knees and stared at the view. Lazily, she thought that she should be changing for dinner, and dismissed the thought at once. Isabel was already in their bedroom, brushing her hair before pinning it up. Isabel was suddenly much more interested in her hair, and her dresses. She could spend an hour rearranging her costume for nothing more interesting than a decorous walk with her sister, and she would sit eagerly over the seasonal fashion sketches sent for Lady Lovell's approval by her favourite couturiers. But in Isabel's case it was worth doing, Amy thought loyally, because Isabel was beautiful. Her dark red hair was smooth and shiny where Amy's was curly and rough, and her skin stayed flawlessly white under the sun when Amy's turned pink and itchy. Isabel looked ravishing in the plain linen day dresses and simple pastel silks for evening that Adeline insisted they wore. Amy was taller, and she felt that she bulged and sprouted from her clothes like an oversized vegetable.

Not that I care, she told herself firmly. At twelve years old Amy would rather watch the intriguing world around her, or even read a book, than spend time on her appearance. She was particularly proud that she could make herself ready for dinner in exactly six minutes, start to finish.

She was just congratulating herself on the fact, which meant that there was a full half-hour yet before she need move, when Bethan came in. Bethan's territory was a little square room beside the front door of the suite. Amy couldn't remember her ever coming into their sitting-room without a discreet knock first, although all three of them recognized it as a pure formality.

As soon as she saw Bethan's face, Amy swung herself off the window seat. 'Something's wrong. What is it? Are you going to be sick? Wait, I'll get a bowl . . .'

'No,' Bethan said. 'There's been an accident.'

Amy whirled around again. Isabel was standing in the bedroom doorway, her hairbrush in her hand. 'Not Richard? Mother?'

'No. At home. In Wales. A pit explosion.' She held out the paper to them. Isabel took it, and Amy wrapped her arms protectively around Bethan.

'I don't know what to do, see. My dad's in that pit, and my brothers. I've got to telephone . . .'

The sisters looked at each other. Bethan was usually so calm, and full of dependable common sense; it was very strange to find her turning to them for help instead.

'Of course you must telephone,' Isabel soothed her, 'I'll go down to the desk. They'll find us the number. Where . . . do you think we should ring?'

Bethan shook her head helplessly.

'We must ask Tony,' Amy said crisply. 'He'll know what to do.'

'You shouldn't call him Tony,' Isabel protested automatically.

'Why not? It's his name, isn't it?'

Richard and his tutor had rooms looking on to the terrace, but on the floor above. Out in the corridor Amy glanced at the lift and saw a knot of languid people waiting for the ornate doors to open. She ran for the stairs instead, taking them two at a time. Raised eyebrows and curious stares followed her. She rapped sharply on Tony Hardy's door, calling at the same time, 'It's me. Something's happened. We need your help. *Please* open up.'

Tony was making himself ready for the ordeal of dinner. He had had to go through it a few times before, in Biarritz and at the Lovells' London house before they all left for France, and they were never comfortable gatherings. Part of the problem was his equivocal position. The tutor was only a family employee, of course, but he was also a gentleman and couldn't be expected to eat with the servants. He could dine alone, which Tony infinitely preferred to do with a book for company, but there were times like this when his presence was expected.

Tony Hardy was in his first year down from Oxford. His fixed ambition was to work in the publishing business but his father, a regular soldier with a limited income, had no contacts in the book world and Tony had had no luck in pursuing his own. The only suitable employment that Colonel Hardy had been able to suggest apart from the army was a year tutoring the son of Lord Lovell, who was a nodding acquaintance from his club.

The tutoring part was easy. Richard Lovell was a clever and interesting boy. It was the rest – being equal but not equal, and living in the tense family atmosphere under its thinly civilized veil – that Tony found difficult. Sighing, he rubbed the soap off his face and went to the door with the towel slung around his neck.

Amy Lovell's vivid face stared back at him.

'Sorry,' she said. 'I didn't know you'd be undressed.'

'I'm not undressed,' he grinned at her. 'I just haven't got my shirt on. What's the matter?'

Amy told him.

'Mmm. Is there a telephone in your rooms? I haven't got one here, of course.'

Amy peered past him at the narrow bed heaped with books and clothes. 'No, I see. Yes, there is a telephone in our sitting-room. We've never used it. Who would we ring?'

'Come on, then. It will be easier to do it from somewhere quiet.'

They ran back downstairs. Bethan was sitting stock-still on a sofa with Isabel beside her, holding her hand. Tony glanced at her and said quietly to Amy, 'You'd better order up something. Some tea, or perhaps a brandy.' He knelt down in front of Bethan and said, very gently, 'What's your father's name? And your brothers'?'

'William Jones. David Jones and John Jones.'

'Right. Now, it may take me a little time to find out for you. It's after six o'clock, you see, so the normal places one might try might not be open. Do you want to go away somewhere quiet with Isabel while I do it, or would you rather stay here?'

'I want to stay.'

'All right. I'm going to begin by talking to a friend of mine, a union organizer. Not in mining, but he'll know just who will give us the quickest answer.'

Tony spoke rapidly to the operator. His French was faster and much more idiomatic than the girls' careful schoolroom language. The three faces watched him from the sofa, Bethan's white one flanked by the intent Lovells.

'I want to speak to Jake Silverman, please.'

He was through to England. Amy's hand reached for Bethan's and held it.

'Hello, Jake. It's Tony Hardy.' Tony explained succinctly what

54

he wanted. The voice at the other end cra
there was a long silence. They waited, not mo
speaking again and then scribbling something

'Thanks, Jake. Yes, I hope so too. Soon, I hope

He replaced the receiver and turned to the girls.
ring the Miners' Welfare Institute in Nantlas. I've got the
here.'

Bethan was trembling. 'I should have known that. I just ca
think. I'm so frightened.'

As Tony was talking to the operator again a maid brought in
a tray. There were dainty tea-things and an incongruous balloon
glass of brandy. Seeing Amy's anxious face, Bethan took the
glass but she stared helplessly at it instead of drinking.

The call to Wales took much longer to put through.

There were long silences, and then sharply repeated instruc-
tions from Tony. At last he straightened up and looked at them.
'It's ringing,' he said.

The voice that answered the telephone had exactly the same
rising note as Bethan's but it was a young man's voice, determined
and crisp.

Tony asked his brief question. 'William, David and John
Jones.' Bethan's knuckles were so white around the fat brandy
glass that Amy was sure it would shatter into fragments.

And then, only a second later, Tony was smiling and nodding
and they knew that it was all right. Bethan's face crumpled and
the tears came at last.

'Thank God,' she said, 'thank God, thank God,' over and over
again. Tony held out the receiver to her but she shook her head,
unable to move.

'Thank you,' he said in her place. 'We're very grateful. Yes,
I'll tell her that.'

'I'm glad for her,' Nick Penry said in the cramped, stuffy office
of the Miners' Welfare. 'I'm very glad.'

Nick was almost smiling when the call ended, the first hint of a
smile for two days. He was taking his duty turn in the little office
of the Welfare building. Usually the Welfare and Rest Institute
was a cheerful place, Nantlas' social focus, where miners came
to talk and drink at the end of their day's work, or to borrow
books from the well-stocked free library, or to attend union

. It had been one long succession
ctuated by visits from white-faced
men asking for help, and money,
gs that were in short supply in
eone some good news was a rare

ckled faintly and then
ing, until Tony was
n his notebook.
. *Adios'.*
We are to
number
n't

ethan. 'The man I spoke to knows
anywhere near the explosion. He
father that he's spoken to you,
and promises you that there is nothing to worry about.'

Isabel and Amy were relieved to see that Bethan was almost herself again. She rubbed her face with a handkerchief and straightened her neat skirts.

'I don't drink, thank you, Mr Hardy, but I will have a cup of tea. Funny, isn't it? Now I know they're safe, I can only think of the other poor men. Before, I couldn't have cared less who might have been down there with them.'

Amy was shaking her head, amazed and horrified now that her concern for Bethan was past. 'It's so terrible. So many men, just to die all at once. Has it ever happened before?'

Bethan said sadly, 'Oh yes. It happens all the time. It's a rare miner's family that hasn't lost someone. My grandfather was killed, and his brother. It's black, dangerous, dreadful work. There's not a man who'd do it if he didn't have to, or starve.'

Tony looked sympathetically at Bethan, and then at the glowing apricot and pink faces of the Lovell girls. So much difference, he thought. Such a huge, unfair and eternally unbridgeable gulf. And then, irrelevantly, he realized that they would both be beauties. Isabel would be a conventional good-looker, but Amy would be something different, and special. Tony didn't generally find women interesting but he liked Amy Lovell.

'I think,' he said, 'that the average death rate for coal miners in this country, over the last few years, works out at about four per day. Every day of the year, that is. If you're not going to drink that brandy, Bethan, I think I'll have it.'

They were late down for dinner, but that didn't matter because everyone else was too, except for Richard.

56

He was sitting calmly in his place, expressionlessly watching the other diners. His light hair was watered so that it lay flat to his head, and he was buttoned up to the neck in a stiff white collar and a short jacket. Richard's appearance was completely unexceptional, but there was something in his face, in the set of his mouth and the light in his green eyes, that was an unexpected challenge from a little boy.

He was watching his father now, as Lord Lovell bore down on the family table. Gerald's grey eyebrows were drawn together in a heavy line, and his pouchy cheeks were untouched by the sun.

'Good evening, Father,' Richard murmured.

God damn it. Why does the boy always irritate me, always, in just the same way? Gerald jerked out his chair and sat down. He didn't want to have dinner with his white-faced son and the too-clever tutor, or with his daughters, half-frightened and half-choked with giggles. Not even with Adeline, who would be bright-eyed with cocktails and full of silly talk about the half-witted people she spent her days with. Not that he particularly wanted to spend any more hours in the Casino, either.

Gerald wasn't sure where he wanted to be.

Perhaps at Chance, except that not even Chance meant the same any more.

'What have you been doing?' he asked Richard without enthusiasm. 'Swimming?'

'I don't like the water much, you know,' Richard answered. 'We went to look at a church. A rather fine one, quite close to here. I made some drawings . . .'

Airlie had swum like a fish, almost from babyhood. Gerald could see him now, at Richard's age exactly, swimming in the lake at Chance, his arms and legs flickering sturdily under the skin of green water.

'You should learn,' Gerald said harshly. 'You'll have to start doing things you don't like at school.'

Richard was to enter Airlie's old prep school in six months' time.

'Yes, I expect I shall,' he answered.

Adeline came next. The grey Chéruit dress was daringly short, a slither of bias-cut satin that almost showed her knees. She wore it with long ropes of perfect pearls, dangling pearl and jet earrings, and a shot-silk wrap with long floating fringes around her shoulders. She had never cut her luxuriant hair, but it was knotted up at the back of her head so that she looked smooth and sleek. As he stood up Gerald noted that she was at the excited, three-cocktail stage, and that she was still very beautiful.

'Have you been waiting long, my darlings? I met Hugh Herbert on the terrace, and he was being *so* amusing.'

In the silence that followed Gerald and Adeline looked at each other, and each of them was wondering what had become of the other.

Isabel and Amy ran as fast as they could to the dining-room doors, and then stopped at the heavy glass panels to catch their breath and compose their faces. Relief for Bethan had made them giggly. They peered through the glass across the acres of tables with their stiff white skirts and little gilt lamps with rose-pink silk shades. The tables were separated by clumps of stately palms in pots, and phalanxes of gliding waiters.

'Are they there?'

'Yes. Both of them.'

'Oh, hell. Come on, then.'

'*Amy.*' Isabel's protest was as automatic as always.

Tony Hardy came up behind them in a dinner suit that had clearly belonged to his father. The door was held open for them by the waiter that Amy had come to think of as her favourite. He was very young, with a dark, almost monkey-like face that split into a huge smile. She grinned sideways at him in answer, and between Isabel and Tony she marched forward to the dinner table.

They slid into their seats, murmuring their apologies. Richard telegraphed them a greeting by dissolving his poker face into a mass of wriggling eyebrows, and then returned immediately to his impassive calm.

It was a dinner just like hundreds of others, Amy thought sadly, as she bent her head over her soup. She wondered why they didn't feel on the inside as they must look on the outside to the people watching them – happy, and comfortable, and like other families. Like her friend Violet Trent's family, for example. Amy could remember, just about, times when they had been. Times when her father had smiled more, and when his gruffness had easily dissolved into affection. When Mother had been more . . . well, just more accessible, and there had been fewer friends and parties and pressing engagements filling her days. Mother was wonderful, of course, she reminded herself. No one else's mother was anything like her. There just wasn't enough of her to go around. Isabel minded that she was so busy too, Amy knew that. Yet Mother could always make time for Richard. He was the special one, to her. But that was quite natural too, of course. He would be going away to school all too soon, and they would all miss him dreadfully. And someone had to make up to him for Father being so harsh. Amy wondered if fathers were always like that to their sons, if it was supposed to make them more manly.

She thought of one of the things that had happened, on this very holiday, one of the odd, dark things that she never mentioned afterwards even to Isabel, but which she knew they all still remembered.

They had been sitting beside the hotel swimming pool one morning, sunning themselves, Isabel and herself, with Richard and Tony. Richard was reading a book with Tony. Amy remembered that it was a book of modern poetry with a yellow cover. Tony was explaining it, talking about how the words made pictures with sounds and also meant things that you couldn't see at first. Mother was still upstairs. She often didn't come down until just before lunch. But unusually, Father had been there, sitting in a chair close by. He was frowning, not quite looking at his newspaper.

Suddenly he had stood up and gone over to Richard. He had said something like, 'Come on, my boy, let's see you do something real for a change.'

Then he had jerked Richard to the edge of the pool. They had balanced there for a second or two, and Richard had gone flailing into the water.

To the other people looking, Amy thought, it must just have looked like a father and son rough-and-tumbling together. But it wasn't really like that at all. Father had been angry and pleading, both together, and Richard had been defiant. Father wanted him to do something and Richard didn't want to do it, not now and not ever.

Then when he was in the water he was just a frightened little boy, because he couldn't swim. There was a moment when they saw his face under the water, turned up with his eyes wide open. And then he was splashing and choking on the surface. It was Tony who slid in beside him and helped him to the poolside, and Father had just watched them with a frozen face. Richard had hauled himself out of the water and gone back to his place without looking at anyone, and no one had ever talked about it again.

Amy could remember other things too, going back over the years, as if Father and Richard had been fighting a silent battle that the rest of them were only aware of for a fraction of the time.

It was peculiar that it should be like that, because Richard was such a funny, likeable boy. He could mimic anybody, from Mr Glass to Violet Trent's mother, and he often reduced Isabel and herself to helpless laughter. Mother enjoyed his mimicry too, but he never ever did it when Father was around. Richard could be serious and sensible, too. He often talked about things much more intelligently than other children of only eight.

Why not with Father? Richard put on his shuttered face when he was present, and Father went on being scornful and angry with him.

Amy asked Isabel why they didn't seem to like each other. It wasn't right, was it, for a father and son?

Isabel had said in her gentle way that she didn't know for sure, but she thought it was something to do with Airlie having been killed in the War. If Father had loved Airlie very much, as he must have done, perhaps it was hard for him to love Richard in just the same way.

'He should be glad to have him,' Amy muttered. 'Is it why Mother and Father don't make each other happy?'

Isabel looked at her. They had never quite put it into words before. 'Perhaps,' she said, very quietly.

'When I marry,' Amy said, 'it won't be like that at all. I shall marry a man who is rich and handsome and witty, and who adores me.'

Isabel was laughing. 'You'll have to find one, first.'

'Oh, that will be easy. We'll both find one. Just wait and see.'

'Amy, will you stop staring into space like a half-wit? Adeline, these children have no manners.'

Another family dinner, like hundreds before it. At last it was over. Mother had looked beautiful, had smiled at them and asked them what they had been doing, and had listened carefully

60

because she really did want them to enjoy themselves. Father had been silent, except for telling Tony that he thought trailing around empty churches was hardly educational. Tony had politely said that it seemed sensible to encourage Richard in what he was good at, like languages and art, and history and architecture, instead of forcing him to do things that he didn't enjoy. Amy and Isabel had talked to fill the empty spaces, and they had probably looked the picture of a happy family on holiday together.

Adeline kissed the children good night, with an extra hug for Richard that crushed the shot-silk wrap against his cheek. Hugh Herbert was waiting for her in the cocktail bar. They would have a drink, and then they would dance again. Adeline had been completely exhilarated by their first one. They had swung out over the floor like ice-skaters. Hugh Herbert was charming and flattering. Why not? Adeline asked herself. Gerald had already gone off, unsmiling, with barely a word for her.

Isabel and Amy went upstairs to their suite. They were not allowed to stay downstairs after dinner. They would sit and read or write letters, with Bethan for company, and at ten-thirty they would go to bed and listen to the music coming up from the ballroom.

Tony's last job of the day was to see Richard up to his room. The boy went uncomplainingly, looking forward to losing himself again in the adventure story waiting beside his bed. A little later Bethan would come up to make sure that he had washed and cleaned his teeth properly, and that his pyjamas were on the right way out. As if it mattered, Richard thought. But then what did matter? It was difficult to decide. Perhaps when you knew just how much importance to give to people and the things that they did, perhaps then you were grown up. Clearly he had a long way to go yet.

Tony Hardy went up to his room and took off his dinner suit, his boiled shirt and his bow tie. He pulled on a jersey and ran his fingers through his hair. Down by the tiny harbour in Biarritz where the fishing fleet came in, there were a couple of little bars where people went to drink *vin ordinaire* and cognac, to listen to Basque songs, and to talk. The chance to be there and listen, to talk a little himself, made all the rest of this worthwhile. Even dinners like the one he had just sat through.

Tony closed his door softly behind him and ran down the

61

broad, shallow stairs with his mouth pursed in a silent, celebratory whistle.

On the morning of their last day in Biarritz, Amy went out for a last walk along the sea front. She left the red and cream pinnacles of the Hôtel du Palais behind her and headed for the narrow cobbled streets climbing up the hilltop to the south.

In the hotel Bethan was busy with their trunks and sheets of crisp white tissue. Isabel was packing too, and they had both begged her to go away. Amy was willing to help, but somehow whenever she packed anything the smooth linens came out ferociously creased, and the fragile underclothes looked as though they had been tied up in knots.

'Leave it to me, there's a lamb,' Bethan said.

Amy was enjoying her solitude. It was a chance to say a private goodbye to the little town. She wasn't altogether sorry to be leaving, because holidays made the family differences seem more apparent, whether they were Christmasses at Chance or summers away like this one. Soon they would be back in England, living a routine again, and that was much easier. The children spent term-times at the London house, and the girls went to Miss Abbott's school for young ladies in Knightsbridge. They saw little of Gerald, who spent much of his time alone at Chance. Adeline came and went according to the demands of the Season and Saturday-to-Mondays at the country houses of her friends. But Amy had enjoyed just being in Biarritz. It was further than she had ever travelled before, and it had an exotic, southern feel that wasn't just French like Deauville or somewhere. It was as if it was on the border between somewhere she knew and understood perfectly well, and somewhere exciting, and mysterious, and completely new.

'I'll be back,' she murmured to herself.

Amy wandered slowly along the wide, white-painted boardwalk between the Casino and the sands. It was busy with couples strolling arm in arm, skipping children, and old men in straw hats taking the sun before the heat became too much for them. The tide was going out, and the sand was smooth and glittering. The great rock in the middle of the bay was uncovered, and on the crest of it Amy could see the silhouettes of people who had climbed it after swimming out there for their morning exercise.

Amy passed an arcade of spruce little shops fronting the walk, with Fendi's at the corner. She would have liked to buy an ice to eat under one of the fluttering parasols, but didn't have any money. Instead of walking on round the headland to where the statue of the Virgin on her rock was linked to the shore by a dizzy span of bridge, she turned inland up the steep streets where real Biarritz people rather than those on holiday lived. The little white and grey houses leaned over her on either side, their twisted metal balconies bright with flowers in pots. There were smells of baking and laundry and cooking oil.

Amy was panting slightly from her climb when someone stepped squarely out in front of her.

'Hello, miss.'

She stopped at once, and smiled.

There was the answering brilliant flash of white in the dark face, and the black eyes shining at her. Now that she had met him, Amy could admit to herself that the real purpose of her walk had been to find Luis and say goodbye to him properly. Luis was the waiter from the hotel who looked like a clever, humorous monkey. The two of them had struck up a tenuous, exciting friendship based on smiles exchanged when Luis served the two girls at their decorous lunches in an obscure corner of the great dining-room. When Lord and Lady Lovell were present the head waiter himself served them, and Luis was relegated to distant duties with the trolley. Amy and Luis had talked for the first time when he brought her a glass of fruit juice on the terrace, and they had met once on the beach. Luis had been swimming, and he was wet and shiny like a dark brown seal. He was always looking over his shoulder for his superiors, and then he would melt away into nowhere while Amy was still talking. He was very lively, quite unlike anyone she had ever met, and Amy was fascinated by him.

Luis was Spanish, but they spoke in French. His was very heavily Basque-accented and it bore hardly any relation at all to Amy's polite English version. Sometimes they used the broken English he had picked up at the hotel. Amy felt that he was the very first friend she had made for herself in the real world, and then yesterday he had whispered that they could not meet again because today was his day off and he would not be in the hotel. So she had set off on her solitary walk, without even admitting to herself that she wanted to say goodbye properly to him.

'You are walking?' he asked her now. 'Without your sister or your maid?'

'I'm not supposed to leave the boardwalk when I'm by myself,' Amy answered. 'But . . .' she shrugged in imitation of Luis's own expressive gesture, and they both laughed.

'I will walk with you, then. In case of kidnap.'

Still laughing, they turned to walk on up the hill together. Luis was pointing into the shops, explaining to her about the people who lived and worked there. At the corner of the street they came to a cave-like little shop full of rainbow-coloured sweets and tiny, unfamiliar-looking pastries. An ancient woman in a rusty black dress was selling a handful in a twist of paper to a little boy, who was carefully counting out the centimes as he handed them over.

Amy stopped to watch and Luis asked, 'You would like?'

'I would love.'

He spoke rapidly in Spanish and the old woman twisted a paper cone for Amy too, scooping one or two of each variety into it. Luis paid her and they walked on, sharing the sweets between them. They were almondy, delicious.

'If you would like,' Luis said with sudden gravity, 'we could visit my family.'

'Yes, please,' Amy said.

One street further on they came to a row of houses so steeply perched that they looked as if they were about to topple over. A little girl was sitting on the step of the end house, playing with a stick and four stones. When she saw Luis she jumped up and ran down to him, calling out in Spanish.

'This is my smallest sister, Isabella.'

Isabella had tight black ringlets and the same eyes as Luis.

'You have the very same name as my sister,' Amy told her. Isabella took her hand and pulled her towards the house.

'Come in.'

Amy followed Luis up the steps and in through the door. The small room was square and windowless. It was cool beyond the shaft of light that fell in through the doorway. When her eyes got used to the dimness, Amy saw that the room seemed full of people. There was an old man with an immense, drooping white moustache, and an equally old woman with a black headdress pulled tight over her head. There was a square-built, strong woman who must be Luis's mother, and children of all sizes. Luis drew Amy forward. My friend, she heard him saying proudly, over and over again.

Do they all live here? Amy wondered. Where do they sleep? Through the opposite door she could just make out the shape of a big bed covered with a bright blanket.

The little house was scrupulously clean, but almost completely bare. The only ornament was a dim, oily picture of the Holy Family with a little light burning in front of it. Amy thought fleetingly of the suite at the Hôtel du Palais with its soft cushions and pretty covers.

She shook hands gravely with each member of the family and felt them touching her gloves gingerly, looking at her pleated dress and her white shoes and stockings.

The señorita was asked if she would take a refreshing drink, and they gave her a coloured glass full of a very sweet, reddish liquid that she drank with difficulty while they watched her.

When it was gone, Luis stood up and said that now he must see his friend back to the safety of the hotel. At once they all stood up, shaking hands once more and smiling now. They ushered her the few feet to the door and watched as she walked down the hill with Luis. At the corner Amy turned back and waved.

When they were finally out of sight, Luis said, 'Thank you. You did us a great honour.'

That made Amy angry. 'Don't say that. I didn't do anything of the sort. They did me the honour, taking me in, didn't they? Thank you for letting me meet them. I wish we could have talked to each other. Perhaps next time I will know some Spanish.'

Luis looked at her, drawing his eyebrows together.

'I like you,' he said.

'I like you, too.' She was silent for a moment and then she said, very tentatively, 'Your family, are they . . . do they have what they need?'

He was still looking at her, and she saw that he was amused now. He knew exactly what she was trying to say.

'If you mean much money, no, none. Not like the people you know. But my father has good job, and I have good job. We are lucky ones.'

Not like the people you know. If you are lucky, Luis, what am I? Amy felt her face going red, hot all the way up into her hair.

They had almost reached the sea front again. Luis took her arm and guided her into a little blind alleyway.

'I will come no further,' he said.

'No. I just wanted to say goodbye, you know. Properly, not like yesterday at the table.'

'Of course. I understand that.'

Luis came close to her. She looked up and saw his smile, and then he kissed her, a proper kiss. She was still thinking *a proper kiss*, and how soft his mouth was against hers, when it was over.

'Perhaps you will come back.'

'I hope so. I'll come one day, somehow. Goodbye, Luis.'

'Goodbye, Amy.'

She walked out of the alley, to the end of the street, and back to the white walk outside Fendi's. She felt as if she was flying, with wings on her heels. Not only had she made a real friend, but he had kissed her. She wasn't a little girl any more.

Biarritz, I love you.

It would be thirteen years before she saw it again.

That night, in the Paris sleeper, Amy whispered to Isabel in the bunk below, 'Are you asleep, Bel?'

'No.'

'Do you know, I went up into the town this morning, while you were packing.'

'I wondered where you'd slipped off to. What were you doing?'

'I met Luis.'

There was a moment of startled silence. Amy smiled in the darkness.

'What happened?' Isabel was intrigued, and envious of the adventure.

'Oh, he took me home to meet his family. He's got about a dozen brothers and sisters. The smallest is a little girl called Isabella. Then he walked me back down to the sea front, and he kissed me.'

'Where?'

'On the lips, of course.'

Isabel choked with laughter. 'Oh, of course. Actually I meant where was it, in front of Fendi's with everyone looking on over their ices?'

'No. In an alleyway.'

'Amy, you are priceless. Kissing waiters in alleyways. I'm two whole years older than you, and no one's ever kissed me.'

'I expect your turn will come,' Amy said airily.

When they stopped laughing Isabel said, 'So, what was it like?'

'Well, to tell you the truth it was so quick that I hardly realized it was happening.'

'Mmmn.'

They lay in silence for a while, listening to the clickety-clack of the train. Amy liked to think of all the towns and villages they were sweeping past, full of darkened houses and sleeping families.

'Amy, do you think we'll always tell each other things?'

'I hope so. Sisters are closer than friends, aren't they? I can't imagine telling Violet Trent about it, for example.'

'I suppose we should be grateful for that. Good night, little sister.'

'Not so little, Isabel dear. Good night.'

Even to Isabel, Amy had not mentioned the smallness and bareness of Luis's home, so full of so many people, or the way he had said *We are lucky ones*. That was something she wanted to think about for herself.

Back at the house in London, Bethan's weekly letter from her mother was waiting for her. Once the trunks had been brought safely in, the clamour of arrival had died down, and Lady Lovell had gone to her room to rest, Bethan took the letter out of her apron pocket and went upstairs to her room at the top of the house to read it.

The letters were a lifeline, stretching between the valleys and her life in service, holding her to the tight, united community even though she could only spend her two weeks' holiday a year as a real part of it.

They have had the Inquiry, such as it was. The Mines Inspector found negligence, and Peris and Cruickshank were prosecuted all right. The magistrates fined them the Great Sum of £5.10s. Half-a-crown a man's life, they're saying here. There's terrible feeling about it, but the pit's still closed and there's talk that Peris won't ever open it no more because it costs him less just to run seams in other pits. Those who are in work like your dad are all with them that aren't but it's hard to think of another strike coming. Nick Penry from Glasdir Terrace and them are all behind it. Your dad says they're right, but I can't see further than no money coming in for weeks on end, myself. Nick Penry's marrying that Mari Powell that came up from Tonypandy, all in a hurry it seems to me. I don't doubt I'll be called up there at the end of six months or so.

Bethan smiled over the cramped, hurried handwriting. Her mother had three men down the pit on different shifts, each one wanting hot water and hot food at different hours of the long day. The tiny back kitchen was steamy with the big pan of water on the fire and the potatoes boiling. In the short night between the end of the last shift and the beginning of the next, an anxious father would often come knocking at the door and Bethan's mother would struggle out of bed and collect her midwife's bag. She had no proper training, only what she had learned from experience and her own mother, but she was vital in Nantlas where no one could afford the doctor.

The letter went on. Bethan was frowning now as she read.

Bethan lamb, when will it be your turn? I know you said you never would after Dai was killed, but it's seven years since 1917. Write and tell me you're walking out with some nice young man and make me happy. We need some happiness, God knows. Well, *cariad*, I must close now. William will be back up just now. God bless you. Your loving MAM.

There never will be anyone else, Bethan thought. She had only wanted to marry Dai, and he had died at Pilckheim Ridge, a year after Airlie Lovell. No. She would stay with Amy and Isabel as long as they needed her, and after that, well, she would find something.

Bethan folded her letter carefully into four and replaced it in her apron pocket. Then she went downstairs where thirty-two pieces of luggage were waiting to be unpacked.

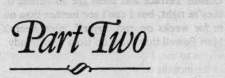

Part Two

4

London, February 1931

Amy was wandering listlessly around the room, picking up a crystal bottle and sniffing at the scent before putting it down again unremarked, then fingering the slither of heavy cream satin that was Isabel's new robe waiting to be packed at the top of one of the small cases.

It was peculiar to think that tomorrow night Peter Jaspert's large, scrubbed hands would probably undo this broad sash, and then reach up to slip the satin off his wife's shoulders. Isabel would be Mrs Peter Jaspert then. Amy wondered whether Isabel was thinking about that too. Didn't every bride, on the night before her wedding? But it was impossible to judge from Isabel's face what she was thinking. She looked as calm and serene as she always did. She was sitting patiently in front of her dressing-table mirror while her maid worked on her hair. Isabel had her own maid now, who would travel with her on the honeymoon, and then they would settle into the house that Peter Jaspert had bought in Ebury Street.

Amy and Bethan would be left behind at Lovell House in Bruton Street. The town house didn't feel as cavernously huge as it had done when Amy was a child, but it could be very quiet and empty, and faintly gloomy. It was all right now, of course, because it was full of preparations for the wedding. But once that was over, what then?

'I'll miss you so much, Bel,' Amy said abruptly. Isabel looked at her sister's reflection in the glass beside her own. She thought that you could tell what Amy was like just by watching her for five minutes. She was so restless, incapable of keeping still so long as there was any new thing to be investigated or assimilated. When there was nothing new or interesting, she was stifled and irritable. Her face reflected it all, always flickering with naked feelings for anyone to read. Isabel herself wasn't anything like that. Feelings were private things, to be kept hidden or shared only with the closest friends. Amy didn't care if the taxidriver or butcher's boy knew when she was in the depths of despair.

She needed a calming influence, and a focus for her days, Isabel decided. A husband and a home would give her that, when the right time came. She smiled at Amy.

'I'm hardly more than a mile away. We'll see each other every day, if you would like that. And I'll be a married woman, remember. We can do all kinds of things together that we couldn't do before.'

Amy dropped the robe back on to the bed. 'Go to slightly more risky restaurants for lunch, you mean? To the theatre unescorted? Will that really make any difference? You'll be gone, and you can't pretend that anything will ever be the same. That's what I'm worried about. You'll be too busy giving little dinners for Peter's business cronies and his allies from the House, and going to their little dinners, and whenever I come to see you I'll be just a visitor in your house . . .'

'That's what wives do, Amy,' Isabel said quietly. 'You don't understand that because you're not ready to marry. And I'm sorry if you feel that my house, and Peter's house, won't be just as much a home to you as this one is.'

Amy was contrite immediately.

'Oh darling, I'm sorry.' She knelt down beside Isabel's chair. 'I shouldn't go on about my own woes when it's your big day tomorrow and you've got enough to think about. They're such little woes, anyway.' She forced the brightness back into her face and hugged her sister. 'I shall love to come to see you in your pretty house, if Peter will have me, and of course we'll do all kinds of things together. I hope you'll be very, very happy, too. If anyone deserves to be made happy it's you, Isabel Lovell. Mrs Jaspert-to-be.'

Bethan came in, her arms full of the freshly ironed pieces of Isabel's complicated trousseau. It had taken two months to assemble it. Bethan's eyes went straight to the robe on the bed.

'The creases! Amy, is this your doing? Isabel will be taking it out of her bag tomorrow night looking like a rag.'

'All my doing, Bethan. I'm sorry. I just looked at it. I'll take it down now and press it again myself.'

Bethan took it out of her hands at once. 'You'll do nothing of the kind. A nice scorch mark on the front is all it needs. Just go and get yourself ready for the party.'

'Do, Amy,' Isabel said. 'They'll need you.' Her maid had finished wrapping the long red hair up in tight papers, and now she was methodically stroking thick white cream on to the bride's face. Amy nodded. Isabel meant Gerald and Adeline. Amy blew a kiss from the door and went next door to her own room, wondering if she looked as heavy-hearted as she felt. If she did, she was not going to be a great asset at the pre-wedding party.

Bethan had laid her evening dress out on the bed for her, and in the bathroom across the corridor that she shared with Isabel everything would be put out ready for her bath. But instead of beginning to get ready, Amy sat down in the chair at her writing-desk. The curtains were drawn against the February dark, but she stared at them as if she could see through and into the familiar street view. She was thinking that for nineteen years, ever since babyhood, she had shared a room with Isabel, or at least slept in adjoining rooms as they did now. They had hardly ever been separated for more than a night or two. And now they had come to the last night, and tomorrow Isabel would be gone.

It was going to be very lonely without her. It had started already. Usually Isabel and Amy would have prepared for a stiff evening like this one together, and then afterwards they would have laughed about it. But tonight the guests were elderly relatives and old family friends who had come up from the country for the wedding, and the party was to be their introduction to the bridegroom. Because Peter was to be there, the bride had to stay hidden. 'What archaic rubbish,' Amy had said, but nobody had paid any attention. The bride was to have a tray in her room, and Amy would have to go down and go through the smiling rituals and the interminable dinner afterwards on her own. There would be Colonel Hawes-Douglas, and the local Master of Foxhounds, and numerous old aunts and second cousins. There wasn't even Richard to help her out. He was supposed to be coming home from Eton on twenty-four hours' leave, but he hadn't put in an appearance yet.

'Bugger,' Amy said. 'Bugger it *all*.'

She went across the landing and ran her bath, then she plunged into the water and topped it up until it was as hot as she could bear. It would make her face as red as a boiled beetroot, but that was too bad. Perhaps the heat would sap some of the loneliness and frustration and irritation out of her.

If it had been different with Mother and Father, Amy thought, perhaps losing Isabel would have been easier to bear. But it wasn't different. It was exactly the same as it had been for years and years.

Hugh Herbert had been the first of Adeline's lovers. It had all been conducted with perfect discretion, and with never a whisper of scandal, but it had been the end of her marriage to Gerald. There could be no question of divorce for Lord and Lady Lovell, but they had simply arranged their lives so that they didn't meet. When Adeline was in London, or staying in a house-party where Hugh was tactfully given a bedroom close to hers, Gerald was at Chance. When Adeline entertained one of her carefully chosen gatherings of amusing people at Chance, Gerald was in London or shooting in Scotland. They were only obliged to meet each other on rare, formal occasions such as family weddings or the girls' presentations at Court. They were always rigidly polite to one another, as if they had just met, and they would be just the same tonight. It was just that sometimes Amy saw her father look at her mother with a kind of baffled, suppressed longing, and Adeline never noticed it at all. She would say, 'Gerald, do you think we should move through into dinner?' but she would never see him properly.

Amy could remember exactly when she had recognized the truth. They had been sitting on the lawn at Chance, under the cedar tree, and a man called Jeremy had been leaning over her mother's shoulder, pointing to something in the magazine she was holding. His hand had brushed her shoulder, and Adeline had smiled like a young girl. *They love each other*, she thought, and suddenly she understood the succession of special friends, always men, who took up so much of her mother's time. She had confided in Isabel, and Isabel had nodded gravely. 'Yes. I think you're right. But you must never, ever mention it to anyone.'

That night Amy had committed it all to her journal, under the big black heading PRIVATE. She was fifteen.

Amy sighed now in her over-hot bath. It was making her feel sadder instead of soothing her, and the prospect of the evening was growing steadily blacker. She stood up to break the mood and rubbed herself ferociously with the big white towel that Bethan had put out for her.

Perhaps Richard would have arrived.

It would help to have him here, even though it was Richard who chafed the soreness between their parents. Amy had witnessed it dozens of times, first seeing Gerald flare from silence into scornful rage at some refusal or attitude of Richard's, and then watching Adeline leap to Richard's defence. They were the only times that her languid, social mask dropped in family gatherings. Gerald would frown angrily and walk away, but there was something in the way he carried himself that betrayed loneliness to Amy. She had tried sometimes to offer him her company, but he always said something like, 'Shouldn't you be in the schoolroom?' or, more lately, 'Haven't you got a party to go to?'

Back in her room Amy put on her dress without enthusiasm. Adeline's taste in her own clothes was impeccable, and so simple as to be almost stark. Her utterly plain sheath dresses worn with a sequinned blazer were much copied, as were her dramatic strokes like wearing a necklace of wildflowers when every other woman in the room was loaded with diamonds. Adeline always had the best idea first. But she preferred to see her daughters in what she called 'fresh, pretty clothes'. Isabel would have looked ravishing in these sweet ruffles, but against Amy's rangy height and firm, high-cheekboned face they were less successful. She hooked the dress up and stared briefly at her reflection.

'Oh God,' she said, and then smiled. Well, the effect wasn't quite so bad when she smiled.

In the long drawing-room on the first floor a handful of elderly guests were already peering mistrustfully into their cocktail glasses. A trio of red-faced men were standing with Gerald in a semicircle around the fire, and their wives were perched with Adeline on the daringly modern white-upholstered sofas. Adeline had had the drawing-room done over, and had banished all the glowering family portraits and brocaded covers in favour of pale polished wood and white hangings. In the middle of it, in her plain black crêpe, Adeline looked stunning. Amy kissed her cheek.

'Darling, such a pink face,' Adeline murmured. 'Thank God you're down. Is Isabel all right?'

'Cool as a cucumber.'

'That's something. Where is Richard, the little beast?'

'I haven't seen him. He can't have turned up yet.'

'That means utter destruction of the dinner *placement*. I was counting on him to talk nicely to Lady Jaspert.'

'Probably exactly why he isn't here. I shouldn't worry about the table. It's only family, isn't it? It's not as though we're expecting the Prince of Wales.'

'No, unfortunately.'

That was a sore point, Amy recalled. Adeline moved on the fringes of the Fort Belvedere set, but HRH had declined the wedding invitation. The Yorks would represent Their Majesties at St Margaret's, Westminster, tomorrow, but it wasn't quite the coup for Adeline that the presence of the Prince himself would have been.

'Do go and talk to people, Amy, before Peter gets into completely full flood.'

Isabel's fiancé was a bulky, handsome man with a high, English county complexion, very sleek blond hair and bright, shrewd eyes. As the eldest son he would inherit in due course, but he was not attracted by the prospect of following his father into obscurity as another country peer. Peter Jaspert was an ambitious City man. ('Metals. Manganese or aluminium or something,' Adeline would say with deliberately affected vagueness. She had long ago given up the cherished dream that Isabel might make the grandest match of all, but still Peter Jaspert wasn't quite what she had hoped for. There were no possible grounds for objecting to him, but Adeline was faintly disappointed. 'Her happiness is all that matters. Anything else is up to you now, darling,' was the only oblique reference she had ever made about it to Amy.)

Peter had also recently fought and won a by-election as the Conservative candidate. He had proposed to Isabel the day after taking his seat in Parliament. He was poised for rapid advancement, and he had chosen Isabel Lovell as the utterly correct wife to help him on his way.

Amy crossed the room to him. He was talking to one of Gerald's ancient, deaf cousins.

'What? What?'

'I said there will certainly have to be a General Election by the end of the year. We can win it, on the National coalition ticket if you like, and then there's nothing standing in the way of tariff reform. Which is the thing the economy needs, as we all know. Hello, hello, little sister. What a pretty frock. Everything ready for the big day, is it?'

'Hello, Peter. GOOD EVENING, Uncle Edward.'

The evening was perfectly orchestrated, perfectly predictable and completely dull. Gerald sat at the head of the massive, polished dinner table, separated from his wife by twenty people. Peter Jaspert dutifully made sure that he spoke to every one of the guests who had been invited to meet him. Amy smiled long and hard and reassured a succession of aunts that yes, Isabel was blissfully happy and yes, they did seem to be very much in love.

Richard didn't put in an appearance at all.

Gerald's face betrayed a flicker of cold fury when they went through to dinner and he saw that Glass had discreetly rearranged the places, but that was all.

It was past midnight when Glass finally saw the last guests into their cars. He left the huge double doors firmly closed, but not locked, and then he walked silently back across the marble floor where the exquisite arrangements of arum lilies stood ready for tomorrow.

Up in her drawing-room Adeline sighed. 'Well, that was rather a trial. Isabel must be asleep by now, so I won't disturb her. Good night Gerald, Amy. Let's pray for not a wisp of fog tomorrow, shall we?'

After she had gone Gerald poured himself a last glass of whisky from the decanter and looked across at Amy.

'You'll miss your sister, won't you?'

She nodded, surprised.

'Mn. Yes. You've been close, the three of you. Things being . . . as they are.'

Amy waited, wondering if he was going to say anything else. If he was going to ask her where Richard was, even mention him at all. Dimly, she felt that he wanted to but couldn't begin, and she was clumsily unable to help him. But Gerald turned away, saying irritably, 'Well. It'll be your turn next, marrying some damn fool who can't even wear proper evening clothes like a gentleman.'

'Everyone wears dinner jackets these days,' Amy said mildly. 'Peter's hardly in the shocking forefront there.' She felt disappointed, as if something important had almost happened and then been interrupted.

'Good night,' Gerald said.

She went to him and kissed his cheek, and felt as she touched him that he was suddenly quite old.

Amy went slowly up the stairs to her room. Her jaw felt cracked with smiling and her head ached. It was a familiar feeling at the end of an evening. She even brought it home with her from debutante dances, when she was supposed to be dancing, and enjoying herself, and falling in love. As Isabel had done, presumably. But Amy doubted that it would ever work for her. Amy had begun her first Season, two years ago now, with all the zest and enthusiasm that she brought to anything new. The dances had seemed amazingly glamorous after the strictures of Miss Abbott's school, and the men she met had all struck her as sophisticated and witty. But then, so quickly that she was ashamed, the idea of another dance with the same band, and the same food, and the same faces, preceded by the same sort of dinner with a new identical partner whose name was the only thing that distinguished him from the last, had become dull instead of exciting. Amy was puzzled to find that most of the young men bored her, whether they were soldiers, or City men, or just young men who went to dances all the time. The few who didn't bore her made her shy, and tongue-tied, and they soon drifted on to the vivacious girls whom Amy envied because they always looked as if they were enjoying themselves so much. Isabel had been one of them. She had the ability to look happy and interested, wherever she was, and she had been one of the most popular girls of her year. Peter Jaspert was lucky to have her.

Amy shivered a little and sat down at her writing-desk again. She pulled her big, black leather-covered journal towards her. She tried to write something every day, even though the aridity of the last months was more of a reproach than a pleasure. Desultorily, before starting to write, she flicked back through the pages. Here were the early days, full of schoolroom passions and rivalries, and long accounts of hunting at Chance. Two years ago came the explosion of her coming-out, with minute descriptions of every dress and every conversation. Here was the night when a subaltern had kissed her in a taxi, and she had felt his collar-stud digging into her and the shaved-off prickle of hair at the nape of his neck. She had thought sadly of Luis, and politely let the boy go on kissing her until they reached their destination.

Amy turned to the day of her presentation at Court. At three o'clock in the afternoon she had dressed in a long white satin dress with a train, tight snow-white gloves that came up over her elbows, and Lady Lovell's maid had secured two white Prince of Wales' feathers in her hair.

> A great day [she had written]. Why was I so nervous? The Mall was one long line of cars to the Palace gates with white feathers nodding in each one. There were people all along the roadside to watch us arriving. Then all at once we were walking down the long red carpets past the flunkeys and there were seven girls in white dresses in front of me, then four, three, two and one, then I heard my name and all I could think was *gather the train up, step forward, right foot behind left, head bowed and down, down, count to three and then up again*. I didn't fall over or drop my flowers. And then the King said something about Father at the Coronation . . .

Someone tapped at Amy's door.

'It's me. Can I come in? I can't sleep at all.'

Isabel came in wrapped in her old dressing-gown, and sat down on the bed.

'Are you scared?' Amy asked, and she shook her head.

'Not exactly. Just thinking how . . . important it all is. How did Peter look?'

'Very handsome,' Amy said truthfully. 'And he was wonderful with Uncle Edward and the colonel and all the rest of them.'

'He is, isn't he? I look at him sometimes when we're with people and I feel so proud of him, and yet I feel that I don't know him at all, and that he isn't the private kind of man he is when we're alone together.'

'Do you know the private man, as you call it?'

Isabel blushed. 'Not . . . not altogether physically, if you mean that. Neither of us felt that that was the right thing to do. But I think I do understand him. When he asked me to marry him, everything seemed suddenly simple, and clear, and I knew that I should accept.'

'I'm glad,' Amy said softly.

They were silent for a moment, and then Isabel asked in a lighter voice, 'What are you doing?'

79

'Just writing in my diary. Or no, not even that. Looking back, instead of facing up to today. I was reading about the day I was presented. It seemed so important then, and so completely pointless now.'

Isabel laughed. 'Oh dear, yes. I remember mine. I was directly behind Anne Lacy, who looked so beautiful no one could take their eyes off her. I could have been wearing trousers and a lampshade on my head and no one would have noticed.'

'Don't be ridiculous. The Prince of Wales danced with you twice, the very same evening.'

'Oh, do you remember? Mother thought our hour had come at last. Now you'll have to marry him instead.'

'Not a chance. I can never think of a word to say. Insipidity personified. I don't know why Mother doesn't try for him herself. She's much more his type.' They were still laughing, and Amy was thinking *Is this the last time we'll do this?* when they heard quick, unsteady footsteps outside.

'Is this a private party, my sisters, or can anyone join in?'

'Richard.'

He was still wearing his school change coat, and his hair and trousers were soaked with rain.

'I walked. From Soho, can you imagine? Tell me quickly, am I disinherited completely?'

'Nothing was said. Father just gave us one of his white, silent looks when he realized you weren't coming.'

'Poor old tyrant. What about Mother?'

'Worried about the table. You were promised to Lady Jaspert.'

'Oh, dear God. Well, too late to worry now. And look, I'm not all bad. I've brought us this. The little man promised me that it was cold enough. Chilled further, I should think, by being hugged to my icy chest.'

From the recesses of his coat Richard produced a bottle of champagne. 'Do you have any glasses in your boudoir, Amy, or shall I nip downstairs for some?'

'You'll have to go and get some. And change your clothes at the same time or you'll get pneumonia.'

'Well now, isn't this snug?' Richard reappeared in a thick tartan dressing-gown that made him look like a little boy again. He had rubbed his hair dry so that it stood up in fluffy peaks. He opened the champagne dexterously and poured it without spilling a drop.

'Where have you been?' Isabel asked. 'It doesn't matter about the party, and I'm glad you've turned up for the wedding itself, but you're much too young to be wandering about in Soho, and drinking. Don't pretend you haven't been.'

'I wouldn't pretend to pretend,' Richard said equably. He had developed the habit of looking out at the world under lowered eyelids that still didn't disguise the quickness of his stare. He raised his glass to his sister. 'Long life and happiness to you, Isabel. And I suppose that has to include Jaspert too. May his acres remain as broad as his beam and his fortunes in the pink like his face . . .'

'Shut up, Richard,' Amy ordered. 'Where have you been?'

'I came up on the four o'clock train like a good little boy. I was going to have tea with Tony Hardy at his publishing house and then come home to change. You remember Tony? As a matter of fact he's coming to the wedding. I got Mother to ask him. D'you mind him being at your wedding, Bel?'

'Not in the least.'

'Good. It will be a help to me, you know, to have an ally amongst the ranks of duchesses. So, I went decorously to meet Tony at Randle & Cates and we talked about an idea I have. Then Tony suggested that we go across to the pub for a drink. Somehow one thing led to another, after that. We had dinner with a jazz singer and a woman who owns a night-club, and about twenty others. It was a good deal more interesting than school supper and study hour, I can tell you. I lost Tony in the course of it all, and when I finally decided to extricate myself I realized that I had laid out my last farthing on your champagne and had to walk all the way back here in the rain. There you are. Nothing too culpable in that, is there?'

'Tony Hardy should know better,' Isabel said.

'Unlike you, Tony knows that I can perfectly well take care of myself.'

'I'm jealous,' Amy told him. 'I've never met a jazz singer in my life. Didn't you look rather peculiar, a schoolboy amongst all those people?'

'I was the object of some interest,' Richard said with satisfaction, 'but no one thought anything was peculiar. That's the point, you see. Everything is acceptable, whatever it is.'

'It's not exactly the conventional way to behave.' Isabel was frowning.

'I'm not conventional. Surely you can't condemn me for that? I don't think Amy is, either. But you are, Isabel, and that's why you're going to marry Peter Jaspert tomorrow in the family lace and diamonds, in front of half the Royal Family and with your picture in all the dailies.' Richard stood up and put his glass down with exaggerated care. Then he went and put his arms around his sister and hugged her. 'I hope you'll be so happy,' he said seriously. 'For ever and ever.'

Isabel smiled at him, her anxiety gone. 'Thank you.'

They drank their champagne, and Amy made them laugh by recounting the excitements of her evening. 'Every time Peter mentioned Ramsay MacDonald or the balance of payments or anything unconnected with horses or crops, Uncle Edward would shout "What? What? Can't understand a thing the boy says."'

At last Isabel stood up. 'I'd better try and get some sleep. I think I'll be able to, now I've had something to drink. Clever of you, Richard.'

'Anything to help. I have to say one serious thing before you go.'

Isabel turned back again, alarm showing in her face.

'What is it?'

'It's a delicate point, but . . . well, someone ought to raise it. Just in case it's been overlooked. Are you quite clear on the facts of life? Bees and birds and so forth? It's just that Jaspert might seem to behave pretty oddly tomorrow night, and you should know why.'

'Richard, you are horrible. I know everything I need to know, and a good deal more than you.'

'I wouldn't be so sure of that,' he said quietly. 'Good night, Isabel darling.' All three of them hugged each other.

After Isabel had gone, Richard said, 'Will it be all right for her, do you suppose?'

'I've no idea.' Amy was heavy-hearted again.

'You'll still have me, you know,' Richard reminded her.

'I don't think I will, by the sound of things. You're already overtaking me.'

'Poor Amy. It must be harder, being a girl. You should do something. Something other than getting measured for frocks and going to lunch, or whatever it is women do all day. The world's full of girls out there doing things. I saw some in Tony's offices today.'

'I know,' Amy said. 'Of course I must do something. I don't think I'm going to find a Peter Jaspert for myself, and I can't sit about here or at Chance for ever. The question is, what could I do? I'm not any use for anything.'

'That doesn't sound very much like you,' Richard said gently. 'It's your life to live, isn't it? Not anyone else's.'

Lady Lovell's prayers had evidently been answered. The morning of Isabel's wedding was bright, and frosty clear. When Bethan got up she went straight to the window. The pavements were shiny wet, but the sky was the translucent pearly white that would later turn to icy blue. The bare plane trees were motionless. There was no wind, either.

'Let's hope it's the same there,' Bethan murmured. She looked at the cheap alarm clock beside her bed and saw that there were a few minutes to spare. A quick note dashed off to Mam wouldn't be quite the same thing as Bethan being there herself, but at least they would know that she was thinking of them.

> All ready here, at last [she wrote]. The coming and going, you wouldn't believe it. Thirty people here for dinner last night, and that just a small party of family to meet Mr Jaspert. Miss Isabel stayed in her room. She is as lovely and calm in the middle of it all as I would have expected her to be. My poor Amy is going to miss her, I know that much. I wish I could have been there with you, Mam, to see Nannon and Gwyn today, but I know you'll all understand. They would have given me time if I'd asked, I'm sure of that, but with having had my two weeks and with Amy needing me, I felt I should stay here with them. But just the same I will be thinking of you at home.
>
> How sad it is that the minister has gone from Nantlas. I would have liked to think of Nannon walking up to the Chapel in her white dress, on Dad's arm, and everyone coming out on their steps to wave, like they used to. It's not so easy to imagine the Ferndale registry.
>
> I wonder what you're doing this minute, Mam? Perhaps you're sitting by the range with Nannon, brushing her hair.

Or no, most likely you're making the sandwiches. Is the Hall up at the Welfare all decorated with streamers, like they used to do it? At least you've got Dad there to help you. Did he understand about the money I sent? I don't need it for anything here. I wish it could have been more, and of course Nannon should have a reception on her wedding day as fine as anyone in Nantlas. I know how hard it is when there isn't the work. I'm sure that things will have to get better soon. Pits can't stay closed for always, can they? I hope Nannon found the bit of money useful too. I'd have got her a present of course, but if she's going to be living with Gwyn's family for a bit perhaps she'd rather have it to spend on herself, instead of pots or blankets. Think of my little sister being married. How glad you must be that Gwyn's in the Co-op and not down the pit. He may be a bit old for her, but he's a good, kind man and I'm sure he'll make Nannon happy. I'll be thinking of you all day, you especially, Mam.

It's fine and clear here, and I pray it is in Nantlas too. God bless you all, your loving BETHAN.

Bethan folded her letter and put it into the envelope. There would be just enough time to run out to the post with it before going down to Amy.

Mari Penry sat back on her heels and stared at the sullen grate. They had let the fire in the range go out to save coal, and now she couldn't get it going again with the dusty slack left in the bucket.

'Are you cold, Dickon?' she asked the child. He didn't answer, nor did she expect him to, but she always made sure to include him in everything. Dickon was sitting in his usual place, close to the range in the little low chair that Nick had made for him. Mari pulled her own thin cardigan closer around her and went to feel his hands. The fingers were cold, but his stomach under the layers of woollens was warm enough.

'Well then,' she said, hugging him. 'We'll wait till your dad comes back, and then we'll go up to the wedding party and leave the stupid old fire, shall we?'

Dickon looked up at her, and rewarded her with one of

his rare smiles that broke his round, solemn face into sudden affection.

'That's my boy,' Mari said. She went through into the front parlour to look out of the window for Nick. It was even colder in here, with a dampness that seemed to cling to the walls and the few pieces of furniture. Mari pulled the lace curtain at the window aside and peered out.

Half a dozen children were playing chasing games from one side of the road to the other, and at the corner a knot of men in scarves and collars turned up against the cold were talking together. There was no sign of Nick in either direction. Mari sighed and straightened the curtain again. She would have liked to make a pot of tea, but without the fire she couldn't boil the kettle.

'Mari? You there?' The back kitchen door banged. Nick must have come the other way, down the back entry. She ran through into the kitchen. Nick had picked Dickon up out of his chair and was swinging him up and down. Dickon was chuckling and pulling at his father's hair.

'I thought you'd left home, you've been gone so long.'

Gently Nick lowered the boy back into his seat. Dickon's eyes followed him as he moved around the room.

'Left home? Hardly,' Nick said, with the bitterness that rarely faded out of his voice nowadays. He looked around, frowning. 'It's too cold in here for Dickon.'

'I couldn't get the fire going again, with that.' Mari pointed to the bucket. 'He's all right, under his clothes.'

'I got half a sack of good stuff. I'll have the place warm in ten minutes. And I called in at the Co-op. Gwyn Jones is off, of course, but they let me have a loaf and some other bits for now.'

Nick had been up at the shut-down No. 2 pit, picking over the slag heap for lumps of coal. Mr Peris didn't allow scavenging, as he called it, around his pits but the managers often turned a blind eye. Half the men of Nantlas were out of work now that the second pit was closed, and for many of them it was the only way of keeping their families warm.

Mari watched him busying himself over the fire.

'I thought we could leave it,' she said. 'As we're going up to the Welfare later.'

Nick shrugged. 'I'd forgotten that.'

'You would forget, wouldn't you? Anything nice that happens, for once? All you can remember is meetings, and committees, and the Federation. Why can't you leave it? You aren't even a miner any more, are you?'

Nick seemed not to hear her. He put a match to a tight coil of newspaper, and a yellow tongue of flame shot upwards. Dickon crooned with pleasure at the sight of it.

'Nick? Please, Nick.' Mari's shoulders hunched up, and she didn't even try to blink the tears out of her eyes. 'What's happened to everything?'

Carefully Nick smoothed a sheet of newspaper across the front of the grate and shut the oven doors on it to hold it in place. Behind it the fire flickered up and began to crackle cheerfully. Only when he was sure that it had caught properly did he turn round to Mari.

'You know what's happened,' he said. 'And you know why. There's no work for me, or for most of the men in this valley. We've eighteen shillings a week to live on, after the rent. The only hope for change in this industry is the lads themselves. We've got to win worker control some day, Mari, and the only way to do that is to go on fighting, through all the meetings and committees, as you call them, or starve to death first.'

'Starve to death, then,' Mari said, 'For all the good any of you are doing.'

Nick's arm shot out and he pulled her around so quickly that her head jerked backwards. 'Never say that. Never, do you hear?' Then he saw the tracks of tears on her cheeks, and remembered how rosy her cheeks had been when they were first married. Instead of shaking her, as he had almost done, he pulled her roughly to him. Her head fitted gratefully into the hollow of his shoulder and he kissed her hair. 'I'm sorry,' he whispered. 'I told you what it was going to be like, that first day down at Barry Island, didn't I? Perhaps you shouldn't have said yes. You could have married anyone you wanted. Kept your job up at the Lodge, instead of losing it because of me.'

'I never wanted anyone else,' Mari said. She rubbed her face against him, solacing herself with his familiarity. She knew all of him, the grim will-power and the stubborn pride just as well as his face and the set of his shoulders under the old coat, and she still loved him.

'Mari,' Nick whispered, 'let's go upstairs for half an hour. Dickon will be all right down here in the warm.'

She hesitated for a second, thinking longingly, and then she shook her head. 'It's too risky this time of the month. Next week, Nick, it'll be all right then.'

'I'll be careful.' He kissed her mouth, tracing the shape of it with his own.

She clung to him, his warmth warming her, but she said 'No, Nick. It isn't safe.'

I couldn't go through Dickon again, she wanted to cry to him. Not the day he was born, nor the time after when we were finding out what was wrong. Not another baby. And if one did come, even if it wasn't like Dickon, how could we care for it, on what we've got? There were too many families in Nantlas with hungry children. No more babies in this family. Not while the world was like this.

But Mari didn't say any more. It was old, well-trodden ground between Nick and herself and she knew from experience that it was less hurtful to let the silence grow between them than to go round in the old, painful circles yet again. Nick let his arms drop to his sides.

'Well. Put the kettle on, will you, my love? Let's pretend that a nice pot of tea will do just as much good. And how could a pot of tea make you pregnant?'

Towards the end of the afternoon, when it was already dark in the valley bottom, the Penrys carefully damped down their fire and set off up the hill to the Miners' Welfare. Dickon could walk almost as well as other children now, although it had taken him years of effort to learn, but he began to whimper with cold halfway up the street and Nick swung him up into his arms without breaking his stride. There were bright lights in the Welfare Hall and groups of people were coming towards it from all directions. Nick and Mari walked in silence, staring straight ahead of them. They quarrelled too often now, and it was growing harder to make up their differences as they would once have done, impulsively.

The Welfare was the heart of Nantlas now that the congregation could no longer afford a minister for the chapel. It was funded by the Federation, and people came to it for company, for books and classes, support and sympathy, and for the occasional celebration like Nannon Jones's wedding that still managed to happen, somehow. The long, dingy green-painted hall was hung from side to side with paper streamers, salvaged from Christmas decoration boxes and forgotten Gala days. On the stage at the far end were the music stands and instrument cases of the choir and silver band, waiting for the climax of the evening when the singing would start. Beneath the stage on a trestle table covered with a white cloth, the wedding cake was given pride of place. Nannon Jones had baked it herself, and put hours of work into the carefully piped white icing. Down the length of the hall were more trestles decorated with red and green crêpe paper, laden with neat plates of sandwiches, pies and cakes. The Welfare tea-urns stood ready, and there were barrels of beer as well, and even bottles of sherry bought with the money Bethan had sent.

The bride and groom stood at the hall door with their parents, welcoming the guests. Gwyn Jones was almost forty, short-sighted and weak-chested, but he was a popular manager of the Co-op. You could always get a bit of help from Gwyn when you were short, the Nantlas women said. Local opinion approved of the match, even though Nannon Jones was hardly into her twenties.

'Well done, well done,' the older guests murmured to each set of parents as they shuffled past. 'And a fine spread, too. Well done to you.'

There was much admiration of the feast set out on the tables. Everyone understood the scheming and saving that must have gone into providing it, and appreciated the generosity of offering it for share. There were no whispers about trying to go one better, or making a show. Hardship had drawn the valley communities closer together.

Myfanwy Jones, the village midwife, stood at the door beside her husband. She was beaming with happiness. At least her youngest had found a good, solid man who would look after her and not ask her to live with the fear that he would walk out of the door one morning in his pit clothes and with his snap-box under his arm and never come back.

She greeted the Penrys with extra warmth as they came in. She never forgot any of the babies she delivered, but she was not likely to forget the night of Dickon's birth.

There had been nothing unusual to start with. Mari's pains had been coming steadily all evening and into the night, and Myfanwy had been reassuring her that the baby would be born soon. Then she had bent over to listen to the baby's heartbeat, and it had gone. Mari's face was suddenly grey against the pillows. The midwife ran to the top of the stairs and shouted to Nick, sitting by the kitchen range. 'Run! Run up for Dr Owen, ask him if he'll come down. She needs forceps.' There had been a flutter from the baby's heart as she listened again, faint and irregular, and then nothing.

The minutes dragged past.

Into the silence came the stumbling crash of Nick running back up the stairs. 'He can't come. His wife says he's gone up to one of the children at the Lodge. Oh God, look at her. Save her. I don't care about the baby, if you can save Mari.'

'I'll save them both,' Myfanwy Jones said grimly. It wasn't the first time that Dr Owen had been unable to come to a house that was unlikely to be able to provide him with his fee. 'You'll have to help me. Hold her, will you?'

Myfanwy knew what to do, although only doctors were supposed to practise it. She even had the right instruments ready in her bag, but only when there was no other alternative could she resort to her own skills.

She took the things out, not looking at Nick Penry's dead white face. 'Hold her properly,' she ordered him harshly.

When Dickon was dragged out into the world his face and hands and feet were blue, and he was completely still.

'She'll do,' Myfanwy said after a brief glance at Mari, and she bent over the huddled baby. She cleared the tiny air passages, and then tried everything she knew to make him breathe.

'Come on, my darling,' she whispered to him like a lover. 'Breathe for me.'

At last, after eternities of time, there was a tiny, thin wail. Mari's eyes opened and fixed on the baby. The blueness began to ebb from Dickon's face and Myfanwy breathed again herself. Only when Mari was comfortable and the baby was wrapped up in his father's arms did she say as gently as she could, 'I think he will be all right for now. But I can't say for . . . later. He went a long time without breathing. Do you understand?'

Mari was too weak to take anything in, and she didn't know whether Nick had even heard her. He sat quite still, with the baby hugged to his chest, staring right through her, right through the wall and out into the street.

Six years ago, that was, Myfanwy remembered. The year after the explosion in No. 1 Pit.

'Hello, my lamb,' she said now to Dickon. 'There's the big boy.'

The child stared back at her. It was impossible to tell how much he understood.

'Is he talking much yet?' she asked Mari.

'In his way.' Mari smiled calmly. Nick had already walked past, down to the end of the room where the men were standing in a group at the foot of the stage steps. 'I will. Thank you,' she said. Someone was holding a plate out to her. She wasn't exactly ravenous, they had eaten something before coming out just so that they wouldn't look too hungry, but paste sandwiches, and cake, were almost forgotten luxuries. Mari took a sandwich and broke it carefully in half for Dickon.

When the food was all gone, and the room was full of a warm, satisfied buzz, Nannon's father pushed through the crowd and went up on to the stage. The bride, pink-faced, with her husband beside her, stood just below. William Jones held his arms up.

'Friends. Neighbours and friends. I'm not going to ask you to stop in your enjoyment for too long. Just to join with me in drinking the health of Nannon and Gwyn, and wishing them everything for the future. And in remembering the friends who can't be with us tonight. My eldest daughter, Bethan. And my boy David, in London too, looking for work. Two boys from the other side of our new family as well, Gareth and Glyn, trying their luck in the Midlands. May they be lucky, and may we start to have some luck here too. Here's to some better times for all of us. Cheers, now.'

He raised his pint glass, his red face glowing, and tipped his head back to it. There was an uproar of cheering and clapping and stamping on the wooden floorboards before he held up his hand again.

'Oh yes. One last thing. We've got a new big man with us tonight.'

Faces were turning in the crowd, and heads craning. Mari realized with a sudden sinking fear that they were looking at Nick.

'We've just heard now, elected Secretary of the Rhondda Branch of the SWMF. Nick Penry, a good Nantlas boy if ever there was one. Give him a clap now, for all his hard work in the past, and to come.'

Mari listened to the clapping, frozen.

It was an important post, although an honorary one. It meant that Nick would be working at a level in the Federation that represented all the pit lodges in the Rhondda valleys. Beyond that it would give him a voice at the top level, on the main South Wales executive. Mari knew that it was the beginning of real power for him, the beginning of real influence, in the world that he cared about. Nick was a Communist because its importance confronted him every day of his life.

And yet, he had never even mentioned to her the possibility of his election. Had they already drifted so far apart that he was sure of her disapproval, certain that she would not put her support behind him?

Mari was proud of him still, but she had lost the ability to tell him so. Just as Nick in his turn seemed to have lost the ability to sympathize with her fears and anxieties.

Mari bit her lips and looked across the room at him.

'Speech! Speech!' Nick was being pushed up on to the stage. She watched him, thinking how much at ease he looked on the platform. He wasn't red-faced and awkward like William Jones, nor was he over-confident and strident. He was just Nick himself, and he smiled down at them as though they were all old and well-loved friends.

'I don't want to make a speech . . .'

'Shame! Shame!'

'Let the man speak, will you?'

'. . . and neither do you want to hear one. I just want to say thank you for voting me into a position where I might be able to join in helping us, and the industry, back up off our knees.'

'That's it, Nick boy. You tell 'em.'

'I'm glad that Nannon and Gwyn Jones have given us something to celebrate together, tonight. This is all we've got left now, isn't it? Staying together, all of us, whether it's this village, or the Rhondda, or South Wales, or the whole community of miners all over the country. And what's more . . .'

The room was quiet now. Everyone was watching Nick.

'. . . that's the only thing that really matters. So long as we're together, so long as every one of us in this room, and in every pit and Welfare Hall across the country, believes that miners and not millionaires should run our pits, well then, we can win. Then our children can go to school in boots again, and our wives can go out to buy food for our families.'

There was a moment of complete silence before the clapping and cheering broke out again.

Oh yes, Nick, you believe it, Mari thought. It's all you care about, except perhaps for Dickon. And standing up there, somehow you can make everyone else believe whatever you want. You've got a talent, sure enough. And you're not the kind of man to waste a talent, are you?

The room was full of the warmth of friendliness. Mari lifted her head, watching her husband.

'There you are,' he said. 'I told you I wasn't going to make a speech. Let's get on now and dance and sing, and forget everything for a few hours. We're here to celebrate a wedding, aren't we? I hope you'll be very happy, Nannon and Gwyn. I hope you'll be as happy as Mari and I have been.'

Nick had ducked down from the stage and was pushing his way through the crowd. She saw his head, taller than the others, looking around for her. In Mari's arms Dickon said 'Da' in a pleased voice and held out his arms to him. When Nick reached her side Mari said, without looking at him,

'Why didn't you tell me?'

'Would you have wanted to know?' As he always did, Nick met a challenge with a challenge.

'Husbands and wives usually mention these things to each other. You make me feel like a stranger, Nick. And why wish that on Nannon and Gwyn? I wouldn't want anyone else to have to enjoy our kind of happiness.'

'You still make me happy, Mari,' he said softly. He put his arms around her and Dickon, and forced her to look up so that he could see her face. 'I'm sorry if I can't do the same for you. I'm still the man you married, you know. Just the same.'

Regardless of the crowd around them he kissed her, warm against her cold cheek. 'I could prove it to you, if you'd only let me. Come on, dance with me. At least then I can hold you close and still look decent.'

'What about Dickon?'

'Give him to your mam to hold, for God's sake. Just this once.'

The band was assembled on the stage, and after the tootlings as they tuned up they swept into a waltz. Couples stepped out on to the creaky floor. Amongst the replete pink faces and careful best clothes there was an atmosphere of revelry almost forgotten in Nantlas.

'Why do you blame me,' Nick whispered, 'for trying to make it possible for nights like this to happen every week?'

'I don't blame you, my love.'

Mari carried Dickon over to her mother. The child allowed himself to be handed over uncomplainingly, but he never took his eyes off his parents.

'That's better,' Nick said. 'And now, may I have the pleasure?' He looked proud, and happier than she had seen him for a long, long time.

Mari saw his arms held out to her, and she smiled. Her eyes met Nick's and she caught his happiness. Suddenly, surprisingly, she felt like a young girl again. Their quarrel was all forgotten. The music lifted her spirits higher and she stood for a second swaying in time to it. Then Nick's arms came around her and they were off across the splintery wooden floor.

Mari tilted her head back so that she could look at him. Nick saw a flush of colour in her cheeks, and a light in her face that turned her back into the pretty, merry Mari he had married. He held her tighter and they spun in the dance together.

'Nick?' she whispered.

'Yes, my love?'

'I'm still the woman I was, you know. And I'm . . . glad you're doing the work you are.'

Nick stopped dancing. His head bent quickly over hers and he kissed her. And all around them the waltzing couples smiled and nodded to each other.

When Mari's eyes opened again they were sparkling. For a moment the world felt a warm and festive place.

'Come on, Nick Penry,' she ordered him. 'Let's dance.'

They moved again, holding each other close. Nick was humming to the music. With her head against his shoulder Mari could hear the sound of it, deep in his chest.

It had been a beautiful wedding. There was no need to cry, Amy told herself. Adeline hadn't cried at all, and the bride's mother was almost expected to do that. Amy thought of her mother at the front of the packed, flower-massed church, her skin like white

93

silk against the black velvet Cossack coat and her hair flaming red under the shako hat. No, Adeline wouldn't have cried. Not in front of the Royal Family, and Lady Colefax, and Mr Baldwin. It had been a great day for Adeline and she had orchestrated it perfectly. Nothing as spontaneous as tears would have been allowed to spoil it.

Amy wrung her facecloth out in cold water and pressed it against her eyes. Just five minutes up here in her room, just five minutes to collect herself, and then she would go downstairs again.

The new Mr and Mrs Jaspert had driven away at last, only a few minutes ago, but the party had barely faltered. Adeline's parties were famous, and the departure of the principals was going to make no difference to this one. Or two, rather, Amy decided. In the huge, long room on the first floor the grandees were dancing stiffly under the chandeliers. There was a buffet supper in the dining-room, where the pink claws and ridged shell backs of lobsters stood ferocious guard around the silver bowls filled with black beads of caviar. In the library the tables were set out for cards. But in Adeline's white drawing-room and further up the house, there were noisier, smarter people. Amy had glimpsed a woman in a man's evening suit, with her hair cropped and brushed flat to her head, and another with her arms loaded from wrist to shoulder with ebony and ivory carved bangles. This party, where the sharp babble of conversation rose to the same crescendos as the jazz, was the one Amy wanted to join. She had been slipping into it, listening to the talk and searching for someone she knew well enough to attach herself to, when Bethan came to whisper to her that Isabel and Peter were leaving. They had gone down to the hall together.

Isabel was standing in a blaze of light while Peter shook the hand of everyone in sight. Her going-away suit was the colour of honey, the ankle-length skirt and slim jacket making her look taller. A cloud of fur framed her face, and a single jaunty feather stuck straight up from the top of her little tilted hat.

'She looks lovelier than I've ever seen her,' Bethan murmured.

The sisters kissed each other.

'I'll be back soon,' Isabel promised. Amy gripped her arms. Perhaps she was imagining it, but she thought that under the soft stuff of her suit Isabel was trembling.

Lord and Lady Lovell, perfectly correct, were saying goodbye now. Peter Jaspert shook their hands firmly, and kissed Adeline on both cheeks. Then the front doors were open and a gust of cold air swept around them. Peter put his arm around his wife's shoulders and hurried her out to the car waiting at the foot of the steps. There was a flurry of waving and shouting and then the car roared away. They were gone, and not even Isabel had any idea where Peter was taking her. Glass, his normally impassive face creased by the faintest of smiles, was shutting the doors again. Amy felt a moment of pure, panicky loneliness. She turned round to see that her mother was already on her way up the great curving staircase. Her black dress left her back completely bare, with an impertinent flat bow at the bottom of the deep V. Gerald Lovell, without a backward glance, was on his way to join the card-players in the library. From now on, the party was Adeline's business.

Amy had run up through the crowded house to her bedroom. The day had gone so quickly, she needed a moment to straighten it out in her head, and to fight back the threatening tears. Even in the silence of her room, she could only see a series of images flashing in front of her eyes. Isabel drifting down the aisle on Gerald's arm, a column of pure white silk and lace, with points of blue light flashing from the diamonds in the Lovell tiara. Peter at the altar, turning back the lace veil to touch his lips to Isabel's. Eight tiny bridesmaids and pages in white satin, all blinking at the press photographers clicking at them. Gerald and Adeline, standing stiffly at the head of the stairs to receive the guests, and Richard's studiedly impassive face winking at her over his starched collar. Isabel's small hands closed over Peter's as they pressed the silver knife into the crenellated cake. And Bethan, sobbing quietly in the corner of Isabel's empty room after the last leather trunk had been carried away. Bethan had cried, on the day when her own sister was being married far away without her.

Amy screwed the facecloth up into a ball and flung it away from her. She faced the mirror and addressed herself squarely.

'Pull yourself together. Isabel's married. Of course Isabel was going to marry. Would you have wanted to stop her? What you should do, Amy Lovell, is go downstairs and drink some champagne. Look for someone to dance with. And tomorrow, find something positive to do instead of feeling so sorry for yourself. Is that quite understood?'

The face that looked back at her was still watery-eyed and pink around the nose, but it was less obviously woebegone. Amy shook her head briskly, and her gleaming hair swung in exotic, unfashionable waves around her face. She picked a brush up from the dressing-table and whisked some colour on to her cheeks. 'Much, much better. Someone might actually ask you to dance now.' As she stood up, Amy thought she caught the faintest drift of Isabel's flowery perfume. She took up her own crystal bottle and squirted it determinedly around her. Then she shook out the folds of her dress, thinking approvingly that the pale lavender colour actually suited her, and marched to the door.

The white drawing-room was packed to the walls.

Amy edged her way slowly into it, listening to the snippets of talk that floated out to her.

'Ninety per cent pure shit, darling, but ten per cent genius.'

'A tonal symphony. Poetic asymmetry.'

'And so we went for a Friday-to-Monday, but there was not a soul there . . .'

'Hello.' Someone pushed out of the crowd and stood squarely in front of her. Amy looked up to see Tony Hardy. He still appeared to have inherited his evening clothes from a misshapen relative.

'Don't you remember me?'

'Tony? Of course I do. Isabel always said I should call you Mr Hardy, not Tony.'

Tony smiled at her. 'I remember. Should I call you Miss Lovell, now?'

'Definitely not.'

'So, Amy, are you looking for someone in particular?'

'Just someone to talk to. I know quite a lot of these people by sight, and a few of them well enough to say how d'you do, but no one at all to attach myself to and ask why I feel like an ostrich in my own home at my own sister's wedding. Except for you, that is. Oh, I could go downstairs and dance with Johnny Guild or somebody, and then go out on the balcony and do some damp embracing. But if I stay up here I thought I might be able to step across to where debutantes don't tread. Like Richard did, last night.'

Amy was conscious that she wasn't sounding quite rational. It must be the champagne. Another of the day's images drifted into her head, of the Duchess of York in the church, floating blue feathers framing her face.

Tony was looking at her levelly. 'You don't look anything like an ostrich. You look . . . extremely beautiful. I always thought you would be more beautiful than Isabel, once you grew into yourself.'

Amy stared back at him. He had very light hazel eyes, and eyebrows that went up in peaks. She felt a faint flush of colour rising in her face.

'Let's find somewhere to sit down,' he said. 'Debutantes never tread anywhere near me, will that do? And I think I can promise that I won't embrace you, damply or otherwise.'

As she followed him, Amy wondered why that seemed to amuse him.

They found a sofa in an alcove. A tall fern in a white marble urn dipped in front of them like a screen. Tony put a champagne glass into her hand.

'Now. What's the matter?' he asked her.

Amy considered. It was partly losing Isabel, of course, but only partly. There was something bigger than that, less tangible and so more frightening. Amy had the growing sense that she was adrift, directionless and isolated. She had watched Isabel dancing through her successful Seasons, aware of the options open to her and coolly accepting them. Isabel had chosen, and today was the celebration of her continuing to walk on down the broad, comfortable path laid down for her from the day of her birth. Amy had never felt at ease in the way that Isabel seemed to. When she looked at her own version of the path it was flat and uninviting, yet the country on either side of it seemed hostile, or impenetrable, or obscured. She was both bored and apprehensive, disenchanted and anxious, and the combination was uncomfortable.

'I . . . don't quite know what to do. Or how to talk about it,' she began.

Tony leaned back and lit a cigarette. 'Is it a love-affair of some kind? Or something awkward like a baby? Surely not?'

Amy laughed in spite of herself, and Tony thought that when her face came alive it was enchanting. Most men, he considered, would find her irresistible.

'No. No, nothing like that. Much less identifiable. I think I'm frightened of not being able to belong. Not to the kind of life that's offered to me, or even to the kind of life that Mother has created for herself. I don't want to find myself a scion of the shires, or a bright hope of the Tory Pary like Peter. The men I meet are all the same, and they make me feel the same. Rather chilly, and hollow.'

'Not very enticing,' Tony agreed.

'So if I'm not going to marry . . .'

'I wouldn't assume that immediately, you know. How old are you? Nineteen?'

'Yes. Old enough to know, I think.'

'Perhaps. Is it likely that you might prefer women?'

Amy held out her glass to have it refilled. She was laughing so much that the froth spilled over her fingers.

'Tony, what d'you think I am? If not pregnant, then a lesbian?'

'I don't know what you are,' he said equably. 'You tell me. I'm just eliminating the worst possibilities.'

'I don't think I prefer women. A man kissed me once, years and years ago, and that meant more to me than all the men I've met and danced with and half-heartedly allowed to kiss me ever since. He was the waiter, Luis, in the hotel in Biarritz, do you remember?'

'Did he now? Yes, I remember him. Go on.'

Amy took a deep breath. 'I want something to do. To believe in, if you like. Something real, and valuable. Richard asked me last night what I do all day, and it amounts to shopping, being fitted for clothes, meeting girlfriends and having lunch, going to parties and staying in people's houses. Helping Father to entertain when Mother isn't here. At Chance, riding and playing tennis. Seeing neighbours and people on the estate. It isn't enough.'

'For many people, you know, it would be more than enough. It would be Paradise.'

Amy's face went a dull crimson. 'I know,' she said humbly. 'Does that condemn me completely?'

'No, it doesn't. Let's try to think. What could you do?'

'Richard says that your office was full of girls doing things. I can speak French and German and a little Spanish. I can paint a bit, and a few other useless things. Could I be a secretary? Could I be your secretary?'

Tony tried not to let his smile broaden. 'I don't think so. Most secretaries have to be able to type and take shorthand, you know.'

'I could learn.'

'Yes. Look, there must be other girls of your class in your position. They must do things to which there could be no possible parental or social opposition. Can't you think of any?'

'There's Welfare work. Charity organizing. That sort of thing.'

'Wouldn't that do?'

Amy's disappointment showed. 'It means sitting on committees for charity balls, and bazaars. Raising money. Addressing envelopes for appeals. I would have liked an ordinary job, perhaps something that might help people. Whatever they're doing out there.' She gestured over the heads of the crowd and beyond the walls with their white silk drapes.

Tony's eyebrows worked themselves into triangular peaks. 'Out there? In Bruton Street?'

'No, damn it. Not Bruton Street.'

'Amy, how much do you really know about ordinary people and the work they do?'

'Nothing. I'm asking you to help me find out. Look, you took Richard somewhere last night. Would you take me out sometimes, too? I'd like to meet some people who aren't anything like these. There isn't anyone else I can ask. If I mentioned it to Johnny Guild, he'd say, "Oh, I say, Amy, what for? I hate slumming." If I could broaden my horizons a little, it might help me to know a little bit better what I'd like to do. Is that reasonable?'

Tony sighed. 'My dear. Downstairs you have the entire British aristocracy. If someone dropped a bomb now we'd have an instant socialist state. Up here is the cream of London's fashionable intelligentsia. One notorious poet there. Two well-known actresses there, ignoring each other. A beautiful divorcee here with very high connections. What do you imagine you are going to gain by hanging around the Fitzroy Tavern with me? Or making little expeditions to gape at conditions in the East End. Or whatever romantic idea it is you've got in your head?'

Amy looked down at her glass. 'These are Mother's friends. The people downstairs are here because Father is who he is. The King's Defender, and all that. I want a life of my own, Tony. A useful, ordinary life with the rewards of satisfaction.' She was crying again. A tear fell and rolled over her knuckles.

Tony Hardy's amused impatience evaporated. He thought that Amy had all the naïveté of her age and class, but without the cushioning of complacency. Her sincerity and her unhappiness were clear, and his heart went out to her.

'Poor Amy. Here, handkerchief. Of course I'll take you out and introduce you to some new people, if that's what you would like. Don't cry any more. Let's fling ourselves into the throes of this party. There are dozens of people here I wouldn't get a chance of seeing otherwise. If I arm myself with you, they can hardly cut me dead. Here's some more champagne, to begin with. And in a week or two, if you would really like to come, we'll go to a meeting organized by a friend of mine. It's a political meeting, and it might interest you. Or more likely it'll bore you to death. But there's usually a kind of party afterwards, and people are certainly different. Different in the sense that they're like one or two of the people in this room before they became fashionable or successful enough to be invited here by your mother.'

Amy missed the touch of irony in his voice, or else she chose not to hear it. Her face was alight. She dabbed the tears away with Tony's handkerchief.

'Thank you. I'd like that very much. Now, let's fling ourselves, if that's what you want to do. Is it the poet you'd like to talk to first? Colum O'Connor comes to Chance for Mother's house-parties sometimes. He used to like me to go for walks with him.'

'I'm sure he did,' Tony said drily. 'Yes, please. Do introduce me.'

Amy went across and touched the poet on the arm. He beamed at her.

'Well now, little Amy Lovell. Perfectly grown up.'

'Hello, Mr O'Connor. How are you? Do you know my friend Tony Hardy?'

Together, they worked their way around the room, greeting and talking. The faces Amy didn't recognize, Tony did. Between conversations, Tony whispered quick, scurrilous histories to her. Amy was distinctly impressed, and intrigued. He seemed to have a far-reaching knowledge of the more colourful sides of London literary and political life.

After an hour, when they had reached their alcove again, Tony winked at her. 'Thank you. That was useful. Now, d'you think we've earned some supper?'

On the way downstairs Amy asked him, 'What do you do at Randle & Cates, exactly? Apart from gossip?'

Tony looked sideways at her, appraisingly, and then grinned. 'Quite right, I do like gossip. I tell myself that it's part of the job, listening to who thinks what and who's doing what. I publish books, as you know. Which books I choose, or more often which books I nose out and coax people into doing, depends partly on what I hear, partly on what I believe in, and wholly on what will sell.'

'Which is?'

'Some poetry. No Eliots or Sitwells yet, but I'm working on it. Some politics. Not Peter Jaspert's sort, I'm afraid. And some novels.'

'What did my brother come to see you about yesterday?'

They came into the supper room. At the far end, at an empty table, was Richard. There was a champagne bottle beside him. His chin was propped on one hand and he was smiling a faint, remote smile.

They paused for a moment. Then Tony said smoothly, 'He came to me with a proposition. Or rather more than that, a partly completed novel. I told him that he was too young even to think about it, let alone to carry it off properly. I also told him I would be interested to talk about it again in five years' time. More than that, I don't think I should say.'

Amy looked across the room at her brother. He waved, exaggeratedly.

'I didn't know Richard was writing a novel.'

'I don't think it's the kind of book you would describe to your sister,' Tony said, inaudibly.

'Shall we go and join him?'

'You found each other,' Richard greeted them. 'Nobody has found me, as you can see. I have consoled myself with champagne, and with imagining edifices of elaborate insults to every dowager that has strutted past the table. Sit down and keep me company.'

'Are you drunk?'

'A little. Just a very little.'

Tony brought them plates of cold lobster and quivering aspic, and the first tender asparagus tips from Chance.

'Tony is going to take me to a political meeting in a couple of weeks, and to the party afterwards,' Amy remarked conversationally as they ate.

Richard glanced sharply from one to the other, and then his eyelids drooped again.

'Is he? How nice. And how nice that you have suddenly developed a political awareness, Amy. I'm sure you'll fit in amongst the comrades with glove-like ease.' There was a small, awkward silence. Richard smiled innocently. 'What have I said? Well now, have we enjoyed the wedding? The tyrants have put on a creditable show, I must say. Look at it all.' He waved at the long table with chefs in tall white toques behind it, the supper tables crowded with guests, and the endless procession of couples between supper and the ballroom where the music was growing steadily more insistent. 'Your turn next, Amy, as they say. Have you danced with a dozen officers?'

'Not one, this evening,' she answered, determined not to let Richard prickle her in front of Tony. She had seen him in this mood once or twice before. 'I was hoping Tony might ask me.'

Richard snorted over his glass. 'Tony doesn't dance. At least, only in louche clubs where you would be very unlikely to encounter him. There's a much more likely candidate on his way over here. I'm sure he'll foxtrot you off your feet.'

Amy looked. Johnny Guild was bustling across the room. He was a captain in a very smart regiment, the same one that Peter Jaspert had once belonged to. Johnny Guild had been part of the guard of honour at St Margaret's. He was in dress uniform tonight, very tight black trousers with a broad cherry-red stripe down the sides, and a cherry-coloured coat frogged with gold.

'He looks,' Richard murmured, 'as if he's just walked out of an operetta. D'you think he's going to sing something in a light but agreeable tenor?'

Amy bit the corners of her mouth, hard. Johnny Guild was the most persistent and most harmless of her admirers.

'Here you are. I've searched high and low. Amy, I was hoping you might have a dance or two left for me. 'Evening, Lovell.'

Amy looked at Richard and Tony in the hope of rescue, but they stood up politely, clearly expecting her to go. She let Johnny take her arm.

'I'll telephone you in a few days, if I may,' Tony said, 'about that arrangement we made.'

102

Johnny led her away to the ballroom.

It seemed to be full of pink faces looming over white ties, tulle skirts that were beginning to droop along with the corsages, and the determined bray of voices against the dance music. Johnny took her in his arms. His hand against her bare skin felt moist and warm.

It was all depressingly familiar.

'Who was that with your brother?'

Amy considered the possible responses, but in the end she simply said, 'He used to be my brother's tutor, years ago.'

'Oh. Well.' *Nobody at all*, she silently supplied for him.

When at last Johnny led her back to the supper room, the far table was empty. Tony and Richard were gone.

In the bathroom of the odd, florid hotel between London and the South Coast that Peter had chosen for their first night together, Isabel wrapped the heavy satin robe around her and tied it carefully. She had brushed her hair until it crackled, dabbed herself with scent, and hung her honey-coloured suit up herself in the fake Empire cupboard. Her maid would rejoin them at Dover tomorrow, before they sailed.

Peter was waiting for her. She had heard the creak of his heavy tread as he moved around the bedroom, but now there was silence.

She breathed in slowly and deeply, trying to ease the hammering of her heart, and walked through into the bedroom.

Peter was already in the wide bed. He had drunk a bottle of wine over their late dinner, and two brandies afterwards. His face looked red against the pillows.

'I thought you were never going to come,' he whispered. He held up the covers, beckoning her in beside him. Isabel hesitated. She couldn't get into bed in her robe, but was he expecting her to take it off?

'Shall I turn out the lights?' she asked.

'No. I want to look at you.' Peter's voice was hoarse.

Obediently Isabel unwrapped the robe again, slipped it off and laid it across the foot of the bed. Her silk nightdress, made for her in exactly the same shade, was cut on the bias so it clung to her, with a translucent lace inset from the mock-demure high neck to the top of her breasts. Peter didn't even glance at it.

'Come here,' he said. 'Get into bed.'

Isabel did as she was told, sliding under the covers and then lying still, trying to make her stiff body relax. Peter's large hands reached out and moved over her, groping for an opening in the folds of silk.

'Take this thing off,' he begged. Isabel sat up again and reached up to undo the tiny pearl buttons. She lifted the nightdress off over her head. Peter groaned, a long *Uhhhhn* sound that frightened her, making her think that he was ill. But he slid across the bed to her, and put his mouth on her breast. He began biting and gnawing at it, the blond stubble on his chin tearing at her skin. Isabel drew in her breath sharply with shock and disgust, and Peter lifted his head.

'Like that, do you? That's good.'

He pushed her backwards so that she was lying flat, and then hung over her. He was naked, and the heat of his heavy, hairy body shocked her again. Peter kissed her, rubbing all over her lips with his mouth and tongue, making little grunting noises under his breath. Isabel's mouth felt frozen, with a choking sensation at the back of her throat as if she might vomit. This was nothing like the times Peter had kissed her before, gently, so that she had wanted to kiss him back and answer his tongue with her own. He had even touched her breasts before, reverently, with the tips of his fingers. Now he was kneading her as if she belonged to him.

You do belong to him, a cold voice reminded her. You are this man's lawful wedded wife.

This bristly, panting creature with a sweating, screwed-up face was her handsome, confident husband.

Now Peter moved his hand down between her legs, parting them with his fist. His fingers probed at her, and then he groaned again.

'Sorry. Can't hold on,' he whispered. His breath burned her ear. He heaved himself on top of her. Something bumped and then stabbed, bluntly. Isabel clenched her teeth to stop herself screaming. There was a jolt of pain and then her husband buried himself inside her. He began to rock up and down, tearing at her inside, and moaning in his throat. Isabel tried not to listen or to feel. She tried to retreat into some cold, white, locked place inside her head.

'Oh *God*!' Peter shouted, and then came a roar, so pain-filled that her arms tightened protectively around him. He jerked involuntarily, his face distorted and drops of his sweat falling on her face.

At last the jerking stopped and his full weight sank on top of her, the roar dropping away into a sob.

Isabel stroked his damp shoulders, staring up past him at the curlicued wallpaper on the ceiling. If it wasn't so horrible, she thought, it would be funny. It was so absurd. And it was pathetic, and hardly human.

Peter slid away, leaving his hot stickiness all over her.

'Was it all right?' he whispered, like a child asking for a sweet.

'Not very,' Isabel said, longing for him to comfort her.

'I'm sorry.' He sounded huffy. 'I was too excited, and I'd had a bit too much to drink You'll like it better in the morning.' He kissed her cheek. 'Good night, darling. I love you.'

Isabel lay very still, listening to his breathing deepening into snores. When he was properly, deeply asleep, she promised herself, she would get up and wash.

At least it was quick, she consoled herself as she waited. At least it was quick.

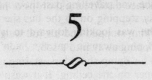

5

Appleyard Street, just off Bloomsbury Square. That was where Tony Hardy had said they were going. Amy peered out of the grimy window of the bus as they rumbled past Selfridges. The lit-up windows were full of spring fashions, print frocks and little straw hats, although the daffodils were barely out in Hyde Park and a week's icy rain and high winds had already flattened them to the grass.

Outside the front doors in Bruton Street, Amy had stood poised on the steps, automatically expecting Tony to wave to a cab. But he had taken her arm and steered her briskly towards Park Lane.

'Only a twopenny bus ride to Appleyard Street,' he said.

'Yes, of course.'

Amy could almost count the number of times she had been on a bus before. Past Selfridges she turned to Tony. He was smoking and frowning over a sheet of typewritten paper.

'What's the meeting about, exactly?'

'Oh, the usual sort of thing. Welcome to new members of the group. A paper, read by one of the old guard. This month's is entitled "From Dialectic to Daily Practice. A Pan-European Approach". Then a guest speaker. Tonight's is Will Easterbrook from the Trades Union Congress Executive. He should be interesting. And then there will be a discussion of arrangements for the hunger march.'

Seeing Amy's blank stare Tony began to laugh. 'You did ask to come.'

'Hunger march?' she asked quickly. 'What's that?'

'Don't you know? This one is one of my friend Jake Silverman's projects. You'll meet Jake tonight. And you'll hear plenty about the march.'

Not wanting to betray any more ignorance, Amy went back to

studying the Oxford Street windows. The shops were familiar but she felt that she was travelling past them into new territory. It was if by simply stepping on to the bus she had set out in a new direction. She was looking forward to what the evening would bring, with an eagerness that she hadn't felt for a long time.

When the bus reached High Holborn, Tony rang the bell and they jumped off together.

Amy had never penetrated into this corner of London before. She peered interestedly at the shops, mostly small grocers, and bookshops with pavement display cases emptied and locked up for the night. There was hardly anyone in the streets, and no traffic at all, but the lights behind curtained windows over the shops spoke of tiny flats full of people.

Appleyard Street was exactly like the others. Tony stopped in front of a bookshop with a smeared window crammed full of haphazardly arranged books. A violently lettered poster stuck to the glass commanded UNITE. FIGHT FOR YOUR RIGHTS. Tony rang the side door bell and then pushed the door open. The hallway and steep stairs facing them were completely bare, and lit by a single bulb with a cracked glass shade.

Tony waved her inside with an ironic flourish. 'Welcome to the Centre for Socialist Studies. First floor. Jake has a flat at the top, where we shall adjourn later. Shall I lead the way?'

Amy nodded. She was very cold, and annoyed to find that she was disconcerted by the bleakness of their destination.

The big first-floor room had three uncurtained windows overlooking the street. It was packed with rows of upright wooden chairs, most of them occupied. At the front was a table covered with a red cloth, with another half-dozen chairs arranged behind it. The room was warm, heated by a glowing gas fire. At the rickety card table beside the door Tony stopped to sign his name in a register. Underneath it he wrote 'A. Lovell. Guest.'

'It's not a public meeting,' he told her. 'You have to be a member, or an invited guest.' Then he guided Amy to a pair of empty chairs, mercifully close to the fire. It welcomed her with a gentle hiss.

Tony smiled at her as they sat down, acknowledging her sense of disorientation, and mocking her a little for it. Amy peeled off her suède gloves and he saw that her fingers were white with cold.

'Poor Amy! Where have I dragged you to?' He took her hands and rubbed them in his own warm ones, and Amy was sorry when the circulation was restored to her fingers and he laid them gently back in her lap. She made herself stop looking at the way his fine, rather long hair fell over his ear, and turned her attention to the rest of the room.

Her first reaction was relief that she didn't look too conspicuous. She had been right not to come in her dinner dress. Amy had dined alone with her father, and as soon as Gerald had left for his club Amy had gone upstairs again and exchanged her dress for a cashmere sweater and a tweed skirt. With a plain woollen coat, low-heeled shoes and a soft hat pulled down to cover her hair, she imagined she looked exactly like any of the girls in Tony's office. If anything, she thought now, she was conspicuous for her ordinariness. A girl just in front of her was wearing her hair wound up in a brilliant green turban with a big fake emerald pinned to the front. Her eyes were shadowed in the same green as the turban. She was talking to another girl with a mass of black curly hair and big brass earrings that jangled as she shook her head. Her skirt was a tight tube of scarlet flounces and her legs, hooked casually over the chair in front of her, flashed stockings in the same colour. Another woman, grey-haired, in a raincoat and a rakish velvet beret, was smoking a man's cigar. The men, much more numerous, had nothing in common from their appearance. One or two, in blue suits and stiff collars, might have been bank officials. Others were clearly working men, with red faces and flannel shirts. The rest were like Tony, somewhere between the two, with an occasional touch of flamboyance. Not a single person wore evening clothes, although it was well after nine o'clock.

Amy's feet were beginning to thaw out, and her interest revived with them. She was looking around the room again when without ceremony a big man stood up and went to the table. He was young, Tony's age or a little older. He had a full black beard that made his lips look very red, a big nose, and glittering dark eyes. He was wearing a red and black plaid shirt, with a red handkerchief tied at the throat.

'Comrades,' he said quietly. Silence fell immediately. 'The meeting is called to order.' He nodded at two or three other men, and they filed up to join him behind the table.

Tony nudged Amy. 'Jacob Silverman,' he whispered. His

108

manner, and the attention given to him by his audience, told Amy that Jacob Silverman was someone to be reckoned with. He welcomed them all briefly to the meeting, greeted new members by name, and added that other guests were welcome too. As he looked along the rows his eyes fixed briefly on Amy, and she knew that Jake Silverman would miss nothing.

A patter of applause met the first speaker who stood up and began to talk, very fast and rather loudly. He had none of Silverman's quiet, commanding fluency. Amy tried hard to concentrate, but her attention drifted away to the rest of the audience, and then to Tony beside her. He was frowning a little, and there was a sceptical twist to his mouth that indicated he didn't think much of the speaker either. It was nice being here with him, Amy thought. The warmth of the room and the monotony of the speaker's voice grew soporific, and she lost herself in comfortable dreams.

The second speaker was a blunt, brusque little man who launched himself into an analysis of trades union power bases. Amy's interest quickened again, in spite of the happy reverie she had fallen into. She knew in theory that two or three extra shillings were important enough so that bargaining over them could go on for weeks, but she had never exactly thought what those shillings would mean every week to a man and his family. Much of the talk was beyond her, but it made her think for the first time about the right to work, its rewards, and the deprivation of those who had none. The memory of her own petulant behaviour on the night of Isabel's wedding made her feel faintly uncomfortable.

The speaker moved on to talk about the power wielded by strikers, making Amy think back to her vague memories of the General Strike. Adeline had gone out in her silliest hat to serve soup to the strike-breakers. The sons of family friends had driven buses, and it had all been regarded as tremendously good fun. Tonight, surrounded by these intent faces, she saw it in a different light. Her feeling of discomfort deepened into shame, and she wriggled lower in her seat. Suddenly she was conscious of the diamond clip fastening the soft brim of her hat.

Before the last part of the meeting, Tony turned to grin at her. Amy saw that he was challenging her, and that the whole evening's expedition was a challenge. He was more or less expecting her to be bored and uncomprehending. How would he judge her when he discovered that she wasn't? Amy was aware that her perceptions were shifting slightly. She wanted Tony to approve of her, but she also wanted to know more about what she had heard tonight for its own sake,

Jake Silverman stood up again.

'Thank you, Comrade Easterbrook,' he said. 'Now. I want to call for the meeting's help in connection with the hunger march. The response from workers between South Wales and here has been excellent. The march will last twelve days, and we have been able to plan overnight stops in places where a school hall or something similar will be made available for the marchers to sleep in. The problem, ironically, arises when they reach London. Accommodation for men without money is harder to come by in this great city of ours. There will be several hundred men by the time the march reaches here, possibly a thousand or more. Even if every comrade here and in the movement offered his home, there would be barely enough room.'

'Kingsway Hall?' someone suggested.

'Salvation Army hostels?' another man said.

'They deserve proper accommodation, and a reception after the petition has been presented,' someone else shouted.

'There's time to raise the money,' the girl in the turban called. 'Let's do them proud.'

Jake Silverman was beaming. He produced a hat and waved it. 'Very well. We'll begin here and now.'

'There's nothing Jake likes better,' Tony whispered, 'than orchestrating enthusiasm.'

The hat was passed along the rows and money clinked into it. When it reached the end of their row Amy fumbled in her crocodile-skin bag for her purse. There were two pounds in it. *Never*, Adeline said, *leave yourself without money for a cab ride home*. The hat reached her and she stuffed the notes into it.

'Will you see me home?' she asked Tony.

He winked at her. 'Of course. It's only a twopenny bus ride back to Bruton Street, after all.'

The meeting proceeded to heated discussions of where the marchers could be most comfortably and honourably accommodated, and how the money was to be raised to do it.

At last Jake Silverman waved his red and black plaid arms. 'Thank you, all of you, very much. Our comrades in the South

Wales Miners' Federation deserve every effort. The meeting is closed now. Join us upstairs, if you can.'

At once, the crowd began to surge out of the room, which had grown uncomfortably hot. Amy had been engrossed and hadn't noticed it, but now she pulled her hat off and shook out her hair. She saw the girl with the brass earrings looking at her.

Some people were clumping back down the stairs to the street door, but most of them were heading for the flat above. Tony and Amy were carried along with them.

Jake Silverman's flat was a series of small, low rooms crowded with books, pamphlets and people. The jabber of talk hit them at the door. Hands were waving and gesticulating, voices were shouting each other down and clamouring to make a point before anyone else could refute it. Amy edged through the crowd in Tony's wake and came to the kitchen. Jake Silverman was standing in the middle brandishing a wine bottle.

'Come and get it,' he shouted and a forest of empty glasses was thrust at him. He looked across at Tony. 'Wield a corkscrew, Tony, will you?'

'Jake, this is my friend Amy Lovell.'

Jake put down the bottle. 'Pour it yourselves,' he called out, and held out a hand to Amy. 'Any friend of Tony's is welcome here,' he said simply, and took her hand in his large, warm one. Amy could almost believe that she felt the crackle as he touched her, he was so charged with energy. Jake's arm enveloped her shoulders and he turned her to where the girl with the scarlet stockings and the earrings was frying sausages over a corner gas ring.

'This is Kay Cooper.' Jake kissed Kay enthusiastically on the mouth. 'And Angel Mack.' That was the turban girl. 'This is Tony's friend, Amy Lovell.'

Kay waved her sausage fork, and Angel said, 'Hmmm. Tony's friend, eh? What did you think of the meeting?'

Amy glanced from one to the other. 'Just that. It made me think.'

Suddenly, both the girls were smiling at her.

'Have a sausage.'

'And a glass of wine. Guaranteed to turn your tongue jet black.'

'Thank you. I will.'

111

Armed with food and drink, Tony took Amy away into the throng. He introduced her to everyone in sight.

'Wait!' she protested. 'I'll never remember who everyone is.'

'You wanted to meet different people,' he reminded her. 'What do you think so far? Changed your social perceptions, has it?'

He was teasing her again, but Amy looked straight back at him.

'Do you know, I think it has, a little.'

She was enjoying the smoky, crowded rooms and the lively babble of talk more than the grandest society party she had ever been to. She thought that she had never met such opinionated people in her life. Or no, that wasn't quite true. Peter Jaspert was opinionated too, but his opinions stood at the opposite pole from those expressed here. She had never found Peter Jaspert particularly congenial, yet she felt perfectly at home here tonight.

Was this, then, where her sympathies lay? For some reason the idea excited her. By listening very carefully to the talk, and by putting it together with what she already knew from newspaper reports, Amy understood that the hunger marchers were miners from the Rhondda, out of work now, who were marching on London to deliver a petition at Downing Street. Sixty per cent of men were out of work in the valleys.

Amy stared at Kay, whose black curls shook with her passionate recital.

'This Depression can only get worse. We're cushioned from it here, you and me and all the rest of us, by our education and because we live in prosperous London. But out there, in the mines and the rest of industry, people are suffering every day.'

Amy thought, who could be more cushioned than me? Bethan came from the valleys, but she had never so much as mentioned these terrible things. How much more don't I know about? How much more have I never thought about, or bothered to enquire about?

'Hello again.' It was Angel Mack, with a jug of wine. 'More of this stuff? Or there's beer, if you'd rather. No cocktails or champagne, I'm afraid.'

Was it really so transparently obvious where she came from, then? Amy wondered.

'Wine, thank you,' Amy said firmly.

'I've never been to a party like this before,' she added. 'Where everyone seems to have so much to say to everyone else.'

Angel laughed. 'Oh yes, there's always plenty of talk. That's half the trouble with armchair comrades like us. Too busy talking about what'll happen when the revolution comes to actually do anything about making it happen.'

'Can it happen without you?'

'Most definitely,' Angel said. 'And what about you? Are you on our side?'

Amy thought suddenly of Chance and the cedar tree shading the cool grass, and of the hunger marchers sleeping in village halls on their endless walk to London. And then of Peter Jaspert and his fluent talk of trade tariffs.

'I'm not on the other side,' Amy said at last. 'Although I've only just discovered that.' At once, she felt that she was a traitor to everything she knew. Quickly, to cover up her own uncertainty, she asked, 'Does Tony Hardy come here a lot?'

Angel glanced curiously at her. 'Tony comes and goes. Got his own fish to fry, as they say. As far as all this goes, he's less committed than some but his heart's in the right place. Does that tell you what you want to know?'

Amy wasn't sure what she wanted to know.

'What about Jake Silverman?'

'Yes, everyone always wants to know about Jake. He's probably much more like you than you would think. His father and the rest of his family are in the garment trade, rather prosperously so. Jake turned his back on all that when he was eighteen. I think he'd describe himself as a full-time political activist now. He supports himself by working in the Left Bookshop downstairs, and writing the odd article for the quarterlies. He lives here with Kay.'

'Kay's his wife?'

'No,' Angel said coolly, 'not his wife. Kay doesn't believe in marriage.'

Amy began to laugh, so that Angel stared at her even harder. She was thinking of Johnny Guild and his friends, and Peter and Isabel in St Margaret's, Westminster.

'I don't think I do, either,' Amy said.

'I imagine not, if you're going about with Tony Hardy. Here he comes now, looking for you.'

In the next room, someone was piling records on to the ancient

113

gramophone. The music was very loud and very crackly, and there was hardly room to move, let alone to dance. Tony bowed gravely and held out his arms.

At once Amy lost track of the evening's progress. She had the impression that the party was in full and noisy swing, and that a telephone had been ringing insistently somewhere. She was startled when Jake crossed the room and turned the music off.

'Sorry, everyone.' Jake grinned at them. 'Complaints department. Either the row stops or the police arrive.'

Tony found Amy's coat for her, and the hat that had been rolled up and stuffed in one of the pockets.

'Good night,' Jake boomed from the top of the stairs. 'See you next time, Tony. And you, Amy Lovell, whoever you are.'

Amy smiled to herself. She wanted to come again. She definitely wanted to come again, and not just because of Tony Hardy.

Out in the darkness she began to walk briskly the way they had come, back towards the bus stop. Then she realized that Tony was still standing at the kerb, and that he was laughing at her.

'D'you imagine that we're going to catch a bus at one in the morning? This way. We'll have to look for a cab towards Oxford Street.'

'You'll have to pay,' Amy reminded him. 'I put my taxi money in the hunger hat.'

'I think I can manage. You may do it next time.'

They found a cab, and Tony handed her into it. In the familiar stuffy interior Amy leaned back in her seat. The wine she had drunk and the relaxed atmosphere between them made her ask, without thinking very hard, 'Angel Mack said something odd. I told her I didn't think I believed in marriage, and she said something like "I'm not surprised, if you're going about with Tony Hardy." What did she mean?'

Amy thought she saw Tony's head jerk round, silhouetted against the street lights rolling past outside. But then he was so still that she thought she had imagined it.

'I've no idea,' he said smoothly. 'Possibly pique because I've never made a play for her myself. Practically everyone else has. But I shouldn't pay too much attention to what Angel says. She works very hard at being modern and hardboiled, and a good deal of it is just for effect.'

'I liked her,' Amy said.

'I like her too. But it doesn't mean I have to trust her, or believe what she says.'

The silence that followed was awkward, and Amy wished fervently that she had kept Angel's remark to herself. In the end Tony said, with his old lightness, 'My views on marriage are the same as yours. So we don't need to mention it again, do we?'

'No. Why should we?'

But neither of them could find anything else to say, and the cab rumbled to a stop in Bruton Street. Tony paid the driver, and they got out and watched it rattle away again.

'Don't you need him to take you home?' Amy asked. 'I don't even know where you live,' she added sadly.

'Not far from Appleyard Street. I'll walk back. I like walking at night. It's my thinking time.'

In the shadow of the front doors, Amy fumbled in her handbag.

'Don't you have to ring to be let in?'

'Not after midnight. I agreed it with Mother. It isn't fair to Glass and the footmen. I've got my own key. Father doesn't know.'

Tony put the key in the lock for her, and the door swung open. He didn't even glance inside at the cavernous hallway.

'You do have quite a lot of freedom, you know. You shouldn't complain.'

'I'm not, any more. Good night, Tony. Thank you for this evening.'

Amy turned to him, and Tony saw the curve of her cheek, and the shadow of her eyelashes under her hat brim. He kissed her, very quickly, just brushing the corner of her mouth with his own.

'Good night,' he answered.

Amy felt a faint, vanishing flicker of disappointment. But what else could she expect from him here in the front doorway?

'Next time I take you out,' he added, 'we'll do something more orthodox. Dinner, perhaps?'

'Yes, please.'

He was turning away when Amy called after him.

'Tony? Are you a Communist?'

He chuckled. 'There are a number of shades of opinion to the left of Peter Jaspert, you know. No, I'm not a Party member. I belong to the ILP. The Independent Labour Party. Good night, Amy Lovell.'

Amy closed the big door quietly behind her, and made sure

115

that the bolts were secure. Then she walked slowly up the great curve of staircase. On the first floor, where in the daytime a high glass dome brought light spilling down into the well of the house, she stopped under a line of portraits. The King's Defenders, back over the centuries. Would Gerald, she wondered, take up the ceremonial sword to defend his Sovereign against Jake Silverman, and Kay and Angel and even Tony Hardy, when their revolution came? And on which side of the barricades would Amy Lovell be standing?

'I've no idea,' she said aloud to the row of impassive faces. 'I've no idea at all. I should start thinking about it, shouldn't I?'

Upstairs, Amy saw that the light was still on in the old night nursery. Bethan was sitting in an armchair beside the fire, knitting. She pursed her lips when Amy came in.

'It's very late, lamb. I was beginning to worry.'

Amy knelt down beside her and put her head on Bethan's shoulder. Bethan hugged her as she used to do when Amy was little.

'Don't worry about me so much. Bethan . . . I wanted to ask you something.' The thought of the Rhondda, and the things that Kay Cooper had told her about the way people were living there, was vivid in her mind.

'What's that, then?' Bethan was rolling up her knitting. Usually Bethan looked to Amy exactly as she had done for fifteen years, ever since she had come to Chance as a sixteen-year-old nursery-maid. She was plumper now, but her round, plain face was as cheerful as it had always been, and she moved with the same quick energy. But tonight Amy saw that her eyes were heavy and dark, and her shoulders sagged. It was almost two in the morning, and Bethan was exhausted with waiting up for her. She realized that she had never glimpsed that tiredness before, and she frowned at the recognition of her own selfishness.

'It doesn't matter tonight,' Amy said quickly. 'You go to bed now. I don't need anything. Bethan?' The maid stopped in the doorway. 'Thank you for looking after us all.'

'Go on with you now.'

Nick Penry reached up for the old khaki kitbag that had been stowed away on top of the wardrobe. He shook it out, and began carelessly stuffing a few pieces of clothing into it.

116

Mari had been watching in silence, her chapped hands gripping the brass bed-rail, but now she said, 'Let me do that. You'll mix everything up.'

Silently he handed the bag to her. Mari refolded the two shirts and the darned pullover and socks. Her eyes were blurred with tears and she shook her head angrily to clear them. Nick sat down on the edge of the bed, staring at the faded linoleum with his hands hanging loosely between his knees.

They had been arguing again.

They had always argued, right from the beginning, but they had always been able to make it up again, fiercely or gently, in bed.

But they couldn't do that now, or almost never. Mari had changed from the rosy-cheeked provocative girl she had been when she married into a white, frightened woman. She was afraid of anything worse happening to them, afraid of anything that might disturb the fragile equilibrium they lived by. She was afraid of another handicapped baby. She was afraid for Dickon, now and in the future when the two of them wouldn't be here to care for him any longer. She was afraid of Nick turning on the Means Test man, who came to peer insultingly at their back kitchen in search of any unexplained luxuries that might point to money coming in beyond the bare minimum they existed on. If there was any hint that they earned money elsewhere, their tiny unemployment benefit would be cut off. She was afraid of any of them falling ill, because there was nothing spare to pay for that. And she was newly afraid of Nick's convictions, the flaring beliefs that made him revile the soft options, the 'company unionism' that was threatening to spread in the hard times, and despise the owners and the government for their agreement that increased the miners' hours to eight a day underground again, instead of seven and a half. She was afraid that Nick would never get a job again. He had stepped too far out of line. His name was known to the owners and their agents.

And all her fear seemed to trigger off the very opposite in Nick, as if he had to stand firm for both of them. He clung harder to what he believed in, to the socialist ideals that earned the nickname 'Little Moscow' for their bleak corner of the bleak, depopulated valleys. It made him angrier, and more determined, and somehow less knowable. It didn't make him any easier to love.

And now he was setting off to march to London, and she was afraid of being without him.

With a sob, she dropped the bag and went to sit beside him. He put his arm around her, warm and protective.

'Have you got to go?'

'You know I do. If I don't, why should anyone else bother? It's something we can do to make people across the country look at us, and think about us. If we can just get public opinion with us, Mari. The Miners' executive are meeting MacDonald again, to try to win him over, make him understood what we want, and why. He's not to be trusted, but Henderson is on our side. The march might make the difference.'

Mari's face was wet with tears. She hated the words. They were too familiar, too impersonal.

'Can't you let the others go for once? Stay here with Dickon and me. We need you more than they do.'

Gently Nick let her go. 'You know I can't do that. It'll only be two weeks. I'll get a ride back somehow.'

He took up a blanket wrapped in a gabardine cape that had belonged to his father. He strapped it beneath the bag, then swung the bag on to his back. It hung there, tellingly almost empty.

'Best to be travelling light,' Nick said. 'It's time to be going, love.'

They left the room in silence. It was very early, hardly light yet, and Dickon was still asleep in the other bedroom, no more than a cupboard at the stairhead. Nick stooped in the doorway and knelt by the low bed to kiss him. When the child was asleep he looked like any other little boy, the liveliness briefly rubbed out of his face by oblivion. Nick looked at him for a long moment, hopelessly wishing.

'You'd better have something before you go,' Mari said flatly.

She went down to the icy kitchen and stirred the fire under its blanket of coal dust. With a horseshoe of solidly twisted newspaper she coaxed up a brief blaze and set the kettle on it. Then she brought the heel of a loaf out of the pantry and sliced it, spreading it carefully with thick dripping out of a blue-glazed bowl.

'I don't need that,' Nick said. 'You and the boy have it.'

'You've left us more than enough money,' Mari said.

That was true. Nick was setting out to walk to London with

hardly more than a shilling in his pocket. He sat down in the armchair to pull his boots on, glancing first at the oval patches worn almost through, and the split already gaping between the sole and the upper.

'You could have done with new boots,' Mari said.

He smiled at her suddenly. 'So could every man setting out this morning, I dare say.'

Mari handed him his tea, in the precious china mug that he had bought for her long ago at Barry Island. The tea was sweetened with a hoarded tin of condensed milk. Dickon could finish the rest. He loved licking the thick yellow stuff off a spoon.

Nick drank gratefully, looking at her over the rim of the mug. 'Remember that day?' he asked, and she nodded. It had been their day together, and the day of the explosion too. There was no happiness without an equal or deeper seam of sadness, Mari thought bitterly. Even if he were to walk twice round the world, Nick couldn't change that.

He was anxious to be off now, like a small boy before an adventure. He bit impatiently into one piece of bread and dripping and wrapped up the other to go into his bag.

'Here,' Mari said. From a drawer she produced two flat bars of chocolate and slipped them into the bag too. She had put by the money for them secretly, buying less food for the week and doing without when Nick was out of the house. Nick didn't try to protest. He understood the gesture and the price of it. He smiled crookedly instead, then put his arms round her and kissed her.

'I'll eat a square a day, and think of you,' he promised. She felt light in his arms, birdlike, and small for the weight of responsibility that he felt towards her and Dickon, dependent on him. Nick suddenly thought of saying that he wouldn't go after all, that he would stay because she wanted him to. But the men were waiting for him at the bottom of the hill. He had to go. He had to act on what he believed in, otherwise how could he justify the belief?

'I won't come down with you,' she whispered. 'Because of Dickon.'

Nick kissed her again and they shivered, held against one another. Then he lifted the bag and the blanket bumped awkwardly.

'Two weeks,' he promised, and walked out into the dark,

dripping entry. Someone had scratched WORK, NOT WALKS on the bricks.

Mari listened to his steps receding into silence, and then stared round the kitchen at his empty mug, and the imprint of him in the armchair where he had bent to lace his worn boots.

It was so cheerless without him that she was almost crying again. When he was here they quarrelled, repetitively and weary-ingly, and when he was gone she couldn't bear it.

Upstairs Dickon began calling her. 'Mam. Maa-am.' He had only a few proper words. The others that he used most were 'Dad' and 'More'. Even Dickon was beginning to understand that there usually wasn't any more, but his endless repetition of it was one of the day's painful refrains. Mari sighed.

'I'm coming, love,' she called up to him.

Nick squared his shoulders beneath the straps and set off down the hill. The wet slate roofs of the houses shone like mirrors, and smoke from the chimneys already hung like greasy bunting over them. The air smelt of coal as it always did, gritty and rough at the top of his lungs, cut through with the rival scents of damp and, very faintly, of frying food. The streets were deserted. Those who had work were already there, and it was too early yet for the knots of aimless men to gather and talk on the street corners.

The arranged meeting point for the Nantlas marchers was the old pit gates. It had never reopened after the explosion, and the heavy padlocks and chains on the gates were rusted over.

As Nick came over the humped iron bridge spanning the railway and the river, he saw that most of the twenty-odd marchers from the village were already there, waiting for him.

Two or three of them waved cheerfully at him, and called out greetings.

'Feeling in good leg are you, Nick boy?'

'Pack up your troubles in your old kitbag . . .' someone else sang in a fine, resonant tenor, and there was a ripple of ironic laughter.

Nick was counting the heads. Two more men joined them, making the full complement. He took a deep breath. It was the setting-off point at last. There had been weeks of planning, with the Fed at first wary of then, finally, co-operative with the National Unemployed Workers Movement and with the idealistic young men of Appleyard Street, London. Letters of encourage-ment had come from Jake Silverman, and funds had been sent by the Communist Party of Great Britain. Jake Silverman had even followed his letters to the Rhondda, and Nick had listened to him talking about the coming of the glorious revolution to a roomful of unemployed miners.

His colleagues on the Federation executive recognized that the hunger marches were as good a way as any of drawing public attention to the mass of unemployed. But Nick himself was more interested in marching the one hundred and fifty miles straight to London and confronting the Prime Minister with the Federation's demands. He had volunteered himself as a march organizer unhesitatingly, with that goal in mind. He had been proud of the idea that he would be part of the deputation of miners that would march on from Trafalgar Square to Downing Street. And yet, now that the moment had come, he felt the wrench of leaving Mari and Dickon. The crowd of men was growing restive. They jostled one another and called out their impatience.

Nick lifted up his arms to quieten them again.

'That's it, lads. Shall we make a start? Don't want to keep them waiting down the valley, do we?'

They shuffled awkwardly into a column. Half of the men had fought in the War, and remembered the discipline of marches. The rest lined up behind them, grinning in embarrassment. There was a ragged cheer of encouragement from the wives, children and old men who had gathered against the railings to watch them go.

'Good luck, boys. You tell 'em, up in London.'

Amidst the renewed cheers, the uncertain column began to wind away along the valley road. At the back of the line two boys were carrying a roll of canvas. They looked at the waving hands, and the erect shoulders in front of them, and then glanced at each other. At once they dropped the canvas roll and unwrapped it. Inside was a green silk banner. It was gaudy with gold threads and the scarlet of a huge dragon, its tail curling back over its head. *Nantlas, Rhondda* was embroidered on it in big gold letters, and the initials *SWMF*. They slotted the supporting poles quickly together and hoisted the banner between them. The wind tugged at the gold fringes and the silk bellied out, making a riveting splash of colour amongst the drab greys.

It was like a signal. From windows and doors up the terraces heads appeared and the cheering was carried up the hillside in thin, insistent waves. Nick glanced back from the head of the

121

line and saw the banner glaring bravely behind him. The march, setting out in hunger and despair, was suddenly festive, like the Galas of the old days. He lengthened his stride and the marchers swung along behind him in the pride of the moment.

The singer was next to him. He looked back too, smiling, and then began to sing again.

> *Hello, Piccadilly, Hello, Leicester Square,*
> *It's a long, long road up from the valleys,*
> *But we'll march, right there.*

Nick joined in, and the song was taken up all along the line until they were singing and marching and the waving and cheering followed them all along the road until the corner took them round the fold of the hillside and out of sight.

The road ran on in front of them, flanking the railway line with its empty, rust-red trucks shunted into deserted sidings. The slag mountains towered on either side of them, and the black scars of the workings bit into the green hillsides. No one glanced at the scenery. Strung out down the valley were more towns and villages like Nantlas. More men would join them from all these places, and they would march on to meet the miners who had come down from Rhondda Fawr, and the others from across the entire stricken coalfield. At Newport, when they were all together, they would turn on to the London road.

And they would walk and walk until they reached Downing Street. It was a long way.

Around him, Nick heard the singing dying away as one voice after another was silenced by the road stretching ahead. They were solemn now, and the sudden burst of high spirits was over. The two boys in the rear let the banner drop again and wrapped it in its protective canvas before running to catch up once more.

'We're on our way, then,' Nick said quietly.

'May it bring us something more than blistered feet,' the singer said beside him, with an absence of expectation that was ominous to Nick.

Tony was as good as his promise. He took Amy out to dinner in Soho, to a cheerful restaurant where Italian waiters with striped aprons wriggled between the close-packed tables, and the owner came out with his magnificent moustaches to sit at the tables of

122

the most favoured customers. Amy ate the highly flavoured food from the thick white plates with clear enjoyment, and drank quantities of Chianti from bottles wrapped in a raffia shell.

A trio of violinists in red shirts came and played insistently between the tables, and Tony and Amy winced and laughed at each other before Amy put a shilling into their held-out plate to make them go a little further away.

'I like this place,' she told him, and Tony smiled.

'I like taking you out. You have the knack of enjoying uncomplicated things. Rather unusual for a girl like you, I should think. I had imagined it would be hopeless if I didn't know where to buy orchid corsages or belong to exclusive clubs.'

'Does that mean you'll go on doing it?' she asked him. 'I'd like to go to Appleyard Street again.'

Tony looked at her. 'I don't know,' he said with deliberate vagueness. He had been evasive when she had mentioned Appleyard Street before.

'When?' she pressed him, and he sighed.

'Look, Amy. Appleyard Street isn't really a suitable place for you. I took you as a once-off expedition for interest's sake. See how the other half, and all that. If I'd thought a bit harder, I wouldn't have done it at all.'

'Why can't I go there?'

'Peers' daughters with connections like yours don't generally mix with Communist sympathizers. It would make a nice little item for some newsman. Think of it from your father's point of view. Or your brother-in-law's.'

Peter Jaspert. Isabel and he would be back in two weeks' time. Amy had begun to admit to herself that she was hurt by the stilted quality of the letters and cards from her sister. She told herself that of course she wasn't expecting detailed descriptions of married life, but she still felt that the closeness that had always existed between them was being denied by the pages of guidebook enthusiasm for Tuscan hillsides or Michelangelos.

The truth was that she was missing Isabel badly. If she saw more of Richard, Amy thought with a touch of sadness, perhaps she wouldn't feel it so much. But even when Richard was home from Eton, although he was as amusing and affectionate as always when they did meet, he was increasingly busy with his own mysterious affairs and he seemed to have no time to spare for Amy.

'Haven't you got a dozen Guards officers to take you dancing?' he would grin at her.

When she protested that she didn't care for officers he would stare at her, mock-surprised.

'Don't you?'

She sighed now and turned her attention back to Tony and the question of Appleyard Street. 'Yes. I see that you can't be responsible for taking me there. Sorry. It's odd, you know. I felt . . . comfortable, there.'

'You made an impression. Angel Mack was asking about you the other day. I didn't tell her anything, of course. Never mind, Amy.' Seeing her face, Tony reached out and covered her hand with his own. 'We'll go somewhere else. Poetry and music at the Wigmore Hall next week? One of my poets is reciting his work. Very avant-garde, I promise you.'

'Can I come with you to the hunger march?' she persisted.

'No. For different reasons, but definitely not. It might not be safe, for one thing. What about the Wigmore Hall?'

Amy submitted to the diversion. She could perfectly well see the hunger marchers alone, after all.

'All right,' she grinned at him. 'Avant-garde verse it shall be.'

His hand rested lightly over hers. Amy liked him touching her. It was odd that she disliked what other men tried to do to her, yet she definitely wanted Tony to kiss her and he never even tried to. It wasn't because of who she was, Amy was sure of that. They were friends, on a clear footing that had nothing to do with social position.

She looked at him now across the table. Tony leaned back in his chair and the sputtering candlelight made dark shadows under his cheekbones. Amy thought that he looked intriguing. Not handsome, but romantic, and clever, and enigmatic.

She was suddenly breathless, and she opened her mouth to breathe more easily. Tony looked back at her, as if he was waiting for her to say something.

Daringly, she tried out the words in her head. *Tony, I love you. Did you know?* At once she felt her cheeks redden. She turned her hand so that her fingers laced with Tony's and pressed them.

He returned the pressure lightly and then laid her hand gently back on the cloth. She felt scattered breadcrumbs rough under her wrist.

'Time to go,' Tony said.

Outside the restaurant the night air was cool.

With his hand at her elbow Tony steered her to the kerb and into a cab. They sat side by side in the darkness watching the lights flick past. Amy's face was turned away and Tony saw the disappointed hunch of her shoulders.

'What can I do?' he asked, wishing there was something.

'Kiss me,' Amy answered without hesitation.

'Oh, Amy.' There was a faint breath of exasperation in his voice and something worse, amusement. But he leant forward and touched her mouth with his own.

I didn't mean like that, Amy thought miserably.

She looked away again, out into the street. At the beginning she had been interested in Tony for the doors that he promised to open. But now he attracted her in a different way that made her feel hot, and awkward, and unsure of herself. He was certainly fending her off. The realization embarrassed her, and she felt her face grow even hotter.

Tony said, 'You aren't very happy, are you? What is it?'

Amy shrugged. She couldn't, in her embarrassment, recite her loneliness for Isabel and Richard and her feeling of uselessness to the world.

'I told you at the wedding,' she said, as lightly as she could. 'I feel a little lost. But I should solve that for myself. Don't you agree?'

The cab was turning in at the end of Bruton Street. Amy looked and saw the warmly lit windows of her home. Adeline had been giving a dinner party tonight, but by now they would all have moved on to the Embassy Club.

'I hope you will find some way of being happy,' Tony said, with odd formality.

The cab drew up. The driver sat stolidly behind his glass panel, collar up and cap pulled well down over his ears.

'Isabel will be back in a day or so, won't she?'

'Yes,' Amy answered. 'Isabel will be back.'

'Until next week, then. At the Wigmore Hall.'

They said their good nights, and Amy went up the steps and into the house alone.

Isabel's new home in Ebury Street looked as clean and shiny as if it had just been unwrapped, Amy thought. The maid showed

125

her into Isabel's drawing-room on the first floor. It was full of pretty pale chintzes and bowls of fresh flowers. There were tranquil watercolours on the blue walls, and a tidy little fire in the polished grate. Silver-framed pictures of Peter's family and of herself and Isabel as children stood on the grand piano at one end of the room.

The door opened and there was Isabel. Amy ran to her.

'Oh, Bel, I've missed you so much.' The girls hugged each other, smiling wordlessly.

Then Amy stood back, holding her sister at arm's length. Isabel was wearing a pale blue dress that matched her room, and her hair waved flatteringly over her ears and was caught up at the back of her head. She looked more elegant than ever, but there were faint, blue shadows under her eyes.

'Bad journey?' Amy asked sympathetically.

'Oh, the night sleeper isn't so bad. But we were glad to be home.'

'Where's Peter?'

'He went to his office for a couple of hours. I think he might be back now. He's probably dressing. Lucky the House is in recess, or he'd have dashed off there too. He was getting very restless, the last few days.'

Amy sat down on one of the sofas near the fire, and Isabel settled herself opposite.

'Well?' Amy asked. 'How was it?'

'Would you like a drink?' Isabel reached out for the bell. The maid came in with the tray, and the sight of Isabel enjoying her hostess rôle made Amy feel more cheerful for a moment or two.

When they were alone again she said, 'Tell me about it. You've been away for six weeks.'

'Didn't I, in my letters?'

'Not really. I could have got exactly the same news from the *Guide Michelin*. Are you happy, Bel?'

Surprisingly, Isabel laughed and the shadows disappeared. 'Oh, I've missed you too. Amy the insistent. Yes, darling, of course I'm happy.'

'Is it what you expected?'

'Rather early to say, after only six weeks. And not very typical wedded weeks, either. It's more than I expected, I think.' Isabel looked down at her wrist, turning her bracelet so that the stones caught the light. 'And it takes a little getting used to, you know. You'll find out for yourself, when the time comes.'

'I expect so,' Amy said noncommittally. She was relieved, in a sense, that Isabel wasn't making wild claims of perfect happiness. Marriage would take some getting used to. Isabel looked tired, and she seemed a little withdrawn, but she appeared to be reacting with all her old calm, common sense. Perhaps the fears that her letters had aroused in Amy were unfounded, after all. Isabel was moving gracefully around the drawing-room now, using the refilling of their glasses as a pretext for adjusting an ornament and straightening a cushion. Suddenly she looked every inch the proud new wife, and Amy smiled.

'Not a lot has happened to me. I've been out two or three times with Tony Hardy.'

'Mmm? I saw him briefly at the wedding. I didn't know he was a friend of yours.'

'I think he is, now. He took me to a political meeting because I was complaining that I never met anyone different. Almost everyone was a Communist.'

'Amy, for God's sake don't say anything about that to Peter. He thinks they should all be clapped into prison.'

They looked at each other apprehensively and then they started to laugh, just as they had always been able to do.

Peter came in. His hair was brushed flat and sleek and he looked even healthier than he usually did, if that was possible.

'Oh dear,' he said genially, 'the terrible twins. Giggling, just like always. How are you, Amy m'dear?'

'In the pink, thank you Peter.'

There was the faintest of suppressed snorts from Isabel.

'I really don't understand you two, you know,' Peter said. He poured himself a whisky in a crystal tumbler and splashed soda into it from a siphon on the tray. He crossed the room to where Isabel was sitting and stood behind her sofa, one hand resting on her shoulder. Amy saw her sister glance up at her husband. It occurred to her that there was a kind of wary anxiety in the look.

Whatever there was, Peter didn't see it.

'Have you had a good day, darling?' Isabel asked him. His hand moved, lightly, to stroke her neck.

'An excellent day.'

They faced Amy now, both smiling, and she thought how

127

handsome they looked. Mr and Mrs Jaspert, comfortably at home.

Amy felt a frown gathering behind her eyes with the sense, still persistent, that everything was not quite right, for all the external harmony. But Isabel went on smiling and Peter's hand tightened affectionately on her shoulder before he moved away again.

They were extolling the beauties of Tuscany, reminding one another of sights and improving on one another's descriptions, when the maid appeared to show in the other guests. Two couples came into the room, exclaiming conventionally at its prettiness. There was another Tory MP, senior to Peter, and his ambitious wife, and a sharp-eyed City man with whom Peter went into a huddle at one end of the room while his wife talked about horses at the other.

A moment or two later Amy's partner for the evening arrived.

She had been vaguely expecting someone in the Johnny Guild mould and the blond young man who shook her hand surprised her a little. He looked hardly older than herself, twenty or perhaps twenty-one. He had a gentle, unassuming manner and Amy could see that he was shy in Peter Jaspert's house. But when, at length, his eyes did meet hers his blue, direct glance seemed at odds with the rest of him.

'Amy, may I introduce Charles Carew? Charles, this is Miss Lovell, Isabel's sister.'

They found themselves sitting together on the sofa, isolated by the conversations on either side of them. Glancing up, Amy saw Isabel talking animatedly to one of the wives about the arrangement of her drawing-room. She looked proud and happy, and Amy felt her anxiety dissolving. Following her gaze Charles Carew said quietly, 'It must be strange, finding oneself married.'

His perception startled her and she asked, absurdly, 'So you aren't married, Mr Carew?'

He laughed, and then tried to smother the sound. For a moment he was so like one of the 'suitable' boys who had been invited as dancing partners to Miss Abbott's school that Amy looked down, half-expecting to see Charles Carew's knobby, adolescent wrists protruding from his shirt cuffs in just the way that theirs had done. But his cuffs were long enough to hide his wrists. She saw that his hands were well scrubbed with long, square-ended fingers.

'No,' he said, his amusement under control. 'I'm a doctor.'

He must be older than he looks, then, Amy thought.

'I'm almost entirely dependent on my father. Surgery is a long training. A wife and family's a long way in the future. If it happens at all, that is.'

They found themselves smiling at each other.

'I think I feel the same,' Amy confided.

When they went down to dinner, Charles took Amy's arm politely, with old-fashioned manners.

The dining-room was filled with more flowers. Isabel must have spent the whole day arranging them. The table was a polished oval reflecting the candlelight and the pink, white and gold of Isabel's wedding china, and the faces around it looked pleased and relaxed. Isabel herself was beaming with pleasure at the success of her arrangements.

Amy felt herself relaxing too, with the laughter and talk and Peter's elegant claret. Suddenly she was enjoying being in Isabel's house, amongst her own generation. It was quite different from being at Bruton Street, or Chance, or one of the formal dinners before a dance. And because of his seeming youth, and his shyness, and the memories that he'd stirred in her, Charles Carew seemed more like a childhood ally than a dinner partner.

Amy looked from Isabel at one end of the table to Peter at the other. Perhaps this was what marriage was. Being in your own house, with your own friends. Perhaps it wasn't surprising at all that Isabel looked strained after six weeks' travelling. Being at home would make all the difference.

If I marry, will it be like this? Amy asked herself. She tried to imagine Tony Hardy at the other end of the polished table, but the picture eluded her. Chianti and sardines at Appleyard Street were the things that went with Tony. The thought of him made her smile.

'Will you share the joke with me?' Charles Carew asked her softly. He had been watching her, she realized.

'I'm sorry, that was rude of me. I was just thinking of a friend of mine and trying to imagine him here.'

'And could you?'

'Not really.' The idea was irresistibly funny, but Amy suppressed it because it seemed inappropriate to be talking about Tony, however obliquely, to this shy, polite boy. To deflect him, she asked, 'Are you an old friend of Peter's?'

'My father was in India with his, years ago. The Jasperts came home when Peter's grandfather died whereas we stayed, but the families have kept in touch. Otherwise my world doesn't exactly touch on Peter's.'

'What is your world?'

'Medicine,' Charles said, as if he was surprised at her need to ask. 'Once I'm qualified as a surgeon I'm going straight back to India. I can be useful there, you see. There's a lot to be done.' The mild expression had vanished.

'I envy you,' Amy said simply, and once again she was aware of Charles Carew's appraising, direct gaze.

She had to turn away, then. On her other side the MP, Archer Cole, was asking her something.

It wasn't until the end of the evening that Amy and Charles spoke directly to each other again. Charles was the first to leave, and he came across the room to say good night to her. They exchanged good wishes and then, thinking of her vacant days, on impulse Amy asked him, 'Would you be free to come and have tea with me at Bruton Street one day?'

She was still thinking of him as a family friend, and also perhaps imagining that he would fill in, in a brotherly way, some of the emptiness that Richard's elusiveness created.

Charles thought for a moment. Then he said, 'I'd like to, very much, but I don't think I can. I'm doing my theatre practice in the afternoons, you see. I have surgery lectures all morning, and at night there's cramming to do. I don't have any free time, really.'

'Never mind,' Amy said cheerfully. 'I'm sure we'll bump into each other again.'

They shook hands. Peter was waiting, and Charles followed him out of the room and the door closed behind them.

Amy didn't think about him again.

Amy was the last to leave. She had stayed behind after the others had gone to have a nightcap with Peter and Isabel.

'I did enjoy myself,' she told them, stretching out on the sofa with a sigh of pleasure. They beamed their satisfaction back at her. Peter took Isabel's hand and held it, and Isabel murmured, 'I thought it went rather well, too. I must tell Cook how pleased we were.'

The fire had sunk to a red glow, warming their faces and making the silver picture frames reflect back a coppery light.

Isabel let her head rest against Peter's shoulder. Her eyes were closed and Amy couldn't guess what she was thinking, but her face was smooth.

It's all right, Amy thought.

She wanted to slip away and let the maid see her out, but they jumped up when she stood up to go, and insisted on coming downstairs with her.

At the street door Peter hailed a taxi for her.

'I hope there will be hundreds more Ebury Street evenings like this one,' Amy said.

'Of course there will,' Peter answered, and Isabel echoed him. 'Of course there will.'

As the cab pulled away Amy looked back at them. They stood side by side framed by the light that spilled out of their front door and down the steps. They lifted their hands and waved to her, in unison.

There was a wonderful, tantalizing smell filling the dusty hall.

The men came filing in, too tired to joke any longer or even to talk, and dropped their bundles against the walls without looking at them, But the smell drew them to cluster round the open door at the end of the hall.

'This way, lads. That's right.' It was the catering contingent who had gone on ahead of the marchers from stop to stop, and had been waiting for them with hot food at the end of every day. Silverman and his friends on the Organizing Council had done well, Nick thought. The soup was being ladled out of big pans into a medley of cups and bowls. Nick was ravenous, but he waited until he had seen all his Nantlas contingent into the line before joining the end of it himself with the other march leaders.

It was the last night.

They had reached the outskirts of London, where new factories were springing up along the Great West Road and rows of neat, suburban houses in their square gardens stretched to the north and south of them. On every street corner here there was a little grocer's shop or a tobacconist's, windows and walls bright with coloured signs. The long column of dirty, exhausted men had tramped silently past the homeward-bound workers, men coming

131

out of the shops with the evening newspaper under their arm and packets of cigarettes in their pockets, and women in bright, spring-like clothes carrying baskets of food.

There had been cheering supporters lining the route, more tonight than on any of the others because the London Workers had turned out to greet them. But in the tranquil streets behind them the ordinary people going about their business had stared in surprise. London looked prosperous, different from any of the other places they had been through. Nantlas with its empty shops, grey streets and hollow-faced men and women, might have been on another continent. Another world, even.

The soup queue in the parish hall inched slowly forward. All around, men were sitting on wooden chairs, intent on their steaming bowls. When he reached the table at last one of the catering volunteers filled Nick's bowl for him, and gave him two generous hunks of bread. It was vegetable soup, thick and delicious. Nick carried his away to a corner as carefully as if it was a bowl of molten gold. The first spoonfuls, so hot in his mouth that they almost burned him, spread warmth all through him.

Along the endless road, and in the villages and towns where they had stopped, there had been surprising support. During the day the farmworkers in the fields and most of the drivers of the cars and lorries that rumbled past them, splashing them with filthy water from the potholes in the roads, had stared and then, when they understood, there had been encouragement and coins dropped into the bags marked 'March for Work. March for Food.'

At nights, when they stopped dead tired in the town halls and even, once, in a huge barn still stacked with hay bales, people had brought food. Sometimes it had been local union representatives, bringing cash donations and messages of support as well as thick sandwiches and urns of strong, sweet tea. But sometimes it was different people, prosperous, middle-class and not workers, as the miners described them. These people looked shocked and sympathetic, and murmured 'We must all do what we can to help,' and they brought exotic pies with rich, crumbly pastry and, on one memorable night, a huge baked ham. He had been eating much better than Mari and Dickon would be doing back in Nantlas, Nick thought painfully.

He finished his soup and the last of the bread, and then reached into his rucksack. He had given most of the chocolate to a boy with a terrible cough who had been struggling to keep up almost ever since they had left Wales, but there was one square left. He had been keeping it to have as a celebration when they reached London, and he unwrapped it now and ate it slowly, thinking about Mari.

It was right that he had come, even though he had had to leave her, Nick was sure of that. The march was running under its own momentum now, already a success. Out of the seven hundred men who had left Newport eleven days ago, only a handful had dropped out, in spite of the official labour movement predictions that the miners would never make it. Even those men had had to be ordered to stop marching because their torn feet or exhaustion were holding up progress. Their dogged determination to reach London was a testament in itself, because the marchers had deliberately been chosen, by Nick and the other organizers, from the poorest and weakest of all the thousands of unemployed men across the coalfield who had wanted to march. Any man still receiving the meagre unemployed benefit or the Poor Law relief had been excluded, because no one could guarantee that he would be able to claim the money again on his return. None of the march organizers wanted to claim the responsibility for another destitute family.

Only those who had nothing were chosen, just because they had nothing to forfeit. Nick put aside the thought that he stood to lose his own benefit. That was something he would have to reckon with if and when it happened. It would have been impossible to act as a spur to the other men and not to march himself.

And the march was a success. People were with them, no one could deny that. The food, and the money in the fighting fund proved it. Best of all was the support that had come not only from workers, often in defiance of their own right-wing unions, but from the secure, middle-class people who need never have bothered to think about unemployed miners. If we can reach them, Nick thought, not the politicians, or the coal-owners, but ordinary decent people with money in their pockets, then perhaps we can get something done for us all.

He unstrapped his blanket once more and found a space to unroll it. The floor was draughty bare boards, but to Nick it felt as welcoming and comfortable as a feather bed. He wasn't hard with working muscle any more after the months of enforced idleness, and the general shortage of food had taken its toll, but he was still fit and strong enough. Yet his legs ached all the way up into his back, and his calves and feet felt leaden with the endless walking. He rubbed the complaining muscles and reminded himself that he was comfortable compared with the older men suffering from pneumoconiosis, and the thin boys transparent with undernourishment from babyhood.

Nick carefully unlaced his boots, afraid that they might fall apart if he handled them too roughly. The sole of the left one had parted company from the upper and the two halves were bound together with rag. Yet some men didn't even have that, and their progress had slowed to a shuffle that threatened to hold up the whole march.

He smiled suddenly. They had looked like the last tattered remnants of a defeated army long before reaching London, but the fire of spirit had burned stronger and stronger all the way. At first the sheer distance had overwhelmed them, but as the days and miles slid past they had begun to sing again, the old songs remembered from Flanders and the Somme, and the favourite hymns from the chapels in the valleys. They had talked, too, endless fiery discussions of political theory, literature, and even philosophy. Most of the men had brought books in their packs. Reading seemed to satisfy a kind of hunger when there wasn't any food.

Nick himself had brought a fat, black volume of *Paradise Lost* borrowed from the Miners' Welfare library. The magnificent, stately rhythms of the verse soothed him even though the thread of meaning was sometimes lost to him. He took the book out now, thinking that he would read a little while there was still light. But he had hardly begun when from down the crowded hall came a low, bass humming, rising and falling like the sea. Nick put his book away again. There would be singing tonight, instead.

The visiting vicar sat down on one of his wooden chairs, and the men in the kitchen stopped clanking the pans and crockery. The hall grew dark while the singing went on, and somebody brought in oil lamps flaring behind their smoky gas mantles.

The final hymn was the one that was always left until last. The singing rose and filled the hall, and drifted beyond it out into the suburban night.

Bread of Heaven, Bread of Heaven,
Feed me till I want no more,
want no more,
Feed me till I want no more.

There was no more, after that. The hall was just a crowded, stuffy room full of tired men turning on their thin blankets ready for sleep.

Nick was smiling when he fell asleep. Tomorrow they would do what they had come to do, and then they could go home.

6

It was raining again, a cold, thin rain that fell straight down from a blank, grey sky.

Amy turned away from the window and went to her wardrobe. She was supposed to be shopping and having tea with her old schoolfriend Violet Trent, and Bethan had pressed her pale grey suit for her and put out her high-heeled grey suède shoes. But Amy had telephoned Violet to say that she couldn't manage tea today, and she put the suit back in her wardrobe. She wasn't sure of the appropriate costume for this afternoon, but it certainly wasn't a Charles Creed suit and a shirt with a pie-frill collar and two dozen tiny tucks in the front.

Amy frowned at the outfits hanging on the rail, each one shrouded in its linen bag and with the matching shoes polished and wrapped in the racks below. The right sort of clothes that she owned were mostly at Chance, and this array only underlined the frivolity of her London existence for her. In the end she put on a pair of dark trousers with the stoutest shoes she could find, and the plain coat she had worn to Appleyard Street. A beret hid her hair, and at the last moment she snapped off her pearl ear-studs and dropped them back into the red morocco box that stood on her dressing-table.

Amy slipped downstairs and out of the house without anyone seeing her. The rain dripped monotonously from the trees in Berkeley Square, and the pavements were crowded with bobbing black umbrellas. She set off down Hill Street, certain of where she was going, and emerged a few minutes later into Park Lane.

Amongst the red buses and taxis sending up plumes of spray she saw a handful of police on horseback plodding towards Marble Arch, their waterproof capes spread out over the big brown rumps of the horses. On the opposite side, beyond the traffic, was a thin but continuous stream of people heading in the same direction. There were more policemen amongst them. Amy crossed the road and with her hands deep in her coat pockets she began to walk too.

At Speaker's Corner the crowd was already a thousand strong and it was swelling steadily as people trickled to join it from all directions. A brass band was playing cheerful music under the trees at the edge of the Park, but the musicians' faces were solemn and no one seemed to be listening to them. Amy edged close to the makeshift platform of piled-up boxes. Most of the people she passed were simply waiting quietly in the downpour, their collars turned up and dark, damp patches showing on their shoulders. There were policemen everywhere, ringing the growing crowd and filtering through it in pairs. Amy wondered why there were so many of them to control this dejected, almost silent gathering of people. The banners and placards held up were smudged and limp, at odds with their defiant messages.

Amy read them as she waited, wishing that Tony had let her accompany him so that he could explain.

'Bermondsey for Workers Control.'

'London Workers Support the Miners.'

'A Job for Every Man.'

Suddenly, in the middle of a knot of people beside the platform, she saw Jake Silverman. His dark head and black beard stuck up above the rest. He was bareheaded, coatless and soaking wet, but Amy could sense the crackle of his liveliness even from where she stood. She was about to run towards him, unthinking, when a motorcyclist came nosing slowly through the crowds. A red armband was fastened around the sleeve of his jacket. Jake's head jerked up at the throb of the engine, and he beckoned the rider forward. Reaching the foot of the platform steps, the man pushed up his goggles and said something to Jake. At once Jake seized his hand and shook it, pumping the man's arm up and down in his pleasure.

Then Jake vaulted up on to the platform. Amy saw Kay there at the front in a bright green waterproof with her hair wrapped in a scarf. She immediately began to look from head to head, searching for Tony, but there was no sign of him.

'Comrades and friends!'

Jake was up at the edge of the platform, beckoning them all forward. The crowd surged forward immediately, pressing closer around Amy. She let herself be carried forward too. Out of the corner of her eye she saw the head of one of the police mounts rear upwards, its harness jingling.

'Friends, we have just had word from the courier here that the marchers will reach us in fifteen minutes.'

Jake's voice carried easily over the cheering that broke out, raggedly at first and then growing in conviction.

'You all know that they have been on the road for twelve days. That on every one of those days comrades and workers have come out to support them. And that their support was often in direct defiance of the Labour Right who have done their best to sabotage this march. Let's give our marchers a welcome now to beat anything they've seen yet. Let's every one of us be proud that we are here to march with them on the last lap to Trafalgar Square. And let's go on from there to Downing Street!'

The cheering was a roar now. Somehow Jake Silverman had drawn the soaking, silent crowd forward and set it alight.

'Today we'll show Ramsay MacDonald that a capitalist Labour government is no bloody good to us. Let's show him that we want work. That we want to control that work ourselves. And that we mean to do it. Let him be warned!'

Jake's clenched fists came up over his head and he shook them, and the cheering rose to meet him as if he was conducting his own powerful orchestra. The forest of placards and banners rose in a wave and the clenched fists defiantly answered Jake Silverman's defiance.

'Be warned! Be warned!'

It was a chant now. Under the trees the band began to play again. Dimly Amy recognized *The Red Flag*, and at the same time, quite close to her, she heard another shout.

'Commie saboteur!'

'Kike! Kike! Fuck off to Russia if that's what you want!'

The surge of the crowd towards it half-turned her around. She saw a big man with a red face ducking away, and the smooth flanks of a police horse as it wheeled sharply in front of her. The horse blocked her view for an instant, and when she looked again a space had opened in the crowd. The margins of it were held back by lines of police with their arms linked tight.

Amy was suddenly cold. Something ugly was flickering here, behind the police helmets and in the London faces milling around her. *It might not be safe, for one thing*, Tony had said when he

138

had refused to let her come with him. What was it that wasn't safe, amongst these people and the half-understood rhetoric of their slogans?

Part of her was detachedly aware that the rain had stopped, and that towards the west beyond the ragged edges of the clouds there was a faint, pale blue line. But with the rest of herself she was listening to the crowd noise, and waiting fearfully for that flicker of ugliness again.

There was more shouting from the roadside now.

'They're here!'

The police, with their arms still linked, were easing the crowds further apart so that a wide aisle opened between them. The cheering and shouting died into an expectant silence and the band sounded much louder.

Amy stood on tiptoe, craning to see. A fat man in a coat much too small for him grinned at her, showing black teeth. ''Ere y'are, my love. Get in 'ere in front.'

In the sudden breathless silence, between the square shoulders of the policemen, Amy saw them coming.

It was a long, black column, with lights bobbing on either side of it. The miners were in ranks of four, swinging smartly along as if they had only set out that morning.

As they came closer, the leaders turning in between the held-back crowds, she saw that the impression of blackness came from their dark, sodden clothes and from their physical likeness. They were small, hunched men with dark faces under their caps. And the lights were miners' lamps. Each man carried his lamp, lit up and swinging to his step.

She was struck by something incongruous about the column as it drew closer. The men were marching like an army, and the band was playing them on. But there was no triumphant ring of well-drilled boots on the metalled road. Amy listened, and the sound she heard caught at her throat and sent a shiver deep inside her.

There was only the muffled flap, flap of hundreds of pairs of broken boots, boots tied up with rag and shored uselessly against the rain with newspaper.

It was the flap, flap that cleared Amy's head and drove her forward against the wall of policemen. She found her voice and she was shouting, shouting the same welcome and greeting that rose in a deafening crescendo around her. She stretched her hand out past the uniform shoulders and waved and shouted as she had never done before.

If men could walk so far in boots like those to ask for help, how badly must they be in need of it? And in her own cupboards at home, polished for her and brushed and carefully stored in bags, there were dozens of pairs of shoes in crocodile skin, soft suède and supple pastel leather.

In that instant Amy knew, with as much certainty as she had ever known anything, which side she was on. She was with these men, with their proud lights and their thin, drawn faces and their terrible boots, and she was with Jake Silverman and his friends. With Tony Hardy, wherever he was. Amy felt as if she had just come home, and yet as if she had cut herself off from everything she loved and understood. Gerald Lovell and Peter Jaspert, Adeline, and even Isabel, didn't belong in this new home because they couldn't or wouldn't see what was happening here today.

Amy was gulping for air that tasted of wet wool, sweating people and horses. Were these people her friends and family, she thought wildly, looking at the strangers surging and shouting around her?

The column of marchers was still passing.

Amy saw a green banner with a red and gold dragon. *Nantlas, Rhondda* it proclaimed. Bethan's home village. Bethan was having a rare day off today. Was she here in the crowd too? Why hadn't the two of them come together? Amy felt dizzy, as if her world had suddenly tilted to one side and changed all her perspectives. Under the Nantlas banner she saw a man much taller than his companions, bareheaded like Jake Silverman and with his black hair flattened to his head by the rain. He was looking over the heads of the crowd and smiling, pleased with what he saw. Amy had time to think, *There, there's someone who knows he's right*, before the man had passed and was swallowed up into the black ranks beneath the platform.

The tail of the march arrived and the aisle held open in the waiting crowd was filled with miners.

There was one brief speech from the platform and then Jake was speaking again, not shouting yet his voice carried to the back of the huge crowd.

'The last lap now. We'll march together to Trafalgar Square.

140

Let's tell our friends from South Wales that we're proud to march behind them.'

There was a great burst of cheering, but there were other shouts too and Amy struggled to hear what the raw voices were threatening. The police horses wheeled round again and the miners raised their banners once more. The dark-faced men in their black clothes turned and led the way along Oxford Street with their lamps swinging and the band playing behind them. Amy let herself be carried forward in the press as the police chain broke to let them through and then she was walking too, past the familiar shopfronts and the curious, staring faces of shoppers on the city pavements. For one odd, hallucinatory moment she thought she saw herself and Violet Trent among them, faces blank under their smart little hats. The gutters were huge puddles after the heavy rain, and Amy's shoes were unsuitable for walking any distance. Her feet and trouser legs were soon soaked, but she was oblivious. She felt as proud as Jake Silverman could have hoped, and she cheered and sang at the top of her voice with everyone else. The fat man with the tight coat was still at her side, and he winked at her. 'We'll show 'em, eh?' He was holding one side of a placard that read *National Unemployed Workers Movement*.

I am unemployed, that's true enough, Amy thought wryly.

They passed Oxford Circus. The police were holding up the traffic and she glimpsed Regent Street choked with stationary buses. At the far end of Oxford Street they turned and streamed down Charing Cross Road. Amy's right shoe had rubbed her heel into a blister, and she thought again of the hundreds of miles from South Wales in boots tied up with rags.

At last they reached Trafalgar Square. There was another, bigger platform here, draped with banners that read 'London Workers Welcome the SWMF Marchers'. The square filled up behind her and Amy found herself pushed closer to the front. Just ahead of her and to the right, on the steps between Landseer's lions, she saw Jake and Kay again. There were still more policemen here, on foot and on horseback, and another brass band playing outside the National Gallery. The cheering and shouting was deafening, and the crowd surged and swayed in pulsating waves, suddenly much bigger. More people must have been waiting for the marchers to arrive in the square.

It was difficult to hear the speakers and Amy strained to

catch the words of one after another of the march leaders and organizers. 'This government . . . be made to see that the failure of private enterprise in our industries . . . chronic poverty and destitution among unemployed men . . . persistent pit closures . . . repeal of the Eight-Hour Day Act . . . iniquity of the not seeking work clause . . .'

Then, as she struggled to hear through the din, she caught the sound of different chanting.

'Commie scum! Commie scum!'

The crowd bulged around her and swayed towards the sound with a sudden, ominous life of its own.

'Dirty reds! Dirty reds!'

Amy glimpsed Jake Silverman hoisting Kay out of the way on to the steps and then plunging forward. The chanting broke up into urgent shouting. Four police horses and a dozen bobbing helmets converged on the spot where Jake had disappeared. From somewhere ahead of her Amy heard a woman's scream, and then as if at a signal the boiling crowd erupted into violence. Right beside her a man's fist came up and smashed into another's face, and a spurt of blood sprang from his nose before he fell backwards under the trampling feet. Amy heard her own scream rising with the others, and then she was propelled violently forward by the fighting breaking out behind her. She stumbled forward, catching at clothes and arms to stop herself being pushed over, and almost fell over another man lying on the ground with his arms up to protect his head and face. Then the high brown flanks of a police horse loomed over her and she saw the great polished hooves only a foot or so from the man's head. She ducked down to try to help him but he was already being hauled to his feet by his friends.

The crowd from the back of the square was still pushing forward to the steps, and Amy felt an instant of pure, panicky certainty that she would be crushed to death or suffocated in this dense, heaving mass of bodies.

The steps, she told herself. Try to reach the steps where she had seen Jake lift Kay up. The next blind surge carried her forward, and she saw that she had come up against the solid phalanx of miners in front of the platform. A lamp was still swinging in someone's hand. The steps were only a few yards away.

Then, right beside her, Jake Silverman was fighting to pull

142

away from two men who held his arms pinned savagely behind his back. A mounted policeman was just behind them with his stick raised. Amy saw the leather thong wrapped around his gloved fist. Then there was a third man right beside Jake with something short and heavy in his hand.

A lead bar. A length of piping. Whatever, it was for Jake.

Amy opened her mouth to scream but he would never have heard the warning. As she watched, frozen, the bar came up and then down. The dull crack of metal against bone and skin made her feel sick to the pit of her stomach. Jake's head flopped forward and he fell like an empty sack.

Horror gave Amy strength. She thrust past the men blocking her way and knelt beside Jake. His face was as white as candle-wax and his eyes were closed. When Amy looked up again to scream for help the three men had vanished and there was nothing in the world except trampling feet and swaying bodies that threatened to topple over them. In feeble desperation she tried to pull at Jake's coat and realized that she would never be able to drag his weight to safety. Then someone else was pulling her aside and stooping beside Jake. She saw the blue scars on the hand turning Jake's unconscious face, and the lamp hooked to his belt.

'Murdering bastards,' the miner said.

Then he bent and scooped Jake up. He hoisted the dead weight over his shoulder as if it was nothing, and began to strike through the tangle of people. Amy looked wildly around for Kay or another familiar face, but there was no one. The police were moving through the crowd in blue lines now, and the violence was ebbing away. Most people were standing still, bewildered, with their arms hanging at their sides. A little path opened in front of the miner with his burden and Amy ran after him, almost sobbing with relief.

He didn't stop or look round until they were clear of the mass in the square. In front of St Martin's-in-the-Fields he glanced back over his shoulder and then very gently swung Jake down and put him on the pavement. His face was so white that Amy was afraid he was already dead. There was a tiny trickle of dark blood at the corner of his mouth.

'Are you his friend?' the miner asked abruptly.

Amy nodded.

'See to him, then. I'll run for the ambulance. Bloody First Aid Post's the other side of the square.'

He was gone immediately.

Amy knelt down beside Jake. He must still be alive if that man's gone for help, she thought stupidly. She undid her coat and took it off, wrapping the soft folds over the crumpled body as best she could. Then she untied her silk scarf and put it under his head. He was so heavy, and there wasn't a flicker of movement.

'Jake,' she whispered. 'What can I do to help you?'

She had no idea. She took his cold hand and held it, bitterly thinking that she was completely useless. She had marched along Oxford Street, singing and shouting and feeling proud of herself, yet now she was needed for something real and she was failing them. Jake was going to die here on the pavement outside St Martin's-in-the-Fields because she didn't know how to save him.

A knot of people had gathered round them, and she looked up at the faces. 'Does anyone know any first aid?'

They shook their heads, sympathetic but unhelpful.

'Nah. Ambulance'll be along just now.'

The seconds ticked by and Jake didn't move. Amy went on holding his hand and found herself praying. Please God, let him be all right. Please God, let him . . .

The miner came back again.

He knelt down on the other side of Jake and felt his wrist, then turned his head to one side. Amy was surprised by the gentleness of his scarred hands.

'I didn't know what to do,' she said, 'I'm sorry . . .'

'Nothing you could do,' he answered without looking at her. 'He needs hospital.'

Almost at once they heard the siren. The ambulance was ploughing up through the crowds on the east side of the square. Amy looked up and saw the high white side of it with the reassuring red cross.

'Thank God,' she said, and the miner looked up and smiled in relief for the first time. I know you, Amy thought.

The ambulance-men came running with their rolled-up green canvas stretcher. They spread it out beside Jake and lifted him on to it, then hoisted his weight up into the dark mouth of the ambulance.

From the folding metal steps the miner jerked his head at Amy. 'You'd better come too.'

She scrambled in and the doors slammed behind them. They sped away in the direction the ambulance had come.

The miner leaned back against the hard wooden bench opposite the stretcher. 'Don't worry,' he said. 'Your man will be all right.'

'He isn't my man,' Amy said. 'I just know him.'

The man was still smiling, and she knew why she recognized him. He was the tall miner who had marched under the Nantlas banner, and had smiled out over the crowds in his enviable certainty.

'How do you know he'll be all right?'

'I've seen enough head injuries,' he answered abruptly.

The ambulance was slowing again. Charing Cross Hospital, Amy thought, and again: Thank God.

Light flooded in at them as the doors swung open. The stretcher was lifted and carried out and they followed behind it into the hospital. Another ambulance had arrived immediately behind them, and the hallway was full of hurrying people in white uniforms. Two nurses came forward to meet Jake's stretcher as it was lifted on to a trolley. His hand hung limply at one side. One of the nurses peeled back the ambulance blanket and Amy's coat. She held it out briskly to Amy. 'Do you know this patient?'

Amy opened her mouth, but the miner forestalled her. 'His name is Jacob Silverman. I am a relative. I will look after his things for him.'

Smoothly he removed a worn leather wallet and a little book from Jake's pocket, and smiled at the nurse.

'I'm afraid you can't do that . . .' she began, and then shrugged.

'We'll wait out here until the doctor has seen him,' the miner said. The nurses wheeled Jake away, and Amy watched them until they disappeared around a maroon-tiled corner.

'Shall we sit down?'

There was a double row of hard wooden chairs down the length of the hall, and they found two empty ones side by side.

A man passed them, supported by two others, his nose streaming blood.

'Quite a fight,' Amy's companion said. He was flicking quickly

145

through Jake's little book, and then through the few papers and notes in the old wallet. He frowned at one piece of folded paper and slipped it into his own pocket, then closed the things up again.

'Did you see what happened?' he asked.

'Two men were holding him. Another man hit him with something that looked like a metal bar. There was a policeman on a horse right beside them. Who'd want to do that to Jake?'

The man was looking at her. Amy saw him looking at her face and hair, and then at her hands. She was surprised to find that she was still clutching her handbag.

'How well do you know Jake?'

'I met him once at Appleyard Street.'

'And what were you doing at Appleyard Street?'

Amy felt a prickle of resentment. Why, after what had just happened, was this man questioning her?

'Just visiting,' she said coolly.

'I see. Just a tourist?' His voice was equally cool.

'I suppose so.' His suspicion aroused her own and she looked squarely at him.

'What did you take from Jake's pocket?'

The miner grinned. 'Can't you work that out? If you know who Jake is, and what he does?'

They sat in silence after that. Amy watched the nurses coming and going, moving quickly but unhurriedly. It seemed a very long time.

At last a doctor came round the corner. A nurse beside him pointed to them.

'Are you Mr Silverman's friends?'

They nodded.

'There's nothing to worry about. He has some concussion, but there is no skull fracture and he should regain consciousness before too long. We will have to keep him here for a few days, of course. I understand you are a relative?'

'That's right.'

The doctor's eyes flicked over the dark clothes and the lamp at the man's belt, but he said nothing. 'In that case, perhaps you would inform his next of kin. You may say that the sister in ward two may be telephoned for news of him in the morning.'

'Thank you.' The man held out Jake's wallet and book. 'I said

146

that I would take care of these for him, but if he's going to be conscious soon he might worry about where they have gone. Will you take them for him?'

The nurse held out her hand and Amy and the miner turned away. Still in silence they went out and stood in the hospital courtyard. The clouds of the afternoon had all drifted away and the sky was the colour of pearl, pink-tinged in the west.

'What time is it?' he asked.

Amy glanced at her watch. 'Half past six.'

'Everything will be all over, then,' the man said. His voice sounded flat and, for the first time, uncertain. They began to walk together, still in silence, heading automatically for Trafalgar Square. When they reached it the crowds had evaporated. There were just the ordinary passers-by, a pair of patrolling policemen and a handful of men dismantling the makeshift platform.

'Which way is Downing Street?'

Amy pointed. There was no sign of the long column of miners, or any of the crowds and placards that had filled the afternoon.

The man turned in a circle, looking all round him. 'Well,' he said, and Amy suddenly saw how tired he was. 'That's that, then. I wonder where they've gone?'

'I read in one of the papers,' Amy said carefully, 'that the marchers were to be put up while they were in London in Bethnal Green Town Hall.'

'Ah.' The man's smile was wry. 'And which way is that?'

Amy pointed eastwards down the Strand. He hitched his jacket around him, still smiling. 'I'd better start off that way, then.'

'Wait.' Amy was thinking quickly. *I'm on your side*, she wanted to say, remembering Hyde Park and the flapping of the boots as the men marched past her. *I always will be, however uselessly.* But there was something about this man that disconcerted her. There were two pound notes in her bag, but he wasn't the kind of man to have money pressed into his hand.

What kind of man was he, then?

'Why did you steal that paper from Jake's wallet?'

The man was much taller than Amy. He looked down at her and she saw that he had unusual grey-green eyes, and that he was amused.

'Steal it? To eat, perhaps? Or to start a fire to keep warm by?

147

Listen, whoever you are. Written on that piece of paper were addresses that are important to us. Addresses of Communist Party organizers, sympathizers, the whole network. Better that the police shouldn't see it if they come to see him and happen to search him.'

'The police?' Amy was going to protest *They wouldn't*, and then she remembered the big horses with their shiny hooves.

The man gestured his impatience with her. 'Of course. Jake Silverman is a dangerous Communist agitator.' Amy bent her head to escape his grey, distant stare.

As she looked down at the paving stones she saw her own polished shoes with their elegant toes pointing at the miner's worn, gaping boots.

Amy forgot his hostility. There was something she could do to help him, she thought. There was no need for him to trudge the last miles to Bethnal Green in those boots, and there was no need either to risk his scorn by trying to give him money. Bruton Street was a big house full of bedrooms that no one would occupy tonight. It was her home, and she could invite this man to stay the night there as her guest. As soon as the thought came to her she looked up and met his eyes again.

'If you haven't got anywhere to stay tonight,' she said at last, 'you could have a bed at my home.'

His eyebrows went up into black peaks.

'Your home? And where's that?'

His coldness angered her. She had made her impulsive offer in a spirit of straightforward friendliness, and she wanted him to accept it in the same way.

'Does it matter where it is?' she snapped.

The miner shrugged. 'Not really. I'm sure it will be better than the Spike. Shall we go, then?'

There was a taxi passing them. Amy flung up her arm and it rumbled to the kerb. The cabbie scowled at the miner, but Amy wrenched open the door and scrambled inside and the man followed her.

'Bruton Street,' she called sharply through the partition, and the driver muttered something about it being fine for some people, as they trundled grudgingly away. The man leaned back and closed his eyes, and she saw the exhaustion in his face. Her anger evaporated, bafflingly.

'My name's Amy,' she said.

'Nick Penry,' he answered without opening his eyes. After a moment he added, 'Thank you. I don't know where Bethnal Green is, but I don't want to walk there tonight.'

'You come from Nantlas, don't you?'

She was aware of his quick sidelong glance at her now but she kept her face turned away, pretending to be watching the streets sliding past.

'How do you know that?'

'I saw you under the banner. At Hyde Park. I . . . know someone else from there.'

'Do you, indeed? That surprises me a little.' Nick Penry's eyes were closed again and Amy continued to stare out of the window, her cheeks reddened. Neither of them spoke again until they rolled into Bruton Street.

Damn you, Amy thought.

She had been wondering what to do with the man once they were home. Where would she put him? What was he expecting? It was not a situation that Miss Abbott's social deportment lessons had prepared her for.

Now she decided. This sharp, unsettling man would be treated just like any other guest in their house. Gerald was at Chance and Adeline was occupied with a new friend. That would make it easier, she thought, and at once felt that she was compromising her new allegiances by being grateful for that.

On the steps in front of the tall doors Amy ceremonially rang the bell instead of using her key. One of the footmen opened the door.

'Good afternoon, Miss Amy.'

Inside, she said crisply, 'This is Mr Penry. He will be staying the night. Perhaps it would be easiest if one of the maids made up Mr Richard's room for him. And Mr Penry has been separated from his luggage. Would you see that some things are laid out for him? We'll be ready for dinner at . . . oh, eight, I should think.'

'Very good, Miss Amy.'

Nick Penry looked up from the marble floor to the high curve of the stairs and the crystal waterfall of the huge chandelier spilling light over them. There was an inlaid table encrusted with gilt with a silver tray on it and the afternoon's post laid neatly out. Amy had automatically picked up her letters. It was very quiet; the muffled, dignified silence of money and privilege.

149

Under the curve of the stairway with a scroll-backed sofa covered in pale green silk beneath it, there was a huge, dim oil painting of a big house. Row upon row of windows looked out expressionlessly over drowsy parkland.

Nick pointed to it. 'That's the country place, is it?'

'Yes, as a matter of fact.' He was grinning at her, and there was a taunt in it that made her angry again.

'Jesus Christ. Who are you?'

'Amy Lovell.'

'Should I be any the wiser?'

'If you aren't,' Amy said, surprised at the tartness in her voice, 'I'll elaborate. My father is Lord Lovell. The Lords Lovell have been the King's Defenders since the fourteenth century.'

'How nice. Does that make you Lady Lovell?'

'Of course not. That's my mother. My title, by courtesy only, is the Honourable Amalia Lovell. My friends call me Amy.'

'I see,' Nick Penry said, pointedly not calling her anything. They stood underneath the chandelier, staring at each other.

The footman came back again.

'John will show you upstairs, Mr Penry. Dinner will be at eight, if that suits you.'

Still the taunting grin and the odd, clear stare. 'Oh, delight-ful.'

'This way, sir.' The footman was carefully not looking at the visitor's gaping boots and the lamp clipped to his belt like a proclamation.

Amy went upstairs to her room. She ripped open the sheaf of envelopes she had picked up downstairs and stared unseeingly at the invitations. Then she remembered that she was supposed to be dining at Ebury Street. She telephoned Isabel and told her that there was an unexpected guest at Bruton Street.

'It doesn't matter,' Isabel said. 'There would only have been us, anyway.'

'Bel, are you all right?'

Concern cut through Amy's preoccupation. Isabel's voice sounded as if she had been crying.

'Of course. Call me tomorrow if you like. I'm not doing anything much.'

Amy hung up, frowning, and automatically set about changing for dinner.

150

In Richard's bedroom Nick Penry prowled to and fro between the cupboards and the bookshelves. He picked one of the leather-bound stamp albums out of the row and looked through the carefully set-out lines of tiny, vivid paper squares. There were dozens of books neatly shelved, most of them on art and architecture, but there were volumes of poetry too. The copy of *Paradise Lost* looked identical to the one that Nick had lost with his pack. The old rucksack had been pulled off his shoulders as he fought to Jake Silverman's side in Trafalgar Square.

The Welfare library would expect him to pay for a lost book, Nick remembered.

Nick had asked the superior footman if he could make a telephone call, and he had been shown into a vast room lined with books. There were little tables with the newspapers and boxes of crested paper laid out, and a wide, polished desk with a silver inkstand and a green-shaded lamp. He had sat at the desk in a green leather chair to telephone Appleyard Street.

He told the girl at the other end what had happened to Jake, and gave her the doctor's message. The sob of relief in her voice as she thanked him suddenly made Nick think of Mari and Dickon, alone in the damp, cheerless little house in Nantlas. He was struck with a sudden, sharp physical longing to hold them both in his arms.

Nick resumed his pacing. There were silver-backed brushes on the tallboy, and in the heavy, mirrored wardrobe there were what seemed like dozens of suits and coats and polished shoes. If Mr Richard was the frowning boy beside Amy Lovell in the silver-framed photograph on the tallboy, he was hardly more than a child. How could a child need so many clothes; own so many possessions? With a sharp clatter, Nick replaced another photograph, this one of a beautiful woman lounging in a basket chair with a spaniel on her lap.

As he stood there, Nick felt the ugly swell of anger within himself. It was a familiar feeling. He had known it since early boyhood when he had caught it from his father. Nick thought of the anger as an infection because it made him helpless while it lasted, and it clouded his thinking. It made him vicious, as he had felt on the night of the explosion long ago at Nantlas No. 1 pit, and that was of no benefit to anyone. It was better by far to be clear-headed. That was a better weapon in the battle that he had inherited from his father and mother. They had died early, of deprivation and exhaustion, but Nick knew that he had enough strength himself to last a long time yet. Nick's father had lived by the Fed, and his son had adopted his faith. As soon as he was old enough to think for himself, Nick had gone further still. He had become a Communist because the steely principles of Marxism seemed to offer an intellectual solution beyond the capitalist tangle that bled dry the pits and the men who worked them.

But yet sometimes Nick couldn't suppress the anger. It came when he looked at Dickon, and when he watched Mari working in the comfortless back kitchen at home. And it came to smother him now in the rich, padded opulence of Amy Lovell's home.

Nick slowly clenched and unclenched his fists, and then shook his head from side to side as if to clear it.

First thing tomorrow, he promised himself, he would be off.

The swell of anger began to subside again, as he had learned it always did. Deliberately he began to peel off his grimy clothes.

He was here, now. There was nothing he could do here, tonight, in this particular house. He didn't know why the girl had brought him here, but something in her ardent, sensitive face worked on his anger too, diminishing it.

He would make use of the house, Nick thought, by taking whatever was offered to him. He found a plaid robe behind the door and wrapped himself in it. He stood his lamp on the tallboy next to the silver brushes and went across to the bathroom that the footman had pointed out to him.

A deep, hot bath had already been drawn. There were piles of thick, warm towels and new cakes of green marbled soap. The brass taps gleamed and the mirrors over the mahogany panels were misted with steam. As he sank into the water and gratefully felt the heat drawing the aches out of his body, Nick was thinking about Nantlas again. In Nantlas, baths were made of tin and they were hauled in from the wash-house and set in front of the fire in the back kitchen. Then a few inches of hot water were poured in from jugs. He sat up abruptly, splashing the mirrors.

How much longer could they last, these gulfs? Between the people who had things and the people who didn't?

Not for ever, Nick promised himself. Not for ever, by any means.

When he put the plaid robe on again and padded back to the bedroom he found that his clothes had been removed. In their place was a dinner suit with a boiled shirt and a stiff collar, a butterfly tie, even a pair of patent shoes that shone like mirrors. Black silk socks. Underwear with the creases still sharp which looked as if it had just been unfolded from tissue.

'For God's sake,' Nick Penry murmured.

It was exactly five minutes to eight. Someone tapped discreetly at the door. He flung it open to confront Amy.

'Um. I thought you might be ready,' she said. Her cheeks went faintly pink. 'I'll come back later.'

Nick jabbed his finger at the clothes on the bed. 'I won't wear this get-up. Where have my clothes gone?'

'I expect they've taken them away to dry them properly for you. What's wrong with the ones they've given you?'

'Everything. D'you really think I'd put all that lot on?'

Amy's face went a deeper pink. She pushed past him into the room. 'I don't give a damn what you wear. Come down to dinner in my little brother's dressing-gown, if that's what you feel like.'

Nick suddenly wanted to laugh. Instead he leant against the door frame and folded his arms. 'A shirt and jersey and an ordinary pair of trousers will do nicely, thank you.' He watched her flinging open drawers and rummaging through cupboards, suddenly noticing how pretty she was without the disfiguring beret that she had worn all afternoon. She had thick, shiny hair that was an unusual dark red, and warm, clear skin that coloured easily. Her eyes were the bluey-green colour that often went with red hair. She was wearing a creamy-coloured dress of some soft material that was slightly too fussy for her, Nick thought, but she had exceptionally pretty calves and ankles that her high-heeled, pointy-toed shoes with ankle-straps displayed to perfection.

'Very nice,' Nick said smoothly. She was holding out a navy-blue jersey that Richard had put away because it was too big for him. There was a plain white shirt too.

'Leave the shirt unbuttoned if it's much too tight,' she said sharply. 'I shall have to go and look for some trousers belonging to my father. Richard's will be far too small.'

'You're very kind,' Nick called after her, laughing when she could no longer see him.

153

A moment or two later she came back with an unexceptional pair of grey flannel trousers. Nick took them.

'His lordship's very own?' he asked, grinning, and Amy snatched her hand away in case their fingers touched. Why did he find her so amusing? It annoyed her. 'Give me two minutes to change. Unless you'd rather stay?'

'No, thank you.'

Amy shut the door behind her a little too firmly, and stood in the corridor wondering how Nick Penry had driven her so quickly into prissy defensiveness. He came out very quickly, a tall man with his black hair smoothed down and Richard's blue jersey tight across his shoulders. Amy had taken the time to collect herself. She was on her own ground, after all. She wouldn't let this man make her feel like a curiosity in her own home. 'Let's go down to dinner,' she said evenly. 'You must be hungry.'

'A little,' he agreed. 'It's so hard to get a decent luncheon on the road. Today's was bread and margarine.'

Amy stared straight ahead of her. 'I think you'll find that dinner will be an improvement on that.'

They went down the stairs in silence. Nick looked up at the portraits as they passed them.

The footman was waiting at the dining-room doors. He held them open as Nick and Amy passed through, and Mr Glass stood waiting behind Amy's chair. The velvet curtains had been drawn against the cold spring evening, and in the warm glow of shaded lamps Nick saw the elaborate plaster cornice-work picked out in cream and gold, the cream and gold upholstered chair seats, the smooth curves of the marble fireplace and the delicate colours of Adeline's collection of early English porcelain shelved on either side of it. A pair of branched silver-gilt candelabra stood on the table, with tall new candles all alight, and an array of silver cutlery, crystal glasses and starched napery.

Nick and Amy sat down, facing each other across the polished gulf of the table. From a white china tureen with curved handles and tiny garlands of gold-painted flowers soup was ladled into bowls so thin that they were almost transparent. On the bowls, and the handles of the cutlery, and worked into the heavy linen napkins, was the same crest, a crowned lion in a wreath of laurel leaves. The footman offered bread wrapped in a napkin folded into intricate peaks, and the butler poured pale gold wine into

154

the glasses. Reflections wavered back at once from the polished wood.

They sat waiting. The servants moved discreetly, making sure that everything was in place. Then the doors closed silently behind them.

Nick looked at Amy. He had been about to say something sharp, mocking, but then he saw how young she was, not more than twenty, and how anxious. It occurred to him that it had been brave of her to bring him here, and sit him down in the face of all this silk and gold. He swallowed the abrasive words and said, 'May I eat this now?'

The anxiety vanished and at once her face was alive with sympathy and humour. 'Of course.'

The soup was thin and clear, yet mysteriously rich with game and brandy. Nick's disappeared in two spoonfuls, and the crusty bread with curls of yellow butter along with it.

Amy was smiling with pleasure. 'Would you like some more?'

'I think I could manage some.'

She reached for the bell-pull, a thick cream silk tassel, and then changed her mind. Instead she ladled the soup herself into Nick's bowl. When all the soup and all the bread was gone, Amy touched the bell-rope. Nick raised his glass of wine to her.

'What shall we drink to? To the revolution?'

Amy glanced up at the gold-traced ceiling and the heavy curtains with their tassels and drapes. 'Not the revolution. Not here and now. I don't think it would be . . . fitting.' She was smiling, but Nick saw that she meant what she said and he felt the first flicker of liking for her. Amy Lovell's loyalty would be worth winning. 'I think we should drink to Jake. To his recovery, and his success.'

'That's more or less the same as drinking to the revolution. But here's to him.'

They drank, looking at each other.

The butler came and took their plates away, and the footman's eyebrows went up a hairsbreadth at the sight of the empty soup tureen. After the soup came fish, as light as foam with a shrimp-pink sauce.

When they were alone again, Amy asked tentatively, as if she was expecting a rebuff, 'What was it like, marching to London?'

Instead of dismissing the question with a shrug, as he might easily have done, Nick said, 'It was a long way. But not as hard as I'd expected. Most days we ate better than we would have done at home, and there are worse things than just being wet and cold and tired. And then there were times when it was all worthwhile. More than worthwhile. Like when the local trades council people came out to meet us even when their executives had directed them not to. We didn't have official backing for the march, you see. It was all supposed to be a Communist manoeuvre. Yet the people came anyway. And other times, like when we made the Spike managers give us special status.' Seeing Amy's puzzled face, Nick put down his silver fork and grinned in the candlelight. He was struck by the incongruity of talking about these things to this girl in her pearls and her elaborate dress. 'The Spike. The workhouse, you see. When there was nowhere else for us to sleep we'd go there. They'd try to put us up in the Casual. The Casual ward, for vagrants. One blanket, usually lousy. Two slices of bread and one mug of tea for breakfast. And in return you surrender everything at the door. No money, tobacco, matches, anything, allowed in the Casual.' Nick laughed at Amy's expression. 'You didn't know? Why should you? It's a fine, proud system. If a man hasn't got anything else, why should he need dignity? But we wouldn't accept Casual status and we took over the wards anyway. And we had fried bacon for breakfast. Then when we marched up Park Lane and saw the crowds and heard the cheering, I'd have done it all over again for that.'

'I saw you, under the banner. Looking out over the crowds as if you were saying *I'm right*.' Amy stopped, feeling her cheeks redden with the sense of having said too much.

But Nick only said softly, 'Oh, we're right. I'm certain of that.'

The plates were replaced again. Now there was breast of duck, thinly sliced in a mysterious peppery sauce, and early vegetables from the walled gardens and greenhouses at Chance. In fresh glasses the wine was garnet red and when Nick drank some it reminded him of the scent of violets.

Amy saw with relief that the tense, aggressive set of his shoulders had relaxed a little, and that some of the exhausted lines were smoothed out of his face.

'You said in the taxi that you knew someone from Nantlas.'

'Bethan Jones. She's been my friend since I was a baby, almost.'

'Your friend?'

'Why not? She's looked after my sister and me as if we were her own children. Is there any reason why I shouldn't think of her as a friend?'

'No reason at all.'

In the silence that followed, as Nick watched her over the rim of his glass, Amy wondered what they were both defending so fervently against each other. And if they were in opposition, so naturally and immediately, why were they sitting here facing each other between the brilliant points of the candles?

'Do you know her?' she asked lamely at last. 'Her mother is the local midwife.'

'Yes, I remember Bethan Jones. And I know Myfanwy well.' Nick thought of Dickon, and the night he was born, and the way he said 'Da? Dada?' over and over again, insistent and uncomprehending, in the cold little house.

Nick's face darkened as he saw himself sitting in this opulent room, enjoying the scent of violets opening up as the wineglass warmed in his fingers. *Da? Dada?*

Seeing his face, Amy could think of nothing to say. The silence spread and seeped coldly between them, and the chance of breaking it receded.

Glass and the footman came in again with pudding in a cut-glass bowl, fruit and cheese and port in a decanter for Miss Amy's strange guest if he should want it. They felt the silence and glanced at each other as they moved between the table and the long sideboard.

'Will there be anything else, Miss Amy?'

'I don't think so, Glass, thank you. I'll ring for coffee if we need it later.'

It was a mistake.

It had been a mistake to bring the man home and imagine that she could do anything to help. It was an interference, no more than that. This painful silence was proof of it. Amy stared dully at the fruit-knife placed beside her plate and unexpectedly the tears pricked in her eyes like a reminder of her weakness. She felt her powerlessness, and her isolation, and the little certainty that she had possessed this afternoon ebbed away. She didn't understand what she wanted to do, nor did she understand why this dark, frightening man was suddenly a symbol of it. She only knew that she had wanted to reach out, and that the simple gesture was suddenly threateningly complex and utterly beyond her.

'I'm sorry.'

The words startled her so much that she jumped. There were tears on her eyelashes and the realization made her redden with humiliation.

'I'm sorry,' he repeated. He stood up and walked all the way round the great table to Amy's chair, and then he put his hand on her shoulder. She felt his fingers resting in the hollow of her collarbone. 'I'm not schooled, like your friends probably are, in masking feelings with manners. Talking about Myfanwy Jones made me think of my son. She delivered him, one night when the doctor wouldn't come out to my wife because we couldn't pay him. Myfanwy saved his life, and probably my wife's too. She did all she could. But the baby was damaged. He'll never be able to do anything much. Nothing, without Mari and me to help him. Thinking about him in the middle of all this . . .' the sudden sweep of Nick's other hand took in the table, the glinting silver and the polished hothouse fruit, the white and gold china and the port waiting in the decanter on the sideboard. 'It made me angry, for a moment. I'm sorry if I upset you. You've been kind, and you were brave in that crowd this afternoon and when you didn't know what to do to help Jake. I would have expected a woman of your class to run away, if she had been there in the first place.'

Amy shook her head to clear the tears. She didn't know why, but it was important that Nick Penry shouldn't see that she was crying.

No wonder his face had frozen her. No wonder she had been unable to think of a light, casual word to break the ice of silence.

The tip of his finger touched her shoulder and then he was strolling away again, back to his place at the table.

'Shall we talk about something else?' Nick asked. 'You could tell me why you were in Trafalgar Square this afternoon.'

Amy looked up. What else was there to say? That she was sorry about his son? That she couldn't help it if she was rich and Nick Penry was poor? That she had wanted to help, and had just seen, humiliatingly, that she couldn't?

158

She shook her head slowly. 'I was at Appleyard Street when they were planning the march. By accident, really. A friend of mine took me because he thought it might amuse me, more or less. But I was interested. I liked the people there because they seemed to believe so strongly in what they were doing. And they were much livelier than a lot of the people I know. What I heard there made me start thinking a little about differences. And asking myself whether it was fair, I suppose. It's partly to do with feeling rather . . . pointless myself lately.' Amy felt that her face was red again. She was making herself sound like a pampered society girl in search of fresh diversions. She didn't think that was the real truth, but what else would Nick Penry think? 'I can't dress it up in the right comradely words, like Jake Silverman would. I just felt that there was more I should know. That I should try to find out for myself, because nobody else was going to show me. I went this afternoon just to see. For a moment while I was there I was sure I knew. I knew what was right, and what I must do, and whose side I was on. It seemed perfectly simple.' Determined to be as truthful as she could, Amy added defiantly, 'It was the boots. The sound they made as you marched. You can laugh if you like.'

Across the table Nick was watching her intently without even a flicker of a smile. 'Go on, Amy.'

My friends call me Amy, she remembered telling him.

'Not ringing out like you'd expect, like soldiers' boots, but flapping and shuffling. I thought, if men can walk so far in those boots to ask for help then they must need it badly.'

Nick said crisply, 'The boots aren't important. Nor were we marching to beg for help. What we want, you know, is what is ours by rights. To work under fair conditions for fair wages. Oh, I know that Jake Silverman and his friends put a different colouring on it for political purposes. But that was what the march was really for. Not begging, but demanding. But for Jake, I would have been in the deputation of men meeting the government committee on the mines this afternoon. Who knows, they might have achieved something by now.'

Amy nodded, realizing again how little she knew and how little she understood. 'I thought I could help in some way. I felt full of glory, marching along Oxford Street. I suppose this evening has demonstrated that I can't. We seem to be in opposition, don't we?'

159

Nick did smile now. 'You helped. You got to Jake Silverman before I did. And you've given me the best meal I've ever eaten, sorry though I am that the rest of them at Bethnal Green haven't shared it. Can I finish it now on temporarily neutral ground?'

Amy was touched and pleased that he should let the Lovells' formal dining-room be neutral ground.

'Please do. Will you have lemon pudding or cheese?'

'Both.'

They smiled at each other. Amy was discovering that under the complicated layers that she had glimpsed this evening, she liked Nick Penry.

'Tell me about something else while I eat this. You said you had a sister. And the room I'm sleeping in belongs to your brother?'

Hesitantly at first, and then more fluently as he prompted her with questions, Amy began to talk about her family. She told Nick about Isabel's marriage, and how lost she felt without her.

'Jaspert the Tory MP?' Nick asked, and she nodded. She told Nick about the way Richard and their father stalked painfully around each other, and about Airlie's death in the War. She talked about Richard's friendship with Tony Hardy, and her own growing one. Nick smiled sardonically. He leaned back in his fragile chair and hooked one arm over the back, biting into a russet apple from Chance while Amy described her mother's confusing appearances and disappearances, and how important Bethan's constancy had been to them as children. She was surprised by how easy it was to talk to Nick.

She told him about the lunches, and the parties and dances that filled her time, and her descriptions of the people she met made him laugh. When he laughed naturally, and the coldness of his stare disappeared, Amy thought how different he looked.

Then, when they had drunk the last of the wine between them and her guest seemed to have finished eating at last, Amy said, 'Well. That's all I've done, up until now. It isn't very much is it? But today did help me to decide something.' As she spoke she felt a bubble of optimism rising inside her. She would tell Nick Penry about the germ of an idea that had been growing since this afternoon, and telling him would help to fix her intentions.

160

'I've never felt so useless, or so helpless, as I did this afternoon. Just sitting on that pavement outside St Martin's with Jake, and not knowing what to do. He might have died there beside me, and all I could think of was wrapping him in my coat. I don't want to feel like that ever again.' Amy took a deep breath and then said, 'I'm going to train to be a nurse.'

As soon as the words were out, she was quite certain that she had found the answer she was looking for.

Nick said calmly, 'And do you think you'll make a good nurse?'

Amy was laughing in the candlelight. 'I'll be a better nurse than a debutante. Do you think it's a good idea?'

Suddenly, it seemed very important that he should think it was.

'I think it's a fine idea.'

'Good. Then I'll do it.'

After that Amy had rung for coffee and they had taken the port decanter up to Adeline's white drawing-room. In the doorway, seeing Nick's raised eyebrows, Amy had said hastily, 'No, not in here. Come up to the old schoolroom.'

Nick carried up the tray and Amy brought in an electric fire and stood it in the hearth where she and Isabel had so often sat over the fire on wet London afternoons. A big, sagging sofa with a chintz cover was drawn up in front of it, and behind that was the double desk where they had sat to do their French translations before going to Miss Abbott's.

'Didn't you go to school?' Nick asked from the depths of the sofa. Amy spun the old wooden globe on its stand.

'Not until I was fourteen. We had governesses until then. And the school we went to in the end concentrated on teaching us Court curtseys and where to place duchesses at dinner. I've always felt rather uneducated, and jealous of Richard at Eton.'

Leaving the globe still spinning, she crossed to the tray and filled the two port glasses. She had drunk more wine than usual this evening, but it had made her feel warm and comfortable, rather than dizzy and remote as it often did. She gave Nick his glass and curled up in the sofa corner opposite him, kicking off her shoes as she settled back. The schoolroom felt safe, and homely.

'It's your turn now,' she said. 'Tell me about Nantlas.'

161

Nick was looking at her. She saw the colour of his eyes agai . and thought that sometimes they looked almost transparent. .ie lifted his hand as if he was going to reach out and touch her, then let it fall again.

'Do you know,' he said quietly, 'that you have very pretty feet? No, don't hide them under your dress. I wasn't going to touch them.'

You can, if you want to, Amy said silently. The lurching awkwardness of the evening, the painful gaps that it had revealed between them and the flimsy structures that they had bridged them with were forgotten for the moment. To Amy, in that instant in the schoolroom, they were equal, and close enough to each other to reach out and touch.

Then Nick was talking again, faster than usual. 'Nantlas. It was a fine place until ten years ago. It worked, as a community. There was a school, and the master was good enough to make us want to go on learning after we all left for the pit at fourteen. There was a choir, and a pit band, and sports on Saturday afternoons. There were two chapels and enough money to support a minister for both of them. They're gone, now.'

'I know.' Amy was looking away at the hard red bars of the fire. 'Bethan told me. Her sister had to go to Ferndale to get married in the registry office.'

'I was at the wedding party,' Nick said. 'There was food, and singing and dancing. Almost like the old days.'

Amy sat beside him in her corner of the sofa, following the outlines of the flowers in the chintz with her fingertip and listening, only half-comprehending. The moment of closeness had crept up on her and then receded so quickly that it was hard to believe it had happened. Nick was talking almost to himself, about the pits that closed one after another, about the system that forced out-of-work miners to walk from pithead to pithead, often covering scores of miles in a week, to get the pit managers' signatures on a piece of paper. The signatures were proof that they had genuinely been seeking work, so that they could claim the dole money. He talked about the soft company unions that threatened the strength of the miners' lodges, the only hope that remained of defending their livelihoods.

'That's why we march,' Nick said bitterly. 'That's why I believe we can do something if we fight them instead of taking what the

162

companies and the government hand out. It's less every time; less even than it was in 1918.'

Nick had been talking for a long time. Abruptly he sat upright, frowning. 'I'm sure all that has bored you to death.'

'It wasn't boring,' Amy said gently. 'Tell me something. You say that you have to prove that you've been looking for work, and that if you can't you lose your benefit. Won't you lose yours now?'

'It's possible.'

'What will you do?'

Nick's frown was black, but he shrugged the question away. 'I don't know. Try to find some work. It hasn't happened yet.'

Amy looked at the fire and then at the familiar chintz flowers, the faded blues and pinks reminding her of summer gardens and the long borders at Chance.

'If . . .' she began slowly, 'if you needed work badly, there would be something at Chance. I could ask my father, and the estate manager. It's a big estate. I don't know exactly what the men do there, but . . .'

As she saw Nick's face her voice died in her throat. His eyes had gone completely cold.

'You're very gracious,' he said.

Amy could have bitten out her tongue. Without warning the gulf had opened up again, deeper than ever.

'Thank you, but no. I'm a miner. I don't want to join the creeping army of Lovell retainers. And even if I'm out of work I've got other things to do in South Wales. As well as a wife and child.'

'I was thinking of them . . .'

'Let me do that. I'm grateful for the dinner and the bed. Even for the kind offer of someone's penguin suit to dress up in like a gentleman. But it doesn't give you the right to patronize me. I don't want charity from you, or people like you.'

His words stung Amy. Half-sensing the painful, damaged pride and the humiliations that lay behind them, she hesitated. Her rational self told her that she should keep quiet, but anger at his harshness overtook her.

'You're a fool, then,' she said hotly. 'It was an honest offer to help. Why should I want to patronize you? Why should you think I'd care enough?'

Nick looked at her, and she felt the full insulting weight of his appraisal. And then he laughed at her.

'As you correctly remarked earlier, you can't help. People like you can't do anything for us. You are the enemy. Go and learn how to wind bandages to fill up your time between parties, if it makes you feel better. But don't imagine that by trotting along to Appleyard Street or marching under a banner with the working classes you're going to change anything. Least of all your spoilt self.'

He stood up, and then yawned ostentatiously. 'I will make use of your brother's comfortable bed, since you offered it. Goodbye, Miss Lovell.'

Amy was shaking with shock and anger. She stood up to face Nick, clenching her fists at her side. 'Have you finished now?'

Nick had half-turned away, but he swung back and stood as if considering something. 'Not quite,' he said.

His fingers closed around her wrist. Slowly he lifted it so that their forearms touched. And then he bent and kissed her. Amy felt the hardness of his mouth against hers and the brush of his tongue. The breath caught sharply in her chest. Savagely she jerked her arm up, bringing Nick's with it, and she bit into his imprisoning hand with all her strength.

'Bitch.' She heard the word under his breath. Nick let go of her at once. He stepped back, rubbing the round red mark among the blue scars.

'Don't ever touch me,' Amy said. Anger was almost choking her, but it was anger with herself as much as Nick. The violence of her own reaction baffled her. It had only been a kiss, and an hour ago she had felt close enough to Nick to want him to touch her.

Nick was looking at her glittering eyes and flushed cheeks with amusement tinged with admiration.

'So they taught you biting at school as well as curtseying. Hasn't anyone ever kissed you before?'

'Of course they have.'

But not like that, Amy thought, remembering the hot, half-drunk boys in taxis. And Tony's distant gentleness. 'I'm sorry I bit you.'

'Oh, not at all.'

This is ridiculous. Amy stood up straight, trying to muster the

164

remains of her dignity. She felt a sudden fatal desire to laugh. 'I don't think there's much point in prolonging this evening.'

'There doesn't appear to be,' Nick said equably.

'Can you find your way to your room, or shall I ring for somebody?'

'Oh, I think I can manage.'

He was perfectly cool now, the amenable guest determined not to let his hostess's outburst mar the end of the evening. The irrational laughter died in Amy as she recognized something. Nick Penry was clever, and formidably quick. With all her advantages, she was nowhere near a match for him. How many masks have you put on tonight? Amy wondered. Which is your real face?

In his turn he was looking through her, as if her own amateurish disguises were transparent.

'Good night, then,' she said abruptly and turned to the door.

Nick watched her go, his hand with the red weal resting on the old chintz sofa back.

In her room Amy found that she was shaking. She dropped her pearl necklace on the dressing-table top with a clatter, stripped off her dress and underclothes and left them where they fell, and slid under the bedclothes to curl up in the safe darkness like a child.

But even there she felt that the man was still staring through her.

'Go away,' she said aloud to the muffled stillness. 'Leave me alone.'

In the morning Amy changed her clothes twice before finding an outfit that pleased her, and then she frowned at herself in the mirror at the thought that she might be dressing to please anyone except herself. She pinned her hair up carefully and made up her face before marching briskly down to Richard's room. She had rehearsed what she was going to say this morning. She would apologize, lightly and humorously, for her double gaucheness of last night, and Nick would apologize in his turn. Then they would go down to the dining-room and she would make sure that Nick had an enormous breakfast before he set out for Bethnal Green. She hadn't yet worked out how she could tactfully pay for him to get there, but she would think of something when the time came.

There was no answer to her knock on Richard's door. The bathroom door opposite it stood wide open.

'Mr Penry? Nick?' There was still no answer. Amy pushed open the bedroom door and looked inside. The bed was as smooth as if it had never been slept in, but on the chair beside it, neatly folded, was the navy sweater, the white shirt and the grey flannel trousers.

'Nick?'

Amy looked again, but she knew that he was gone.

Without faltering, and with her chin firmly up, Amy went down to breakfast on her own.

There was a single place laid at the table. If Adeline was at home she would be having breakfast on a tray in her room. Adeline never appeared before midday.

Mr Glass was standing at the sideboard in front of the silver-domed hot dishes.

'Good morning, Miss Amy.'

'Good morning. My guest, Mr Penry, did he have breakfast?'

'Mr . . . . ah, Penry left the house two hours ago. He said that he wouldn't be requiring breakfast. He left this for you, Miss Amy.'

It was an envelope with the Lovell crest, with a single sheet of crested writing paper inside it. Amy looked at the few words. Nick's handwriting was firm, black and confident. Educated writing, she thought, and knew that she should have expected it.

> Thank you for everything last night. Even for the job offer. I'm not a fool, you know. Neither are you. Learn to be a nurse, but try to be a real one like Myfanwy Jones and not a society girl filling in time. Then when the day comes you may really be able to help. Good luck. Nick Penry.
>
> PS. Do some more kissing. You might get to like it. The bite is healing quite nicely.

With a smile lifting the corners of her mouth, Amy refolded the paper along its crease and put the envelope safely in her pocket.

Mr Glass lifted the silver cover off one of the dishes.

'Eggs and bacon, Miss Amy?'

She sat down in her place, with her own pink and white china breakfast cup laid in front of her, just as always, and her napkin in one of her silver christening rings. Just as always.

Well then, Nick Penry had disappeared as quickly as he had materialized. But Amy felt that he had lifted the pall of the last weeks for her.

She knew what she was going to do.

breakfast cup laid in front of her, just as always, and her napkin
in one of her silver christening rings, just as always.
Well then, Nick Penry had disappeared as quickly as he had
materialized. But Amy felt that he had lifted the pall of the last

7

The interview with the matron of the Royal Lambeth Hospital,
when it finally came, was almost an anti-climax.

As she sat down facing the grey, starched martinet in her office
lined with bound copies of nursing journals, Amy thought that
whatever was coming it couldn't possibly be as complicated as
the course she had steered to get even this far.

Amy had first of all confronted Adeline with her plan, on the
morning of Nick Penry's departure. She had found her mother
sitting up in bed, her breakfast tray pushed to one side. With her
uncoiled mass of dark red hair fanned over the shoulders of her
dove-grey silk robe, Adeline looked about eighteen years old.
The white bedcovers were strewn with her morning post, engraved invitations and scrawled notes and long, intimate letters
from abroad. The morning papers were still folded neatly as her
maid had laid them out. Amy kissed her.

'Darling, you look very pretty. What are you doing today?
Shall we have lunch together? I'm going to the Carlisles' this
afternoon, but we could have a tiny lunch, couldn't we? Or are
you booked?'

Amy had picked up the newspapers and was staring at the
headlines.

ANTI-COMMUNIST DEMONSTRATORS AND HUNGER MARCHERS
IN TRAFALGAR SQUARE BATTLE
HEAVY POLICE PRESENCE CONTROLS OUTBREAKS OF VIOLENCE
17 INJURED, 27 ARRESTS IN TRAFALGAR SQUARE

There was a picture of the dense swaying crowd and the police
horses massed in front of the platform that brought the taste of
packed bodies and fear back into Amy's throat. Nick's head
was somewhere in that dark throng, and her own, and Jake
Silverman's with the frightening sticky patch on his skull. Could

she telephone the hospital this morning to ask how he was?

'Amy? Darling? Share the fascination.'

Suppressing a guilty start Amy waved vaguely at the headline.

'Mmm. The traffic was a nightmare all afternoon. Where did you and Violet go? You would think that people could rally somewhere a bit further off without disrupting all of London.'

Heaven forbid, Amy thought with a moment of savagery, that the hunger march should make any of us late for the hairdresser. The thought made her come out with what she wanted to say more coldly and abruptly than she had intended.

'I want to talk to you about something important. I've been feeling for months that I don't do anything. Anything worthwhile,' she added firmly, seeing Adeline's surprise. 'I want to take up nursing. A proper nurse's training at one of the London hospitals, not voluntary work.'

Adeline's reaction had been to laugh, and then to be sympathetic when she saw that Amy was serious. It was a whim, of course. Perhaps a boy had disappointed her and this was her way of working off her troubles.

Adeline said consolingly, 'Well, darling, I do know that sometimes one needs a change. London can get very stale. Perhaps we should have a holiday? We could go – oh, to Venice. Or Egypt, what about that? Bobbie would come, I'm sure, and we could ask the Carlisles, or Mickie Dunn. Wouldn't it be fun?'

Amy sat down on the edge of the bed, wondering how to explain to her lovely worldly mother that she didn't want a life like hers. Adeline had had her own unhappiness, Amy knew that, and she knew equally well that her antidote to it had been party after party, dancing and dining and travelling and dangerous, discreet liaisons. Amy loved her mother dearly but she was filled with a sudden, puritanical aversion to her world.

'It would be lovely to have a holiday with you, Mama, but if everyone else came along too it would be exactly like here, or Chance, and we might just as well stay at home.'

Mickie Dunn was a witty, middle-aged dandy with a sharp tongue who was one of the stalwarts of Adeline's circle and the Carlisles were young, rich and fast. All the signs were that Bobbie was Adeline's newest interest. It wasn't a party that Amy could even pretend to relish.

'My love, how could we go on our own? What would we do?' Adeline was genuinely surprised and Amy smiled at her.

'Well, I suppose it wouldn't be all that much fun. Anyway, it isn't a holiday I need, it's just the opposite. I want to work, Mama. I want to be of some use in the world. No, don't . . .' Amy reached out to hold her mother's hand, preventing her from impatiently waving the idea away. 'Please hear me out. I'm fit and strong, and I'm not stupid. I'm bored, that's what's the matter with me, and ever since we were little you've told us that boredom is a sin. If there was a war on, I'd be doing something useful.'

'That's hardly the same thing,' Adeline said faintly.

'Why should it be different, if we're just talking about me? It's not a whim, I promise. I've been thinking about what I should do ever since the wedding, although I've only just realized exactly what.' Amy took a breath now and faced her mother squarely. 'I want to train to be a nurse. There are always sick people everywhere. I can do something helpful. Something useful, not just go to parties and wait to get married. I'd be a good nurse, you know. I'm not afraid of work.' Amy let Adeline's hand go, ready to defend her decision. 'And I like people. All kinds of people.'

Adeline sighed. 'I don't think you're afraid of anything,' she said. Looking at the set of her daughter's chin Adeline thought how mulish Amy could be when her mind was made up. All through their childhood it was Isabel who had been the pliant one. But then, perhaps Amy would do best in the end. She had a little core of self-will that gave her a sparkle lacking in Isabel.

Adeline marshalled herself to dissuade Amy from this latest idea, but she suspected that the battle was already lost.

'Darling, it would be such a terrible waste. You're young and pretty, and you don't have a thing to worry about. I want you to enjoy yourself, Amy. Do you have any idea how hard nursing would be for you? It would be all wounds, and bedpans, and people dying every day. All the horrible, ugly things that you needn't even think about now.'

'I don't know yet how hard it would be,' Amy said, thinking of Jake Silverman and the dark, sticky softness at the back of his skull, and her own fear. 'I'll find out, if you will let me.'

Seeing her face, Adeline shrugged and swept the litter of her correspondence into a haphazard pile. If the child was set on it, perhaps it wouldn't do her any harm to spend a few weeks coming to appreciate her own good fortune.

'Amy, I can't pretend that I'm delighted by the idea. But I won't forbid it absolutely. You must also talk to your father about it.'

Amy's delighted hug enveloped her. 'Thank you, darling. You'll see in the end that it's the right thing, I promise you.' And now, Amy decided as her mother's hair brushed her cheek and she smelt her expensive gardenia scent, she had better give her version of last night before Adeline heard about it from one of the staff.

'I wished yesterday that I wasn't so helpless,' she said quickly. 'I was in Trafalgar Square yesterday afternoon. A man was hurt beside me and I helped to get him to hospital.' As lightly as she could, she told the rest of the story.

'A coal miner?' Adeline repeated, as if Amy had said *aborigine*. 'Here?'

'He was tired and hungry, and he had nowhere else to go.'

'Did Glass see to him?'

'Well, no. As a matter of fact we had dinner together, and then he slept in Richard's room. He went off first thing this morning.'

Adeline stared for a moment, and then her famous, enchanting smile flickered. If Adeline was amused, there was no need for Amy to worry about the episode.

'I suppose we should thank God that Gerald wasn't here. I can't imagine what he would say over breakfast to a coal miner brought home as a house-guest by his daughter. And I hardly dare to think of you in all that violence. You might have been hurt yourself. Did Violet adopt a miner too and take him home to Lady Trent?'

'Violet wasn't there. It was just me.'

'Dear me, Amy. Don't make a habit of being so unconventional, will you?'

No, Amy thought, there wasn't any likelihood of it becoming a habit. With sudden regret she realized that Nick Penry really had gone, and there was no reason why she should ever see him again.

The matron put on her rimless spectacles and ran her fingers down Amy's letter of application.

'You have your parents' consent, of course, Miss Lovell?'

'Yes, ma'am,' Amy said meekly.

She had telephoned Gerald at Chance, imagining him picking up the receiver in the gun-room where the installation had eccentrically placed it. The leather-bound game books going back to the turn of the century were shelved beside it, and Gerald often turned back the pages, frowning over the day's bag of twenty years ago. In the last entry under his name, one of a small party of guns out after grouse, Airlie's total was eleven birds. He had been a fine shot. Richard had refused even to be measured for his guns from Holland & Holland.

'I'm not interested in slaughtering small animals for the fun of it,' he had insisted, white-faced against his father's scorn.

'Well, Amy, what is it?' Gerald demanded. He disliked the telephone, and avoided it wherever possible. Amy sensed him listening impatiently as she explained. She had barely finished before he cut in.

'Sick-nursing is a servant's job. It's not a suitable occupation for a girl of your sort.' The tone of his voice was final. Amy was glad of the distance separating them as she took a deep breath and prepared for battle.

'People of our sort have done it in the past. Lady Trent was a VAD in the War. They used the ballroom at their London house as an orthopaedic ward and hung the walls with bolts of material to protect the gilding. She often talks about it even now.'

'That was wartime,' Gerald said sharply. 'That will never come again.'

'War or peace, does it matter? I feel that now I'm grown up I would like to contribute something. If I have got anything to offer, don't you think I should be allowed to do it?'

From the silence that followed Amy knew that she had struck a chord.

In a different voice Gerald answered at last, 'Perhaps you're more of a Lovell than I give you credit for. More than Richard will ever be. Airlie is the one you take after. He had something to offer, and he did it without stopping to think. He was a fine boy, Amy. I only wish you could have been older and known him better.'

172

Amy closed her eyes, ashamed that even unconsciously she had adopted a stratagem that touched on Airlie.

'I remember him,' she said quietly. 'I'm not brave like Airlie was. I just want to do a job that might be some use to somebody. I don't even know why I'm so sure, but I know that job should be nursing.'

'What does your mother say?'

'Ummm, she agrees that I can try it with your consent.'

'Is she there? I'd better speak to her.'

'No, she isn't here now. She's away for a Saturday-to-Monday.'

'With?'

'I think . . . the Earl and Countess of Carlisle.'

The silence was longer this time and Amy waited, feeling the weight of distance and formality and failures of understanding that separated them.

'Very well, Amy. If you want to be a nurse, and God knows why you should, you have my permission. Now, let me get on with what I'm doing here in peace, will you?'

Amy replaced the receiver and stood for a long moment thinking. She had felt it before Isabel's wedding, and again now. She had almost reached her father, almost seen him as he really was, and then at the last moment he had put up the angry, impervious screen again and shut her out.

'Good,' said the matron. 'Now. Educational background. Adequate, I'm sure.' She was filling in a form in very fast, spiky handwriting.

Amy told her about the governesses, and Miss Abbott's school, and she nodded.

'You will have to work hard, like all our probationers, to keep up with lectures and clinical studies in your off-duty hours. Do you understand that?'

Amy said yes, she understood, and the matron capped her pen with a decisive snap. 'Your age and level of education are suitable, Miss Lovell, and you look more than strong enough for the work. Your background is a disadvantage to you, because there are not many girls of your class amongst our students. I won't make a secret of the fact that it's an advantage to us, because we are trying to attract more girls from better families into the profession. But I must make it clear from the start that

173

you can expect no special treatment or privileges because of wh[o]
you are. You will be treated exactly as the other girls, and yo[u]
will be expected to obey the same rules.'

'I understand, Matron.'

Rapidly the matron began to outline the conditions of Amy'[s]
entry. She seemed to do everything at top speed, as if there wa[s]
not a second to be wasted. Amy felt intimidated and energize[d]
by her in equal proportions.

'You will be enrolled as a nursing student of this hospital fo[r]
three years, after an initial trial period of one month. You wi[ll]
receive free board and lodging, and you will live in the nurses[']
hostel like the other girls. You will work a one-hundred-and-ten
hour fortnight, which will include full day shifts, split day shift[s]
and night shifts in accordance with the rota system. Lectures an[d]
study will be in addition to those hours, and you will be permitte[d]
three weeks' holiday per annum. Your salary in the first yea[r]
will be twenty-five pounds, thirty in the second and thirty-fiv[e]
thereafter. You will be provided with free uniform dresses[,]
aprons and caps but you will be required to provide your ow[n]
regulation stockings and shoes. Laundry bills will be deducte[d]
from your salary. The next intake is in four weeks' time, Mis[s]
Lovell. There is a waiting list for studentships at this hospital
but for the reason I explained I am prepared to waive it in you[r]
case and offer you a place at once. Do you wish to accept it
under the conditions I have outlined?'

Amy remembered the red and cream corridors she had bee[n]
hustled through to reach the matron's office and the glimpses o[f]
long wards with straight, white rows of beds. She smelt the ree[k]
of disinfectant and heard the squeak of hurrying rubber-sole[d]
shoes, the crackle of starched skirts and the clang of mop-bucket[s]
in cupboards stacked with harsh soap and hospital towels. Thi[s]
would be her world for fifty-five hours a week, one hundred an[d]
ten hours a fortnight, and with three weeks' holiday a year.

She took a deep breath. 'Yes, I accept. And I would welcom[e]
the chance to start as soon as possible.'

The matron almost smiled, the first glimmer of cordiality tha[t]
Amy had glimpsed in her. 'Welcome to the Royal Lambeth, Mis[s]
Lovell.'

As she retraced her steps towards the outside world, Amy sa[w]
the hospital quite differently. Passing the wards, she peered i[n]
and saw the people in the beds, old men and children and on[e]

174

room lined with babies' cots, all different and all needing different things. She looked at the nurses' preoccupied faces under the stiff white pleats of their caps, and wondered if any of them would become a friend. A senior doctor with a flotilla of juniors behind him brushed past her, and one or two of the young men glanced back curiously at Amy.

The hospital wasn't just a grim Victorian pile smelling of illness. It was a world in itself, occupied with the realities that she knew she was missing at Bruton Street. In four weeks' time she would be joining it.

Outside there was a single circular flowerbed crammed with egg-yolk yellow wallflowers in the macadamized strip that separated the hospital from the busy main road. Amy beamed at the hideous flowers and then up at the building's red-brick height towering above.

'I'll be seeing you soon,' she said aloud and then she turned and almost danced out of the gates into the traffic.

The hospital was across the river, in a part of London she hardly knew. No one she knew had ever had any connection with the hospital or the area it served, and it was for those reasons she had chosen it, although Matron must never know that, Amy reminded herself. Matron, of course, believed it was the Lambeth's distinguished reputation that had attracted her.

A cab, heading back to the West End and civilization, accelerated towards her. Amy almost hailed it, and then she stopped herself.

'Begin as you intend to continue,' she ordered. She let the cab sweep past, and then with her hands in her pockets she began to walk towards Westminster Bridge. The sun, with the first heat of summer in it, shone on her head, like a blessing.

On the evening of Amy's interview at the Royal Lambeth, Isabel was sitting alone in her drawing-room at Ebury Street.

She looked up at the clock on the mantelpiece. It was a pretty clock with an enamelled face, a wedding present from one of the Jaspert cousins.

Eleven o'clock.

She folded up her embroidery without glancing at the soft blues and purples of the pansy she had completed this evening. Peter hadn't telephoned, but that could mean anything. If he had

175

gone to the House he might be attending a debate, or meeting colleagues from any of the committees he served on. If he had gone on to his club from the City, he might be drinking with his friends, and simply have forgotten the time. Either way, she would not wait up for him. It was a decision Isabel was making increasingly often, and as it always did it brought both relief and a twist of regret.

Slowly she went upstairs and made herself go mechanically through the routines she had laid down for herself, creaming her face and hands and brushing out her hair until it crackled under the bristles. When she had finished Isabel looked at her face in the mirror. It seemed that the roundness of girlhood had disappeared and the new face was hollower, and sadder. Perhaps if she had her hair cut off, so that she looked as sleek and shiny as enamel, it would give her back some of the confidence that seemed to be ebbing away with every day of her marriage.

Isabel glanced at the door of Peter's dressing-room, connecting his bedroom to hers, and suddenly heard the silence of the house. It had been with her all evening, ever since the solitary formal dinner she had eaten with Peter's place laid and unoccupied at the other end of the table.

Yes, she would have her hair cut off.

The silence stretched on, mockingly unpunctured by her small decisions. It wouldn't make a fraction of difference, Isabel thought, whether she cut her hair or not.

She was lonely here, amongst her pretty furniture and her china and pictures and flowers.

Isabel hung up her robe and got into bed, and then lay quietly looking round the room before turning off her light. It was all just as she had expected it would be, and yet in the midst of all the things, nothing like it at all. Usually when her thoughts ran on like this Isabel forced herself to turn them aside, but tonight a new fear made her want to confront them.

She had never tasted loneliness before she was married, and she had never dreamed that it would be lying in wait for her. She had believed, in all her innocence, that marriage would be a communion between herself and Peter for ever. She had imagined that they would live in their lovely house, well provided with friends and families, but still within a core containing just the two of them.

It wasn't like that, Isabel had discovered. The core was rotten.

When she wasn't lonely, when Peter was with her, what she mostly felt was fear.

She made her racing thoughts slow down so she could consider that.

She was afraid of her own husband, and she had been afraid of him since their wedding night. The fear bred the loneliness, and the loneliness increased her fear. It had grown all through their time in Italy. The loveliness of the place had made it worse for her because the beautiful days only faded and brought the nights again.

None of the careful descriptions she had read, nor Adeline's little talks, had prepared her for those nights. When she had imagined it, Isabel had thought that married love with Peter would be gentle and slow, a tender expression of his feeling for her. He had been careful of her during their engagement. And yet, once she was in his bed he took her body as if it was his by right. And her body recoiled from the coarse touch of his hot flesh, from the taste of his breath and the weight of him pinning her down, and his painful, blunt invasion of it.

At first she had tried to tell him that the things he did hurt and frightened her. Embarrassment, and a reluctance to hurt him, made her explanations vague and faltering. Peter had been embarrassed too, and his embarrassment made him angry. Isabel began to see that he didn't know how to control himself when he was aroused, and he simply deflected with anger and impatience all the questions they might have asked one another.

Worse, as the weeks of their honeymoon went by, Isabel understood something else about him. Her very reluctance, and the way she shrank from his big body, only aroused him further. When he saw that she was afraid, he seemed to need to take her more violently still. She knew that he would never admit that, even if he understood it himself.

So Isabel protected herself with a barrier of passivity, a pretence that she felt nothing. Now that they were at home again she had devised a set of wifely rules that she made herself obey every night. If she could do everything she was supposed to do in preparing for bed, without hurrying or skipping anything, and still be asleep before he lumbered into her room, well, then, that was perfectly fair. But she mustn't pretend. If she was still awake when he came to her, she would let him, and she would stare over her husband's shoulder into the soft darkness. She would lie still and try to fight back the nausea, and suppress her longing to scream out and struggle away from underneath him.

In the beginning, the daytimes were better. There were enough times when they were comfortable together, as they had been before the wedding. Peter was simply her husband, as she had dreamed he would be, on the evenings when they entertained successfully, or sat quietly together in their drawing-room with the clock ticking. At those times Isabel had felt that their lives could, after all, be salvaged. Then the nights came, and the weight of her guilt at her sexual inadequacy and her revulsion, inextricably connected, came down on her again. There weren't many comfortable times now.

They couldn't talk about it. It seemed, already, much too late. There was something else too.

Isabel had always thought that she would be pleased, when the time came, and proud. Yet the probability ahead of her loomed like a threat tonight. If she had a baby it would be born of the secret, hideous core of her marriage that she was trying so hard to conceal.

Isabel started guiltily. The silence was broken. Downstairs the front door slammed and she listened for and then heard the sound of Peter's steps. It was too late to turn the light off. He would have seen it from the street, and anyway it was against the rules she had set for herself.

Hastily she picked up a copy of *Vogue* from her bedside table and began to flick through it, listening. Peter came heavy-footed up the stairs and then went into his bathroom down the corridor. Isabel heard the lavatory flush and waited, discovering that she was holding her breath. Once or twice Peter had gone straight into his bedroom and, from the sound of it, gone to sleep immediately. But tonight the footsteps sounded too firm and steady for that.

A moment later her door swung open. Peter was red-faced and his black tie was crooked, but his eyes were steady as he stared in at her.

'Waiting up, eh? That's heart-warming.'

Isabel put her magazine down and said in a neutral voice, 'You're very late, darling. Have you been somewhere important? I was rather expecting you for dinnner.'

Peter steadied himself on the way with a hand out to Isabel's spoon-backed chair and then plumped down on to the bed. Isabel moved her legs away from the weight of him. He was frowning as he bent to untie his shoes.

'Don't for God's sake start cross-questioning me before I'm in the house. I've been to the Coles' for dinner, if you must know. Met him at the club and then went back on the spur of the moment.'

'Couldn't you have telephoned?' Isabel asked mildly. 'I would have liked to come too.'

Peter flung his shoes into the corner and then stripped off his jacket and shirt. 'You made no secret of not liking them when I did take you. Why go through the performance again?'

It was true enough, Isabel thought. Sylvia Cole was strident, and Peter's close friend Archer Cole was an ambitious politician whose climb up the parliamentary ladder had left him no time for finesse or social graces except when it suited him to switch them on.

Was an evening with Peter in their company preferable to being left at home alone? Isabel didn't know, any more. At least she would have been with her husband, as a wife should be. And now he was turning on her with his bright blue eyes reddened with food and drink and the vein in his neck throbbing beneath his ear.

'I'm glad you're still awake,' he said, his voice changing from belligerent to conciliatory. 'Come on.' His arm came round her neck and he lifted her off the pillows to kiss her. His mouth felt hot and spongy against hers and Isabel tried and failed to make her own relax.

'Peter.' She twisted her face aside. 'My head aches tonight.'

His fingers grasped her chin and turned her face beneath his again. 'I'll stop it aching,' he said. He was pushing her down underneath him, half lying across the bed and reaching down inside her nightdress. The fear that was always lurking inside Isabel now sprang up, suffocating.

'I don't want to,' she gasped, struggling to free herself.

'Well, I want to.'

He was very strong. Isabel rolled her head sideways to look at him, trying to gauge what stage he was at. Peter had a weak head for alcohol. Even when they drank together, glass for glass, she could see the signs of it in him before she felt them herself. When he was drunk he was oblivious of anything except getting what he wanted. But when he was drunk it was very quick, and she could bite the fear back and count, saying the numbers very clearly in her head like a litany, until it was over.

She didn't think he was drunk tonight. Usually that was worse. It took longer, and he wanted things that made her shiver and the fear was mixed with humiliation and disgust. The fingers of one of his hands were winding themselves in her hair, and the others were fumbling and stroking, trying to coax her along with him.

'Lovely Isabel,' he murmured. 'Do something, will you?' He was wheedling her now, and that was even more frightening.

'What?'

'Roll over. Look, like this.' Pulling and pushing at her, he made her roll over so that her face was pressed into the lace pillow. Then he was on top of her and she felt a shock of disbelief and then a wave of terror as she realized what he was trying to do to her.

'No,' she whispered into the muffling pillow and then, almost screaming, 'No.'

His face was over her shoulder and she glimpsed the fine, blond hairs of his moustache pricking against the lace ruffle.

'Let me try,' he coaxed her. 'I'll be so gentle.'

And all the time he was pushing at her, trying to force his swollen self into the wrong place.

Isabel writhed from side to side, trying to escape him. But the more she struggled the tighter he held her. He was suddenly deaf and blind to the fact that she was Isabel, and the fighting, clawing creature that she had become seemed only to excite him further. His eyes were screwed tight shut and his face was drawn up into a scarlet pucker.

Isabel felt the disgust hardening inside her like a stone.

Peter was murmuring 'Oh yes you will, oh yes you will,' over and over again. Now he almost had her where he wanted her. Her wrists were imprisoned in one of his hands, and with the other he kept her head pressed down into the bedclothes. The weight of his torso pinned her down and his thick, muscular legs between hers kept them forced wide apart.

The murmuring stopped abruptly as he hoisted himself for an instant and then forced himself into her.

Isabel screamed, once. The pain was so severe that she thought she was split in half, but worse than the physical pain was her humiliation. That Peter should do this to her. That a man who

...ad told her he loved her and promised to honour and cherish
...er should treat her like the lowest, filthiest object.

If this was love, this and the other nights separating her from
the day of her marriage, then she couldn't bear it.

At that moment, something snapped inside Isabel. The tears
burnt her eyes, but she felt as if some vital part of herself had
escaped from the body lying on the bed with Peter Jaspert jerking
above it. She still felt the pain, and the tearing at her inner flesh,
but she could stand outside herself and watch it happening with
icy detachment.

She both felt and saw Peter slithering in his own sweat against
her back.

She felt her tears, and saw her wet face against the white
pillow. And then, when his shout came and his big body bucked
over hers, she watched his contortions with cold, cold careless-
ness.

As soon as he had finished with her Peter rolled away and lay
exhausted on his back with his forearm over his face.

Isabel was sobbing, and as soon as her body was her own again
the blessed detachment from it was lost to her. She was just
Isabel again, crying with fear and pain and revulsion. Where
would she go from here? What would happen to them both now?

At last, without moving his sheltering arm or trying to touch
her, Peter said, 'Isabel, don't make a thing about it. It isn't so
very terrible, you know. Lots of men need to do it like that.
Don't pretend it hurt you more than it really did.'

She heard the blustering, defensive note in his voice and knew
that he was ashamed. It had happened before, to a lesser degree.
He wouldn't admit anything, but he would try to be gentler with
her now and she would be reminded of the man she had dreamed
into existence before her marriage.

Taking a deep breath to control the sobbing, Isabel said, 'You
have no right to force me. You can't force me to do what disgusts
me.'

She sensed him wincing at the word, and then he said coldly,
'There is no force in marriage, Isabel. You are my wife.'

'Not your possession,' she bit back at him. But she knew that
Peter wouldn't hear her. He sat up and pulled the cover carefully
around him. Except when he was excited, Peter was conscious
of his nakedness.

'I don't know what to do with you, Isabel. God knows, I've

tried hard enough. I've never known a woman as stiff as you. I thought it was just maidenly decency before we were married, but now I'm beginning to wonder.' A note of vindictiveness crept into Peter's voice. 'It's like poking a bolster for all the response you make.'

And this was her husband, Isabel thought. Saying these things, hurting her like this.

'What . . . what am I supposed to do?' she asked.

'You are supposed to enjoy it. Other women do, believe me.'

Isabel flinched and stared down at her fingers twisted in the ribbons of her nightdress. Peter had known other women and they had enjoyed it. Of course he would have done before they were married, Isabel thought. She was not so naïve as to imagine he was as innocent as herself. But then, if exactly the same things had happened to other women and they had enjoyed them, then clearly it was herself who was at fault.

Fleetingly she thought of Adeline and the physical pleasure she had suspected lay at the heart of her mother's changing friendships and then, as always, she sheered away from the hint of coarseness in that.

'I don't, Peter. I . . . can't.'

Help me, she was going to say. Try to be patient. But he gave her no time for that. Peter made a small, angry noise. He stood up and gathered his scattered clothes and then banged through the door into his dressing-room.

For a long time Isabel lay dry-eyed in the crumpled bedclothes, staring at the closed door. As the pain and humiliation receded, a little of the detachment came back to her. The man who came to her bed wasn't the man she had married. He wasn't even the man who lived the other hours in the well-ordered house with her. He was another person, a stranger, and she would have to learn to exist with him. At the prospect of the years ahead Isabel went stiff in the sheets that still smelt of him.

In the morning, Peter had gone out long before Isabel came downstairs and she was glad of that. The mornings were difficult enough at present anyway.

Taking her cup of weak tea and lemon with her, she went into the drawing-room and dialled her doctor's number.

Yes, the secretary confirmed. Of course Mr Hardwicke would see Mrs Jaspert this morning. Would eleven-thirty be suitable?

Peter's Daimler and chauffeur were at Isabel's disposal in the mornings, but instead of ordering the car round she slipped out of the house and took a taxi to Mr Hardwicke's consulting rooms in Devonshire Place. At eleven-thirty exactly she was shown into the doctor's room.

It was time to have her suspicions confirmed.

Mr Hardwicke was Adeline's doctor and he had attended to the childhood ailments of all three Lovell children. The big room with its waxy floral arrangements, polished desk and green leather examination couch were so familiar to Isabel that she didn't even glance around her. Mr Hardwicke had crossed the room to greet her and now he was shaking her hand. She forced herself to smile and focus on what he was saying.

' . . . since you were married. Congratulations, and so forth. How time flies. It hardly seems a year since you were a little girl down with that nasty bout of measles. Dear me. Sit down here, now.' Behind his desk again the doctor folded his hands and beamed at her. 'Well, Mrs Jaspert. What can we do for you today?'

Carefully Isabel took off her cream leather gloves and laid them on her lap, smoothing the fingers flat. The big solitaire diamond in her engagement ring flashed at her.

'I think I'm pregnant.'

'Well, well. That's very suitable. Well done. I'm sure you're right. Tell me the symptoms, will you?'

Isabel told him, keeping her eyes fixed on her folded hands.

'That sounds like it to me. Well now. We'll do a couple of little tests, and I'll examine you to make sure everything's in perfect order. Then you can go home and tell Mr Jaspert the good news. I'll call in my nurse, and perhaps you would slip behind the screen there and undress and then put yourself on the couch so we can take a look at you?'

Isabel did as she was told. She stretched out on the white towel laid over the green leather and the nurse put a blanket over her. The doctor's face was wreathed in smiles as it loomed over hers, hovering unnaturally close and then dissolving back again with the light flashing off the gold-rimmed spectacles.

Isabel fought against the nausea and the faintness. The doctor's voice boomed in her ears.

'Try to relax. Just a little examination.'

The blanket was taken away and Isabel almost screamed as his gloved fingers touched her thigh. It took all the shreds of her

183

will-power to force herself to lie still while the fingers explored her.

At the end of it, inexplicably it seemed, Mr Hardwicke was still smiling. Was it possible that he didn't feel her shuddering? Isabel wondered.

'There now. That wasn't so very terrible, was it?' He was peeling off his gloves, and the nurse tucked the blanket back again. 'How long have you been married?'

'Three months.'

'And I can confirm that you are at least two months pregnant. Nothing at all amiss there. You're very lucky, you know. Some young people have to wait for ever. Boy or a girl, would you like? Boy first for Mr Jaspert, I expect? You can get dressed now, my dear.'

Isabel was thinking of the hotel room in Florence with the view of the Duomo from the balcony, the high white bed and the nights with Peter. On one of those nights, then, it had happened.

'Mrs Jaspert? Would you like to get dressed?' The nurse was holding her clothes, one hand stroking the soft furs with unconscious envy.

When she was dressed again and sitting opposite the doctor at his desk, Isabel felt the nausea releasing its grip.

Mr Hardwicke was writing her notes, nodding and smiling. 'You're a healthy young lady, Mrs Jaspert. I foresee no problems at all, but perhaps you would like to consult an obstetric specialist? I can give you the name of the best man, or perhaps Lady Lovell will have some advice for you as far as that goes. Nearer the time of your confinement, perhaps? That will be in mid-November, so far as I can judge. During your pregnancy you should continue to live as normally as possible, eat a healthy diet, and take as much rest as you feel you need. Not too many parties, crowded rooms and late nights, eh?' His eyes twinkled at her behind his spectacles. 'Any questions you want to ask me?'

Isabel's fingers tightened on her gloves. 'Yes,' she said abruptly. She knew what the question was, but she hadn't tried it out in her head. She had been too busy concentrating on not fainting. 'What about our . . . married relationship? Might it be dangerous for the baby to . . . to . . . Surely that should stop, until afterwards?'

Mr Hardwicke leaned forward reassuringly. 'Your married life can certainly continue as long as it is comfortable and pleasurable for you both. Some young couples stop in the last few weeks, others continue right up until the time of confinement. It's a matter of personal choice.'

Isabel stared at him. She had been certain that she would be able to take her pregnancy back home with her like a shield.

'But . . . I'd be afraid. For the baby, you know.'

The doctor was looking at her more carefully now. 'There really isn't any need to worry. Mother Nature has arranged things as logically as she always does. But if you do feel particularly anxious perhaps the best thing would be to discuss it with your husband, explain what you feel, and ask him to be extra gentle with you. It is his baby too, remember. Or would you prefer it if I spoke to him? I couldn't recommend months of complete abstinence for a newly married couple.'

'No,' Isabel said hastily. 'No, I'll talk to him myself, of course.'

Automatically she reached for her handbag and pulled her fur around her shoulders.

'Are you quite happy,' the doctor asked gently, 'with the physical side of your marriage?'

Isabel stood up. Her chair rocked precariously for a moment before she reached to steady it. 'Yes. Perfectly happy.'

Mr Hardwicke's smile had faded a little as he walked round his desk to open the door for her. 'It does take a little time, you know.'

As he stood there, kindly and familiar, with his fingers not quite touching the doorknob, Isabel almost told him. She opened her mouth and moistened her lips, and saw his eyebrows go up a fraction as he waited. But his expectancy touched her reserves of pride and she squared her shoulders against him.

'Like all kinds of other things in life,' Isabel said brightly.

The doctor nodded, as if conceding a point, and opened the door for her. Isabel went down the wide, carpeted steps to the street, pulling on her gloves and smoothing the leather over each finger as if the fit of them was her most important concern.

Peter was home early, for once. Isabel was finishing her five o'clock cup of tea in the drawing-room when he came in. He stood awkwardly in his City clothes, his newspaper in one hand, not quite looking at her and waiting to see how she would receive him. It was as if part of him wanted to apologize for the night before, but his stubborn truculence wouldn't allow it. If Isabel was prepared to be civilized and pretend that nothing had happened, then he could do the same, but if she was still angry he could use that as an excuse to let his own anger flare up again.

Looking at him in the coolness of her new detachment, Isabel thought it was odd that Peter could handle his constituents and colleagues so expertly in his overbearing way, yet had no idea how to deal with his own wife.

Isabel smiled. 'What sort of day did you have today?' she asked him.

Peter shrugged with relief. So last night hadn't happened.

'Quietish. I may have to fly to Berlin tomorrow for a day or so to close a piece of business.'

Isabel nodded. She knew that Peter's trading on the metal market was currently concerned with armaments, but she didn't enquire beyond that.

'Shall I ring for a fresh pot of tea?'

'No, this will do.'

'Cream?'

She gave her husband his cup and watched him sit down opposite her. The paper, already folded to the financial pages, lay beside him. She knew that he was itching to pick it up, but he was prepared to extend the truce a little further.

'What about you?' he asked stiffly.

Isabel looked down at her rings. 'I have something to tell you. I went to see Mr Hardwicke this morning, and he says that I am two months pregnant.'

The clatter startled her and she looked up. Peter had put down his cup and stumbled forward from his low chair. Now he was half-kneeling, half-crouching in front of her. She saw that the polished black toe of his shoe had rucked up one corner of the pale rug.

'Oh, darling. A baby?' His big hands hovered and then came down over hers in her lap. Isabel looked at him and saw that his face was suffused with simple pleasure, all the self-sure imperviousness gone for the moment. She hadn't expected that he would be so pleased.

'In November, he says.'

Peter's hands tightened over her fingers. 'And is everything all right?' After the shock of pleasure had come anxiety. Not for her directly, Isabel saw, but for the baby. It was his baby that

186

would be important. Isabel had guessed that was how it would be, but she had underestimated how much it would mean to him. Now she revised the full value of what she possessed. She lifted her chin and stared straight into Peter's eyes.

'Mr Hardwicke says that I must be very careful.'

The anxiety in him intensified at once. 'Careful? What's wrong? If there's anything, we'll get the top man . . .'

'Nothing's wrong, Peter,' she said smoothly. 'He just talked about rest.'

'Rest? Of course you can rest. You don't do anything . . .'

'And he forbade any kind of physical stress. Anything like that, until after the baby is born.'

Peter met her stare now, and his hands were heavy on hers. He was no fool, Isabel knew that. He understood at once what she was saying. She was offering his heir, whether or not the doctor's warning was genuine, in exchange for her physical inviolacy.

For a long moment they went on looking at each other. It occurred to Isabel that they were locked in position like a tableau of a Victorian proposal, and her irrational desire to laugh was vaguely disturbing.

At last Peter stood up. 'If there's anything not quite normal, I think we should see a specialist. Hardwicke's no more than a GP.'

'I don't think there's any need for that,' Isabel said firmly. 'Mr Hardwicke has looked after us since we were babies, and I trust him absolutely.'

'I see,' Peter said, and she knew that he did. He turned away abruptly and Isabel felt confidence waking up and beginning to grow inside her again like the baby itself. Her hand rested protectively over her stomach. 'We shall have to abide by Mr Hardwicke's strictures, of course. Somehow or other,' he added threateningly. Isabel suspected that he would go looking for physical gratification elsewhere, if he wasn't doing it already, and in the relief of her first victory she couldn't have cared less. The longing to laugh grew even stronger.

Then, with his characteristic ability to put what he didn't choose to consider further right out of his mind, Peter was swinging around the room smiling again. 'It will be a boy, of course. God, but the old man will be pleased. Have you told anyone?'

187

'Of course not, darling. The father should know first.'

'The father. Quite right. I'm going to telephone.' As he passed her, he stroked her shoulder awkwardly. He looked, Isabel decided, just as he must have done when he was picked for his school eleven. He was halfway through the door before he said, almost pleadingly, 'Well, we must have been doing something right, wouldn't you say?'

'Something,' Isabel echoed expressionlessly.

'We'll make it work, after the baby comes. Just wait and see,' he promised her.

Alone once more in her drawing-room, with her hand still shielding her stomach, Isabel stared at the enamel clock on the mantelpiece.

At first sight, Amy didn't recognize her. She was sitting waiting for her sister at a corner table in the Ritz dining-room. The lunchtime ritual was at its height, and the big room was alive with the muted buzz of greetings and conversation. Isabel was late, and Amy had begun to watch the doors as the maître d'hôtel swept forward to greet each new arrival. Even so, as the woman in the pale tweed Vionnet suit was ushered towards her table Amy glanced once and then away again. She looked like any one of a dozen other women lunching today, but she didn't look like Isabel.

But then she stopped beside the empty chair and the waiter drew it back for her. Amy started in surprise and then collected herself.

'Bel, darling, I'm sorry. I must have been miles away.'

'I'm sorry too, for being so late,' Isabel said. She smiled, but her face was tired. 'I don't know exactly what takes up so much time nowadays, but I'm always late. And I used to be so well organized. Forgive?'

'Of course.'

It wasn't just the new, intimidatingly elegant clothes. Isabel had always enjoyed shopping and fittings, whereas Amy hated them, and as Peter Jaspert's wife Isabel could certainly afford to dress at the top couturiers. The cut of Isabel's tight-waisted suit was perfect to a hairsbreadth, and the soft blue-grey tweed fitted her like a second skin. The silvery grey of her blouse with its extravagant bow-tied neck exactly matched the cloud of grey

188

fox-fur around her shoulders, and there was a little hat in the same shade, tipped forward with a wisp of veiling.

'Isabel, your hair.'

Amy was too surprised to hide the dismay in her voice. Isabel's rich mass of dark red waves, her best feature just as it was Adeline's, had been brutally cut back. Under the pert little hat was a hairstyle exactly like every other woman's in the room – stiff-looking ridges drawn back to a flat little chignon at the nape of the neck. At a single stroke, Isabel had reduced herself to chic ordinariness.

Isabel was leaning wearily back in her chair and looking around her. 'I know. What do you think? I thought it would make a difference. I forget now what kind of difference, but it doesn't seem to have done in any case.'

It wasn't just the hair, Amy thought. Isabel looked exhausted, as if all her old liveliness had been drained away. Her face was thinner, with a new, shuttered look to it.

Anxiety gripped at Amy. *Whatever's wrong?* she was going to blurt out, and then from the corner of her eye she saw the black height of the head waiter, hovering. Isabel had picked up her menu but she was twisting it in her hands, unopened.

'What shall we eat? I'm famished,' Amy said, with an attempt at cheerfulness.

Isabel shrugged. 'I don't know. I'm not very hungry.' Then suddenly she smiled, a thin approximation of her old smile. 'D'you know what I'd really like? A glass of milk, and an apple. One of the russets, from Chance.'

'I don't suppose that would tax the Ritz kitchens too severely,' Amy said. She was about to summon the waiter, but Isabel's smile had already faded. 'I'll just have a plain omelette,' she said tonelessly.

When they had ordered and they were alone again in the discreet bustle of the dining-room, Amy put her hand out to cover Isabel's. The big square diamond her sister wore sat cold and hard under her palm.

'Isabel, what's wrong?'

A trolley with a huge silver dome perched on it was wheeled past, followed by a phalanx of waiters with silver dishes balanced at shoulder height. Isabel turned her head away from the smell of the food.

'Please, Isabel? Won't you tell me? I know there's something.'

189

Isabel forced herself to focus on the starched white tablecloth, her sister's hand warm over her own at the middle of it.

'Nothing's wrong. I'm going to have a baby.'

Relief flooded through Amy. So that was it. It explained everything, the tiredness and the secretive look. It even explained the hair. It was a pregnant woman's whim, and of course it would grow again.

After the relief came unalloyed delight. The news would please everybody. Both families. There would be a new baby for Bethan to look after . . . Amy wanted to run round the table and hug her sister, but she contented herself with squeezing her fingers.

'How wonderful, how wonderful. A baby. I should have guessed. When?'

'November, apparently.'

'And how do you feel?'

'Sick,' Isabel said, and the comical mixture of expressions in Amy's face brought back the urge to laugh. For some reason Isabel felt that she should suppress the laughter.

'Oh, Bel, why didn't you say something? You shouldn't be sitting in restaurants. Let's go home right away.'

'There's no need. I'm all right, really I am. Life can't stop just because you're pregnant, can it? Anyway, I want to hear all about you and the nursing. When did you decide and when do you begin?'

The anxiety flickered again in Amy. Surely, as well as feeling tired and unwell, Isabel should be pleased with herself? The few expectant mothers that Amy had encountered positively glowed with pride. She could see nothing of the sort in Isabel's thin, closed-in face.

'Later. Tell me more about the baby first. Peter must be thrilled?'

'Oh yes. He's being marvellous.'

Marvellous meant that her husband came home nowadays and went straight to bed. She didn't any longer have to lie shaking and listening to which way his footsteps would turn. Peter left her alone except for an indirect solicitousness that made her feel like a biological machine temporarily housing his baby. It was hard, Isabel discovered, to think of her pregnancy in any other way. There it was, growing and protecting her every day.

After it was born, what then? Isabel bundled the thought up hastily and pushed it away from her.

'Do you feel all . . . fulfilled, and ripe, like pregnant women always look as if they feel?'

What she mostly felt, Isabel reflected, was cold, and empty. As detached from what was happening inside her as from everything else.

'It's early days yet, you know,' she answered with forced brightness. 'Wait till I'm huge and lying on a sofa all day, and then ask me. Do you have any free time when you're a nurse? Will you be able to come and sit with me? I'll miss you, Amy,' she said with a sudden rush of real feeling. Amy was going off to do a proper job, moving into a world that Isabel would have no insight into, and she felt suddenly that Amy was her only link with normality.

'Whenever I have an hour, I'll come,' Amy reassured her. 'I miss you, too.'

Their food was laid ceremoniously in front of them. Isabel picked up her fork and prodded her omelette with it. 'It doesn't look edible at all,' she remarked. 'More like a piece of folded underwear.' Then she began to talk very rapidly about her last fitting at Vionnet, and how her *vendeuse* had remarked on how slim she had become. 'Not for long,' Isabel added flatly.

The whole lunch was like that. Amy felt that they were moving elliptically around each other, almost touching before Isabel swung away again in her own eccentric orbit.

Isabel ate nothing at all.

Amy forced her food down, ordering more than she wanted to keep up a pretence of normality. To stop the talk from dying away into awkward silences she found herself chattering too brightly about her enrolment at the Royal Lambeth, then about Jake Silverman and the afternoon of the hunger march, and how Tony Hardy and Appleyard Street had led her there, and then at last about meeting Nick Penry and taking him home to Bruton Street.

A flash of the old Isabel followed that. She laughed almost naturally. 'Amy, I don't know anyone else in the world who would have done that.'

'He had nowhere to go.'

'You could have helped him to find somewhere. What made you decide to take him home?'

'I didn't decide. I just did it. He wasn't the kind of man you

191

hand out money or charity to. He was too . . . important for that.'

'You liked him, didn't you?'

Amy shrugged. 'Yes, I suppose I did. Although he made me angry, too. For being so arrogant. No, not arrogant, exactly. Dominating, rather.' But she saw that she had lost Isabel again. Her sister was looking away, and her face had gone taut.

'Name any man who isn't,' she said, in a voice so low that Amy had to lean forward, and then wasn't sure if she had heard correctly.

'Tony Hardy,' she said at once, but Isabel wasn't listening. 'Why do you say that?' Amy persisted. 'Is it Peter?' *Peter Jaspert*, she thought. *If you are doing this to Isabel . . .*

'Oh no,' Isabel said deliberately. 'Peter's fine now.' She was gathering up her gloves and handbag. 'Do you mind very much if we leave? I think I'd like to go outside for a while.'

'Of course.' Amy found herself stumbling after her. The uniformed doorman sprang forward as he saw them coming and handed them out under the colonnade fronting Piccadilly. There were early flowers in the baskets hanging under the arches and Amy caught the sudden scent of them. If only they were safely at Chance together, she thought irrelevantly. The doorman's piercing whistle brought a cab to the kerb. Isabel was about to step inside with Amy following her when she turned abruptly aside.

'You take it,' she ordered. 'I'm going to walk somewhere.' Amy found herself bundled inside, the door was slammed on her and the cab was swinging away. She turned to look out of the little rear window and saw Isabel, perfect in her modish clothes, hesitating under the arches as if she didn't know which way to turn. But then, with a little shielding gesture that drew the soft furs up around her throat, she began to walk slowly westwards. Amy's last glimpse before the traffic swallowed her up was of Isabel walking unevenly, as if she was playing the old, superstitious childhood game of not stepping on the cracks. Amy remembered how they had chanted the rhyme on town walks with Bethan.

> *If you step on a crack, you'll marry a Jack,*
> *If you step on a square, you'll marry a bear . . .*

The anxiety that had nagged Amy all through lunch redoubled.

192

Something was badly wrong with Isabel, and the shutters seemed to have come down between them just when her sister might need her most.

Amy frowned out at the afternoon bustle of shoppers crowding the pavements, thinking of Isabel walking blindly through them, alone.

Well then, if Amy herself couldn't help, perhaps Bethan might. Somehow, she vowed, she would see that Bethan was installed at Ebury Street.

Bethan wouldn't allow any harm to come to Isabel.

Amy was still thinking about Isabel and Peter as she let herself in through the front door at Bruton Street. The wide hallway was empty and shadowy. The house seemed as quiet as always. Amy sighed as she peeled off her gloves. She took her hat off and threw it on to a stiff-backed chair, then ran her fingers through her hair and wondered what she was going to do with herself for the rest of the afternoon. Then she cocked her head to listen. The house wasn't perfectly quiet after all. There was music playing upstairs somewhere, loud, brash dance music.

She was standing with her face turned upwards when Richard appeared at the head of the stairs.

Amy's face lit up and she flung her arms open wide.

'Richard! I can't tell you how pleased I am to see you.'

He ran lightly down the stairs and across the marble floor. Amy put her arms around him and hugged him with delight.

'Such a warm welcome,' he murmured. 'Do I deserve?' But Richard was smiling too, and he returned her hug with equal warmth.

Amy stood back to look at him. Her little brother was growing up, she decided. He wouldn't be tall, but he was built neatly and he moved with fluid elegance. His half-closed eyes gave his face the same enigmatic expression it had worn since childhood, but Amy thought there was a new zest in Richard, a new relish for life. Adulthood would suit him.

'I didn't know you were coming home,' she said. 'Are you supposed to be here? Richard . . .'

'Perfectly legit, sister dear. Mid-term break, y'know. Where are the tyrants?'

193

'Father's at Chance, of course. Mama was here yesterday, but I think she's gone off to the country for a few days.'

Richard glanced at her. 'All on your own, eh?'

'I've just lunched at the Ritz with Isabel.'

His glance sharpened. 'And?'

'She's expecting a baby.'

Richard hunched his shoulders, a comical gesture of resignation.

'What could be more normal and natural? The primogeniture of a whole new generation of Jasperts? One can hardly be surprised, even though one may not view it with unalloyed pleasure. I have to say that any baby gives me the positive shudders. The smell, you know. But I dare say that Peter and Isabel are bursting with happiness and pride?'

Amy's smile had faded now. She didn't try to hide her concern as she blurted out, 'I think Isabel's unhappy. I'm worried about her. She . . .'

Richard held up his hand.

'Wait. I'm ravenous. Starved to death. I can't tell you not to worry until I have eaten five pieces of cake and drunk three cups of tea. On second thoughts, I shall probably need cucumber sandwiches and anchovy toast as well. Before you arrived I was going to ask for it to be sent up to the schoolroom. I was playing the gramophone up there, all alone, rather melancholy. Now you're here we can have tea together and talk afterwards.'

'Tea first, then. In the schoolroom.'

'Race.'

Amy was protesting but she was already running too. They reached the stairs and pounded up them as if they were children again.

Later, when Richard had finished the last crumb of his last slice of cherry cake and had poured himself a third cup of tea, he settled a cushion behind his head and leant back in the depths of the battered sofa.

'Now,' he said.

Amy sat looking out of the window at the familiar view. Isabel and she had sat over their lessons and looked out at the same jumble of chimneys and rooftops. She explained her anxieties and Richard listened carefully, not interrupting her once.

'I'm afraid that she won't talk to any of us,' Amy said. 'I'm afraid that she will cut herself off. She's proud and stubborn, you know, under that pliant exterior. She wouldn't let us know if it had gone wrong.'

Richard looked full at her now. 'If what had gone wrong?'

Amy made a little, awkward gesture with her hands. 'The marriage. You know.'

Richard pursed his lips. 'Not really. I make no claim to know anything whatsoever about marriage. As a perfect outsider, judging by the two or three occasions on which I've been at Ebury Street, Isabel's marriage looks quite ordinary. Keen young politician, pretty wife to charm the constituents. A lot of mutual pleasure in their silverware and so forth.'

Amy nodded. 'Yes, I've seen that too.'

Richard put down his cup and went over to the gramophone. He sorted through the scatter of records and slipped one on to the turntable. The dance music crackled again and he held out his hand to Amy. She let him draw her to her feet and put his arm around her waist. They were almost the same height, she noticed. They began to dance a slow foxtrot, their heels clicking on the ink-blotted boards of the schoolroom floor.

'Dear Amy,' he murmured. 'You have such strong feelings yourself, and concealment of them is utterly beyond you. You love, and fear, and rejoice, and plunge into gloom and glee all in the space of half an hour.'

'You are not so very impassive yourself.'

'No. But Isabel is different. I think you must let her follow her own course.'

'Are you telling me that I should mind my own business?'

He brother swept her through a flourishing turn before he answered her.

'No. I'm not telling you to stop worrying, either, because from what you say I believe there's cause for it. All you and I can do is let Isabel know that she can confide in us and that she can trust us because we love her and support her and we always will, whatever Jaspert is or does.'

Amy smiled, then. 'I wanted to hear you say that. I know quite well that's all either of us can do. But it's quite a lot, isn't it? I know how much I rely on Isabel and you. How important you are to me. Will you . . . will you try to see her oftener? I may not be able to, so much, from now on.'

Richard looked squarely at her again. 'Yes. I'll do that. I'm

195

sorry, Amy. I know I'm not much company for either of you. There are all kinds of things one does, you know . . .'

'What kind of things?'

His eyelids drooped again. 'Just things.'

Richard is much better at concealment than I am, Amy thought. She realized how much she loved him, and wondered a little jealously about his life.

The music stopped and they faced each other more happily.

'May I have the pleasure of another dance, Miss Lovell?'

'If you change the needle first, and choose something a bit livelier.'

When they started up again Richard asked, 'And what about you, my dear ardent Amy?'

She grinned at him. 'I have got news. I have enrolled myself as a student nurse. And I start at the Royal Lambeth Hospital in ten days' time.'

He whirled her around in a wide circle so that her hair spun around her face. 'A nurse? Starched cap? Night duty? Cocoa in the Nurses' Home?'

'Most definitely.'

'I'm very, very glad. And I am proud of you.' He kissed her, lightly brushing her cheek. 'You'll be a fine nurse. The Florence Nightingale of Berkeley Square. You know, Amy, you're the only one of us with any real decency. If I had my hat on, I would take it off to you.'

His approval was so sincere and so valuable that Amy felt tears behind her eyes. He was the only one of her family who had understood what she wanted and believed in it. Even Isabel had received her news with polite bafflement.

'I'm glad you think it's a good plan,' she said softly.

'Well, now. What shall we do to celebrate? We could see a show and have dinner somewhere risky afterwards.'

Gratefully Amy seized on the idea. 'I'd love to. Don't you have to do anything else?'

'One doesn't have to do anything.' Amy let the evasion pass. 'And I've got another suggestion. Before you start nursing, why don't you come up to the Fourth of June? I'll introduce you to the Captain of the Eleven. Perfect specimen. Tall, broad shoulders, Apollo in flannels. No brain, of course, but you can't have it all ways.'

Amy was giggling in the way that only Richard could make her. 'Not my type. Not at all.'

He tucked her arm under his. 'Never mind. Come anyway. I like to show you off.'

With his free hand Richard lifted the arm of the gramophone and then they went companionably down the stairs to change for the theatre.

8

~~~~

Thick black stockings, blue dress with a starched collar and a
maddening row of eighteen tiny buttons, heavy black shoes,
bib-fronted apron crackling with starch from the brown paper
package delivered to her room every Monday, the bow at the
back to be tied just so, cap the same, set exactly straight and
pinned over her tightly coiled hair . . .

Feverishly counting the seconds remaining, Amy peered at
herself in the tiny square of mirror over the shelf that doubled
as work desk and dressing-table, judged that her appearance
would be acceptable even to Sister Blaine, the head nurse of the
ward, and ran for her life.

Seven minutes to six a.m. and she was due to present herself
on the ward, correct to the last button, at six o'clock precisely.
She was aching in every limb and joint from twelve hours on her
feet yesterday, twelve the day before and the day before that,
and her eyes were heavy with sitting over textbooks late into the
night. Of all the things she had learned to do since arriving at
the Lambeth, Amy found waking up at five in the morning the
hardest.

The stairs and corridors of the nurses' hostel seemed ominously
deserted, and then Amy heard the sound of pounding feet behind
her.

'Glory, Lovell, we'll be late again. Sister Blaine will kill me,
that's for sure.'

Student nurse Moira O'Hara was pinning her cap on as she
ran, hopelessly tucking the wiry strands of hair in at one side as
they escaped on the other.

'Come on, Moira. We can make it.'

They chased down the stairs into the narrow, dirty street,
ducked down an alleyway lined with dustbins, and came round
a corner to the nurses' entrance to the hospital. Once inside,

hospital discipline made them slow their pace to a brisk walk and Amy couldn't help laughing at the anguished glances Moira shot back at her as they climbed the scrubbed stairs. They reached the ward door, with seconds to spare, and found Sister Blaine waiting inside them.

'I was wondering if prize nurses Lovell and O'Hara were planning to grace the ward this morning. O'Hara, go and fix your cap and don't ever appear on my floor improperly dressed again. After that you will attend to the sluice-room. The night staff have left it looking like a battlefield. If you are quite ready, Lovell, you can begin with Mrs Marks.'

Amy marched away down the ward. She wasn't exactly afraid of Blaine, although most of the other juniors found her terrifying. The sister's cruel tongue was her chief weapon against the generally fumbling inadequacy of her new recruits, and her vitriolic criticism simply made Amy try harder in order to show the old witch just what she could do.

'Hello, Mrs Marks. How is it this morning?'

'Murder, bleedin' murder. Me legs is like red 'ot bolsters.'

Her first patient of the morning was a cheerful Cockney grandmother whose arms and legs were grotesquely swollen, taut and tender to the touch. She was the salty commentator on everything that happened in Blaine's ward, and Amy liked her very much.

'Come on, then. I'll give you a cool wash, and then we'll see if we can make your bed more comfortable.'

There were five more patients to attend to before seven-thirty, when Amy and Moira had a ten-minute break during which they made toast and gulped tea in the tiny staff kitchen off the ward.

'God forgive me, but I hate her,' Moira murmured as Sister Blaine's ramrod figure passed the door.

'She sounds worse than she is.'

'She just likes you, Lovell, because you're grand. She's a bloody old snob, as well.'

They grinned at each other over the last mouthfuls of toast, brushed away the invisible crumbs and scurried back to the ward.

There were forty-five minutes for lunch, which according to the rota organized by seniority often didn't come around for the juniors until three p.m. After that, depending on their workload, another ten-minute tea-break might be squeezed in before the shift ended at six.

All through the rest of the day, Amy went to and fro under

the orders of the sister and staff nurses. The juniors did the dirtiest and least rewarding jobs. All the bedpans, the cleaning and scouring that didn't fall into the ward maids' duties, the lifting and washing of inert patients, were delegated to the newcomers. Amy was perpetually exhausted, but she had never felt more alive in her life. She liked and admired the stoicism of the Lambeth's mostly working-class patients, and the proper nursing duties that were the province of the staffs and senior students fascinated her. She watched everything she could, and remembered how it was done. She resented all the wearying scrubbing and polishing and mindless routine as much as every junior but when she was given something more interesting to do she found it so absorbing that she forgot all the drawbacks of the work.

To her pleased surprise, Amy discovered that the theoretical and written work came easily to her. She could remember the lists of procedures for care of septicaemia, the treatment of infantile diphtheria, and the bones of the leg and foot almost effortlessly. She was physically clumsy and uncoordinated and would never be as quick and deft as little Dorothy Hewitt, a clerk's daughter from Clapham who was destined to carry off all the prizes of their year. But she was streets ahead of the unlucky Irish girl, Moira O'Hara, who had become her closest friend. Moira was always late, dropped things, and could never remember a list of five classic symptoms for more than half an hour at a time. The other nurses would cover for her surreptitiously, and coach her for tests in their short dinner-breaks.

The sense of companionship and solidarity among the girls of her intake was like nothing Amy had ever experienced before.

When she had first arrived, in the bewildering early days when life had seemed reduced to exhaustion, confusion and the fear of doing the wrong thing, the other girls had treated her with suspicious reserve. They would sit with their heads together at hostel canteen meals, and when Amy joined them they eyed her warily. In the rare free hours they looked curiously at her clothes and Amy was suddenly acutely conscious of her glove-soft hand-made shoes, her cashmere sweaters and silk scarves. She had felt isolated and awkward, but instead of trying to compensate by being over-friendly Amy had simply behaved as naturally as she could, and slowly the reserve had been broken down.

Dorothy Hewitt had obligingly shown her how to fold and tuck in the bedclothes at the end of a hospital bed in exactly the way that Sister Blaine favoured. Amy had never made a bed or polished a floor in her life, and it was the simple household tasks, so familiar to most of the other girls that their tutors didn't bother to explain them, that were her major pitfalls.

In her turn, Amy had told Sister Blaine that Moira O'Hara had taken a pail to the sluice-room when really she was late back up the stairs from dinner.

'You said that?' Moira gasped when Amy slipped out of the ward doors to greet her with an empty pail.

'Ssshh. Quickly.'

'Oh God, but you are a friend in need. I could not have lived through another roasting.'

Moira, from a village in County Cork, had dreamed of nursing at a great London hospital ever since she was old enough to dream of anything. But as soon as she arrived, she was crippled by homesickness which made it hard for her to keep up the demanding pace. Amy, who was also homesick and as much at a loss in Lambeth as Moira, warmed to her at once, and after the sluice-pail episode they became friends. The unlikely pairing attracted the attention of the other girls, and they stopped assuming that Amy was a stuck-up snob because her father was a lord and she had crystal scent bottles on her bedroom shelf.

By the end of the first month they were saving a place for her at the draughty corner table next to the canteen service hatch that belonged to the newest intake. The hostel corridor became a friendly place where girls tapped on her door in search of a stamp, or to borrow one of her scarves or blouses for a special evening, or to invite her to feast on buttered toast and cocoa whilst perched in a row on somebody's bed.

Hospital food was sparse and tasteless, and they were all perpetually starving. Amy had never been so hungry; she had never thought about food before except as something that happened automatically, and on her days off at Bruton Street the size and sheer splendour of the meals was newly surprising. She ate ravenously, enjoying the subtle flavours and the freshness of the ingredients.

'Darling, are you sure you won't get fat?' Adeline asked faintly.

Amy smiled cheerfully at her. 'Not a chance. I've never worked so hard, and I'm getting thinner and thinner.' It was true. The waistbands of her uniform dresses were hanging loose.

Before going back to the hostel she would take a basket down to see Cook, and fill it with hothouse fruit, cold chicken, cheese and cakes. When she returned Moira and the others who lived too far away for regular home visits would fall on the basket with cries of delight.

When their studentships were confirmed after the first month, Moira's with a stern warning from Matron that she must do better, Amy felt as if she had known her companions for the whole of her life, and that some of them were almost as close to her as Isabel.

There were only one or two exceptions to the rule of friendship and mutual support. Mary Morrow, a doctor's daughter from Hampstead and consciously a social cut above the rest of the group, took an instant dislike to Amy. Usually she took the trouble to disguise it, and Amy was irresistibly reminded of acquaintanceships struck during her debutante years when girls would appear to be friendly whilst actually checking the pedigrees of her dress, her jewellery, and Amy herself, as well as the number and quality of her partners in the course of the evening. It wasn't Amy's fault that Mary chose to measure herself against her in some kind of battle of social standing and found herself losing on every count. But she discovered herself beginning to meet dislike with dislike, and the two girls tried to keep as far apart as possible in the claustrophobic world of the wards and hostel.

Amy was opening one of the first Bruton Street baskets when Mary's narrow, watchful face appeared in the doorway. Her eyes went straight to the crested white linen napkins that had covered the impromptu picnic.

'What has Lady Bountiful brought back for the deserving poor today?'

Amy went bright scarlet. She looked down at the basket at her feet and suddenly saw how her well-meant gesture might be interpreted.

Moira looked up from the cheerful scramble around the food. Deliberately, she recited, 'Chicken with a sauce straight from Heaven itself. Pineapples and strawberries, and a real cake thick with cream and chocolate that I'm sure won't taste of hospital bandages like every other thing I've eaten today. Now, I'm deserving enough, and I'm glad Amy took the trouble to bring the stuff back to us. What's more, I'm going to eat it and enjoy it without you staring down on me like a squinty old sheep. Sit down and share, will you, or get away with yourself.'

'I'm going home myself tomorrow, thank you very much,' Mary said stiffly. She turned away from the doorway and disappeared. Amy was still standing, rooted by the basket, wishing she had never even thought of bringing the food.

'I didn't mean . . .' she began, but Moira put her arm briskly around her shoulders.

'No, you didn't, and we all know that. Sure, she's an old cow that one, and you're not to take any notice of her.'

'Sheep or cow, which?' Amy said, laughing with Moira in spite of herself.

'Auch, who cares. Pass me that chicken, now, will you?'

'Moira's right,' quiet little Dorothy Hewitt said. 'You shouldn't pay any attention.'

Amy took their advice, but Mary's covert hostility remained a wrinkle in the days which grew smoother as her confidence increased.

As she grew more adept at the tasks set for her, Amy found brief intervals in between them during which she could stop and breathe, and talk to the patients. She began to distinguish between them as individuals instead of thinking of them as so many beds to be made, so many blanket baths to be given or so many cupfuls of hospital food to be spooned into slack mouths. It was especially true of night duty.

Sometimes, the twelve-hour darkness shifts were terrifying. Often, because of staffing shortages, a whole ward might be left under the supervision of a third-year student nurse with only Amy and one other junior student to assist her. When these nights were busy with new admissions from the accident department, or when there was more than one dangerously ill patient, Amy was too rushed to be frightened at the time, but afterwards, retrospective fear of the responsibility would make her feel almost faint.

It was on one of the busy nights that her first patient had died.

'Nurse! Nurse!' a woman had called her urgently from one bed as she passed. 'You'd best take a look at the old gel over there.' Amy whirled round to the opposite bed. It was an old woman who had only been admitted that afternoon. She had been dozing quietly only a few minutes before. Now her head had lolled inertly forward and her arms were slack over the bedcovers. Amy lifted one of the ancient, fragile wrists and felt a single flutter. Then she heard a faint sigh, almost politely regretful, and the pulse was gone. Amy dropped the arm and opened the nightgown on the thin, yellowish chest. She put her head to the old woman's heart, but there was nothing. Desperately she turned and ran, against all the hospital rules, up the ward to the senior nurse. The senior was busy at another bedside where a younger woman was moaning softly and rolling her head against the pillows.

'Bed eight,' Amy gasped. 'She's . . . dead.'

The other nurse glanced at her.

'Sure?'

'Yes, I'm certain.'

The nurse turned back to her own patient. There was a kidney bowl waiting beside her with a syringe and she was swabbing the flesh in the crook of the patient's arm with antiseptic. Calmly she picked up the syringe and checked the volume of the contents.

'Would you hold her steady, Lovell, while I administer this.'

'But . . . .'

'There is nothing we can do for Mrs Hughes now. When you have finished helping me here you can draw the curtains round her and ring down for the mortuary porter. Now hold, please.'

The needle slid smoothly into the vein and within seconds the patient was quieter.

'Come with me, Nurse Lovell.' On their way up the ward they took the pillows from the old lady's back and laid her flat, and then pulled the curtains across to shield her. Amy thought that she would never forget the open, sightless eyes, but the older nurse had closed them with perfect composure.

In the privacy of the ward office the senior said with brisk sympathy, 'Was that your first?' When Amy nodded miserably she touched her shoulder. 'It's part of the job, you know that. And remember that once a patient is dead, your immediate responsibility is to those who are not. Go down and make yourself a cup of tea now, we can spare you for a few minutes. You can bring one up for me, too.'

But not all the nights were busy.

Sometimes there were long, quiet hours when there was nothing to do at all except the routine chores that would assist the day staff. If any of the patients were awake and well enough to talk, the nurses were not exactly encouraged to do so but it was allowed, provided that every bowl and jar in the sluice-room already shone like the sun.

It was on just such a quiet night that Amy first talked to Helen Pearce.

'Nurse–Patient Demeanour' was the title of one lecture in the introductory series attended by Amy and the rest of her group. From it, as her notes reminded her, she had learned that 'a nurse must at all times be cheerful, reassuring and encouraging to her patients. She must be sympathetic and approachable, but she must remember always that it is a professional relationship and she must never, under any circumstances whatsoever, allow it to progress beyond that. Over-familiarity with any one patient is ultimately as detrimental to that patient as to the others under the nurse's care.'

'I am sure,' Amy recalled the sister adding darkly, 'that I do not need to caution you girls further, except to say that particular vigilance is necessary in the case of male patients.'

At least Helen was female, but Amy broke all the other rules as soon as she met her.

Helen Pearce was lying in one of the six beds in the corner of the L-shaped ward. She must have been admitted or moved in from elsewhere during the day because the bed had been empty the night before. Amy went to the foot-rail and glanced at the chart clipped to it. She read the girl's name and saw that she was nineteen, born in the same month as herself. Under the bare statements of name and status were the scribbled clinical notes, still almost unintelligible to Amy, and beneath those the temperature graph dipped and soared again.

Amy looked up and saw the girl watching her. She had been lying so still that Amy had imagined she was asleep but now saw that she was wide awake. She had very dark eyes, unnaturally large in her hollow face. The cupboard beside her bed was empty, with no personal possessions except for a snapshot with curled edges propped up against the hospital water-jug so that she could see it clearly.

'I'm Helen Pearce,' the girl said.

'Nurse Lovell,' Amy said automatically, and thought how distant it sounded. 'Amy,' she added.

'When can I go home?' The question was level, but Helen's eyes were fixed on Amy's face. 'When?' she repeated, when Amy didn't answer.

'I've only just come on duty. I don't know about you, but I'll go and find out and come straight back.'

The night's senior nurse on duty was a staff nurse Amy had never worked with before.

'Helen Pearce, the new patient in the side wing, is asking when she may go home.'

The staff sighed. 'Dear me, she's only just got here. She has a tubercular left lung, she needs rest and a good diet. More than that only Dr Davis and God can tell her. Ask her if she would like a sleeping draught to help her settle.'

Amy went back. Helen hadn't moved even a fraction.

'You need to rest,' she told her reassuringly as she moved to plump up her pillows. But something in Helen's stillness stopped her. She caught sight of the photograph again and saw that it was of two children, sitting side by side on some steps outside an open door.

'Rest?' the girl repeated unbelievingly. 'I only came in to see the doctor in the Free Clinic for some medicine for the cough. I wanted to go home straight after.' Any knew that the people in the streets immediately surrounding the hospital came to the voluntary accident department when they couldn't afford any other medical treatment. 'I've had some medicine now,' the girl added.

'One dose won't help much, you know,' Amy said gently.

Helen turned her penetrating stare on her at once. 'I know that, don't I? I could've taken it with me in a bottle. I'm not a baby, am I?'

No, you're not a baby, Amy thought. It seemed to be part of the Royal Lambeth's policy to try to turn you back into one for as long as you lay in one of its beds. She glanced over her shoulder. Here in the corner of the ward she was out of sight of the senior nurses as long as one of them didn't choose to come down on a tour of inspection. She sat down on the edge of Helen's bed.

'You know that you're ill, don't you?' she asked.

'Of course I know. I wouldn't have come in for the medicine otherwise, would I?' For the first time Helen's gaze left Amy's face as she looked sideways at the photograph. 'TB, is it?'

'Yes. They can cure it nowadays, you know. Or at least control it. But you have to do exactly what the doctors tell you.'

'And how long does that go on for?'

'I haven't been a nurse for very long. I'm not much of an authority. But I think it can be quite a long time. Months, or perhaps even longer.'

Suddenly Helen laughed, a spontaneous bubble that made her thin shoulders twitch. 'They want me to lie here for months?'

Then Amy understood why she had been lying so still. The laugh changed into a cough, a terrible, almost silent cough that doubled her over so that her dark hair fell over her face and her fists clenched and unclenched convulsively on the sheet. Amy put her arm around her shoulders and held her until the spasm subsided. Helen leant back again and reached for the enamel sputum bowl on the cupboard top. She spat into it, and Amy saw that the greenish blob was streaked with blood. She took the bowl away from Helen at once and covered it up, then went down the ward to the sink and brought back another bowl of cool water to sponge her face.

'Better?' she asked at last and Helen nodded, exhausted.

When she had made her as comfortable as she could she asked her, 'Why is it so important for you to go home?'

Warily Helen inclined her head towards the snapshot. 'I've got our Aunt Mag to look after them tonight. Well, she's not an aunt really. But she's got enough of her own to think about. I can't leave them for any longer than that.'

'May I?' Amy picked up the photograph. The children were clearly Helen's younger brother and sister, with the same dark eyes and hair. She judged that they were about eight and ten. The two of them looked as if their faces had been hurriedly wiped and their hair straightened for the photographer, but their clothes were the same assortment of mended hand-me-downs that all the children in the nearby streets wore.

'Not a bad picture, is it? The photographer came down our way with his camera on one of those stands and a black cloth to go over his head and all. A shilling, he charged. Some of the women down our street made their kids change into their Sunday best. All stiff, they were, done up like twopenny hambones.' The two girls looked at each other and smiled, and through Helen's eyes Amy suddenly saw the street and the travelling photographer and the groups of stiffly posed children in their Sunday suits. 'But I thought our two looked more themselves just in the things they stood up in.'

'You were right, too,' Amy said as she replaced the photograph. 'And I can see that you must be worried about them. Is there . . . no one else in the family to help?'

'Not really. Mum died four years ago, and Dad had done a runner years before that.'

Amy thought that the street slang came out of Helen's mouth in faint inverted commas. She sounded as if she was practised at using it to make herself fit in, but knew all along that she didn't. Then Amy heard the purposeful squeak of regulation nursing shoes coming down the main ward. She jumped up hastily and began to straighten the covers.

'You should stay here as long as you possibly can, for their sake, then. There is a hospital almoner, you know, who might be able to help. I'll ask the staff to leave a message for the day sister.'

'Thank you,' Helen said simply. 'I mean for telling me the truth.'

'I probably shouldn't have done.' Out of the corner of her eye Amy saw the starched peaks of the staff nurse's cap progressing towards them. In a louder voice she asked, 'Would you like something to help you to go to sleep?'

'No.' Helen Pearce would be mutinous when she didn't want something, Amy saw. 'But I'd like it if you would come back and talk to me later.'

'I'll try,' Amy whispered, and was whisking away with the used sputum bowl just as the senior nurse said majestically, 'Thank you, Lovell. I will attend to Miss Pearce now. Take a bedpan down to Mrs Marks, would you?'

Later, after she had done everything that could possibly be expected of her and all the other patients were asleep or at least comfortable, Amy went back. Helen was still lying in the same position.

'Would you like me to turn you over?'

'No, thanks. Just sit and talk, if you're allowed. Can I call you Amy?'

'Of course. What are their names?' Amy nodded at the picture.

'Freda and Jim. They're very good. Jim wasn't much more than a baby when Ma died, but Freda helped me with him right from the beginning. She looks after him now when I'm working.'

'Do you have to support all three of you?'

Helen grinned. 'Who else d'you think would do it? I go cleaning offices over the river. You have to be there early in the morning,

208

and then back in the evening to do others. It means I'm out when the kids go off to school, and I have to go straight back after I've given them their tea at night. But – ' Helen shrugged – 'I've been doing it for a long time, and the supervisor's good to me. She sees I get time off if Jim's ill, or they need me at home. I might not be so lucky somewhere else.'

Helen's hands lying loosely on the sheet looked grey with work against the whiteness. Amy thought of the endless mop-buckets and scrubbing brushes they must have carried, and her own recent experience of them heightened her sympathy.

'Will the supervisor cover for you if you stay in here for a few days?'

'I suppose so. It's Jim and Freda I'm worrying about. I'd never have gone to see that doctor downstairs if I'd known he was going to make me stay.'

'Try not to worry,' Amy said with all the authority of health and strength. 'There must be something the hospital can do to help.'

'What about you?' Helen asked, as if she was bored with the topic of herself. 'Got a boyfriend, have you?'

Amy found herself going faintly pink. 'Not really. There's someone I like, but not a boyfriend. His name's Tony Hardy.'

'That's nice. Sounds like a film-star.'

'He doesn't look much like one,' Amy said, and they laughed. 'Have you?'

'Nah. They're all like stupid kids. If someone a bit older and a bit richer were to come along, that'd be different, but they're a bit thin on the ground round our way. Where does this Tony Hardy who isn't your boyfriend take you? I can tell you're not from round here. You belong up West, I should think, don't you?'

'I did,' Amy said shortly, 'but I'm a nurse now, and I live in the hostel round the corner. Tony takes me to political meetings, sometimes to concerts or poetry readings.'

'Doesn't sound all that much fun,' Helen said, sniffing. 'Why did you want to be a nurse?'

'Because before this I wasn't doing anything much, and I started wanting to be of use to somebody.'

Helen's glance flickered. 'Bit of a luxury, then, is it? If you don't have to do it?'

Amy stiffened defensively, but she knew that Helen was right.

Nursing was a kind of luxury for her because she was using it to assuage her prosperous, privileged guilt. Helen was unusually clever, she thought. No one else at the Royal Lambeth had put a finger so quickly on the truth. She hadn't even admitted it as clearly to herself.

'Yes, you're quite right.'

Helen smiled. 'Don't look so worried. You're a good nurse, aren't you?'

'I don't think the sister would necessarily agree.'

They were laughing again, pleased and a little surprised by the intimacy that had sprung up between them in the darkened ward.

Amy sat beside Helen for a little longer, talking quietly, until Helen closed her eyes. 'I think I could almost go to sleep now,' she said.

There was one more terrifying coughing fit during the night, but when Amy went off duty at six Helen was asleep, with the skin around her eyes and over her cheekbones so tightly stretched that it looked almost translucent.

Amy thought about her all through the two lectures that followed breakfast, and while she tried to write up her notes afterwards until her head nodded over the desk and the hand-writing blurred in front of her eyes. Even while she was asleep she dreamed that she was nursing not only Helen but little Jim and Freda too, and the three of them were crammed into the hospital bed while Amy tried to hide them all from Sister Blaine.

When she went back on duty Helen was propped up against her pillows. She looked noticeably less exhausted, and a glance at the chart told Amy that her high temperature had dropped a little.

'I've been asleep half the day,' Helen greeted her. 'When I'm not asleep they're bringing me meal after meal.'

'That's the treatment. Food and rest.'

'Do you know what that Sister has arranged? The one with more frills on her hat than anyone else and a face like a brass poker?'

'Sister Blaine?'

'There's a holiday place by the sea near Bournemouth, for kids whose parents are ill or who can't look after them for a bit. It's a charity, did you know?'

'I thought there must be something like it.' Amy remembered now that Princess Mary Holiday Homes for Children was on

Adeline's list of favoured charities. There had been a ball for it a year or so ago, and Adeline had gone in a cloud of gold tissue with gold butterflies in her hair. The outfit had started a minor craze for butterfly ornaments. Under duress from Adeline, Amy had done a dull stint of selling tombola tickets. It was nice to think of the money going to pay for Freda and Jim's seaside holiday.

'They're going there for two weeks. They came in to see me with Aunt Mag this afternoon, just after I'd heard from the sister, and I told them. They were both so excited that they couldn't sit still. They've never been to the sea. Neither have I, come to that. It seems a shame to be stuck in here.'

'Better for you,' Amy said firmly. The change that simple relief had made in Helen was striking. Her eyes had lost some of their staring intensity, and her body no longer looked as if it was strung on taut wires that hurt when she moved. But when she reached out to grasp Amy's wrist her fingers felt dry and hot.

'Will you be on every night? They're so busy during the day they don't have time to look round, let alone talk. I'll never see you.'

'Nurse. Nurse Lovell?' The staff nurse was calling. Amy knew that she had already spent longer than she should at Helen's bedside.

'I'll be on for five more nights,' she whispered. 'Two days off after that, then back on day shift. Don't worry, we'll see each other somehow.'

'Nurse!'

Helen's fingers released her, and Amy scurried away.

'There are other patients on the ward, Lovell,' the staff nurse reminded her tartly.

Over the next nights, Helen continued to improve dramatically. Her face seemed to fill out and the coughing fits stopped almost completely. She slept a great deal but she was always awake and waiting when Amy came in.

'Look,' she said one evening, 'I've had a postcard.'

It was propped up beside the photograph, a bright blue sea under a bright blue sky. *Dear Helen, haveing a fine time here and hopeing you are getting better. Your loving Freda and Jim.*

On the quieter nights, Amy made certain of odd half-hours when she could sit and talk to Helen. She listened to her wryly funny stories of the people in the crowded blocks and neighbourly

211

Lambeth streets. She had lived there all her life and had only rarely gone further afield, but she had still acquired a level of maturity that reached far beyond her circumstances. Quite often she made Amy feel that her own attitudes were naïve and ill-informed.

In turn, once she realized that Helen wasn't remotely critical, Amy told her about Chance and Bruton Street and her life outside the hospital.

'My God,' Helen breathed. 'A real butler? I thought they were only in films. Will you take me home with you some time?'

'Of course I will.'

On the last night before her days off, the ward was busy and Amy hardly had time to talk. Just before she left she leant over Helen's bed.

'Have you got to go?' Helen asked abruptly, startling her.

'I don't want to, but I must. I want to see my mother, and my sister who isn't very well. I'll be back on the ward in two days.'

'Promise?'

'Cross my heart.'

Suddenly Helen reached up and hugged her. 'It's only you coming in that's kept me alive in this place. I've never had a friend like you before.'

Amy looked down into the pale face with its sharp, premature lines. 'Neither have I.' She hugged her back and then let her go, afraid that the coughing might start up again. 'I'll see you in two days,' she repeated. She knew that Helen's eyes followed her around the corner, and that she was listening as her footsteps receded up the ward.

'Well,' Tony said, 'I have to hand it to you, Amy my love. I thought you'd hate it, and that it would disturb you. But here you are, prettier and happier-looking than I've ever seen you, and coping perfectly.'

'It does disturb me,' Amy told him, thinking of Helen again. 'I haven't learnt professional detachment yet. I'm not sure that I want to. And it's bloody hard work, like nothing I'd ever imagined. Sometimes at the end of the day my arms and back ache so much that I can't eat because the knife and fork seem too heavy to lift. But yes, I am happy. Doing it makes everything else, everything outside, look quite different. I don't feel so guilty any more.' She faced Tony squarely as she said it. Since Helen had identified her luxury so clearly Amy was admitting it as openly as she could.

'Nor should you.' Tony smiled at her and lifted his glass. 'Here's to you, Amy.'

She sighed with pleasure and leaned back in her chair. They were having dinner together in the little Italian restaurant in Soho that Amy always enjoyed and begged to be taken back to again. The waiters in their striped aprons and the noisy, vociferous diners were exactly the same, and now she felt that she wasn't just a sightseer but a part of the cosmopolitan bustle herself. She had her own work to do, just like Tony and the girls in his office, all the people in the restaurant crowded around the checked tablecloths, and like Jake Silverman, and Kay and Angel.

Amy had found her way back to Appleyard Street once or twice on her evenings off. If Tony wasn't going to take her, she decided, she would go on her own. Usually she made the long bus journey in her black stockings and navy nurse's cape. If any newspaper columnist might be remotely interested in Peer's Daughter at Communist Meeting, no one would cast a second glance at Lambeth Nurse in the same place.

On her first visit she had been apprehensive, not even sure whether she would be recognized or allowed into the upstairs meeting room. But as soon as she arrived at the top of the dimly lit stairs she saw Jake's huge, bear-like shape and immediately he bellowed, 'Amy Lovell! So you've turned up again so that I can say thank you!'

He was wearing the same red and black checked shirt, and as he hugged her she remembered the bulkiness of the body she had tried to drag away from the horses and the trampling feet.

'I know I do have something to thank you for. I don't remember a damned thing, but I'm told that you plunged in when I went down, and then stuck with me all the way to the hospital. I'm grateful, Amy.'

'I didn't do anything. I didn't know how to. It was the miner who carried you out, Nick Penry.'

'I know Nick was there.'

It was odd to hear someone else saying his name when she hadn't spoken it herself since he had left Bruton Streeet. She had thought about him and isolated him into a private experience of her own, and now she felt a quiver of something that might

213

almost have been jealousy. She wondered too how much he might have told Jake about where she lived. Amy felt the importance of preserving her anonymity at Appleyard Street.

'He's a friend of mine,' Jake went on. 'He wrote, and said you found him a bed for the night as well.'

If that was all he had said, Amy thought with relief, then Nick Penry knew how to be discreet despite having disapproved so sharply of everything she stood for.

'Kay, look who's here.'

Kay came up behind him. 'Why haven't you come before this?' she demanded fiercely, but her smile was full of warmth. 'We tried to find out where you live from Tony, but he was very cagey about you.'

'I'm a student nurse now,' Amy said quickly, gesturing at her cape. 'I don't have very much spare time.'

Kay put her arm through hers. Jake was greeting someone else at the top of the stairs. 'Thank you for looking after him. He's as strong as a horse and he got better very quickly, but he could have died there in the bloody square.'

'Why did it happen?' Amy asked.

'Oh, it probably wasn't completely deliberate. They're frightened of Communists. They think we're going to crush the capitalist machine. We are, of course.'

Kay was laughing and shaking her head so that her huge brass earrings jangled. Amy liked her infectious enthusiasm and good humour. Kay pulled her into the room, and across it Amy saw Angel Mack, her eyes extravagantly made up in glittering green, waving a greeting at her.

'Come and sit down. It's "Europe and the Threat of International Fascism" tonight. You'll enjoy it.'

As at the other meetings she attended, Amy sat quietly and listened to the fervent discussion. As always, she was impressed most of all by the compelling force of Jake Silverman's convictions. When he spoke, she believed every word he said. Otherwise she tried hard to understand the theories and counter-theories that flew over her head, and accepted the pamphlets and poorly printed booklets that were handed out. She took them back with her to the hostel and read them scrupulously when she could find a spare moment. She also thought carefully about what she had heard and read for herself, usually when she was buffing brass sink-taps to a blinding shine or folding and counting linen supplies in one of the store-cupboards. Amy was still far from believing with the Appleyard Streeters that the only way ahead lay in the complete destruction of capitalism and the restructuring of life along rigidly Soviet lines. She was too caught up in her new-found satisfaction, and the way of life that she knew and understood was too deeply and unconsciously ingrained in her for that. But the things she saw and heard every day on the wards made her ever more sharply aware of the separation between herself and her family and friends on one side, and the patients of the Royal Lambeth and all those who were like them on the other. It must, Amy thought, be possible to devise some system by which all the wealth and comfort and privilege need not be bestowed just on a handful of people who happened to be born to it. The Appleyard Street doctrines were much harsher than Amy's own tentative ideas, but still something drew her back there yet again and compelled her to sit listening quietly as she struggled to understand what their revolution might mean.

'*Grazie, bella mia.*' The waiter with the most luxuriant moustache put Amy's plate in front of her with a flourish. She was ravenously hungry and the glistening heaped-up *spaghetti alla vongole* smelled exquisite. She sighed again at the sheer pleasure of being waited on, and there was silence as she attacked the first mouthfuls. When she looked up again Tony was watching her.

'You're rather a sensual person, aren't you?'

'Whatever do you mean? I've never had a chance to find out.'

Tony laughed. 'Not necessarily in the sexual sense. Although I'm sure you'll enjoy that too.'

Amy hadn't drunk quite enough Chianti to have the courage to say *Why don't we try it then?* although she was longing to. She was thinking how attractive he was as she sat across the table from him trying to twirl her spaghetti like an expert. She liked the downward curl of his mouth. It would have been nice to lean across and kiss it, tasting the wine on his lips as well as her own.

But whenever Tony kissed her he did it ironically, as if kissing at all was faintly ridiculous.

'No,' he was saying. 'I was thinking of the way you enjoy everything. You like tasting and touching and smelling things. Ve-ery uninhibited. Almost pagan. You were the same even when you were quite a little girl. I remember the summer I was tutoring Richard, seeing you at Chance kneeling by the lavender

215

border with your face buried among the flower spikes. And then at Biarritz, standing with your eyes closed taking tiny cat-licks at a pistachio ice-cream from that place on the promenade.'

'Fendi's.'

'Isabel was quite different. She thought more, and enjoyed things less.' Seeing Amy's face, Tony asked, 'How is she?'

'I don't know, exactly.'

As soon as she had arrived home the day before, Amy had telephoned Ebury Street. A maid had told her that Mr and Mrs Jaspert had just left for the country. It was perfectly natural and a good thing, Amy thought, that Peter should have taken Isabel away from the lifeless heat of London in August. It would be quiet at the Jasperts' family home in Wiltshire, and Isabel would be able to rest. Peter would be with her too, instead of pursuing his complicated business and political affairs and leaving her alone at Ebury Street. But when she had tried to telephone her sister at West Talbot, Amy's uneasiness stirred again. Although she told the butler quite clearly that she wished to speak to Mrs Jaspert, after a long wait it was Peter who came to the telephone.

'How is she?' Amy asked, anxiety sharpening her voice.

'Perfectly well,' Peter said smoothly. 'Tired, of course, but quite in order physically.'

'I wanted to speak to her, particularly.'

'I rather think that she's asleep. Shall I give her a message for you? Or you could speak to Mama, perhaps?'

Amy had the sudden sense that Isabel had been captured by Jasperts. 'I'd like to speak to Isabel,' she said distinctly. 'When will she be awake, do you think?'

At last, after two more calls, Amy was successful. Isabel's voice sounded thin and distant, as if she was only half-attending to Amy's questions.

'Yes, I'm fine. I'm supposed to be resting.'

'Did Mr Hardwicke say so?'

'Yes.'

'Is Bethan with you?'

'Yes.'

At least that was something. Bethan would take care of her, however cut off they were by Jasperts.

'Can I talk to her?' Bethan could also be relied upon to tell the plain truth about Isabel. The response Amy heard might have been a laugh, but it wasn't like Isabel's old laughter.

216

'Of course not. Do you remember when the King and Queen came to Chance?'

Amy remembered. There had been a retinue of thirty-seven attendants, and a rigid formality had descended on the house that made the sisters wonder how anyone managed to breathe at Court, let alone to live.

'Well, it's like that here. Except that there's only family in the house. One spends one's whole life changing.'

And so Bethan would be firmly placed below stairs, and definitely not available for talk on the telephone.

Isabel had stayed at West Talbot before her marriage, and she and Amy had laughed gently at the pomposities of Lady Jaspert's household. But now the whole pitch of Isabel's voice had changed. Amy was frightened for her.

'Bel? I wish I could come down and be with you. But I can't. If I hadn't enrolled until after the baby . . .'

Isabel cut her short. 'There's nothing you could do. I'm well looked after. In any case we may be back in town soon. I don't know what's going on, Peter doesn't tell me much, but he spends half his day on the telephone here and the rest sitting over papers in the library. It's some crisis. Something to do with lending money to Germany, and the run on the pound. Do you understand that? Peter says the Government may collapse.' Amy had been thinking how vague and remote her sister sounded, but now Isabel added with sudden vehemence, 'It looks as if he's waiting to pounce. You can almost see him licking his lips.'

Amy frowned into the black bakelite mouthpiece, trying to conjure up Isabel's face. She sounded, suddenly, as if she hated Peter.

'Will you come back with him?'

'I suppose so. Nothing could be worse than staying here alone.'

'Come back. Then I can see you and make sure that you're all right. West Talbot is too far away. Isabel?'

'Yes?' The thin, listless voice was back again.

'If there was anything, anything wrong, you'd tell me, wouldn't you?'

'There's nothing wrong.'

At a loss for anything more to say, Amy had hung up after repeating her warnings that Isabel was to rest, to take care of herself and not to worry. When her sister was back in London, perhaps she would be able to probe deeper. But if it was Peter

217

who was the trouble, and she was increasingly afraid that it was indeed Peter, then what could she possibly do?

Amy looked back at Tony across the restaurant table. 'I don't know,' she repeated. 'I think well enough, as far as the baby goes. But she sounds unhappy. She . . . said something to me on the telephone, something about Peter. She sounded as if she didn't like him at all.'

They had finished their meal, and the waiter had brought them coffee in thick white cups. Tony was stirring his, first one way and then the other, waiting to see if Amy wanted to talk about what was worrying her.

'She said he was licking his lips, waiting to pounce. She made him sound like a predator.'

Tony put his spoon down with a tiny clink. 'How much do you know about Peter Jaspert?'

Amy shrugged, puzzled. 'I know who he is in the family sense. Vaguely what his political interests are, even more vaguely his business ones. Why?'

'I know a little bit more than that. I hear things, here and there. You pointed out once that I'm too fond of gossip.' Tony smiled sardonically. 'Jaspert's a clever man. He uses that pink bluffness as a mask. He's a director of Massey & Dart who have made considerable investments and loans to Germany over the past few years, some of it raised in France. Now, the French don't like their money being used to help Germany and they've called in the loans. There's a financial collapse in Germany and the London bankers' money is frozen there. To meet their obligations Jaspert and his friends have persuaded the Bank of England to let them draw on gold reserves, and those have run out now. So they've turned elsewhere, notably to the United States. But foreign governments won't lend unless the house is tidy. The bankers and the big money men in the City are insisting that the Government sweep up and tidy away the balance of payments deficit to help them out.'

'How?' Amy asked, aware of her blithe ignorance.

'You've read about the May report?'

Amy nodded, vaguely remembering, although the only reading she had done in the last week was textbooks of anatomy.

'Five rich men who recommended that a national deficit of nearly a hundred million pounds be met in the simplest and most painless way. Not by increasing taxation, because that hurts rich

218

men. No, by putting a stop to government waste. That's prudent housekeeping, isn't it? And the biggest waste of all, of course, is unemployment benefit. So they want to cut that by twenty per cent. A nice, round figure. What could be simpler?'

Amy could hear another voice, rising and falling with Tony's. It was Nick Penry, up in the old schoolroom at Bruton Street, talking about Nantlas. There was no chapel singing on Sundays now, because there was no minister. There was none on Saturday nights in the Miners' Rests any more, because no one could afford the beer that fuelled dry throats. There was no warmth, no medicine, and precious little food because the benefit didn't stretch to it. And now they wanted to cut that by twenty per cent.

'It's cleverer than that, even,' Tony went on. His thin, quizzical face was stiff. 'The City men know that they can win MacDonald round because he can't do anything else. He'll carry half the Cabinet with him. They'll get the benefit cut, even if not by twenty per cent. But the rest of the Labour Cabinet, the Party and Bevin and the TUC, they won't support it. So there'll be a split, and a collapse of the Government. My guess is that they'll opt for a coalition for the duration of the "National Crisis". It will be the end of MacDonald in real political terms, and at the next general election, when everyone is tired of the crisis, why, a Conservative victory. It's neat for Jaspert, isn't it? I'm sure he is licking his lips. It's financial salvation and political expediency all in one package. I hear that he can expect to be a junior minister in the next government.'

'You hate him, don't you?' Amy said quietly and Tony's stiff mask dissolved. He put his hand over hers.

'I hate what he stands for, and so would most of the people I call my friends.'

Jake, Amy thought. *And Angel, and Kay. And Nick.*

'So long as there are men like Jaspert entrusted with the running of it, this country will always be as bitterly class-divided as it is now.' Tony's fingers tightened. 'Do you believe that, Amy? Do you believe that there is a war between people like us, sitting here, and him?'

Amy followed his stare past the looped curtains at the plate-glass restaurant window. Outside in the street a man was standing at the kerb. He was wearing a cloth cap and a torn coat, and he was playing a whistle. At his feet stood an empty tin cup. The

219

passers-by streamed past him, on their way from Shaftesbury Avenue in search of dinner, and they never heard the whistling. Behind him in the street a taxi roared past, and then a low open tourer driven by a man in evening dress.

Amy looked away, back to Tony's fingers covering her own. She thought of Helen lying in the Royal Lambeth, and then of Nick and his handicapped son. Her thoughts always came back to Nick.

'I believe it,' she said heavily. Tony's thumb was stroking the side of her hand, very gently, to and fro. 'I just don't know how I'm supposed to fight in it.'

Tony didn't answer that, nor did she expect him to. As they sat, preoccupied with their own thoughts, a little silence beat between them.

After a moment Tony sat upright again and lifted a finger to the waiter to refill their coffee cups.

'Anyway, to answer your question properly, no, I don't hate Jaspert himself. How could I? I don't even know him. All I do know is that there are dozens of other men just like him, and quite a lot of them are happily married to girls like Isabel. His business and political lives may be one thing and his personal self quite another. He's probably a model husband and father, and kind to animals and his old mother as well.'

'Or he may be just as predatory at home as elsewhere.'

Tony looked sharply at her over the rim of his cup. 'You shouldn't assume that.'

'Why not? I know that something is making my sister unhappy, and I think it's him.'

'Oh, Amy. You may be right. But when two people are married they are accountable to each other. It's a contract between consenting adults. By definition. If I were you I'd leave them alone, unless Isabel comes to you.'

Tony was the one who was right, of course. Isabel was a Jaspert herself now. It was absurd to think that she was trapped by them.

Suddenly, Amy felt that she was on the verge of tears. She was worried, and tired from the incessant work. And the insistent, hopeless whistling from the street was filling her head. The cheerful restaurant bustle and clatter was grating.

'Tony, do you mind if we go now? Perhaps we could walk a little way.'

'Of course.'

He paid the bill and steered her out into the street. At the kerb Amy fumbled in her bag but Tony was quicker. He dropped a coin into the tin cup and then took her arm in his.

'Let's walk up to the square.'

It was a warm, still night and through the pall of soot and smoke came the scent of moist earth and leaves. Amy had never spent August in London before, and she realized as she sniffed the air how much she was missing the wide green spread of Chance.

As they came into Soho Square a burst of dance music and laughter drifted into the quiet, and was swallowed by the netted black leaves of the plane trees against the indigo sky. They walked slowly, arm in arm, with the lights of an occasional car picking them up and then letting them fall back into the dark. Through the trees and over the rooftops was the faint acid glow of light from Oxford Street where the late buses were still clanking past. It was soothing to think of London spreading all round, for miles and miles in every direction, full of separate lives that would never touch on hers, full of people settling down for the short summer night. It wasn't all men whistling hungrily in a gutter, any more than it was all dances in Berkeley Square. Amy smiled at the thought that her own particular London, Society London, was scattered abroad and to the depths of the country, and yet the city hummed on unnoticing. In the stillness Amy felt her anxiety dropping away. Instead she felt a kind of languid fatalism. She could do nothing more than she was doing now, and it was pointless to try to drive herself beyond it. And if going on just as she was meant walking on beside Tony Hardy, then she was happy with that too. They were almost the same height and they moved perfectly in step, hip to hip. Tony's arm and hand felt warm against hers, and she saw the quick turn of his profile as he looked away across her at the mottled columns of the trees.

'Tony?' she heard herself asking, 'why aren't you married?'

Without letting the smoothness of their steps falter, he said, 'Because I don't, personally, believe in it.'

'Why?' she asked, and then he did stop and turn to stand squarely in front of her. In the shadow of the trees it was almost completely dark. Out of the corner of her eye Amy caught the movement of a blacker shadow still, and then saw it was a cat prowling across the fenced-in grass.

'I couldn't make it work,' Tony whispered. Then with the tip of his finger he turned her face so that she had to stop watching the cat, and counting the beats of her own heart, and look full at him instead. His eyes were almond-shaped, she noticed, and there was an expression in them she had never seen before. He moved again, and his face was so close to hers that she felt, rather than heard, him say, 'Although there are times when I could almost believe it might work.' The tip of his finger traced the curve of her cheek and then the corner of his mouth touched hers.

Amy closed her eyes. They were standing very close. Very slowly Tony put his arms around her and she felt him touching her, as if he was gauging the weight of her against him. His mouth moved over hers, exploring, stiff at first and then softening.

At last, she thought, and there was a moment of relief as Soho Square stood utterly silent and dark, and Tony kissed her as she had longed for him to do. His hand slid from the small of her back up the length of her spine, then to the bare nape of her neck, and his fingers touched the thick waves of her hair, pinned up with tortoiseshell combs. He touched one of the combs experimentally and then pulled it out. The waves of hair fell loose at one side. Amy laughed and shook it back over her shoulder but Tony was still touching it, lifting the thickness of it almost unbelievingly.

'Amy,' he said in an odd voice. 'Why are we doing this? We were good enough friends already, weren't we?'

The shock was like a splash of icy-cold water.

Because I love you. Don't you love me?

She almost said it, and then heard the bewildered plaintiveness that the words would have held, like a little girl denied a promised treat. The soothing darkness had turned hot and threatening, and full of invisible pitfalls.

Tony was tucking her hair back into place, and pulling her wrap around her bare shoulders again.

He didn't love her, she understood that. He wasn't going to love her either, however long she waited and watched the beguiling curl of his mouth. Humiliation and a fierce longing to be by herself almost choked her.

'Of course we're good friends.' She forced the lightness into her voice, hearing the words coming through her clenched teeth. She kept them bitten shut to stop the other things from spilling

222

out, so that at least he would never know how she was feeling now.

'Shall we walk up and look for a taxi?' Amy said pleasantly. 'I should get back home. I have to be on duty by noon tomorrow.'

Tony took her arm again and they strolled on under the spreading branches as if nothing had happened at all.

Amy was glad to be going back to the Lambeth. Neither Gerald nor Adeline was at Bruton Street, Richard was staying with Eton friends and the big house felt empty and hollow. With Isabel immured at West Talbot, and after last night, there was nothing to be at home for. Amy decided as she put her things back into her bag that the bleak hostel would be friendly and welcoming by comparison.

At the bus stop she bought a newspaper. She scanned the tall, black banner headlines and saw that Tony's prediction had been correct. The Labour Government under Ramsay MacDonald had divided and collapsed over the question of reducing unemployment benefits. A coalition National Government was being formed under the Prime Minister's leadership, with a Cabinet composed of four Labour members, four Conservative and two Liberal.

From the paragraphs of close type under the heading Amy learned that one of the new Conservative Cabinet ministers was Peter's friend Archer Cole.

'Dear God,' Helen Pearce greeted her on her return to the ward. 'You look about as cheerful as a wet Monday morning at the hock-shop. Didn't you enjoy your leave? Had a fall-out with Tony, did you?'

'Not really.' Amy smiled at her in spite of herself. 'Everything with Tony is just the same as it always is. You look a hundred times better than you did.'

It was true. Helen's face was rounder, there was a glow of natural colour in it instead of the unnatural flush of fever, and she was sitting confidently up in bed with none of the old, strained immobility.

'I feel it,' she said proudly. 'The doctor says I can go home for when Freda and Jim get back from Bournemouth.'

'I'm glad. But I'll miss you on the ward.'

Helen looked away and said casually 'Well, p'raps you'll come

223

and see us at our place? It's only round the corner, you know. And the little ones would like it.'

Amy beamed at her, delighted. 'Of course I will. I'll come and make absolutely sure that you're taking care of yourself. And we'll be able to talk without Sister watching to make sure we don't get too friendly.'

'Nurse Lovell.' It was Sister Blaine, like a starched battleship.

'See what I mean?' Amy mouthed over her shoulder as she scurried away to do what she was told.

In the week after her evening with Tony, Amy discovered that the easiest way to cope was to absorb herself in hospital life. She fixed her attention firmly on the wards and on her classes, and even earned a word of commendation from Sister Tutor.

Isabel remained at West Talbot, and in her few free hours Amy went once to the cinema with Moira to see a new Laurel and Hardy film, and spent the rest of the time in the hostel. It was easier, in the enclosed atmosphere where the hospital was the sole topic of conversation, not to allow herself to worry about Isabel or to relive the humiliation of Tony turning away from her. If they really had been such good friends, she reasoned with herself, then Tony didn't want them to be more than that because he didn't find her attractive enough. She knew it was her vanity that was suffering, but that didn't make the hurt any less.

There was something more, too. She hadn't seen Tony particularly often, but she had always looked eagerly forward to their few times together. Now that there was no daily anticipation of seeing him, and imagining what might happen, there was a small, black void in the centre of her life. Amy began to fill the void with work, and with her deepening friendship with Helen Pearce.

As he had promised, Helen's doctor allowed her to go home on the day that Freda and Jim came back from Bournemouth. Two days after that, on her free afternoon, Amy set out to visit her with the scrap of paper on which Helen had carefully written the address folded in her pocket.

It was the very beginning of September, and the first smoky tang of autumn was in the air. Although the streets were still hot and dusty, the leaves of the single spindly tree at the corner of Helen's street were crinkle-edged with yellow. As Amy walked down past the houses, searching for the numbers on the peeling doors, a horse pulling the water-cart clopped slowly past her. The man up on his seat in front of the big brass-bound barrel sat lazily with his hands loose over the reins. The horse must know every street and where to stop in each one. Two women carrying pails that slopped dark patches in the dust came past and stared curiously at Amy.

'Looking for someone?' the younger of them asked.

'Number seventeen. Helen Pearce.'

More friendly now, the woman jerked her head. 'That one. Green door.'

Outside No. 17 a dozen children were skipping and singing a complicated rhyme. As Amy slipped past one of them detached herself and stared up at her. Amy saw Helen's pointed chin and dark, wide-set eyes.

'You must be Freda.'

'Yes, miss.' The child bobbed awkwardly.

'I'm Amy. Helen's friend, from the hospital.'

'She's waiting for you indoors. There's been a bigger fuss than if the Queen was coming. Jimmy!' A very dirty little boy scuffled towards them. 'This is our kid.'

Their skin was tanned and glowing from their weeks at the sea, making them stand out from the pale faces hopping around them. Amy held out her hand and Jim shook it gingerly. Watching approvingly, Freda took a deep breath.

'We wanted to thank you, miss. For looking after Helen when she was bad.'

Amy smiled, but her throat was stiff. 'We were glad to. Everyone in the hospital. Your sister is someone special.'

But having done their duty, the children's eyes were already turning back to the game. Amy said, 'I'll go in and find her, shall I?'

Helen must have been waiting inside the basement door. As soon as Amy knocked she flung it open and said formally, 'I'm so pleased you could manage it. Won't you come inside?'

The formality persisted as Helen showed her from the cramped, pitch-dark lobby into the low, square room.

'This is it,' Helen said abruptly, gesturing around her. Amy moved at the same time and they bumped awkwardly together. Stepping back in embarrassment, Amy saw a table covered with an oilcloth, three upright chairs and an armchair beside the small, empty grate. There was a truckle-bed against one wall, covered with a bright knitted blanket. Over the mantelpiece a piece of red plush was draped, and in the centre was a sepia wedding

225

photograph which was probably Helen's parents with the picture of Freda and Jim propped up beside it. A flowered screen stood in one corner and Helen pulled it aside to show a little gas ring and a tiny, scoured sink with buckets of fresh water standing beneath it. The kettle was already filled and Helen lit the popping gas.

Except for the photographs the room was bare of any kind of decoration, but it was the cleanest place Amy had ever seen. Every surface shone as if it had been individually polished, from the glass shade of the single light to the faded linoleum.

'Me and Freda sleep in there,' Helen said. Through the doorway Amy glimpsed a double bed that almost filled the cupboard-sized room. 'And Jim in here.' She pointed to the truckle-bed. 'Well, now you've seen it,' she said defiantly. 'Except the privy. That's out the back.'

Amy looked at her and saw that her friend's face was stiff. Something mattered to her very much, although she didn't want to show it. It was important that Amy should see where she lived and belonged, but she didn't want the poverty of it seen against the imagined splendours of Bruton Street to make any difference to their friendship.

Amy opened her mouth to say something, anything, to show that it wouldn't. But the words didn't come. Instead she felt her eyes go hot and sudden tears prickled in the sockets.

Everything was wrong with the world. It was all, all of it, wrong and iniquitous.

'I don't know what you're crying about,' Helen said. 'It isn't you who lives here.'

Stupid shame flooded through Amy. Helen was right, as always. They looked at each other for a moment and then Amy shook her head helplessly. Helen put her hand out and Amy took it, and then they were hugging each other, half-crying and half-laughing.

'God help us,' Helen said at last. 'Let's have this tea, now you're here. There's penny buns as well, if you want.'

Helen insisted that as she was the guest Amy should have the armchair. She sat down in one of the upright ones herself, poured out the tea, and they began to talk.

They were still talking at six o'clock, with the teapot cold between them. Amy thought that she had never talked as easily or openly to anyone, even to Isabel.

When Freda and Jim came in at last, Amy knew that she had found a friend for life.

'Where's our tea, Helen?' the little boy said plaintively.

The two girls blinked at each other, and laughed.

'That's never the time, is it?' They stood up, together.

'I've got to get back,' Amy said reluctantly. 'But I'll be back. When can I come?'

'Whenever,' Helen said simply.

The three of them came with her to the top of the area steps, and then stood waving until she reached the end of the street.

Looking back from the corner, she saw the thin girl with the little, healthy replicas of herself on either side of her. Suddenly Helen looked fragile and too small against the gaunt height of the old houses.

Biting her lip, Amy made herself smile and wave one more time.

Then she turned the corner and walked slowly back to the hostel.

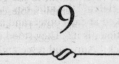

9

In the warm, pin-neat Ebury Street basement kitchen, Bethan looked at the tray and sighed.

There was clear soup in a gold-rimmed bowl and bread cut transparently thin. A little dish of green-gold grapes was set beside a wedge of creamy cheese. As she watched, Cook smoothed the starched cloth and carefully positioned a long-stemmed wineglass, then brought a decanter and filled the glass with red wine.

'That will put some heart into her,' Cook said with conviction. 'When I was with Lady Kiftsgate and she was in the same condition, I always made sure she drank wine.'

Bethan had heard enough about Lady Kiftsgate, and she was afraid that all the wine in France wouldn't change Isabel's heart now. But she said, 'Thank you, Cook. I'll take it up now, and we'll just hope she eats some of it.'

At Isabel's bedroom door Bethan knocked, and when there was no response she knocked louder and pushed the door open Isabel was lying on the day bed in the window, exactly as Bethan had left her an hour before. Her eyes were closed and her hands were hanging awkwardly at her sides as if she didn't want to clasp them over her mounded stomach.

Bethan put the tray down on the table beside the day bed. 'Mrs Jaspert? Isabel, love, are you asleep?'

Isabel's eyes opened and stared, wildly, before they focused at last.

'Not sleeping. Trying . . . trying to think.'

'What have you got to be thinking about?' Bethan tried to soothe her. 'All you've got to do is rest, and not let yourself get worked up again. Here, now. Cook's made some special soup for you. Try and eat it for me, will you?'

She put her arm behind Isabel's shoulders and eased her upright.

'Please eat some,' Bethan whispered, trying to reach out to the Isabel she had always known, to the gentle child within the correct little girl, and the vulnerable adolescent who had sheltered in the self-possessed young woman. But all the familiar faces of Isabel had vanished in the last weeks, shrivelling away into this wild-faced stranger who seemed to have lost all touch with her own world. Bethan felt that there was a household conspiracy – Peter Jaspert, Lord and Lady Jaspert, the staff of Ebury Street, all of them seemed wilfully set on ignoring Isabel's distress. Yet she ate almost nothing now, and sat all day in her room staring as if she was looking in fear into her own head. And yesterday, Bethan had found her crying. The tears came silently, unstoppably, and they had gone on for hours. Bethan had been on the point of telephoning Mr Hardwicke when Isabel fell into an exhausted sleep.

With an effort now, Isabel leaned forward and tasted the spoonful of soup that Bethan held out for her. It felt thick on her lips, like blood. She shivered and swallowed against the nausea. The thin triangle of bread was as dry as ash and her throat closed up against it.

Instead she made herself concentrate on Bethan's arms around her and the soft, Welsh voice begging her just to talk a little.

Hopelessly Isabel shook her head. The warmth of Bethan's shoulder, her innocent scent of soap and toilet water, brought back the very first time that Bethan had comforted her. A long, long way off, like a tableau spotlit at the end of a dark tunnel, Isabel saw the nursery at Chance and the bars of sunlight sloping over Airlie's rugs. A weight was crushing her, squeezing the breath and life out of her.

'I'm afraid,' she said. 'I'm so afraid.'

'Oh, there.' Bethan's arms tightened. 'There's no need to be afraid. The doctors all say so. They won't let you have a bad time. It isn't like that nowadays, all the wonderful things they can do.'

But Isabel only shook her head again.

How could she explain to anyone that it wasn't the birth that was frightening her? She wasn't frightened for herself, for the physical pain or the risks that women whispered about and Mr Hardwicke soothingly never mentioned. She wasn't afraid for the baby, either. The weight of it sat broodingly within her, sometimes like a cold, heavy stone that had nothing to do with her own flesh and blood. At other times it was turbulent, writhing inside her as though it had taken over her system and reduced her to a dry husk.

Just by looking at herself in the mirror, Isabel could see that was what really was happening. With her arms as thin as sticks and the bones knobbed at the base of her neck, and the huge, swollen pod in front of her, she knew that she was grotesque. The baby possessed her, branding her and reminding her of how it had come there.

She wasn't afraid for herself, nor for the baby because it was a hundred times stronger, and a Jaspert.

It was everything else that frightened her. The bright, busy jigsaw of the world had shaken and the neat, familiar components of it had clicked out of place one by one and spiralled away. Isabel frowned, trying to recall what the pieces of it had been. She only dreamed about them nowadays, long vivid dreams of parties where she laughed as she danced and the men's white-gloved hands correctly holding her never wandered or turned hot, pink and fleshy. She dreamed of walking with Amy at Chance, hiding in the hollow heart of the great box-hedge in the formal gardens, and then of riding her mare at a canter up and over the long ridge that sheltered the estate.

The dreams were more vivid than life, now. Life had become fear, and watching, and waiting.

Am I ill? Isabel wondered.

There were nightmares, too. Peter came to her in them, and she felt the hot, stifling weight of the bedclothes, and the guilt of terrible secrets. There were other men in the nightmares, too. There was Mr Glass. Even, once, her own father. *I must be ill.*

'Isabel, dear, couldn't you talk to me? Or Amy? I'll tell you what, I'll ring Amy at her hospital and ask her to come to see you.'

'No,' Isabel said sharply. 'Don't do that.' Amy shouldn't be here in this place. Amy shouldn't be contaminated by it. She was trapped herself, but it must never happen to Amy.

'Or Lady Lovell, then.'

'She's abroad.' The baby wasn't due for another three weeks. Lady Lovell would fly back from Morocco in good time for the birth, of course. Isabel was wondering vaguely at the note of

230

triumph in her voice. Did she want to be so isolated, then? How much of all this weight of despair was her own doing?

'Where's my husband?' she asked, feeling briefly pleased with the normality of the question until she saw Bethan looking at her.

'It's Election Day. The twenty-seventh of October. Don't you remember? Mr Jaspert'll be in his constituency.'

'Of course he will.'

She had forgotten. Peter's was a solidly safe Conservative seat, but he had campaigned vigorously in the three weeks since the last Parliament had been dissolved. Isabel had been excused by her condition from sitting beside him on platforms, applauding his speeches and smiling, smiling. But she would be expected to do it next time. Peter had married a politician's perfect wife, and he would see to it that she functioned as one. At the thought of it, at the very idea of after the birth and the demands that would be placed on her again, Isabel's skin crawled. She turned and smiled a bright, tight, skeletal smile at Bethan's worried face. 'Leave the tray, Bethan. I feel quite hungry now. I won't need anything else tonight, thank you.' She felt suddenly cunning. Of course she could hide the disgusting food somewhere, and pretend that she had eaten it.

Reluctantly Bethan stood up. 'Well, if you're quite sure . . . you will ring for me, if you need me, won't you?'

At last, Isabel thought, she was alone again. She was levering herself upright, intending to slop the soup and wine into her hand-basin, when something that had been obscenely stretched inside her burst wide open. Water seeped and then splashed. Her dress was soaked, and the pale green watered-silk of the day bed showed a dark, spreading stain.

'*No*,' Isabel whispered. But even as she said it she felt the first low pull of pain, as definite and undeniable as gravity itself.

Peter Jaspert was comfortably pleased with the day. It had been a long, arduous one during which he had been driven from one makeshift street-corner hustings to the next to rally the last of the undecided into voting. It had hardly been a fight even from the beginning. There was no Liberal candidate, and the Labour man, a muddled MacDonaldite, had never stood the ghost of a chance in a squarely middle-class constituency. But Peter had spared no effort in making his victory as emphatic as it could possibly be. All day he had been shaking hands, and smiling confidently, and exhorting voters to choose the man who was so incontrovertibly right for the job.

When the polls closed he had had an excellent dinner with his constituency agent and the committee at a rather good local hotel, and then they had driven to the Town Hall where the count was taking place to await the result.

They had had to wait until one a.m., but the result when it came was well worth it. Peter had increased his majority by six thousand votes.

In a mood of mellow elation he decided that he would drive back to town at once instead of putting up for the night at the hotel. That way, he could be certain of seeing Archer Cole first thing tomorrow morning.

As Peter came up the stairs at Ebury Street he saw that Isabel's light was still burning. The habits of the last months dictated that he should ignore it and go on to his own room. But tonight he felt so pleased and happy that he decided that he would go in and share the good news with Isabel at once. The door swung open and he marched inside.

His wife was lying on her day bed in the window, and her face was as white as the pillow.

Peter saw that she had bitten her lips so hard that there were bloody punctures in them. He saw the tray beside her, where spilled wine mingled disgustingly with bread and congealed soup, and then the other spilt wetness on the silk underneath her.

'What's happening? Why haven't you called anyone?' His voice was harsh with fear and accusation. He knelt beside the day bed and touched the stain, and then looked at his fingertips. Not blood, then. Some water was normal, wasn't it? 'Why haven't you?' Isabel's head rolled just a little to one side, and Peter noticed how brittle and thin her white neck looked. His fingers stretched and clenched, and then he stumbled to her bell and rang and rang. Bethan came flying, with her hair wound up in curl-papers.

'I've just come in,' Peter blustered. 'And look at her.'

Bethan was kneeling beside her now, one hand feeling for Isabel's pulse and the other resting over the bulge of the baby.

'Ring for Mr Hardwicke,' she said. 'And the other man, the obstetrician. Sir.'

She pushed aside the mess of the tray, and folded her hand over Isabel's damp forehead. 'Why didn't you call anyone, love?'

'It isn't time for it to come yet,' Isabel said clearly. 'I don't want it to come yet.'

The doctors arrived with surprising speed. They brought leather bags, nurses in white aprons, and an atmosphere of steady reassurance.

Mr Hardwicke ushered Peter and Bethan out of the room. 'Nothing to worry about. Not a bit. She's just got a bit of a head start on us, that's all. If I were you, Mr Jaspert, I'd go downstairs and have myself a large whisky.'

Peter went, and Bethan slipped down to the telephone in the butler's room. She fumbled inexpertly through the directory pages until she found 'Royal Lambeth Hospital. Nurses' Hostel'. Then she dialled the number and waited. The ringing went on for what seemed an eternity, and then someone answered. 'Lambeth. Nurses' Hostel porter.' The voice was thickened with sleep, but there was no mistaking the fury in it.

'I want to speak to student nurse Lovell. Please.'

There was a brief, incredulous silence. Then the voice said acidly, 'This is not a message service for nurses. It is an emergency number, for use in the case of fire, or war. I suggest you contact your friend through the normal channels.' There was a click, and then the dialling tone again. Bethan could have cried. She had no idea what the normal channels might be. All she knew was that Amy would have the strength and determination to stick by Isabel as long as she was needed. She would know how to cut through Mr Jaspert's bluster, and the doctors' smokescreens.

But Bethan didn't know how to reach her. She reached out to the telephone again, but her courage failed her. Instead she turned around and tiptoed back up to her room, to wait.

Mr Hardwicke's colleague, gloved to the elbows, leaned over and looked into Isabel's face. 'You've got to help us, my dear. You've got to push the baby out. You're both ready now, and then it will be all over.'

Isabel was shaking, and her teeth were chattering, but she was buoyed up by the sudden, intoxicating feeling of power. The pain had been like torture, but now she felt that she was floating somewhere above it, beyond the reach of the tearing fingers. She smiled through the terrible shivering, and could almost have laughed. She was in control of herself after all. The baby wouldn't be born, because she didn't want it to be. Even as the thought came, she seemed to float higher and away from herself, as if it was someone else's body submitting to the agony on the bed beneath her.

Isabel saw the nurse's face swim closer to her, and had time to wonder 'Is she up here with me too?' The muslin masking the lower half of the nurse's face looked just like a shroud.

'Come on, dear. Be a brave girl and push for us.'

Isabel did laugh now, although it came out sounding cracked. The doctors exchanged glances across the bed.

'She isn't co-operating,' the specialist said. Mr Hardwicke was frowning, trying to put the docile, responsive girl he had known together with this mute, staring woman. Something had happened to Isabel Lovell.

'If she won't, she won't,' the other doctor said irritably. 'We'll have to take her in. Can't risk the baby any longer. Nurse? Ring through to the hospital, will you? Perhaps you'd speak to the father, Hardwicke.'

After that it was all noise and jarring movement for Isabel. Her room was suddenly and inexplicably full of people, and they were pulling her off the bed where she was floating so comfortably and dragging her on to a narrow canvas stretcher where the fingers of pain dug themselves into her all over again. She was swaying down the familiar stairs feet first and the thought came to her that she was dead. She wanted to laugh again, but found that she couldn't now. At the door she saw Peter and she knew from the mixture of fear and rage in his face that she wasn't dead at all. It was fear for the baby, and anger with herself. There was only noise and pain after that, a bell shrilling somewhere and agonizing bumping, then bright lights overhead and pink face-blobs that kept coming and going. A vile-smelling rubber flap came down over her face and she knew that she was going to be sick, and then there was only delicious, peaceful dark.

'A fine chap,' someone was saying over and over again. 'Yes, a fine little chap. Look at his face, he's got Jaspert written all over him.'

Isabel opened her eyes. She remembered that she had been awake before, but there had only been nurses and white sheets and welcome silence. Now the first thing she saw was a hazy blur of colour with a dark column towering beside it. When her eyes focused the colour turned into flowers, banks of them all around, with Peter in a City suit standing in front of them. He was leaning over a white crib, smiling with satisfaction. Isabel felt the skin at the back of her neck prickle, then down the length of her spine. She wanted to shut her eyes again and plunge back into the safe darkness. Then she saw another face, closer to her. It was Amy, sitting beside the bed.

Isabel tried to turn to see her better, and then she felt the burning slice across the middle of her. At once, she understood what they had done. She had refused to have his baby for him, and so they had sliced her open and pulled it out of her anyway.

A fine little chap.

Inside Isabel's head someone who wasn't herself at all began helplessly screaming.

'Bel, darling? Are you awake now?' Amy was leaning forward. Her hand touching Isabel's felt solid and warm.

'Am I awake?'

Peter swung round at her. 'You are, aren't you? Look, he's all right. It was touch and go, but you needn't worry now. You mustn't blame yourself. Come on, look at him.' He was lifting a white bundle, pushing it towards her.

'*No.*'

Amy moved protectively in front of her. 'She's barely out of the anaesthetic. She should rest, Peter. Perhaps if you come back this evening, she'll be more alert to the baby.'

Reluctantly he lowered the white shape back into the crib. 'Peter George Jaspert,' he murmured. 'Peter George Lovell Jaspert, if Isabel insists. Well then, I'll look in later if I can. I have to see Archer Cole again. It's an important time for me now. There are all sorts of things in the wind.'

Covertly Isabel watched him go. When the door closed the scream in her head faded a little.

Amy didn't try to talk. She sat beside Isabel holding her hand and concentrating on keeping the anxiety out of her face. Her sister had lost a good deal of blood and had taken an unusually long time to rally from the anaesthetic. It was only because she was a nurse herself that they were allowed to be alone together, and still one of the hospital staff came in every five minutes to check on her. The baby, almost nine pounds of him, big-boned and lusty, was in perfect health. Amy had never seen Peter

Jaspert look so pleased with himself. It was as if he had produced the big pink baby alone and unaided, seeing it spring direct and untainted from healthy Jaspert stock.

She looked back at Isabel and saw that she had drifted into sleep again. Amy had gathered from the doctors' euphemisms and from the half-heard professional murmuring that Isabel had fought against the birth up to the point when they had taken the choice away from her. She could only guess at why, but from Isabel's face when she looked at him she knew that Peter was at the hidden root of it all. Somehow, Amy resolved, Isabel would have to be kept away from him until she had recovered herself. Somehow it would have to be done. Adeline would have to know, and perhaps together they could find a way of rescuing Isabel.

It took Adeline twenty-four hours to reach London after receiving the cable in Morocco. She came to the hospital the next morning, tapping into Isabel's room on high, tapering heels. She was wrapped in silvery furs and there was a little round fur hat perched on her beautiful hair. Her eyes were very blue and wide, and Amy thought as she hugged her that her mother looked no older than she did herself.

'Mummy, thank God you're here.'

'Thank God I'm here,' Adeline echoed in her famous drawl, and Amy smiled at her.

Amy had spent the night with Isabel, dozing in the chair beside her bed, and now she was due back on duty at noon. She felt exhausted, but her mother's determined sparkle was as much of a tonic as always.

'The poor invalid,' Lightly Adeline stroked Isabel's forehead. 'She's terribly white and thin. How do they say she is? Have we got the best man?'

'Yes. She'll be all right, with rest and proper treatment.'

'And my grandson?' Adeline moved gracefully to the crib. 'Mmmn. He's enormous.'

'There isn't any problem with the baby,' Amy said quietly.

They looked at each other, and Amy saw that her mother understood and was thinking quickly. Under all the frivolity and fashionable detachment she knew that Adeline loved the three of them dearly, and would defend them fiercely against the world. And she was as shrewd as anyone Amy had ever met.

'And so what shall we do?' Adeline murmured.

Isabel had retreated into the safety of sleep yet again. Amy took her mother's arm, smelling how the perfume that clung to her furs overpowered even the massed blooms around the bed.

'I think we should talk. There's a little private sitting-room across the hall.'

And there, with Adeline wrinkling her nose over the hospital's attempt at China tea with lemon, Amy told her why she was so frightened for Isabel's sake. She told her about the strange lunch at the Ritz, about Isabel's growing remoteness and the tautness that had replaced her old even composure. She described Isabel's extraordinary physical denial of giving birth, and the expression in her eyes when Peter held the child out to her. She remembered everything, even the colourless letters from the Italian honeymoon, and as she recited it the evidence seemed to mount damningly. Isabel was unhappy with Peter. By her very nature, because she was loyal and steadfast and proud, she wouldn't be able to leave him, or even admit it to anyone. And the lonely pressure of it, together with the stress of her pregnancy, had made her ill. Had unbalanced her, somehow.

There, it was said. The worst of Amy's fears was that her sister wasn't normal any more.

Adeline was looking at her exquisitely manicured oval finger-nails. Her rings flashed blue sapphire light.

'Do you know they aren't happy?'

'Not for certain. I only imagine it, from the man he is and the way Bel has changed.'

'And do you know that all marriages are not automatically happy? That peaceful and equable solutions can be found to the problem that don't involve hasty, dramatic gestures or public scandal or stories in the newspapers?'

Adeline was still studying her fingers. In all the years she had never, never, even obliquely, referred to the meaningless façade of her own marriage. Amy thought briefly of Gerald immured in solitude at Chance, and wondered if the solution was peaceful and equable for him too.

'Yes,' Amy said softly. 'I know that.'

'Do you also know that in a marriage it is the two married people who matter, and interference from outsiders, however well they mean, can be an impertinence?'

Tony Hardy's words, almost exactly. 'I know that, too.'

'So what are you suggesting, Amy darling?'

237

From the look in her eyes, and Adeline's half-smile, Amy knew that her mother was with her.

'Just that we rescue her from him, somehow or other. So that she can recover from all this and then decide in peace whether or not she wants to go back.'

'Ah. Well, that seems quite rational, except that the idea of rescuing her is just a little extreme. Isabel is twenty-one years old, you know.'

Amy nodded meekly, and said nothing about the strong sense she had had of Isabel being trapped among the Jasperts at West Talbot.

Adeline sighed, and then said, 'You know that I was never exactly ecstatic about the match. Would you know what I meant if I said that Peter Jaspert is a perfect example of one of those blunt, jabbing Englishmen who can't stay up and don't care that they can't?' Adeline's smile broadened enchantingly, and Amy blinked at her. 'Perhaps not. Just say that they're not ideal husband material. But she would have him, you know.'

Amy remembered Isabel's calm certainty before the marriage that she was doing the right thing. Surely that must make the shock of what was happening now even more profound?

'He's just the sort of man that Isabel would choose. She's . . .' Amy faltered tellingly ' . . . such a rational person. If you wrote a list on paper, Peter would have all the right qualifications.'

'I'm guessing wildly, of course, but if the trouble between them is what I suspect it is, it's the very thing that none of us can work out on paper. How easy life would be if only one could.' Adeline smoothed the silver-white points of her fur, first against the lie of the pelt and then flat again so that it gleamed like silk. 'So, what shall we do for Isabel?'

Amy took a deep breath. 'I think you should say, insist, that Isabel must come away on a long holiday with you. And then take her off somewhere safe and just see how she is.'

'Safe? Jaspert may be an oaf, but I don't think he's dangerous.'

I do, Amy suddenly thought. *Oh, I think he's dangerous.*

'But, as you say, Isabel will need a long holiday. Where shall I take her? Do you know, it might be the very best of fun. Couldn't you come too, dear heart?'

Amy made a wry face. 'I can't even find six spare hours, let alone six weeks or six months, or however long you can spare for Isabel.'

238

Adeline stood up and smoothed her tight skirt over her hips. She was still as slim as a girl.

'And what about my huge grandson?'

'There will be a nurse, and Bethan, and from the look of it Peter will be a besotted father.'

'Yes,' Adeline said meditatively. 'And I'm sure that Joan Jaspert will do everything possible to help, if only to demonstrate to me how maternally remiss I am. Very well. We'll do it. As soon as Isabel is well enough to leave here I'll sweep her off to the sunshine somewhere. If she'll come, that is. Does that make you happy?'

'I think she'll come,' Amy said. 'Yes. Just a little bit happier.'

They crossed the hallway again and looked in at Isabel. She was still lying with her eyes shut, apparently asleep.

She was safe. She could hide. Hide from Peter and the baby in its crib. And from the concerned faces that were a reproach rather than a comfort.

It was easy to retreat into the darkness at first, but as the hours passed and then the days began to crawl by Isabel found that the precious oblivion was harder and harder to achieve.

Sleep wouldn't come and she lay with her eyes shut, hunched over her aching breasts, and listened to the screaming in her head. Her body felt as if it was being stretched tighter and tighter until she was certain that the livid pucker of the red and purple scar would split open again and she would fall in half.

The tears, when they came, were a relief and then they wouldn't stop. They soaked her chic hair so that it lay lank and flat against her head, and the pillows, and the ruffles of her crêpe-de-chine nightdresses.

The nurses were soothing at first, then baffled, and then, helplessly, Isabel sensed their impatience. She was healing physically, but with every day she felt herself slipping further out of control of herself.

Peter came and sat by her bed, talking significantly and at length about how the Prime Minister had made Archer Cole his Home Secretary. Isabel lay completely still, feeling the skin prickle along her arm again at his proximity. One morning he strode in and announced that his own appointment had been confirmed. He was to be a junior minister in the Home Office.

'I knew Archer had something for me. It was a question of how far up he could bring me in. I'm still a new boy to most of them, of course. There's a lot to be done, Isabel, but with a minister like Archer there's no telling how far we might go.' He went on, talking and talking, and looking out of the hospital window towards Westminster.

The tears ran down Isabel's cheeks and Peter's face tightened with anger.

Mr Hardwicke came, and said, 'A little depression is very common after the birth of a child. You'll be as right as rain as soon as you are back in your own home with your beautiful baby.'

All of them tried to thrust the baby on her. The nurses asked, 'Will you try to feed him yourself for a week or so?'

'*No*,' Isabel said, and they shrugged and gave him a bottle. She saw the bony little gums clamp round the teat, and shivered.

When they made her hold him she looked into the tiny face, closed-up and calm, and sensed all the reserves of power and strength in it. She knew that she had none. Yet she was getting better. It was as if her own body was defying her, gathering its own strength out of the hospital air. They made her get up, dressed her in one of her pretty robes, and sat her in a chair in the window. She could see the tower of Big Ben, so she drew the curtains on it and sat in the dimness until the nurses came and pulled them back again.

Adeline came to see her every day, always exquisitely dressed and always just on her way somewhere, or else hurrying home to change to go somewhere else. She was talking gaily about travel plans and Isabel stared uncomprehendingly at her. Even Gerald came. He looked like an old man now, and walked arthritically with a stick. He approved of the baby's big, healthy pinkness. 'He's a fine boy,' he said to Peter. 'The first grandchild should be called Airlie.'

'Airlie? Don't be ridiculous. His name is Peter George. We've already announced it. Archer Cole has agreed to be a god-father.'

Amy was the only visitor Isabel didn't shrink from. Amy didn't say much, nor did she coo and cluck falsely over the baby. She simply sat, sometimes holding her sister's hand, and tried to will some of her own strength into her.

Once, just once, Isabel felt a flicker of the old life.

Richard came and found the two of them sitting together.

'Darling sisters,' he said, and raised an eyebrow at the room filled with flowers and presents and messages. 'I knew, Bel, that you would be showered with tributes and I had no idea what offering to bring. And then I was passing through Covent Garden . . . don't ask me what I was doing there because I won't tell you . . . and I saw this.' From a pocket Richard produced a tomato. 'It is the most perfect tomato in London. Don't you think? It's very important that whatever you bring should be the best,' he said seriously.

The tomato was large, and evenly and floridly red. He put it reverently on the bedside locker and kissed Isabel. Richard was wearing a tight-waisted pale jacket and a Windsor-knotted emerald silk tie. His hair was slicked back and he looked taller, and more elegant than the schoolboy they had last seen. But the defensive humorousness marked his face as strongly as ever.

'Well. Where is the infant?'

Amy pointed and he peered into the crib. There was a moment's silence.

'Oh dear,' he said at last. 'Do you know, I always thought that all the stuff about the child being father of the man was romantic piffle. Now here is the living proof that old Wordsworth was perfectly right. This child is Lord Jaspert down to the very last wrinkle. How does it feel, Isabel, to have given birth to your own father-in-law?'

'Richard.'

It was Amy's exclamation, but Isabel felt a ripple of laughter spreading inside her. For the briefest of instants they were together again, Amy and Richard and herself, sparring and giggling around the fire. The ripple spread and lapped outwards and more followed it. She was laughing aloud but suddenly it wasn't the right sort of laughter any more, and the happy moment had gone. Amy was staring at her as she laughed louder and then abruptly the sobs came to choke her and she was blind to her brother and sister and she knew that she was lost to the old safe world for ever.

Over Isabel's cropped head Amy and Richard looked at each other. The white knobs at the nape of her neck stood sharply out.

'I'm sorry,' Richard said awkwardly. 'I'm very, very sorry.'

The terrible crying was unstoppable. At last Amy called a

241

nurse who brought Isabel a sedative and sent the two of them out.

'I could cut out my tongue,' Richard said as they walked slowly away together. 'An all-too familiar feeling.'

'It wasn't your fault. Isabel's ill.'

Richard looked sideways at Amy. 'Head ill?'

'I think so. Mummy's going to take her away for a while.'

She sensed his shrewd glance again. 'Away from Jaspert?'

'Yes.'

'What a very good idea.' They stopped at the corner of the street. 'I have to go back now.' Richard made a quick, disgusted face. 'I'm in bad enough trouble as it is. And don't ask me about that, either. But you'll stay with her as much as you can, won't you? I love you both.' He touched her wrist quickly and then walked away, leaving Amy to watch until he was out of sight and wish that she knew her brother better. For all his whimsy Richard was tough, and it would have helped to have him with her now.

After three weeks the doctors judged that Isabel was strong enough to be allowed home. After another two weeks, they said, she might travel in easy stages with her mother and a nurse to Spain and then, perhaps, to the sun in North Africa. The flowers in Isabel's room had withered and the presents had been taken home with the folded-up greetings and telegrams.

The tomato had stayed on the bedside locker until the bracts curled and blackened like a spider, and the red skin puckered. Then a nurse threw it away.

Isabel was taken home in the Daimler, tucked up in a fur rug. Bethan took the baby separately in his voluminous white wrappings.

The Ebury Street bedroom was bright and warm. The day bed was drawn up beside a low table where a cloisonné bowl filled with pot-pourri gave out a cloud of spicy perfume. The flowers had been carefully arranged, shaggy bronze and white and gold chrysanthemums and heady forsythia from the hothouses at Chance. There were new books and magazines on the table too, and Isabel's embroidery laid out neatly in its frame.

Adeline and Amy had been carefully preparing for her return, Isabel thought, but instead of welcoming her the warmth and bright colours and scents made her feel her own chill brittleness more intensely. She moved slowly around the room, touching the green silk coverings and the stiff curve of a chrysanthemum petal, then with horrified fascination the handle of the door leading into Peter's dressing-room. Isabel was shivering, and the high, thin screaming that plagued her constantly was much louder here. Ebury Street didn't feel like home. Everything was too light and bright and shiny. It attacked her senses, making her feel even thinner and colder and more isolated than she had done in hospital. Isabel made another circuit of the room. It occurred to her that she was looking for somewhere to crawl into and find shelter in, and her own bedroom offered nowhere.

I don't live here. I can't stay here. Where can I go?

She couldn't think of anywhere, and she felt like a small animal caught in a box. Adeline had talked about travel, of going south in search of the sun, and she shrank from that idea too. The sun would probe her and shine through her raw skin when she longed for darkness and silence.

From the other end of the house, where Bethan and the trap-mouthed night nurse appointed by Lady Jaspert shared the nursery suite, Isabel heard the baby Peter crying.

The two screams, internal and external, merged and became one.

Please stop. I want to be quiet. Please stop.

When Peter came home he was exhilarated by the first of a series of committee meetings under his own chairmanship. Archer Cole had appointed him to head a vital and timely investigation of public order and the processes of police control. Peter was in complete agreement with the Home Secretary that street political demonstrations and mass displays posed a threat to public safety, and he was looking forward to drafting legislation that would forbid them, and to increasing police powers to deal with them when they did erupt. Peter believed that politics were the rightful and hereditary affair of his own class, and that any attempt by the remaining masses to involve themselves was an intrusion.

He found Isabel's room in semi-darkness, and his wife in the farthest corner of it. Her white face half-turned towards him, and Peter thought impatiently that she looked like a cringing animal. After the committee he had stopped in for a drink with Sylvia Cole, who had poured out whisky and flattered him with political gossip and assurance of how very highly Archer valued him. Sylvia was electrically charged by her husband's new power and prominence. She was wearing red lipstick with her fingernails varnished the same colour, and her bright scarlet cocktail frock showed off the tops of her full breasts. As he watched her striding up and down her drawing-room talking and laughing and waving her cigarette-holder, Peter was reminded of an exotic tropical bird. When she drank, Sylvia's mouth left a red print on her glass and Peter could hardly take his eyes off it when she put it down on the tray again.

When he stood up he had to control an urge to pick the glass up and press his own mouth to it.

Compared with Sylvia's brilliance his white, trembling wife seemed hardly alive at all. Her helplessness suddenly made Peter angry, and when he was angry he was brutal.

'Welcome home,' Peter said. 'It will be nice to have a wife again. Now that we've got the boy safely.' He caught Isabel's wrist, and it felt like a stick. He pulled her towards him so that her head jerked back, and looked down into her face. Isabel's skin was drawn and there were dark, unhealthy circles under her eyes. He thought with impatience that his wife was losing her looks faster than he could have believed possible, and her eye-catching, windflower beauty was one of the main reasons why he had married her. Angrily his fingers tightened on her arm and he kissed her, his mouth open over her compressed lips. She was shaking so much now that her head wobbled, and Peter thought it was like kissing one of the wax-faced clockwork dolls in his sister's collection at West Talbot. The idea disgusted him, and he pushed her away so that she half-stumbled against the bed. As if the touch and sight of it galvanized her Isabel backed away from it, her hands to her mouth.

'What's the matter with you?' Peter hissed at her. 'What? What? Look at it all.' He gestured wildly at the pretty room. 'You've got everything, every damned thing, and you look like a scared nanny goat. What do you want, Isabel? I know what I want. I need a wife. I need a wife like other men have, like Sylvia Cole. You can't even smile at my table and open your legs in bed at night. Look at you.' Isabel saw the spray from his mouth as Peter swung round and swept the cloisonné bowl and the books and papers and sewing off the table. The pot-pourri scattered in dry, aromatic dust and the bowl, unbroken on the rug, rang with a single resonant note.

244

The hum of it and Peter's shouting pierced Isabel's skull and even cut through the screaming. Her hands moved from her dry mouth to her ears as she tried vainly to block out the din. She shook her head in bewilderment.

'I can't . . . be . . . like . . . Sylvia Cole. Never.' Was that her own voice? Isabel wondered within a corner of herself. Were the words really coming out of her mouth, or was she just imagining herself saying them? 'And you ask me what I want. I want you not to touch me. You make my skin crawl. The things you . . . the things you do to me are disgusting. I hate them. I hate you.'

She really was saying the words. Isabel knew it from the disbelief and then the blind anger mounting in her husband's face.

'You're mad,' he told her. 'I've wondered, and now I know. You're insane.'

Isabel pressed her hands flatter to her head.

'Don't say that.' Her voice was rising. 'Don't say that. Don't tell me I'm mad. It's your fault. You did it . . .'

'Stop screaming.' Peter's hand flashed up and down and the blow caught the side of her head and rattled the bones of her jaw. 'Do you want all the bloody servants to hear you?'

Isabel fell against the bed and then lay huddled half on the smooth green cover and half on the floor. She heard the door close and the sound of Peter walking away towards the nursery. He was going to see the baby, of course. Their two strengths, the one male and blunt and brutal, and the other primeval, mysterious, but none the less male, would meet and reinforce each other. Meanwhile her own strength had bled away into nowhere.

Oh, please, just let there be quiet. Where can I go?

Isabel lay for a while listening, unable to distinguish whether the scream was really the baby's or her own, internal one. Then, when she felt strong enough, she stumbled to the door and locked it. She locked the dressing-room door too, and with her breath coming a little more easily she went and lay down on the bed again. She stayed wide-eyed in the darkness listening to the domestic sounds of the house, and when they subsided at last into the silence of night she was still lying, waiting and listening.

When she judged that everyone must be asleep she levered herself upright. She was stiff and cramped from lying so long in one position, but she knew exactly what she must do and she moved quickly.

The key turned noiselessly back in the lock, and she slipped out into the darkness beyond her room.

The noise. The screaming. If only I can just stop it, everything will be all right. There must be something the matter with the baby for it to scream like this. It would want me to stop it, wouldn't it?

The door of the nursery suite was closed, and she turned the knob breathlessly and inched it open. There was a little lobby linking the three rooms, and one of the doors stood ajar. A dim light filtered through, and Isabel blinked at it after the total darkness.

Wait until you can see properly. That's better. Oh, the terrible noise. Put it right.

Stealthily, with her hand out in front of her to guide her, Isabel crept forward. Inside the nursery the nightlight was lit. In the middle of the room was the white crib under its white canopy hung with ribbon and lace. She moved towards it, one tiny step at a time. The room was all white, fresh and pure. *It's nice here, except for the noise. Why doesn't anyone else hear it, Bethan or the nurse? I'll stop it myself now. Then everyone will be happy.*

Isabel reached the foot of the white crib. Taking a deep breath, she leaned over and looked inside. To her surprise, the baby didn't look as if it was crying at all, although the sound of it was deafening. The eyes were shut in the autocratic little face, and it was motionless.

Frowning a little, Isabel looked around her. There was a folded blanket on the nursing chair beside the crib. She picked it up and folded it again into a neat square and then she pressed it over the baby's face.

Is it so strong then? The scream hardly faltering. As strong as Peter himself. Of course.

Isabel leant on the blanket with all her strength and at last, after so long, the screaming dropped in pitch and suddenly choked on itself.

The blessed silence.

'Madam? What are you doing?'

Isabel let go of her blanket and turned round. It was the nurse, the one with the mouth like a steel trap. She was staring at Isabel in shocked disbelief.

'The baby was crying,' Isabel said calmly. 'Couldn't you hear it? I was quietening it. We can't let it scream like that all night, can we?'

The nurse ran forward and leaned over the crib. She gasped and snatched up the white bundle and held it against her shoulder. There was a choking sound and then a thin, shuddering wail.

Isabel saw the woman's face sag with relief, and wondered vaguely why. The nurse wrapped her arms around the baby and after an instant's hesitation she ran, carrying it with her.

Isabel stood listening gratefully to the silence.

It didn't last long. Within seconds a door slammed, and there were raised, urgent voices and hurrying feet coming towards her. She looked around and half-retreated behind the white-draped crib. Peter burst into the room. His face was red and seamed with sleep, and he looked even bulkier in his striped dressing-gown. At the sight of him Isabel shrank and tried to slip behind the crib hangings. But he was coming for her, and his arm reached out and gripped her like a vice. Over his shoulder Isabel saw the nurse still staring at her in horror. Standing a little to one side was Bethan, and she was crying, tears pouring silently down her cheeks. Only then did Isabel understand that something terrible had happened.

Peter could hardly speak. Something was strangling his voice in his throat. 'You. *My son.* A baby. Helpless. You are mad, Isabel. You should be locked up.'

Isabel raised her free hand to try to ward him off but he was too close. She tried to twist sideways, meaning to run to Bethan as she had done as a child. Bethan's arms opened to her, but Peter held her tight. There was no escape, and Isabel's arm crooked to protect her head.

'Not mad,' she whispered. 'Not. Just couldn't bear the noise, any more.'

'Is the baby all right?' Peter asked harshly and the nurse nodded.

'I reached him almost at once.' She wouldn't look at Isabel now.

'We'll wait until morning to speak to the doctors, then. Come with me.' He pulled Isabel across the room so roughly that her foot caught in the hem of her robe and she almost stumbled. He jerked her upright again.

'Let me stay with her until the morning,' Bethan pleaded. 'She'll be all right with me. Won't you, love?'

Peter wouldn't hear her. He propelled Isabel back to her own room and pushed her inside. She fell forwards and lay with her cheek against the rug, wide-eyed in the pitch blackness. There was a moment of relief as she heard Peter slam the door between them, and then she heard the click of the lock.

Her door wasn't locked against the world any longer.

It was locked on the outside, and she was behind it.

She was imprisoned with herself, and the memory of the nurse's horror beside Bethan's helpless tears and outstretched, empty arms.

Isabel lurched forward and rattled the unyielding door. At the same moment she heard the bolt on Peter's side of the dressing-room door slide home. Her hand came up to her mouth and she bit into the heel of it until the pain made her feel dizzy and she tasted the warm, salty blood.

Then she knelt down and leaned her forehead against the door. The draught through the crack sliced down the side of her face like a knife-blade.

Amy sat bolt upright in bed. She was shivering and sweating, but the black fingers of the nightmare were already losing their grip. Isabel had been running towards her, shouting something, and there was a chasm between them that zigzagged wider and wider as Amy tried to warn her. But she was fully awake now, and she couldn't remember what Isabel had been shouting, nor what she herself had been trying so desperately to warn her against.

Amy reached out for her alarm clock, breathing deeply to try to stop her teeth from chattering. A quarter to five in the morning, and she was due on day duty again at six. It was almost time to wake up in any case. She turned on the overhead light and looked around the little room. Her uniform dress was ready on its hanger behind the door, and her textbooks were piled up on the shelf exactly as she had left them the night before. It had only been a bad dream and she couldn't even remember exactly what had been happening, but still the atmosphere of it clung round her. She was still afraid, with a dull knot of anxiety that sat in the pit of her stomach. Isabel was slowly recovering, she was safely back home at Ebury Street, but Amy was frightened for her. Why, so vividly, now? Was it just the effect of the nightmare?

Amy pushed back the covers and gathered up her things for

the bath. There were only two bathrooms in this part of the hostel, and there were always queues to use them. She would go early and relax for a few minutes in the hot water, if there was any, and then she would make a cup of tea and perhaps take one along to Moira . . . But the routine plans failed to calm her nerves. Amy was still shaking, and the thought of Isabel running desperately stayed obstinately with her. Instead of heading for the bathroom Amy went quickly to Moira O'Hara's door and tapped urgently.

'Dear Lord,' she heard Moira murmuring. 'Is that you, Lovell? Do you have any idea what the time is?'

Her friend came shuffling to the door and opened it, blinking.

'Moira, will you do something for me? Will you tell Blaine that I'm sick and can't come on this morning?'

'Are you ill? You look white enough.'

'No. I'm worried about my sister. I want to go home and see her. Will you tell Blaine?'

Moira looked doubtful. 'Sure I will, but they'll come down here and check on you, you know. If they find you out it'll be big trouble.'

'I'll risk it. I might be back before they notice I'm gone.'

Amy ran back to her room and pulled on her clothes. To fool the porter in his cubicle by the front door into thinking she was simply going on duty early, she wrapped her nurse's cape around her and slipped out of the hostel. The street was dark and deserted, with the few lit-up hospital windows reflected icily in the puddles. The air tasted raw and cold, with a sour lacing of smoke and the dustbins in the yard at the side of the hospital. Amy glanced up and down. There was no hope of a taxi, of course, and she thought that it was probably much too early for a bus. Grateful for the heavy warmth of her cape, she pulled it around her and began to walk north towards the river.

By the time she reached Lambeth Bridge her feet were soaked and she was chilled through by the raw November air. But on the corner of Marsham Street a cab stopped right beside her and disgorged two couples in evening clothes. One of the women, in a silver lamé dress with a little fur shoulder cape, stumbled and the two men caught her, laughing. Amy ran past them, waving to the driver. He stared doubtfully at her nurse's cape and her damp hair loose and clinging to her face.

'I said Ebury Street. At once,' Army repeated sharply. Hearing the authority in her voice, the driver jerked his head to motion her into the cigar-reeking interior.

The house in Ebury Street seemed to be in forbidding, total darkness but as Amy came up to the area railings she saw a light in the basement kitchen window. She ran down the area steps and, through the half-drawn curtains, she saw that it was Bethan inside, sitting alone at the square scrubbed table. Her face was buried in her hands. Bethan's head jerked up in fright and Amy saw the tears.

The anxiety tightened its grip within her.

'Bethan. It's me. Let me in, will you?'

A second later the area door swung open and the two women stood facing each other in the tradesmen's lobby.

'Oh, Miss Amy, thank God.'

'What's happened?'

'He's locked her in. Why should she try to hurt him? The little mite was asleep. But her poor, white face, Amy. She didn't know what she was doing . . .'

Bethan's incoherence was enough to tell Amy that something was terribly wrong. She fought against the infectious panic and gripped Bethan's arm firmly to steer her back into the kitchen. She made her sit down and drew her own chair up so that they sat knee to knee.

'Now. Tell me slowly.'

'I didn't hear anything. The nurse woke me, with the baby in her arms. She said . . . she said that Isabel had tried to kill him. By smothering him with a blanket. She said that she heard her, and saw her.'

'That can't be true.' But even as she said it, Amy knew that it could be. *Isabel.*

'I saw her too. She didn't look like our Isabel at all. She was as white as death, and her eyes stared like stones. She said something like she wanted to stop the noise. But he was asleep, Amy. There wasn't a whisper of noise.'

Amy stood up. Somehow, she discovered, the months of training on the wards had given her a kind of quick-thinking calm. It helped her to suppress the pity and horror welling inside her and ask levelly, 'Where's Isabel now?'

'In her room. Mr Jaspert locked her in, he wouldn't let me be with her. He said that she should be locked up. He's going to bring the doctors in in the morning.'

250

They both looked up at the white-faced kitchen clock. Not quite six a.m. 'He said that she was mad, Amy . . .'

'She's ill, that's all, and she needs help. We'll get it for her.' Amy was already at the door, wrapping the anonymity of her dark cape around her.

'Where are you going?'

'To Bruton Street, to get my mother. We'll come back and take Isabel away with us.'

Outside it had begun to rain, and it was at least another hour before the beginning of the winter dawn. Incredibly, or so it seemed to Amy, another taxi was unloading a party of late revellers. One of them looked a little like Johnny Guild, and she smiled bitterly at the remoteness of that other world now. The taxi swept her on through the streets that were already beginning to come alive with delivery boys and shop workers, and deposited her on the steps of Bruton Street. Amy hadn't thought of bringing her own key and it took prolonged ringing to summon a faintly dishevelled footman to open the huge door.

'Good morning, Miss Amy, ah, Miss Lovell.'

Amy brushed past him and into the hallway. 'Is Lady Lovell at home?'

'Yes, I believe so, miss. Ah, Parker usually takes up her tray at nine-thirty.'

Amy was taking the steps of the great curving stairway two at a time. She ran under the glass dome and past the ranks of portraits to her mother's suite. Her private sitting-room was empty, but there were two glasses on a little tray beside the dead fire. In her dressing-room one of the mirrored doors along its length had swung open to reveal the skeletal shoulders of dresses on their padded hangers. The bedroom door was closed. There wasn't a thought in Amy's head except Isabel, and taking Adeline to her as quickly as possible. Amy knocked lightly on the door and pushed it open at once, intending to tiptoe in and wake her mother gently. Her first confused sight was of a man's forearm forcibly pinning Adeline against the pale peach bedcovers. She saw black hair on the pillow, and the glowing red-brown of her mother's tangled with it.

As Amy realized that her mother was asleep in a man's arms, Adeline woke up and stared at her. Her blue eyes were clouded with sleep at first, and then they snapped open wide. For the first time in Amy's life, she saw her mother at a loss. The man beside

251

her stirred and murmured something, and then he was looking at Amy too, frozen into immobility.

If it hadn't been for her anxiety for Isabel, Amy might almost have laughed. It was an absurd rôle to find herself in, to be the innocent daughter discovering her mother in bed with a lover. And yet. Although she had known for years that Adeline had lovers, to be so brutally confronted with it shocked her. Amy took a faltering step backwards, pulling her cape up around her throat as if she was the naked one. It didn't take long for Adeline to collect herself.

'You know, darling,' she drawled, 'it's never advisable to burst into people's bedrooms unannounced. Or is the house on fire?'

'It's Isabel,' Amy blurted. 'She's ill. I came to get you.'

'I see.' Adeline was sitting up, drawing the covers around her smooth, creamy-pale shoulders. 'If you'll go back to your room, darling, and ring for some tea, I'll join you in a tiny tick.'

She came almost immediately, wrapped in a slither of pale peach silk that fell around her like sculpted marble. She had tied back her hair with a peach satin ribbon, and her skin glowed.

Does sex make you feel wonderful as well as looking it? Amy wondered, with an odd, wild tinge of bitterness.

'Tell me,' Adeline commanded. She listened intently as Amy told, her head bent, letting the folds of silk fall in ripples through her fingers.

At last she nodded. 'Yes. I'm not altogether amazed. Clearly she is ill, and we must go and fetch her. We'll take her to Chance, to begin with, while I make arrangements. Then to Switzerland, perhaps. There's a clinic outside Lausanne.'

'Peter won't like it.'

Adeline sighed. 'Quite probably not. He is her husband, and therefore her next of kin. I suspect that that might be crucial. We shall have to deal with that when we get there.'

'Quickly, then,' Amy begged her and Adeline smiled.

'I'm not going to run wildly out into the night half-dressed and looking more than a little crazy myself. I'm not like you, Amy. I'm going to drink my tea and then have my bath. Then I shall dress, and say goodbye politely to poor, embarrassed Bobbie, and then I shall ring for the car and we will drive calmly round to Ebury Street. From what you say, I don't think Isabel will be going far this morning.'

Amy was half-wild with impatience, and with a certain convic-

252

tion that they should race back to Isabel at once, but she knew better than to argue with Adeline. She passed the interminable waiting time in pacing up and down her room, up and back again. Incredibly, it was ten o'clock before Adeline sailed in. She was wearing a dark grey tailored costume with a black Persian lamb collar and her maid had coiled her hair up under a Cossack hat of the same fur. She was pulling on her gloves and smoothing the black suède over each fingertip.

'And now, let's go to Ebury Street,' she ordered regally.

Her chauffeur, in lavender-grey breeches and tunic with a double row of silver-gilt buttons, was waiting with the car at the steps. He took his peaked cap from under his arm with a flourish and pulled it low over his eyes, then handed them inside. Adeline's car was a rakish cream Bentley, and every inch of chrome on it, from the radiator grille to the wheel spokes, was polished to a sparkle. As the long cream bonnet nosed out into the street the traffic seemed to hold respectfully back for it.

Amy glanced at the thick glass partition behind the chauffeur's head.

'I'm sorry I rushed in this morning.'

Adeline was still smoothing the ruches of suède at her wrists. 'Yes. You know, I wouldn't dream of bursting into your bedroom, whatever the circumstances.'

The idea made Amy smile, but it was an uneven, bitter smile. 'You wouldn't see anything unexpected, even if you did.' A thought struck her. Was she jealous of her mother, then? Jealous of her free spirit and her prime concern for her own pleasures? Or simply of her good time?

'Oh, I don't know,' Adeline murmured. 'What with bringing home coal miners, and going to strange meetings and dinners with Mr Hardy.'

'How do you know about the meetings?' Amy was surprised, and curious.

'I know all kinds of things,' Adeline answered. 'But you shouldn't worry about whether I do or not, my darling. You have your own life to lead – and only one life, after all.'

They were in Ebury Street, and the long cream car was stopping at Peter Jaspert's door. Standing at the kerb ahead of them was another car, a discreet black one. Adeline frowned at the sight of it.

A scared-looking maid ushered Amy and Adeline into the

upstairs drawing-room, and after a long moment Peter came in. He was freshly shaven and immaculate in morning dress with a gold chain looped across his waistcoat. Amy thought he looked as if he was about to preside over a wedding rather than his wife's collapse. Adeline kissed him elaborately on either cheek.

'Peter, my dear, I'm so sad and worried about Isabel and the baby. I think she should have a long, complete rest. And, if this terrible story of Amy's is true, some proper medical attention. I'll take her home to Chance with me now, and then we can talk about sending her to Dr Ahrend's clinic in Lausanne. Will you ring for her maid to begin packing for her? Just a few things. The trunks can follow later, of course.'

Peter was standing stiffly, like a wax model of himself. 'The terrible story, as you call it, is perfectly true. Isabel tried to smother the baby. I appreciate your concern, of course, Lady Lovell, but it won't be necessary for you to make any arrangements. I have already done so. The doctors are examining her now, and the car is here to take her to an excellent rest home. In Chertsey, as it happens.'

'Chertsey?' Adeline was incredulous. 'If it has to be in England, surely somewhere nearer home? There is someone in Harley Street who specializes . . .'

Peter cut her short. 'I'm afraid I have already made the arrangements for my wife. She is going to Chertsey this morning.'

'Peter,' Adeline said in her soft, dangerous drawl. 'What are you doing? Are you planning to certify my daughter?'

Amy thought that Peter might waver, but he stood his ground. 'The papers have to be prepared. Nothing can and nothing will be done in haste. But in the meantime, it will be best for her to be somewhere secure. For her own good, as well as the child's.'

Adeline stood facing him. To Amy it was clear that she was already being forced to fall back on her second line of attack.

'The baby will stay here with his nurse and Bethan, of course. We'll just take Isabel, and as soon as she is well again, she can come home to you both.'

My daughter for your son, in other words. The bargain was clear to all three of them.

'Isabel is going to Chertsey this morning,' Peter repeated.

'You can't do it.'

'I'm afraid,' he said evenly, 'that it is already as good as done. I cannot risk my son.'

254

Amy had jumped to her feet ready to launch herself into a protest, but then she saw Adeline's shoulders drop and knew that if her mother was giving up the fight so quickly, then they didn't stand a chance at all. Peter was Isabel's husband and her lawful guardian now if she had lost the precious responsibility for herself, and he held all the cards against them.

'I want to see her,' Amy demanded. As she spoke, they heard dragging footsteps come slowly down the stairs. Adeline wrenched open the door and Isabel confronted them. She was wrapped in a blanket and there was a nurse on either side of her, holding her arms. A doctor was coming down the stairs in the wake of the procession.

'Isabel,' Amy said, but her sister barely looked at her. Her hair was matted around her face and one cheek was swollen and puffy, the eye above it watery and blank. 'I just wanted to be quiet,' she explained to them all in a thin, childish voice.

Adeline made as if to go to her, but Peter caught her arm and the nurses gestured her back.

'I'm afraid it isn't advisable,' the doctor said. 'Any excitement, or sudden movement. In any case, we're not sure that she knows who anyone is. We've given her a sedative, and she will be quite calm shortly. If you will let us through?'

They stood in a huddle in the drawing-room doorway, watching in silence as Isabel was led shuffling away, her head hanging like a convict's. Peter shook himself and followed the little group down to the street. The door of the black car opened and swallowed Isabel, and then it drove away from them and disappeared.

Amy heard her mother utter a single, black obscenity. Peter came slowly back into the house and Adeline raised her chin and swept past him without a glance. Shaking, with her legs almost giving way underneath her, Amy followed her. She was aware of Peter closing the door on them and on his wife being sped away somewhere to a discreet, distant and unmentionable locked room.

Amy sank into the car beside her mother and the Bentley purred off in the opposite direction.

All Amy's calm was gone and she turned to Adeline and begged her, like a child, 'Mummy, what can we do? If we had been earlier . . .'

Adeline's face was turned away, out to the busy, everyday streets.

'It wouldn't have made any difference. He owns her, don't you see? He is her husband, and her keeper. Oh, we'll get her back in the end, but it will take time.'

There was a long silence, and then she said fiercely, 'Don' marry, Amy, will you? Do anything else you like, but don't marry anyone.'

10

'And how long will they make her stay there?' Helen asked.

'I've no idea,' Amy said. 'I don't think anyone has.'

They were sitting together in Helen's clean, bare room. In the corner beside the grate was a fire-bucket filled with sand and swathed with red paper, with a fir branch stuck firmly into it. The spiky green arm was liberally hung with paper decorations, cut out and coloured by Jim.

It was the week before Christmas and in pride of place on the mantelpiece next to the photographs were the presents that Amy had just bought for Helen and Freda and Jim. The glossy wrappings and the determined effort at a tree made an almost festive glow in the colourless room.

Amy tried to smile over the rim of the best tea-cup, but the smile failed and Helen looked sharply at her.

'It's me sitting here, you know, Helen. I thought we were friends. You don't have to be cheerful if you don't feel like it. Have a bloody cry, if you feel like that. I probably would, if it was my sister in the loony-bin.'

The smile did come now, even if it was a slightly twisted one. 'Sanatorium and Rest Home, Helen. They would shudder to hear it called anything as honest as loony-bin. And I've done enough crying. It won't help Isabel, will it?'

The room was warm, with a small fire lit in honour of her visit, but the chilly fingers of Thorogood House, Chertsey, seemed to reach out and touch Amy even here and she shivered involuntarily.

The secure rest home that Peter Jaspert had chosen precipitately for Isabel was in a quiet road lined with similar gloomy Victorian houses standing in huge, dripping gardens. There was a cramped attempt at a carriage drive leading from the locked iron gates to the locked front door, and the raked gravel was

257

overhung with laurels and rhododendrons. While visitors waited for someone to peer through a slot in the door before undoing the locks, they stood on the stone steps listening to the rain drumming in the evergreens and breathing in the scents of sour earth and prowling cats. When the door was finally inched open, visitors were ushered into a little green-painted room off the dark panelled hallway. From there they were summoned either to the communal sitting-room or to the discreet suites on the upper floors, depending on the patient's health. Isabel's doctors were advising complete rest and calm. On the few visits Amy had been allowed to make, Thorogood House had struck her as the most depressing place on earth. How could anyone get well, surrounded by so much ugliness and gloom?

Isabel seemed to have retreated so far into herself as to be almost unreachable. She was quiet and docile, and so the staff let her sit for hour after hour beside the window in the day room, staring out at the dank, mottled leaves. She hardly ever spoke, and when she did it was with faint, puzzled politeness.

'There's no need for her to be in that place,' Amy said now, with sudden violence, 'if Peter hadn't gone so wild. He signed everything there was to sign, just to keep her away from the baby and out of the papers. He wanted her taken away, there and then. If he could only have been patient and calm, she could have been in Lausanne now, where Adeline could go and stay with her. But he was so afraid that he couldn't think. I despise him for that more than for anything else.'

Helen reached over and peered into the teapot. The sudden movement made her cough, and she sat still to let it subside. 'Here,' she said. 'Have a fill-up before it gets stewed. So what happens? Can't your ma do anything?'

'Eventually. She's got plenty of influence, but she wants things done discreetly as much as Peter does. Madness isn't chic, is it? Isabel will be moved somewhere, probably to the Lausanne clinic. But without Peter's help it will take time. And I'd have gone mad already myself, locked up in that place for so long.'

Helen shook her head sympathetically. 'I'm sorry. But she will get better, won't she? In the end?'

'Oh God, I hope so.'

They were silent for a second or two. Then Amy shook herself deliberately. 'I shouldn't be unloading my problems on to you.

258

I will have some more tea, please. And if you're not going to have any cake I'll eat it myself.'

Amy had brought a dark, rich fruit cake glistening with cherries and peel, and a big bowl of oranges that made another splash of colour in the dimming firelight. Helen sliced the cake and put one piece on a plate.

'Aren't you going to eat anything?' Amy persisted.

'Nah. I'll save the rest for Freda and Jim.'

'There's plenty.'

'I don't want anything,' Helen said, with the stubborn air that Amy now knew better than to argue against. She drank her tea and ate her own cake, and noticed that Helen's hands were thin and veined under the rough skin.

'Let's talk about something cheerful,' Amy said to break the silence. 'What about Christmas? What do you do?'

'On Christmas Eve, after the carol singers have been along the street, we all go down to the boozer. Only the one on the corner, you know? Kids and babies and all. There's an old joanna in there and someone thumps on that and we sing all the old songs. I had rum toddy last year. Got quite tiddly. On Christmas Day we go to Aunt Mag's for our dinner, we've always done that even before Ma went. Mag makes plum pudding you'd die for. There's presents and a tree and all that. But we'll open yours before we go.'

Amy had bought a soft, jade green cashmere jacket for Helen. It was feather-light and folded up almost into nothing, but it was as warm as a heavy coat. For Freda there was a bright red knitted skirt with matching mittens and cap, and a perfect scale model of a Hispano Suiza for Jim that ran jerkily on a wind-up clockwork motor.

Helen stood up and went behind the screen that hid the sink. She came out with two packages wrapped in holly-sprigged paper and laid them awkwardly beside Amy's plate.

'These are for you. This one's from me.' A soft parcel, carefully sealed. 'And this is from Freda and Jim.' A small, bundled-up package that rattled. 'It isn't very much, but make sure you think of us on Christmas morning.'

'I will,' Amy said softly.

'So what do you do?'

'Almost exactly the same thing every year, ever since I can remember.' Although that wasn't quite true. Amy could just remember Airlie's last Christmas, and that had been magical and glittering in a way that none of the others had ever matched. But Adeline loved Christmas as much as any child, and she threw herself into the preparations and the celebration itself with infectious excitement. But what celebration could there possibly be this year, without Isabel? Amy had half-expected, even half-hoped, that she would be on Christmas duty. But when the duty rota had been pinned up and the students crowded round it, she saw that she was one of the half-dozen lucky ones who had been given leave. She was free for five whole days, from Christmas Eve.

'Lovell's got the time off, of course,' Mary Morrow had said sourly. 'Wouldn't you know it?'

And so she would be going to Chance, to join her family, and Adeline's traditional house-party.

'On Christmas Eve,' she told Helen, 'there is the servants' dance. It's a big party for everyone who works in the house and on the estate. There's a tree, specially chosen from the fir copse and brought up to the house on one of the wagons. Isabel and I and our governess used to decorate it. There's a present underneath for everyone. My mother does that. She's very clever at knowing who enjoys a drink and who would rather have silk stockings than linen handkerchiefs. For the dinner, long trestle tables are laid up in the servants' hall, covered with white cloths and decorated with wreaths of holly and ivy, and my father sits at the head of one and my mother at the other. It's a proper Christmas dinner, with turkey and bread sauce and plum pudding to follow.'

Adeline thought that the traditional meal was hideously vulgar, and at her own Christmas table family and guests were served game, and the finest beef that the estate could offer, and her own favourite pudding, syllabub in crystal cups.

'After the dinner the tables are cleared away and everyone dances. My father leads off with the housekeeper, and my mother with Glass, the butler. Isabel and I take our chances with the footmen, who are always so rigid with embarrassment that they can't dance at all.' Amy paused, smiling at the thought. 'They can't wait for us to go, and leave them with the maids. My brother Richard dances with the old woman who does the plain sewing and makes her roar with laughter. Then my father makes a little speech thanking everyone for a wonderful evening, and wishes them all a merry Christmas and we tiptoe away. The party goes on for hours after that. Isabel and I . . .'

Amy broke off and looked across the table at Helen. Her friend was listening, open-mouthed with fascination. There was no trace of envy or rancour in her face. 'Go on,' she ordered. 'It's just like in a film.'

'Isabel and I walk across the park to the church. The gravel and the grass is always crackling with frost, but the church is warm. The verger has banked up the coke stove ready for early service. There are white and gold flowers on the altar, and around the pulpit and the font, and there's always a nativity scene made by the estate children with a doll in the crib and a woollen donkey. It's so quiet, utterly silent, and there's that religious smell of candles and flowers and cold stone. Last year it was just before Isabel's marriage. I remember praying for her to be happy. Oh damn.' Amy's hand came up to shade her eyes, but not before Helen had seen the tears. She heaved herself out of her chair and came to put her arm round Amy. 'Tough, isn't it?' was all she said, but Amy felt the depth of her unspoken sympathy. It comforted her at once, but at the same time shamed her. The physical touch made Helen's emaciated fragility so obvious, and yet the strength was all flowing the wrong way.

'Oh, bugger it,' Amy said, sniffing.

Helen laughed at once and let her go. 'And you supposed to be a real lady. I wish I had something stronger in the house than bloody tea. Look, it's nearly half past. Shall I yell for Jimmy to go round to the Jug for sixpenn'orth and we'll have a Christmas toast?'

Regretfully, Amy shook her head. 'I can't. I've got to be on at six. Blaine'll flay me if I get there late and reeking of drink as well, Christmas or not.'

They stood up and Helen turned on the single overhead bulb as Amy groped for her coat. The fire had burned low and they had been sitting in semi-darkness. They both winced now at the harshness of the light.

'It'll be a week, then?' Helen asked casually.

'Five days. I'll be back to see in the New Year with you.' Amy kept her voice equally casual, but a new anxiety was stabbing at her. In the bright light she saw that Helen looked ill. There were red patches on her cheekbones, and grey hollows under her eyes.

Amy suddenly thought of the fresh, sharp air at Chance and the soft beds in firelit rooms, and the tables abundantly heaped with the best of everything. How good a few days of that would be for Helen. It wouldn't be enough, but it would be something. She reached out and grabbed Helen's thin, hot hand.

'Listen. I should have thought of it before. Why don't you come with me? You, and Jim and Freda. I've taken guests for Christmas before. It won't be . . .'

'Not like us, you haven't.' Helen was laughing again. 'Are you soft? How could you turn up there with us lot? Thanks, but no. We wouldn't know where to stand or sit, and I'd be ill with the fright of it. Take me to your London house one day when there's no one about and let me have a good stare. But not to stay, love.' Seeing Amy's face she added, 'Look. You can't change anything. I'm me and you're you, and we're friends. That's enough. Don't try and pretend we're the same. We both know the difference. Just count yourself lucky you're on the right side of it.'

There was no bitterness in her words. Helen was simply matter-of-fact. Amy started to say something fierce, but Helen was quicker. 'Aw, I know you think you can do something, with all your meetings and leaflets.' Amy had told her about Appleyard Street, and had shown her the pamphlets until Helen had dismissed it with 'Your Commie tendencies are all guilt, y'know.' Helen went on now. 'But you can't. The gap's getting wider, not narrower, didn't you know? I appreciate the gesture. But I can't come home to the manor with you for Christmas.'

'I didn't ask you as a political gesture,' Amy said stiffly. 'I asked because you are my friend.'

'Nor did I refuse as a political gesture. I don't believe in politics. But it's there, isn't it? And you're my friend, as well.'

'I'd better go.' Amy pulled her cape around her.

'Here.' Helen held out the holly-wrapped packages. 'Don't go without your presents.'

In the doorway, suddenly, they hugged each other.

'Happy Christmas.'

'Happy Christmas.'

As she fled down the street towards the hospital Amy heard Helen coughing, as if she had managed to contain the spasm all the time she had been with her.

The Christmas rituals at Chance were all performed with a kind of mechanical cheerfulness that depressed Amy deeply.

The house was full of the usual shifting crowd of guests who came and went over the holiday. Gerald had mustered a quartet of friends for shooting and cards, three of them equipped with fading, powdered wives who sat in the drawing-room after dinner and listened with fascinated disapproval to the fast, cliquey gossip of Adeline's women friends. Adeline's set smoked and left the ashtrays full of lipsticked butts and drank complicated cocktails. They talked a great deal about people called Bunny and Buffy and Tiger, and laughed in flurries that baffled their powdered rural counterparts. Watching them, in her depressed mood, as they turned their long necks to listen to a new story or to sip at a champagne glass and their diamonds flashed, Amy was reminded of so many hooded cobras.

It seemed inevitable and yet sharply painful that her parents should pretend that everything was normal and as it should be. Adeline sparkled and clapped her hands to demand charades, or Clumps, or forfeits, and Gerald drank and gambled and went out all through the frosty days with the guns. She reflected that they were adept at it, after all. The keeping up of carefully controlled appearances must be more than second nature after so many years. Isabel's absence, glaring at Amy through every minute of the day, was neither spoken of nor questioned. Peter Jaspert was never mentioned either. The acceptable match and the glittering marriage might never have been made.

The cobras knew, of course, all of them. But not a word was spoken.

It was almost worse, Amy thought, the way that Isabel had just been allowed to fade away, than if they had all been talking about her. For her sister she was there in every stone of the great house and every white-rimed blade of grass across the park.

'I miss Isabel. Don't you?' she answered sharply, when Adeline complained of her long face. Surprisingly, they found themselves alone in the drawing-room in the mysterious hour between tea and the appearance of the first Lanvin sheath and white waistcoat before dinner. Amy was sunk into the depths of one of the sofas with an unopened book beside her, and Adeline was writing a letter, covering sheet after sheet of crisp blue paper with her leggy, energetic scrawl.

'Of course I miss her. So what shall we do, sit in darkness and silence until she's well again?'

'No. Just not be quite so determinedly gay, perhaps.'

263

With an exasperated shrug Adeline screwed the cap on her gold pen and folded up her letter.

'Gaiety is all there is. Without it, you might as well be in the grave, my darling one. Stop looking as if you're carrying the cares of all the world on your shoulders and who knows? You might even find that you're enjoying yourself. Not doing so won't help Isabel, in any case, will it?' When Amy didn't answer, Adeline said more patiently, 'Why don't you go and find the boys? They were making you laugh last night. I saw them. At least twice.'

By 'the boys' Adeline meant Richard and Tony Hardy. To Amy's surprise, Richard had turned up on Christmas Eve with Tony. Clearly Adeline had been expecting them both. Amy found herself placed next to Tony at dinner. They had seen each other two or three times since the night in Soho Square, but the old easiness between them had faltered a little. Yet on Christmas Eve in the ambiguous atmosphere of the servants'-hall party, Amy found herself liking him as much as ever.

The boys had indeed made her laugh. After the family and house-guests had left the dancing the three of them had gone upstairs and drunk quantities of brandy together. Richard was a natural mimic, and he had honed to perfection the set-piece of Gerald thanking the staff for another year: 'Ah . . . the family here at Chance . . . and we are a family you know, all of us, working together. Except for me, that is . . .'

Tony was the perfect, dry foil for Richard. Watching them over the rim of her glass, and all through the hours of Christmas Day with the dry headache that the brandy had given her, Amy understood why Richard's antics seemed more frenzied than ever. He didn't talk about her, but Amy knew that he was trying to fill the void that Isabel had left.

He could make everyone laugh, the cobras and their husbands and the powdered wives. Everyone except Gerald.

Now, on Boxing Night, Amy decided that Adeline was right. She would go and find the boys, and they would have a stiff drink together before the ritual of dinner. She kissed her mother, who nodded absently and went on with her animated scribbling.

Amy left the drawing-room where the footman had just stirred the fire to a fresh, scented crackle and crossed the panelled height of the hallway. The family Christmas tree stood here, a blaze of white and silver light in the dimness, tipped with a diamanté star.

A handful of unopened presents remained from the great heap that had circled it yesterday, and at the sight of them Amy put her fingers up and touched her necklace. She had unwrapped her holly-sprigged packages alone in her bedroom. Helen had hoarded discarded woollens and had painstakingly unpicked them, choosing the gentlest blues and greens that blurred together, and had knitted them up into a soft scarf. Amy wore it to church on Christmas morning. Her present from Freda and Jim was a string of blue and green glass beads to match the scarf, carefully threaded by Jim and fastened with a pretty clasp that Freda had found and saved.

Amy was thinking of the three of them now as she hesitated by the Christmas tree, and wondered if their Christmas at Auntie Mag's had been a happy one. Happier than her own at Chance, despite all the music and the exquisite food under the silver-domed dishes and the warmth of the crimson-throated log fires? Amy shivered a little. To find Richard and Tony, that was the thing, and share a large drink with them.

Instinctively she left the hall by the south door and walked quickly down a long, carpeted corridor where a colonnade of arched doors opened in summer on to the terrace. The arches were shrouded with heavy drawn curtains now and the corridor was filled with a muffled, undisturbed silence that seemed to cut it off from the rest of the great house. At the end of the corridor was a pair of intricately carved double doors that led into the orangery on the south side of the house. Amy paused, frowning slightly as she found herself in front of them and wondering why she had come here instead of any of the more obvious places.

But in the silence she pushed one of the carved doors and it swung smoothly open. At once the scent flooded out to her, a sharp reminder. Isabel and she had played for hours in the orangery as children. Breathing in the memories, Amy slipped inside.

The Chance orangery had been built in the eighteenth century in a severely classical style, with a long span of white-arched columns echoing the corridor that led to it. The house wall was lined with niches for prim classical statuary, and the floor was tiled with severe black and white marble blocks. But overhead the arches soared into a magnificent ogee-shaped glass roof, and in summer the sun poured into the orangery with almost tropical splendour. The Lovells who had built it had intended a fashionable adjunct where the ladies could parade gently in inclement weather, the trains of their dresses swishing gently on the marble floor, and it had stayed that way for almost a hundred and fifty years. But Gerald's Victorian grandfather had been a traveller and a plantsman, and he had made the orangery his own. Over a long lifetime he had filled it with his botanical trophies until the arching fronds of palm trees brushed the glass roof, and the strange tendrils of sub-tropical creepers snaked treacherously across the floor. The old man had designed the ingenious stove-house that heated his domain, and in the warmth the orchids with strange, sticky, pungent blooms flourished alongside weird growths that oozed with resinous gum. A family of greenfinches twittered and swooped in the thickening jungle.

Amy prowled down the central avenue, absorbing the scents of rich, dark earth and dripping leaves. The thick foliage swallowed the sound of her footsteps and the glass space around her was alive with other noises, the rustle of unfurling leaves and peeling bark, and the flutter of the finches. Like all the rest of the festive house the orangery was brightly lit, electric lamps flaring in sconces on the house wall. But the greenness dimmed it, and outside the pitch darkness pressed against the glass, misted and dribbled with condensation. Amy was about to turn away again, out of the oppressive air, when somebody spoke.

She looked, and saw them in the little bay at the end of the orangery. There was a white-painted scrolled iron seat under a tree that hung green fingers down to hide it. Beside the seat was a stone statue of Pan, holding the pipes to his lips, with green moss clinging to the stone furrows of his beard.

Tony and Richard were facing each other, as if they had just stood up to continue their stroll and had paused to exchange a last remark. Amy opened her mouth to call out to them, and then she felt the hair lift at the nape of her neck and in the heat a cold, slow trickle run down her spine.

'I don't give a damn where we are,' Richard said clearly. 'Or a bugger, for that matter.'

'I know that,' Tony said. His voice was low, but something in it reminded her of Soho Square and the plane trees black against the indigo sky. By contrast the orangery felt clammy and the reek of it suffocated her.

266

'Well, then,' Richard said, and Amy heard Tony's answer, 'Not here.'

But they were still standing facing each other, and Tony reached out for Richard's wrist and held it, and then he pressed the inner side against his cheek. Then, with a small movement as if his head and neck hurt him intolerably, Tony turned his face so that his mouth was pressed against the veins of Richard's wrist. Richard was looking at Tony as she had never seen him look at anyone before, with all the posturing animation drained away, as vulnerable as a child and yet not a child at all any longer. With his free hand he touched Tony's bent head, and then Tony looked up and their eyes met.

Amy stood rigid, listening to the whispering leaves and the insistent drip of condensation. She was aching to move, to be anywhere else in the world, but she was transfixed. She was longing to be blind and deaf, but every movement and sound was painfully magnified.

The chink of green air between the two familiar profiles had closed. She saw Richard's hand again, with the crested gold ring he wore on his little finger, moving to touch Tony's cheek in a gesture of almost unbearable tenderness. It was the most fleeting of kisses, but it was the longest second Amy had ever known. When it was gone, everything had changed. It was as if the orangery with its snaking tendrils and weird blossoms had shaken, and all the world beyond it, to jolt the pieces of a puzzle she had only been able to glance at. The shudder had slid the pieces into place, and Amy saw the picture now with all its depths of shade and rolling contours. What had been flat and coarsely black and white before was suddenly grained with infinite subtlety. In all the surge of feelings that followed, she tasted humiliation at her own hopeless, naïve yearnings for Tony Hardy, and the opposite relief of understanding at last why he had seemed to reject her.

But Richard? What did it mean for Richard? The new landscape lurched, threateningly steep, as Amy thought of her father, and then without warning of Airlie, proud in his Sam Browne belt.

Amy looked past the vivid picture and realized that Richard and Tony were watching her. Richard was angry and in Tony's face she read sympathy and an echo of her own relief. She lifted her chin and squared her shoulders deliberately.

'Don't think I was spying on you. I wasn't. I'm going now. I didn't see anything. I don't know anything about it.'

She turned and walked back up the green-arched aisle to the carved doors, and she closed them firmly behind her. Her hands and legs were trembling as she walked on. *Was that the right thing to have done? Was that what they would have wanted?*

As she retraced her steps down the silent corridor and past the glittering tree Amy felt the layers of security and comfortable childhood assumptions drop painfully away. She was afraid suddenly that she didn't know anything, or anybody. Not her own sister and brother, certainly not her mother and father, or any of the truths that mattered about Tony Hardy, or Moira O'Hara, or any of the people who filled her days. All she knew were little, trivial things, and attitudes solidified in her through privilege and habit. Helen Pearce in her dim basement room, existing on her terrible diet of penny buns and tea, knew a thousand times more than she did.

Amy went slowly up the grand staircase, feeling the smooth-rubbed wood of the banister curve and twist upwards under her hand. She opened the door of her room and saw the folds of her evening dress laid out ready by the maid. Her evening slippers stood side by side, ready for her to step into them. Amy wanted to laugh, but she wanted to cry even more. She knew, as she stood there staring at her satin shoes, that she was experiencing her first moment of adult loneliness. There was nowhere to hide, or anyone to run to so that her hurt could be rubbed better. She had only herself, and here and now.

Amy wasn't going to let herself cry.

Instead she went to her jewel case and took out a pair of diamanté pendant earrings that she had dismissed as too flamboyant. She clipped them on to her ears and then she wound her hair up to leave her long neck bare. She put the pretty pastel-coloured dress back in her wardrobe and took out a slim black one that flared around her calves. Sitting in front of her mirror, she painted her mouth and rubbed colour on to her cheeks with the little pink puff from its gilt case. Then she looked at herself once more in the mirror, seeing a red-lipped stranger with very bright eyes, and went down to the drawing-room for cocktails before dinner.

Later, fortified by gin and wedged in her place at the dinner table, she looked down the polished length of it and saw Richard, relentlessly amusing his neighbours. Tony was opposite her, turning his glass round in his fingers. She smiled at him, a smile of perfectly normal friendliness, and gave her attention back to her neighbour on the left-hand side. From her place at the foot of her table, Adeline nodded her approval of her daughter's bright new demeanour.

Gaiety is all there is. Well, Amy thought. She would give it a try.

She had understood something tonight, and understood it with startling clarity. She couldn't live Isabel's life for her, or Richard's for him. She had only her own. And with the knowledge of that, to compensate her for the new, chilly loneliness, Amy thought that she had gained the first, durable shell of maturity.

In the morning she went into the billiards room where Richard and Tony were lounging against the big green table, and kissed them both goodbye. Then Adeline's chauffeur drove her to the local station in the Bentley and Amy caught the London train. From Euston she plunged into the grimy clatter of the Underground with her thoughts already fixed on the Royal Lambeth.

There was always work, Amy told herself.

For the next weeks, with the rest of her set, Amy worked an eighteen-hour day. The crucial first batch of examinations was looming ahead of them.

'I'll never make it,' Moira groaned. 'I might just as well head back to Mother Ireland now. Perhaps I could get myself a little job in the draper's in Portair.'

'Don't be so spineless,' Amy retorted. 'And if you're not going to do your own work, at least shut up and let me get on with mine.'

'I don't know what's come over you, Lovell. You used to be such a normal person. Got to come top, have you?'

'I just want to pass these exams,' Amy told her with an attempt at patience. 'I need something to go right, just now.'

Moira looked shrewdly at her. 'How's your sister?'

'The same.'

Isabel didn't want to leave Thorogood House. Adeline showed signs of winning her battle with Peter Jaspert for Isabel's guardianship, but when she had mentioned Lausanne and Dr Ahrends, Isabel had said in her quiet, firm way, 'I want to stay here.' She

269

had made a friend of one of the other patients, and they sat in the day room together and walked in the grounds under the dripping rhododendron trees.

Amy and Richard went to see her, and came away silenced by Isabel's remoteness. They travelled back to London and had dinner together at Bruton Street, but they never mentioned the orangery. Yet Amy felt that Richard held her less firmly at arm's length than before. As their concern for Isabel drew them closer Richard tried less hard to be witty and surprising and let her occasionally glimpse his inner, reflective self. Amy loved her brother very much. Resolutely she had convinced herself that it wasn't abnormal for boys to have love-affairs with other boys. The judgement made her feel sage and mature. It was a phase that Richard would surely grow out of, and then he would marry and have children like everyone else. More than like everyone else, because Richard's children would be Lovells. And Tony Hardy wasn't difficult to love. She knew that, painfully well, herself. If Tony was truly homosexual – well, he had his own life too. Even with her new maturity Amy couldn't bring herself to speculate beyond that. After Christmas at Chance Tony didn't write to her or telephone again, and she accepted it sadly as she had accepted her loneliness.

The weeks dragged and then accelerated past towards the examinations. Amy had worked to the point where she felt nauseated by the sight of her file of lecture notes and dreamed at night of burns that she had forgotten how to dress and boils that swelled under her fingers.

There was little time for anything, even visiting Helen. In the few, snatched times that they spent together Amy was distressed by Helen's listlessness and by the cough that had taken hold of her yet again.

Once, not expected, she came plodding down the street through drifting snow that piled against the steps and capped the black area railings. The door to Helen's basement room was ajar and she was pushing it open as she heard Helen shout, 'Look at it. Get out, will you? Go away. Don't come back. I hate you. All of it.' Thoroughly alarmed, Amy went in. To her astonishment there were only Freda and Jim, white-faced, and Helen at the table with her head in her hands. On the rubbed, faded linoleum were the tracks of dirty, melting snow that the excited children had tramped in with them. Hand in hand they pushed past her and escaped into the harsh white light again. The door slammed dully.

Amy went behind the screen at the sink and brought out a bucket and a floorcloth. Carefully she dried and polished the floor, and when she had finished she went and put her arm around Helen.

'I don't hate them,' Helen said, her voice muffled by her hair and hands. 'They're everything in the world, and I bloody yell at them every hour of the day. They'd be better off on the parish, anyway.'

Amy stroked her hair back, feeling how hot she was. 'Hush. You're tired. And ill, you know that. I think you should be in hospital again.'

'No.'

'Please, Helen.'

'It's winter, or haven't you noticed? Who's going to find the money to feed them and keep them warm while I lie in bed?'

'I will,' Amy said quietly.

'No, thanks.'

Helen hadn't even paused to think and the abruptness of her rejection stung Amy.

'Why not? Don't be so selfish. Why kill yourself out of pride?'

There was a long, quiet moment. Then Helen said, 'You don't know everything, do you? If pride was all you had, you'd know better than to say that. People like you make me laugh.'

Then Amy understood how close to the edge Helen had come. She bit back the sudden fear and said gently, 'Don't argue with me as well. Shall I put the kettle on?'

Helen shrugged with exhaustion. 'There isn't any milk.'

Amy went out to the dark, cramped and pungent-smelling shop at the corner and bought a basket of supplies. When she came back she made Helen a cup of tea sweetened with condensed milk, just as she liked it, and a piece of bread and butter that her friend didn't even touch. Amy said nothing, but, remembering what Helen had done once before when she was there, put a hambone with some chopped carrots and onions in a pan and left it on the ring to simmer for soup. There would be something for Freda and Jim when they came in again, and perhaps the savoury smell would tempt Helen.

271

'Where have they gone?' Amy asked, and Helen smiled lop-sidedly.

'Mag's, I should think. Oh, they won't be huddled in a doorway somewhere, if that's what you're thinking. They can take care of themselves, if they have to. Don't worry.'

'It isn't Jim and Freda I'm worrying about.'

'Thanks.' Helen didn't even have the energy to smile.

When the time came Amy had to force herself to leave and make her way up the deserted street once more. It was snowing again, wet flakes driven cruelly by the wind. She would have to come much more often, every day if possible, and at least she could bring food. Helen had accepted the first basket, that was something.

If pride was all you had, you'd know better than to say that. The words dinned in Amy's head as she put on her starched uniform again.

The exams came, almost an anti-climax after the build-up that the students had given them. Amy wrote her papers, ruthlessly clearing her head of everything else before each one. She went through her practical tests under the granite stares of Blaine and the sister tutor, never confusing a pressure dressing with a burn dressing and bandaging crooked legs in perfect overlapping layers.

The results appeared with surprising speed. The sister pinned up a typewritten list on the faded green baize-covered board in the study hall ante-room. Dorothy Hewitt's name headed it, to nobody's surprise, but Amy's was immediately beneath.

'Well done, Lovell,' breathed Moira O'Hara in awed admir-ation.

Mary Morrow was standing nearby, looking at her own name halfway down the list. She turned sharply towards them. 'Are congratulations really in order? If they've got themselves a precious candidate like Lovell, they're not going to let her come bottom, are they now?'

'I would have thought so, just to prove their egalitarian prin-ciples,' Moira retorted. 'Lovell doesn't get any privileges. She's scrubbed as many sluice-rooms as you.'

Amy put her hand on Moira's arm and dragged her away still protesting over her shoulder at Morrow.

'Why didn't you speak up for yourself?' Moira demanded indignantly. 'I've never heard anything like the old cow.'

Amy shrugged, pretending indifference. 'Why bother?' But she had seen the naked resentment in Mary Morrow's face and it had shocked her. It was hard, Amy thought, to be hated just for being in the place you had been born in, and not for anything to do with yourself at all.

Amy was given a silver pin for her apron, and Dorothy Hewitt received the gold one from Sister Tutor herself. New student intakes were already coming up behind their set, and the drudgery of hours spent carbolizing bedsteads and brushing mattresses passed to them. There was more proper nursing, and less numbing exhaustion from sheer physical overwork. Even Moira O'Hara could begin to believe that she might, after all, reach the dizzy grandeur of State Registered Nurse.

Not very many nights after receiving her silver pin, Amy woke up to someone knocking on the door of her room. It was an insistent tapping, not loud enough to wake anyone else, and although she ached to plunge her head back under the pillows, Amy was already awake enough to know that it wouldn't stop or go away until she answered it.

'Moira?' she mumbled. 'Sa'matter?'

The tapping went on. She would have to get out of bed and open the door. Amy stumbled to it and jerked it open, ready to hiss a protest at whoever it was. Standing outside was a girl from her set, fully dressed in uniform and with her cape wrapped around her. She glanced up and down the corridor as if she was afraid that she might have been followed and then gasped, breathless with running, 'I'm on nights on Talbot. I've come over in my break. There's a friend of yours been brought in and she's calling for you.'

The corridor went cold, and the blackness seemed to thicken around them.

'Helen,' Amy said mechanically. 'Is it Helen?' In her head she was already planning what she would have to do. Dress in her uniform, pull her cap on. Duck across and into the hospital as if she was on duty, and up to Talbot on the sixth floor. Talbot was the isolation and fever ward. Why was Helen there, instead of down on the chest ward?

'Pearce, her name is,' the other nurse told her. 'She's bad. I

273

thought I'd better come. Lovell, I've got to get back now I've told you . . .'

'Wait. Who's the staff on Talbot tonight?'

'Corcoran.'

That wasn't so bad. Corcoran was slow-moving, and kind-hearted. Amy had worked with her and earned her approval.

'Tell Helen I'm coming.' The other nurse was already running, skidding out of sight around the angle of the corridor. 'Thanks,' Amy whispered after her. Her heart was thudding as she pulled on her uniform and her breath was tangling in her chest as she wrestled with the ridiculous buttons. *She's bad. She's bad.*

The hostel night porter was asleep in his cubicle. Amy ran through the icy wind and reached the hospital nurses' entrance, and then made herself slow down as she reached the second porter in his box. She put her fingers up to the starched wings of her cap and then breathed in to steady her voice. The porter glanced up at her curiously, knowing that no one came on or off duty at two in the morning.

'Two short on Talbot tonight,' Amy said. 'So they've pulled me in. And I've already done eight today.' The man nodded, commiserating, and turned back to his folded newspaper. Amy walked briskly past him, and once out of sight she ran at the stairs counting the steps blankly in her head. *Sixth floor. Which way?* Her friend was hovering at the double doors, a box of fresh dressings in her hand.

'Isolation four,' she directed her. 'Corcoran's down the main ward. I'm supposed to be watching your friend.'

Amy glided past the grim isolation cubicles until she came to number four. Inside the bare box Helen was lying on her side, her thin hand hooked like a claw over the white sheet. She didn't speak or move her head. Amy knelt at the side of the bed so that their eyes were level and they looked at each other. Helen's eyes were like dark holes and the blood had sunk out of her face to leave her lips as white as the sheets. Gently Amy touched her hand. She realized at the touch that Helen was going to die, here in this bare cream room, without even the photograph of Freda and Jim beside her.

Impotent fury flared in Amy as she looked wildly around. There was nothing on the locker except a covered sputum bowl. She snatched up the chart from the foot of the bed and read off the height of Helen's fever. Dr Davis had been in at eleven-thirty

274

and had gone away again, almost certainly to bed. There was nothing they could do for Helen, and so they had left her out of the way here, alone. But for a junior nurse who had broken the rules to run for Amy, Helen would have died as isolated as she had lived. Amy knelt again and looked into the white face. Helen's eyes were filmed, and she couldn't be sure that she even knew Amy had come at last.

'Helen,' she whispered, 'it's Amy. Don't go.' The eyes didn't even flicker.

Cold anger made Amy feel stiff and dry. She knelt in silence, her back rigid, listening to the night noises of the hospital and thinking it was like a great unsensing machine. She hated the hospital, and everything outside it as well for the waste of Helen Pearce.

Footsteps squeaked up to the door of the room, but Amy didn't turn her head and they retreated again after a moment's pause. Gently Amy slid her arm under Helen's shoulders so that her head was cradled, and laid her own head close to it. Helen seemed to be looking nowhere, staring at blankness. The minutes passed slowly, and Amy felt the anger solidifying inside her like a rock. There would be no starting again for Helen, no hope that tomorrow would be happier, or different, or fairer. No anything.

Her head lay heavily on Amy's arms, and the circulation tingled and shot tiny points of pain into Amy's fingers, reminding her bitterly of her own vitality.

Amy felt the spasm as it first stirred in Helen's chest. It gathered force terrifyingly, shaking her as if the bed, the whole room was moving instead of just the emaciated body lying in it. The cough never broke free of the tattered lungs. Instead the blood came, first a black gob of it that slid between Helen's lips before her mouth opened and the red bubbled out, flecked with foam and spreading over the pillow and into her black hair.

Amy never moved.

The pool of bright blood engulfed them both, soaking the starched cuffs of Amy's uniform and trickling warm and sticky under her cheek as she held Helen in her arms. Outside the room the night noises of the hospital went on without faltering until at last the blood stopped rushing. Amy felt the last, shallow flutter of breath.

She looked into the dark eyes again and saw that Helen was still staring into blankness. Slowly, with infinite gentleness, Amy

275

slid her arm from under the head that had suddenly grown unbearably heavy. Blood had soaked her sleeve and glued her fingers, and her hand felt bloated and heavy with cramp. Carefully Amy wiped her hand clean on her crackling apron and then with white, creased fingertips she closed Helen's eyes. 'I'm sorry,' she said, and her own voice shook her in the infinite silence contained inside the shabby cream walls.

Behind her the cubicle door opened. As if from a long way off, Amy heard the crisp rustle of uniforms. 'Who's this? Nurse? Lovell, what are you doing on the ward?'

It was Staff Nurse Corcoran, followed by a sister, a nurse Amy didn't know. Behind them Amy glimpsed Mary Morrow, shocked fascination and righteous expectation mingled in equal parts in her expression. Morrow must be the other junior on duty tonight. It was Morrow who had brought the staff and sister, of course.

'Lovell?' It was the sister. Hospital discipline was affronted. Amy would have to explain herself. The inappropriateness of it, with Helen's closed face still warm under her hands, made the core of anger set still harder.

'She's my friend,' Amy said. 'She's dead.'

The staff nurse was already moving, lifting Helen and turning her in the soaked scarlet mess of sheets. The sister stared at Amy as if she was struck dumb by the towering height of her misconduct.

'She's dead,' Amy shouted. 'What do your bloody petty rules matter?'

'Lovell,' the woman repeated sharply, 'before you leave this room you will tell me exactly what happened with this patient.'

They were laying Helen flat. Mary Morrow was bending over her, putting her arms straight and then covering her poor face with the sheet. Amy wanted to drag them away from her bedside, to wash the blood herself and then to sit with Helen in the silent room. But they wouldn't let her do even that. Of course they wouldn't let her.

In a hard, unwavering voice Amy told them what they wanted to know. The sister nodded, her little mouth pursed even tighter.

'Very well. You will come with me to my office while I put this in the night book. You will sign the report, and so will I and Staff Nurse Corcoran. Then the front hall porter will escort you back to the hostel, and you will stay there until you have seen Matron . . .'

The little recital went on. Amy closed her ears and found she could just control the anger. The black rock was swelling inside her and threatening to burst out. *She's dead*, her own voice echoed in her head, silently answering the sister. *She's dead, curse you all* . . .

Amy carried the rock with her to the sister's office, and then back through the freezing darkness to the hostel. Once she was alone in her room she sat down on the upright chair, her head bent. She was staring down at her sleeves and apron where the blood was drying, brown and stiff.

'Helen,' Amy whispered again, 'I'm sorry.'

She was apologizing for the indignity of death in the Royal Lambeth Hospital, and for her own part in that. Much more, she was apologizing from her heart for the unfairness that had left Amy sitting warm and alive while Helen's face was covered by a hospital sheet. The great, unfair gulf had always been there. Helen had seen it and she had never resented it, while Amy had naïvely tried to pretend that it didn't exist. They would never bridge it now. Amy remembered that she had never even taken Helen to Bruton Street as she had promised. She had, after all, allowed their friendship to lie in its watertight hole as if she was ashamed of it.

'No,' Amy said angrily. 'Never.' The first tears fell on her apron, and darkened the brown blood all over again.

Amy had fallen asleep at last in her soiled uniform. When the terrified new student came in the morning to summon her to the matron, Amy had to change her clothes. Instead of hurrying she moved deliberately, as if each familiar action was of vital, separate importance. She stood in the matron's office for half an hour. All she could remember afterwards was her feeling of incredulity that this catalogue of her professional shortcomings was being delivered in the face of Helen's death.

Amy was warned that her failure to report Helen's haemorrhage to the senior nurse was gravely negligent. Her very presence on the ward, unsupervised, was an act of sabotage.

'Do you have anything to say?' the matron asked.

Amy checked the thousand things that might have spilled out. 'She was my friend,' she said. The matron's expression didn't flicker. So friendship didn't count then. At length Amy heard

277

that the Royal Lambeth Hospital was not proposing to deprive her of her studentship. She was to hand back her silver pin, and she was to forfeit so many days' leave. That was all.

A student nurse had broken all the rules and had been reprimanded and punished. The great machine that was the Royal Lambeth sailed majestically on.

And Helen was dead.

Helen was buried in the churchyard of St Saviour's Church, Lambeth. Amy couldn't attend the funeral. It took place at three in the afternoon, when she was on the afternoon shift.

At six o'clock, when her duty ended, she put on her cape and left the hospital, walking rapidly through the freezing slush. The church stood in an unlit cul-de-sac off a much smaller side street, the bulk of its tower black against the livid city sky. The graveyard gate was open. It was a small enclosure, surrounded on three sides by crowded terraces and separated from a bare playground on the third by a rusting wire fence.

The graveyard was almost full. Amy walked past the headstones to the last row, where there was a mound of raw earth and ice. There were two or three bunches of flowers on the earth. One was a little posy, its label already sodden with damp: 'To our dear Helen, ever your loveing Freda and Jim.'

Amy stood with her head bent. She had brought no flowers.

Somewhere close at hand a train rattled by. It would be full of office workers on their way home, looking forward to food and their firesides after another day.

No more days for Helen.

Amy bent down to feel the earth. It was heavy and sticky, and the cold seemed to touch through to her bones. For a moment she crouched there, frozen herself, and then another train passed. This time Amy glimpsed the chain of yellow lights between the houses. Stiffly she stood up again. It was still anger rather than grief that weighed her down. But there was nothing to keep her in the sooty graveyard. Helen had gone. Amy turned away from the icy earth and the chilled flowers and walked back between the headstones to the gate and the roadway.

The old street where Helen had lived was close at hand. Amy came down the area steps and saw that there was a light in the window. She tapped on the door and it was opened a crack by a small, wiry woman who stared defensively out at her.

'I'm Helen's friend, Amy Lovell. I couldn't come to the church this afternoon.'

The crack widened a little, but not enough to let her in.

'Are you Aunt Mag? I came to see if I could do anything. Are Freda and Jim there?'

At last Mag opened the door and Amy followed her into the room. Freda and Jim were sitting side by side on the truckle-bed. The blankets had been removed and were folded in a neat, threadbare pile. Glancing into the cupboard room beyond, Amy saw that the big bed Helen and Freda had shared was similarly stripped. The mantelpiece was bare of its plush cover and the precious photographs. Even the glass shade had been removed from the single light.

'What's going to happen?' Amy asked.

Mag stuck her hands in the pockets of her print apron. 'I won't let them go on the parish,' she said. 'Not in that orphanage. They'll come 'ome with me for as long as I can manage. Freda'll be old enough to bring in a bit herself, soon.' Mag saw Amy's troubled glance at their dismantled home. 'They can't stay 'ere, can they?'

Amy tried to look at the children. They shrank closer together, not wanting to meet her eyes. Jim's face was grimy and reddened where he had rubbed at the tears with his knuckles.

Amy had been Helen's friend, not theirs. To them, in spite of the presents, the glass beads and the clockwork car and the red cap and skirt, she belonged to the other side. She represented power and authority just because of the way she looked and spoke, and all three of them were wary of her. It was hard, Amy thought, with sudden bitterness. She remembered Mary Morrow and then with vivid clarity she saw Nick Penry, with his black hair and blue-scarred hands, in the nursery at Bruton Street.

'I'd like to help,' she said abruptly. None of them looked at her. 'If money would help . . .' The clumsiness of it stirred her anger again.

'Nah,' Mag said quickly. 'We'll manage, won't we? Freda? Jim?'

It was exactly the same rapid rejection that Helen herself had dealt her. People like you make me laugh, Helen had said. And: If all you've got is your pride . . .

Amy opened her handbag and took out a piece of paper. She wrote on it her name and the hostel address, and the address of the Bruton Street house as well, and then she folded it up and gave it to Mag. Mag put the paper in her apron pocket.

'If you change your mind,' Amy said into the silence.

She turned to go, looking around the room for the last time. The screen that Helen had used to hide the sink was folded up, exposing the buckets and a little zinc bath. On the floor in the middle of the room was a cardboard suitcase, open, with Helen's few clothes folded in it. On the top was the green cashmere jacket.

'You gave her that, didn't you?' Mag said. 'Do you want to take it?'

Amy stood stock-still. The anger that she had carried with her since Helen's death was suddenly gone. It was futile to be angry, with the hospital or the world outside it or with Helen herself for leaving so abruptly. And in place of the anger came grief, swooping and choking.

She shook her head blindly. 'No. You wear it. Helen would want that.' Somehow she crossed the room, passing the truckle-bed. She wanted to hug Freda and Jim but their hunched shoulders and averted faces rejected her still. Instead she reached and just touched Freda's tangled hair with her fingertips. 'Goodbye Jim, Freda. If you need me . . .'

Amy knew that she wouldn't see them again. She reached the door, opened it and closed it again, and climbed the steps into the streaming street.

In the darkness she cried. The wind whipped the tears and stung her face as the grief took hold of her and she cried for the pity of everything. It seemed to Amy then that the quicksands were engulfing Helen and swallowing her up as if her years had never been. In a single day the home and everything she had fought and scrubbed for had been folded into a suitcase and carried away.

Nor was it just Helen that Amy cried for. It was for Isabel and the baby Peter, for Richard and Tony, her mother and father, and for Nick Penry and his wife and child.

And then she heard Helen's voice, as clearly as if she was walking beside her huddled against the wind.

'Tough, isn't it? At least you're on the right side of it.'

That's what she would have said. They were still there, Freda and Jim and Mag and Amy herself, and so they were on the right side of it. Nor had the quicksands swallowed Helen. They would remember her. Amy could only grope at the idea through her sorrow, but she already understood that for the rest of her life at times that truly mattered she would act or think in a particular way because that was what Helen Pearce would have done.

Amy reached the hostel door. The porter peered at her and then reached for his book for her to initial. Amy was not allowed to be out after eight o'clock without the matron's specific permission. Tonight she signed herself in without having to swallow her usual anger at such pettiness. She was still shackled by the fact that Helen was dead.

In her pigeonhole a batch of envelopes was waiting for her from the afternoon's post. They were thick, cream or white envelopes addressed to the Honble Amy Lovell in confident black handwriting and mostly forwarded from Bruton Street. She knew that they all contained invitations, engraved and gilt-edged, for dances and dinners. Usually Amy wrote her well-schooled formal refusal. Tonight she picked up the sheaf of them and dropped them into the waste-bin unopened. Then she went on up the dingy stairs to her room.

Part Three

Part Three

11

Nantlas, 1933

Mari climbed the steep stairs, lifting each foot as if it hurt her, and ducked under the low lintel into Dickon's tiny room. He hadn't moved since she had left him to go down and warm his food. Mari sat down in her place beside the bed and stirred the contents of the bowl, then held a spoonful out to him.

'Come on now, Dickon *bach*,' she coaxed. 'Eat this for your mam, will you?'

The little boy's head seemed too heavy on his thin neck for him to lift it off the pillow, but when the smell of the potatoes reached him he pushed the spoon away. Mari stared at him, dry-eyed with desperation.

'You must eat something, lovely. You won't get better if you don't eat.'

Dickon made no response, but he kept his eyes fixed on his mother. Even before his illness he had been small for his eight years, and now his body was shrivelled and brittle. His eyes seemed to have shrunk into a bony helmet.

'Dickon?' She held the spoon again, invitingly.

Mari knew from the long years of caring for him that Dickon understood what she was saying. His way of answering had always been by look and touch, even though he had proudly mastered a dozen or so important words as well as 'Mam' and 'Daa-ad' and 'More'.

In the last years, under her patient, repetitive tuition, Dickon had learned to feed himself and even to keep himself clean and dry. Mari had begun to hope that against all the odds he might go on improving, might even one day be capable of living a sheltered life of his own. But with the illness he had slipped back into helpless infancy. Mari had to boil the old copper every day for the heavy washing, and she fed him in slow spoonfuls like a baby.

285

Dickon was looking at her now, and telling her explicitly that he couldn't eat the food. She glanced down at the waxy chunks of potato in the thin, greyish liquid and felt a surge of exhausted anger. She didn't want to eat it herself, and she was fit and well. She put the bowl down, out of sight beside the bed, and straightened the pillows behind Dickon's head.

'All right then.' She smiled at him brightly. 'I'll make us both a cup of tea. With conny milk, just like you like it best. There's a tin that your nan brought.'

'Yes.' Dickon said in his slurred voice. Mari knew that he wanted to agree, to please her. She turned away abruptly so that he wouldn't see the tears. Fear of losing him had begun to possess every hour that Mari was conscious, the fear even stronger than her impotent anger and bitterness.

'Here's your dad,' she called from the top of the stairs, hearing Nick's boots in the entry.

'Daa-ad.' There was pleasure in the child's voice. When Nick went up to him, he would hold out his arms for his father's hug. Mari was Dickon's limbs and tongue, but Nick was the sun in his sky. Mari woud once have smiled at the thought, but now her face was stiff and cold.

'How is he?'

Nick was standing aside from the foot of the stairs to let Mari come down, because there was no room for them to pass in the steep space.

'The same. He's eaten nothing.'

They passed without looking at each other, and Nick went up the stairs. Mari made tea, spooning condensed milk recklessly into Dickon's special cup. When she took the cups upstairs she found Nick sitting with his arm around Dickon while with his free hand he drew charcoal pictures on the backs of old handbills. Dickon's face was faintly flushed with pink and he was laughing his funny, braying laugh. Mari silently gave them their tea and drank her own downstairs while she was waiting for the washing water to boil on the reluctant fire.

When Nick reappeared she was in the tiny scullery, feeding wet sheets from a tin bucket through the wooden mangle.

'He's asleep. He seems better today,' Nick said carefully. When Mari didn't answer he went on. 'I think he's on the mend. Perhaps that doctor didn't know what he was on about.'

'He knew what he knew,' Mari said. 'And that was that he

couldn't do anything for him. And that he won't get better without the specialist.'

It was old, painful ground. They had covered and recovered it a hundred times. Mari had wrapped Dickon in an old shawl, Nick had lifted him, too easily, and they had carried him to the Ferndale bus. At the end of the journey, after gritting their teeth at every jolt, they had seen an old doctor, a friend of Myfanwy Jones, the midwife. Nick and Mari had watched anxiously as the doctor examined Dickon, running his square hands over his tiny body and peering into his mouth and eyes with a small light.

After the examination, the old man had frowned and eased himself upright, pulling the points of his waistcoat down over his stomach.

'I'm a country quack, that's all,' he told them. 'I'd say it's a kind of progressive blood deficiency, some form of pernicious anaemia perhaps.' He had explained again quickly, using simple words in case they hadn't understood him, and Nick had frowned at the assumption. Mari had touched his arm warningly.

'But you shouldn't take my word for it,' the doctor rumbled on. 'Anyway, I couldn't treat him properly. With children like this, any diagnosis and treatment is complicated. There's a big man in Cardiff now, a blood specialist. I could write him a letter for you. I don't know how you're placed . . .'

And the kindly doctor had broken off and looked at the shawl Dickon had been wrapped in, at Mari's tight dress that was faded under the arms and at the seams, and at Nick's decaying boots.

'Thank you,' Nick had said stiffly. 'We'll manage. If you would write the letter for us. And your own bill, if you would . . .'

The doctor had turned away to wash his hands. 'There's no charge. I'm glad to do it, for Myfanwy Jones.'

So Nick and Mari had wrapped Dickon up again and carried the uncomplaining bundle back on the bus to Nantlas.

The doctor's letter in its stiff, white envelope still stood on the mantelpiece, tucked safely behind the Barry Island china mug. They had as much hope of finding the money to see the big man in Cardiff as they had of retiring in comfort to the Gower peninsula.

'He seems better today,' Nick repeated. He was struggling to convince himself, Mari knew that. She had tried the same thing herself, and she had failed. The truth was that Dickon wouldn't get better, not without the help that they couldn't afford. She didn't answer, and went on turning the handle of the mangle so that the wooden rollers clamped on the sheets and sent the water dripping and splashing into the enamel bowl set underneath.

Nick stood awkwardly for a moment with his arms dangling at his sides, and then took a single step so that he was beside her. He put his arms around her waist and rested his cheek against her hair, pulling her towards him.

'Mari,' he murmured. 'It will be all right. Dickon will be all right.'

His wilful blindness pierced Mari's shell of control. She let go of the handle of the mangle and it swung backwards, clanking. The sheets fell and dragged on the gritty floor, and she just let them lie. Her resentment of him, her bitterness and her despondency boiled up inside her and it seemed for an instant that she hated Nick Penry and all their life together. She snatched at his sleeve, her white face frightening him.

'Come here,' she hissed at him. 'With me.' Still gripping his sleeve, Mari dragged Nick through the back kitchen to the foot of the stairs. Half-pulling and half-dragging, she made him follow her up to Dickon's room. Only when she had knelt down beside the low bed did she let him go, because she was turning back the sheet and worn blankets that covered the sleeping child.

'Look,' she whispered to Nick. 'Just look at him. You think he's getting better?'

Her hands were shaking as she undid the buttons of the child's pyjamas. They were Nick's last pair, cut down, and they flapped pathetically as the boy stirred in his sleep. Mari pulled the folds of them away from Dickon's chest. The ribs stood out under the white skin as sharp as knife-handles.

Mari did up the buttons one by one, and covered him up again. Then she stooped and picked up the bowl of cold potatoes.

'See this? See? He hasn't eaten anything for two days. Two days, Nick. And are you surprised, when this muck is all I have to give him? He should be having eggs, and fruit, and little bits of chicken and rich gravy to tempt him, and proper soups full of goodness, not this old dishwater . . .'

Watching her, Nick thought with shocked detachment that the old, sensual vitality he had loved in his wife had drained down into this one lascivious recital of all the good things that they couldn't give to their sick son.

'We're lucky to have what we've got,' he said quietly. 'Some don't have even that much.'

'I don't care about some. I care about us. No, not us. Not you, Nick. I care about Dickon. I don't want him to die just because of you.' Mari was almost screaming, the high, hysterical note in her voice cutting through Nick like a wire. Behind her, he saw Dickon's wide-open terrified eyes.

'Don't frighten the boy,' he said.

Mari broke off at once and knelt down to soothe Dickon. 'There, lamb,' she murmured. 'Your dad's set me off again. You go back to sleep and take no notice.'

Dickon's eyelids fluttered as he drifted into sleep again. Silently they crept down to the kitchen and Mari closed the door on the stairs.

'What do you want me to do?' Nick asked.

Mari smiled, a thin, down-turning smile that aged her already lined face. 'Where have you been?' she demanded.

Nick sighed, knowing what was coming. 'Mari . . .' he began, but she cut him short.

'Where?'

'I've been to a meeting. The Associated Collieries rate per ton is being cut again. For God's sake, they'll be asking the lads to pay for the privilege, next, of dragging the bloody coal out of the ground for them. Half of the lads want to sit down and take it because any rate is better than nothing, and they're drifting away into the pit unions faster and faster because they think they'll hold on to their few shillings that way. Christ, Mari, the Fed's all we've got and we've got to make them see that nothing will ever get better for us unless they stick to it. It matters more than ever now.'

The fervour for workers' solidarity that had always galvanized Nick still reverberated in his voice, but Mari read the bleakness in his face. Even Nick was beginning to lose heart. He was seeing the decay spreading across the coalfields as clearly as anyone as the world markets for coal contracted, as the pit owners cut more corners, and as thousands of men struggled humiliatingly for jobs and were paid less and less for the back-breaking hours underground.

Nick had seen his share of it. He had queued hungrily in the dark of winter mornings with dozens of others hoping for a day's casual pit work, only to be turned away when he reached the lighted pit-top and the managers saw who he was. Once or twice he had even been taken on, and had deliberately been given the most menial of tasks, a bitter insult for a skilled worker like Nick. More recently there hadn't even been the hope of casual work. For two years, since the hunger march, Nick hadn't worked in the pits at all. His meagre unemployed benefit had been stopped because, as the official put it, he 'wasn't looking hard enough for work if he could spare the time to wander off to London'. The Penrys existed on the few hours of odd jobs that Nick managed to find for himself, on tiny and irregular hand-outs from depleted union funds, on whatever their relatives could spare, and on Co-op credit.

All through it, until Dickon's illness, Nick had never flagged. He devoted the hours of unwelcome freedom to the Miners' Federation, and to the individual causes of his members. He was a popular labour organizer and a charismatic speaker, liked and respected all through the valleys. He would walk miles and then spend hours with a single miner, trying to persuade him not to leave the Federation for a toothless, powerless company union. Even the dwindling numbers of his own men, the bleeding away of the strength which he believed was their only hope, had not weakened Nick's convictions.

Until Dickon's illness.

Seeing the boy's new helplessness as the illness sapped his meagre strength, and left the ribs showing through his thin skin, Nick asked himself if it was worth hanging on. If anything in the world was worth seeing Dickon suffer any more than he did already. He heard the answer clearly, his first renegade thought. No, nothing was worth that.

Mari wouldn't look at him. The down-turning smile was bitter. 'So, what do you want? Another strike?'

'If needs be,' Nick said quietly.

The lines around Mari's mouth deepened. She stared past Nick, and back down the years stretching behind them. The strike of 1921, when her family had got by on what she and her mother could earn. 1926, the year of Dickon's babyhood when they were discovering that he would never be like other children, the General Strike and the long, bitter summer that followed it with the miners straggling back to work when the winter cold began to bite. 1928, 1931, the dreary repetition of hardship, and all for nothing. People like Nick and herself had nothing, and they never would.

Angry resentment was alive inside her, and it focused suddenly on Nick.

'Another strike, is it?' she murmured. 'You think you're such a big man, Nick Penry, don't you? You with your meetings, up on the platform telling the men with their wives and children back home to lay off work and fight the bosses. Telling them to go another week without money coming in, all for the cause. Well, I'll tell you something. You're not a big man. You're not a man at all. What kind of man is it who can't bring home food for his child who's dying? Dickon can't eat pamphlets, can he? We can't pay the doctor in Cardiff with workers' solidarity, can we?' Mari's mouth was working although the words had stopped coming. There was a white fleck on her lower lip, and the cords in her neck stood prominent.

'I hate you,' she whispered. 'I hate you, and everything you've done to bring us to this.'

'I haven't done it,' Nick said softly. 'Capitalism has done it.'

Mari moved so quickly that the stinging slap almost caught his face, but Nick was quicker. He held her wrist as she tried to twist sideways to escape him.

'So what do you want me to do?' His voice turned hard and cold.

'I want you to get a job. Leave here, go wherever it is that there's work.'

Leave the valleys, leave the struggle that's taken everything since you've been old enough to think. Leave what you believe in and the people you care about and go anywhere you can to earn the shillings that will save Dickon.

The unspoken words were tangible between them, sharp and pointed like little flint arrows.

Nick let go of Mari's wrist and turned away. He took his coat and cap off the peg behind the back door.

'I'm going for a walk,' he said. 'Don't wait the tea for me, will you?' That was an ironic shot. For months there had been only one meal a day for the Penrys, and they had already eaten it.

Mari waited, motionless, until the door had banged shut before she let the hot tears spill over.

It was the middle of June. At the end of the covered backs,

daylight shone in an oval of blue and gold. Nick left the passage, with its smell of damp brick that never evaporated even in the driest weather, and walked out into the sunshine. The terrace was noisy with the shouts of children who were running after a ball as it rolled away over the steep cobbles. A miner was coming up towards Nick with two whippets straining on the leash. He nodded calmly and strolled on. With so little work to be done, the pace of Nantlas seemed to have slowed to a dawdle. Only the children bothered to run, or to shout to one another.

Nick turned his back on the motionless winding-gear at the valley bottom and climbed upwards. Beyond the last row of houses and the ugly hem of brick-and-slate privies, makeshift sheds and rusting corrugated-iron shelters, was a line of allotments. Half a dozen men were working there, moving to and fro between the tangle of greenery and orange-scarlet flowers that scrambled over the beanpoles. The men straightened up from their hoeing and nodded to Nick as he passed. No one spoke. 'Going for a walk' was a recognized way of filling time in a workless day, although until today Nick himself had almost always been too busy to need to contemplate it. Beyond the allotments was bare, open hillside. Nick scrambled upwards, leaving the sprawling black gash of the tips away on his right.

He didn't stop until he reached the hill crest, panting slightly from the steepness of the climb. A little way below the ridge was an outcrop of rock that made a rough shelter. Nick and his friends had smoked their first cigarettes here when they were boys. As he sat down with his back against the sun-warmed rock Nick smiled a little at the memory of the coughing that had followed. He would have given anything for a cigarette now, but he couldn't remember when he had last had the money for tobacco.

The sun was almost too hot. Nick took off his jacket and eased his shoulders under the thin shirt that had belonged to his father. It had been a little too small when he had inherited it from the old man, but since he had been out of work the hard muscles of his shoulders and upper arms had softened down and the old shirt, carefully patched by Mari, fitted perfectly now.

Nick had climbed the hill to think. He stared down at the familiar view. Along the valley, at the pit that was still working, he saw a full truck heave into sight and disgorge itself at the pithead. The rumble and clatter reached him a full two seconds later on the heavy, still air. Further away he saw a tiny white signal arm quiver and drop beside the railway line and a train of trucks began to inch forward behind the busy engine. He heard a shrill whistle and the clash of couplings with perfect clarity.

Work.

He had come up here to think but now, with the hopelessness spread neatly out in front of him and the blue-purple roof of his own house in the centre, he knew that there was nothing to think about.

If there was work anywhere, he would have to take it. It went against the grain of everything he believed in and hoped for. It was giving up, and running away when he knew he was needed, but he would do it because it was for Dickon. Nick thought of the rough crest of hair at the crown of the boy's head that wouldn't lie down however hard Mari brushed it, and the square shape that his mouth took on with his strange laughter, and his body ached with the pity of it.

Work. Nick knew where he would try first.

He had often thought of Amy Lovell and the great, quiet house in Bruton Street where the servants padded to and fro and where there was not a wrinkle or stain in the soft, shining expanse of luxury.

He would write to the Honourable Amalia Lovell, and ask her politely if there might still be some work for him on her family estate. Nick bent his head at the thought of sitting down to the letter, but the pang passed quickly enough. Swallowed pride wasn't all that palatable, he thought, but he was getting more than used to the taste.

There was a chance, of course, that Amy Lovell would have forgotten all about him. But somehow, recalling her still face and the hurt in her eyes when he had refused her help, Nick didn't think she would have forgotten. And if Amy Lovell couldn't, or wouldn't help him – well, then, he would try the Midlands, where light industries were burgeoning, or he would try the car manufacturers. He would go anywhere, except to London. There were enough men from the valleys in London already, walking the streets in search of something they could do.

So the decision that wasn't really a decision at all was made, but Nick went on sitting with his back against the outcrop of rock. As the light changed the blue sky faded to pearl grey with a rim of pink softening the hills to the west. Nick kept his eyes on the horizon, never glancing at the black smudges of houses and workings in the darkening valley.

It was completely dark when he stood up stiffly and began the scramble down to Nantlas. As he passed along the terraces most of the lights were already out, and his own house was black and silent when he reached it. The thin curtains were drawn tight across the upstairs window.

Nick let himself in and crossed the back kitchen, sniffing the familiar scent of carbolic soap and brass polish with the knowledge that he would have to leave this and everything he cared about. The realization gave him a moment of sharp physical pain.

He trod softly up the stairs and pushed open the bedroom door.

In the dimness he saw that Mari had taken Dickon into bed with her. Her arms were wrapped protectively round the boy, who was restless in his sleep. His bottle of medicine, a patent tonic, stood with its spoon on the table by the alarm clock. Slowly, Nick turned away.

He stopped at Dickon's doorway and lay down on the child's bed, too frozen even to take off his clothes. This is how a marriage ends, then, Nick thought. In the dark, cold and silent.

In the morning, as soon as it was light and before Mari and Dickon were awake, he sat down at the kitchen table and wrote to Amy Lovell.

Amy found the letter in her pigeonhole at the hostel, forwarded with the rest of her mail from Bruton Street. It was the end of a night shift and she was yawning and looking forward to tea and toast in the nurses' canteen before going upstairs to sleep.

She recognized the strong black handwriting at once.

Nick's request was straightforward. If there was still a job on her family estate, as she had once mentioned, he would be grateful for it now. *Yours, Nick Penry.* Amy folded up the single sheet of paper, wondering. The hauteur with which Nick had rejected her offer in the first place still stung. It must have been hard for him to come back and ask, after that. But Amy had heard enough from Bethan about the way things were in Nantlas to be able to guess why he had had to do it.

Instead of going up to her room Amy went to the telephone in the common room and, after a short delay, she was put through to Chance. She could see her father's irritable frown as he answered her.

'The labourers on the estate are Mackintosh's business. I won't interfere with that.' Mackintosh was the estate manager.

'This man saved the life of a friend of mine, once,' Amy said. 'He's my friend too, in a way. Could you make an exception with Mr Mackintosh, just once?'

'It sounds very unsuitable.' Gerald was stiff. 'And we have enough trouble finding work for our own people nowadays.'

'Please.'

Her father loved her, awkwardly and mutely, Amy knew that. At length, shaming her a little and masking his capitulation with gruffness, Gerald said, 'All right. I'll speak to Mackintosh. If he has anything, your friend will be offered it. Don't ask me to do anything of the kind ever again, because I won't.'

'No, I won't ask again.'

A week later, a letter in a crested envelope arrived for Nick. The brief, uncordial missive under the heading 'The Estates Office, Chance' stated that at his lordship's direction, and subject to a satisfactory trial, the post of under gardener on the estate would be offered to N. Penry at a wage of twenty-eight shillings a week. If Penry would present himself to Mr Mackintosh at the above address as soon as possible he would receive his directions. Accommodation would be provided on the estate.

Nick looked down at the thick paper, the neatly typed words. He was thinking about Amy Lovell and the smooth machinery she must have set in motion. So much for a naïve, impulsive, pretty girl to be able to do so easily.

Without speaking, Nick gave the letter to Mari. She was sitting in the chair by the range with Dickon on her lap. His head was resting on her shoulder, and Nick saw the sharp chain of bones running from the nape of his neck.

Mari read the letter and stared at Nick over Dickon's crest of hair.

'At his lordship's direction? How?'

Nick had never told her about Bruton Street, or the girl. The gulf between that polished place, he had reasoned, and the things

295

that Mari had to make do with was cruelly wide enough without pointing it up further.

'Does it matter? The job's on offer. It's the wages that count. Not over-generous, but there you are.'

'It's twenty-eight shillings more than we're getting now.'

'Exactly. I'll be able to send you almost all of it.'

Mari's eyes were fixed on him. Instead of the relief she had expected to feel she was cold, and suddenly vulnerable.

'You're going to go, then?' she whispered.

Nick was cold, too. Leaving Nantlas. Leaving the Fed. He could do that, even though it would hurt. But to leave Dickon. And to leave Mari. Even though the love had gone, and all the warmth and softness and the sweet smell of her with it, Nick didn't know how he would live without her.

'Of course I'm going. Isn't that what you wanted?' He was adding up swiftly in his head. 'Ask the doctor in Cardiff if you can pay him weekly. With not having me to feed, and even with the extra bits of good food for Dickon, you should be able to manage.'

'You'll need to eat.'

'I expect there'll be plenty of rabbits on his lordship's acres.' Nick smiled slightly. Rabbits were as scarce as tigers in the valleys nowadays.

'It says here as soon as possible.'

'It won't take me long to get myself ready.'

There was a moment when either of them might have said something else. Might have changed everything. Dickon rolled his head against his mother's shoulder and moaned fretfully. The silence spread between the three of them, unbroken.

'I'll go down and see the Committee,' Nick said at last. 'I'll need to do a bit of explaining about resigning the secretaryship.' He had done the voluntary and important job for years, and it was hard not to feel like a renegade now.

'Yes. You should do that,' was all Mari said.

They hardly spoke again for the single day that it took Nick to prepare himself. He knew that the other stalwarts he had worked with thought he was deserting them. They accepted his resignation stiffly, and there were none of the votes of thanks and congratulations due to outgoing officers.

At seven the next morning Nick was ready to go. The cardboard suitcase that had belonged to his father was packed. He had arranged a ride in a delivery van as far as Newport. After that he would walk, hitching lifts where he could, eastwards to Chance.

He put his empty cup down on the kitchen table and Mari snatched it up at once and took it to the sink. Her hands were shaking and the cup rattled as she rinsed it. Nick knelt down by Dickon in his seat by the range. He ruffled the crest of hair and then lifted the boy in his arms. He smelled unhealthy, faintly of soured milk, and his limbs were like knobby sticks. Nick kissed him, closing his eyes for a moment to seal the memory within himself, and hugged the frail weight against him. Then he folded Dickon back into his blankets.

'Be a good boy for your mam until I get back.'

Mari followed him to the back door. She was still in her nightdress, with her hair hanging loose over her shoulders. She looked like a young girl until she stopped and he saw the deep lines around her eyes.

'Good luck,' Mari said simply.

Nick nodded. She didn't turn her face up to be kissed, and he didn't try to put his arms around her. He touched her hand instead, but their fingers didn't grasp at each other.

'I'll write,' he promised. 'When I send the money. Take care of you both.'

Nick almost ran down the passage, out into the street and down the hill to where he had arranged to meet his friend in the van.

He didn't reach Chance until the middle of the next day. Rides were hard to come by, and after he had slept the night burrowed into the prickly warmth of a haystack he knew that he looked rumpled and disreputable. At last, a baker's van set him down at a crossroads.

'Down that road,' the driver directed him. 'A mile or so, you'll come to the gates. You can't miss it.' He was chuckling as he drove off.

Nick trudged the distance down the quiet green road and understood why. The high stone wall that the road had clung to gave way to tall iron gates topped with the increasingly familiar crest. He stopped and peered through them, and then whistled. It was so big. The great house stood on rising ground in a wide space of shimmering parkland. A long driveway, swept and raked, curved away towards it from the gates. A little stone lodge stood beside the driveway with lavender and hollyhocks in the trim garden.

Nick put his suitcase down to push at the gates, and they creaked reluctantly open.

A man came out of the lodge at once and hurried towards him. 'That'll do. You've no business here.' He looked more closely at Nick's case and added, 'No work either, if that's what you're after.'

'I have a job here,' Nick said coldly. 'I am to see Mr Mackintosh.'

The lodge-keeper frowned at his Welsh voice, unmollified. 'Mr Mackintosh? Then what are you doing here? This is the carriage drive. For the family.'

Nick was amused to hear the man uttering the word with the same reverence as for God, or the King.

The keeper pointed to the road curving onwards with the wall. 'Follow this into the village. There are tradesmen's gates there, and the estate buildings. I'll telephone to Mr Mackintosh . . .'

. . . to check up on me, Nick thought, as he plodded away.

It was hardly a welcome to the vast acres of Chance, but he hadn't expected one in any case. He was thinking of Amy as he walked on, and the way that she had taken him home without ceremony. She had been welcoming, he thought, and generous as well.

But then, she could afford to be.

Two weeks, Amy told herself cheerfully. Two glorious, sybaritic weeks off. Fourteen mornings to lie in bed until she felt like getting out of it, with the prospect of nothing to do that wasn't thoroughly enticing for the rest of the day. She rolled up her discarded apron and stuffed it into the laundry chute and sent her cap and cuffs rustling after it.

For the next two weeks there would be lipstick instead of starch, champagne instead of lysol. 'Thank God,' Amy murmured. She glanced at her watch. Adeline was sending her car to the hostel for her. It was time to go down and see if the chauffeur was standing in his lavender-grey breeches at the porter's cubicle. Amy had stopped worrying about whether the

298

other girls might judge her for her rank and money. She knew that Moira O'Hara didn't, and nor did the others of her circle of nursing friends. And if Mary Morrow chose to hate her, well, then that was Mary's privilege.

Amy picked up her belongings and ran down the stairs. The chauffeur was waiting. He bowed slightly before taking her bag, ushered her out to the Bentley and handed her in. The car's patrician nose slid out between the buses and tradesmen's vans and then they were bowling north towards the river and freedom. Amy sighed with pleasure. She didn't even glance backwards as the Lambeth vanished behind her.

Her love-affair with nursing had died with Helen Pearce.

The old, urgent longing to be of help, and the pleasure in it that soothed all the other anxieties, had vanished with her. Amy had never regained the silver pin. She knew that she was a competent nurse, and she did her job as well as she could. But the tedious formality of hospital procedure irked her, and she still felt the callousness at the heart of the machine that healed or failed to heal in about equal proportions. A little of that callousness, she thought sometimes, had rubbed off on her. Either that or she had adopted it for her own protection. Probably, she decided coolly, she was a better nurse for it. Whatever the truth was, there never would be another Helen Pearce.

After her precious leave, Amy would return as a third-year student, with only a year separating her from the examinations of State Registry. And after she was registered, near-freedom beckoned seductively. She could live outside the hostel, even have some say in regulating her hours of duty. There were only twelve more months of slavery. And in the meantime, there was her annual fourteen days in the old world.

Adeline was waiting for her in the white drawing-room. There were lilies everywhere in tall white porcelain vases. The white blinds were lowered against the midday sun, so that the light in the long room was pearly-soft.

'Darling.' They hugged each other. As their cheeks brushed Amy felt her mother's taut shoulders and with a little shock she saw the fan of tiny wrinkles at the corner of her eye. 'Darling, you do smell of hospitals. I've got some perfectly delicious new bath scent. Want to try? Be quick if you can, there's a dear old friend of mine for luncheon. And Richard has promised to come, so we'll be four . . .'

299

Adeline was anxious, and that was unusual. Mildly, Amy said that she was sorry about the hospital smell and of course she would change because she hadn't expected there would be guests. Adeline was wearing a Schiaparelli dress and jacket in black and fuchsia pink, as sharp as a gleaming blade in the pale room. As Amy left the room a maid brought in a tray with the cocktail shaker and chill-frosted glasses. Perfect, she thought, as she went up to Adeline's bathroom. A dry martini, talk, a long luncheon with more talk and nowhere to hurry away to, and afterwards . . . perhaps a nap on her own wide bed without having to shake herself awake too soon to go on duty all over again. She was smiling as she drew the fragrant bath, and still smiling when she wrapped herself afterwards in one of her mother's thick white robes and sat down in front of her dressing-table mirror to look at herself.

Amy felt that she had grown into her own appearance lately, as if her features had knitted together into a coherent whole at last. She thought critically that her mouth didn't look too large and wobbly any longer, nor did her eyes seem to be set too far apart. They stared back into the mirror, blue-green, direct. Amy reached for one of Adeline's pots and deftly brushed gloss on to her eyelids. She chose one of the array of gilt-cased lipsticks and lightly painted in her mouth. Her hand hovered over the other brushes and jars, and then rejected them all. Her skin was pale from long hours in the wards, but it still had the faint apricot glow from which the freckles had faded at last. Her hair had been cut short because that was the easiest way to wear it under a starched cap, but it also showed off her long neck to the fullest advantage.

Amy stood up and let the robe slip off her shoulders. The pale, glowing skin was flawless from shoulder to toe. She was slim and taut from two years of hard, physical work, that could equally have come with tennis and dieting. Only her hands, with rough skin around the short nails and reddened knuckles from disinfectant scrubbing, betrayed her as something other than the society girl.

She had brought a plain black linen dress with her, with deep Vs at the front and back that showed the smooth skin. Amy slipped it on and then frowned at herself. On impulse, she walked back to Adeline's dressing-table and opened her jewel case. Every night her maid locked the case in the safe, but during the day the nested velvet layers lay ready for Adeline to choose from their glittering contents. Amy lifted out a dark blue tray where pendant earrings sparkled, and peered into the recesses. There they were, the pieces she was looking for. She took out the two identical bracelets and slipped one on each wrist. They were bands of diamonds, as heavy and as wide as handcuffs.

It was too much for a family lunch party, but at the same time it looked exactly right. Just as Adeline herself, with her flair for unpredictable statements, would have looked. Amy picked up the hairbrush with AL in rhinestones on the silver back and smoothed her hair once more. And then, she judged, she was ready.

In the drawing-room Adeline was pouring a martini for Richard. Her own glass was already refilled. Richard was lounging against the white marble mantelpiece. They both glanced up at her as she came in trailing her waft of Chanel, and then they stared. Richard's perpetually half-closed eyelids blinked just once as he glided forward.

'Is this how one looks when one comes of age?' he demanded. 'I can't wait for it to be my turn, if it is.'

Amy had celebrated her twenty-first birthday four weeks earlier. Her party had consisted of bottles of wine and an iced cake from Bruton Street, shared between shifts with the other nurses. There had been no time for anything else.

She returned Richard's kiss on both cheeks, and then held up her wrists like a pugilist.

'Do you mind, Mummy? May I wear them? It struck me when I was dressing that it's exactly what you would have chosen to wear with this nothing frock.'

Adeline wasn't staring any longer. She was nursing her drink and smiling, but there was a small quiver of apprehension in it that hollowed her cheeks.

'Of course you may, my love. They'll be yours some day. I'm glad you've discarded the wholesome nurse look for a few hours. The . . . the old friend who's joining us for lunch . . . it wouldn't appeal to him at all. And I'm enough of a mama to want to be absurdly proud of you all to people who matter to me.'

'Who is he?'

Behind her mother Amy saw Richard raise one eloquent eyebrow and blow a kiss into the empty air.

Adeline was touching her hair, an uncharacteristic gesture of anxiety. She didn't answer Amy and an odd silence deepened between them, as if they were waiting anxiously for something.

They didn't have to wait long.

A moment later the maid opened the door and announced 'Mr Roper, my lady.'

'Jack.'

Adeline stood up and held out both her hands but the tall, broad man who had swept in ignored them and wrapped his arms around her. He rocked her so that she swayed on her fuchsia suède heels and then turned her face up so that he could look squarely into it before he kissed her.

'Beautiful Adeline,' he said. 'And not a day older.'

'Several thousand days.' There was a glow in her cheeks that had nothing to do with the martinis. 'How many years is it? Too many, anyway.' She shuddered a little theatrically. 'Jack, I want you to meet my two younger children. Amy, and Richard.'

The man turned to look at them. Amy saw close-cropped fair hair that was beginning to turn silver, a mouth marked by lines that might indicate either laughter or very strong will, and bright, clever blue eyes. She judged that Jack Roper was about fifty years old, and from the timbre of his voice rather than his accent she knew that he was American. His hand as it shook hers was warm and firm, and he held it for seconds longer than he need have done.

'Amy?' he said musingly. 'When I last saw you, you were hardly more than a baby. It was your sister who promised to be the beauty then, I thought. I see I was wrong.'

Amy felt a faint, unmistakably pleasurable shiver. Whoever he was, Jack Roper was somebody special. Unplaceable, and so a little threatening, but special.

'Isabel is very lovely . . .'

'Isabel is married with a baby of her own, now . . .' Amy and Adeline spoke together and then broke off, falling silent. Jack Roper was still holding Amy's hand. He lifted it and touched the knuckles with his mouth. She saw his eyes flicker at the rough skin, and then narrow with calculation. It was a reaction as automatic as blinking. Mr Roper would miss nothing. Amy found herself wondering how much he had deduced from their quick, bright mentions of Isabel.

'And Richard?' He relinquished her hand at last, and she knew that he had registered that she wore no rings.

The men shook hands. Again there was the sharp, blue glance,

302

and Richard countered it with his hooded stare. Adeline's hand shook a little as she handed Jack Roper his glass, but her smile was under control again.

'To old times?' Adeline proposed, lifting her glass to him, and he echoed politely, 'Old times.' But Amy as she watched him knew that Jack Roper wasn't a man who would care much for the past. The future might challenge him, but it was the present he lived for. She felt the little shiver again.

Adeline and her guest were talking about the years of their friendship. They had met almost twenty-five years ago, in London during the glittering Season before Adeline had married Gerald Lovell.

'Your mother was like the fairy on top of the Christmas tree, then,' Jack Roper said.

'And still is,' Richard murmured. He was reluctantly impressed by the stranger, and so unusually quiet.

Jack Roper bowed. His pale grey suit was perfectly cut, smooth as a second skin across his broad shoulders. 'Of course. But in those days, every man who saw her fell in love with her. Including me, of course. I was crouching underneath the tree, hoping to catch a sequin falling off her skirt.'

Adeline was laughing. 'You were too busy making money and making yourself known,' she corrected him. He made his ironic bow again, smiling.

'We were two Pittsburghers, both of us with our way to make in the world. By the time I had paved mine a little, you were Lady Lovell.'

'Yes,' Adeline said softly. From the brief glance that passed between them Amy guessed that, at some inevitable time during the years between, her mother and Jack Roper had been lovers.

'Good to be back in London,' he said after a pause. 'I always feel at home here.'

'And where's home when you aren't feeling at home in London?' It was unlike Richard to sound waspish. Amy wondered a little at the complex currents eddying around her.

'All over. New York mostly, for the last few years. Trying to put my business back on its feet after 1929.'

Somehow Jack Roper didn't have the look of an unsuccessful man.

'What is your business?' Richard asked.

'Construction. What's yours?' The blunt deflection made Rich-

303

ard laugh in spite of himself. He spread his arms out along the marble mantelpiece.

'Eton, for far too long. I'm not going back for the next half, though. I've decided to launch myself as a man of letters. It sounds agreeable as well as impressive, don't you think?'

'I've no idea.'

They were all laughing when the maid came in again and whispered to Adeline. Adeline stood up and said gracefully, 'Shall we go through?'

It was an agreeable lunch, to begin with. There was lightly poached salmon with a purée of sorrel and champagne sauce, and then wild strawberries in a silver dish. Amy ate with a small sigh of contentment that earned her another of Jack Roper's blue glances, followed by a quizzical smile. She was sitting beside him and had to turn slightly to see his profile. His beaked nose gave him a forbidding air, until he too turned and looked at her again. Amy felt suddenly that her curled fingers were damp around the stem of her glass.

They had all been talking, Adeline leading them in her pretty drawl, her face alight with vivacity and her eyes brighter than usual. But when she saw the look, and Amy as lovely as a flower with the diamonds cuffing her wrists, the mask slipped and sagged.

She held out her glass to be refilled and then, when the servants had gone again, she motioned to Richard to do it once more.

One by one the three of them saw it and felt it, looking back at Adeline across her perfect table. In the course of a single meal Adeline had grown haggard.

The talk limped on. Amy and Richard had to lean heavily, for the moment, on Jack Roper's urbanity. He had an admirable fund of London gossip and he gently pushed the tastiest titbits across the table, trying to tempt Adeline back into the circle. He had dined the night before with the Channons.

'And do you know what Honor told me about Sylvia Ashley?'

Richard glanced sideways at his mother, and then his hand slid to cover hers on the polished table top.

At length, Adeline collected herself. There were sudden deep lines at the side of her mouth, showing under the peachy-pale make-up that had once hidden everything.

'I think we've all had enough of this luncheon, darlings. Shall we go and have a little cup of coffee?'

Her voice was slurred, a drawl within a drawl. They walked slowly back to the white drawing-room, with Richard and Jack supportively on either side of her as if she was an old woman.

Amy came behind them, caught short in miserable confusion.

Adeline sat in the corner of one of the sofas. She smoothed the black and fuchsia folds of her dress around her and then she lifted her hand to shade her eyes a little.

'Sit here, beside me,' she commanded and Jack Roper sat down. He went on talking smoothly about New York and London, and about old friends, as Richard poured coffee into little gilt-rimmed cups. Adeline drank two cups and then, seemingly as quickly as she had let the mask slip, she was herself again.

'I'm sorry,' she murmured to Jack Roper. In answer he took her hand and smiled at her, and the lines in Adeline's face were invisible again. Watching the two of them, Amy understood that Adeline would always command devotion from the men who had loved her. Even from Gerald. Perhaps especially from Gerald, and that was part of his sadness.

Surprisingly, the lunch party ended as cheerfully as it had begun.

Richard went over to the liqueurs tray and raised his eyebrows at them. 'I'm going to have some of this green chartreuse, for no better reason than that it matches my tie. Mama? There isn't anything pink, I'm sorry to say. Amy? Mr Roper?'

Adeline fluttered her fingers. 'Not a single drop more for me. It makes me feel so lugubrious today.'

Jack Roper had a brandy, and smoked a cigar. Amy leaned back against the cushions and sniffed appreciatively at the mingled scents of flowers, cigar smoke and Chanel.

'I'm so pleased to be home,' she said, and Adeline looked round meditatively at her.

'I wish you were here more often. It wouldn't come as such a shock, then, to see that you have grown up.'

At length, Jack Roper stood up to say goodbye. He kissed Adeline, turning her face so that his lips met the corner of her mouth. She bent her head, and touched one finger against the grey lapel of his suit.

'Amy, perhaps you would see Mr Roper downstairs for me?'

Amy wasn't sure that she wanted to be left alone with Jack Roper, but she nodded obediently as the men shook hands and then she walked with Jack beside her, under the well of light that splashed the line of Lovell portraits and to the head of the stairs. He was much taller than she was, and the bulk of him was a little intimidating.

As they paused before the long sweep downwards, he asked 'What do you do, Amy? Are you a nurse?'

His quickness unsettled her.

'Yes. How do you know that?'

'Ah.' They began to descend, their muffled footfalls losing themselves in the still space. 'I didn't think, from your enjoyment of the little things, that today was quite ordinary for you. And your hands look as if you do more than go to parties. So does your hair. And nursing is the kind of thing a girl like you might do. Even though you like diamond bracelets as well. Or perhaps because of that?'

His finger on the truth reminded her of Helen. The memory pained her, as always.

Abruptly Amy said, 'I work at the Royal Lambeth. I am home for my two weeks' leave.'

They reached the foot of the stairs and crossed the marble floor to the front door. At once a footman materialized, holding the visitor's hat. Jack took it, and waited until they were alone again.

'Two weeks,' he said thoughtfully. 'That doesn't give us very long, does it?'

Amy said nothing. She had the sudden feeling that she was holding a conch shell to her ear, listening to the sea surging within the pearly folds.

'May I telephone you?'

Amy looked directly at him now. There were darker flecks in the bright blue irises. 'I don't think so.'

Jack Roper smiled. 'Your mother and I understand each other. Ask her, if you don't believe me.' She opened her mouth to say something that would imply she didn't understand, and then she thought better of it. She realized that Jack Roper habitually left out the intervening, polite sentences that ordinary people might have mouthed for form's sake.

'I don't want to hurt her,' Amy said clearly. 'I don't know quite what happened this afternoon . . .'

He interrupted her. 'Oh, I think you do. You should talk to Adeline about it. She has an unusual capacity for friendship. Particularly, I would think, with her own children.' They stood

306

for a moment looking at one another. Then, in quite a different voice, he said, 'Diamonds suit you. With a neck as beautiful as yours you should be wearing diamond earrings. Long, extravagant ones that glitter as you dance. I know that it was your twenty-first birthday a month ago, becaue I remember the day you were born.'

Suddenly, the deep-sea roaring in Amy's ears threatened to deafen her. The blood pounded like Atlantic surf in her head.

'I shall buy you a birthday pair, and I will present them to you over dinner the day after tomorrow.'

'No . . .' Amy said weakly, and he raised one eyebrow as he laughed at her.

'Amy, where do you imagine all your mother's jewels in their chic Cartier settings came from? Those diamond handcuffs, for example? They're not musty old Lovell heirlooms, are they, not like those monumental family rubies that look like drops of bullock's blood?'

Amy was too afraid of the new, terrifying idea that had swept down on her even to speak. Jack Roper went on: 'They were given to her. By men who loved and admired her. You should be prepared to accept tributes in the same way, Amy.'

He turned his hat in his fingers, preparing to put it on. 'Until the day after tomorrow.' Then Jack Roper opened the door and strode down the steps, settling his hat on his silver-fair hair. Amy had a last glimpse of him walking purposefully away towards Bond Street before she closed the door and leant briefly against the safe barrier of it.

It was a long moment before she walked back up the stairs to the drawing-room. Adeline and Richard were sitting on the sofa. Richard's arm was round his mother's shoulders and their heads were close together. As soon as Amy came in they looked up, their expressions changing. Amy saw that her mother had been crying. One of Richard's schoolboy handkerchiefs was crumpled in her fingers.

How close they are to each other, she thought, with a little shock. Much closer than I am to either of them. How alike, too. I've never noticed that before.

'Thank you, darling,' Adeline said. 'That wasn't such a brilliant luncheon, was it? I love Jack dearly. I always have. But seeing him after so long made me realize that I'm old. I've always hated old age. Ugliness. Being alone . . .' She faltered, and then her face crumpled once more. Richard drew her close again and murmured against her hair as Amy stood helplessly by.

'You are just forty-two years old. You will never be ugly. And people will always love you, because you are you.'

After a moment Adeline sniffed self-derisively. She blew her nose on Richard's handkerchief and stood up, frowning at the creases in her silk dress. 'I think I will go upstairs and have a tiny nap. Quite probably everything will look different afterwards. One shouldn't drink immoderately, at my age.'

They watched her to the door, and then turned to each other. Richard pursed his lips in a long, slow whistle.

'So what did you think of him?'

'Mr Roper?'

'Who else, darling?'

'I thought he was . . . impressive. And attractive, I suppose.'

'So did I.' He smiled his wry smile as Amy tried to put aside the fear that had closed round her in the hallway.

'Did you mean what you said, about not going back to Eton?' she asked, to distract them both. 'And being a man of letters?'

'Yes,' Richard said airily. 'Eton and I hold nothing for each other now. I would prefer to leave before they ask me to. And I've written a novel that's going to make me rich and infamous. Tony Hardy says it needs completely rewriting, and it will take me a year, but it will do in the end. Hasn't he told you?'

'I don't see much of Tony nowadays.'

It was a mark of their closer relationship since the orangery that he acknowledged her friendship with Tony. But they had never spoken about what had happened there.

'Too busy bandaging?' he asked.

'Something like that,' Amy responded with equal lightness. 'You know, I think I might follow Mama's example and lie down this afternoon. I'm not very used to wine in the daytime.'

But although she lay on her bed and stared up at the ceiling, sleep didn't come. She was thinking, instead, a knotted and insistent tangle of thoughts that coiled around the reality of Jack Roper.

Adeline was out to dinner that evening, and absent from the house all the following day. Amy found her at last at seven o'clock, in her room changing for another evening.

'Come in, dear heart,' Adeline called out in response to her knock. 'See? Do you think this will make me look too much *en fête*? Too tinselly?' She held up a short slip of pearly-grey dress and the straight, silver-sequinned jacket that went over it.

'Like the fairy on the tree? Why not? No, I don't think so, anyway.' Amy put her head on one side to consider it, but Adeline had already hung the dress up.

'Jack said that. Rather romantic, for someone who claims to be so hardboiled. D'you think he meant it?' She laughed, not waiting for an answer. 'Did you like him?'

'Yes.' Amy was hesitant, now that the moment had come. 'I wanted to talk to you about him. He said I should. I thought . . .'

Adeline sat down in one of a pair of velvet-covered armchairs and pointed to the other. She was wearing a peach-coloured robe trimmed with ostrich feathers, and more feathers trimmed the toes of her high-heeled slippers. 'Go on,' she ordered.

'I wanted to ask you if Jack Roper might be my father.'

For a brief, frozen moment Adeline stared at her. *It's true*, Amy thought, and then Adeline threw her head back and laughed. In confusion Amy looked at her mother's smooth white throat and the feathers drifting around it. She had expected anger, or shock, or an admission of the truth, but not so much obvious amusement. Adeline had a rich, musical laugh. At last it died away and she sat upright again.

'I'm sorry to laugh. But it *was* rather funny. Amy, your father is your father. Isabel's and Richard's too. I loved him distractedly until the day Richard was born, and even for quite a long time after that. But when Airlie died all those years ago something died in Gerald too. It was the part of him I loved, surprising and secretive, and it left me with the dry, British shell that I didn't. That's all.' Adeline shrugged to dismiss the pain. 'I'm not very good at being brave, or soldiering on alone and all the things one is supposed to do. I found other people to love, and to love me. You know that, of course. Jack wasn't the only one. But he was special, in a way. We shared the same roots, you see, even though they grew on different sides of the tracks. We were both adventurers, in our own ways. And we both needed to enjoy ourselves, because we couldn't see the point in living otherwise. We don't believe much in duty, and honour, and doing what is right, like you British.'

You British, Amy thought, and then: yes, that's fair, I suppose.

'That's why I made such a damn fool of myself yesterday. The terrible mistake of one cocktail too many, like any old dowager trying to convince herself through a haze of gin that she's still dynamite. It hurt, a little, to see Jack Roper look at you in that particular way, and not at me. I dare say it comes to every mother of daughters.'

Amy felt that she was smiling, just a little vacantly, still digesting her relief that after all Jack Roper was just a man like any other.

'I'm sorry.'

'Don't be. I wouldn't want you to look like the back of a cab, would I?' Adeline changed her tack, suddenly brisk. 'I want you to enjoy yourself too, darling. Not to spend all your best years up to your elbows in some dreadful old lady's operation. This nursing game has gone on altogether too long.'

'I am a nurse, it's not a game,' Amy said automatically. 'And they're not dreadful at all. But I feel, just a little, that the time might have come for some fun after all.'

'Thank God. So. Did you like Jack Roper as much as he liked you?'

'I liked him,' Amy said quietly. She wouldn't admit to Adeline how much, nor exactly what she had thought, even in the face of her lurid imaginings that he might be her father.

'I imagine he might suit you better than, what's-his-name, the stuffed shirt in the army?'

'Johnny Guild.'

'Or Mr Hardy.'

'I don't think Tony Hardy would do at all, actually.'

Adeline was dressing now. She slipped the grey dress over her head and stood up straight. It showed off her perfect legs, as smooth as a girl's.

'Mmmn.'

'Jack Roper asked if he might telephone me. He asked about dinner, tomorrow night.'

On went the silver-sequinned jacket. There was a white gardenia for the buttonhole.

'So, will you go?'

Amy crossed the room in two steps and wrapped her arms around her mother. She smelt the familiar scent of her, that from her childhood had breathed glamour and the romance of adulthood.

'May I?' she said.

Adeline's arms came round her in response and they stood, cheeks together, reflected almost like twins in the long mirrors.

'Listen to me. I would rather see you with Jack Roper than almost anyone else in the world. And I would rather see you in love and free and true to yourself than married to a man like Peter Jaspert. Do what your heart tells you, Amy. It's a sensible heart and not a poor romantic one like Isabel's. I was beginning to worry that it was just a little too sensible.'

Amy stood still for a moment, letting her mother stroke her hair as if she was a girl, conscious of the unfamiliarity of being on the brink of happiness.

'Thank you,' she whispered.

Amy waited all through the next day, refusing to admit her anxiety, but refusing also to leave the house in case she missed him. The telephone rang incessantly, but always for Adeline or Richard.

At six o'clock she was sitting in the library leafing unseeingly through the *Illustrated London News*. She had stared irritably a dozen times at the silent telephone on the table beside her, but when it rang at last she jumped like a rabbit.

'Amy Lovell speaking.'

'Shall we say eight o'clock?' he asked without preamble.

'Eight-thirty,' she said crisply, and hung up smiling.

She was ready for something to happen.

No matter what.

12

Within five days, Amy was Jack Roper's mistress.

From the first evening they spent together, a pattern was set for what Amy came to think of as *Jack's time*. He lifted her out of the world of the Royal Lambeth and introduced her to another, so remote from it that it might have belonged to another universe.

On the first evening he came in his bright scarlet Lagonda and drove her to an impeccably proper dinner at the Savoy, just as Johnny Guild might have done. But when they had eaten and his cigar smoke was curling around them, he produced a midnight-blue velvet box from his pocket and slid it across the table towards her.

'Happy birthday,' he said.

Inside, nestled in the white satin folds, were the diamond earrings. Amy lifted one and cradled it in the palm of her hand. The stones shone back at her, a thousand facets of light in their white-gold settings. Then she looked up to see Jack watching her, with one slightly raised eyebrow. In the soft lighting he looked tough, and handsome. He was stroking the side of his jaw, meditatively, with his thumb. Amy realized that she wanted him to stroke her too, and she looked down again at the diamonds in her hand so that he wouldn't read it too clearly in her eyes.

'Do polite manners dictate that I should say *Oh, Jack, I couldn't possibly . . .* I don't want to. They're so beautiful.'

She looked up again and they both laughed.

'If you do, I'll take them away again.' He reached out for the earrings, handling them like trinkets. 'May I?' Gently, touching the softness of her ear-lobe first, he fixed the earrings in place. Then he turned her chin with his forefinger so that he could look at her, and traced the line of her neck down into the hollow of her collarbone.

Clavicle, Amy recited to herself with blind irrelevance as all

312

her bones, with all the names she had learned for them in another world, melted within her.

'You are very beautiful,' Jack said softly. 'I was right about the diamonds. And now, do you think we should go on to Ondine's? Would you like that?'

'Yes,' Amy said. 'I've never been.' But she had heard of it, and she was impressed, even though from what she already knew of Jack Roper it was inevitable that he would be a member. Ondine's was the night-club for the innermost of London's circles, not just for the titled and the very rich, although many of its members were both. The clever and the famous, in almost any field, so long as they were fashionable, might also be invited to join. Ondine's had the reputation of being both smart and raffish, lavish and louche at the same time as rigidly exclusive. And she knew too that the very grandest night-club patron of all made regular appearances at Ondine's.

Jack drove the Lagonda to Mayfair at breakneck speed.

'Why so fast?' Amy gasped, and he turned to grin at her, shouting over the engine's roar.

'Bad habits die hard. In my day I was an amateur racing driver. Not any more, sadly. Reactions too slow, now.' The street lights streaked overhead and then they swerved and the big headlamps cut through the dimness of a deserted side street. 'Didn't you know? Hasn't Adeline told you anything about me?'

A touch of vanity, there, Amy thought. 'I'd never heard of you until the day before yesterday.'

'I don't know whether or not to be flattered by that.'

She was profoundly relieved when the Lagonda drew up at the bland façade that fronted Ondine's. The little street was solidly lined with cars. Jack took her arm and led her in through the anonymous front door.

The dance floor and the packed tables that surrounded it were in the basement, and must have extended through the cellars of several houses on either side. As they came down the steps into the club, the talk, the music and the décor assailed Amy simultaneously. The room was solid with people and the décor was Egyptian as Egypt had never been. The doorways and panels around the walls were obelisk-shaped, and the negro band, in glittering priests' robes, was playing on a dais surrounded by silver pyramids. On the wall opposite Amy was a huge, blindly staring reproduction of the mask of Tutankhamun.

'It aims to be exotic but is in fact perfectly cosy,' Jack murmured beside her.

The club's owner saw Jack as soon as he reached the bottom step, and undulated forward to greet him. Ondine was wearing a sheath of glittering green, and her eyes were made up to echo the stare of Tutankhamun over her head. Even though her dress was only just held up over her breasts by a huge scarab pin, Ondine was rumoured to be a man.

Jack kissed her on both cheeks.

'Zhack Ropaire, *chéri*. You are at ze table tonight?'

'Madame Ondine. Yes, if you please.'

Ondine guided them to the booths against the wall away from the band, where round tables and red velvet chairs were separated by more pyramids. Jack held out one of four empty chairs in the most secluded of the booths, and Amy sat down. A moment or two later champagne in an ice-bucket materialized beside them. Jack's head bent and almost touched hers as he gossiped amiably about the dancers revolving in front of them. Amy knew one or two of the faces from her mother's drawing-room, others from the newspapers, but most of them were strangers. As she watched she had the feeling that this was a stratum of society that would be as interesting as the debutante dances of Berkeley Square had been dull.

Amy was excited, alive with every fibre of herself, and more wide-awake than she had felt for months.

'Couldn't we dance?' she asked Jack. It would be an added pleasure to feel his arm around her, and the weight of his hand in the small of her back.

'Would you mind if we go on sitting here for a moment?' he answered. Jack was glancing at his watch with the first hint of anxiety she had glimpsed in him. He was waiting for something.

'Of course not,' Amy murmured. She drank her champagne, and watched the kaleidoscope turning in front of her.

A moment or two later Amy felt rather than heard the ripple that washed through the room. It was like a little wave that gathered its own momentum into a crest before breaking away into whispers of foam around the room. And when she did look to see where it had come from, it was the woman of the couple approaching their table that she noticed first. She was tall and stately, with dark hair drawn back in smooth waves from the centre. She had full, reddened lips and dark eyes, and she was

314

wearing a perfectly simple dress of gleaming topaz satin. It was Thelma, Lady Furness, one of the celebrated Morgan twins. The man at her shoulder was the Prince of Wales.

Jack Roper stood up and bowed and Amy stumbled to her feet beside him.

'Good evening, Sir. Thelma, how lovely you always are.' Jack took Amy's hand. His was firm and dry and perfectly cool, unlike her own.

'Sir, may I introduce Amy Lovell?'

Memories of Miss Abbott's school came flooding mercifully back to her. Not a formal Court curtsey on a private occasion. One foot gracefully behind the other, and dip into a small, controlled bob.

'Good evening, Sir.'

'Adeline's daughter?'

'Yes, Sir.'

They were sitting in their red velvet seats again around the intimate little table. Just wait, Amy thought irreverently, until I tell Moira O'Hara. And then she thought how much Helen Pearce would have enjoyed the reflected glory. She had sustained an odd, admiring awe of the Royal Family, and the Prince especially.

He drank whisky, and smoked incessantly, cocking an eyebrow through the wreaths of smoke. As soon as he had stubbed one out he lit another, tapping a staccato rhythm with the butt on his cigarette case. Amy found herself leaning forward, straining her ears. His light, clipped voice was difficult to hear and the Prince kept turning sideways to Lady Furness for confirmation of what he was saying. Only Jack seemed perfectly at ease now that the moment of waiting for the royal arrival was safely past.

After a few minutes' conversation, the Prince turned to Amy. 'Miss Lovell, would you like to dance?'

'Thank you, Sir.' They were on the dance floor, and Amy was conscious of the covert stares of every woman in the room. How odd it is, she thought. Her partner was just a small-framed, dandyish man with a sad, almost monkey-like face. He was exactly like everyone else, and yet could never be because people were never quite themselves with him. Amy felt that her own face was stiff, and a ripple of sympathy disconcerted her.

The Prince said very little, and then only pleasant trivialities, but he danced like a professional. Amy frowned, concentrating on keeping up with him. At last, her partner said, 'Shall we rejoin our host?' and she felt quite giddy with relief. The band finished the number with a triumphant flourish, and she was restored to Jack. He grinned at her over the rim of his glass. The Prince was leaning forward attentively to Lady Furness, his duty clearly done.

'Would you like to dance again?' Jack asked.

'Yes, please.'

It was quite different. No one was looking at them and pretending not to. They were alone, with Jack's height a bulwark between them and the world. All Amy's physical being seemed focused in her fingers, laced with his. The rest of her felt as light as if she could float up off the sprung floor.

She looked up and saw the amusement in Jack's blue eyes.

'Silenced?' he asked.

She laughed, and let her head rest against his shoulder. 'Not quite. Deeply impressed. Are you a close friend of his?'

'No. He doesn't have many of those. We just like the same things. Adeline, for example. And Thelma and I have known each other for years. We Yankees have to stick together, after all. Tomorrow,' he promised her, 'we'll do something quite different.'

Amy nodded, her head still against his shoulder, content with that.

His Royal Highness was disposed to enjoy himself. Amy's impression of the evening began to run together into a blur of smoke and dimming lights, of the Prince's monkey-sad face and the shimmer of Thelma Furness's topaz dress. Jack's arm around her and the insistent music seemed the only reality.

It was very late when the Prince stood up to leave. Madame Ondine came forward to escort the royal party to the entrance of the club. In the dark the Prince's car slid up to the steps at once.

He bowed over Amy's hand. 'Perhaps Jack will bring you out to the Fort, one of these days.'

On my afternoon off from the Lambeth? she thought hilariously.

The Lagonda nosed forward and the leather seat swallowed her up. The street lights swung overhead again, and Amy saw as they reached Bruton Street that the sky was grey with dawn.

Jack leaned forward and just touched her mouth with his.

316

'Is tomorrow evening much too soon for you to see me again?'

'No. It seems a long time off.'

This time his mouth was harder. Amy reached up and touched his cheek.

'Until tomorrow, then.'

He came at the stroke of eight, but Amy had been waiting for an hour. On her breakfast tray that morning she had found a little note from Adeline.

> Darling, I do hope you will enjoy yourself. I know that Jack will take care of you. But, somehow, I don't feel quite brave enough to stay and watch. Am I too silly? I have gone with Mickie Dunn to Venice for the d'Abres ball. To Paris first for a frock fitting.
>
> I love you.

I love you too, she thought.

Amy had always considered Lord and Lady Carlisle to be her mother's friends. When she had thought about them at all, it was to regard them as rather intimidating and exclusively fashionable. They were legendary party-givers and party-goers. But with Jack beside her, she discovered, it was different. There was a dinner for twenty-four people at the house in Green Street before the party began, where the talk licked wittily around the table. As Adeline's daughter and Jack Roper's partner a place seemed to open quite naturally for Amy. She had, she discovered to her pleasure, a talent for making her fellow guests laugh. It was nothing like Richard's ability, but it made her feel happy and comfortable. She liked these clever, agreeable people who were devoted to nothing more complicated than enjoying themselves, Amy decided.

It was time she enjoyed herself, too.

Across the table she caught Jack's blue gaze, and smiled at him so that the diamonds swung and sparkled in her ears.

She was also the focus of envy, she discovered.

The women withdrew briefly to Caroline Carlisle's drawing-room.

'God, isn't Jack Roper divine?' breathed a girl of her own age with round, saucer eyes. 'I'd give my best pearls for a single evening, truly I would. How d'you manage it?'

'He's a very old friend of my mother's,' Amy answered demurely.

The house was already flooding with people. The party began like any other, with a band playing and a river of guests flowing up the stairs to where the long windows of the first-floor drawing-room stood open to the hot, velvety summer night. But at midnight, Caroline Carlisle came into the drawing-room waving a thick sheaf of papers. She jumped on to a low table and clapped her hands.

'Scavenger hunt! Scavenger hunt!'

At once there was a roar of approval and a forest of hands stretching for the pieces of paper.

'Wait till I say. Cheats will be disqualified. Ready, steady, go.' Lady Carlisle flung the papers up in a white whirl and at once the room was a boiling mass of people snatching and running. Amy felt one of her wrists clasped in Jack's iron fingers. In his other hand he brandished the paper.

'Run.'

They pounded down the stairs amongst the eddying crowd and out into the street where the Lagonda crouched at the kerb. As they vaulted over the gleaming red sides another couple pressed in with them.

'Do be an angel, Jack. Let us come too.'

'Hold tight, all of you. Amy, what's top of the list?'

She read it breathlessly. At least a dozen items.

One diamond butterfly
One bicycle lamp
One evening slipper of Madame Ondine's
One sandwich from the porters' bar at Covent
    Garden . . .

'Adeline's got a diamond butterfly,' she gasped. 'She had it made up for a charity ball. And I think one of the footmen rides a bicycle.'

Jack was already racing, with their passengers clinging on behind and waving to the less fortunate running for cabs.

The bizarre items began to pile up safely in Amy's lap.

'On to Ondine's!' Jack shouted. He was possessed with the

318

excitement of the hunt. Amy saw how much he needed and enjoyed the competition. Perhaps everything, even herself, was part of his need to win. She didn't mind that. She was glad to be a prize for Jack Roper.

At Ondine's he left them at the club door. A moment later he was back, bearing a sequinned slipper, surprisingly large.

'We're not leading yet,' he shouted, as they swung away again. 'She was only wearing this one. And God knows what sort of shape her dressing-room's in. There were about a dozen people scrimmaging at the door.'

At Covent Garden the tea-stall was besieged by imploring people in evening clothes, to the astonishment of the handful of porters.

'It doesn't matter a damn what sort of sandwich,' a man with a monocle was shouting.

At Marble Arch tube station more people were hunting through the litter for discarded tickets. *One tube ticket*, and the Underground was closed for the night. It was the maddest, funniest evening Amy had ever spent.

The chase took them down to the river, in search of a lifebuoy. From the river Jack drove like a demon to Soho where an ancient theatrical outfitter living over his shop came blinking to his door in answer to the fusillade of knocks. He took the crisp five-pound note that Jack held out and came shuffling back with a comic-opera policeman's helmet.

'It doesn't say it has to be a real one,' Jack beamed as they roared off into the night again. 'Oh God, where can we get a cricket bat? Is Lord's open after midnight?'

'Chap who shares my digs plays cricket,' said the man perched in the back of the car, and they were off again.

At last, bearing their trophies, they shot back into Green Street. Amy glanced up and saw Caroline Carlisle in her silver dress out on the balcony waving them on.

But from the opposite direction someone else was running, head down, like a rugger player. A policeman's helmet was jammed on his head and the handle of a cricket bat protruded from under his arm. Jack saw him and vaulted over the side of the car. He was running too, with Amy and their friends of the evening at his heels, but not even Jack was fast enough. The boy streaked up the stairs and fell at Lady Carlisle's feet, scattering his treasure all around her.

When Amy caught up with him Jack was leaning against the door jamb, gasping and smiling. 'Beaten into second place by a damned sprinter,' he complained. 'But what a race.'

She put her arms around him and kissed him, laughing. 'We should have won.'

From outside they heard someone shouting, 'The Betts have been arrested for assaulting a police officer.'

'What is a scavenger hunt if one or two of one's guests aren't clapped into the cells?' said Lady Carlisle philosophically.

It was daylight when Jack walked Amy home again through the silent streets. The pavements were misted with the damp that clung in rainbow beads in their hair, and their breath clouded milkily ahead of them. Amy thought that she had never seen London look so polished clean, so perfect. It was the first moment, in all the hectic, sparkling hours since she had met him, that they had been alone and quiet together. She felt her happiness real enough to reach out and touch it.

At Bruton Street Jack kissed her fingers, one by one.

'I have to do some business today. Shall I come for you at eight tonight?'

'Another party?'

He smiled at her. 'The very best kind of party.'

For the best kind of party Amy chose to wear her most elegant, plainest black evening dress, and extravagant long black gloves. The dress left her shoulders and throat exposed and creamy-pale, and from Adeline's wardrobe she had borrowed a cape of floating white feathers to wrap herself in.

When Jack saw her standing like a black and white column under the huge chandelier he stopped for a moment. Then he reached almost awkwardly to touch her cheek.

The Lagonda was waiting outside. Jack drove them to Chelsea, to a neat white house in a pretty terrace.

'Who lives here?' Amy asked curiously.

'I do,' Jack answered.

Inside the quiet house he put his arms around her and turned her face up to his. Beside them a rococo gilt mirror reflected their stark black and white back at them, and Amy thought for a giddy instant as she saw it that they were already fused, already part of one another.

'Are you hungry?' he asked formally. 'I could cook you some dinner, so long as it's scrambled eggs.'

Amy smiled at the contrast with their other nights together. She felt privileged at last, to be here with him alone.

'No,' she said clearly. 'I'm not hungry for food.'

The gentleness was suddenly gone. Jack took her hand and led her abruptly upstairs. In his bedroom there was a wide bed with a black silk cover. Roughly he kissed her throat and then lifted one of the damp white feathers where it clung to her skin. The feather cape dropped on to the black cover, and the drifting fronds settled lazily into stillness.

Jack peeled off the long black gloves, first one and then the other. He knelt to kiss the blue threads inside her wrists. Looking down, Amy saw the silver glitter in his fair hair and laced her fingers through it. His mouth moved upwards to the warmth in the crook of her arm, then to her shoulder and her lips again. His tongue moved against hers and for Amy the whole world slipped a little and then dissolved beyond them. There was only Jack now, only his hands and mouth and the expanse of rippling black silk. He undid the tiny buttons at the back of her dress and it fell in folds at their feet. Amy stepped out of it in her high-heeled slippers and he unhooked her stockings and touched the soft skin inside her thighs.

'Jack,' she whispered as her hands reached out for him. She saw his blue eyes half-close as the ribbon of his black tie unwound and dropped between them.

'My love. My pretty, wicked love.'

They were both smiling as he kissed her again and her mouth opened wide to him. The last of their tangled clothes fell and he laid her back against the smooth silk. The kiss of his warm skin against hers was almost chaste in its sweetness, yet it excited her so that she moaned aloud and laced her fingers tighter, pulling him to her.

'Jack,' she whispered again, imploring now. His hand explored the heart of her so that she felt the petals already unfolding. He hung over her for a second, poised, and then with the arrogance of certainty he came inside her.

The pain and the pleasure were simultaneous, infinite, and then the pain was gone and there was only the pleasure as they moved together, opposite parts of the whole that had eluded her and now, at last, was here in all its simpleness for her to touch and taste.

The tide of sweetness overtook her and washed the breath and

321

heat and anxiousness out of her, and then receded as mysteriously as it had come. It left her lying with Jack Roper in her arms, his eyes closed and his silver-fair hair darkened with sweat. The silence that wrapped around them was as warm and calm as the tropical sea. She smiled, crookedly, with her lips against his cheek, and stirred a little. He lifted his hand and found her fingers, and wrapped them in his own. Amy looked outwards, from the folds of black silk around them to the white walls, the curtained windows and the pattern of London beyond. The world knitted together and she felt whole and calm, as smooth and rounded as an egg and as powerful as a breaking wave. The world had let her into a secret at last and she was alive with it.

So that's what happens, Amy thought. Her virginity was gone and she was glad, as if Jack had given her the answer to a question that had nagged at her for months. The intimacy of the moment seemed so natural and so tender that she felt she understood, at last, the mystery of love. It laced the world together, and illuminated it as well. Amy understood it for herself and Jack Roper, and it made her wonder why the same happiness had been denied to Isabel. Suddenly she knew that it was true that sex hadn't completed any circle for Isabel. It had broken her down instead, and she been led away, helpless, between the nurses from Thorogood House.

It wasn't fair, Amy thought. Why should there be the difference?

She opened her eyes and saw that Jack was watching her face. She was so close to him that all she could see was the net of tiny wrinkles at the corner of his eye and the little, tender fold of his eyelid. Jack was her friend, and he had shown her the secret with ease and grace and she loved him. That was all. The difference was between Jack Roper and poor Peter Jaspert.

Amy reached up to touch Jack's cheek with her fingers.

'Thank you,' she said softly.

'In the normal run of things,' Jack told her, 'I am supposed to thank you.'

Amy lay back so that her hair spread in red-brown feathers over his chest.

'You know why,' she murmured.

'Yes,' he agreed. 'Well? Did you like it?'

Amy rolled over so that she could see him, touching her finger to his mouth and then looking down at the curled, greying hair

322

on his chest and the tanned, muscular belly, and his long legs still wound around hers. He made her own body look soft and glimmeringly pale by comparison against the rumpled silk cover. Amy bent her head so that her face was hidden.

'I thought it was wonderful.'

She felt the rumble of laughter. 'Oh, Amy, my darling. I'd sworn that I wouldn't ever make the comparison, but you are so exactly like Adeline was.'

'I don't mind you comparing,' Amy said honestly. She was thinking of her mother's generosity and vitality and her determination to be happy. She knew that Jack was wrong, because she wasn't the same as Adeline. 'I'd be proud, if I thought that I really was like her.'

'I don't want to think of anyone at this minute but you,' Jack said fiercely. 'And anyway, one shouldn't. It's most discourteous.'

Passion veiled with flippancy, Amy thought, dreamily. Oh yes, I like that. I do like you, Jack.

He reached for her and kissed her so that she twined her legs more tightly in his and stroked his shoulders and the curve of his flank where it tapered into his hips. How wonderful it is, she thought, to be so hungry and to be fed exactly what you want. And how clever, and how beautiful, bodies are when they fit together.

'Would you like to put on your exotic black dress again so that I can take you out to supper?' he murmured.

Amy shook her head slowly. She forgot Isabel, and Adeline, and everything in the world except Jack. 'I want you to make love to me again. Will you?'

He wound his fingers in her hair and pulled her down on top of him. 'I'm forty-eight years old, my love. I should have known you when I was eighteen.'

Her hand moved, stroking, and then found him. 'You can,' she said simply and she heard the brief bubble of laughter again.

'Yes. I can.'

Much later, they went out to supper together. Amy's long black gloves were restored, and the floating white feathers enveloped her to the point of her chin. The diamonds shone in her ears again and her hair was as smooth as when she had left Bruton Street. But Amy was different. As the maître d'hôtel guided them through the packed tables to their shaded corner, the diners looked up at them. They saw the brilliance of Amy's eyes and her pink cheeks, Jack Roper's confident height and her fingers tucked under his arm, and they sighed enviously.

At their table the maître d' murmured, 'And will the beautiful madame sit here?'

Amy had been told that she was beautiful before, and the idea had made her nervous. Tonight she knew that she was beautiful, and that she had achieved something that she would never forget.

Across the white tablecloth Jack raised his glass to her, with the bubbles rising and bursting in it like stars.

'To you,' he said.

There was no going back to Bruton Street. Amy fell asleep in the little Chelsea house with Jack's arms around her, and he was still asleep beside her when she woke again in the morning.

She lay quietly, watching the bars of sunlight move infinitesimally slowly across the floor.

Jack stirred and opened his eyes. He was fully alert at once. He always crossed the barrier between oblivion and consciousness with perfect ease. His arms tightened around her now.

'How long have we got?' he asked.

Until she had to be a nurse again. 'Only a week,' Amy said sadly.

'And how long will it take you to be packed and ready to go abroad?'

'A couple of hours, I should think.'

'Let's do it, then. I want to see you in the sun.'

They flew from Croydon Airport to Nice. Amy had never travelled by air before and the ease of it enthralled her. Jack grinned at her indulgently, as if she was a child with a coveted new toy. By eleven o'clock they were dining overlooking the harbour at St Tropez, where the lights of the moored yachts reflected in skeins off the black water and the music drifted out over the ripples.

All through the hot, still days of their holiday Amy basked in the sun. Her skin turned gold, and her hair shone with copper lights. She swam with Jack in the warm sea, fighting to keep up with him as he forged ahead of her with powerful strokes sending up glittering plumes of spray. In the evenings they hopped from café to café with the surging crowds of friends, and danced on yacht decks under the strings of coloured lights. Then they went to bed, and reached out for one another all over again.

324

Amy had never felt so vibrantly happy, nor had she ever had the same sense that everything she looked at or touched was brighter than usual. The whole world seemed charged with a new electricity, from the crystalline sand under her feet to the feather of pink clouds against the evening skyline. The South of France was painted in its exotic colours by the physical pleasure that she shared with Jack. It wrapped around them so that their hands had only to touch to make them stop short and stare at one another, the dancing that drew them close and separated them was almost a torture, and the kisses lightly exchanged under the blue-black night sky grew deeper until they melted against one another and fled hand in hand from the noisy parties to be alone again.

The short summer nights seemed hardly long enough. But Amy felt stronger on the lack of sleep than she would ever have believed possible at the Royal Lambeth.

'Do you think,' she asked Jack once as they lay in bed in the ash-pale moonlight, 'do you think it's wrong to enjoy this so much? Isn't there a word for it?'

The moonlight drained the colour from everything and his eyes were grey as he laughed at her.

'The word you're thinking of is quite inapplicable to you. You have a perfectly normal, natural appetite and I love it.'

He saw that Amy's face was suddenly touched with sadness, and he reached out to hold her. 'What is it?'

'I was thinking about my sister.'

Isabel and her sadness had been often in her thoughts.

Jack was waiting. He knew about Isabel, as he seemed to know about most things. He even included Peter Jaspert among his huge circle of acquaintances. But he had almost never spoken of them.

'Jack,' Amy said abruptly, 'when we get back home, will you come to Chertsey with me to see her?'

'Of course.'

The last golden day came. Twenty-four hours before Amy was due to present herself to Sister Blaine once more they swam in the sea for the last time, and then drove back to Nice between the oleanders and the bougainvillaea.

Amy sighed. 'I've never been so happy,' she said softly. 'Thank you.' And then, in Jack's tanned, familiar face, she saw anxiety briefly flickering. She put her finger on his wrist, knowing how the golden hairs on it thickened on his arm under the white shirtsleeve. 'It's all right,' she told him. 'I think I understand the rules.'

'Not rules,' he corrected her. 'Except, perhaps, in the sense that a game has rules.'

It was a game. Amy had sensed from the beginning that what was happening with Jack Roper could hardly lead to their engagement, and her picture in the *Tatler* in a demure dance dress with a rope of pearls. It had been an invitation and a step into a new, exotic world for Amy, and she was grateful to Jack for the graceful way he had done it. It was as if he had given her a present of herself, rich and intact, and a million times more precious than the diamonds. But for Jack himself, she knew with perfect clarity, it was a diversion amongst many others. He would be her lover, she hoped, for a little while longer yet, and he would be her friend for ever.

They leaned back in their seats in the aeroplane, and tightened the seat buckles across their laps.

'I wish,' Jack said softly, 'there were more girls in the world like you.'

The engines spluttered and roared, and then they were taxiing.

'I loved it all,' Amy said. 'Being with you, and going to the parties, and the scavenger hunt, and the Prince of Wales, all of it. Who could ask for two happier weeks?'

She had intended to reassure him that she was safe, and playing the game with as much assurance as Jack Roper himself. But he was looking away from her, out of the tiny porthole window as the huddle of airport buildings vanished behind them. There was a folded copy of the London *Times* lying in his lap.

'I'm glad, Amy. There may not be so very many more years of parties to come.'

Amy sat very still. 'What do you mean?'

'Chancellor Herr Hitler. German rearmament.'

Appleyard Street and its slogans, the *threatening march of Capitalism* and *Comrades against Fascism*, seemed to Amy at that moment to belong to another world. The plane was airborne now and climbing steeply. Far below her Amy glimpsed the curve of coast and the blue-green sea with its tiny white fringe as they banked in a slow curve and turned inexorably northwards. A slow, cold shiver touched her spine as the Mediterranean swung and vanished behind them.

The Lagonda was waiting for them at Croydon. Jack's mood had changed again and he grinned at her as he slid behind the wheel.

'Shall we drive straight to Chertsey? Why not?'

England seemed lushly green and shady, although the roads were white with dust in the mid-August sun. Even Thorogood House looked merely cool and solid amongst its shrouding evergreens that allowed shafts of sunlight to flicker over the lawns.

Isabel was sitting in a white wicker chair against a high rhododendron wall. Another chair was drawn up close to hers and she was reading aloud to a thin man in a grey woollen shirt. His long, thin grey-flannelled legs stretched out in front of him. Amy was unsurprised by the sight. Isabel and her friend were almost always together.

Isabel saw them coming towards her across the grass and stood up, blushing slightly. She looked pale beneath the pinkness after the tanned St Tropez faces, but she seemed composed enough.

'Darling.' The sisters hugged each other. Amy glanced down at the book that Isabel had hastily closed up. It was Kipling, she saw.

'This is Jack Roper, Bel.'

As they shook hands Amy saw her sister look from Jack's face to her own. There was a flicker, and the pink flush over Isabel's cheekbones deepened a little. She saw at once, Amy knew that. Isabel's vagueness had gone, and sometimes she seemed almost herself again. But she had withdrawn into the protection of Thorogood House, and the world beyond it was a threat that she had no wish to confront, as yet. After her brief home visits she went back to Thorogood House with a relief that was clear to them all.

At Chance, Isabel spent her days sitting quietly reading in her room or in the gardens. When she was at Bruton Street, Bethan brought the baby Peter to visit her. At Adeline's insistence, Bethan was part of the rigid Ebury Street nursery hierarchy. Peter Jaspert and his mother tolerated her presence, and the visits to Bruton Street were permitted so long as Isabel was carefully watched at all times. They need not have worried. Isabel would play politely with the baby for an hour or so, as if he was the child of a rather distant cousin, and then Bethan would bear him away again, anxiety and incomprehension creasing her kind face.

Amy herself could just understand that Isabel had cut his baby out of her consciousness in the same way as she had excised Pete Jaspert himself, because it was her only, distorted, hope of survival. But to Bethan it was a mystery. Loyalty to Isabel on the one hand, and on the other to the little boy under her care even though he was a living replica of all the other Jasperts pulled Bethan painfully in two opposite directions.

Isabel would go happily back to Thorogood House after her visits so that her treatment could continue. For months Amy had known that the reason for her sister's tranquil acceptance of the grim nursing home was the thin, grey man beside her.

'How do you do, Mr Roper?' Isabel said pleasantly. 'May introduce Captain William Parfitt?' She glanced back at the red-brick house as confidently as if she was the mistress of her own house. 'I'll ask them to bring us some tea out here, shall I?'

They sat down in a circle in the rhododendron shade.

'You look so well, Amy,' Isabel said. 'So pretty.'

'Jack and I have been in St Tropez. It was so hot there.'

Isabel shivered a little. She glanced quickly away, her shadowed eyes flicking over the mown grass until they fixed on Captain Parfitt.

Amy bit her lip. It had been a mistake to come here with Jack. A reassurance, selfish, for herself and a cruel statement to make to Isabel. It was the insistent memory of Isabel as her best friend and her equal that made her want to share her happiness with her even now.

The tea-tray arrived, white china arranged on a blue linen cloth.

'It's been so hot here, too. Hasn't it, Bill?'

'Oh, yes. So hot.'

They smiled at each other, and Isabel put a reassuring hand on his sleeve before she turned to pour the tea.

Captain William Parfitt had been so severely shell-shocked that he had been invalided out of his regiment in 1918. For most of the years since then he had been institutionalized. Until Isabel came to Thorogood House he had spent his days sitting alone shaking, almost completely mute. Now, companionably, they spent their days together. Bill Parfitt followed Isabel everywhere

He could talk again, but he turned to Isabel for confirmation of every word. And Isabel was proud and protective of him. Sometimes, even now, Bill's eyes would fill with tears. Isabel would simply take his hand and wait until his face was in control again. They read aloud to one another and walked in slow circuits between the dank evergreens.

Now they sat side by side across the tea-table facing Amy and Jack. The talk moved on from the hot weather to cricket, and Larwood's bodyline bowling that was causing a storm in Australia.

'Damned un-un-un . . . unsporting,' said Bill Parfitt and Isabel nodded her encouragement.

'Oh, I don't know.' Jack was reasonable. 'The man's a fine cricketer.'

The two men plunged into discussion, and animation began to shine in Bill Parfitt's thin face. Isabel watched him for a moment, and then turned a smile of gratitude on Amy that was startling in its warmth and naturalness.

'Bill misses the chance to talk about cricket to someone who understands it. I don't, although I try for Bill's sake.'

So Jack was accepted, in spite of the threatening, unthinkable implications that surrounded him, because he could talk to Bill. Amy smiled back, but anxiety nagged at her.

They sat talking mildly for another hour. To an onlooker it might have been a tea-party on the lawn of a big house anywhere in England. Madness seemed far removed from the sunny order of things, and so it was hard to believe that this Isabel wasn't exactly the same sister that she had always known. The sense of loss and futility boiled up inside Amy while she talked neutrally of France and London.

When she stood up at last to leave with Jack, Isabel hugged her warmly. 'I like your friend,' she murmured. 'And Bill does, too. Will you bring him down again?'

It was time to go. When she turned back for the last time to glance at them from the corner of the house, Amy saw that Isabel had already picked up the volume of Kipling and she was reading again. Bill Parfitt was listening, one hand held up to shade his face from the sun.

Amy was very quiet on the drive back to London.

At length she said abruptly, 'Isabel really doesn't need to be in that place any more. She's well enough to be at home, or in

329

Switzerland, or anywhere that would do her good. She only want
to stay there because of Bill Parfitt.'

Jack looked sideways at her, quizzical creases showing at th
corners of his eyes. 'Haven't you considered that Bill Parfi
might do her more good than anything else?'

'Why?' Amy sensed her own anger.

'Just because he needs her. Because she can feel stronger tha
he is. I'm not a brain-doctor, but I'd guess that's just what Isabe
needs. Love the healer, and so on. Don't you think so?'

'Do they love each other?' she snapped at him. 'Surely, afte
Peter Jaspert, after what's happened to her, Isabel wouldn'
want . . .'

Jack laughed at her. 'Oh, Amy. Why shouldn't they? Yo
don't imagine everyone loves in the same way as you, do you
White-hot and body and soul? Isabel could do worse than lov
poor Bill Parfitt.'

Amy's knuckles went white as she gripped the leather seat
'That's just it, Poor Bill Parfitt. Isabel is Isabel, and she's lovel
and clever and capable of all kinds of things. She's just been ill
that's all. There's everything that she should do, if she's wel
again. Not . . . not just sit there, vegetating, with him.'

Jack said nothing, and Amy glared at him. 'How can you sa
that she ought to stay there?'

He was still silent, as if to let her listen to her own words, an
then he said, 'Nobody can say what Isabel ought to do, if sh
really is well again. That is for her to decide. If she's happy, an
she looked happy to me, shouldn't you accept that? Sh
isn't you, my love, and nor are you Isabel. You're differen
people.'

Amy wanted to shout at him for his arrogant reasonableness
Then she remembered how patiently he had talked to Bill Parfitt
waiting for him to form the stammering commonplaces, an
Isabel's radiant smile of gratitude.

Impulsively she reached and hugged him. The car swerve
violently.

'Don't kill us both, Amy.'

'I love you.'

He swung the long scarlet nose of the car straight again, an
then drew up at the roadside so that he could put his arms aroun
her.

'I love you too.'

330

It wasn't a pledge, or any kind of a promise. It was a simple, satisfying statement of a simple truth.

Eighteen tiny buttons on the uniform dress. Over it went the apron, starched so stiffly that it crackled. Then the frilled cap that hid the sun-bleached copper lights in her hair.

In ten minutes, she would be on duty. Amy smiled ruefully as she straightened the seams of her black stockings. She had already forgotten the smell of the sun on the sea and the blossoms that had overhung their balcony. The hospital smelt just as it always did, obliterating everything else. But yet, not quite. Jack had brought her back to the hostel, sliding right up to the door in the gleaming car and kissing the tip of her nose.

'Telephone me,' he had ordered imperiously, 'as soon as you have your barbarous duty hours quite clear. Then I shall come and take you away from all this for a minute or two.' Then he had waved and tooted the horn, and driven away in a blaze of scarlet.

The first person Amy saw was Moira O'Hara.

'Holy Mother, Lovell. You look like a foreigner. Where've you been?'

'I've been to the South of France. With a lover. Just wait till I tell all. It beats cups of cocoa and *The Primer of Nursing*, believe me. It's vile to be back. Except for seeing you, of course.' And in her exuberance Amy swung Moira around until they stumbled against each other, giggling.

'God, I could do with a lover. Is he rich?'

'And handsome. And a friend of the Prince of Wales.'

Moira asked in sudden alarm, 'You're not going to pack it in, then, are you? Be a lady, after all?'

Amy laughed. 'No. I can't marry Jack. I shall stick it out here with you, through thick and thin.'

'Speaking of which, it's thin for you all right. You're under Blaine this week.'

'Oh no.'

'Oh yes.'

'Oh damn and blast. I'd better go, I'm late . . .'

Jack Roper was true to his word. When Amy was off duty he would come purring up to bear her away to a party, or to a

331

night-club, or to a dinner *à deux* where he would fill her up with oysters and caviar and laugh through the smoke of his cigar at her groaning descriptions of hospital food.

Once there was a great fancy-dress ball in a country house where three marquees were decorated as circus rings, and the hostess presided as ring-master on a towering white stallion. Two plane-loads of flowers had been specially flown in from Paris for the ball, and the lake beyond the house was carpeted with floating petals.

Amy, in her tiny spangled trapeze-artist's costume, was awed by the profligate splendour of it all.

'It's the beginning of the last fling,' Jack said, with his touch of grimness. Fear flickered in Amy again, even more coldly because now she understood some of the reason. She had been back to Appleyard Street again, and found it seething with anti-Fascist feeling. Jake Silverman had been arrested and was still in gaol after leading some violent street battle against the Fascist sympathizers. Kay Cooper and Angel Mack were bitter and cold, with the old dilettantism bled out of them.

'I wish I was a man,' Angel declared. 'I could fight then, instead of just waiting and stuffing pamphlets through letterboxes. Why is it that everything that happens is by and because of men?'

Amy began to see the parties and the night-clubbing against an increasingly sombre backdrop. She felt like a schizophrenic as she shuttled from Jack and Bruton Street and the noisy glamour of that world, and back to the wards again, and then on to the quiet tension of Appleyard Street.

Autumn turned slowly into winter, and the happiness that the summer had brought to Amy seemed to fade a little with the sunshine.

Christmas came, and this time Amy had only a short leave. Jack came with her to join the house-party at Chance. Isabel was home too, for a whole week. She was as pleasant and withdrawn as always, nowadays. She seemed content to sit and read or to watch the boisterous party games that Adeline insisted on. There was never any question that Isabel might join in.

'Bill's gone to his sister at Broadstairs for a few days,' she explained to Amy. 'He's really so much better. They think he might be able to live outside, soon.'

Remembering the day of her visit with Jack, and the way that he had reprimanded her for her judgements, Amy simply nodded. 'I'm glad,' she said.

The Christmas rituals were performed with the enthusiasm that Adeline insisted on. It should have been a happy time for Amy. Isabel was here, at least, and Richard was home too, in the highest possible spirits. She was with Jack, who prowled along the dark passage to her room as soon as the huge house had settled for the night. 'Shh . . .' he whispered, with his cheek against her hair so that she felt rather than saw his brilliant smile. 'I can hear Gerald stalking with his twelve-bore . . .'

He could make her forget everything, as always, when he lay beside her. But afterwards, when he had padded back to his own room, Amy lay staring up into the darkness, feeling the melancholy gathering around her.

On Boxing Day, almost the whole of the party went off to the local meet. Jack had been mounted by Gerald on a big, nervy bay.

'At least the fellow can handle a horse,' Lord Lovell had muttered. 'I've never seen that he's good for anything much else except driving damned noisy cars.'

Jack had looked more handsome than ever under the black brim of his top hat. He bent down to kiss Amy on the cheek as the cavalcade moved away. She smelt the familiar scent of saddle soap and horses with a quick lift of excitement, but somehow she didn't have the heart to ride out herself today.

Instead she put on her boots, and the scarf that Helen had knitted for her two years ago, and set off to walk across the park.

There had been a heavy frost, and the grass was crackling white as she walked away from the house and under the branches of the huge cedar tree. In the circle of its shelter the grass showed its thin winter colouring. Amy shivered, and her breath hung in front of her in a misty plume. The cold was biting and she began to walk faster in an effort to keep warm. She took the neat gravelled walk beside the wide curving herbaceous bed that was the glory of the gardens in summertime. The earth was bare now, spiked here and there with frost-blackened stalks. The gardeners had industriously cut everything back, and carried the debris away to bonfires and compost heaps. There was nothing here to remind her of the languid, scented warmth of summertime. Amy went on walking, head down against the cold, thinking. She followed the gravelled walk beyond the grey stone wall of the gardens and down the ridge towards the little huddle of houses at the village gates. The smoke from one of the chimneys made a blue-grey smudge against the colourless sky.

The high gates were locked, and the village street beyond them was deserted except for a tabby cat lifting its paws off the frosty stones. Amy turned around again and glanced at the little houses. Behind the trim curtains the men were at home with their families, enjoying their Christmas together. The estate office was locked too. Peering through the window she saw a calendar on the green wall and Mr Mackintosh's bare wooden desk.

She was thinking about Nick Penry.

In the months since he had written to her, she realized, she had almost forgotten him. In her hours off the wards there had been Jack, and the parties and dancing and champagne bottles clinking in their silver buckets, and the nights when she had submerged herself in him and forgotten the whole world.

Now, suddenly, Nick Penry was as clear in her mind again as if he was standing beside her. Amy swung around, half-expecting to see him watching her. But there were only the blank eyes of the office windows, and she knew each of the families who lived behind the curtains of the others. She didn't even know for sure whether Nick had come to work at Chance at all, and she had never bothered to find out.

Amy felt that the cold was cutting right through her and into her bones. As she stood hesitating, remembering Nick's face and quiet voice and the well-shaped hands with the livid blue scars, one of the cottage doors opened. She started with pleasure, a smile of greeting already beginning, and then saw that of course it was only Mrs Wathen, the gamekeeper's wife.

'Good morning, Miss Amy. Merry Christmas to you. Would you like to come indoors now for a cup of something warm? You look half-starved out there.'

The smile was fading into disappointment, and Amy forced it politely back again. 'Merry Christmas to you too, Mrs Wathen. I came out for a walk, but it's much colder than I thought. I think I'll just walk straight back up to the house, thank you very much.'

With the smile that she didn't feel, Amy retraced her steps, following the marks that her feet had made in the frost. Sadness and a sense of emptiness that she couldn't have explained folded around her. There was an image of Nantlas in her head, vivid from what Nick and Bethan had told her as if she had seen it all herself. It stayed with her all day, and it was still there when the riders came crowding back, exhilarated and red-cheeked from the gallop.

'We killed over at Collyer's Copse,' Gerald announced.

'You should have come,' Jack smiled at her. His hands were wrapped gratefully around a brandy glass. 'You look sad. Why's that?'

Suddenly Amy wanted to tell him.

She wanted to talk about Helen Pearce in the desolate grave-yard beside the railway line, and about Nick's handicapped son in Nantlas, and the men she had seen swinging bravely up Park Lane with their lamps at their belts and their worn-out boots. And then she could have told him about the day she went back through the little Lambeth streets to Mag's, looking for Freda and Jim, only to find that Mag had moved away and taken the children with her, leaving no address. People like Mag often moved away and were swallowed up, untraceable. Amy knew that. Then she could have described the Royal Lambeth to Jack and the people who came in and struggled and died in the high iron beds, night after night. But he had never asked her about that. Never, except to find out when she would be free again to come with him to yet another party. It was a part of her life, a half of her that was just as important, but it might never have existed.

Amy looked back into Jack's level, bright blue eyes and knew that she would never talk to him about any of those things.

Jack believed in living and enjoyment and in finding happiness wherever possible, just as her mother did. And he was wrong about Amy herself, because half of her wasn't like Adeline at all.

'I do feel sad,' she said. The hollowness around her was vast and frightening. She had lost her sense of happy unity with Jack. She liked him still, but she knew with sad clarity that she wasn't in love with him any longer.

'Don't,' he said cheerfully. 'There isn't any need. Listen, Adeline's got a scheme for this evening ... .'

Stiffly, Amy turned away. 'I don't think I want to,' she said.

She was remembering Nick Penry again, and wondering

whether he was still here among the trees and meadows of Chance.

It was a month later that Jack told her he was going back to New York.

'There are some things I have to see to there,' he said, with an expression of faint distaste. Just as he never spoke of Amy's work, he never mentioned his own business either. It was better, Amy had discovered, not to enquire too closely into how he had amassed his fortune.

There had been no change in their relationship, and Amy liked him just as much as she had always done. But on one or two of her free evenings lately Jack had not been there. Without having to ask she knew, as she had guessed would happen some day, that he had found someone who did not have to get up at dawn to be on duty at six a.m., and who didn't yawn with tiredness just as an evening was fizzing to its high point. Amy didn't know if the new somebody was American and so made New York important again, and she didn't ask that either.

She simply said, with perfect truth, 'I'll miss you, Jack. Life will be very grey without you.'

'I'll miss you too,' he said, and tilted her chin up so that he could kiss her.

Amy knew that even her mouth tasted sad, and she thought back regretfully to the summer when she had felt strong enough to take on the whole world.

Jack was to sail on the *Mauritania* at the end of February. On their last night together he took Amy to Ondine's again. The decorations had grown endearingly familiar, and Madame Ondine greeted Amy as a favoured regular.

'Such a crowd in tonight, darling. They haven't had quite enough for me to take a firm line with them, but I will if it goes a single step further. I'd move your table if I could, but there isn't a cranny anywhere else.'

There was a big group of a dozen people at the table next to theirs, and several pushed-back chairs revealed that more of the party were in the throng on the dance floor.

Jack and Amy sat down. Jack leaned back with one arm hooked over his chair and his eyes half-closed against the smoke of his cigar. There was a loud burst of laughter from the next table, and the sound of breaking glass followed by more laughter. Out of the corner of her eye Amy saw Madame Ondine undulating towards the source of trouble.

When they could hear themselves again Jack said musingly, 'I wonder whether your brother-in-law is being deliberately indiscreet? I should say that he is treading on the very thinnest of thin ice.'

Amy's hand stopped with her glass halfway to her mouth. She followed the direction of Jack's lazy stare, and saw Peter Jaspert.

Peter was dancing, his high-coloured face brick-red and his eyes closed. He was moving slowly, not quite in time to the music, and his partner was bent against him like a bow. Her face was hidden against his shoulder. One of Peter's big hands held her hips against his, and the other had drawn their twined fingers in against her breast.

Amy felt the colour rising in her cheeks at the thought that she and Jack might ever have looked so openly, nakedly in possession of each other.

The band had been playing a sweet, slow arrangement of 'These Foolish Things'. The music stopped on a long drawn-out note, Peter turned his partner, and they stopped with a tipsy flourish.

Amy recognized the woman then. It was Sylvia Cole. She put her glass down again and looked away.

As Peter and Archer Cole's wife rejoined their noisy party she heard several of their friends ironically clapping their performance. Amy bit her lip and stared down at the tablecloth. Peter was the last person she wanted to see, but it was already too late. With euphoria and whisky clearly buoying him up, Peter blundered over to their table.

'Well. My little sister-in-law. Hello, Amy. Can't I have a kiss, as family? Mmm. There. 'Evening, Roper.'

'Jaspert.' Jack nodded coolly.

'We're having a party. Join us; you must know Talbot and Harrington, and Sylvia, of course you know Sylvia.'

Amy found her voice. She looked up at Peter. 'Thank you, but Jack and I are having a very quiet evening. We shall be leaving soon, and we wouldn't want to break up your party for you.' She could feel the heat of him from where she was sitting. He was like some big, steaming animal still hot from a chase.

The thought of Isabel's remoteness and pallor came back to her, and she shivered a little.

'Dance, then,' Peter begged her. 'Just one. You won't mind, Roper, will you, if I take her off for just one dance?'

Jack inclined his head very slightly. 'Amy?' he asked drily. Jack wouldn't decide anything for her, of course. Amy would have refused Peter Jaspert whatever he asked her, but then she thought with a sudden wave of exhaustion that it would cause less trouble to do what he wanted. She stood up, and Peter held out his arm to her. She took it, and he pulled her with a flourish on to the dance floor. His breath smelt of whisky and was hot enough to burn her cheek. She would have pulled away, but he was holding her too tightly. Even in the early days of dinners at Ebury Street, Amy had seen Peter the worse for drink, but he seemed much coarser, and heavier now. She felt her flesh grow chilly under his hands.

'It's a pity,' he was mumbling, 'that it's all come to this. I like your mama, you know. And you, Amy.' He pulled her a little closer, if that was possible. 'But that was a terrible thing that Isabel did, y'know. Apart from all the other things I could tell you about. What'm I to do? How can a man trust a wife like that? There can't be a divorce, of course. Not in my position. Wouldn't help my chances. Bad enough as it is.'

Amy went stiff with anger. The combination of cold dismissal of Isabel and amorousness towards herself disgusted her.

'Isabel had a breakdown,' she said coldly. 'I don't know exactly what drove her to it, but I could guess. How can you talk about trust? While Isabel sits in her nursing home, you are at a night-club sprawling all over someone else's wife.'

Surprisingly, Peter Jaspert chuckled. 'Sylvia and I are good friends. The best. And this is a private club. What goes on here is nobody's business. I would have thought that you of all people would see that.'

'What do you mean – of all people?'

He was still chuckling, insinuating. 'I mean you and Jack Roper. Look at you. You're humming with it. You know what it's all about, Amy, so don't put on the wide-eyed debutante act. What am I supposed to do, with a crazy wife locked up in a mental home? Turn monk?'

Amy stopped dead. Peter, still blundering with the music, tripped over her feet and almost stumbled.

338

'Good night, Peter.' She turned her back on him and began to thread her way through the dancers.

'Anyway,' she heard him say, too loudly, determined to have the last shot, 'Isabel's got her own fish to fry in that home. Don't think I don't hear.'

With her chin up, looking straight ahead of her, Amy reached the table. Jack stood up and drew out her chair for her. Then he saw that she was trembling. His warm hand covered hers.

'I shouldn't have let you. He was tight. What did he say to upset you?'

Amy's smile was bitter. She was thinking about the difference. 'He didn't upset me.'

The physical intimacy that she had discovered with Jack had seemed so natural just because he was Jack. His ability to piece together fragments into a satisfying whole had been her good fortune. Isabel had had nothing of the kind. Amy could still feel the heat of Peter Jaspert's hands on her, and she understood.

'Jack, I'd like to go home.'

'Of course.'

Peter Jaspert's arm was around Sylvia Cole's shoulders again as Jack shepherded her away. He didn't look up as they passed.

In the car Jack asked her, 'Bruton Street or Chelsea?'

'Chelsea,' she answered. She wanted very much to be with Jack tonight.

In the quiet little house Jack poured a tumbler full of brandy and put it into her hands, then drew her down on the sofa beside him.

'Why did that upset you so much? Couldn't you tell me?' he persisted.

'For Isabel. When he touched me . . .' Amy shivered, and took a gulp of her brandy. 'I don't know why. He isn't ugly, or even particularly obnoxious. He's just . . . poor Isabel. I didn't understand before. Do you know what he said? That a divorce would be out of the question, in his position. And that Isabel has other fish to fry.'

Jack made a face at her, so full of comical shock and distaste that there was almost a smile in Amy's eyes again. 'Didn't I tell you that Isabel is better off where she is? I'd rather live with Bill Parfitt than Herr Jaspert, any day. And I love *his position*. Horizontal on top of Sylvia Cole, did he mean? I can't believe it's the way to get on, publicly rogering your Minister's wife.'

339

Amy did laugh now. 'It doesn't seem to be doing him any harm. I heard he's a great success. Do you think Archer knows?'

'He can't do. Yet.' Jack leaned against the cushions, stretching out his long legs and settling Amy's head against his shoulder. Gently he stroked her hair. 'Mmm. That's better. It won't be long before Archer Cole does find out. I wouldn't put any big money on Jaspert's further advancement.'

Amy settled herself so that her cheek rested against the pleated front of his shirt.

'Why do you call him Herr Jaspert?'

'Oh, partly because Massey & Dart are still heavily involved in German loan deals. They must be very good friends of Hitler's by now. Particularly as he's using the money to rearm as fast as he can. Archer Cole and his Cabinet pals refuse to see it, of course. The Red menace is the only thing that worries them.'

'Jack,' Amy asked very quietly, 'will there be another war?'

'Yes. Not yet, but it's coming.' He sat up abruptly and reached out for the brandy bottle. 'So let's gather our rosebuds while we may.' When he sat back again his hand moved to stroke Amy's breast.

The room was silent except for the soft whisper of ash falling from the glowing log fire and the slow ticking of a gilt clock.

'What's the other reason?' Amy asked at last.

'Do we need a reason? Oh, about Herr Jaspert, d'you mean? I'd hoped we could forget him. The man's a Fascist. An out-and-out Mosleyite, and beyond. Of course all the Conservatives have been dithering about whether to jump right or left, and Jaspert's chosen to jump about as far right as you can go. As you rightly said, he's making a big success just now because they're all so terrified of Reds. His law-and-order and Trots-off-the-streets-and-into-the-cells policies are going down well with certain segments. It won't last. He can't help his temperamental inclinations, but they've led him to make the wrong choice. When it comes, the fight will be against Fascism. Look at Italy and Spain, as well as Germany.'

Amy sat watching the fire and thinking. She had heard her brother-in-law's name mentioned often enough at Appleyard Street, most recently by Jake Silverman only a few days before. Jake was out of gaol again, his face pallid under the black beard but with his fervour burning more brightly than ever.

Tony Hardy had kept her secret loyally. None of the comrades had any idea of Amy's connections. She listened silently to their denunciations of Peter Jaspert along with Mosley and his sympathizers. Her own dislike of him enabled her somehow to disconnect the memory of his relationship. Tonight, and the insinuating heat of him, had fanned it alive again. It was an ugly thought.

She turned her face against Jack's shoulder. 'Let's not talk about him any more.'

'By all means.'

'Jack?'

'Mmmm?'

He was very warm, and close, and she longed to cling to the protection he had given her. But that wasn't possible, any more.

'I know we've come to a kind of end, together. Do you remember, right at the beginning, I said that I understood the rules?' Jack moved to put his fingers lightly to her mouth, but Amy turned her head aside. 'I wanted to say thank you. For giving me what you have done, and for making it happy. That's all.'

'Oh, my love.'

Jack stood up and took her hands. He led her up the stairs and laid her down on the black silk cover, and Amy looked round for the last time at the familiar place before he bent over her.

She saw the light glitter on his hair, and the little, tender creases at the corners of his eyes. He kissed her mouth and undid the buttons of her dress, sliding it off so that he could kiss her shoulders and her bare breasts.

Jack had given her her physical self, whole and miraculous. *Thank you, for that.* Amy let her head fall back. He put his hands up to her face and held it, looking into her eyes. And then he lay down beside her, holding her and stroking her until she moaned deep in her throat and turned imploringly to him

He tore off the smooth satin of her underclothes and ran his hands over her skin. She reached out for him in her turn, impatient, and she felt his restraint as he guided her, directing her pleasure, as he had always done.

She begged him, *please.*

At last he fitted himself within her and she wound her arms and legs around him, holding him. They lay still, their faces together, for a long moment of silence. And then they began to move together and Amy forgot their parting, forgot the world itself beyond the bedroom walls. For the last time they belonged together, and there was no more consideration than their bodies' delight.

Later, in the safe darkness, Amy let her head rest in the hollow of his shoulder. Her eyelashes were heavy, glued together with dampness, and behind them the hot prickle of tears was starting. Amy stared straight up and blinked them back again.

'May I come with you to Southampton? I'll wave you off at the dockside.'

And then, in the silence that followed, she heard the sound of solitude.

'No, my darling,' Jack said softly. 'I can't bear shipboard goodbyes. Let's say it just as if you were going off to the hospital for an ordinary day.' The warmth of him curled round her, but she knew that Jack was already gone. His mouth brushed against her forehead. 'Good night, my love.'

After a moment, with the heat burning her eyes, she whispered, 'Good night.'

Then there was only work.

The days and nights seemed longer and harder without Jack to look forward to when her duty spells ended. Amy felt wearier than she had ever done after the strenuous night-clubbing and party-going. She went mechanically through the rituals of living as the cold, wet winter dragged interminably on and then grudgingly slipped into a damp, chilly spring. There was little else for her to focus on, and even if there had been anything outside the hospital and hostel walls to tempt her away she could scarcely have afforded the time. For all the nurses of Amy's set, the final examinations for State Registration loomed in May.

When she came off the wards each day Amy would sit over her textbooks and her lecture notes, anxiously aware that her mind seemed to be working only at half pressure. She seemed to be forgetting even the simplest facts that she had known for years. The anxiety nagged at her, and even though she was perpetually exhausted she slept badly. She had no appetite either, and she lost so much weight that the bones showed too sharply in the planes of her face.

Adeline was concerned when she saw her. She sat on one of her white sofas, with a posy of waxy-white overpoweringly scented stephanotis in a bowl beside her, and took Amy's hands.

'I can't bear it, Amy. You look so ill.'

The scent of the flowers was making Amy feel sick. She tried to smile at Adeline. 'I'm working hard and sleeping badly, that's all. I'll take a holiday after the exams. I'll go to Chance and stuff myself with butter and eggs.' Her stomach heaved at the mere thought of it. Adeline's face suddenly went stiff.

'My dear, I don't want to pry, of course. But is it possible that you are *enceinte*?'

Amy smiled crookedly at her mother's delicacy. After her own stints on the Lambeth's labour and maternity wards she had acquired a matter-of-fact view of the female mysteries.

'No. I'm certain of that.'

When she had first started sleeping with Jack she had trusted him so implicitly that she had left the responsibilities to him. Later, at the height of her happiness, she had believed that she would be glad to bear him a child. Yet nothing had happened, and Amy knew that she wasn't pregnant.

'At least that's something. Darling, it rends me to see you so sad. I wish I hadn't ever introduced damned Jack if he's done this to you. But you do understand, don't you, that that's the man he is? Gloriously here, and then not here and a vale of tears left behind him?'

'Yes. I always knew that. It's all right, I promise. I'm not in love with Jack. Just let me get these bloody exams over . . .'

'Amy.'

Even though Amy was conscious of being absurdly and unnecessarily on the verge of tears, Adeline comforted her. Her gaiety was like a rock.

The week of the exams came. Amy fumbled through them, panic alternating with dull apathy. By the time they were over, she was convinced that she had failed. On the night after her last paper, she went to bed with a headache that was almost blinding her. She woke up again at five in the morning shivering uncontrollably, and soaked in her own sweat. She pushed back the bedcovers and tried to stand up and her knees buckled beneath her. Somehow she crawled back and lay down. She was puzzled by the illusion that she seemed to be floating somewhere above the narrow bedstead, and almost amused by the way that the room changed its dimensions around her.

343

Amy had no idea how long it was before her door opened and someone leant over her. A hand that felt as cold as ice touched her forehead. After that Dr Davis appeared. Amy tried to struggle respectfully upright, certain that he was on ward rounds and had caught her asleep on an empty bed.

'I'm sorry,' she murmured. 'I'm so sorry. It was a silly mistake.'

After that, time was confusion. Night and day came at unpredictable intervals, and her head and chest hurt unbearably. Once or twice Amy woke up and saw Bethan knitting at her bedside. It convinced her that she was a little girl again, and she turned her head on the pillow towards Isabel. She called for her, and then cried when she wouldn't come.

Then, one morning, she woke up and found herself in her own room at Bruton Street. A nurse she didn't recognize was opening the curtains on a fresh, pale blue summer sky.

'Hello, dear,' the nurse said brightly. 'Are we feeling ourself this morning?' She took Amy's hand to feel her pulse. Amy tried to struggle upright, and felt her physical weakness.

'What is the matter with me?'

'Nothing that won't mend. Don't worry yourself. Mr Hardwicke will be in later to see you.'

Sure enough, the family doctor came with his leather bag and a watch-chain looped across his waistcoat front. For a moment Amy was disoriented again, wondering if she was still a little girl with measles, and everything else no more than a dream.

'What's the matter with me?' she repeated, hearing weak petulance in her voice.

'Mhmm. Mhmm.' Mr Hardwicke was examining her. He took the stethoscope out of his ears. 'Well now. You've had a nasty bout of influenza. I think you were a little run down before it, so it laid you particularly low. There was a touch of chest infection which worried us all for a day or two as well, but I think you've got the better of that now. You'll be up and about in no time. Nurse?'

He was talking to the attendant who had woken her up, but Amy felt herself jump automatically to attention at the summons. She laughed weakly, with a touch of hysteria.

'That's it,' the doctor said benignly. 'Soon be your old cheerful self.'

After Mr Hardwicke came Adeline, perfumed and jewelled and like a breath of summer in the sickroom.

344

'Have I been very ill?' Amy asked in bewilderment. Adeline put her arms round her to hide her face for a moment. When she had it under control again she answered, 'My darling, for twenty-four hours at death's door. I actually went down to St Margaret's and said a prayer. Can you imagine? Me?'

Amy lay back against the pillows. The room was light and bright, washed with pale sunshine. The sun touched her pictures and the tattered covers of her girlhood books and the flowers, and shone on her mother's dark red hair. Outside were the windows of the houses opposite, clear sky, and the rumble of London. The world was beautiful. She felt calm, and warm, and glad to be in it.

It was two weeks before Amy was well enough to go to Chance. When the day came she tottered down the stairs, supported by Mr Glass and one of the footmen. Adeline sailed ahead to where her chauffeur was waiting with the Bentley. They lowered Amy into her seat, and wrapped the fur rugs around her legs as gently as if she might break.

'I can manage,' she protested, half-laughing. 'And it's June. I don't need rugs.'

'Don't argue,' Adeline said.

Chance soothed her as it hadn't done for years.

As the long summer days began to slip past Amy got better by steady leaps. She had been recuperating for almost a week when the letter came from the Royal Lambeth. She had passed. She was almost at the bottom of the list, but she had passed. She was a State Registered Nurse at last. Amy tucked the letter into the pocket of her dress. It was completely unexpected because she had been so certain she had failed, and the good news gave her more quiet pleasure than anything since Jack's time. Feeling the slight, stiff crackle of it as she walked, Amy wandered through the sunlit house. For no particular reason her feet led her down the long carpeted corridor to the carved double doors that closed off the orangery.

Thinking of Richard and Tony she slipped inside, her soft shoes noiseless on the marble floor. The morning sun slanted obliquely through the glass roof and the tangle of leaves and strange blossoms cast distorted shadows over the statues in the wall niches. The heat was almost tropical, and it drew the scent

345

from the dampened earth and from the throats of the brilliant flowers.

Amy sat down on the seat at the end and let the warmth wrap its soothing languor around her. Then she heard water dripping and looked up to see one of the gardeners working. He was bent intently over an orchid, feeling the earth with his fingers. Amy saw that he was bare-armed and bare-throated in the heat.

She knew the shape of his head, and the way that he stooped, even in the high orangery, as if he was too used to cramped places.

She knew that the hands stroking the petals of the orchid were marked with blue scars.

It was Nick Penry.

346

13

In the same instant, Nick looked up and saw her. A girl with dark red hair cut short around a thinner, paler face than he remembered. The blue-green eyes were the same, watching him, unstartled.

Nick put down his watering-can and half-straightened, on the point of greeting her like a friend. As he moved, one of the greenfinches fluttered noisily from the fronds of the tallest palm and began to peck at the scatter of crumbs that he brought in every day for them. No one but the gardeners ever came to the orangery, and he had welcomed the birds' company. Now the sound reminded him of where he was. He turned the warm flash of recognition into a distant nod, and stooped to his work once more. Amy went to him, brushing the glossy leaves aside impatiently. She stood beside him, forcing him by her closeness to look up and acknowledge her again.

'Hello,' she said quietly. 'Don't you remember me?'

He remembered her. He remembered her with perfect clarity from the soft silence of her house in Bruton Street, and since he had come to Chance he had glimpsed her again, even watching for her with a kind of perverse fascination. He had seen her walking slowly on the terraces with her father, and once riding a big brown horse, her hair in a net under her peaked cap. He had seen her last Christmas, when he had brought a barrowload of red-berried holly up to decorate the hall for the servants' party. She had been kneeling under the half-dressed tree, holding up a silver star. The last time had been on Boxing Day, standing in the middle of a knot of wheeling horses whose breath clouded the air. A man in white breeches with a top hat shading his handsome face had leaned down from his saddle to kiss her on the mouth. Nick had turned sharply away into the emptiness of his Christmas holiday.

'You look different,' he said defensively.

'I look better than I did.' Suddenly she was grinning at him. 'I've been ill. I've been sent home to recuperate. I don't quite know what to do with myself, actually.'

After the surprise of seeing her Nick was in possession of himself again. He was standing politely waiting for her to finish, the picture of a deferential servant. Amy heard as clearly as if he had said it aloud his ironic *Will that be all, ma'am?* She felt a slow, red flush spreading over her cheeks. 'What are you doing?' she asked, to cover herself.

'Working.'

The single word held all the weight of difference between them. The work he had needed so desperately, and she had held in the palm of her hand. The need to go on at it, whatever came, while Amy rested and recovered. The difference, again.

'Do you like it here?' she asked. She sounded like Royalty visiting a hospital, she thought, or her mother gracing a local church fête.

'I like the flowers.'

Amy turned round in surprise. Nick was bending over the cream and gold petals of the orchid again, his thumb just touching the bloom of the inner lip.

'What's that one?' she asked, clinging to the hope of a safe topic.

'Don't you know?' His dark eyebrows went up, mocking her. 'It's the Brazilian orchid, *Epidendrum fragrans.*'

'My great-grandfather was the only plantsman in the family. He brought all these things back from his travels.' Amy gestured around at the moist greenery, the aerial roots that curled and looped and the heavy-scented, florid blooms. She was conscious of the hothouse heat under her hairline and the dampness gathering in the small of her back and at the cuffs of her dress. She saw that there was a faint sheen of sweat in the hollow of Nick's throat where the dark hair showed at his open collar. He saw her looking.

'I'm very sorry.' The stiffness momentarily dispelled by the orchids' beauty was back again. 'Mr Dawe doesn't permit the gardeners near the house without collars and ties. But no one ever comes in here.'

Mr Dawe was the ancient, formally trained head gardener. He regarded every flower cut from his beds and borders as a sacrifice. Amy smiled faintly at the thought of him.

'It doesn't matter to me,' she said, 'I'm a nurse now, you know.' She had meant to imply that she was a matter-of-fact, hard-working person herself, but it had come out instead sounding as if the sight of a man's bare chest was a familiar one. Amy felt the colour deepening in her already flushed face. Nick Penry was standing watching her, his respectful attitude only a veneer over the challenging mockery. Amy remembered the anger he had stirred in her on the day of the hunger march, and she swallowed it down again, determined to be friendly. He could laugh at her if he pleased, but she wouldn't give him the satisfaction of seeing that she minded.

'Do you know a lot about flowers?'

'I didn't, until I came here. Not much grows, down the pits,' he said drily. 'When I came here, they started me off in the gardens as a handyman. Digging, forking manure, that kind of thing. Easy work, but not exactly interesting. Then, not long afterwards, one of the lads went off sick and they pulled me in to work in the cold houses. It was fascinating, seeing all the cuttings standing up in those little pots as if they would wither and die for sure, and then coming back and seeing that they'd taken, with all the white roots curled in the pot like threads. Mr Dawe said I had a talent for it, and kept me there. Then a couple of months ago he put me in charge of this place.' Nick glanced up at the curve and swell of glass roof rising to the central ridge. 'I'm going to put the blinds down on the sunny side,' he said.

On the house wall a system of metal rods was connected to a polished brass handle. Nick began to wind it round and with grudging squeaks of wire against metal faded rolls of green canvas unfurled against the glass. When one side of the ogee roof was covered, a mysterious green shade fell across the jungle of plants and dimmed the strident blossoms. Amy felt the coolness fall across her face and looked up gratefully. The orangery felt like a rain forest instead of a tropical island.

Nick had gone back to his flowers. She was afraid, from his absorbed expression, that the moment of confidence was over. But after a moment he began to talk again, almost to himself.

'I like the orchids best. Look at this one.' He reached out to touch a dark pink flower with a soft lip that turned downwards and out like a woman's mouth. 'Did you ever see anything so lovely? So uselessly and extravagantly beautiful?'

In the dim, scented heat Amy felt a little shiver puckering her skin. If you come from Nantlas, she thought, seeing in her mind's eye the grey stone and black dust and the cold curtains of rain, then the flamboyance of orchids would strike your eyes like a torch in the darkness. She thought they were sinister. Her own preference was for the flowers of the cottage gardens, the grey and blue of lavender and the spikes of lupins, and the innocence of daisies and sweet peas.

'I started reading about them. There are the records in the estates office. I went into town, to the public library. But there are only two books on orchids there, neither of them much good.'

Amy remembered that behind the metal-latticed doors of the Chance library there was almost a whole wall of botany books. 'I think there must be some of my great-grandfather's in the library here,' she said. 'I could look them out for you.'

Nick picked up his watering-can again. 'That would be very kind,' he said.

Don't, Amy wanted to beg him. Don't make me be Lady Bountiful. It doesn't have to be like that.

'How is your son?' she asked.

'Well enough, thank you. He had a kind of blood disease and we were badly worried. But he's getting treatment and he's almost back to normal now. He won't ever be right, because of what happened when he was born. But it seemed hard that he should have to suffer even more than that.'

Amy thought of the Lambeth, and some of the things she had seen in the children's long-stay wards. 'Yes,' she said quietly.

Nick was working, apparently eager to be alone again with his flowers. Amy only knew that she wanted to go on talking to him.

'And your wife?' she persisted. 'Don't they miss you at home?'

He jerked round so that he stood squarely in front of her. His height was suddenly threatening, with no trace of a submissive stoop left now.

'Why do you want to know?' he snapped. The odd greeny-grey of his eyes was hard and opaque.

'I . . .'

'My wife is well. They are both fed, thanks to you, by what I send back from here. Is that what you want, for me to say thank you? Why don't you come right out and ask me? "I'd like you

350

o show some gratitude, Mr Penry." Well then, thank you. My son's alive, my wife's got food and clothes and a fire in the grate. All thanks to you, Miss Lovell. Will there be anything else, miss?'

Amy stepped back as if he had struck her. The air suddenly felt leaden, as if a thunderstorm quivered overhead.

'Why do you hate me so much?' she asked.

Nick stood for a long moment without moving, and then let the watering-can drop sharply so that the metal clanged on the marble floor.

'Ach.' There was despair as well as disgust in the guttural little sound. 'I don't hate you. I don't care enough. It doesn't matter, either way.'

'I don't believe you,' Amy said hotly. 'Not about me, but you do care. You care about things, all right. That's what's the matter with you.'

Then she turned and walked away, slowly and with measured steps, denying him the satisfaction of seeing her run.

The heavy, carved doors closed firmly on the rampant jungle and Nick was left alone with the finches.

He stood in the same position, staring ahead of him. When a whirr of green wings brought another of the birds down to his crumbs, Nick wearily lifted his hand and rubbed his face.

Aloud, he said something in Welsh. *Mae'n ddrwg geni.* I'm sorry. And then, bending to his work again, 'The Honourable Amalia Lovell, wasn't it? *But my friends call me Amy.* I expect you've got plenty of those. You don't need another.'

Amy went back along the silent corridor, faster now that he couldn't see her, almost running until she reached her room. The nurse who had come to look after her was smoothing the white cover on the bed.

'Miss Lovell? Are you all right? Here, sit down.'

Amy shook her head. 'I'm just breathless. I walked too fast up the stairs. There's no need to stay. I'll just sit quietly for a while.'

At last, the woman went away and left her alone. Amy sat down on the seat in the deep window embrasure. The glass was cool to lean her burning face against. Beneath her the mown grass of the park rolled away to the huge cedar tree, and almost in the shade of it a man was working, raking up the folded swathes of cut grass into neat piles.

Abruptly, she turned away from the sight.

The morning's papers and a new glossy magazine were laid ou on her table. Tony Hardy had sent her a package of new novel when she was ill, and the coloured spines glowed invitingly. Amy picked one out and flipped through the pages. Nothing was right Nick Penry's opaque eyes stared out insultingly.

Amy stood up again. She would go and find Gerald. Since she had been at home a kind of easy companionship had developed between them. She had begun to suspect that he even enjoyed having her with him. She would look for her father. Perhaps he would come and walk with her, or ride up over the ridge and gallop down the other side into the cool wind.

Outside the offices of Randle & Cates at exactly one p.m. a taxicab drew up. A young man in a white linen jacket with a loosely knotted, pale pink tie sprang out, paid the driver and dashed up the steps.

Tony Hardy, watching from the window of his first-floor front office, drew back a little and frowned.

A moment later his secretary came in to announce the visitor 'Mr Lovell.'

Richard breezed in immediately. 'Tony. Here I am. It looks divine, you know. I'm thrilled to death. Everyone will buy it, I'm quite certain.'

'Everyone will talk about it. That isn't quite the same as shelling out the necessary for a copy, I assure you.'

Tony picked up a book from a little pile of identical volumes stacked neatly on his desk. The jacket was plain pale grey, and the title stared out in bold black type. *The Innocent and the Damned.* Beneath, in smaller letters, it proclaimed itself *Nearly a Novel, by Richard Lovell.*

Richard came to stand beside Tony, admiring the effect at arm's length.

'So un-innocent looking. It could so easily have looked like a cheap romance, don't you think? And I think we were so right not to go for some fussy picture that would have lessened the impact.'

Tony sighed. 'I'm not worried about the impact it will have.'

Richard rounded on him at once. 'What's the matter? Losing your nerve?'

'Not on our behalf. It won't be the first risk I've taken, nor

352

the first *succès de scandale* we'll have suffered. I was thinking more about the effect on you, as it happens.'

Richard laughed delightedly. 'My dear, just look at me. Do I look too fragile to cope with a brickbat or two?'

Tony did look. Richard Lovell had grown from the detached, clever little boy he had tutored into an even less knowable adult. And Tony thought that he probably knew him as well as anyone else in the world, outside his family. Richard had cultivated his flair for the ridiculous to the point where he was an invariably amusing companion, the expected life and soul of any of the unconventional gatherings he chose to frequent. He was determinedly cheerful, and seemed dedicated only to enjoying himself. In that respect he was like his mother. But Tony knew that behind his half-closed eyes Richard hid a much more complex nature. He was adept at disguising himself. Even his age was difficult to guess at. With his cultivatedly weary, cynical or occasionally puckish manner Richard, at nineteen, might have been taken for anything between twenty and thirty.

And now there was his extraordinary, risky, pyrotechnic novel. Thousands of copies of it, delivered this morning to the Randle & Cates warehouse from the carefully indemnified printers.

'Well?' Richard prompted. 'Do I?'

'No,' Tony said. 'I don't think you're too fragile to cope with whatever they fling at you. What about your family?'

'Amy already knows that I have written a novel. I don't think, given what she knows about you and me, that she will be shocked into insensibility. Adeline loves me to the point of idolatry and would continue to do so even if she heard I was a mass-murderer. I don't think poor Bel is in a position to care.'

The omission was all too clear.

'And Lord Lovell?'

Unusually for Richard there were two or three seconds of silence before he answered. And then his voice was measured, without the light sparkle of flippancy. 'I hate everything that my father stands for. I don't hate him, although I easily could. I can't take any responsibility for what Gerald might feel.'

Tony replaced the new book on the pile.

'And the other risks?'

Richard was growing impatient. 'It's rather late, isn't it, to be beating our breasts about all this? If you mean the *gendarmes*, I don't intend to hang about for long enough to be clapped in the

353

cells. And I'm still a minor, remember, and so the innocent party. Your own lawyers have assured us that I have been as discreet as fiction demands about the less innocent. Enough.'

Tony was putting on his tweed jacket that had been hanging on the back of his office chair, and glanced at Richard's turnout as he did so.

'You don't exactly dress discreetly.'

'Oh dear.' Richard fluffed out his pink tie. 'I am in the kennel today. And I thought we were supposed to be celebrating. I shall pretty myself up as much as I please. It's one of life's least damaging pleasures, and one that you, in those frightful tweeds, clearly don't take enough account of. Tony, you know that you are my dearest friend, and I am grateful unto death for what you're doing. But just sometimes you can be just a little too much the old maid. Now, let's go and have this famous publisher's lunch. I've struck everything else out of the diary for the rest of the day.'

'God help us,' Tony murmured, as they went down the stairs together.

In the restaurant Richard ordered champagne 'to begin with'. He watched the waiter pouring it and then leant back, stroking the side of his glass.

'Are the review copies out?'

'Of course. Two hundred of them. I've tried to make sure that enough have gone to people likely to be sympathetic.'

'The old queers' network? I don't want sympathy.'

'Don't be a fool. You want good reviews.'

'And the bookshops?'

'Are taking copies in cautious quantities. Waiting for publication and the reviewers' reactions.'

Richard lifted his glass. 'One more thing. You've never really admitted it. Is it a good book?'

Tony smiled and picked up his own glass. 'It's a brilliant book. It'll probably land us both in gaol, even so.'

'Thank you. Here's to publication day, then.'

'To next week,' Tony said, and they drank together.

Gerald was reading the newspaper on the shady side of the long terrace at Chance. His leg was propped stiffly on a footstool in front of him. Amy sat down close to him on the stone balustrade, feeling the warmth of the pitted stone under her fingers and the tiny, crumbly yellow lichens.

'Is your leg bad today?' she asked.

Gerald rustled his paper. 'The same.' He was curt in discussing what he regarded as physical weaknesses.

Amy tried again. 'Is it well enough for us to have a walk together after lunch?'

He put the newspaper down and folded it up with an air of patience in the face of constant interruption. 'A walk? A walk to where?'

'Just across the park. Over the ridge, if you felt like it.'

'Felled a lot of oaks, over the other side. Sign of the times.' Gerald sighed gloomily and took his watch suspended on a gold chain out of his waistcoat pocket. 'Time for luncheon. I'll see how much I've got to do afterwards.' But when he had heaved himself upright he offered his arm companionably to Amy and they strolled back into the house together.

The route to the dining-room took them through the long, brown-leather and faded gilt expanse of the library. Amy glanced up at the heights of shelving and the thousands of books in their locked cases.

'Papa, where are the botany books? The ones Great-grandfather collected? I remember we used to look at the paintings of orchids when we were children.'

'End bay, on the right, I believe. Why do you ask?'

She thought quickly, and decided on the truth. 'One of the gardeners is working in the orangery, and wanted to read some more about the plants. The orchids, in particular. I thought they might help him.'

'Don't go lending the books to the damned gardeners. They can't read, half of them, anyway.'

'Oh, this one can,' Amy said.

After his lunch Gerald demanded abruptly, 'What are you sitting about for? Let's have this walk, if we're going.'

He took his stick, but he made a point of only using it to swish at the grass as they walked. Amy was quickly out of breath, and so their slow pace was perfectly matched. In the sunshine they climbed the gently rising parkland to the crest of the ridge. When they reached it Amy and her father stood still, arm in arm. On one side of them was the dappled green patchwork of woodland, and on the other the grassy slope dipped down to the great grey house set amongst its terraces and flowers. In the distance was the sweep of high wall that enclosed the park, and the domestic huddle of houses at the village gates. The sky was a perfect, impervious blue, and under it the countless shades of green and gold shimmered in the haze of heat.

Amy blinked at the tears in her eyes, and then they came rolling down her cheeks. Since her illness she had cried easily, sometimes inexplicably. But today it came with the unexpected wave of love for the acres of Chance, pulling inside her like a bowstring.

'It's so beautiful,' she said, turning her face away from her father.

'As beautiful as any woman,' he echoed her. 'It's all here for you children. The three of you.'

And there it will end, Amy thought, with a moment of clairvoyant certainty. She almost stumbled as Gerald turned them away from the ridged back of the hill and down the slope again.

'Steady,' he murmured. 'Tell me. What're you going to do with yourself, when this little illness is all behind you?'

'Go back to nursing. That's what I am, now. A nurse. State Registered,' she added lightly.

Gerald gave his characteristic snort. 'I don't understand you damned children,' he complained. 'But I suppose this nursing idiocy is better than marrying some fool or other.'

Breathlessly Amy groped for the words that would let them begin to talk about Isabel, even about Richard. But awkwardness and apprehension drove all the possibilities out of her head. They never would talk, she realized. It was too many years too late. If only Gerald could have talked to his children, to his wife, even, Amy thought sadly, how different everything might be.

'I don't think I'm going to marry anyone,' she told him honestly.

'Delighted to hear it. Now then, I want to go down and see Mackintosh in the office.'

'I'll walk down there with you.'

They crossed the park in a long diagonal, and came to the estates office at the gates. Mr Mackintosh, a sandy-eyebrowed Scot, was working at his desk. Amy sat outside in the sun while Gerald despatched his business and then, when he limped off to

356

see another of his staff, Amy slipped in to see the estate manager. He bobbed up from behind his desk at once.

'Good morning, Miss Amy. It's grand to see you well again. We heard you were very bad at one time.'

'Thank you, Mr Mackintosh. I'm quite all right again now. Tell me – Mr Penry, one of the gardeners. I met him working with the orchids, and he seemed so interested in them that I offered to lend him some books from the library. Where shall I take them?'

'That's really very good of you, Miss Amy. Penry shouldn't be troubling you. If you would like me to come up to the house for the books, I'll see he gets them. And takes care of them,' Mr Mackintosh added.

'It's no trouble. It was my suggestion to him,' Amy said pleasantly. 'I'm sure I'll bump into him again in the orangery.' She turned away, and then as an afterthought she asked, 'Where is Mr Penry living?'

The sandy eyebrows went up by the merest fraction. 'In the empty keeper's cottage up on the north side.'

'All the way over there?'

Amy knew the tiny cottage. It wasn't easy to settle any of the estate families in it because of its isolation.

'Penry seems to prefer it,' Mr Mackintosh said with a touch of grimness. Amy gathered that Nick wasn't exactly his favourite amongst the men, and smothered a little smile at the thought of them confronting each other.

'Thank you, Mr Mackintosh.'

'Thank *you*, Miss Amy. You'll find his lordship on the stable side with the farrier.' As she walked out again into the late-June warmth, Amy knew what she would do.

It took her most of the evening in the library to find the books she wanted. The botany collection belonging to the fifteenth Lord Lovell had hardly been touched for decades. Amy found the brown-leather Victorian volumes dealing with orchids, with the minutely detailed, almost erotic paintings of columns and labellae, bulbils and fleshy aerial roots that had vaguely disturbed her as a child. But something else tugged at her memory, and she went on searching.

It was late when she made her discovery, standing on the

357

highest level of the mahogany library steps. The big, square books, bound in calf, were tucked in at one end of the highest shelf, almost hidden by the frame of the case. Amy took them out, three of them, and blew the dust away. Then she carried them to one of the big tables and laid them carefully in the light of a lamp.

Inside the flyleaf of the first, in a vigorous script that time had faded to faint sepia, was written 'The journal of my travels through South America. George Lovell, 1854–1856'.

Turning the pages, Amy began to read the matter-of-fact accounts of plant-hunting expeditions into tropical rain forests or up the inhospitable rock-faces of unclimbed mountain peaks. Her great-grandfather had clearly been a dedicated and stoical traveller. On one page she read with horrified fascination how one of his native bearers had accidentally shot himself in the thigh with a pistol, and how George had performed the operation to remove the bullet himself, with only the first-aid kit to help him. A little further on came the description of how a troublesome wound in his lordship's own leg was refusing to heal and how he 'feared that gangrene might develop and so hold up progress entirely'.

The unemotional account of his self-cauterization with only brandy to dull the pain made even Amy shudder.

But the adventures and obstacles were only incidental to the real purpose of the expeditions, the discovery and categorization of rare plants. The appearance and habitat of every one was minutely described, and the pages were full of long botanical names and tiny, immaculate sketches of leaves, petals and stamens. A regular entry was *N.S.* for *new species*, or with occasional uncharacteristic tentativeness, *?N.S.*

Amy read on, intrigued by her relative's obsession.

The big, domed clock on the library wall told her that it was nearly one in the morning when she closed the last book.

Tomorrow she would take them to show to Nick. She knew that the stories of how the orchids had been found and brought home to the orangery would fascinate him.

It would be a peace-offering.

The next afternoon Amy went riding with Gerald. They hacked slowly over to his nearest neighbours' damp manor house where they had tea and fruit cake on the lawn and deplored the state of the country, and then rode back again. Gerald was a fine horseman in spite of his leg, and considered the round trip of ten miles hardly a ride at all. Amy was relieved to discover when they reached Chance again that she was barely tired. She was recovering rapidly.

They ate an early dinner in companionable silence while Gerald peered at a bloodstock magazine, and then he went off to his rooms and left her alone. Amy put on her jacket, then searched for and found a basket big enough to carry the explorer's journals. She went out of the terrace doors, down the steps to the lawn, and set off towards the north side of the estate.

It was dusk, and the blue-grey light seemed almost thick enough to touch. As she silently crossed the grass, she saw the occasional glimmer of a moth's wings, and once the black swoop of a bat against the sky. She caught the scent of honeysuckle from the gardens, and the succulent richness of damp earth.

It was more than a mile to the keeper's cottage and Amy walked slowly, shifting the heavy basket from arm to arm and enjoying the stillness. At last she saw ahead of her the dense black line where the woodland encroached on the park and a tiny square of yellow light standing out against it.

For the last hundred yards she walked even more slowly, listening to the faint squeaks her flat shoes made in the wet grass, and the distant burr of a car on the lane beyond the woods.

The cottage window was uncurtained, and she stopped on the doorstep with her hand raised to knock. Nick was sitting at the wooden table, reading by the yellow glow of a paraffin lamp. Amy had just time enough to see the sadness in his intent face before he sensed her eyes on him. His head jerked up just as she rapped on the door.

'Come in,' Nick's Welsh voice, firm and unstartled.

Amy pushed the low door open and stepped inside. A moth fluttered around her head and was drawn at once to the glass mantle of the lamp.

Amy stood on the stone-flagged floor and looked at the bare lime-washed walls, and unlit black range and the tiny steep staircase that corkscrewed up to the single room overhead.

How lonely it must be here.

How long had Nick lived in this little house, a mile from anyone, more than a hundred miles from Nantlas? A year. Over a year. *I've never thought*, Amy reproached herself.

Nick was looking steadily at her, one eyebrow raised a fraction.

'This is an honour,' he said. 'So far, so late at night.' Amy wasn't certain, but she thought she saw the flicker of a smile. 'And alone? Or did you get one of the grooms to bring you over?'

Amy put her basket on the table. The room was so small she only had to stretch her arm out to it from the doorway.

'Please,' she said. 'Don't let's begin like this again. Can't you see me just as a person? Just as Amy, and nothing to do with Chance or any of the rest of it?'

There was a small moment of silence. 'I'll try,' Nick said, and now his mouth did twist up into a smile. 'What's in the basket?'

'A peace-offering. Can we call a truce?'

He laughed now. 'If you like.'

Amy lifted the books out one by one. 'My great-grandfather's journals. The history of your orchids.'

He reached out and took them, laying them on the table under the lamplight just as Amy had done the night before. He began to turn the pages, glancing at them and then leaning forward with his head bent, absorbed. Amy stood quietly in the doorway watching him, and then she saw that he had forgotten her. She looked aound the room. The beams were so low that Nick must have to stoop under them. The only furniture was the table and chair, and a black oak settle at right angles to the range. On the table beside an empty plate was a pile of books, and a scatter of papers, letters and pamphlets. Amongst them Amy recognized the familiar style of pronouncements from Appleyard Street. Clealy Nick was still politically active, for all his isolation at Chance.

Amy crossed the room behind his chair and sat down on the settle, drawing her knees up beneath her chin to make herself comfortable on the narrow seat.

Nick was smiling as he read.

'Here it is,' he said. 'The one you were asking about.' He hadn't forgotten her, then. 'The Brazilian orchid. "A fine specimen. Placed it in the peat bag with the greatest of care and entrusted it to the boy to carry back to the camp. There being an hour before dusk, I went on up the ravine, but found nothing of note. May 17, 1855."' He touched the two unopened books as if gauging the mass of information that they contained. 'Thank you for bringing them,' he said simply. 'I shall enjoy reading it all.' This time he was smiling at her, and the warmth dissolved the harsh lines in his face.

Amy was conscious of the yellowness of the lamplight and the shadows on the bare walls, the park stretching silent and moist beyond them, a moment of waiting, as if for something inevitable. She looked around her again, at the tiny room with the fluttering moths and Nick at his table, his hands resting on the old journals.

'Who did you say he was?' Nick asked, and she jumped.

'Who? Oh, my father's grandfather.'

'I like the sound of your father's grandfather. He must have been quite an adventurer. What happened to him in the end?'

'He died safely in his bed here at Chance, as far as I know. At least, he's buried in the church along with everyone else. Except for my brother Airlie, who died on the Somme.'

'Mine too,' Nick said. 'I thought I'd be a pacifist after that. I'm not so sure, now.' There was another moment of silence. One of the moths drawn to the lamp found the top of the mantle, settled for an instant and then plunged. There was the faintest sizzle as the papery wings burned.

Amy thought of Airlie, and of Nick's brother, and then of her own time vanishing as irrevocably as the moth's. She was possessed by a sense of loss and transience, and by the certainty that if she didn't reach out and hold it something vital would be gone too.

Then she looked up and saw Nick watching her, and she thought that she knew his face better than anything else in the world.

'Why did you come?' he asked softly.

'To bring you the journals. As a peace-offering.'

Nick stood up and came over to the settle. 'Why did you really come?'

He was forcing her to answer, uncompromising, but Amy saw the flicker in his face that betrayed him. So Nick was vulnerable, and needy, too. Suddenly, the precious something she had been afraid to lose was there, within her grasp. The closeness and importance of it made her heart knock in her chest.

'I came because I wanted to see you.' She shouldn't look away, covering herself. Amy met his eyes. 'I'm afraid of you, but I want to be with you.'

That was the truth. She didn't understand yet, but she was certain that she wanted to be with him.

Nick stooped, and then knelt in front of the settle. He was

very close. 'Don't be afraid,' he said. He took one of Amy's hands, lying clenched in her lap, and held it. And then: 'I'm afraid, too.'

Amy understood that he had stopped fencing with her. He was no longer taunting her with the distance that separated them, and he was admitting the question that had hovered between them since the night at Bruton Street.

Amy's heart was hammering so that she was sure he must hear it. The breath caught in her chest and her mouth opened to draw in the air. She saw Nick's high cheekbones and wry mouth, and the chameleon eyes suddenly clear under the black brows, and she knew that she was seeing Nick himself, unguarded.

'Don't be afraid,' she whispered.

Very slowly, he bent his head. His mouth brushed against hers as lightly as the moth's wings.

'Amy. *My friends call me Amy*,' he murmured, and impatiently she turned her head a fraction so that their mouths met again. His hands came up to cup her face, tilting it to his, and then he kissed her.

Amy closed her eyes, and against the velvet blackness she saw the yellow halo of the paraffin lamp, bright and dim, image upon image, receding into the dark. Stillness folded around them, their own stillness, inviolable.

Nick.

His mouth opened against hers, wider, bruising her lips with its insistence. She tasted the quick movement of his tongue and answered it with her own.

Nick's hand moved, down to the buttons of her thin jacket and then to the loose bodice of her dinner dress. His fingers found the fastening and opened it, and then his hand enclosed her breast. His palm moved gently against the nipple's hardness.

Amy opened her eyes. He was looking at her with a kind of disbelief, urgent and tentative at the same time. His eyes went to the copper light in her hair, and the tilt of her head on her long neck, the pearls in the hollow of her throat and the swell of pale skin under his hand.

She saw how much he needed her. And just as quickly Nick drew down a veil somewhere. They were kneeling on the bare flagstones now, facing each other with their fingers interlaced, and he leaned back a little.

'Is this what you came for?' he asked her. 'It's been a long

362

time. A very long time – ' she heard the huskiness in his voice – 'but I can do this if it's what you want.'

Taunting her, she thought, and testing her. Testing himself, and his power to resist as well.

If he would just ask her, Amy thought, she would gladly lie down there and then on the bare stones and give herself to him. And knowing that, she was past pride. If he thought she was voracious, well then, she would prove herself to be other things too.

'Not just for this,' she told him, struggling for the truth. 'To be able to look at you and talk to you, as well. I told you, I wanted to be with you. I don't understand what else, quite, yet. But yes, I wanted you to touch me. That's the truth, Nick. Won't you tell me the truth too? Don't you want it too?'

She saw it flash in his face, and heard it in the harsh edge in his voice. 'Oh yes,' he whispered. 'I want it. I want you. Ever since I saw you . . .'

'Nick.'

The veil had dissolved again.

Nick, I'm here.

Amy felt as if his kiss would swallow her up, and as if her answer to him would wash them both away. His height bent her backwards, and she felt the weight of his body over hers as his mouth moved to her throat, and then to her bare shoulders where the dress had slipped. The stone was cold under her thighs. His dark head dipped again and she saw how black it was against her own white skin, and then he kissed her breast, moving his tongue in a slow circle so that she quivered and felt Nick's trembling answering her. She drew him closer and he rested his head against her, letting her cradle him in her arms like an infant. As they knelt in the sweet silence Nick looked across the room to the uncurtained window.

At once in her own head Amy saw the cottage as she had walked towards it from the park, a black shape against the dense woods with the little square of light picking it out. Picking them out, to the eyes of the night.

Let the eyes look, she told herself, but Nick lifted his head. Gently he slipped the soft stuff of her dress to cover her shoulders. He knelt back on his heels, watching her as if to imprint the sight of her inside his head. Then he reached out and touched her cheek, and with the palm of his hand, he smoothed her hair.

363

'Why?' Amy asked him.

'Think,' he said. She heard the sadness, and she wanted to reach out to him and kiss it away. But Nick picked up her jacket from where it had fallen and wrapped it around her.

'I don't care,' Amy said. 'None of it matters, out there. We can cover the window.'

And then there will be just us. Nick, I only want there to be us.

He smiled at her. 'You're very honest, Amy.'

He stood up and began to move around the little room, looking back at her as she knelt beside the hearth as if to convince himself that she was there.

'I want you to think, first. Think about out there, of course, about your life and mine. But I really meant think about in here. About what would happen. If it does begin, you know, it won't be easy to undo.'

He was warning her, holding off his own need for her benefit.

He was right, Amy knew that. There would be no undoing it. It was the thing that she had been afraid of losing, and the same thing that had seemed so easy to grasp, and so sweet when she had briefly tasted it. It was big now, so that it cast a shadow and hid everything else.

Amy stood up stiffly. She nodded, a quick jerk of her head.

'All right,' she promised him at last, in the certainty that there would be no avoiding what would happen, and even now no going back. 'I will think. But I don't need to. I know, already. I'll come back. You'll be here, won't you?'

Nick was sitting in his place at the table once more, touching the cover of the journal with his fingertips.

'I'm not going anywhere,' he said.

She looked quickly at him, afraid that he might have retreated into bitterness again. But he was simply stating what was true, and telling her that, yes, if she chose to come back he would be here.

Amy went to him and put her arms over his shoulders to touch his hands, resting her cheek against his hair. His arms tightened on hers, pulling her closer.

'It wouldn't be just me taking his lordship's daughter to bed. It would be more than that, wouldn't it? I wasn't sure that I'd ever want that again. Knowing what it costs, in the end.'

To Amy he seemed almost to be talking to himself. She wasn't

364

afraid of whatever it was ahead of them, because she had no experience of it. But Nick did, and Nick was afraid.

'Why don't you go home, any more?' she whispered against the black warmth of his hair.

'Because we hurt each other. I stay here, and I send her the money every week for Dickon. Once in a while she writes to me to tell me how he is. That's all.' And then, so quietly that she had to strain to catch the words, he said, 'Amy. Amy, is anything that might happen between us worth the risk of any more hurt? Putting everything else aside, that is?'

Amy thought. Everything else was Chance, and her father and Mr Mackintosh and the orangery, Nantlas and the pits and Mari and Dickon. Leaving herself and Nick. She turned her cheek against his head, closing her eyes. It would be impossible for her to walk out of the cottage now and leave him, and whatever it was he held in his hands for both of them.

'Yes,' Amy said fiercely. 'Yes. I know it's worth the risk.'

Nick stood up abruptly, turned to face her and pulled her against him. He looked down at the dark patches illness had left under her eyes, and at the hollows in her cheeks. His fingers clenched in her hair but he was gentle as he kissed her. For an instant, so that she was almost giddy with it, she felt the hard line of him against her. Then, just as gently, he let her go again.

Moving like a sleepwalker, Amy crossed the stone flags to the low doorway. She opened the door on to the blackness and the damp fragrance of the night air filled the room.

'Have you been lonely here?' she asked.

Nick smiled slightly. 'I've been as lonely as you have,' he answered.

Amy was briefly startled, and then she knew that he was right. For years she had been lonely, and tonight she wasn't lonely any longer.

'Would you like me to walk with you back to the house?' he asked formally.

Amy grinned her happiness at him. 'Nothing can happen to me at Chance. I'm perfectly safe.'

'I wonder if your father would agree with that, after tonight?'

Amy's smile was brilliant. 'I'm twenty-one years old, I don't need my father's safe-keeping any more. Good night, Nick. Think of me.'

Nick was standing beside his paraffin lamp, the shadows it cast

365

black across his face. 'I will.' She had already turned away when he called after her. She heard the crackle in his voice. 'You think,' he ordered.

'Yes.'

Then she was gone, closing the door behind her with a soft click of the latch. Nick went back to his chair, looking down at the books she had brought for him. 'Thank you for the orchid journals,' he murmured. Against the dull brown covers, watching him, he saw Amy's vivid face with her eyes as bright as stars.

Outside in the darkness Amy was running. Exhilaration bubbled up inside her like a spring and carried her towards where the lights of the big house sailed like a liner across the park.

The house was silent when she reached it, but as she passed the library door, the telephone began to ring. Knowing that her father would already be asleep, she went in and picked up the receiver. 'Chance,' she said automatically.

'Amy, my darling love, this is your erring brother.'

'Richard?' He sounded drunk, and triumphant, with an edge of apprehension that reminded her of when he had misbehaved as a small boy.

'The same.'

'Where are you?'

'At Bruton, at this very moment. Dear old Glass keeps the door so well against the vulgar columnists that it seems the sensible spot. And Mama is being a perfect archangel, too. Shocked to the core, of course, but just a tiny bit proud as well.'

'Richard, what are you talking about? You're tight, aren't you?'

'Fractionally. Oh dear, this conversation has come out completely back to front. I'm telephoning to say that the balloon has gone up, and all that. Keep your dear head down, and watch out for the old man.'

'What?'

'It's my novel, dearest. Just out this week, and I have to say attracting attention from every quarter. Respectable literary notices, but some thoroughly prurient bits of gossip as well, and seedy-looking fellows hanging round the back door reading the laundry lists. The news hasn't penetrated to the rural depths of Chance yet, then?'

Amy frowned as she tried to take in what Richard was saying. He had talked about a novel, of course. She even knew that he

366

had finished writing it. But she had never taken seriously the idea of its publication. Clearly that had been a mistake, Amy thought with a touch of grimness. Knowing her brother as well as she did, it was hard to believe that his novel would be particularly good news for the family.

'What's it about?' she asked cautiously.

'About me, of course.'

Amy closed her eyes, wondering if there was any way that the whole thing could be kept from Gerald. There wasn't, of course. He would hear about it in the end.

'I'll send a copy down for you to read, Amy. I'll be interested to hear what you think.'

'I know what I think already,' she snapped. 'Couldn't you have found a rather less cruel way of telling him?'

To do Richard justice, there was a moment or two of awkward silence before he answered, a shade too brightly, 'No, I don't think so. Did you really expect me to pop down to Chance and confront him over a game of billiards? "My cue, I think, Papa. By the way, I've been meaning to ask you. Do you know that I'm queer? No? Well, there it is. Nothing to be done about it, I'm afraid. Oh I say, good shot." Do you think that's how it should have been?'

Amy sighed. Clearly there was no use in trying to find out any more from him now.

'I'd go to bed, if I were you, Richard. I'm coming up to town in the morning and I'll see you then. Don't say anything to Papa yet, will you? Has there been anything in *The Times*?'

'No. Literary mags and scandal sheets.'

'He's not likely to see any of those, thank God. Until tomorrow, then, damn you.'

'Looking forward to it.'

'Good night,' Amy said coolly. And damn Tony Hardy as well, she thought, as she hung up.

Amy went slowly up the stairs to her room. The curtains were tightly drawn, her bed had been turned down and her night things laid out for her. On the table beside her bed the nurse had left her dose of tonic, and her sleeping draught already mixed. Amy picked up the little glass of cloudy liquid and looked at it, then poured it away. Sleep was irrelevant tonight. She didn't want to fall asleep and lose the thread of closeness that linked her to Nick across the silent park. She sat down in her armchair and

367

leant back with her eyes closed. At once he was there, with his head bent in the lamplight, and then with his face so close to hers that she saw the muscles move at the corner of his mouth.

If Richard chose to make his life into a matter for public gossip, then that was Richard's own business. She would do what she could when the time came to soften it for Gerald, but she couldn't change the truth. The anxiety for them both was real but it was pale tonight beside the brilliance of what she had discovered. She felt as exhilarated as if she were drunk herself.

'Nick,' she said softly.

She had to do what she had promised, and think about what loving him would mean. She could do that as easily in Bruton Street as here. More easily, perhaps, without the constant hope of seeing him in the garden or the orangery.

And then she would come back to him. She was as certain of that as if she had already done it, and the thought of it filled her with soft, quiet happiness.

Amy smiled. She was still smiling when, curled up on the bed in all her clothes, she fell dreamlessly asleep.

When she arrived the next day, the house in Bruton Street looked perfectly normal. Even if she had only half-expected to see a rabble of gossip columnists besieging the door, it was a relief to find that there wasn't one. Glass was his usual impassive self as he ushered her inside.

Amy went up to Adeline's white drawing-room. Her mother, in a perfectly draped Mainbocher dress, was sitting on a sofa reading a magazine.

'Darling!' she exclaimed. 'The drama, you would scarcely believe. Richard is so wicked. I guessed, no, I knew, of course, not that it matters nowadays except for the sake of the inheritance. But to put it all in a book, Amy, for everyone to read . . .'

And there, on the table beside her, was Richard's novel.

'Where is he?' Amy asked, picking it up.

'Lunching somewhere. The attention is turning his head. He does nothing except go out, come home to change into even more flamboyant clothes, and go out again.'

Amy could almost have smiled. There was the faintest note of pique in Adeline's voice. Her description of Richard's day was exactly the kind of programme she enjoyed most herself.

Adeline held out a white folder. 'And here are the press cuttings and reviews. The things people have said . . .'

Amy waved the folder away. 'I think I'll just read the book itself, first.'

'Do. And to think I was so approving of that Mr Hardy of yours, Amy. This is all his fault.'

'He's not mine, Mama. And it's Richard's fault. Tony Hardy's a publisher and a businessman, and he will do whatever his acumen suggests. I'll go down and read it in the library.'

'Some of the reviews are really very good,' Adeline called after her. 'He's a talented writer, you know.'

Adeline wasn't angry, Amy thought, as she went back downstairs. She adored Richard, and from childhood he had been her favourite. Nothing he could do, however injudicious, would ever change that.

The green shades in the library were drawn against the hot sunshine. The room was cool, and smelt faintly of dust and leather. Amy sat down at the wide desk. Just for a moment, she closed her eyes and thought of Nick. He might have sat in this chair to scrawl the note he had left for her after the night of the hunger march. *Do some more kissing*, he had written. *You might get to like it.*

I do, Amy thought, smiling.

Then she remembered what she was sitting in the library for. With a faint sigh she opened Richard's novel and began to read.

The Innocent and the Damned was short. Amy read it all, sitting in the quiet room, without looking up once. Then, when she had finished, she closed the sombre grey covers and sat quite still, staring unseeingly ahead.

It was all perfectly recognizable, yet painfully distorted because it was seen through Richard's eyes.

'Queer's vision,' she heard him say. They were all in it: the beautiful and sociable mother and the pretty sisters with their escorts. And the father, savagely drawn, cruel to the boy and remote from the man. Richard's innocent moved in a world they all knew. It was a world of the Fourth of June, the Eton and Harrow match, Henley Regatta and country house-parties and tennis. And then, as the innocence was eroded, another, parallel world emerged. It was a black world of corruption and degradation, pursued in the alleyways of Soho and the tattered streets of the East End. The knowing young man pushed deeper and

369

deeper into it in search of what he wanted, and needed. The end came abruptly. No longer innocent, he was stabbed to death by his lover of that night in a deserted bar.

That was Richard's metaphor for the progress of life. Light into dark, innocence into depravity, unstoppable. The bleakness of the vision frightened Amy. Was that what Richard thought, behind his smile and his flow of banter?

His book was sad, and also funny in macabre, characteristic bursts. It was brave, and a considerable achievement. And Amy thought that reading it would break her father's heart.

The telephone rang on the desk beside her, startling her. She realized that she had been sitting in the same position for hours, and she was stiff from head to foot.

'May I speak to Mr Lovell?' an unrecognizable voice asked.

'I'm afraid not. He's out at lunch.'

'Am I speaking to Lady Lovell?'

'No. I'm Mr Lovell's sister.'

'My name is Corbett. The *Evening Voice*. We're all very admiring of your brother's novel, here. Perhaps you can tell me why he describes it as "nearly a novel"? It's an unusual vision for a young man to conjure up, wouldn't you say? Especially for the son of Lord Lovell? A future Defender of His Majesty, as it were? Of course, if it is fiction, but an imagination so strong . . .'

'I can't comment,' Amy said coldly. 'You would have to talk to my brother in person. Good afternoon.' She hung up sharply, and then sat staring at the telephone, fighting the feeling of being invaded. So that was what Richard had meant by seedy fellows reading the laundry lists. She could only hope for Gerald's sake that the lists weren't too revealing.

The library door opened and Richard himself peered round it. 'Ah-ha. Mama told me you were lurking down here. Was that one of the vultures?'

'Yes. A horrible, insinuating man.'

'Dear me, how they love a whiff of corruption in high places. "Peer's Son charged with Immoral Behaviour". They are positively fainting with delight at the prospect.'

'Will it come to that?' Amy asked in alarm.

'Of course not. I'm far too circumspect.'

'Your book isn't circumspect.'

'It's fiction, darling. And it isn't, technically, obscene either. What did you think of it?'

370

Looking at him as she framed her answer, Amy saw that her brother looked, oddly, more substantial, as if his overnight success suited him. And she also saw that he was anxious. He didn't write to please, clearly, but he wanted approval. From her, at least.

'I thought it was impressive,' she said carefully. 'Scabrous, but impressive . . .'

'So kind,' he trilled at her, covering his pleasure with flippancy, as always.

' . . . and it will hurt Papa terribly.'

Richard's face stiffened. 'Our father has never thought about me,' he said, 'from the moment it sank through his hide that I couldn't be Airlie all over again. I can't adjust my life to please him, Amy. Truly I can't.'

'I suppose not,' she said sadly.

Dismissing the thought, Richard put his arm through hers. 'Come on. Let's have some tea and I'll tell all. I meant the book when I wrote it, deeply heartfelt and all that, of course. But it's been the most wonderful tease since it came out. I wouldn't have missed it for anything. Nervous, respectful reviews here, trying to convey the book's essence without mentioning the dread word *buggery*. Darling, I'm so glad you're a nurse and know all these things, tending those poor sailors down at Lambeth. It makes you so much easier to talk to.'

'You're thinking of Greenwich,' Amy protested.

'No, I'm not. I know my sailors. Anyway, po-faced rejections there saying it's not a book they could review in a family publication. The literary crowd in two camps – no, don't laugh – and every party one goes to divided right down the middle between people queuing to shake hands and people who can't snub one fast enough. Who would have thought anyone cared? Imploring letters from old queens and violent threats from purple brigadiers pouring into Randle & Cates by every post. Tony's been such a tower, the dear boy.'

'What's Tony's reaction to all this?' Amy asked, laughing in spite of herself.

'Unbridled delight. It's all shillings in the coffers, after all.'

As he always managed to do, Richard disarmed her. There was no point in judging or moralizing, because Richard was his own law.

He insisted on taking her out to dinner at the Ritz.

'I've got lots of cash. Do let's spend.'

He commanded, and got, the best table. 'See?' he crowed. 'Word has even spread here. They know I shall be filthily rich on the proceeds of my writings and they're looking to the ten bobs of the future.' He was already mildly drunk, and Amy knew from experience that it would be a long, bibulous evening. She settled back in her seat, prepared to be her brother's audience of one.

'I shall be rich, of course,' he assured her.

'And what will you do with all this wealth?'

'Oh, stay around here for a little while. People keep asking me to do things. Reviews, articles, that kind of thing. Do you know, I met a dear little choreographer the other night who wants to turn it all into a ballet? Can't you see it, all black and silver leotards and very, very stark lighting? And then, if things are a little warm here and I detect suspicious men watching me, then I might go to Paris for a little while, or even Berlin.'

Amy frowned at him. 'Berlin? Would you really want to go there?'

'How political you are. Other things go on in Berlin, darling, as well as Herr Hitler.'

'Oh, of course.'

Richard filled her glass to the brim, although she had barely taken two sips from it. 'And you, my sister?'

'I shall stay here for a day or two. And then go back to Chance. To . . . be with Gerald, for a while, until your little cloud has blown over.'

After an evening of Richard's company, it was easy to find oneself talking like him. He leaned across the table now, suddenly shrewd. 'Who is he?' he asked.

'What do you mean?'

'Don't fence. Whoever he is who's making you look the way you do. As if you can't quite hear and see what's going on because something much more important is blocking it out. I remember the feeling. Hasn't happened much lately.'

'No one you know,' Amy said quietly.

Richard put his hands over hers. 'He's very lucky, whoever he is.'

Later, Tony Hardy came across the room to join them. Richard was clearly expecting him. He jumped up at once and put his arm round his shoulders.

'It's fair that Tony should celebrate with us, don't you think?'

Even Tony looked a little sleeker. His shapeless evening clothes were at least well brushed, and his thin, quizzical face seemed to have filled out. Amy had a renewed sense of time passing, and leaving her.

Tony kissed her. 'Well?' he asked.

'I can see that it's a good enough book for you to have to publish it. Whether Richard should have written it in the first place is a different matter.'

'Dearest, don't start all over again. Another bottle, I think?'

Later, they went on to a night-club. It was a far less grand establishment than Ondine's, and Richard and Tony seemed to be habitués. As soon as Richard came in he was surrounded by an admiring knot of people.

'The literary lion!'

'Darling, I must paint you. Say yes, won't you?'

Leaving him to it, Tony led Amy on to the dance floor. Peering through the gloom, she saw that more than half the couples were men dancing together. The enclosed space was a forest of feathers and sequins and glitter. Reading Amy's expression, Tony murmured, 'Well. I suppose it is rather louche. Do you mind?'

'I'm flattered you should think me sufficiently one of the boys to bring me here.'

He laughed and hugged her. 'I bring Angel Mack, sometimes. She always pretends to despise it, but she dresses to the nines and has the time of her life.'

Amy rested her head on Tony's shoulder as they went on dancing. If it weren't for Tony Hardy, she would never have gone to Appleyard Street.

And so would never have known Nick.

The fragility of chances stretched backwards, and onwards. Don't miss the chance of happiness, however fragile, Amy knew instinctively. And the thought of Nick made her throat tighten. She lost the rhythm of her step and stumbled against Tony. He steadied her and they stood still for a moment in the crowd. Tony stared straight into her face.

'You look different,' he said.

'So people keep telling me.'

373

'Or no, not exactly different. As if you're certain of something.'

'Yes,' Amy said. 'That's it exactly. I am certain, at last.'

She stayed at Bruton Street for another three days. She fielded the telephone calls for Richard, growing adept at evasion. She lunched and shopped with Adeline, and went for fittings for clothes she didn't need. Adeline's tame expert did her hair, and she had tea with Violet Trent, now married, and dinner with one of Johnny Guild's old set. She went to *The Marriage of Figaro* and a charity dance. She did everything calmly, watching herself parade through the days, and every moment she thought of Nick.

She knew, with certainty, that she wouldn't be coming back to any of this. Whatever might happen to them together he was already powerful enough to have stopped it all for her.

She said a measured goodbye, and then she went back to Chance.

There was the familiar single taxicab waiting in the hope of a fare at the station. Amy had known the driver for years, and he tipped his hat to her.

''Afternoon, Miss Lovell. Up to the House, is it? A fine day for coming home.'

Coming home, she echoed in her head.

The park was midsummer green, patched with the shade of the old trees. Amy looked towards the dark fringe of woodland on the north side. The cottage was hidden in its remote hollow.

She paid the driver and walked into the cool of the hallway. One of Gerald's spaniels flopped down from a chair and came to be fussed over. Amy rubbed the silky ears. 'Where is he, boy? Show me.' With a flurry of its tail the dog bustled away, its toenails clicking faintly on the oak boards.

Amy found her father in the gun-room. He was sitting with his back to the door amidst the dead season's clutter. He had been re-reading the old game books from before the War.

He put his hand out to the spaniel before acknowledging Amy.

'Down, Pollux.' When at last he did glance up at her it was clear that he knew. The change in him was startling. The vertical furrows were pulled deeper in his cheeks and the corners of his mouth turned down with a new bitterness. Worse than that was

374

Gerald's bewilderment. He had aged ten years, and to Amy he looked on the verge of senility. His hand grasping the leather arm of his chair was shaking.

Amy went quickly and knelt beside the chair.

'Daddy . . .' she began, and he turned to stare at her. The old, piercing look that threatened explosions had turned milky and unfocused, and it frightened her far more.

'Daddy, he . . .'

Gerald might not have heard her. 'So. I hear my son's a bugger,' he said. Even his voice had aged. It was thinner, without its old resonance.

'Have you read the book?' she asked gently.

The violence of the shaky hand's gesture made Amy start backwards.

'I don't want to read that sort of filth. Hearing about it was enough.'

'Who told you?'

'Morton.'

Of course, it would be Morton. He was her father's country solicitor, a malicious and small-minded little man whom Richard had often cruelly mimicked. Morton would consider it his duty to inform his lordship of what was being vulgarly bruited abroad. Amy could hear the very pompousness of his words and his measured, judgemental cadences. Gerald could hardly have received the news more damagingly.

'I have read it. Only since I've been away. I didn't know anything about it before. It's a good book, Papa. It's very sad, and honest. Richard shouldn't have done it, for your sake, but for himself I think it was brave. I don't think he chose to be the way he is. It can't be . . . particularly happy for him.'

Gerald's taut mouth showed his disgust.

'So it's not Richard's fault? Of course, it couldn't be. I suppose you want to say it's mine? Or your mother's. Yours and Isabel's too, perhaps.'

Perhaps, Amy thought. *All our faults. Even Airlie's.*

But she shook her head. 'No,' she said sadly.

Gerald screwed up a loose sheet of paper and flung it away from him. 'I don't want to see him. Never again, never, in my house. If the estate wasn't entailed on him I'd will it away today. You and Isabel could have it.' He put his face in his hands. 'Poor Chance. When I'm gone your brother will fill it with bum-boys

375

and dancing niggers and scum. He'll cut down my trees to pay their bills.'

Even as he spoke, Amy could hear Richard parodying Gerald in the very same words. It was cruel, and cruelly ironic that her father's vision of a bleak and corrupt modernity was not so far removed from Richard's own pessimism. The realization stirred sour laughter in Amy.

'Damn him. Damn him to hell.'

Gerald was crying with his face in his hands. Never, since the day Airlie died, had Amy seen him cry.

'Daddy. Don't.' She put her arms around him, trying to offer some comfort, but he wrenched himself aside with a strength that frightened her again.

'Leave me alone, can't you? Damn you, too.'

Slowly, stiffly, Amy stood up. 'I'm here if you need me,' she said, but she wasn't sure if Gerald even heard her.

As she shut the gun-room door he was already talking to himself. 'Every coronation since Crécy. The King's Defenders. And see us now.'

The bitterness in him stabbed deep inside her.

Amy went and sat in one of the state rooms. It was called the Tapestry Room after the dim Flemish hangings that darkened it still further.

As she stared at the heavy family portraits on the fireplace wall and the stiff tapestry seat covers worked by docile Lovell women over the years she felt the weight of the house and its symbols hanging around her like chains.

She had no idea how long she sat there, but it was almost dark among the embroideries when she stood up again. She walked out on to the terrace and saw the buttery evening light and the swifts dipping and circling over the grass.

Outside the sombre house Amy felt free.

She didn't want to be a Lovell tonight. It didn't matter who she was, or who Nick Penry was or where he had come from. It only mattered that they were themselves.

Amy walked down the stone steps, past stone urns filled with flowers and past stone statues guarding dark clipped hedges. She began to walk faster and then she was running, running north towards the line of woodland and the little cottage at its edge.

376

Under the trees and out again, running faster, Amy heard her footsteps pounding in her head. Her breath came raggedly, the sound of it magnified in the soft silence of the park.

Ahead of her she saw the cottage at last, the windows dark and the door tightly closed.

If Nick wasn't there? How would she bear that?

But he was there.

Amy half-fell against the little low door, and it swung open at once. Nick had been sitting at the table, and now he stumbled to his feet. Amy knew from his face that he had been waiting, not hoping, and she saw the resignation give way to incredulity that she had really come.

'Nick.' Her voice was distorted, caught in her throat. 'I was afraid you wouldn't be here.'

He moved too quickly and his chair overturned, the wooden crash amplified by the stone floor. He stood in front of her and his hands reached out to grip her arms. 'I'm here,' he said.

Slowly, stiffly, Amy let her head drop forward. Against her forehead she felt the rough stuff of his work shirt, and the warmth of his body through it. Still more slowly, as if she was afraid that at any moment he would shake her off again, she let herself relax against him. At last he held the weight of her in his arms. They tightened around her and she pressed her face against his shoulder.

'It's all right,' he murmured, and she felt his mouth move against her hair. 'It's all right, now you are here. I thought you wouldn't come. I was sure you wouldn't come.'

Amy smiled and her mouth caught against the folds of his shirt. They stood for a long moment, holding on to one another. Half-dazed, Nick went on breathing in the scent of her hair until he was convinced that she was real. Then he loosened his arms and she looked up at him, anxious again.

377

'Come here,' he ordered. He led her to the black settle and made her sit down. The old oak was worn smooth and slippery. Amy wanted to hold on to him but he said 'Wait,' smiling at her.

Outside, the light was fading. Nick hung a heavy curtain across the tiny window. Amy couldn't remember having seen the curtain before. For a moment the room was in blackness and she blinked, turning her head as she heard him moving. Then a match struck a circle of bluish light and Nick lit the paraffin lamp. At once black shadows wavered and settled on the bare walls.

'There,' he said.

'I don't want to hide,' Amy told him defiantly. 'I don't care who sees, or knows.'

'You should care,' he told her, with a touch of his old sharpness. 'Here and now, tonight, concerns us and no one else. It will have to go beyond here, this safety, soon enough. I told you to think about that.' Nick rubbed his face almost wearily, rubbing away the prospect that Amy couldn't see for the wild happiness of the moment. 'Let's keep it, just for now,' he whispered.

It didn't matter who she was, or who Nick was. Names and places had lost their significance. It only mattered that they were together. None of Nick's forebodings touched her.

'Come and sit here,' she begged him.

He came, and they sat looking at one another in the cramped space between the high wooden arms.

Nick's hands and forearms were brown from the outdoor work, and his shirt was tight across his shoulders where the muscles had filled out again. Amy saw that the soft light rubbed out the lines of bitterness around his mouth and eyes, and the anger that marked his face had faded away. In that moment he could have been her own age; younger, even.

'I . . . don't know what to do, now I'm here,' she confessed. 'I could only think of getting here, and finding you.'

Nick took her hand, and fitted her fingers gently between his own. Amy saw how smooth and white her fingers looked, even after all the ward work, held in his. Abruptly she lifted their two hands to her mouth and kissed the roughness.

'I imagined what it would be like if you came through the door, looking like you did,' he told her. 'It seemed so unlikely I didn't think any further.'

378

They smiled at each other, dazed by the unlikeliness and the certainty that had brought them together.

'New territory, then,' Nick said very softly. Leaning forward so that his dark head blotted out the light, he kissed her.

Amy closed her eyes. He was so close to her, as close as if she had known him for ever. And yet he was completely strange, and everything else with him. She had the sense of a new world waiting, a world she had longed for and which would have to be explored, and mapped, and made their own.

The thought was almost unbearably exciting; she shivered, and realized that it was partly from fear because her bearings were gone and she was irrevocably adrift. Her fingers tightened impulsively on his shirtsleeves.

She opened her eyes again and saw that Nick was looking at her, holding her focused in the very centre of his odd, green-grey stare so that she knew that for him, too, there was nothing else to see or consider.

'And so?' Nick was challenging her, she understood that. There would be no easy following his lead, with Nick Penry, as she had been able to do with Jack.

'And so here I am,' Amy said simply. 'Whatever.'

'Whatever comes? Are you brave enough for that?'

'Yes,' Amy said unhesitatingly. 'I'm brave enough.'

Nick's face was soft now. With his fingertips he traced the length of her neck and the hollow at the base of her throat. 'I think you are too, Amy Lovell,' he said.

He kissed her again and she answered his kiss, and in the dark tangle of trees behind the little house they heard an owl hoot.

After a long time still holding her in his arms, Nick said, 'I want to make love to you.'

'I want you to.'

'Are you sure?' The challenge again. She must commit herself, an equal and opposite stake.

'Surer than I've ever been of anything.'

They stood up together, and at the foot of the tiny, steep stairs that led up to the room above Nick stood formally aside, with a touch of his old mockery, to let her go first. Behind her he carried up the lamp and Amy saw their shadows, a single huge shape, thrown on the wall above.

The tiny bedroom had a little low window covered with the same curtaining. A single thick oak beam supported the roof.

The bed was freshly made and the sheets were linen, crisp with laundering. She reached out to touch them.

'And you say that you didn't think beyond my coming through the door?'

'A man can dream,' Nick answered, laughing. He glanced around the room. 'It's not exactly my lady's chamber . . .' he began, but Amy put her hand to his mouth to stop him.

'Don't,' she ordered. 'I'm glad. Do you understand?'

'I hope so.'

Their shadows were moving again across the ceiling, separate and then coming together. 'May I?' he asked, formal for an instant again, and Amy nodded as he reached to undo the buttons of her dress. He peeled it off her shoulders, and the slippery lace and satin underthings with it. Amy stood in the lamplight naked to the waist, and Nick stroked her hair and her shoulders, and then held her breasts in his hands. Suddenly the formality and the challenges were forgotten.

It was Nick in her arms, her own man now, his head against her skin and his mouth so hard that she almost cried out. He knelt in front of her as his fingers fumbled at her waist, and then her dress fell loose and she stepped out of it without a glance. Still kneeling, as gently as a lady's maid Nick unhooked her stockings and unbuckled her shoes, holding her bare foot in one hand to look at the arch of it and the slender ankle.

As he lifted his head to kiss the secrecy of her inner thigh, Amy saw how black his hair looked spread against the white skin.

With her clothes lying in a heap on the bare floorboards, Nick lifted her and put her on his bed. She lay very still, unashamed, so that he could look at her. From his face, almost unbelieving, and from the way that his hands touched her, Amy knew that she was beautiful, as beautiful tonight as she would ever be.

Nick was trembling violently now, and she felt the heat of him as he leaned closer. 'You are so lovely,' he said.

Amy held out her arms.

Briefly the rough corduroy and flannel of his working clothes prickled her, and then Nick pulled off his shirt, tearing one of the buttonholes so that the button rolled away, and unfastened the brass-buckled belt of his breeches. Amy reached to help and their fingers touched and then clasped fiercely together. In a moment he lay against her, with all the longed-for sweetness of skin against bare skin. She stretched up so that their mouths could meet as he pulled her to him.

'Nick.'

She didn't even know whether she had said it aloud or whether his name reverberated silently through her. The arm that held her was deeply scarred with a bluish pucker under the brown skin and she touched it with her lips, then the other faint blue scars on his hands and wrists.

'Amy.'

His voice was fierce. He rolled so that he leaned over her, poised, and Amy thought that she loved every line of his face. He caught her wrists in one hand, pinning her beneath him. 'I want you.'

'Yes.'

His hand found her, and Amy lifted herself, giving herself to him. Need made him violent and she was glad, tasting the joy and pride that he should want her so much. There was a moment's stillness, waiting silence; and then Nick groaned low in his throat. He entered her, deep with a single stroke, and Amy felt the stirring of her own response. The little room and the oak beam overhead, the cool sheets and the curtain at the window and the owl in the woods outside were all obliterated by an urgency that she had never known with Jack Roper. Their bodies arched together, yearning to be closer still, and Amy knew an instant of intense pleasure.

But Nick had been alone too long in the isolated cottage, and he was too quick for her. The muscles in his shoulders knotted under her fingers and his face was buried against her hair as he stiffened and she felt the quick pulse of him inside her.

Amy kissed his closed eyes and held him until the stillness wrapped around them again. She looked at the bare room, at the few clothes hanging behind the door and the book on the chair beside the bed, and thought how beautiful, and how simple, everything was.

'I'm sorry,' Nick said at last. 'I was like a boy of sixteen.'

More overwhelmed, he thought, than he had been with Mags Jenkin years ago in Mountain Ash. And he was a grown man now, thirty-three years old and saddened by all that had happened in the time since, so that he couldn't have believed he would ever again feel so strong and weak at once, and so exposed as if all the layers of skin and experience had been stripped away together.

He had never known anyone like this girl who held him tight in her arms. It wasn't just her lovely face and the softness of her miraculous skin, or the way that her hair shone as if it had been polished, or the lemony scent that clung all over her. There was a fierce strength somewhere in Amy Lovell, a survivor's strength that had nothing to do with her father's acres or her mother's millions. Her defiance met his own. Nick recognized it, as he would have done in any kindred spirit, and he loved it in her.

Amy was laughing, stretching herself out against him and then leaning back a little so that she could see his face.

'Good God. Is that what sixteen-year-olds are like?'

Her happiness was absurd, infectious. Nick found himself laughing back at her.

'Worse. Even quicker. At least, I was. It takes practice.'

Amy leaned over him imperiously. 'Practise with me.'

Nick looked down at the slim length of her, and fitted his arm around her narrow waist. Her small breasts with their hard nipples brushed his chest. It was a woman's body, for all her youth, not a girl's.

'I don't think you've got all that much to learn.' He had intended it light-heartedly, but he was overcome by a sudden surge of jealousy for all the times that she hadn't spent with him. 'Have there been many others? Other men?'

'Just one,' Amy said softly.

'The grey-haired man with the haughty face who kissed you? Sitting up on his big horse, here, on Boxing Day?'

Startled, Amy looked at him. 'Yes. Jack Roper. I didn't see you. Why didn't I see you? After they'd all gone off I walked down to the estates office. I was thinking about you. Looking for you. Where were you, Nick?'

'Watching you from the back of the crowd. I stayed long enough to see your friend kiss you.'

'Don't be jealous of Jack Roper,' Amy said. 'There isn't any need.' And as she settled against him, tucking her head comfortably against his shoulder as if it belonged there, Nick knew that there truly wasn't any need.

'And you?' Amy asked him. She had a strong sense of Nick's life, years of it already behind him, separate from her, and she felt her own shiver of jealousy.

'There hasn't been anyone, except my wife, since I was married. Almost ten years.' Ten years, and Dickon, and the kind of hardship that was hardly imaginable here in the fertile richness of Chance.

The shiver intensified itself in Amy, and she made herself lie still and quiet so that he wouldn't sense it.

'Do you still love her?' she asked. Honesty, Amy told herself. It's important that we should be honest with each other, always. I can bear it if he does, so long as I know.

After a moment's silence Nick said, 'It isn't very easy to love, in Nantlas. Mari's my wife, and mother to my son. I'm here because of them, so they can eat and keep themselves warm. But, since you ask, ours isn't a real marriage any more. It hasn't had a chance to be.'

So I still don't know, Amy thought. The happiness of a moment ago seemed utterly remote, and the little sheltering room was suddenly cold, and no shelter at all. Impulsively she turned her face to him, blotting out the light against his shoulder, and he stroked her hair, soothing her.

'What shall we do, Nick?'

'I don't know.'

For a long time they lay in silence, and gradually the shivering inside her stopped. Nick was here with her now, and that was as much as she could ask. They had time yet. Time enough, even if not for everything.

They began to talk again, in low voices, in the innocent, intimate circle of warmth that their bodies made together. There were wide, blank spaces between them that had to be filled with the little jigsaw pieces of recollection and description. They found that they were hungry for the smallest, irrelevant details that would draw them together, and they came spilling out with the important things, mixed in the flood of words.

Amy talked about the hospital, and the life that she had been led to after she had leant helplessly over Jake Silverman's unconscious body.

'Trafalgar Square,' Nick said. 'And you, looking like Lady Somebody caught up in the fray on the way to a garden party, pulling at Jake to get him away from that brute on a horse.'

'I thought I looked so inconspicuous,' Amy admitted. 'I had no idea what I was doing there. Full of the glory of the march, drunk with fervour.'

'I thought you were a society bitch, but brave as anyone.'

'I was terrified to death. Of you, mostly.'

They laughed, and kissed each other again.

She told Nick about the importance of her friendship with Helen Pearce, truth she had never shared with anyone else. She told him how Helen had died in the Royal Lambeth, and he hugged her close to him, murmuring 'Poor Amy. Poor love.'

'Poor Helen,' she answered. 'I was lucky to be on the right side. She told me that.'

In his turn, Nick told her the story of how he had come to Chance. At first, rigid with resentment and pride, and despising what he had regarded as the soft life on the fertile land, he had held himself aloof from the other men and refused the overtures they made to the new workman. He had settled himself into the isolated cottage, and had found himself utterly alone.

The head gardener had discovered his talent with everything that grew and had put him in charge of the weird orangery. His fascination with it had helped him to keep going. There was the money, doled out to him every Friday by Mr Mackintosh as he stood in line with the other men. Almost all of that was sent home, and it had helped to make Dickon well again. The big man in Cardiff, specialist in Dickon's blood disease, was pleased with his progress. The little boy would never be like other children, but he wasn't going to die.

It was Amy's turn to hold Nick, murmuring her sympathy.

Nick told her how he had watched for her, without admitting it to himself, even, and had seen her riding, and walking arm in arm with her father on the terraces.

'Nick,' she said fiercely, clenching his fingers in hers, 'so much time wasted. If only . . .'

But he stopped her, kissing her again. 'It doesn't matter. We have the time now.'

With some of the exultant happiness creeping back, Amy let the beat of anxiety and regret die within her. Nick's arms wrapped round her and his hand touched her breast. She felt her blood move quicker, and her mouth widened under the insistence of his tongue.

Nick was the leader now, and she had no option but to follow him. He drew her on, further and further into a world of his own creation where there was nothing that mattered but his mouth and hands. In Nick's world she opened out to him with innocence and honesty and he guided her, and held her back, and then led her on again until she felt that she could fly with him, and begged him to launch himself with her. Gently this time Nick fitted himself within her and they were like two halves of an ancient, simple puzzle, perfect at once in its intricacy. Then came the moments of such intense, exotic pleasure that Amy heard herself cry out, a long way off like a sea bird, and then they were spiralling together, gulls over a cliff top.

It was a long time before they moved again. Outside, unseen, the hunting owl swept low over the grass in wide, silent arcs.

Her head was heavy against him, and Nick savoured the weight of it. At last he smiled, and Amy felt even the tiny movement. She lifted her head to look at him, and saw the tenderness in his face. She was surprised to remember that she had once thought he was bitter and hard. With the corrosive shell of his loneliness melted away Nick looked as he must have done as a child. Amy knew that he was happy at this instant and she seized on her own happiness and offered it to him.

'I love you,' she said.

He took her hand and kissed the inside of her wrist where the veins showed blue under the thin skin.

'I love you,' he answered, but awkwardly, as if he was trying out the forgotten words on his tongue. As he spoke he saw Mari in their bed at home, asleep with her back turned on him and the warmth of herself protectively curled around Dickon. Now Amy was here in the painful space that Mari had left. She was the embodiment of everything he had despised and fought against, and yet she was as desirable as life itself. *I love you.* Nick didn't know what love meant, any more. But he did know, with utter certainty, that he couldn't let Amy go.

'Stay with me,' he implored. The urgency in his voice made her look anxiously at him.

'I can't stay,' she had to say at last. 'Not every minute. Because of my father, you see. I . . .'

The reality of the distance separating them filled the silence.

'I'll come whenever I can. Until . . . until we know what we must do.'

Nick had warned her, of course. There was no going back now, nor would she have wanted to. Somehow they had found one another, and somehow they would be together. They clung together now, listening to the night sounds beyond the cottage.

As if to signal the intrusion of the real world, there was the distant hum of a motor-car winding along the lane beyond the woodland.

'Are you hungry?' Nick asked her. Instinctively they both shied away from saying, or thinking, any more. Amy realized that she had eaten nothing since leaving Bruton Street, and she was ravenous.

'Are you going to cook dinner for me?' she asked, smiling at the thought.

'Most certainly. Do you think I can't?'

Reluctantly they left the cocoon of the tiny bedroom and went down the corkscrew stairs again. Beyond the downstairs room tacked on so that it was almost under the line of trees, was a kitchen with a stone floor and a sloping roof so low that Nick had to keep his head permanently bent as he moved around.

There was barely room for an old green-painted metal meatsafe with a white enamel top. Nick took out a bowl covered in white muslin, and tipped the contents into a saucepan that he had lifted down from the single hook on the wall. As the soup heated on the little stove, he produced a loaf from an earthenware bread-crock, and a dish of butter from the meatsafe.

Amy stood in the doorway watching him, because there was no room for them both to be in the kitchen together. She saw that everything was neatly organized, and scrupulously clean.

When the soup was hot, Nick tipped it into bowls and carried the simple meal through into his front room. He pushed aside the litter of books and papers and laid two places at the table. There were two bottles of beer, but only one glass. He put out a mug for himself, and Amy saw too that there was only one knife.

Nick held out the chair for her with a flourish, and when she was seated, he drew up an upturned box for himself. He glanced at the table as he sat down. 'It looks strange to see two plates. No one has been here before.'

Amy dipped her spoon into her soup. 'I'll bring another glass and some more plates and cutlery.' The acknowledgement that they would share other meals warmed them both, and they smiled at each other.

The soup was thick with vegetables and rich stock, and fragrant with herbs. Amy buttered a slice of brown bread and sighed with pleasure.

386

'You can cook, too,' she said admiringly.

'Of course. My ma died when we were kids, and when my dad and brother were down the pits and I was still at school I used to keep house for us all. Do their snap tins at night, ready for the next day, and everything. What you would call their luncheon boxes,' he added, seeing Amy's mystified face. 'It's easy here. I've made a little vegetable patch, outside there, and I grow more than I can eat. I get eggs and cheese from the wife of one of the other gardeners, who feels sorry for me, and the odd boiling hen too. There's the remains of one in this soup. There are plenty of rabbits, and trout now and again as well. I expect you know where from.' Nick was grinning at her, proud of his self-sufficiency.

'I expect I do,' Amy said. It was easy to imagine Nick in a poacher's capacious coat, slipping out into the dark to see what he could bring home.

'It's an easy life on the land. I don't need to buy anything except a pint of beer once in a while, newspapers and soap. I send everything home to Dickon.'

And Mari, of course, Amy added silently for him. She was unintentionally wistful as she said, 'I'd starve to death. I wouldn't know how to catch a rabbit or a trout, or grow a potato. And even if I did I couldn't cook them. Not much good, am I?'

Nick put his protective arm around her. 'I know enough about surviving for both of us. You can do other things. You can nurse people. Do you remember, at your house in London, I sneered at you for being just a society girl learning how to wind bandages to salve her social conscience and fill in time? I'm sorry I said it. You didn't deserve it. I admire what you've done, Amy. It can't have been easy.'

Amy had been thinking about that other evening too, and the one other meal that they had shared. There had been all the ceremony of Bruton Street then, and flawlessly elegant food laid out on the crested china among the crystal and the silver. She smiled at the contrast. She had never eaten a meal as perfect or as satisfying as this one, off the chipped plate in the light of the paraffin lamp.

'I did deserve it. Or most of it. I was very young and silly then. I don't think I'm quite such a fool now.'

'You aren't a fool,' Nick said softly. 'Here. Have some more bread.'

She took it, even though the soup had filled her, because the

387

sense of him offering it, caring for her, was so pleasurable. More pleasurable, in its homeliness, than all Jack Roper's generous, expansive gestures had ever been.

They sat for a long time over the empty plates, talking in low voices, and sometimes not even talking, but just looking at one another.

At length Amy gestured at the books and pamphlets at the opposite end of the table and asked, 'You're still working with Jake Silverman?'

On her last visits to Appleyard Street she had noticed how drastically the atmosphere had changed. There were no parties any more, no sausages and Chianti, and no arguments for the sheer pleasure of arguing. The people who came to the increasingly crowded meetings talked as grimly as if they were already at war. The discussion topics had changed from the abstraction of Communist theory to the latest street confrontation, the most recent arrests, the threat of Fascism manifesting itself in London. And Germany and Herr Hitler, and Italy, and Spain, again and again.

Since his spell in prison Jake himself was thinner, and his eyes glittered less with geniality than with fanaticism. Watching him speak, with a fleck of foam at the corner of his mouth, it had occurred to Amy that Jake was frightening. Kay Cooper was thinner and paler too, and as Jake made his speeches she watched his every movement, nodding her agreement.

'Yes,' Nick said. 'There's plenty to do. And it helps, to feel that I haven't run away entirely from what I believe in.'

Amy saw the lines of bitterness deepen again and she said, 'You haven't run away.'

Nick stood up and began to clear the table. 'Perhaps not. But I'm not in Nantlas with my family, and the union, where I belong. Or even in London, working for the Party. I'm nowhere, here, eating good food every day and watching the flowers grow.' The plates clattered as he picked them up. 'And now there's you.' His voice changed suddenly. 'God knows why you're here. I don't deserve you, but I want you so much.'

Amy stood up and went to him, putting her hands on his arms and resting her forehead against him.

'I'm here because I love you.' As she spoke, Amy wondered sadly whether happiness was always knotted up so painfully with guilt. 'I know what we'll do.' She began by putting conviction into her words that she was far from feeling. 'We can go away from here. To London, Nick. The hospital allows me to live outside, now I'm qualified. I can find a flat somewhere and we'll live together, if you want that. I'll go on nursing, and you can find a job somehow so that you can look after Mari and Dickon, and you can work at Appleyard Street as well, and we can be just like everyone else.' Amy had succeeded in convincing herself. The prospect suddenly glowed in front of her. They would have a home together in a street like the ones she had passed through with Tony Hardy on her first visit to Appleyard Street. They would do the work that they both believed in, and they would come home at night to the curtained warmth of a shared life. They would be like Jake and Kay, knitted together without the need for marriage. Tony Hardy would come to visit them, and Richard, and Moira O'Hara, and at last she could put down the exhausting burden of duality that she had carried from the day of meeting Nick.

'That's what we'll do,' she said triumphantly.

Nick looked down into her vivid face and smiled. Amy still possessed the autocratic belief that if she wanted something it could, and would, be done. And yet her enthusiasm tugged at him until he let himself believe in the rosiness too.

'Perhaps,' he said softly. 'If jobs in London really grow on trees like you must think they do.'

'We'll find a job tree,' Amy promised him. 'Just wait and see.'

And they stood with their arms around each other, Nick's head bent over hers, tasting the strong flavour of hope.

At last Amy said, 'I think I should go back to the house now.' It was past one in the morning. The nurse who had come to look after her had been discharged now that she was well again, and Amy knew that there was no one to see at what time she slipped back into her room. She thought longingly of the little beamed bedroom over their heads, and of the luxury of falling asleep in Nick's arms. But they both knew, tacitly, that that was impossible at Chance.

'What do you imagine your father will say to your setting up home in London with one of his gardeners?' Nick was only half ironical, and Amy snatched at the acknowledgement that they might even do it.

'It would hurt him very much,' she answered honestly. 'And he's hurt enough already. He needn't know about it.'

'And your mother?'

'She won't be utterly thrilled. But I think she'll accept it in the end, to see me happy. She once said to me, "Don't ever marry. Do anything else you like." Her own marriage hasn't brought her much happiness.'

But in truth she was thinking about Isabel, and Peter Jaspert. She turned inwards with a shiver to the reality of Nick. 'Anyway,' she went on, lifting her chin, 'I'm twenty-one, and self-supporting. Or I could be.' She checked herself with the recollection of her tiny income from nursing, and the generosity of her allowance that multiplied it by almost ten. There were Jack Roper's diamonds, she remembered. She could sell those, and the proceeds would probably keep Mari and Dickon, and Nick and herself as well, for months on end. Amy almost laughed with the light-headed sense of everything changing.

'We'll manage,' she promised him again. 'You'll see. So long as we're together.'

Nick echoed the word, and he kissed her so that their mouths clung together and the impossibility of the walk across the park and separation silenced them.

'I'll come back tomorrow night,' Amy whispered at last. 'It's only a few hours.'

'I'll walk with you,' Nick said. 'Just to the edge of the formal garden.'

He took his coat from behind the door and draped it protectively over Amy's shoulders. Outside the cottage door the bleached brightness startled them. The moon had risen, almost full, and the silver grey of the turf deepened the blackness beyond the line of trees. The breeze had dropped and there wasn't even a whisper in the stillness. Amy shivered and pulled the coat closer around her. Nick was beside her but not touching her as if, ridiculously, whatever poacher or prowler who might be watching them from the shelter of the trees would be deceived by the little distance.

They had left the cottage, and even in the night's silence they were exposed. They couldn't stay at Chance. London would welcome them with its anonymity.

Yet for all their unspoken fear of being seen, they reached the clipped yew hedge that marked the garden boundary and stood reluctantly, watching the highlights and black hollows that the moonlight threw in one another's faces. Amy's hand reached out to touch Nick's and suddenly he pulled her to him and kissed her so that their bones jarred together. Then, just as abruptly, he let her go again. The iron gate under its yew arch swung slowly open and Amy went through it, her arm outstretched so that her fingertips touched Nick's until the last second. Then, when they were separated at last, she turned and ran. She passed the statues and the flowerbeds where the moonlight froze the anemones into silver cups, and up the terrace steps into the muffled silence of the house.

That was the beginning of the unreal times. The days as they passed were given their unearthliness by a joy so intense that Amy wondered whether she had been alive at all before she knew it. Amy and Nick took the hours in the cottage and turned them into voyages of discovery that mapped their bodies and minds. When they were there together the world stopped, disregarded.

Kneeling beside her on the bed, Nick cupped Amy's face in his hands and told her 'I love you more than all the world.'

And Amy answered, 'There isn't any world but you.'

It was the height of summer. When Amy thought back to the seemingly endless blue days she always remembered the sun hot on her hair, and smelt the scent of flowers all over again.

Nick was sent out to the haymaking, and he came back at night with sunburnt skin that made his green-grey eyes look piercingly pale in the lamplight. Amy caught the freshness of mown hay in his hair, and sometimes she found tiny yellow stalks of it caught in her own clothes where she had clung to him.

The sweet, still summer nights, from dusk to just before dawn, were their own territory.

Amy spent her days with her father, and her concern for him heightened the precarious, other-worldly happiness she fled to at night.

The storm of publicity that Richard's book had generated raged on without any signs of dying. *The Innocent and the Damned* had run quickly through five printings and Tony's publishing house had another in hand. Much of the real furore was confined to London, where Richard was mobbed at night-clubs and, once, booed by the audience at a West End theatre as he sauntered into the stalls wearing a sugar-pink, fully-blown rose in his lapel and with the satin lining of his opera cape dyed to match it exactly. But the reports of his flamboyant embrace of fame featured in all the national newspapers, and the stories never failed to mention that he was Richard Lovell, heir to one of the oldest of England's baronies and the hereditary King's Defender.

'How,' one paper asked with typical rhetorical relish, 'can our Gracious Majesties possibly be reacting to the prospect of protection, however symbolic, by the young author of a book of this kind?'

Never mind, Amy thought, that their Gracious Majesties had already been proudly defended by her impeccable father, and that the Prince of Wales himself had almost certainly never given a thought to whether or not he would welcome the same service from Richard.

For all that they were immured together in the isolation of Chance, it was impossible for Amy to keep everything from her father. He saw the papers before she could pretend to lose them, and Mr Morton and the less tactful of his country neighbours kept him fully informed of everything that she managed to hide away.

At first Amy tried to talk to him about it, hoping to put Richard's point of view as gently as she could. But Gerald cut her short with a terrible outburst of anger. His voice rose almost to a scream, and a thin thread of moisture hung at the corner of his mouth so that he jerked at it with the back of his hand.

'Don't mention his name in my house. Never, d'you hear me? Or I'll turn you out. He's dragged my name into the filth. Not just mine. My father's, and grandfather's. Every one of us.'

Gerald Lovell's face was red and white in blotches, and the cords in his neck stood out like strings. Amy's hands gripped the red velvet padded arms of her dining chair as she shivered under his fury.

'You and Isabel, too. Both of you coupled with that perverted mire.'

Amy felt her own face reddening. 'It isn't perverted. Necessarily,' she stammered, between fear and anger. 'He didn't choose it, and if he's brave enough to hold up his head . . .'

'Brave?'

Gerald's hand came up in the air like a claw, and she was sure that he was going to hit out at her. He seemed to choke on his words and then his hand dropped again to lie on the table. Gerald stared at it as if it was something inanimate, unconnected with him.

'You call that brave?' he repeated. 'Your half-brother was brave, my girl. Airlie was brave and straight as a rod, and he was proud enough to die the same way. Think what your precious Richard has done to him.'

Amy sat rigid in her place.

'He has done nothing to Airlie. Nothing at all.'

Gerald moved jerkily as if he was going to push back his chair and lunge round the table towards her. Amy felt herself tensing to accept the blow. But then her father's head fell wearily forward.

'Airlie,' he whispered. 'Airlie. If you had lived. There would have been none of this.' Gerald's heavy hand took in the great oval table, their two places pitifully isolated by its expanse. *There would have been a family*, Amy understood. *We wouldn't have been cut off, each one of us. We might have been able to help each other*.

Very slowly, as if he was half-crippled, Gerald stood up and slid his chair back so that it stood in the line of others facing her like so many red velvet shields. He walked painfully away from Amy. He said something as he went, something that might perhaps have been *my fault*.

Amy let him go, and sat for a long time staring at the panels of the closed door.

Later she intercepted the butler carrying her father's mid-morning tray of China tea and carried it to him herself. He was shut up in the gun-room that had become his lair in the centre of the huge house.

Amy put the tray down on the stool beside him. Her father was sitting at the old bureau that served as his desk. She saw that he was sorting papers, and that there were balls of screwed-up paper lying on the floor. Then she leant over his shoulder and realized that he was actually staring at photographs. There was a faded sepia one on the top of the heap, with Airlie smiling like Apollo in the middle of a group of boys in cricketing clothes.

Fear clutched at her, and sorrow, as she realized that her father was living in the past with increasing intensity. His life had become the gun-room with its memories encapsulated in the game books, and his hoard of photographs of the son who had never grown up.

'I've brought your tea,' she said softly.

'Thank you.'

Amy stood awkwardly for a moment, and then she went to him and laid her cheek against his hair. It was sparse and grey-white now, and she saw that the scalp showing through was furrowed.

'I won't say anything else. I'm sorry to have made you angry.'

Stiffly, one of Gerald's hands came up to cover hers as it rested on his shoulder.

'I'm sorry we've all disappointed you,' Amy whispered.

Gerald's head turned now so that his cheek touched her fingers. 'You haven't.'

Only because you don't know. Guilt whipped at Amy again and she jerked her head up to free herself of it. It was her own life, and she couldn't live it without Nick.

'Go on now, and leave me alone.'

Obediently, Amy padded away and left him with his photographs, closing the door silently behind her.

'What sort of book?' Nick asked. He had seen the tense lines in Amy's face as soon as she reached the cottage door. At first she had shaken her head at his questions, refusing to bring the day's anxiety with her.

It was the moment of the evening when the sky was changing from translucent blue to thicker grey, and there were swallows dipping and swooping over the grass. Nick and Amy sat down outside to to watch them on a rickety wooden seat against the cottage wall, hidden by the hollow that sheltered the cottage. Nick had grown sweet peas at the edge of his vegetable patch and Amy breathed in the scent of them as she leaned her head back against the warm stone. Between the moments of intense passion that they shared there were other intervals like this one, of utter tranquillity, that gave her almost more happiness.

She had intended to say nothing about her father, but Nick persisted, with a gentle concern that broke down the last of her defences. Haltingly, she began to tell him about Richard, and about the devastating effect his book had had.

'What sort of book?' Nick repeated.

394

Amy hesitated. She turned to look at him and saw the curve of his eyelid and the hollow under his sun-browned cheekbone. He was watching her intently and she saw his black brows and eyelashes and the muscles move at the corners of his mouth as he spoke. Suddenly, grateful relief flooded through her. She wasn't alone any more.

Slowly at first and then more fluently, she told him about *The Innocent and the Damned*.

'It's a bleak story, and funny in places as if it was Richard talking off the page. Nothing happens in it that most people don't already know about, but Richard . . . uses words and describes things that you don't read about in books. It's too soon for it, that's all. In twenty years' time everyone will admire it, I know that. There's nobody like Richard,' she finished loyally. 'You'll meet him, Nick. I know that you will like him too.'

Nick was smiling crookedly at her. 'How many of England's aristocratic families are like the Lovells?'

Amy felt some of the tense stiffness dissolving as she smiled back at him. 'Dozens. Most of them are as mad as hatters.'

'Centuries of inbreeding and overprivilege, you see. The whole system should be abolished. There wouldn't be all this hue and cry about your brother's tastes if he came from Glasdir Terrace, Nantlas, would there?'

Amy was laughing now. 'No, I suppose not.'

'And next week some upper-class sprig will do something else that will fill the newspapers, and your brother will be forgotten again.'

'I hope so,' Amy said. 'For my father's sake.'

Nick hugged her close to him, and over his shoulder she watched the skimming swallows in the dusk. She felt their happiness again, tangible in the face of all the odds.

'Thank you,' she murmured.

'For?'

Amy searched for the right words, and then knew that it didn't matter anyway. 'I've never been as happy as this,' she said simply.

They reached for each other again, urgently now. Nick had drawn her to her feet and the cottage door had already swung open in front of them when they heard the swish of grass.

Nick's arms dropped to his sides at once and Amy looked around, bewildered. She was aware that they were standing guiltily too close together, but it was too late to move apart. A woman carrying a basket was coming down the gentle slope towards the cottage.

''Evening to you, Mr Penry,' she called. And then, as she reached them through the twilight, Amy saw her little start of recognition.

'Good evening, Miss Lovell. I didn't realize . . . I've just brought some eggs for Mr Penry, I hope I haven't . . .'

In her turn, Amy recognized the intruder. It was the wife of one of the men, the one who supplied Nick with butter, and cheese, and eggs.

Briskly, too briskly, she said, 'That's perfectly all right. I've just brought up some books for Mr Penry. Botany books.' And too late she realized that there was no need for her to justify her visit to the wife of a gardener.

The woman held out the basket to Nick and then backed away. 'I'll say good night. Miss Lovell, Mr Penry.'

She was almost running as she turned and disappeared the way she had come.

Nick's face was black. 'Damn it to hell,' he muttered. He took Amy's wrist and led her into the cottage, drawing the bolt on the door and hanging the curtain over the window so that no chink of light could shine through it.

'Just four nights you have been coming here. And if the whole village doesn't know about it already, they will tomorrow.'

'I don't care,' Amy said. 'I'm not ashamed, Nick.'

He turned on her. 'And your father? All your concern for him?'

'No one will tell my father. They wouldn't dare.'

They confronted one another, almost angry.

'You know why she was here with her eggs, don't you?' Amy demanded. 'At nine o'clock at night? She wouldn't have been, if you were some old boy with a wooden leg, and his washing needing to be done, and . . .' Absurdly, hot jealousy surged up inside her. 'How many times has she been up here before?'

Nick frowned, uncomprehending, and then his face creased into an unwilling smile as he rubbed his hand over it.

'Dear God, I hadn't thought of that. All that butter, and it never occurred to me to kiss her even once. Those are the last eggs, then. And she'll tell every soul in the place, out of pique.'

They were both laughing now, their shoulders shaking helplessly.

'Amy, come here.'

The laughter died as his mouth moved against hers, gently and then insistently.

His arms tightened and Amy felt the hard length of him against her.

'We can't stay in this place,' Nick murmured. 'And I can't be without you. I can't.'

'We'll go to London.'

The cottage, thick-walled and sheltered by the woods, seemed suddenly an oasis in a desert of hostility.

'Just one more week,' she begged him. 'Here in the cottage. Then I'll go back to the Lambeth, and I'll look for somewhere for us to live. Then you can come.'

It would mean a separation, unthinkable, but nothing mattered as he held her except her need for him.

'A week,' he answered.

It was like a sentence. Pushing the threat of it away from them, they let the waters of passion close over their heads. The twisting staircase was too far away, the bedroom overhead unreachable.

Amy's head fell back as Nick's mouth reached her throat. His fingers were deft with her buttons now, and her skin glowed apricot in the light of the lamp. The flagstones of the floor were damp and cold, but they might have been the softest feather mattress for all that Amy and Nick cared about them.

'I love you.'

'With all my heart.'

'Stay with me.'

'I'll never leave you.'

The days passed, bright blue and gold and shimmery with heat. For all their loveliness, Amy greedily watched each one fade into twilight because the short summer nights brought her to Nick. She knew already that she loved him as she would never love anyone else.

Forcing herself to think beyond the week that they had allowed themselves, Amy sat down and wrote to the matron of the Royal Lambeth. She thanked her for the generous sick leave and convalescent time that she had been granted, and said that she would be fully recovered and ready to return to her work on the wards in one week's time. She sealed the flap of the crested envelope, addressed it, and left it with the others on the silver tray for the post. The square finality of it stared up at her and she turned quickly away.

As she sat in her room or on the terrace, Amy made herself plan how she would look for a simple flat in Bloomsbury, so that Nick could be near to Appleyard Street. Perhaps Tony Hardy might be able to help him find some work. Then he could come quickly to London to join her. Amy knew, instinctively, without ever having mentioned it, that Nick wouldn't come unless he could support himself. He wouldn't let Amy provide for them both.

Amy spent almost all of the long, hot days alone. Gerald had become increasingly withdrawn, transformed into a stooped, visibly aged figure who shuffled between his rooms on the first floor and the gun-room at odd, unpredictable hours of the day. Accustomed all her life to her father's military correctness, Amy was shocked to glimpse him in his dressing-gown on the stairs, unshaven, with another sheaf of newspapers in his hand. Sometimes he failed to appear for meals, and Amy sat at the great polished oval alone, with the butler serving her from the big silver dishes and then closing the double doors behind him to leave her to her soup, or fish, and her cutlery chinking in the silence.

'Isn't his lordship coming down?' she would ask, and they would tell her, 'A tray has been sent up to his room, Miss Amy.'

Once or twice, unable to face the solitary formality, she had asked for a tray too. She ate sitting on the window seat in her room, looking towards the hollow that hid the cottage.

The very stillness of the days seemed to hold time at a standstill. There was never a cloud to change the skies, and the gardens were at the moment of midsummer perfection when it seemed impossible that autumn would ever come to wither the massed spires of delphiniums, or turn brown the froth of late-blooming roses that fell over the crumbling brick walls of the rose-garden.

As she walked through it, Amy thought that Chance had never seemed as beautiful as it was in that last week. Every flower in the gardens made her think of Nick, bending intent over the blossom. The house was full of flowers too. Amy ordered the housekeeper to arrange them, thinking that the magnificence might lift her father's spirits. The gilt-framed mirrors and polished tables endlessly reflected the tall arrays of white and pink and gold. Even the tapestries and panelling and dim portraits seemed to capture some of the brilliant light that danced outside and glowed in the long rooms.

Amy walked slowly to and fro, touching a bronze statue or looking at her own face reflected in a greenish mirror under the portrait of an eighteenth-century Lady Lovell in a stiff brocade dress.

And then the evening would come, the fading light setting her free to slip through the protective shadow to the cottage. Nick would be waiting for her, and his dark face would break into a smile with the pleasure of seeing her.

Even for all the differences that separated them, Amy found it was so simple to be with Nick. The hours of talk drew them closer and closer, and then they lay down under the oak beam and took possession of each other all over again.

It was on the second to last night of the week that they had granted themselves that Nick said softly, 'Haymaking's nearly done. I'm to work in the orangery tomorrow.'

Amy was lying with her tawny hair fanned out over his bare chest. Her eyes were closed so that he thought she was drifting into sleep, but she smiled and whispered, 'Now I remember. There's a particularly favourite orchid of mine that should be just coming into bloom. I must go and look at it tomorrow. And I can take some books along, in case I meet that gardener who's interested in botany.'

To her surprise, Amy met her father at breakfast. He had already finished, and was standing with his hands on the back of his chair, looking eastwards out of the long windows over the terrace. The massive trees that dotted the park threw pyramids of shadow in the early light.

Amy went to him and kissed him. Her spirits were high with the hope of seeing Nick in minutes rather than hours, and they lifted further at the sight of Gerald. She might almost have believed that he was his old self again, except for the deep furrows that marked the corners of his mouth. His face was close-shaved, and his sparse hair was smooth. He was dressed, with precision, in riding clothes. His boots shone and his jacket was impeccably sponged and pressed. The knot in his tie lifted his chin to jutting point. Only his hands on the carved chair-back were shaking.

Amy smiled at him. 'You look well this morning, Daddy.'

He seemed not to hear her, but after a moment he turned amiably enough, and said, 'I'm going to ride this morning.'

Amy said instantly, 'I'll come with you. It's a perfect day.' On she wouldn't be able to see Nick. But Nick would understand, sh knew that.

'No,' Gerald said sharply.

Amy stood still, startled by the vehemence. Awareness of seemed to touch Gerald only seconds later, and he mumble 'Rather be on my own today, I think. Going over the ridge, an then towards Blackstone. That was Airlie's favourite ride, yo know. Always was. Took him on his first pony.'

He touched Amy on the shoulder, very gently. Then he square his shoulders in the soft tweed coat and walked away. Am noticed that he wasn't limping any more, and he had left his stic propped against the table. He was marching, almost soldierly.

The heat in the orangery was intense. Nick's shirtsleeves wer rolled up to show the puckered blue scar. Amy's crêpe-de-chin summer dress stuck to her between her shoulder-blades, an Nick touched the damp patch with his fingertips so that sh longed for him to press his mouth to it. But they only stood an stared at one another, and the high, tangled leaves threw a gree shadow over their faces.

'Amy,' he said softly. 'Don't look at me like that here.'

She made herself turn away and look out through the arch of glass, and she heard the greenfinches fluttering overhead.

A man was running, diagonally towards the house, across th close-mown grass. In that instant Amy was four years old agai watching the telegraph boy bicycling the long way up the we drive to the main door. The image merged with the memory Mr Glass running too, and the spider crawl of his shadow reachin ahead of him. This man was waving his arms, and Amy saw M Mackintosh appear in the archway at the top of the steps tha led down into the rose-garden.

'Something is wrong,' Amy said.

Nick came and stood at her shoulder, and then he put dow his watering-can and wrenched open the doors that led outside He had covered the distance before Amy was even halfway, an he reached the rose-garden arch at the same time as the othe man. Amy saw Nick's head, and Mr Mackintosh's as well, jerk sharply round to follow the man's finger pointing to the ridge.

Amy's breath was coming in sobs and pain was stabbing in her chest as she stumbled up to them. The man pulled at his forelock, but he wouldn't look at her. She recognized him just the same. He was a farmer who lived just over the ridge, beside the Blackstone Road.

'What's wrong?' she asked sharply. She saw Nick's hand reach imperceptibly to touch her, and then fall again. 'What's happened?'

Mackintosh said, 'I'm sorry, Miss Amy . . .'

'Tell me at once.'

'There's been an accident. His lordship has had a fall. Griggs here found him, and came running.'

'Where? Quickly.'

'It's an isolated spot, that. I saw the horse first, with his bridle caught in the hawthorn. I ran and it took a while to find him.' The man was turning his flat, greasy tweed cap round and round in his fingers. 'He's bad, miss. I left the lad with him while I ran. I didn't know what else . . .'

'You did well,' Amy said. She was fighting for her own breath, and then looking at Mr Mackintosh she saw with despair that he was helpless with fright. But Nick had hold of the other man's arm.

'How far?' he snapped.

'Two mile, by the road. More, maybe . . .'

'Can we get a motor wagon up there?'

'Not within half a mile.'

'We'll have to do what we can from there. Where's the timber wagon?' Nick turned to Mackintosh. With a moment of giddy relief Amy realized that Nick knew what to do.

'Outside the estate office.'

'Thank God. We'll need another four or five men, whoever's closest. Fencing poles, blankets and rope. Amy . . . Miss Lovell, could you bring blankets and cushions, anything soft, from the house?'

Amy was already running. The gun-room was the nearest room she could think of where she would find everything. She snatched up the faded chintz cushions from the old sofa, picnic blankets from the cupboard and a folded dust sheet. A second cupboard, filled with discarded junk, yielded two sets of cricket stumps.

They must have been Airlie's, Amy thought wildly, as she ra
again. Richard had never played cricket.

Outside again the sunshine seemed cruelly bright. She saw th
timber wagon, rolling over the grass, with men scrambling in
the high, open back. She reached it, with no idea how she did
heaved her burden into the back and began to climb up over th
tailgate. Mr Mackintosh's sandy Scots face loomed in front
her.

'I should stay here, Miss Amy. It might not be . . .'

'For God's sake, man, I'm a nurse.'

Nick was driving the wagon. She could see the back of his hea
through the oval window in the rear of the cab. The wor
pounded in her head as she looked upwards at the ridge lurchir
towards them. *Thank God he's here. Please let Daddy not de
Thank God Nick's here. Please . . .*

They were over the ridge and bouncing down a rutted trac
Amy saw the farmer pointing ahead, and Nick tilting his head
hear over the whine of the engine. They stopped with a jolt th
tipped them all forward at the top of a steep wooded bank.

Nick scrambled out with the engine still running and pulle
the two fencing poles out.

'Blankets. Rope,' he ordered, and the men ran instinctively
do what he told them. The blankets were laid on the poles ar
lashed into an impromptu stretcher. 'Down this way? Run, now
Shouldering the poles, Nick plunged down the slope.

In another vivid instant of recollection, Amy thought of Beth:
at Biarritz, and Tony Hardy telephoning for news of her fami
after the pit explosion. For every day of the year, four mine
were killed. That's what he had said. Of course Nick knew wh
to do. How many stretchers had he carried before?

With her hands balled into fists so that her nails dug into h
palms, Amy plunged down the steep slope behind him. Lo
branches tore at her face and brambles caught around her legs

There in the dry earth at her feet, she saw the deep imprir
of slithering hoofprints. At the bottom of the slope was a ditc
dry and clogged with nettles so that she couldn't see how deep
was, with a hedge rising almost straight out of it. At the sour
of their crashing approach a white-faced twelve-year-old b
wriggled through the hedge and shouted.

'Over here. He's here.'

After the panic and noise it was very quiet beyond the hedg

402

Gerald Lovell was lying on his back in the long grass. His head lay twisted at an angle under the lush fringe of cow parsley, and his face was ash-grey.

Amy dropped to her knees beside him. He was breathing, shallow irregular breaths that seemed to cloud his face with pain.

She knew that Airlie's cricket stumps that she had brought for splints were useless, and the dust-sheet bandages were useless too. Another shadow moved over her, Nick's, and she glanced up into his face.

Nick knew that there wasn't any use either. But he laid the fencing poles in the grass and deftly smoothed the blankets under their web of ropes.

'Six of you. Two each end. Two in the middle. Take his head, Miss Lovell. Gently lift him.'

They lifted Gerald up and laid him on the stretcher. With Amy walking beside him, they carried the heavy burden to the field gate and the long way round to the track and the waiting wagon.

One of the men half-glanced backwards in shocked disbelief. 'He never tried to jump that, did he?'

But Gerald had tried, knowing that he couldn't clear it, and the horse responding to his urging had tried as well. Gerald was a fine horseman.

As they reached the field gate there was a single shot. Mr Mackintosh had brought a gun for the horse.

As the gate opened the stretcher lurched, and one of his lordship's arms fell and dangled, inert. Amy lifted it and placed it across his chest. The flesh felt as cold as clay, although the pulse fluttered under her fingers.

They might as well have brought a gun for her father, she thought.

15

It took Lord Lovell nearly a month to die.

He was completely paralysed, and he lay against the pillows in his massive carved bed motionless and speechless.

Amy nursed him, spooning his food into his slack mouth while his eyes watched her. She knew that her father's spirit still flickered inside the helpless shell and that he didn't want the food, or to be nursed, but simply to be left to die. Although she turned him in the bed so that the sheets wouldn't chafe his skin into sores, washed him and fed him, she was only waiting with him. At night she slept in a room across the corridor, to be within the night nurse's easy reach. The matron of the Royal Lambeth, 'in consideration of Miss Lovell's sad family circumstances', had granted her further leave. Unpaid leave, the letter reminded her stiffly.

'How much longer?' she whispered to Nick as he held her close against him. 'Who could have believed that he would have so much strength?'

'It can't be much longer,' Nick answered. 'If he wants to die.'

'I know he does. He wanted it to be when he took that fence, not lying on in that bed like a helpless animal. I wish I could do it for him.'

The tears stung and wet her cheeks. Nick brushed them away with his fingers and kissed her eyelids. Amy couldn't have survived the black time without him, although they managed to snatch only a few hours together. The brilliant midsummer week of happiness already seemed months away, but she clung to the memory of it, and to Nick's comfort now.

Adeline had come down from London as soon as she heard about the accident, and she prowled the house uncomfortably. From time to time she came to sit in Gerald's room, settling in a chair on the opposite side to Amy and watching her husband's expressionless face. There was no telling what Gerald thought because he couldn't even turn his head to look at her, but the mixture of fear, impatience, pity and repugnance was clear to read in Adeline's face. The sickroom atmosphere disturbed her, and she bore the unvarying, anxious monotony of the days with difficulty. Amy, with a specific rôle to play and the advantage of knowing she was comforting her father, survived the time better. And she had Nick.

One day, seeing her mother's sharpened features and restless hands, she said, 'There's no need to be here, Mama, if you can't bear it. It will only make you ill in the end yourself. It might . . . take a long time, you know. Why don't you go back to Bruton Street? I'll telephone the minute there is any change.'

Adeline swept up the Patience cards that she had only just laid out, shuffling and cutting the pack without looking at it. They were sitting in the little salon that they used when they were alone, and she stared through the doorway towards the great staircase that curved up to Gerald's room. Amy saw that there were tears in her eyes, but she wouldn't let them fall.

'He's dead already,' Adeline said, 'except that we can't bury him decently. I can't stand to see him lying there, knowing nothing.'

Gently, Amy said, 'Go back to Bruton Street.' She believed herself that Gerald knew everything, as much as they did themselves, but she would spare her mother that.

Adeline began to lay the cards out all over again, snapping them mechanically off the pack. 'I can't go. I owe it to him to stay. Funny that I should feel that now, isn't it, and not while he was alive?' Her fingers fumbled over the cards and she dropped them, pattering in a blur over the inlaid table-top. Adeline stared down at them for a second and then her face contorted. She stumbled to her feet and Amy watched her as she fled towards the door with her hands over her eyes. Her mother was wearing silk stockings with arrow-straight seams, and high, tapering heels that clicked on the floor as she ran.

The end of the fourth week came. As she sat in the chair beside her father's bed Amy saw that the trees outside were touched with yellow. The sunlight slanted through them, and it seemed that it was already thickened with mist. Suddenly she smelt woodsmoke, damp earth and leafmould, the unmistakable scent of the year's downward turn.

At the same instant, as if he had smelt it too, her father said clearly, 'You must be all the Lovells now.'

Amy sprang forward at once, leaning over him with her hand gripping his. Hope leapt up, wild and irrational.

'Say it again. I'll be whatever you want if you say it again.'

But his face was immobile, as it had been for so long, and his eyes were closed.

Amy waited, willing him to speak again with all her strength, even a single syllable. But he gave no sign and at last she sat down in her chair again, although her shoulders were still rigid with the effort of waiting, and listening. The afternoon crept past into evening, and at length she wasn't sure whether he had really spoken, or whether she had conjured the sound out of the air.

At seven o'clock the night nurse came in to relieve her. She came briskly to the foot of the bed and glanced at Gerald, then came closer to look at him more carefully. Amy moved stiffly.

'Do you see a change, Miss Lovell?' she asked. 'It looks to me as if he might be slipping into unconsciousness. His pulse is slow . . .'

Amy knew. Although he hadn't moved the shutters had come down over her father's face.

'Yes.'

Awkwardly the nurse said, 'Shall I call Dr Pace?'

Amy stood up, weariness in every joint. 'If you would. I will go for my mother.'

Adeline came and sat in her place beside the bed. The doctor arrived with his bag, although he knew as well as the nurses that he could do nothing except wait with them. He had been up all the night before with a difficult breech birth, and he thought longingly of his home and supper table. But Lord Lovell was Lord Lovell.

The house was silent. Downstairs the butler snuffed the candles that had been lit on the dinner table ready for Adeline and Amy and the silver dishes were carried back to the kitchen untouched. At the corner of the kitchen table one of the maids was sitting in tears, and the cook moved round her grim-faced, listening like all the rest of the house.

At ten Richard arrived from London. He stood at the bedside for a moment looking into the stiff, grey face and then turned abruptly away. He took a chair in the farthest corner of the room.

Just before midnight, Gerald's shallow breathing stopped

406

Listening to the silence, they heard nothing, and then one more breath, like a sigh.

The doctor stooped over him, but there was nothing else.

'I'm sorry,' he murmured, straightening up. 'Your ladyship.'

Amy rubbed her eyes. *Thank God. Thank God, at last.* But even in her relief for him, she knew how deeply she would miss him.

Richard came from his corner. 'I'm sorry,' the doctor repeated. 'Your lordship.'

Richard's face was chilly, the eyelids drooping. They snapped upwards for a moment as he stared at the doctor and then there was a short, painful bark of laughter.

'Yes,' Richard said. 'I suppose so.' Then, without looking at any of them, he left the room. If Richard would grieve for his father, he would do it alone.

'Of course I will come. How could you imagine not?'

The same autumnal sun that had slanted gently through the trees at Chance was swallowed by the dripping evergreens at Thorogood House. Amy had come to Chertsey the next morning to break the news to her sister, and now she was shivering in the dampness of the visitors' forbidding sitting-room. But Isabel, in a soft woollen dress that suited her and with her hair, grown long again and wound around her head so that she looked older, almost stately, was pink-cheeked and comfortable. She had taken the news well.

'Poor Papa. But if it was a release, as you say . . . It would have been terrible for him to lie there, paralysed, for years and years. Do you remember how he used to frighten us, as children? One moment playing with us, and then those terrible, irrational rages . . . No wonder.' Isabel smiled, faintly.

'No wonder what, Bel?'

'Oh. Nothing, I suppose. He was such a horseman, Amy. That it should be a fall from a horse.'

Amy nodded. There was no need for Isabel to know more than that.

'I'm glad Bill doesn't ride,' her sister added, and her pink cheeks glowed again. 'He won't mind my being away at the funeral. In fact, he'll say that I must go. He knows I will come back, after all.'

407

Amy nodded again, acquiescent. If Isabel wanted to come to Chance for her father's funeral, then no one could stop her. The reception order that the doctors and Peter had prepared on her committal to Thorogood House had never been renewed, and her specialists insisted that she was fully recovered from her breakdown. Her prolonged stay at the sanatorium was accepted to be for Bill Parfitt's sake.

After they had packed a small suitcase for Isabel they went to look for him. He was sitting in the sanatorium library, his long, grey-flannelled legs crooked awkwardly under the table. Isabel put her arms over his shoulders and he grasped her wrists at once and looked up at her, smiling his pleasure.

'Bill, my sister's here. She's going to drive me home for the funeral.'

Bill uncoiled his legs and stood up, although it was an effort for him to unlock his eyes from Isabel and shake Amy's hand.

'My s-s-sympathies,' he said. 'Isabel t-t-told me. T-t-t-t-tragic.' Only her name came out easily, proudly.

They exchanged a few more conventional words, and Amy noticed how her sister watched him as he spoke, willing the completed words out of him and beaming with approval when they came. Amy remembered that Captain Parfitt had been almost totally dumb, and understood some of Isabel's triumph.

Why shouldn't they love each other, Jack Roper had asked, if it makes them happy? Only that Isabel was still married to Peter Jaspert.

'B-b-bring her back soon,' Bill Parfitt was saying.

'On Monday, Bill. It's Thursday today, and I'll be back on Monday.'

'I'll th-th-think about you.'

Amy turned away briefly as they held each other, and Bill stroked her sister's newly luxuriant hair as if it was spun gold.

They drove away from Thorogood House with Isabel's suitcase on the seat behind them.

'How will you feel,' Amy asked carefully, 'if Peter appears at the funeral? He might feel that he's obliged to be there, you know.'

Isabel turned to look at her. She said, 'Peter can't hurt me any more.'

408

Amy nodded and then, keeping her eyes fixed on the road, she asked, very gently, 'Bel, what are you going to do? Now that you're well again?'

After a moment Isabel laughed. To Amy's ears the laugh sounded natural and unstrained and she relaxed a little.

'Amy, you're such a doer yourself. Not everyone else is the same, you know.'

With sudden happiness, Amy realized that the old current of affectionate understanding was beginning to run between them again. Quickly, before the mood changed, she said, 'You can't stay at Thorogood House for ever. When you come home for good, will you divorce Peter?'

'I think about him sometimes,' Isabel said. 'Not like he is now, making one or two formal visits. He's like a stranger, now. A lawyer, or a distant cousin of someone's, not important at all. It's strange to remember how it was then, when we were at Ebury Street. He . . . made me very unhappy. He was brutal to me, you know. But it wasn't all his fault. Perhaps if I'd been stronger, or less cringing, anyway, I could have made it different. I just didn't know, you see. I didn't know anything at all.'

Amy waited, watching the empty road ahead and the yellowing tunnel of leaves that hung down over it.

'I can't divorce him. He wouldn't allow it, because of his position, you know. His political career. And I feel that while I'm still his wife I might . . . I might stand more of a chance of seeing little Peter once in a while. I can do that much, as his mother, can't I?'

Amy reached for Isabel's hand, squeezing her fingers in hers. 'Yes, Bel. You can.'

Isabel seemed to gather confidence as she talked. She went on, more quickly now. 'When Bill is well enough I'll find a house somewhere, perhaps at Chance, and another for him nearby. I can look after him. That's what I want to do, you see. Bill needs me absolutely.'

In the silence that followed Amy could almost hear her sister's happiness at being able to meet that need.

'I'm glad,' Amy said simply.

Isabel leaned across and kissed her cheek. 'You are the best sister anyone could have.' The declaration reminded them both so strongly of their girlhood that they laughed in unison, as they used to do long ago. 'It's true, Amy. And I admire you. You . . .

have the courage to take risks, and the sense not to make bad mistakes.'

Amy thought of Nick, his dark face, and the cottage at the edge of the wood. 'I don't know,' she said, so softly that it was almost to herself.

When she looked sideways at Isabel again she saw the calmness in her face. 'I wish Papa could have seen you today.'

Isabel bowed her head. 'I wish he could, too.'

The funeral was the next day, September 21st. The tiny church at the edge of the estate was banked with white lilies and over the edge of each of the carved wooden pews there was a pall of heavy black crape. In the village the curtains of all the houses were drawn, and a single bell tolled over the rooftops, hour after hour. The coffin already stood at the chancel steps with a thick white candle in the holder at the head of it. As she followed her mother and sister down the aisle, Amy saw the bright point of light the flame made in the dimness. Adeline's head was erect and her back was straight under her black furs. Since Gerald's death she had been in perfect control. She had made the necessary arrangements with dignity, received the condolences of neighbours and staff, consulted with Mr Morton. Her air of calm gravity suited her. Even widowhood suited her, Amy thought, like everything her mother did. Adeline was good at adopting the necessary part, and she was playing Lord Lovell's widow as she had played his wife. Her real feelings were as difficult to gauge as they had always been.

Amy took her place beside Isabel at the front of the church. Behind the family pew and Gerald's friends and close country neighbours, the pews were packed with estate workers, stiffly turned out in their Sunday clothes, heads awkwardly bent. She wondered if Nick was among them, watching the back of her head, and felt a shiver touch her spine. Isabel knelt beside her, her hand in a black suède glove shading her eyes. Isabel, too, was calm and grave. She looked unassailably beautiful in her tight-waisted black costume with a Victorian jet brooch at the throat.

Peter Jaspert had sent a message of condolence to Adeline. Political business prevented him from being at Chance for the funeral, he regretted, but his wreath lay with the mass of others that would cover Gerald's grave.

At the last moment Richard slipped into his place next to Amy. He kept his eyes fixed on the pink and amethyst lights of the rose window above the coffin. Of all of us, all Gerald's family, Amy thought, Richard is suffering most. She wanted to reach out and put her hand over his, covering his fingers and the gold signet ring. But the rigidity of his arm and shoulder fended her off.

The rector of Chance came slowly past them with his surplice starched over the black cassock and turned at the chancel steps.

Amy only half-listened to the sombre, magnificent words. Her father was gone, and the burial service comforted her only in that it was done as Gerald would have wanted it. It was the same as it had been for his own father. The plain oak coffin was the same, and the pews were filled with the silent, respectful sons of the same men who depended on the hierarchy of Chance. Their lives were as much bound up with it as Gerald's had been, and they regarded the Lords Lovell as kings in their own kingdom. The thought made Amy glance upwards. The space over their heads where the black and gold banner had hung had remained empty since the day Gerald had torn it down.

If Richard ever marched at a coronation to defend his Sovereign, it would be without the old symbol. He was standing beside her, staring straight ahead. Suddenly, with the emptiness above and the rustle of Sunday best around her as the congregation knelt to pray, Amy felt a cold wind blowing. Beneath her feet instead of the firm church floor there was sand, and it was shifting treacherously. Everything was changing, slipping past behind her, blown by the wind or swallowed up by the sand. She wanted to reach out and hold on to Richard and Isabel, but their profiles on either side of her were distant and cold.

Chance had always stood like a secure fortress on Amy's horizon but now, with the oval of candlelight in front of her flickering in the wind, Amy understood that without her father Chance would vanish. Her conviction on the day that she had walked up to the ridge with him, that it would all end here, with Isabel and Richard and herself, froze into certainty. Everything was changing. The sand shifted and slid beneath her until Amy had to put out her hand to the pew-front to steady herself and she shivered in the cold blast of rushing air. The terrifying sensation persisted as the pall-bearers, six men from the oldest

Chance families, stepped forward and lifted the coffin. Amy was shaking as she followed Adeline and Richard down the aisle behind it. Beside her Isabel whispered, 'Are you all right?' and Amy nodded, clenching her teeth to stop them chattering. She searched the huddle of people at the graveside with her eyes, looking for Nick's dark height among them, but she couldn't see him. The coffin was lowered into the hole, and with her sister and brother she stepped forward to drop in a handful of earth. But it wasn't earth that spattered on the polished oak; it was sand.

The fear was still with her as she shook hands with murmuring neighbours who came up to the house after the burial, and as she sat with Adeline and Isabel through dinner. Richard had done what was expected of him all the afternoon, but he didn't come down to eat with them. And the fear was still with Amy when Mr Morton came to read the will the next day.

There was nothing in it to surprise anyone. The estate and the house passed to Richard, as Gerald had said it must under the terms of the entail. *He'll cut down my trees to pay their bills*. The bitter words cut at Amy again as she glanced at Richard's closed face. There was a proviso that Lady Lovell should be able to occupy a portion of the house, if she should wish to do so, until her death. There was a sum of money each for Isabel and Amy, not large, because Gerald had little disposable income. The real money had always been Adeline's. The remainder of the bequests were small sums of money and personal mementoes for Gerald's servants.

At the end Mr Morton folded up his documents and eased the pince-nez off his nose. Amy had seen Richard mimic the same gesture in the past.

The old solicitor stayed for a glass of sherry with the family. He shot a curious, malevolent look at Richard.

'Will your lordship be living at Chance now?' he asked.

Richard turned from the window where he had been studying the park. 'At Chance?' His eyebrows went up as he considered Mr Morton for a long moment. 'No, I won't be living at Chance. I am leaving in a few days, to live in Paris.'

'And the estate?' the solicitor asked grimly.

'Will be managed by Mr Mackintosh. I will make whatever decisions are required from abroad. The house will be kept open for Lady Lovell and my sisters, I imagine.'

The four of them sat in silence, looking at Richard. As if their quietness faintly reproached him he added, 'I'm not my father, as you know. I could not possibly lead the life my father led. The best thing that I can do is to pursue my chosen existence as far from here as is both possible and convenient.' Calmly he lifted the decanter from the tray. 'More sherry, Mr Morton?'

Amy went to bed early, and lay staring at the familiar ceiling of her bedroom, still shivering with cold. The thoughts revolved persistently and chillingly in her head. *He'll fill my house with bum-boys, and dancing niggers, and scum.* Gerald had been wrong. Richard wouldn't fill Chance with anyone. The house would stay empty and silent. Adeline wouldn't come, and nor would Isabel. *You must be all the Lovells now.* Not even Amy herself could come. Loving Nick, Amy knew that she had already thrown in her lot with him. She couldn't be all the Lovells, any more than Richard or Isabel could be what Airlie had been born for.

I'm sorry, she whispered, and the thoughts revolved again, veering to Jake Silverman and the prophecies of Appleyard Street, and to Jack Roper who had told her it would come when she had asked him about war. Then on to Airlie, and back to her father again, and there was no warmth or solid ground to be found anywhere except in the thought of Nick.

I love you, she repeated, but she was still shivering when she fell asleep.

Amy heard the news of September 22nd before Nick did. She was sitting in the little salon on Sunday morning listening to the radio that Adeline had installed. Her mother and Isabel had gone to church, but Amy had thought of the mound that they must pass in the churchyard, covered with flowers wet from the night's rain, and felt herself shaking again.

'I'll go to evensong,' she said. She was restlessly turning the dial, frowning at the waves of static, when suddenly she heard the announcer's sombre voice and stood still. There had been an explosion at a colliery at Gresford in North Wales. More than two hundred men had died. The pit was considered to be so dangerous that the bodies were unrecoverable. It would be sealed up, and the shattered workings would become their grave.

'No.' Amy stared at the domed shape of the radio, as if she

could will it to swallow the words out of the air again. Then, without stopping to think, or to put a coat on over her dress, she went out to Nick. The late September wind was cold, and it whipped strands of her hair across her face as she walked. He was standing at the table slicing vegetables, and she felt a clutch of longing to be with him, simply living and preparing meals together, sharing like married people did.

Nick saw her face and laid his knife down on the table. He drew her to him, stroking the hair back from her cheeks.

'It's over now,' he tried to comfort her. 'He's dead. No more can happen.'

'Listen.' Miserably she turned her face up to him, and told him what she had heard.

Nick didn't drop his hold, but she felt him go stiff. At last, in another voice, he said, 'Makes it look different, doesn't it? Your father, at the end of his comfortable life. He probably never went short of anything, except children from his sons. As against two hundred men in the middle of their lives, murdered. Leaving their wives and children helpless. Pit owners and managers murdered them. I've seen it in Nantlas.'

Amy could find nothing to say. She nodded, mute with misery, her cheek against Nick's shoulder. After a moment he let her go and gestured wearily at the table.

'I'm cooking some food. Will you stay and share it with me?'

'Yes.'

Amy thought of the dining-room table across at the house, and the footmen standing against the sideboard, and her mother in her artlessly simple black dress, and Richard's face hidden behind his lowered eyelids. She believed that she belonged here, at the cottage kitchen table, with Nick. Without saying any more she picked up his discarded knife and began slicing the carrots again.

They sat down together at the table. Amy realized that she hadn't cared or even noticed how cramped the space was in the intensely happy days before her father's accident. Soon now they would have to go to London together. They couldn't stay here any longer.

'Were you in the church?' she asked him. 'I tried to see you, but I couldn't.'

Nick shook his head. 'I felt that would be . . . intrusive.'

When they had eaten the frugal meal Nick touched the back

414

of her hand, almost diffidently. 'Let me make love to you. Just once more, here.'

Because soon they would be going to London, Amy thought. She nodded, knowing that Nick would make her warm again, and perhaps shut out the tortuous, persistent thoughts for a brief moment.

They lay down in the little bedroom and wrapped their arms around each other, their mouths and the length of their bodies touching. Amy knew from looking into Nick's eyes that he loved her, and that he read the answering love in her face. They were gentler with each other that autumn afternoon than they had been in the short, wild summer nights, but the satisfaction that he brought to Amy was deeper than anything she had ever known. When they were finished at last she lay still in his arms, drifting into sleep. The shivering inside her had stopped.

Amy didn't know whether she had really slept or not, but when she was fully awake again she stretched like a cat, and asked him, 'When can we live together in London? Like this?'

There was only the smallest moment of silence. Then Nick said, 'I can't come to London, Amy.'

She listened to the words, trying to make them mean something else, and then she said sadly, 'Did you never mean to come?'

'I let myself believe that I could, because I wanted to so much. Please, Amy, don't look at me like that.'

So Amy laid her head against his shoulder where he couldn't see her face, and watched the light on the flaking ceiling while he talked.

'I had a letter a week ago from a man I know well and respect. He's a powerful man, in an unobtrusive way, and the purpose of his letter was to tell me that if I wanted to apply for a full-time job on the Executive, which is the controlling body of the South Wales Miners' Federation, then he could almost guarantee that it would be mine. I'd have to be voted in, but with the right backers I'd get the men behind me. I know the work. And I know damn well they couldn't get anyone to do it better. Even though I packed up and came here, for Mari and Dickon.'

Levelly, Amy said, 'So it's your chance to go home. Would they pay you?'

'Hardly a princely sum. But yes, it would be a salaried job.'

'So, when do you go?'

'I haven't answered the letter yet.'

415

'Why ever not?'

'You know why not.'

Amy closed her eyes. She did know why, but she was unable to keep the bitterness out of her voice. 'You must go, of course.'

For all their physical closeness they were apart, quivering with the sense of distance that had opened between them.

'Yes,' Nick said softly. 'I think I must. I'll tell you why. It isn't because I want to go home, although I miss the valleys like I'd miss my two arms. It's because I'm soft, and useless, here.'

Except to me, Amy could have bit back, don't I matter to you? But she kept her eyes tight shut, and lay in silence.

'I can do something valuable in Nantlas. What you've just told me about Gresford and the poor devils down there has made me sure of it, surer than I've ever been. I know that bloody pit, Amy. I've talked to men who work there. It's a non-union colliery, or as good as, because if you're a miner in that part of Wales it's your only chance of a job. There's nowhere else to go. So the lads don't join the union because they're frightened of being victimized. Deprived of their nine shillings a day. Their bread and butter.'

Amy heard it then, the fire in Nick's voice that she had heard in the old nursery at Bruton Street. And she knew that she should never have hoped to possess all of him.

'Because there's no one to stand up and fight them, the managers and the owners flout every safety rule there is. Then the day comes, like it did yesterday, and there's an explosion. They seal up the hole and say how sorry they are, and then they open up another pit or part of a pit and send down some more men from the inexhaustible flood of those who are willing to work anywhere, however close to hell, because they and their families need to eat.

'I want to try and stop them doing it. And the only way is through the unions, Amy. By galvanizing our people to fight just a little harder for a little longer. If we organize now, and put the heart back into the Federation, we'll have our bargaining power again.'

Then they lay silent, listening to the sound of one another's breath.

'I'm sorry,' Nick said at last. In that moment Amy decided that if Nick was to be part of her life, and she couldn't imagine

416

a day of life without him now, she would have to accept what he had told her. She would have to share him with his convictions, without rancour or opposition.

'You don't have to be sorry.'

He pulled her closer to him then and kissed her, and she saw how the fierce and hungry light that she remembered, missing in the inactive months at Chance, had come back into his eyes again.

'Will we see each other sometimes?' she asked sadly.

'Often. I'll be in London for delegate meetings, conferences. And whenever else I can. We may not be able to spend every night of our lives together . . .'

Like you and Mari did, Amy thought bitterly. Like married people do.

' . . . but we still belong together. If you want that.'

'Oh yes,' Amy said softly. She put her arms around his neck and rested her cheek against his. 'I want it.'

Later, when the light of the already wintry-looking sun was making fingers of shadow through the trees to lie on the wet grass, Amy and Nick hesitated at the cottage door.

'I won't walk with you, any more,' Nick said.

'Why?'

'Someone – one of the men – said something about you. A sly, sniggering little hint, that's all.'

'And so?'

Nick laughed, sudden amusement lightening his face so that Amy's heart lurched with love. 'I hit him. Not very hard, as it happens. But you should know that the tittle-tattle has started, and it won't stop now.'

'Especially if you fight everyone who mentions my name. What made you do it?'

'Love,' Nick said simply. They stood looking at one another and the wind brought the first yellow leaves spinning over the grass towards them.

'It doesn't matter,' Amy said. 'Walk with me anyway.'

Nor did it matter, now that Gerald was dead. It was Gerald's feelings she had cared about, and his death had set free her pride in Nick.

They began to walk, not touching, watching the scudding leaves.

'I shall have to go back to the hospital almost at once, in any case. Nick, can you leave Chance soon? Could we steal just a few days in London together before you go to Nantlas?'

He looked at her, regret and love and sympathy all mixed together in his glance, and said, 'Yes. Let's steal just a little more time.' Their hands touched now, and Amy was smiling. They had gone barely a hundred yards further when Amy heard a dog barking. Turned her head, she glimpsed a black streak that resolved itself into one of Gerald's retrievers leaping towards her. She stood stock-still as the dog whirled around her in a flurry of greeting. It was an instant familiar to her from earliest childhood, and she waited for her father to appear in his shooting jacket, with his gun under his arm. But the man who came strolling towards them was Richard, and Amy felt her loss sharpen again.

'Damned animal'll pee in the gun-room if it's not taken out,' Richard said. 'Hello.'

She took a deep breath. 'Richard, this is my friend Nick Penry. Nick, this is my brother Richard.'

She saw Richard's quick, sharp glance at both of them, and then his shuttered amiability descended again. He held out his hand, and after a second Nick shook it. Against Richard's slightness he looked tall and powerful and, with his dark, watchful face, a little threatening. 'In fact,' Richard was murmuring, 'I brought the dog because I thought he might track you down. There was the slightest concern when you didn't show for lunch. Glad to see you are perfectly safe.'

Very quietly, before Amy could interrupt that she was old enough to absent herself from the lunch table if she chose, Nick said, 'Amy will always be perfectly safe with me.'

The two men faced each other.

'Yes,' Richard said. 'I see that. Good. Well now, shall we all go back and have some tea? Mama is lying down, but you could come and meet Isabel. Or perhaps you're friends already? Do come and liven us up, Nick. Such gloom, you wouldn't believe.'

Suddenly, Nick was grinning at him. 'Thank you, but I think tea in the bosom of the family would be going too far. Amy, I'll turn back now.'

Instinctively she went to him and kissed the corner of his mouth. To answer her Nick touched the curve of her cheek, just brushing it with his fingertips.

'Tomorrow?'

'Tomorrow,' they promised each other. Richard sensed the crackle of desire between them, and he stared dully down at the dog now sitting patiently at his feet. Then Nick had turned around and was walking away across the park, with long, quick strides, his hands buried in the pockets of his corduroy breeches. When he was gone Richard whistled, a long rising note that had nothing to do with the dog but which set the creature bounding in circles around them again. They began to walk towards the house, Amy staring straight ahead of her.

'Who is he?'

'I told you. Nick Penry. My friend.'

'What else?'

'Why do you want to know? He works in the orangery. He has a natural gift for plants. He lives in the keeper's old cottage, over by the wood.'

She heard a sudden spurt of Richard's cynical laughter. 'Well, at least the old man was spared that. Seeing you walking out with one of the gardeners. Is that what you call it?'

Amy bit the inside of her cheeks to suppress her anger with him. 'No, I don't, since you ask. Not that it's any of your business. I call it loving him. Wanting him. What men and women do for each other, normal and natural and . . .' There was a long, jagged pause. She had meant that it transcended accidents of birth and material endowment, but anger had driven conscious thought and careful expression out of her head. 'I'm sorry, Richard. I didn't mean to say that.'

He bent down and picked up a dead stick, hiding his face for a moment, and then he flung the stick high in the air, end over end, so that the dog raced away for it.

'That's all right. What I do may not seem normal and natural to you, but it has its enjoyable aspects. Although I've never felt anything like you two, standing there with your fingers touching one another's faces.'

They walked on together in silence, and the dog came bounding back with the stick for Richard to throw again. 'Tell me some more about your Nick,' he said.

'He's not really a gardener. He's a miner from the Rhondda. I asked Father to find him a job here because there aren't any in South Wales and he needed money. He's going back there soon because he's going to work as a union organizer, in the Miners' Federation. He's a Communist, one of the Appleyard Streeters.

He doesn't believe that there should be people like us, living in places like this.' Amy jerked her head up to look at the west front of the great house ahead of them, blinking at the rows of windows reflecting back the blaze of the sun. 'I think I agree with him.'

'He seems to believe in you.'

'Yes.' Amy smiled, almost bewildered. 'I don't want anything else. Richard, I should have said thank you. For shaking hands and asking him to tea and not looking at him like a gardener. I suppose I would have expected it, if I'd thought, but it was nice when it actually happened.'

They had reached the edge of the garden, and they stood sheltered by the clipped hedges. Amy smelt the damp must of bonfire smoke from where the gardeners were clearing the borders and burning the dead summer flowers.

'Why not? D'you imagine that I only associate with chaps I was at school with? I liked your Nick Penry. I'd be glad to see him anywhere.' Richard put his arm lightly around her shoulders and they turned towards the terrace steps together. 'Apart from which, he's also absurdly beautiful. How lucky you are. D'you realize?' When Amy said nothing, he probed again, more seriously. 'Are you happy? Does he make you happy?' So Amy lifted her head, and under his arm Richard felt the squaring of her shoulders.

'Yes,' she declared. 'I'm very happy. Happier than I've ever been.' As she spoke, she felt the tears in her eyes to contradict her, and turned her head so that Richard's shrewd glance would catch no trace of them.

'And will you marry him?'

'No,' Amy answered, 'I can't do that. Nick's got a wife and child already.'

'Be careful, then,' Richard warned her. 'Be very, very careful.'

Within two days, Amy was back at the Royal Lambeth. There was change here, too. The old hostel was fully occupied by new students; Moira O'Hara was sharing a flat in Streatham with Dorothy Hewitt and two other nurses. Moira bore Amy off to a canteen dinner on her first evening back.

'Such larks, Lovell. The joy of not being locked in that bloody hostel every night. God alone knows how we get here on duty every day. Even Dorothy's found herself a boyfriend who works in a shipping office. If only you hadn't been ill, you could have been the fourth instead of Ellis. Still now, there's the box-room if you don't mind a squash, and you can keep your things in my cupboard. Come home with us tomorrow night and take a look.'

Amy smiled, but she felt that her face was stiff and she knew that in the months she had been away she had slipped sideways, away from Moira and her hospital friends.

'I can't go anywhere for a while. Ask me again in a week or two.'

'It's a chap, isn't it? Don't think you can keep it quiet. Not that Jack back again, is it?'

'No,' Amy said. 'It's somebody else.' That was all. She wouldn't meet the expectant glance.

'Oh well. I dare say we'll hear about it in the end.'

But Amy knew that she wouldn't talk about Nick.

The work was different, too. On her first day she found herself the senior nurse on the ward, only reporting to the floor sister. The new probationers eyed her anxiously, and flattened themselves perceptibly against the wall as she passed by. Amy sat in the glass cubicle in the corner of the ward and wrote the day reports, and under her eye the juniors hauled the heavy horsehair mattresses and scrubbed the walls with carbolic solution, and then escaped to giggle in the sluice-room just as Moira and she had done three years ago. Even her uniform had changed. Amy wore a dark blue dress now, made of smoother, finer stuff, and there was an extra row of starched pleats on her cap to proclaim her a staff nurse.

At the end of her shifts Amy went back to Bruton Street. Mr Glass served her a solitary dinner each night. Adeline had gone abroad, and Isabel back to Thorogood House and Captain Parfitt. Richard had disappeared somewhere.

Nick had given a week's notice to Mr Mackintosh and in a few more days he would join her in London.

Amy focused her attention on the problem of where they could go together. Bruton Street was clearly impossible, and the two or three little furnished flats that she was able to look at depressed her unreasonably with their cramped, utilitarian ugliness. If they were only to have a few days, she would find them the best possible place to spend them.

In the end, it was Moira's casual mention of Jack Roper that

421

gave her the idea. Amy found the New York address that he had given her before he sailed, and she sent him a cablegram. Within hours, Jack was on the telephone.

'Are you all right, Amy?'

'Perfectly all right.'

'I'm sorry about your father.'

'Thank you.'

'So what do you want to talk to me about?'

Amy remembered his voice so clearly. It was firm and resonant and confident, even through the hum and distortions and an ocean's distance.

'I want to ask you a favour, Jack.'

'You can ask me anything you like.'

'I . . . want you to lend me your house in Chelsea. Just for a few days.'

'It's yours for as long as you like.' He gave her concise directions for collecting the keys from the caretaker. 'Have you got all that written down?'

'Yes. I'm very grateful. I'll take great care of it.'

'Don't worry about that. It's only a house. Amy, are you happy?'

That question again. Because Jack was so far away, it was easier to answer him truthfully. 'Not yet. I don't know what's going to happen, but I've got to try, you see. Anyway, should loving someone very much equal happiness, do you suppose?'

Again the humming transatlantic pause, and then Jack said, 'Not necessarily. Rather the opposite, I think.'

Amy knew that he was thinking, just as she was, that they hadn't been in love but they had made one another happy.

'Who is he?'

'Nobody you know.'

'Try me. I know almost everybody.'

'I don't think you know Nick. Thank you for the house, Jack. I'll return the keys in a few days.'

'If you need anything, you know where to reach me.'

So Nick and Amy came one evening to the little house in the quiet side street. Amy had come earlier in the day and filled vases with white and gold chrysanthemums, and she had put food in the cupboards and wine in the silver cooler. As they stepped

422

into the house it smelt of flowers. Nick put his old cardboard suitcase down in the mirrored hallway and wandered from room to room. Amy tried not to watch him anxiously. He turned the lamps on under their pearly glass shades and looked at the soft pools of reflected light lying on the marble and glass and polished wood surfaces. From the top of the grand piano he picked up the bronze trophy of a winged maiden that Jack had won racing at Brooklands, and turned it in his fingers.

'Is this Jack Roper's house?'

He was too quick for her, and she smiled. 'Yes. Do you mind?'

'No. It's very luxurious. It feels odd, that's all. I haven't spent very much time in places like this. Amy, what are you doing here with me?'

Quickly, Amy said, 'Here isn't important. It's with you I care about. We haven't got a lot of time to spend together. I wanted it to be in somewhere comfortable, somewhere we didn't have to worry about. If it's Jack you're thinking about, it doesn't matter to him. And I didn't love him, you know. I love you. We needn't stay here if you don't want to.' As she blurted out the last words Amy realized that her eyes were full of tears.

Nick came at once and put his arms around her. 'Of course we'll stay. I'm sorry to seem unappreciative.' His fingers smoothed the hair back from her face, and tilted her chin to make her look at him. 'The lives we've got behind us both don't touch at all, anywhere, you see. It is as odd to me that you should be able to command a house like this as it's strange to you that I should question it. It will take a little time and patience to put bridges over the gap, that's all.'

Amy stood close to him, feeling the solidity of his arms and shoulders, and the way that his bones and muscles knitted smoothly together under the skin. His reality reassured her, and made the distances seem an illusion.

'Show me the rest of this miniature palace,' he grinned at her. 'Let's put it to full use.'

In the kitchen Nick peered admiringly into the blue depths of Jack's Frigid-Aire. Amy rapped ice-cubes out of the trays and clinked them into tumblers of whisky.

'I love whisky,' Nick confessed.

They chased each other upstairs like children, and in the bathroom they turned on the brass taps to send hot water foaming into the big bath.

423

'You mean I could lie in a hot bath and drink whisky with ice in it?' he asked, only half in mockery of the sybaritic life she seemed to take for granted.

'I could get into it with you.'

They undressed each other and lay in the hot water, and the steam clouded the brass and mirrors and the ice in their whisky slowly melted. Then Nick lifted her up and wrapped her in a bathrobe and carried her into the bedroom. He drew the thick velvet curtains and they lay down together. At once they forgot where they were, and the space between them that the smart little house had emphasized all over again, and all the world, except for one another.

For a week they lived in Jack's house, and saw nobody. Amy went on duty, and when her day was finished she would find Nick waiting outside for her, and they would take the bus back along the Embankment to Chelsea. They shopped together, and cooked dinners and ate them by candlelight at the oval dining table. Sometimes they went down the street to the smoky public house on the corner, and sat drinking their beer and watching the people come in and out. Afterwards they would walk down the streets to the river, looking in through the lighted windows at family evenings as they passed. The river smelt thick and mud-brown and chains of barges strung with glowing lamps passed beneath them, and they would turn to lean against the railings and look at the jumble of chimneys and the silhouette of the power station against the thin, green glow of the last daylight. They talked voraciously, greedily filling in the blanks of the past. And they made love, with the same intensity but with a new easiness with one another that spoke of firmer ground, and deeper understanding. Afterwards they slept dreamlessly with their arms wrapped round each other, and woke up again, smiling. Except for the spectre of the future, which neither of them dared to confront, or even to mention other than obliquely, saying, 'when we're together again', Amy could have believed that loving someone with such intensity did, after all, equal happiness.

After exactly a week, Nick said that he must go back to Nantlas in two days' time to present himself to the voters.

'I don't know when I can come back. As soon as I possibly can. I wish I could stay here with you for ever.'

You could do, she might have answered, but she knew that

424

that wasn't the truth. She nodded silently. The thought of being without him, even for a day, made her feel cold to her bones.

It happened that Nick's second to last night was the evening of the regular Appleyard Street meeting. Amy's instinct was to keep him to herself, staying alone together as they had been all week, but a self-protective need to soften the blow of absolute separation by sharing him beforehand with other people made her suggest that they go together. Nick looked at her speculatively.

'How often do you go there?'

'I used to go quite often, after I met you. I liked to listen and watch. And it seemed the strongest link I had to you, I suppose. I . . . became interested for its own sake later. They haven't any idea who I am. Except for Richard's old tutor, who first took me. I'm just a nurse. A rather reticent one.'

'I'd like to see Jake Silverman again. Will you mind appearing there with me?'

Amy might have answered that she would go anywhere on earth if he was with her, but all she did was shake her head. In the early evening they took the bus to Bloomsbury, Amy still in her black stockings and her dark blue dress under her nurse's cape. They walked the last few hundred yards to Appleyard Street, and Amy recalled how she had imagined living with Nick in rooms over a bookshop or a greengrocer's.

The first-floor meeting room was packed with people, many of whom Amy had never seen before, and the noise of talk was almost deafening. As she glanced around she had the impression that there was new blood flowing here, faster than it had done before. Angel Mack was sitting at the rickety table beside the door with the signing-in book.

She grinned cheerfully as soon as she saw Amy. 'Hel-lo. We thought you'd given us up.'

'I was ill for a while, and had to go away. But I'm back now.'

Angel's glance had already travelled beyond her to Nick. Amy saw her eyes widen under the heavy green shadow.

'Nick Penry? Do you know each other?'

Nick scribbled his signature in the book. 'I've known Amy for years.' As he took her arm and guided her along the rows of wooden seats Amy saw Angel Mack's unmistakably jealous stare. She sucked in the corners of her mouth to hide her smile. There had been something distinctly unegalitarian about Angel's expression. Did all women want Nick as much as she did herself?

The memory of the gardener's wife and her eggs at Chance came back to her, and Amy's smile broadened. Nick directed a mock-reproving stare at her levity. At the end of a row they met Kay Cooper. She greeted them both with a flicker of surprised curiosity, but she was gentler than Angel and made no open comment.

'Where's Jake?' Nick asked pleasantly. Kay stared at him now.

'Don't you know? He's back in gaol. It happened two days ago. They came in the middle of the night, when we were in bed. They searched everywhere. They found all the posters and pamphlets, and seized them as dangerous propaganda. There were the plans for the anti-Fascist demonstration, and they took those as evidence of incitement to riot and violence.'

'They? The police?'

'Of course. And on top of the lavatory cistern, tucked in under the ceiling, they found two guns. Little, snub-nosed things wrapped in chamois leather. And so they took Jake away too. He doesn't have a firearms permit. He wouldn't know which end of a gun to fire.'

Amy listened, horrified. Fury and bitterness made Kay look older, pinching in her round cheeks.

'They weren't Jake's guns?'

'No. Any more than the pamphlets are dangerous and the demonstration would end in violence, unless the bloody Black-shirts are responsible for it.'

'Did the police have a warrant? Who signed it?'

Wearily Kay said, 'They did it under a general warrant. It's supposed to apply only to the Armed Forces, but the judge who signed it wasn't deterred by that. Nor is that damned bloody bastard at the Home Office.' Amy felt Nick's hand under her elbow, a warning signal that she didn't understand. 'Anyway,' Kay went on, 'he's waiting for trial now. No bail this time.'

From the trestle table at the end of the room, a bald man was calling the room to order.

'Comrades! Comrades! Your attention to the floor now, please.'

Nick steered them into the nearest seats and a shuffling, expectant silence descended on the crowded room. Amy was watching Kay's profile diagonally across from her, and seeing how the bitterness had drawn downward lines beside her mouth.

The speaker raised his hand.

'Comrades and friends. You will all know by this time what has happened to Jake Silverman, the chairman of this branch of the CPGB, at the hands of the police. And, through their agency, at the hands of this National Government of ours.'

Amy glanced around her as clapping drowned the speaker's words for a moment. The old atmosphere of lounging, pipe-smoking, casualness was gone. The people were sitting on the edges of their chairs now, galvanized.

'This government, masquerading under the name of National although it is a bastion of Conservatism and capitalism, and is now moving ever closer to Fascism and the legalization of violence for its own ends. This government, which is proud to number professed Mosleyites amongst its Ministers . . .'

Nick glanced at Amy and saw that she was listening intently, her expression unchanged, ' . . . and which in the wake of the violence inflicted by Blackshirts against anti-Fascist demonstrators has produced the Incitement to Disaffection Act. This Act, brothers, that allows peaceful citizens like Jake Silverman and Kay Cooper to be pitched out of their beds in the middle of the night, their private belongings to be searched and confiscated, and' – he lowered his voice and glanced at the rows of faces in front of him – 'worse than that. It condones the planting of illegal weapons so that our comrades can be bundled without ceremony into gaol. This, in the name of democracy and the keeping of the peace in our country.

'Well then, I say this. If the outrages against free speech and liberty inflicted on Jake Silverman – and through him on our members and our Party itself – if this is the price of peace, then we don't want their peace!'

The clapping and cheering was almost deafening now. The speaker was shouting over the din.

'The time has come for a common front, comrades! The time to join hands with our friends in the Labour Party, and the ILP, and the Trades Unions, and all the workers' groups, to create a common front. And with that united force to fight against the threat of Fascism and war!'

Amy sat silently amidst the applause. There was a new mood at Appleyard Street. The atmosphere in the stuffy room was charged with a violent excitement that frightened and repelled her, and she wondered suddenly what she was doing here. Over the years she had come to meetings because she had believed strongly that she, and others like her, should work towards a fairer distribution of money and resources. She believed that work should be rewarded with sufficient money, and that there should be work for everyone who needed it, as Nick's trades union principles seemed to dictate. Now, looking at the faces around her, Amy realized that her own groping ideas were as weak and vague as milk and water beside the ideals that flared here.

In the past the talk at Appleyard Street had centred on Germany and Italy and Spain, debated with academic detachment along the prescribed Comintern lines. Now Sir Oswald Mosley and his British Union of Fascists had brought the battle home to all of them. All through the summer, with her heart and mind occupied at Chance, Amy had read the newspaper reports with concern, but a concern that was detached from the real events. There had been fighting in the streets of London between Mosley's Fascists and anti-Fascist demonstrators. With sudden vividness Amy remembered the newspaper photographs of the aftermath of one street battle. They showed huddled figures in makeshift bandages and one man with his face blurred black with blood from a razor slash. Almost certainly, Amy thought now, some of the people in this room had been part of that. She could feel the anger and the violence concentrated around her.

Amy shivered on her hard wooden chair, wondering whether she hated violence more than she hated Fascism. And then she thought of Helen Pearce, the way that she had had to live and the night that she had died in the Royal Lambeth. Neither the polemic nor the violent bloodshed would, in the end, have much effect on the Helen Pearces. Amy could hear her saying, with her wry smile, 'It wouldn't, would it?'

Nick was sitting immobile beside her. His face was creased into its familiar, faintly sardonic lines. Amy thought that somehow, for whatever precise reason, Nick's heart wasn't in the upstairs room at Appleyard Street tonight any more than her own was.

Another man stood up at the red cloth-covered table in front of them. He was younger than the first with a thin, dark, clever face. He looked a little like a pared-down version of Jake, almost a younger brother. When he started to speak his voice was quick and impatient. He lacked the first man's oratorical style and he was angrier. Anger tripped his tongue so that he stumbled over his words, banging his fist on the table in frustration. It was only after a moment or two that Amy began to listen to what he was saying instead of how he was saying it.

'It is a personal vendetta,' he shouted. 'He hates Jake Silverman, as well as what he stands for. The man is a Mosleyite, confessed and overt. More than a Mosleyite, because Mosley doesn't go far enough for him. He's a Nazi sympathizer. He was at Nuremberg, comrades, as a privileged guest of Hitler himself. He is an anti-Semite, and he has used the privilege of his position to attack Jake Silverman, not just the Party. He must be removed, friends and co-workers.' The table shuddered under the impact of the young man's fist.

Amy stared at the jerking figure behind the red tablecloth.

'This poison must be bled out now! Before more laws, more Acts like the Incitement to Disaffection, are passed to tie and gag us, and before the working people of this country are trampled beneath the boots of the police!'

The audience was applauding all over again. Across in front of Amy Kay Cooper was nodding in agreement.

It had taken Amy until that moment to realize that the man was talking about Peter Jaspert. She didn't move, even turn her glance from Kay Cooper's unhappy face, in case it attracted attention to herself. The young man sat down in his place, reluctantly.

The hum of words went on. The debate settled along lines that were familiar even to Amy and her breath began to come more easily. Little by little her horror at finding herself so clearly staked out across the divide ebbed away. None of her sympathies, either personal or political, lay with Peter Jaspert. But he was still her sister's husband and the fanatical words of the speech came back to her, alarming her.

What am I doing here?

Her allegiances were closer to these people than to Peter Jaspert and his friends, but she had never joined their Party.

If Gerald had known even this much . . . Amy shivered again. She was here with Nick. Because of Nick, her commitments lay with his. And yet they were hiding in Jack Roper's opulent house together, living on the allowance that her family gave her, condoning what they professed to despise, both of them . . .

I'm a cross-breed, Amy thought. Belonging nowhere. As sterile as a hybrid orchid. I'll never be truly part of either camp. A weary longing for simplicity possessed her and she closed her eyes on the rows of heads in front of her.

Firmly, so that she started at his touch, Nick's hand closed over hers. Her eyes opened again to see his, very bright, watching her.

'I think we should leave now,' he whispered.

Obediently Amy stumbled to her feet and they tiptoed along the cramped row towards the door. Kay Cooper didn't look round, but Angel nodded coolly to them as they passed. Then they were in the chilly darkness of the hallway, and walking out into the road where the light from a street-lamp shone on the exhortatory posters in the dingy bookshop window. WORKERS UNITE! SMASH FASCISM!

They turned away and began to walk over the rain-shiny pavements towards the West End.

'I don't seem to know as much about my own brother-in-law as the rest of the world does,' Amy said at length.

'He's not the only one,' Nick answered. 'Plenty in even higher places share Peter Jaspert's views. These people think Mosley's just another Conservative like themselves, but with the courage of his convictions. It doesn't matter all that much.'

'Doesn't it? To Peter's family? Jake? Jake's friends?'

'Oh yes, in personal terms, to individuals. I didn't mean that. It doesn't matter in the political sense. Mosley's day is over. The "Fascist threat" won't come to anything in this country. It's a useful rallying point for the comrades back there, and for the Left generally, that's all.'

'I thought you were one of them.'

'I am because I believe that the only hope of improvement for my people lies with them. But I'm a Rhondda Communist, not an Appleyard Street pamphlet-fed Marxist. There are dozens of caucuses, you know, even within the CP. Politics is never simple. That's what makes it fascinating.'

Nick was walking bareheaded under the street-lamps, his face alternately in shadow and then raked by the yellow light. He was smiling, and his eyes still reflected the brightness that she had seen in the upstairs room. The meeting had stirred him, even though he hadn't supported it. He was looking forward to going back, to Nantlas and his people and real work. Nick was a political animal, she realized, with a kind of forlorn bitterness. And she herself was not. She cared about individual people and what happened to them, and that obscured her view of the bigger things. It was a fault, she knew that, but it was still the truth. She was thinking, as they walked on, of Peter Jaspert, and his pink-faced pleasure in his house and table at the first dinner she had been to in Ebury Street. She remembered how he used to frown in bafflement over the things that made Isabel and herself laugh. And how he had hung over the baby Peter's cradle with unalloyed delight. Amy didn't like her brother-in-law, but at the same time she knew he wasn't the cold-blooded villain that the young man at the meeting had made him out to be.

'What about Peter?' she asked Nick now, more because she wanted to share her thoughts with him than because she expected Nick to know.

'I suppose he'll have to jump one way or the other soon. Either back into the Conservative fold, or out into Mosley's Union. He can't flirt with the Fascists for ever.'

'Do you think it's true, that he's out to attack Jake personally?'

Nick thought for a moment. 'It would certainly be within his power to authorize a police raid like that. Jake's a prominent figure, and so an easy target. I'm sure Jaspert gains the approval of his masters, whoever they actually are, if he can keep Jake locked up in Pentonville with at least a semblance of legality. With the Hyde Park rally coming up.'

Amy nodded wearily. That had been the next item on the meeting's agenda. Mosley was to address another huge Blackshirt rally at Hyde Park, and the evening's discussion was probably even now focusing hotly on which anti-Fascist speakers should face the crowds from which of the four platforms.

'And the guns?'

'Might have been put there by the police. They could just as easily have belonged to Jake or one of his friends. I don't suppose anyone knows except Jake himself and the police who searched the place. And whoever gives them their orders.'

Amy took a deep breath. 'Nick, that second speaker. The one who talked about Peter and said he should be removed. I thought that was frightening. It made me afraid for Peter.'

Nick stopped walking and swung round to look at her. Then he caught her wrists and pulled her closer to him. 'You want everyone to be happy and safe and comfortable, and it hurts you that they can't be.'

431

Amy smiled crookedly. 'I suppose that's true. Not ideologically crisp, is it?'

'It's human.'

'Do you think Peter Jaspert's in danger?'

'In danger of making a political gaffe, almost certainly. I wouldn't know about anything else.'

'Do you . . . do you think I should go and see him? After what we heard tonight? And tell him to be careful, perhaps?'

'Oh, Amy.' Nick was laughing, and she knew that he was right to laugh at her. 'Go and see him and tell him to be jolly careful about his political line because your friends don't like it? Or to watch out for bogeymen with pistols? Either way, he'll tell you to jump in the river.' He kissed her, and he felt the drops of rain beading her hair wet against his cheek. 'Let's go home to bed. Peter Jaspert and Jake Silverman can fend for themselves.'

Amy saw the bus stop a hundred yards ahead of them, with a line of people huddled in mackintoshes beyond it. Then she heard the rumble of a taxi behind her. She turned on her heel at once and flung out her arm.

'Taxi!'

The cab trundled to a halt. Amy scrambled inside, holding the door open firmly until Nick climbed in beside her. Then she slammed the door so that the panels rattled and sank back into her seat. The raindrops trickling down the window splintered the light and shook her view of the patient bus queue into fragments.

'What's wrong?'

'Nothing's wrong. I didn't feel like the bloody bus tonight, that's all.'

Thirty-six hours later they were standing on the platform at Paddington Station. The vast, grimy glass span of the roof dwarfed them and kept the stagnant air heavy with steam and smoke. Amy could taste the staleness of it in the back of her throat. In their last hours together she had been irritable and strained at the prospect of being without him. Nick had been gentle with her and she loved him the more for it. Now that the moment was here she wanted him to go, and leave her to learn how to be separate.

'I hate station goodbyes,' she said. Hissing steam drowned her words, but Nick heard them.

'I know. It was selfish of me to want you to come.' He looked at her, trying to imprint the vividness of her behind his eyes. But with her soft hat pulled down to hide her bright hair and her big, dark coat Amy seemed already indistinct, as if she was slipping away. He jerked her to him, seeing the vulnerable whiteness of her throat, and kissed her. Behind her the doors of the train were slamming, ricocheting dully down the length of it.

'I can't bear to leave you,' he whispered. She was so familiar now, the height and breadth of her fitted against him. 'But I have to do this work. Do you understand?'

Amy nodded. She understood too that he wanted to do it, and nothing would stop him. The brightness she had seen in his eyes at Appleyard Street was still there. The guard at the end of the train was holding the flags as if he was at a parade.

'You'd better go.'

Nick's old suitcase was already stowed on the rack above his third-class seat. It was only with difficulty that Amy had persuaded him to let her buy him a train-ticket at all.

'I'll come back and see you as soon as I can,' Nick promised desperately. 'Write to me, Amy.'

He had given her the address of the Federation office. She had asked him where he would live and he had shrugged. 'I'll find somewhere.'

The guard's green flag was raised. Nick wrenched open the nearest door and scrambled inside. 'I love you,' he said. Amy stood watching, silenced, her fists clenched in her pockets. Steam rose in a wet curtain between them, and the train began to shudder forwards. As soon as it had carried him away she wanted to run, her hands outstretched to catch the outline of him that she could still see through the smoke. But the train was gathering speed and sliding past her, until there was nothing left to stare at but the baleful red eye of the light on the last coach, swinging jauntily from its lamp-iron and then dwindling into the distance. Amy's head was flooded with the words that were now too late, and she was crying. She lifted her clenched fist to wipe the tears away, and turned towards the black mouth of the Underground.

The last leg of Nick's journey was on the little train that ran up the Rhondda Fach to Maerdy. He knew the outline of every black and sharp-edged slag mountain and the place of every

433

gaunt pit-wheel that poked up from the valleys between them. It seemed to Nick as he watched his landscape unfolding past the train that it was as beautiful, with its dirt scars and the wrinkles of narrow terraces clinging to the hills, as it had ever been. The green and gold cornfields and meadowlands of Chance had never held him in iron fingers like these grey and black valleys did, with their stone and slate and rain-damp shine, their smoky air and their wild, mysterious flashes of untamed mountainside that glowered beyond the man-made, industrious tangle.

Nick left the train at Maerdy and walked up the Nantlas road. Ahead of him the pit-wheel of Nantlas No. 1 was turning against the colourless sky. They were starting to wind up the day shift, and in a few minutes the streets would fill with pit-black men, fanning out from the colliery gates to comb up the cobbled streets in weary lines.

There were plenty of men in the streets already, men with hollow, clean faces under their cloth caps, and mufflers neatly knotted around their necks. They walked with loitering steps. The No. 1 was the only pit working in Nantlas now. Nick turned up the steep street away from the big gates. The cobbles were uneven under the soles of his boots. Several of the men he passed recognized him and stopped to speak. Nick greeted each one of them cheerfully, but he kept pushing on upwards to the terraces above. There were children of families he knew well playing near the front step of his own house, but the children seemed to have grown by much more than he'd expected in the short time he felt he had been away. His boots rang briefly in the dripping entry, and then he came into the yard space that linked the backs of the terraces.

Dickon was sitting in a wheeled truck that must have belonged to bigger boys. He was pulling at the rope that turned the wheels from side to side, and making engine noises deep in his throat. A blue balaclava helmet was pulled tight over his head, and a coat that was much too big for him made him look forlorn. He was utterly absorbed in his private game. Nick put down his case and knelt in the dirt beside him.

'Dickon?' he said very gently. 'Dickon, I'm here.'

The child's head turned and the clouded eyes looked into Nick's for a long moment. Then came his funny, braying laugh.

'Da!' he shouted. 'Da! Da!'

Nick swept him out of the truck and into his arms, almost

crying with the joy of holding him and with happiness that the boy remembered him. The blue wool of the helmet rubbed against Nick's face as he kissed him, and he could have crushed the light, frail body with the weight of his love.

'Nick? Nick, is that you?'

He looked up, and over Dickon's head as they crouched with their arms around each other, he saw Mari standing on the back step. She was wearing her house apron, faded print with a crossover front, and there was a cloth in her hands. Her hands fell to her sides, and the cloth fluttered.

'Why didn't you write and say? Nick, is there something wrong? Tell me, now.'

Slowly he stood up, and took Dickon by the hand to lead him into the house. 'No, there isn't anything wrong. I've just come home. Can I come in, Mari?'

She had been standing in the doorway as if to defend it, but now she stepped aside to let them pass.

The back kitchen wrapped its familiarity around him, the linoleum floor with its worn patches in front of the sink and at the feet of the four chairs grouped around the table, the black-leaded range grate and the Barry Island china mug on the mantel above it. It was smaller, shabbier, but he knew it as intimately as if he had never left it, and as he looked around Nick felt the beginning of a pull inside him that he knew would gather strength and gather strength until it pulled him in half. Dickon was beside him, tugging at his coat to show that he wanted to be picked up. Nick lifted him and held him.

'Is he all right?'

Mari was standing at the sink, awkward, not looking at him.

'Yes. Thanks for the money. Why have you come back?' she asked abruptly. Nick knew that the sharpness masked anxiety and fear.

'To work for the Fed. I'm to be put up for the Executive.'

Mari's chin jerked upwards. 'You're back to stay, then?'

Gently Nick put Dickon down on the floor again and went to her. He put his arm around her shoulders and felt the prominent bones. Her face was turned down, away from him. He saw that her hair was thin, and it had lost its shine and colour, and her skin was unhealthy, without a trace of the rosiness he had loved.

Nick closed his eyes against the sadness. She was still Mari.

'It won't make any difference. The money'll even be better than

435

an estate labourer's. I'll get a room down the valley somewhere.'

'You don't have to do that,' Mari said quietly. 'This is your house.'

Slowly Nick let his face rest against her hair. At once he was possessed by Amy's vivid presence, as if it was Amy in the old kitchen instead of Mari, and he was watching her cream skin and the russet of her hair, and meeting the intense stare of her blue and green eyes.

'I don't know what to do,' he said, and through the pain of the pull inside him he felt surprised that he had confessed it aloud.

'Dickon and me sleep in our old room now,' Mari said. 'We . . . needed each other's company. You can sleep in his little room, if you want. Just until you see how things turn out.'

Mari wanted him to come back, Nick knew it at once, and that she was too proud to say as much. He thought briefly of the comfort that had been his marriage, and the way that the two of them had knitted together before the bad times came. Then, painfully, he straightened up and let her go. Between them Dickon looked up blankly from face to face.

'No, Mari. I'll get a room down the valley somewhere. I'll . . . be going to and fro a lot. Work, and meetings.' And to the hurt and bewilderment of love self-disgust was added.

Mari's hands still hung at her sides, and she was still holding her cloth. Now she folded it carefully and put it beside the sink.

'I see,' she said softly. 'Well then, I'll put the kettle on and make us some tea. You can stay and have some tea, can't you?'

16

~

October 1935

The little boy sat quietly between Amy and Bethan. On the train from London he had been excited, dashing from one side of the compartment to the other, exclaiming and pressing his face against the window until Bethan said, 'Don't do that, Petey. You'll get black soot all over your face and your clean collar.'

Now, in the car that was taking them from the station to Henstone village, he was subdued. Amy smiled down at him and took his hand.

'Nearly there, now. Then we can go and see those kittens in the barn.'

Isabel's son nodded his fair head politely, but he said nothing.

A moment later the car came to the top of a ridge and the road dropped ahead of them into a little valley. The village lay in the middle of it, a cluster of stone houses around a church, skirted with brown and ochre fields and the dark clumps of old woodland. Most of the houses in Henstone belonged to the Lovell estate, and Richard had given one of them to Isabel. She had left Thorogood House a week ago to settle into her new home.

Amy pointed. 'Look, Peter, that's Mummy's house, the one standing to the side with the tall chimneys.'

He bobbed up to rest his chin on the seat in front and watch as they wound down towards it.

Isabel had been waiting for an hour, walking through the rooms and breaking off from one little task to begin another, listening all the time. As soon as she heard the car, long before it pulled up at the gate, she ran to the door. She stood looking into the thin October sunlight, shading her eyes with one hand against its sudden brightness.

As the car swept towards the house Amy saw her sister framed in the doorway. With her hair loose, and her simple jumper and skirt, Isabel looked like a young girl again. Her hand dropped from her eyes and she waved, a little gesture of excitement, and then she ran down the path to the gate.

Bethan and Amy clambered out of the car with Peter between them. Isabel opened the gate, her eyes fixed on her son. Peter had put his hand in Bethan's and now he glanced up at her for guidance.

'Go on, lamb,' Bethan said softly.

Peter took one tentative step towards his mother, and then another. Without taking her eyes off him Isabel crouched down. When she was at his level, with the hem of her tweed skirt trailing in the mud, she held out her arms to him.

'Hello, Peter.'

He almost ran the last steps to her, and Isabel's arms went round him. He put his head awkwardly on her shoulder and Isabel hugged her to him.

'Hello, darling,' she whispered.

Amy felt a hard lump in her throat. Abruptly she turned away to pay the driver. When she looked round again, Isabel and Bethan were kissing each other. Isabel held out her hand to draw Amy into the little circle.

'I'm so glad you're all here,' Isabel said. Her voice was shaky and they both smiled. The sisters stood for a moment with their hands linked, and little Peter looking up at them.

Then, in a much brisker voice, Isabel said, 'Let's go inside. I want to show you my house.'

The little house was fresh with new paint and pretty chintzes. Amy recognized some of the smaller pieces from Chance, familiar yet unexpected in these low-ceilinged rooms. There were bowls of chrysanthemums in Isabel's sitting-room, and a portrait of Adeline in an evening dress with an Elizabethan ruff that stood up to frame her face.

'Mama has been wonderful,' Isabel said. 'The house was all ready, and we just went to Chance to choose some things, and bought everything else I needed in one huge shopping spree. She found Mrs Moffatt to be my cook housekeeper, and I've got a parlourmaid who comes in from the village when I need her. So here I am, with everything I could want in the world.'

Her eyes were on little Peter who went running on up the steep stairs ahead of them.

'It's lovely,' Amy said softly.

They came to the end of their tour on the upstairs landing. With Amy beside her Isabel stood with her hand resting on the doorknob of the last room. The long window at the end of the landing faced westwards over open country. Amy knew the shapes of all the fields and the outlines of the hedges and copses. Chance lay less than four miles away, beyond the ridge.

'It feels like home,' Isabel said. 'Do you remember hunting across here, years ago?'

'Yes, I remember.'

Isabel opened the last door. 'This is your room, Peter.'

The little boy scrambled past them to look at it. There was a little bed with a bright cover, curtains printed with bold scarlet soldiers, and a painted chest. On top of the chest stood a row of toy wagons, complete with little wooden horses in the shafts.

Peter made for them with a cry of pleasure.

'What do you think, Peter?' Isabel made her voice light, but Amy heard all the anxiety and longing that underlay it.

Peter took the wagons down carefully, one by one, and then rolled them across the floor. The three women stood watching in the doorway, his pleasure reflecting back in each of their faces.

He looked up at them at last. His hands still held the wagons safely and Amy saw the two likenesses, his mother's and his father's, printed on his round face. The child considered gravely for a moment, and then he smiled back at them.

'I like it here,' he said.

They settled down, all four of them, to play with the wagons on the floor. As she watched her kneeling intently beside him, Amy thought that the growth of Isabel's love and need for her son was the surest sign of all that she was well again. At last she could see the little boy as his own self, and as her son, instead of just an embodiment of his father. Peter was almost four years old. It had taken a long time, but Amy believed now that there was every chance that the boy would grow to love Isabel as much as she longed for him to do. And with the thought Amy found herself wishing for a son of her own. It was a sudden longing so intense and physical that it almost doubled her over. She stood up, and heard herself saying 'Let's go down to the barn and look at the kittens,' so abruptly that Isabel and Bethan glanced up at her, startled.

In the end all four of them went down the lane to the barn belonging to the neighbouring farm. The farmer's wife came out into the yard in her apron, and greeted them as Miss Isabel and Miss Amy, as if they really were girls again.

The kittens were a warm squirming mass of black and white fur nested in an angle of the stacked bales of straw. Peter eyed the mother cat and then gingerly put his hand out to pick up one of the tiny creatures.

'Look at this one,' he whispered. 'It's got a black eye-patch like a pirate.'

'If you like that one, Peter,' Isabel said, 'we can take it back to my house as soon as it's old enough to leave its mother. It will be your very own cat, waiting here for you whenever you come to see me.'

'Can I have him?' he breathed, his eyes as round as saucers. 'Can I really? My father says that we can't have any animals to live with us at Ebury Street, you know.'

They walked companionably back to the house in the sunshine. Before lunch Bethan took Peter away to wash his hands and tidy his hair. Amy and Isabel sat with their glasses of sherry under the portrait of Adeline in the sitting-room.

'Thank you, Amy,' Isabel said. 'No, don't shrug it off. It can't have been easy to persuade his father to let him come. It . . . was so important that he should be able to visit me, you know. Even this morning, I wasn't sure that it could really happen. I kept going up to look at his room, and telling myself *you're a fool, arranging his bedroom and buying him toys, as if he belonged to you.* And now he's here, it feels so natural. Not at all like those stiff, awkward meetings we used to have at Bruton Street.'

'Yes,' Amy said, wondering how it did feel to have a child.

Amy had made the arrangements that allowed Peter to come and visit his mother. She had gone to see Peter Jaspert at Ebury Street one evening. They sat facing one another in the pretty blue drawing-room. It looked almost the same as it had done when it was Isabel's domain. There were no flowers, that was the only difference. Amy hadn't seen Peter for some time. Usually, when she came to see Bethan and little Peter in the nursery, she chose a time when Peter senior was unlikely to be at home. Looking at him now she thought that he had put on too much weight. His big face was flushed dark red and he was drinking steadily, topping up his glass from the whisky decanter on the low table beside his chair.

They had talked briefly about Isabel leaving Thorogood House, and about her new home at Henstone.

'I think she will be happy there,' Amy said. 'It's near to Chance. People know her, and she will be among friends.'

'Isabel can live where she pleases,' he had answered curtly, 'so long as it's a respectable arrangement. I've suffered enough talk about her being in a mental home. It will be a relief to have her quietly at Chance.' Peter shifted in his chair, and the whisky slopped in his glass. 'What about her friend?' he demanded.

'Captain Parfitt is still at Thorogood House,' Amy said coolly. For the moment, that was the truth. There was no need to mention Isabel's plan to find him a house near to her own.

Watching her brother-in-law, Amy decided that she had better broach the main reason for her visit before the whisky overtook him.

'When she is settled at Henstone, Peter, Isabel would like it very much if little Peter could go with Bethan to visit her. I'll go up there with them too, if I can.'

Peter's first response had been an angry refusal, but Amy had been prepared for that. Persuasively, she set out to make him see that it was in little Peter's interest to be allowed to see his mother as a loving friend, and not as a strange creature who was shut away and never spoken of, or, even worse, as someone who had abandoned him.

It took a long time, but at last she gained Peter's reluctant consent. 'Bethan Jones must always be there with him. I know at least that I can trust her.'

'Thank you, Peter,' Amy said meekly.

'She won't ever get more than that, you know,' he shouted. 'Never.'

Peter adored his child. To the father who would never forget the terrible night in the nursery, Isabel would always be a threat. Amy understood that, and she nodded. 'Just to be allowed to see him from time to time, at Henstone instead of Bruton Street, that's all she's asking.'

Amy had stood up to leave then, feeling oddly sorry for the big man reeking of whisky, slumped in his armchair. Something was going seriously wrong for Peter Jaspert, but it wasn't Amy's place to ask him what it was.

Sitting in the bright room in her sister's cosy house, Amy thought that it was Isabel who seemed the strong one now. But she must be warned that little Peter's visits were unlikely to be very frequent occurrences.

'I don't think . . . his father will ever be prepared to let Peter go, Bel. You must be prepared to have to fight for every time he comes here.'

Isabel looked down at the little flute of her empty glass, turning it in her fingers.

'I know that,' she said in a low voice. 'I know that you forfeit everything if . . . you do what I did. But I can go on seeing him sometimes, can't I? Just so long as I can see him . . .'

They heard his voice then, calling out to them, and the sound of his running feet in the hallway.

'It makes the house feel like a real home, doesn't it?' Isabel said with sudden happiness and Amy had to look away quickly, out into the garden where the autumn leaves were beginning to drift down on to the grass.

All through lunch, and in the afternoon when they took little Peter out for a walk and Bethan produced sugar cubes for him to feed to the old carthorse in the opposite field, Amy tried to keep her sadness out of her face. She knew how important it was that no anxiety should touch Isabel today, and she made herself smile through her deepening sense of isolation. But it was impossible to ignore the feeling that she didn't belong here, in the affectionate domestic circle. Isabel's pleasure and wonder at Peter's presence was visibly deepening as he began to respond to her, and Bethan watched the two of them with beaming approval. Amy knew that she was jealous, and the inappropriateness of what she couldn't help feeling increased her sadness.

By tea-time she couldn't bear it any longer.

She stood up, pushing aside the tea-tray on its low table, and said as cheerfully as she could, 'I don't think you three need me here, do you? I think I'll go back to London tonight, after all.'

Isabel's face clouded. 'But you said you'd stay till tomorrow.'

'I know, Bel, but I think I would rather go back. I've been so busy at the hospital . . .' She broke off and they looked anxiously at her.

'Well, if you must go,' Isabel said uncertainly.

Once she had fixed on the idea, Amy found that she couldn't wait to leave. The thought of home pulled at her like a magnet until she almost danced with impatience. Home was her flat in Pimlico, and it was where Nick came when he could make the time for her. She was expecting him the next day, but she was suddenly obsessed by the idea that he might be there already, waiting for her.

While she waited for the car to come to take her to the station, Amy went out into the kitchen with Bethan. They cleared the tea-tray together and Amy put the jam and butter away in the little larder.

Suddenly, clattering the dishes, Bethan asked, 'Is it your work that's tiring you, Amy, love?'

For a moment, Amy could have let anything spill out to her old friend. She could have told her about Nick, for the luxurious relief of talking about him to someone who knew him and Nantlas. More, she could have blurted out, 'I want a baby, and I'll never have one.'

But all she did was stand silently with her hands on the draining board, thinking that there was nothing Bethan could say or do that would help, and so it was unfair to burden her with any more worry.

At length she said, 'It is work, I suppose.'

'Is it too much for you, lamb?'

Amy smiled. 'No. Oh, no, I'm tough enough. It's just not as exciting as it once was. I've got the measure of the work, I suppose. I know I can do it. And hospital routines for nurses are very rigid, you know.'

'You'll end up as Matron,' Bethan said loyally, and Amy laughed again.

'Not a chance. I wouldn't want to be Matron, anyway. It's all administration. Looking after patients is what I like, and what irks me is the way that sometimes comes second to smooth counterpanes and lined-up beds.'

That much was true, Amy thought. She would have let her work absorb her if she could, but she was more often irritated by the rules she was forced to abide by. And as she often did, she thought now of Helen Pearce and the night of her death.

Bethan said, 'Nothing would make me happier than to see you settled with some man good enough to deserve you, and a family of your own.'

Amy bent her head. The dishwater swirled in the stone sink and drained away. 'I've made my choice,' she murmured. 'There's no changing it.'

443

Bethan looked sharply at her, but neither of them said any more.

The car had already drawn up in the lane. In the twilight Isabel and Bethan stood at the gate to wave, with Peter swinging between them and the house lights making cheerful golden squares over their heads. Amy waved and kept up her smile until the car rounded the corner, and then she turned her face towards London.

The train was an hour late reaching Paddington. For the last miles it had crawled through thickening fog. Amy sat unmoving in her seat, staring out at the rolling brown clouds.

At last they reached the platform. With impatience beating inside her Amy ran for the Underground. Even in the stuffy depths of it she could smell the tang of the fog. When she emerged at the other end she climbed the steps to the street and it closed around her, shutting her up in its shrouded world. Amy put out her hand and felt the damp chill of the railings, giving her her bearings. The street was so quiet under the fog blanket, and the opposite side of it was invisible. Somewhere close at hand a car was travelling very slowly, but she couldn't see it or guess which way it was going. As she stood thinking what to do, a man loomed out of the grey.

'Thick one tonight,' he said, and the quiet made his voice unnaturally loud.

'It's better back there.' Amy looked past him into the fog in the direction he had come from. The way to her flat. As she stood by the cold iron railings she had been mapping the way home in her head, street corner by street corner. It would be quicker to walk than go by taxi, even if she could find one to take her. With her hand outstretched so that her fingertips touched the bars of the railings, Amy began to walk. She came to the end of the street and saw that the road beyond was clogged with traffic. She saw the lights of the cars probing a hopeless tunnel through the darkening pall before the fog released the noise of idling engines. She was right to try to walk, then. Amy pushed on, focusing on the grid of streets that she must cross, not daring to let her attention wander.

Although the fog was acrid in her mouth and it stung her eyes until they watered, the weird isolation and the pitch of concentration was exciting, almost exhilarating. Amy began to smile, moving faster, her shoes ringing on the paving stones.

Other pedestrians materialized and passed her, glancing back briefly at the bright-faced girl before she was swallowed up again. The fog lifted once and Amy ran, past the familiar landmarks that brought her almost home, and then without warning, it wrapped itself around her again, so densely that she stood in the middle of the road, suddenly utterly disorientated. Panic gripped her and she groped in blindness to the edge of the kerb, then to the railings, and to a corner where she half-read and half-traced a street sign with her fingertips. A flood of relief warmed her again and she turned to the left, counting the steps, another corner, and then her own Pimlico Street, invisible and silent.

The fog was still thicker but Amy ran headlong, counting the numbers on the porticos in her head rather than seeing them as she passed. She reached some steps leading up to a front door. The bold black numerals on the pillars beamed at her. She was home.

Amy lived in a big house that reminded her of a jilted bride's wedding cake. Its white icing was slowly cracking and crumbling from grandeur into forgotten decay. Once a huge family house, it was now divided into a warren of flats for increasingly bohemian tenants, and Amy felt happy and comfortable in it. Her sitting-room occupied the width of the house and at the front it looked out over the plane trees of an elegant little square. At the back she had a close-up view of the houses behind, a vista of irregular windows and drainpipes leaning at crazy angles. The contrast pleased her, and she never noticed the cramped bedroom and the inconvenient kitchen.

Amy wasn't thinking about her rooms as she ran up the uncarpeted stairs to her floor. There was only one thought in her head. She was gasping for breath as she reached the top and looked down the dark landing. There was a strip of light showing under her door.

Amy's smile was brilliant in the blackness. She stood still, allowing herself a moment of anticipation before she put her key in the lock and let herself in. He was there, standing at the street window looking out, but he swung round at once.

'Nick. I knew you'd be here. I just knew. I almost ran, all the way from the tube station. Oh, Nick . . .'

He reached her in two steps, pulling off her hat to show threads of red-gold in her hair, frowning and smiling and eager all at once.

'Thank God. I thought you were lost. I thought a tram had run over you. I was about to set off and look for you. Amy, Amy . . .'

Her arms wound around his neck, pulling him to her. Nick tasted her cold mouth and the fog damp in her hair and chilling her skin and rubbed his face against her longingly. It was a month since they had seen each other, a month of letters and waiting and wanting.

'How long have we got?' Amy asked now.

'Two days,' he reassured her. 'At least two days, longer if the Committee stage spins itself out . . . Amy, let me look at you. I was frightened something had happened. I thought you were dead . . .'

And Amy's eyes were sparkling as her mouth reached for his, as greedy as Nick but teasing him with her happiness at being together. 'It's only a fog. I like fog, it's exciting. I wasn't frightened. I knew you were here even though you said tomorrow. I've been seeing Isabel and little Peter at Henstone.'

Nick's eyes were closed, his hands reaching under her coat. 'Damn Henstone. Damn the fog, and the Fed, and the Royal Lambeth, and everything that keeps us apart.' His tongue touched hers and Amy felt the warmth in her bones, warmth powerful enough to dispel the fog, and even to drive away the cold that lingered threateningly from too many days apart, too many hours of not knowing what he was doing, and too much longing for him. Her head fell back and his kiss reached further, deeper.

'Which first, d'you think?' she murmured, still teasing him. 'Food, or bed, or whisky?'

'Bed,' he answered, not lifting his mouth from hers. 'Bed. Oh, bed, please.'

The bedroom was so small that her bed almost filled it. Amy had taken the flat in one of the sad times in the year that had passed when she realized that Nick and she would never live together, not as she had dreamed romantically at Chance. Yet when Nick did come to be with her, like now, she knew that she loved him enough almost to make the weeks in between bearable.

They lay down now, still half-dressed, so hungry for one another that their fingers were sharp and their mouths bruised each other. They knew that they were too quick, and yet they were unable to wait. It was always like this when they had been

446

apart. It took time to learn the finesse of love again, and they had so very little time.

'I love you.' Amy's words caught in her throat in the instant that her body and her controlling mind lost touch with one another, and there was only her body, calling *please, please,* and Nick's answering it with his own until she cried out, and the shock waves of pleasure were almost like violence, and left her weak, and washed clean like a seashell.

Then, looking at Nick as she held him, and seeing and feeling his pleasure that was so close to pain, Amy was afraid of the passion that locked them together. Nick felt it too, because he asked her, 'Did I hurt you?' and she answered, 'No. Never.'

She closed her eyes then, thinking of the fog outside, and imagining the house as a tall ship plunging through the waves of it. And when she opened her eyes again she wasn't frightened any longer, because it was just Nick lying beside her and watching her, holding her in the dead centre of his grey-green stare. Amy touched his arms with the tips of her fingers, stroking the dark hairs and the blue-white irregular patches of scars where the hair didn't grow. Then she turned lazily to look at the swell of muscle across his shoulders, and the breadth of his chest before it tapered in to his waist. She saw the way that his hair grew at the nape of his neck, and over his ears, and the dark shadow where his beard grew over his jaw.

She knew that she loved the physical reality of him, safe and reassuring, and that the otherness drew her as well, because it was inimical, male, and remote from her. Amy thought that there was no point in being afraid, because she couldn't help loving him, and there was nothing she could do to change it.

Later, Nick leant on one elbow and smiled at her. 'Whisky now, I think, don't you? Keep still, I'll get it.'

Amy lay drowsily under the blankets, listening to him moving around in the kitchen on the other side of the thin wall. When he came back with the whisky bottle and glasses he was carrying a plate as well, and they propped themselves up against the pillows and fed each other with cheese on toast, and with the small stories of their weeks apart.

Nick talked about his work, full of enthusiasm, licking melted butter off his fingers. 'We're going to set up a ballot vote, I reckon, after this Special Conference. A strike ballot, Amy. We'll get the advance yet.'

The two shillings flat-rate increase for every miner that Nick and the Executive were battling for had become known as the Miners' Two Bob. Amy had come to think of the Two Bob as a rival, with whom she had to fight for his attention.

'Damn the Two Bob,' she echoed him, 'and everything else that keeps us apart. D'you really think you'll get it for them?'

'Yes.' He was smiling, and then he kissed her.

That was the pattern that had been set between them. Nick spent most of his time in Nantlas and the valleys, working endlessly to restore the miners' faith in their Federation, so drastically eroded over the bad years that in some places it hardly existed at all. Sometimes conferences or committee meetings were held in London or the north, and then he came to Pimlico en route and on his way back, or best of all stayed with her for a handful of nights. Then it was back to the Rhondda again, and the pain of parting from him grew rather than diminished.

Amy remembered how he had looked when she had taken the news of the Gresford explosion up to him at the cottage at Chance. Almost a non-union colliery, he had said, and because of that two hundred and fifty men had died. She remembered it, and she never questioned his need to do what he was doing. Yet she couldn't help but feel a kind of resentment. Her helplessness in the face of it made her wonder whether Mari had felt the same, and whether it had driven a wedge between Nick and his wife. And once she was thinking of Mari, Amy began to wonder how often Nick saw her and Dickon, and how much of his Nantlas time was spent with them. Except for his work, Nick hardly spoke of it at all. She knew that he had taken a room in a village down the valley from Nantlas, because he had told her as much. But she would imagine him, on a Sunday afternoon, perhaps, when she was alone in Pimlico, walking up the valley at that moment, to Nantlas. Perhaps he would be carrying a present for Dickon, and walking quietly without looking at the familiar terraces and railway sidings and clogged industry that Amy had never seen. Mari would be waiting for him in their house. Perhaps they would take Dickon out for a walk, or perhaps they would just sit and have tea beside the fire – like families do, Amy thought.

At once she would feel crippled by her own mean-spiritedness. She hated her jealousy, but it was squarely there inside her. She was afraid, too, of losing him altogether, some day, to the valleys and the Fed, and Mari and Dickon, who could claim him so much more strongly than she could herself.

Amy knew that fear and jealousy were poor footings to build anything on, but she couldn't stop herself from suffering them.

Yet just when she had begun to believe that the distance between Nick and herself was wider even than the chasm that separated Chance from the Rhondda Fach, he would appear, just like tonight, out of the fog, and everything would change again.

When he was sitting beside her, like now, laughing at some story she had told him about the hospital, and holding out the last piece of toast to her, Amy wouldn't have asked for anything else in the world.

Nick loved her, she was certain of that because she read it in his eyes, as irrevocably as she loved him. Amy thought back to the summer days of more than a year ago when they had lost themselves in one another. The passion that they had uncovered then remained with them, but out of its intensity their friendship had grown too, and now she knew that they were friends as much as they were lovers. She believed it was their friendship that would endure. They would go on together, somehow, because they were both strong enough to endure the loneliness of separation. And there was no point in being afraid because there was nothing she could do.

For three days out of that October, the Pimlico flat was home for them. They compared its improvised amenities with the luxury of Jack Roper's house where they had first lived together, and laughed, as they always did. Nick spent the day at his conference, and came back at night bright-eyed with the pleasure of doing battle. Amy raced back from the hospital, and they were happy together, not thinking beyond the hours immediately ahead.

On one of those evenings Tony Hardy called to see them. He produced two bottles of wine, with a flourish, from under his coat, and stood them on the tablecloth.

'Can I stay?' he asked, and Amy smiled at him.

'Do stay; stew for dinner. Poacher's stew, Nick calls it, with rabbit. Even though I bought the rabbit from the corner butcher.'

They were both pleased to see Tony. Nick had known him a little from Appleyard Street and when Amy had brought them together they had quickly become friends. For her own part,

Amy was grateful for Tony's acceptance of herself and Nick without question or even apparent surprise.

Tony installed himself in an armchair looking out over the square. The light was fading rapidly, and the sky was a clear indigo blue. The fog might never have existed. Amy handed him a full glass of wine and he raised it to her.

'Your health. You look very pretty, Amy.'

'Doesn't she?' Nick called from the kitchen. He was a far better cook than Amy, even now, and he enjoyed the rituals of preparing food. She took his glass through to him and he leaned over to kiss her, searching for the warmth of her neck under her hair.

'I'm happy,' Amy said simply, telling the truth for that moment. She wandered between the kitchen and the living-room, laying the table with plain white plates and tin cutlery. The room was dim but she resisted turning on the lights, enjoying the yellow brightness coming through the kitchen door and the sound of Nick humming over a saucepan, and the sight of Tony's beaky profile against the lighter square of the window.

It was evenings like this that she had imagined when she had planned a life with Nick in some flat near Appleyard Street. Evenings when one or two friends came to eat with them, and they shared a bottle of wine, and then the friends went home and left them alone together again. She had this much, Amy thought. Not every day, or nearly often enough, but she had this at least.

When Nick had finished what he was doing he came and sat in the chair opposite Tony. Amy leaned back in hers with her legs tucked up beneath her, and tilted her wine in her glass with a luxurious sigh.

'What news from the Secretary of Mines?' Tony asked. His interest in the miners' leaders' plans was genuine, and he enjoyed the inside edge that Nick's stories gave him.

Nick grinned. 'The old bastard said in the House today that he's pressed the owners continually with his view that the selling side ought to be reorganized, so that coal can be sold at a better price and wages improved. Not before, you understand. It's all hot air, anyway. Nothing much else can happen until after the Election. So the Conference is more or less over.'

Tony said, 'Polling day will be November 14th, I hear.' He glanced at Amy and then he added, 'I've got a piece of news for you. Peter Jaspert isn't standing again. In fact, he's already resigned. He's going to join Mosley because, so the story goes, he claims that he can do more outside Parliament than in it.'

Amy stared at him. 'I saw Peter only a few days ago. He looked terrible, but he never mentioned that he was resigning.'

'No. Well, I don't think he would have done, under the circumstances.'

'What circumstances?' Amy demanded, and Tony shrugged apologetically.

'D'you mind me saying this about Isabel's husband? I heard that he was forced to resign, rather than that he chose to. He's been sleeping with Archer Cole's wife. Somebody brought the fact to Cole's attention, and to the attention of various other important persons, in a rather deliberate way. A nasty scandal threatened, which would hardly help the Government just now. Baldwin and Cole have done some hushing up, with Rothermere's help, and it looks as if it will all be kept quiet. The price was Jaspert's resignation, of course.'

'I knew,' Amy said. 'I saw them in . . . a night-club once. I never thought of that.'

'It just won't do, that sort of thing, will it?' Nick said, in tones of mock-horror, and Tony was laughing with him. They had no time for Peter Jaspert, and Amy understood it. But she couldn't forget the Peter she had seen last at Ebury Street, with his red, puffy, puzzled face and his tumbler of whisky. He hadn't wanted to be left alone with himself. She remembered him as he had been before his wedding, a new MP. He had been a big, high-coloured, confident man, the perfect product of his class and time.

What a mess we make of things, all of us, Amy thought sadly. Is nothing in life ever straight and clear, the way children see it? Then she heard Helen Pearce's voice answering her. *It couldn't be, could it? Not* real *life.*

The pendulum of her mood swung down again, and on downwards. She was oppressed by a sense of futility, and at the same time she was painfully aware of the fragile preciousness of the lives they had all constructed for themselves. Not just herself and Nick, but Richard and Tony, Isabel and Bill Parfitt and Adeline and on outwards, in concentric circles, futile and unbearably precious at the same time.

When it was completely dark outside they sat down at the table and Nick lit some candles so that the dishes and knives and the

451

white cloth were held in a little yellow circle in the shadowy room.

Amy tried to listen to what Nick and Tony were saying, but there was a weight of sadness like a stone inside her, pulling her down and away from them. Over her head the words went on and on, resolution and amendment, wage demand and bargaining and concerted action, tariffs and League of Nations, Mussolini and Abyssinia, an avalanche of words and theories, and all of it meaningless to the small lives around her and the fear and love for them that gripped her.

Without warning, still deep in talk, Nick reached out his hand to hers and covered her fingers as they lay loose on the tablecloth. His touch was the final breach. The tears came into her eyes and ran down her cheeks, dripping on to the front of her dress. She felt a sob rising, and distorting her mouth, until it forced its way out of her, an ugly, ragged sound.

'What is it?' Nick asked her in bewilderment, and Amy shook her head. She couldn't have found the words to confess to Nick how much she wanted him, a home together, children; ordinary, humdrum, womanly things, while the men talked.

She pushed her chair back, scraping it noisily.

'I hate politics,' she said wildly. 'Where are the people, Nick? Where?'

Amy stumbled across the room to the window and stood looking out into the dark square. But all she could see was her own dim, distorted reflection in the cold glass. Nick came after her, and she saw his reflection too. He was awkward, for once, silenced by her misery. He put his arms around her and hugged her, stroking her hair and turning her head so that it rested on his shoulder. He was murmuring comforting, disjointed words, as if she was a baby.

Sombre-faced, Tony Hardy slipped out of his place and picked up his coat. The door closed with a soft click behind him.

'What is it, my darling? Don't cry so much, don't cry, my love.'

Amy screwed up her face, pulling away from Nick and pressing the heels of her hands up to her temples.

'I feel so sad. I don't understand anything. I can't be like you want me to be. I'm frightened . . .'

He took her arms, tightening his hold insistently so that she winced. Amy saw him look at her, reckoning and wondering, and the light dawning in his face. 'Amy, listen to me,' he ordered. 'Tell me. Are you going to have a baby?'

The tears felt as if they were burning her cheeks. She couldn't even do that for him.

'No. I'm not going to have a baby. If only I was.'

She broke away from him then and wrapped her arms around herself, hugging the emptiness to her while she cried.

At last, Nick soothed her into silence. When the terrible tears stopped he made her lie down on their bed, and stretched himself out beside her. He was as gentle and patient with her as he was with Dickon, and he rocked her and whispered to her until she felt heavy with exhausted sleep.

'I'm here,' he said. 'Amy, I'm here. Don't cry any more.'

She did sleep, feeling the weight of his arm around her. But the next day the Conference closed, and within a few hours Nick was on his way back to Nantlas and she was alone again.

Part Four

Part Four

17

London 1936

Amy opened her eyes reluctantly and looked at the clock. She always woke with difficulty nowadays, as if oblivion was a welcome shelter. It was ten minutes past five, and still dark, but it was time to get up. The fingers of the day's consciousness tightened their hold, and she rolled on her side in an effort to escape them for a moment longer.

She had been dreaming, a happy dream that she had already forgotten, but the carefree essence of it stayed with her. The day's reality was cold by contrast. Nick was still asleep. She burrowed against the warmth of him, trying to capture his closeness, and keep it, and bury it inside herself against the time when he was gone again. He stirred and folded his arms around her, drawing her against him so that they fitted together. Amy recalled the times when she woke up like this and still, half-dreaming, believed that he was there. She would curl up against him but the warmth would fade, and when she stretched out she found that she was alone.

She closed her eyes against her unhappiness. Today he was going again.

Amy hated her own weakness. It was destructive, spreading through her like a disease that attacked her bones. And she could do nothing to stop the march of it. 'What time is it?' Nick whispered into her hair. Amy went stiff, protecting herself in advance. If she gave herself up to him now, it hurt so much more when he was gone.

'Late,' she said. 'I've got to go.' Defensiveness made her voice cold. She wanted to unsay the words, but couldn't.

'Amy, come here.'

She was already up. The floor was cold under her bare feet. She said nothing, but picked up her robe and wrapped it around her. She went into the little bathroom behind its partition and closed the door. When she came back Nick was sitting up in bed. Sleep had tousled his black hair into points. He watched her, dark-faced, as she began to dress.

Just like any couple, Amy thought, except that they weren't.

'Why are you angry?' Nick asked her.

'I'm not angry.'

The staleness of the exchange was tiresome to both of them. Nick pushed the bedclothes back impatiently and went into the kitchen to make tea. Following him with her eyes, Amy thought how the shape of him filled her landscape, how she saw things only under the slant of his opaque eyes, how the only real feeling leapt in her under his surprising, finely shaped hands. She loved him too much, her need for him frightened her, and her dependence on him undermined her old will to survive.

Amy hadn't imagined that love would be like this.

She pulled her clothes on roughly and her skin felt raw under her stiff uniform dress. Nick came back with two cups of tea and put them carefully on the table before going to the street window. He stood with the curtain drawn back, staring into the beginnings of grey light. He looked as if he was already anxious to be gone, Amy thought bitterly.

'It's going to be fine,' Nick said. 'That's good. The turn-out will be bigger.'

'Don't go.' Her voice came out thin and cold.

The curtain dropped back into its folds, shutting out the dawn again.

'I have to go. I want to go.'

'Those are one and the same thing, Nick.'

They stared at one another, suddenly a thousand miles further apart than the bare yard that separated them.

'What do you want?' he asked her, exasperated, and Amy shook her head. They were too far apart for her to run to him and confess that she wanted ordinariness, a husband and a home and children. And that the denial of that made her cling to Nick too desperately, shaming her with her weakness.

'Amy,' he said, 'I love you.' They were both standing very still and there was an odd, proud, yet vulnerable light in Nick's face. 'I love you under that damned starched dress so that I want to pull it off you and lie down with you. I love your heart and your soul and your brave spirit because you are truthful and original

458

and generous and good. You are the loveliest woman I have ever known or seen. Sometimes when I look at you I can't believe it, and I think you are going to turn on me and snub me for my presumption, the miner from Nantlas. I love you now, and I will always love you. Can't that be enough?'

Amy looked at him through her tears. Her jaw was locked rigidly, and there was a sour, frightened dribble in the back of her throat. She wanted to tell him that it wasn't enough, that the fiercest and truest love in the world didn't compensate for loneliness, and the ache of days and weeks without him. She knew that if she were truly brave, like Nick believed her to be, it would be enough. But she wasn't brave or generous; love made her selfish and afraid for both of them. She wanted to be Nick's wife, and he had a wife already. She wanted to bear his children, and she was denied that. She wanted to be equal with him, one with one, and the years of their lives behind them made that impossible. The hopelessness of it was like a knife in her side. Amy lifted her head so that she looked straight at him.

'Yes,' she lied. 'It is enough. I love you too.'

'I know that,' Nick said tenderly. 'Come on. Drink your tea before it's too late.'

He moved around the room, putting his possessions together. Amy wouldn't watch him. Tonight he would carry them back to Nantlas. And in the meantime, there was today.

'Don't go,' she said again.

'I have to meet Jake,' he answered absently. He had told her what he felt, with his unfailing honesty, and now his quick mind had moved on.

'I don't want you to go. You might be hurt.'

'I won't be hurt.'

Suddenly Amy's precarious control deserted her. She swung around to him, spilling her tea without noticing it. She hit his chest with her clenched fist, and then again, pounding at him. 'You don't have to go, damn you. The anti-Fascist movement won't founder if Nick Penry misses its demonstration.' She shook her head blindly. 'I don't want to worry about you all day. Why do you care so much more about issues than about people? Why do causes matter so bloody much?'

As if a spark jumped between them, Nick caught her anger. She saw it take hold and begin to blaze.

'Because they are more important. You're too pampered and

privileged to understand that. You try, oh, you try to understand, because you feel you should. But you truly can't see, can you, that if we don't fight with every fibre of ourselves for what is right our children will suffer in just the same way as our fathers did? All right, not your father, Amy Lovell, or your children. But most of them. My son will. My wife and family and friends. Working people everywhere.

'I can't expect you to understand that. I appreciate that you try hard. But causes are more important than people. More important than you and me, and our loves and hurts and little concerns. That's why I'm going to do what you don't want me to do today. If I get hit by a brick or police baton meeting the Blackshirts today, it doesn't matter in the least, because I will have been there, demonstrating what I believe in. I've told you what I feel, Amy, and it's the truth from my heart. Don't ask me for anything more because there isn't any more to give. And don't ask me to deny or give up what I believe in, because I never will. Even Mari understood that.'

Amy felt the misery like a claw. They were his family, Mari and Dickon. They were his people, away in Nantlas. She had taken all he had to give her. And she hated herself for it, but it wasn't enough. As if he read her thoughts, Nick said, 'You cannot possess people, Amy. Not me, or anybody. We all owe our allegiances to a dozen different thrones.'

Amy's head jerked up, and he saw the flash of her old defiance. He loved her, and he felt the physical response to her stirring inside him.

'Go on, then,' Amy flung at him. 'Go to your rally and your crowd-raising rhetoric. I don't believe that brawling in the streets helps any cause. Men are like children, they want a show, the quickest, loudest answer. Here, take them away.'

She was bundling his belongings into his arms, pushing him, stumbling over her words in her anger. He hesitated, almost wanting to pull her arms behind her and push her down to the bed, but he turned sharply away. He was angry too, baffled and impatient and angry.

The door slammed, and Amy heard his boots on the stairs. She stood still, one hand rubbing at her arm where his fingers had dug into her.

'Nick?' she said dazedly. 'Nick?'

But he was gone. She turned, slowly, and saw that in his hurry

460

he had left an old jacket hanging over the back of a chair. She picked it up, feeling her fingers stiff like an old woman's, looking down at the criss-cross threads woven together. Then, with a sound that was more like the cry of an animal than a sob or a moan, she buried her face in the folds of it.

In the early hours of the same morning, October 4th, the narrow streets of the East End of London were almost as busy as they would have been at an ordinary midday. The crowds were almost all men, cheering and chanting, but there were women and even children amongst them too.

Every so often a figure detached itself from the crowd in front of a boarded-up shop window, or a bare brick wall. In foot-high chalked letters the words THEY SHALL NOT PASS appeared. Louder cheering always greeted the words, and the chanting took them up and carried them on through the streets like a war cry.

Sometimes a van nosed its way past, and bundles of pamphlets and handbills were passed out to waiting groups of men who stacked them on upturned boxes. They beat a tattoo of encouragement on the roof of the van as it eased its way forward to the next delivery point.

The atmosphere was rippling with defiance, and with excitement, as if it was the night before a carnival. People greeted each other eagerly under street-lamps, putting arms round one another's shoulders and stamping their feet in the chilly dawn. And as the light strengthened the flags began to appear, hanging from upstairs windows and fluttering from telegraph poles, tied to shop awnings and doorknobs and drainpipes, hundreds of red flags against the chalked slogan, THEY SHALL NOT PASS.

The Fascists and their leader were to meet that afternoon near Tower Bridge, and then form four columns to march through the teeming East End to Stepney, Shoreditch, Limehouse and Bethnal Green. The men in the streets were anti-Fascists, Communists, ex-servicemen, trades unionists and Jews, and they were gathering to stop them. On a soap-box at one corner an organizer from the National Unemployed Workers' Movement was rallying his crowd.

'We'll stop them in our streets, brothers, at any cost. We'll stop them with a human barricade if need be, and pile it up with bodies until their jackboots fill with blood.'

461

At the storm of cheering that greeted him he blinked, half in surprise and half in gratification, and then lifted his clenched fist to wave it back at the forest of clenched fists swaying in front of him.

By breakfast-time the Commissioner of the Metropolitan Police, Sir Philip Game, was already at his desk. His senior officers were grouped in a half-circle around him, reading the reports of the night's activities.

The Home Secretary was waiting near his telephone, and the Mayors of Bethnal Green, Stepney, Shoreditch and Poplar were waiting too. They had taken their anxieties to the Home Office days ago, begging for the march to be forbidden, or at least diverted, and they had been told that matters were well in hand. But there had been no announcement, the day itself had come, and the shabby streets had fallen to an anti-Fascist siege. The crowds continued to flood in, carrying their banners that proclaimed SMASH FASCISM TODAY, and in the police stations across London the Metropolitan Police were preparing themselves in their thousands for the day.

Jake Silverman was sitting in an all-night café in Whitechapel. He was bulky in his red and black plaid shirt behind the rickety wooden table. There was a plate of eggs and bacon in front of him and he was reading the top one from a stack of newspaper first editions, nodding and smiling in satisfaction.

One of the van drivers came in and stood beside the table, like an NCO reporting to the commanding officer in the field.

'That's the lot. The lads'll distribute them through the crowds this morning. Every bugger there will get a CP handbill.'

Jake grinned at him. 'We're winning, mate. Get yourself some grub and come and sit down. Might as well, while it's still quiet. Where's the rest of them?'

'Coming.'

Sure enough, the steamy café began to fill with people. Most of the faces would have been familiar to Amy from Appleyard Street. They ordered hot breakfasts and mugs of tea and crowded round the tables, shouting with the keyed-up eagerness of troops before a long-awaited battle.

Nick Penry was walking slowly up the road towards the café, his hands in his pockets and the collar of his coat turned up. He was frowning at the boarded-up shopfronts with their pleas painted on the boards, DONT TOUCH WORKERS SHOPS, at the red flags stirring in the wind, and the surging, expectant people.

When he reached Lenny's Café on the corner he glanced up at the sign, draped defiantly in its own red flag, and pushed the door open. The jangle of the bell mounted behind it was drowned by the babble that swept out to him. The air was thick with steam and grease and food, but Nick could smell sweat and tension and threat in it too, and the frown made his dark face blacker. Jake Silverman saw him and brandished a long arm to beckon him over.

Nick stood at the end of the table, his hands still in his pockets. 'It looks like bloody Madrid out there. This is London, for Christ's sake.'

'Unless you want it to be like Madrid,' Jake shouted at him, 'that's how it's got to be. The Fascists will not walk these streets, Nick, whether they're Franco's, or Hitler's or Mosley's. We have to stop them, all of us who believe in freedom.'

'Spare me the rhetoric,' Nick said coldly. 'I'm not a rally of the faithful. Tell me, does this have to be conducted like a war? People are going to get hurt and probably killed out there today.'

'In war people get killed. This is a war. I'm sorry if you don't like it.'

'Oh, Jesus.' Nick was angry at the provocative display of threats from the people he sympathized with, and he was apprehensive of the violence to come. But he knew from years of experience that it was useless to argue with Jake. He jerked out a chair and sat down, and Jake beamed at him.

'That's better. Why are you here, anyway, if you're going to be an old woman?'

Nick opened his mouth to answer, and then thought better of it. 'Amy's on early shift at the hospital. I wouldn't be here otherwise, believe me.'

Jake's ribald chuckle was cut short by the arrival of a fresh contingent of his workers, hungry for breakfast and congratulation and the fuel of encouragement.

The morning passed, and thousands more people came to swell the crowds. It was a fine, sunny day and Nick thought as he walked gloomily among them that they were treating it as a holiday outing. But the tension was mounting perceptibly as the march time drew closer, further stirred by the loudspeaker vans touring to and fro and imploring everyone to unite, and fight the Fascist menace. Nick glimpsed the red and black of Jake's shirt in one of the vans, although the loudspeaker distorted his voice beyond recognition.

By the early afternoon the atmosphere was electric. All along the four routes that the marchers would take there were blue lines of policemen. The police had cordoned off the side streets to everyone except those who lived in the area, but still the swarming masses of demonstrators managed to pour in. Nick found himself in Cable Street. The roadway was a dense packed mass of men and police and at the far end Nick saw another contingent of police on their horses with batons swinging at the ready. His frown deepened as he listened to the low, angry murmuring of the crowd, like surf on a dangerous beach. The Blackshirt column would be swept up and engulfed when it appeared.

Nick found himself pressed into the doorway of a boarded-up shop. Glancing up, he saw the three brass balls of a pawnbroker's sign and smiled crookedly. He eased himself back against the splintered wood and settled to wait for the marchers.

Neither Nick nor anyone else in Cable Street knew that Sir Philip Game had decided to intervene at the last instant. Sir Oswald Mosley had arrived to meet his supporters at Tower Bridge, resplendent in a new uniform of black military jacket, breeches and jackboots. He had been met by police and Home Office representatives, who informed him that due to conditions generated by anti-Fascists throughout the East End, the march could not take place. The Blackshirts and their leader had been turned away westwards along the Embankment, and had safely dispersed.

But the news hadn't travelled quickly enough. As Nick stood watching in Cable Street the violence broke out and spread as fast and frighteningly as fire in a forest. A builder's yard stood open opposite the pawnshop and men began to stream out with wood and poles that they threw into a tangled mess in the middle of the road. A lorry standing by the yard entrance was overturned and people swarmed over it like ants. Bricks, corrugated iron and glass and even paving stones were thrown on to the barricade.

Nick saw the first fusillade of stones fly over the great heap of rubble as the police charged from the other side.

The air was suddenly filled with hoarse shouts, the rattle of falling rocks and the high, thin shrilling of police whistles. Nick ran, without any thought except to reach the barricade. Over the top of it he saw the detachment of mounted police wheel at the street end and turn to charge. There were hooves clattering on the cobbles and deafening shouts and then a pattering sound as a hail of marbles bounced off the stones. Two of the police horses stumbled and fell with whinnies of fear and the riders' helmets rolled away into the gutter. The others came inexorably onwards and the long batons swished in the air. Away to Nick's right a man was caught by one and he toppled sideways, his arms folded up over his skull.

Nick stood at the centre of the barricade and all around him there were faces distorted with anger, and fists waving broken bottles, and sticks and pieces of brick, and the swarming blue jackets of policemen. The fights coalesced into a battle that raged the long length of the street. Then, looking back the way he had come, Nick saw a man standing in the same pawnbroker's doorway that had sheltered him a moment ago. The likeness startled him even in the mêlée, and then he realized that it wasn't a mere likeness. The man really was Peter Jaspert. He was standing quite still, his hat pulled down half over his face and his collar turned up. He seemed to be watching the vicious fight with perfect impassivity.

For a brief moment Nick wondered whether Peter Jaspert was spying. Perhaps he had come to judge the strength of anti-Fascist support for his new masters.

Nick wasn't the only one to recognize him.

The barrier heaved under the weight of people swarming against it and Nick toppled forwards. As he fell he caught a glimpse of a red and black shirt, and a tight knot of pale faces that he half-recognized.

Then, unmistakable even in all the rest of the clamour, he heard a single shot. Nick was pitched painfully forwards on to his hands and knees, and when he wrenched his head round again to look, Peter Jaspert was sunk into a huddle in the doorway. His face was invisible beneath his hat, but there was a bright splatter of blood on the shop boards beside him.

The pounding of horses' hooves thundered a foot away from Nick's head and he rolled over and over to escape them. Rough hands seized him and then he felt himself being dragged to the kerb and dropped in a heap with half a dozen other men. The big, gleaming brown horses wheeled together again, stirrup irons jingling under the riders' black boots as the police regrouped for another charge. Nick levered himself upright and looked down the street. A man was lying in the gutter with a dark puddle of blood beside him. Another was sitting on the kerb with his head in his hands, and further away two men were dragging a third out of the path of the horses. His heels clattered unevenly on the cobbles.

Peter Jaspert was still hunched in the pawnbroker's doorway, and Nick knew that he was dead.

The barricade was abandoned and the street cleared magically in front of the charge. The horses slowed to a walk and the police riders returned the batons to the leather holsters. Then at a whistle summons they rose to a trot again and turned away to the next street. In their place the roadway filled with police on foot, pouring over the barricade towards the wounded men and the sullenly murmuring anti-Fascists at bay at the far end.

Glancing quickly around him, Nick saw that there was no sign of Jake or his companions. He stood back against a shopfront as the first of the police pelted past him, and watched a pair of them stop short and then stoop in the pawnbroker's doorway. Peter Jaspert's hat fell off as they moved him, and rolled out on to the pavement. Nick saw the damaged head and straightened abruptly. A glance up and down the road told him that Jake and his companions had vanished. Nick turned and melted away down a side alley. The din of shouting and whistles and the rattle and crash of stone-throwing was muffled immediately by the overcrowded houses. Except for one or two inquisitive children peering from doorsteps and the eyes of old women staring fearfully from behind shabby curtains, there was nothing here to tell of the battle raging a few yards away.

Nick stood listening for a moment and then began to walk quickly, westwards.

Amy had worked non-stop from the moment she came on duty in the reception ward. It was always the busiest department in the hospital, and today the tide of sick and injured seemed to flow more strongly than ever.

Then, just before noon, she heard two ambulances swing into the hospital yard with their bells shrilling. As the sister on duty

466

it was her job to receive them and Amy nodded briskly to the third-year student who was assisting her.

'Finish this off, Nurse, will you?'

At the doors she met the ambulance crews with two stretchers. 'Burns,' they told her. 'Paraffin.'

On the stretchers lay a mother and her ten-year-old daughter. They had been trapped in their rented room when a stove blazed up and set fire to the flimsy curtains. Amy was already moving. Not running, because that was never allowed. But even before the constable who had accompanied the ambulances had finished his report, the cubicles were prepared and Amy was ready.

'Will you call Doctor Frobisher, please?'

The junior nurses scuttled to do her bidding and Amy turned to her work. Until the doctor arrived from elsewhere on the ward, Amy was in charge.

Burns victims were all too common at the Lambeth. The crowded tenements in the surrounding streets were all fire traps, and the first autumn chill brought out the rusty heaters and stoves.

From watching the treatments Amy had begun to be interested in the new techniques for keeping burns sterile, and in the methods for helping them to heal. She had even begun to think of it as 'her' speciality, and now she began, coolly but with the utmost gentleness, to separate the charred remains of the little girl's clothing from her burned flesh. Amy gave herself up to her work, and there was no space to think or remember anything else.

Then, a moment later, the doctor came.

'Thank you, Sister,' he said briskly and Amy stepped aside. As she had begun to do more and more often, she felt the pinprick of regret that she couldn't do what the doctors did.

'Sterile dressing packs, Sister, please,' Dr Frobisher ordered.

'Beside your left hand, Doctor,' Amy murmured. The child was beginning to moan and Amy felt her hands ache to reach out and help her. But the student nurse was waiting to attract her attention to the next necessity, and Amy went quickly to do what she had been trained to do, and await the doctor's readiness for the next patient.

It was two hours before Amy had time to slip away to her office and drink a cup of cold tea, standing up.

Outside her door she heard two of the juniors whispering, as Moira and she had once done. 'Bloody hell, what a day.'

'Could be worse, duck. We're lucky not to be in the London, or one of those East End hospitals. I bet they're worked half to death. There's a big riot with those Blackshirts and the Commies.'

Anxiety stabbed under Amy's ribcage like a knife, all the sharper because she had forgotten it as she worked.

Nick, she thought. Isn't there enough pain and suffering? Why do you add to it by violence? Or let it come to you, by being there?

Fear for him made her whirl out of her office and speak with unusual sharpness to the whispering nurses.

The afternoon wore on. Amy went to and fro from cubicle to cubicle. The burned child was too ill to be moved, and they were waiting to see whether she would rally a little before attempting further treatment.

Just before the day shift ended one of the nurses came back to Amy. 'Sister, there's a . . . gentleman waiting to see you outside.'

It doesn't matter if I get hit by a brick or a police baton. That's what Nick had said. Suddenly Amy smelt smoke and heard the clatter of running feet and the confused shouting that brought back Trafalgar Square and the sight of Jake Silverman helpless under the horses' hooves. Five years ago, and more. Perhaps Nick was lying in some cubicle in an East End hospital now. Perhaps a constable had come to bring her the news of him, somehow, perhaps . . .

'A policeman?' she asked, and the nurse stared at her.

'No, Sister, just a man.'

It was Nick standing in the gloomy corridor.

Amy saw him and relief and weariness made anger surge up inside her.

'What the hell are you doing here? You can't just drop in when you're tired of street fighting . . .'

Nick took her arm. 'I've got something to tell you. Is there somewhere quiet we can go?'

Amy's relief was painfully short-lived. She turned to Nick white-faced. 'Is it Richard? Mummy? Tell me, Nick. Not Isabel?'

The door of a little waiting-room stood open behind them. Nick guided her in and closed the door, then made her sit down on a wooden bench.

'It's Peter Jaspert,' he said quietly. 'He was shot this afternoon. I saw it happen.'

Amy was staring at him, her mouth slightly open. 'Shot? You mean with a gun?' Nick nodded. 'Is he badly hurt? I mean, gunshot wounds can be . . .' Amy heard her own voice babbling, and then Nick's bitten-off words cutting through it.

'He's dead. I'm sorry, Amy.'

She shook her head unbelievingly, and then knew that she must believe it. 'Oh God. Who did it? Who shot him? Who would want to kill Peter?'

'I don't know who shot him,' Nick said, truthfully. 'I don't know if anyone ever will know. It was in the middle of a street riot, down in the East End in a place called Cable Street. There was a police baton charge. I saw Peter standing in a doorway, I heard a shot, and when I looked again he had fallen in a huddle. I don't think anyone else saw anything.'

Amy turned her head a little to look straight into his eyes. Very softly, she said, 'You sound relieved.'

There was a long, long moment of quiet before Nick answered her, and Amy was sure that he had waited to choose his words carefully.

'I'm not relieved. I didn't like Peter Jaspert, but that didn't mean that I wanted to see him murdered.'

'I meant, relieved that nobody but you saw anything.' Amy's gaze was very clear, unwavering, and although Nick met it squarely he had nothing to say.

'How many others were hurt?' she asked, stopping with her hand on the knob. 'How many Fascists? How many anti-Fascists? A satisfactory score for the forces of the left?'

Nick's head was bent now, and there was as much bitterness in his answer as in Amy's question. 'There were no Fascists. They were turned back before they reached the East End. The riot was our friends, fighting the police.'

'Friends.' Amy was thinking of the day at Henstone, and Peter and Isabel waving to her from the gate. 'Friends. Our friends have left little Peter without a father. For what? What have we gained today, Nick?' Amy's thumb rubbed over the smoothness of the doorknob as her fingers turned it one way and then the other. Nick's hand reached out, but in the end it didn't quite reach hers.

'We haven't gained anything. We've lost a very great deal. I'm

469

sorry, and I'm ashamed, Amy. But if there were to be another Blackshirt rally tomorrow, I'd go out to try and stop it in just the same way.'

They stood looking at each other for a long moment then, with the clatter of the hospital behind them. Amy hesitated, then seemed to give way to one of the forces pulling inside her.

'Thank you for coming all the way down here to tell me.'

'I wanted you to know before you saw a newspaper placard on the way home.'

'Thank you,' Amy repeated tonelessly. 'I have to go and hand over to the night staff now. Will you wait till I come off duty? I must go to Henstone, to Isabel, and then I must make sure that Bethan and little Peter are all right.'

'I'll wait if you would like me to.' Nick's dark head was still bent, and she couldn't see his face.

When she reached the reception ward again one of the nurses told Amy that the little girl had just died. The mother was likely to survive if she could pull through the next few hours.

Amy wanted to lay down her head and close her eyes. But she simply stared ahead of her and said, 'I see. I will be in my office, Nurse, preparing the reports for the night sister.'

Nick was standing on the steps of the hospital when Amy came out in her cape. Her hair was flattened where her cap had been pinned to it, and her face looked grey with strain. They turned in silence and began to walk towards the Underground station. Their footsteps echoed in ironic unison, and Amy thought that she had never felt so far apart from him. There was a cold, barren space between them, and it made her want to reach out and snatch at him, pulling him close again, because she loved him and she needed him and the fear of losing him threatened to choke her. Yet she did nothing, and they walked on through the homegoing rush, unspeaking.

Outside the station, between the street barrows with their glowing mounds of fruit and a man selling chestnuts roasted over a brazier of red cinders, there were the news placards.

Amy read them, with the sour taste of disgust in her mouth. Nick bought a paper, she glimpsed the headline STREET BATTLES RAGE, and looked away again. Down in the depths of the Underground a group of young men ran past them, chanting in unison. 'They did not pass! They did not pass!' The train rattled in and they raised their voices over its roar. 'They did not pass.' The pinched faces of the commuters turned to stare blankly at them. There were more of them at the mainline station and the chanting seemed to echo through the smoke and gather like a threat under the glass and iron arches overhead. Nick's face set in hard lines. These people had been among the thousands surging around Cable Street.

'They're fools,' he said. 'They're trying to believe that they've won something today, instead of losing almost everything that's important.'

To Amy, the station was an inferno of noise. She didn't even look at Nick. 'You were there yourself,' she said coldly. 'You were part of it, as much as them. A millionth part of Peter's death is your fault.'

The train for the little station that served Chance was at the platform. Amy swung herself up into the nearest carriage, and a porter jostled in front of Nick to slam the door. Amy hauled on the thick leather strap to lower the window, and secured it over the brass stud. Nick's face was turned up to hers.

'Do you believe that?' he asked her.

The din of whistles and shouting and escaping steam buffeted them. Slowly, beneath Amy's feet, the pistons clanked and the great wheels began to turn. Nick was sliding away behind her.

'I don't know what I believe.' Her mouth was stiff, and she didn't know if Nick had even heard her.

She stood in the swaying corridor until the station was gone and tall tenement windows with their bleary lights looked in at her instead. Then she found a seat in the crowded carriage and leaned her face against the cold black glass. The outside world was reduced to chains of lights, fainter than the packed seats reflected back at her from the depths of the glass. Her thoughts shuttled over and over, suspicion to disbelief to sadness and fear and then to love, hopeless and consuming, all at once, over and over, to the monotous rattle of the wheels across the points.

October 4th, the battle of Cable Street and the death of Peter Jaspert, marked the beginning of a different time. To Amy, years afterwards, the mass violence and the unexplained murder of a man who was no longer important came to symbolize the spectrum of changes that 1936 brought. The world seemed to spin faster, and then faster again, piling people and events on top of one another in a random and threatening jumble. Kings were whirled off as well as humble people, and everyone spun helplessly from times in which war was unthinkable into times when war was a reality, first in one corner and then everywhere, roaring and blackening the skies like the apocalypse.

The news waves that followed Peter Jaspert's death were never as high as those generated by the riots themselves, and within a week they had fallen away into ripples. The storm over law and order and the legislation following it raged on, and left was pitched even more bitterly against right, but Peter Jaspert himself was quickly forgotten. The police investigation proceeded, but there was no evidence for them to work on. No weapon had been found, and no witnesses to what had happened outside the pawnshop ever came forward. In the first few days, government ministers paid tribute to Peter's early promise, and the British Union of Fascists' leadership praised his bravery and his single-mindedness, and described him as a martyr to their cause, but after that there was nothing. Peter's death was only truly significant to the stricken old people at West Talbot, to Isabel and her family, and to little Peter. Amy wondered if even Sylvia Cole was not distantly relieved. Archer Cole was in the Foreign Office in Baldwin's Cabinet, and his handsome wife appeared with him at a diplomatic function on October 6th.

After Cable Street, the Appleyard Street cell was broken apart. The Public Order Act was being hurried through Parliament, and Jake and his friends agreed that it was no longer safe to have the headquarters of the group somewhere that was so well known to the police.

In early November Amy recognized that gatherings of the innermost circle were taking place at her own Pimlico flat. It had begun with Jake and Kay calling in to see her, bringing bottles of wine and surprising her with their friendliness. They had appeared again on another evening, bringing a trio of friends with them. Nick had been there that night, and Tony Hardy too, and they had sat talking around Amy's rickety table until three in the morning. It was on that night that Amy first heard the words *International Brigades.*

Three days later, there were a dozen people sitting around the same table. Nick had gone back to Nantlas. Amy sat holding in her black fear of separation from him, and her jealousy of his other life that didn't admit her, and tried to listen. Jake was leaning forward, his black beard thrusting at them and his eyes glowing.

'How many men can we muster?' he asked. 'Who else will go?'

'I will,' a thin, consumptive-looking man said, and there was a murmur around the table and two others said, 'I'll go.'

Across the table from Amy, Kay Cooper's face was white and stiff. She never took her eyes off Jake, and she nodded slowly as he spoke.

They were volunteering to go and fight in Spain.

The civil war was already four months old, a bloody and vicious battle between the leftist forces of the Republican government overthrown by the rightist and military forces under Franco. Republican-occupied Madrid was a siege city, and German and Italian planes, despatched to the aid of the Nationalists, were bombing the Republican supply ports.

Under Comintern direction, the International Brigades were being mustered from all over Europe, even from Canada and the United States, to support the Republican armies.

Amy's own Republican sympathies strengthened as the days passed, and the meetings became an important focus for her too.

Jake was smiling, triumphant, his teeth a white slash in the black beard. 'Four of us from this one room, then. How many more?' He seized a wine bottle in his big, dark fist. 'Let's drink to it. Let's drink to the death of Fascism everywhere.' The dark red wine trickled into smeared glasses, and to Amy it looked like congealing blood. She lifted her eyes again and met Kay's. There was fear in Kay's face, but her words denied it.

'Death to them,' she echoed.

Early one morning in the middle of November, Amy woke up to the sound of her doorbell ringing, in sharp bursts, as if someone was jabbing at it with an urgent forefinger. She stumbled down the dusty stairs and found Tony Hardy on the doorstep. His finger was still on the bell, and he was carrying a newspaper folded open at an inside page.

'I'm sorry,' he said, seeing her dressing-gown. 'I know it's early. Have you seen this?'

Amy glanced at the paper. 'Of course not. I don't read that rag.'

Tony didn't smile. 'I thought I'd better come and show you myself. It's my fault, indirectly. Can I come in?'

Amy led the way upstairs. She went into her kitchen cubicle,

473

yawning, and filled the kettle. Once it was on the gas she said, 'What're you talking about? Show me.'

There was a short paragraph in the centre of the page, headed PEER'S SISTER AND THE PIMLICO REDS. Amy quickly scanned the sentences.

Just who is the quiet hospital nurse who loans her Pimlico flat for Communist meetings? Our informant tells us that she is none other than the beautiful Lady Amy Lovell, daughter of Society's darling Adeline, Lady Lovell, and former friend of Jolly Jack Roper. Red Amy, we hear, is hostess at almost nightly meetings of the London Branch of the Communist Party of Great Britain, whose luminaries include twice gaoled admitted anarchist Jacob Silverman and a dozen other sworn enemies of the British Monarchy and democracy. That's odd enough for any girl of Lady Amy's pedigree, but odder still for the sister of Lord Lovell, who is the hereditary King's Defender. Not that Lord Richard himself is exactly a conventional young man. He is, readers will remember, the author of that very strange book *The Innocent and the Damned.*

Amy dropped the paper in a heap and went to attend to the shrilly whistling kettle. A moment or two later she came back with a tray with a coffee pot and two cups on it.

'They even got my honorary title wrong. I'm not Lady Amy anybody. Will you have some coffee, Tony?'

He sat down heavily in one of the armchairs, reaching out for the cup she held out to him. 'Doesn't this muck worry you?' he asked.

'It would if Gerald was still alive. Adeline won't be particularly pleased. But I don't see that it matters to anyone else, does it?'

There was a defeated note in her voice that was quite unlike Amy. Tony saw that her face had grown thinner, and there were dark patches beneath her eyes. She sat with her fingers wrapped around her coffee cup, as if she was trying to draw the warmth out of it and into herself.

'Amy,' he asked gently, 'is it making you so very unhappy?'

She smiled, a sardonic smile that couldn't hide anything. 'I'm doing it to myself. I'm making myself unhappy by asking Nick for more than he can give me. Have you ever been jealous, Tony? I'm jealous of Nantlas and the Rhondda, and I've never

474

even set eyes on them. I'm jealous of the Fed, and the Two Bob. I'm jealous of Mari and Dickon, God help me. He's here with me as much as he can be, as much as he ever promised, but it isn't enough. I'm afraid of losing him to them, every minute. And I'm guilty because I know he belongs to them. However much we love each other. I don't even know what it's like there, Tony. I don't even understand why he has to fight so hard. Why it means so much to him. How could I?'

'What do you want, Amy?'

She stared at him, and then laughed a little wildly. 'To be ordinary. To be Nick's wife, and have somewhere to live together, and go on doing our work, and to come home to one another at the end of the day.' Not to their children. That wouldn't happen, she was convinced of that now. Amy stared fiercely ahead, forcing herself to go on talking. 'But Nick is there, not here, and – ' she pointed at the discarded newspaper – 'I'm still *Peer's Daughter and Sister*. Not that any of that matters.' She shrugged helplessly. 'It isn't just loving Nick the way I do. It's the darkness of everything, all around, from horizon to horizon. Do you remember when we first went to Appleyard Street together?'

'I remember. You were very young then, Amy.'

'It has all gone murky, hasn't it? Men fighting and maiming one another in the streets of London. Murdering Peter like a rat in a shop doorway.'

Amy was still staring straight ahead, but the muscles in her throat and cheeks contracted, pulling her mouth into the shape of a silent cry.

'Viciousness and blood are disgusting to me too, Amy. But you are a political innocent. Radical change is almost always contaminated by them. And so is the struggle to prevent it, according to which side of the barricades you are standing on.'

The barricades again, Amy thought. She remembered her certainty as she had marched down to Trafalgar Square years ago.

'Like in Spain?' she said.

'Civil war is the bitterest of all wars. But the fighting in Spain is important for every one of us. For the old Appleyard Street causes like workers' rights, and workers' solidarity, that we both believe in. And for the big, cloudy issues like democracy, and freedom. I believe in them, and so do you.'

'So will you go to Spain with Jake and the others?'

His face twisted. 'Without the coward's caveat of having a business to run, on which other livelihoods depend as well as my own? Yes, I would go. All of us who call ourselves socialists, communists, whatever, should go. It is a war that we must win.'

Amy was chilled, and she felt fear in her stomach. 'Nick too, then,' she whispered.

The lines of sympathy in Tony Hardy's face deepened, but there was nothing to say.

Amy looked down at the newspaper still lying on the floor between them. At the top of the page there was a picture of the King opening a new hospital that was named after him.

Tony followed her glance. 'There might be some more stuff about you,' he warned her. 'It depends on how hungry the papers are, I should think. If you're lucky the Mrs Simpson story will break and *Peer's Sister* will be completely forgotten. Otherwise you might find gossip-page writers on your front step, or even calling on your mother. Can you take a few days off and go away somewhere?'

'I don't want to go anywhere in case Nick comes. He does, sometimes, unexpectedly. Everything nowadays is waiting for Nick to come. Then when he's here I can't do anything except dread the moment of his going again.'

With determined briskness Amy stood up and put their cups of cold coffee back on the tray. 'I'm going to Bruton Street to see Adeline today in any case. There's something to do with the custody arrangements for little Peter. I'll show her the little paragraph here. It's not likely to be anything like Richard's *scandale,* is it?'

They smiled at each other, without much real amusement.

'No. It won't be anything like that. I miss him, don't you?'

Richard had lived in Paris for a year. He was deep in a new book, but his work seemed to leave him ample time for dinners, and parties, and a succession of lovers. To Amy he seemed happier than anyone else she knew. His letters brightened up her otherwise grey week.

'Yes, I miss him.'

Amy was holding the newspaper. The picture of the King caught her attention again. He looked years older than when she

476

had danced with him, as the Prince of Wales, in the glittering cavern of Ondine's.

'I feel sorry for him,' she said softly. 'He looks so sad.'

When Amy came into the drawing-room at Bruton Street Adeline was sitting at her escritoire to scribble one of her utterly characteristic notes to a current ally.

'Darling, just one minute. How *sans culotte* you look in that hat and coat.'

Amy sat down to wait, smiling at the scribble and dash of her mother's handwriting and the stab of the pen nib into exclamation points. Adeline sighed with satisfaction and folded up her missive, licking the envelope flap with relish and dropping the letter on to a pile of others waiting for the footman.

'What's the latest?' Amy asked dutifully. The subject of the King and Mrs Simpson was overpoweringly fascinating to her mother and her circle. Nothing else had been talked about for weeks.

'Chips and Honor Channon dined at the Fort two days ago. The King was doing his boxes or talking on the telephone or something, and Wallis sat in his chair to offer drinks and apologize gracefully for him exactly as if she's already Queen. Emerald says she has never seen anything so coarse as the way Wallis flaunts her hold over him. I know that she's been doing it ever since he installed her. She did it to the Duchess of York, even, at Balmoral.'

'What does the King do?' Amy asked patiently.

'He worships her. Every enamelled inch of her. He can't take his eyes off her. He can think and talk of nothing but Wallis, and he looks like a cringing little spaniel in the fear that something might displease her. It's too sad, really.'

'But he can't marry her.'

Adeline pursed her lips with relish. 'Don't be so sure. Chips says that Wallis righteously refuses to make any pronouncement at all, but the King is dead set on a morganatic marriage. Parliament won't stand for that and neither will the country. If he wants her he'll have to abdicate in Bertie's favour. And I'm certain that he wants her. I've never seen a man so helpless and besotted with love.'

'What a shame,' Amy said sadly, 'that love won't accommodate itself more tidily.'

Her mother looked sharply at her. 'Why are you wearing that hideous hat, Amy? You look as if you don't care about yourself any more. You look so unhappy, I can't bear it.'

Amy knew that her mother's irritable outburst only masked her true anxiety. 'I'm sorry. Hats don't seem so important, just at this minute.'

'Hats are always important,' Adeline snapped. 'Do you need money?'

'No, I don't need money. I have more than I need . . .'

'. . . more than your Communist friends think you need, don't you mean?'

Amy smiled crookedly. 'Speaking of which, you'd better look at this.' She held out Tony's newspaper and Adeline read the paragraph, the neat arcs of her eyebrows drawn tightly together.

'Well,' she said when she had finished. 'It's no more than you should have expected. What are you making a fuss about?'

'I'm not. I'm anxious for your feelings, that's all.'

Adeline shrugged gracefully. 'After Richard's *tour de force* in scandalizing all our friends, nothing that any of my children do is capable of disturbing me in the slightest. As far as the newspapers go, at least.' Suddenly her voice changed. She leant towards Amy and put her fingers to her daughter's cheek. 'But it disturbs me to see you unhappy, darling love. It hurts me. For a year – more than a year, now – I've said nothing about your handsome, hard-faced miner. But if he's going to make you miserable, Amy, I will kill him.'

Amy had told her mother about Nick a year ago. She had done it almost out of exasperation, to explain to Adeline why she wouldn't marry and why she wanted to be left alone to lead her own life. She had even introduced them once, in an awkward meeting at Pimlico.

Amy's head jerked up. 'Don't talk about killing anyone ever again, do you hear me?' Adeline started, and the hysteria in her own voice surprised Amy.

Adeline tried to soothe her. 'I'm sorry, darling. They weren't very well-chosen words.' Neither of them mentioned Peter Jaspert, but for a moment his big, flushed face was there between them.

'I can't do anything about Nick,' Amy said at last. 'Even to please you. He's all the world. I suppose I feel like the King must do.'

Her attempt at a smile was almost more painful to Adeline than anything else.

'All right,' Adeline said briskly. 'Now, I'm going to ring for cocktails and then we'd better talk about the boy.'

Adeline's cocktails were mixed to her own stringent rules, and they were cold and very strong. Amy felt the gin like steel in her stomach, and it helped.

They began determinedly to discuss little Peter Jaspert's future.

His father hadn't left a proper will, and his financial affairs were in a tangle that would take months to unravel. But amongst his papers a hand-written instruction had been found to the effect that if anything were to happen to his father, the boy's trustees were to be two old schoolfriends of Peter's and, to Amy's intense surprise, herself. His physical guardianship was to be shared equally between Lady Jaspert and Lady Lovell.

There was, of course, no mention of Isabel. But the issue was complicated now by Isabel's undoubted recovery and by her increasing longing to have her son with her. She had taken the news of Peter Jaspert's death with calm sadness, almost as if he were a distant public figure rather than her husband, and she had barely spoken of it since the day that Amy had travelled to break the news to her.

Bill Parfitt was still technically a resident at Thorogood House, although more of his time was spent with his married sister, and an increasing proportion of it staying as a house guest at Chance, where Isabel spent every day with him.

Little Peter had gone with Bethan and his governess to his paternal grandparents, and the house in Ebury Street had been closed up before being sold. But there were signs that a healthy five-year-old boy's presence in the house was uncomfortably disruptive of the measured, formal routines at West Talbot. Isabel had asked, very circumspectly, if the child might be allowed to spend more of his time with her at Henstone.

Her fellow trustees could be won round, Amy thought, and she believed that Lady Jaspert would probably be relieved to be rid of him.

'The question is, then,' Adeline said, 'whether Isabel is really well enough to have charge of him.'

Or whether, the unspoken, unnerving words echoed between them, she might try to do harm to him again.

Amy thought of the pathetic eagerness in her sister's face as

479

she watched the little boy playing at Henstone when she and Bethan had taken him to visit. He was her child, conceived and carried by her all through the terrible months before her breakdown. But the time was over now, and poor Peter was gone. The little boy shouldn't exist for his mother as only a symbol of what was past.

'I know how badly she wants him,' Amy said. 'I think he should go to her.'

Adeline smiled her satisfaction. 'And so do I. Most definitely. The clear solution is that he should always go with Bethan Jones, and she can stay with him and look after him at Henstone just as well as anywhere else.'

Amy sighed. 'I'm sure that would be ideal. Has anyone thought of consulting Bethan herself?'

'I have,' Adeline said triumphantly. 'And for that very reason she's waiting downstairs with Cook.'

A moment later Bethan was shown in by the footman. She made a respectful bob to Adeline, but she hugged Amy as if she was her own daughter.

'Will you do it for us, Bethan?' Adeline asked. 'For all of us?'

Bethan's round, rosy face seemed hardly to have aged at all. As it always did, the nearness of her took Amy back to the security of the nursery.

'Of course I will, my lady. I'll stay with the poor little lamb just as long as he needs me. And going to Miss Isabel's – why, what could be more natural than he should go to his own mother now she's well again?'

'That's settled, then,' said Adeline comfortably. 'Peter will go to Isabel as soon as he comes back from wherever Joan Jaspert has taken him on this gloomy holiday of theirs. Thank you, Bethan.'

After the nanny had gone, Adeline held out the cocktail shaker again. 'Do have another one, darling. Clearly it's done you good. There's even a tiny flush of colour in your cheeks.'

But Amy shook her head. 'I must go, too.' She kissed her mother, and smelt the scent and face-powder and the less identifiable, expensive scents of an indulged life. 'I love you.'

'I love you, too. Don't be unhappy.'

Amy wanted to catch up with Bethan. She found her turning the street corner, wearing a thick mackintosh that reached almost to her ankles and carrying a huge umbrella.

'Bethan! Wait for me. I haven't had a chance to say hello.'
Bethan turned round at once and beamed at her, and in the
warmth of her familiarity Amy said, 'I wish you'd come and look
after me.'

'You look as if you could do with it, Miss Amy.' Bethan was
stern. 'Living a rackety life, are you?'

'Not really. Which way are you going? Shall I walk with you?'

They began to walk towards Park Lane together, talking about
little Peter and the plans to take him to his mother at Henstone.

'He needs it, the poor little mite,' Bethan said. 'After that
terrible, terrible thing happening to Mr Jaspert. Lady Jaspert's
a decent soul, but she doesn't understand children. Just look at
the way they've taken him off to a great, stuffy hotel in Switzerland, or some such place, where he'll have to be on his best
behaviour from morning till night. And I should be there with
him, not that governess they've got in for him who doesn't even
know what bodice to put on him in the mornings.'

Amy smiled. Bethan had always set great store by warm
underclothes. She imagined that the frugally minded Lady Jaspert
had judged it unnecessarily extravagant to take two attendants
to Switzerland.

'Still,' Bethan sniffed, 'it means I've got a holiday. I'm off
home to Nantlas, you know. Going to stay with my mam. My
sister Nannon's got a new baby I haven't even set eyes on yet.'

They had just come out into Park Lane. Beyond the scarlet
blocks of buses and the busy columns of cars, Amy could see the
yellow and brown of the last leaves on the trees in Hyde Park.
In another week they would all be gone, and there would be only
the bare branches against the sky.

She stood stock-still, staring at them.

Then she said, 'Can I come with you?' Not daring to look
at Bethan's face, breathlessly she reminded her, 'Don't you
remember, when Isabel and I were little, you used to say that
you would take us home and show us the valleys? I could take
some leave now, and I could come and meet your family, and
see Nantlas.' And when Bethan didn't answer she begged her,
in a low voice, 'Please.'

18

At the big station at Cardiff the platforms were being swept and scrubbed. The station signs were being washed, and the staring white moon-faces of the clocks were already polished.

From his office, where the roll of red carpet that had done duty for royal visits since the station was built stood ready in the corner, the stationmaster was watching the men at work. They were miners, mostly, men who snatched at the chance of two days' casual labour whatever it was. He nodded his satisfaction. The royal train wouldn't arrive until early the next morning, and by then every crevice of the station would be shining.

Across on the opposite platform from the stationmaster's office the London train came hissing to a standstill. Amy and Bethan climbed down. They had only brought a small suitcase each, and Bethan's huge umbrella. They had no need to look for a porter so they crossed the iron footbridge immediately to the little train that would take them on up the valley.

Bethan stepped around a trio of men with long brooms. 'Cleaning up for you, you see,' she said. 'They'll be at it all the way up to Nantlas. There'll be flags too, I should think.'

'For me and the King,' Amy replied, and they laughed.

It had been awkward, at first, crossing between their old relationship and the new, holiday one. When they had met at Paddington she had still been 'Miss Amy', and Bethan had even preserved a little, formal distance between them that was usually never there. But as the train ploughed westwards Bethan's holiday excitement had risen and lifted their spirits with it, and now that they were in Wales together they were suddenly laughing like children off to a treat.

'That's our train.' Bethan pointed. There was a little, fussy mountain engine and two coaches. 'Be quick, now.' They ran like schoolgirls, with their cases bumping against their legs.

Bethan had reacted to Amy's plea to be taken to Nantlas with a mixture of reluctance and pride.

'It won't be comfortable for you,' she had said. 'There's only my mam's little house, and you'd have to share a bedroom with me.'

'We've shared a room before,' Amy reminded her. 'At Chance.'

'There's not much to see, except pits, and not so many of those, nowadays.'

'You told me years ago that the valleys are beautiful. I'd like to come.'

Amy had fiercely swallowed down her self-dislike at using Bethan's home and hospitality to take her to where Nick belonged. Her longing to see the people and places that held him more strongly than she could was a craving now, and must be appeased.

At last, Bethan's pride had overcome her reluctance.

'We-ell, if you don't mind slumming it. My mam'd be so pleased, you know. And we'll be going at a fine time. You'll even be able to see the King.'

Their stay was to span the King's two-day visit to the stricken Welsh coalfields and steelworks. As their train began to climb they did indeed see flags, hanging in the rain-darkened and dejected streets beyond the station palings. Bethan was talking volubly, pointing out the places as they pulled past them, but Amy could do no more than half-listen. Her eyes were fixed on the crags of bald grey rock rising out of the lava of scree and grown-over tips, the wrinkled lines of houses, tiny and identical and defiantly clinging to the hillside, the rearing black and rust-red machinery that the train threaded through along the valley bottom, and the green slopes and curves and hollows that held the coal deep in their hearts. The green was so sharp against the black that it had spawned that it made Amy blink.

This, then, was the country that held Nick. It was like him, she thought. It was remote, and contradictory, and powerful. It made her feel a stranger, and an interloper.

'Here we are now,' Bethan said, as the train clanked into a tiny station. Beyond it there was a criss-crossing wilderness of railway lines and empty brown trucks. 'Are you all right?'

483

'Yes, I'm all right. It's bigger, and grimmer, and . . . wilder than I'd expected.'

The land was ruled by iron girders and great wheels spinning, but it was wild just the same.

'Oh, it's homely enough when you get used to it,' Bethan said comfortably.

They stepped out under a peeling yellow- and brown-painted canopy. At once she waved to someone beyond the ticket-collector's booth.

'Gwyn! Gwy-yn! There, it's Gwyn come down to meet us in his van.'

Bethan's brother-in-law was a middle-aged man with sparse hair. His smile showed a row of long teeth. He kissed Bethan, and shyly pumped Amy's hand up and down.

'Pleased to meet you,' he said, 'I'm really pleased to meet you.'

They wedged themselves into the front of a van with *Co-operative Society of South Wales* painted on the sides, and set off up the potholed road towards Nantlas. The hillsides crowded closer and higher on either side, and Amy saw little flocks of wiry, grey-backed sheep grazing amongst the tips. Everyone they passed in the roadway waved a greeting to the Co-op van. Bethan pointed ahead.

'There it is. There's Nantlas. The old place doesn't change, does it, Gwyn?'

'I wish it would,' Gwyn said. 'It couldn't but be for the better.'

Down the slope of the inhospitable mountain flowed the terraces, down to the narrow bottom where the road ran and the towering winding-gear of Nantlas 1 and 2 seemed taller even than the bald ridges surrounding them.

This was Nick's valley, and the pits and the people he was working for. Amy longed for him so much that her hands curled involuntarily into fists and her nails dug into the palms of her hands. She was here, now, but it brought him no closer.

Gwyn swung the wheel and they bumped over the cobbles, pressed back against their seats as they climbed the almost vertical streets.

At every corner they passed there were three or four men with their hands in their pockets, some of them with a thin, wretched dog crouched at their heels. The two shops that the van passed were closed, with dusty blue blinds lowered behind the tin advertisements in the windows. A bigger group of men stood outside the barred doors of the pub with its frosted-glass windows offering BILLIARDS and SMOKE-ROOM.

Gwyn turned along one of the terraces and a scatter of children ran away from in front of the van, faces pinched with the November cold staring out at them from under their knitted caps. Bethan jumped out and waved to them.

'Go on now, is that you, Billy Parry? You've grown a yard since I last saw you.'

Prim lace curtains at the windows on the street had lifted and dropped again. Now women in aprons with their hair scraped back under scarves began to materialize on their scrubbed front steps.

'Your own taxi-service, is it, Bethan? There's posh you are.'

'Back from London, Bethan? And bringing the King with you?'

The laughter, defiant by its very existence amongst the greyness, rippled along the doorsteps. Amy climbed out into the sudden quiet as the eyes fixed curiously on her. She breathed in, taking into her lungs the mixture of mountain air, coal smoke and the smell of food frying on a black-leaded range.

'Come on in now and see Mam.' Bethan drew her away from the inquisitive Welsh faces.

Bethan's mother was waiting for them, with strict formality, in the tiny, icy vestibule beyond the front door. They trooped inside, bumping one another in the confined space.

'I'm glad to see you, Miss Lovell. Come in the parlour, will you?'

The parlour, where the thick lace curtains shut out the last of the afternoon light, was dim and even colder than the vestibule. But Amy could see that Mrs Jones had a plain, intelligent, sensitive face, an older replica of Bethan's own. The hand she held out was square and capable, a nurse's hand, and Amy thought of the hundreds of Nantlas babies that Bethan's mother had helped into the world, Dickon amongst them. She shook the hand in both of hers.

'I'm glad to be here. Won't you call me Amy?'

'Well then, I'm Myfanwy. Sit down, Amy, and I'll get you some tea. No, Bethan, that's all right. You stay here with your friend. Gwyn will give me a hand, won't you, Gwyn? Nannon

485

would've been here, but she's looking after the shop for Gwyn. I've got the baby asleep in the back kitchen by the fire.'

Alone for a minute, Amy and Bethan peered at each other through the gloom.

'We'll have to sit in the parlour for tea,' Bethan whispered. 'It's the best room, and you're company. After tea we can all sit in the back kitchen and get comfortable.'

Myfanwy came back with a tray loaded with triangles of bread and butter and plum jam, curranty black bread that they told Amy was *bara brith*, all arranged on the best china. The four of them sat stiffly on the edges of their slippery, horsehair-stuffed chairs and talked about the King's visit, leaving the starched and embroidered antimacassars smooth on the chair backs, and their breath hung in faint clouds in the parlour air.

When they had eaten everything, as custom clearly demanded, Bethan jumped up and seized the tray. 'Come on, then. Let's go in the back.'

The warmth in the kitchen enveloped Amy like a fur wrap. The back room winked cheerfully with polished brass and copper, reflecting the flames in the old range, and the dry linen airing on the long rack hanging from the ceiling smelt fresh and sweet.

'This is only where we sit ourselves,' Myfanwy said reluctantly. 'The parlour's for company, Amy.'

In the warmest corner of the kitchen there was a wicker basket. Amy became aware that they were drawn towards it, although out of politeness the family kept their attention focused on her.

'Is that the new baby?' she asked. 'Can we see her?'

At once, she was drawn into the circle. They crowded around the little crib together. The baby had been asleep in her nest of pink and white blankets, but she obligingly opened her eyes now and curled her hands up into little fists. She was lifted and passed from arm to arm, and Amy hugged the tiny bundle. At the softness and warmth of it she had to shake her head to keep back the tears.

Myfanwy said proudly, 'Sleeps like an angel, she does. She's no trouble to you and Nannon at all, is she, Gwyn?'

A moment or two later Nannon herself came in through the back door, bringing a sharp slice of cold air with her. But the parlour was forgotten. Bethan's sister was as friendly and natural as the rest of the family, in her white shop overall under her coat, and they were drawn together, all of them, by the pink and white

486

baby. Another pot of tea was made, the clock ticked in its walnut case on the mantelpiece, and Amy was part of the family.

Nor was it just family who came to Myfanwy Jones's house. All evening, after Nannon and Gwyn had taken the baby back to their own home, knocks at the back door would announce friends and neighbours dropping in to talk. They nodded shyly at Amy and then settled at the table or in the armchair by the fire to draw up the threads of news and gossip. The house was a Nantlas centre as much as the shop or the Miners' Rest. The frugal food was shared out cheerfully, more tea was brewed, and Amy listened to the workings of a community that had nothing, neither work nor pleasure, except the willingness to help one another.

One woman came to tell Myfanwy about a sick child in a house further down the village where there was no fuel. Myfanwy promised that she would call on them in the morning, and a burly miner listening from across the room said he would 'take a bag o' bits down first thing'.

Another visitor mentioned an old lady living on her own who couldn't get out any more, and Myfanwy asked briskly whether one of those 'great louts of boys' from the same street wasn't doing her bit of shopping for her. 'I'll see to them if they aren't,' she promised the company.

It would be hard living in Nantlas, Amy thought, grindingly hard and grey, but it wouldn't be lonely, at least.

It was almost eleven when the last caller left.

Myfanwy wound the clock up, stretching to her last inch to reach it.

'My husband always used to do the clock,' she told Amy. 'It was his job, ever since we were married. When he died, I thought I wouldn't know what to do with myself. But the time passes, you know. There isn't any use feeling sorry for yourself.'

'No,' Amy echoed her sadly, 'there isn't any use in that. I can't imagine you feeling sorry for yourself in any case.'

They went upstairs to bed. Bethan and Amy were in the front room, with its little low window looking over the street and over the rows of rooftops and chimney pots falling down the valley below them. Bethan glanced out at the black outlines and the last lights in bedroom windows and then drew the thin curtains.

'It doesn't change,' she repeated, 'the old place.'

Amy heard that Bethan fell asleep almost at once in the

familiarity of home. But she lay awake herself for a long time, thinking. She had made the decision to come home with Bethan impetuously, out of an unconfessed longing. But Bethan's warmth made it seem natural that she should be here amongst her family. Amy thought how long it was since they had last slept side by side like this, in the night nursery at Chance. Almost twenty years ago. Amy lay listening to her friend's even breathing, happy to be so close to her again.

Nantlas. Nick was here, somewhere, close at hand. He was working for Bethan's *old place* like Myfanwy. Seeing Nantlas, and the faces of the men on the street corners, and feeling the bonds pulling in Myfanwy's kitchen downstairs, Amy thought she understood him a little better. She curled herself into a ball around her longing for him, and she fell asleep at last.

The morning was icy cold. When Amy woke up she saw that there were frost flowers blooming on the inside of the window-pane. She pulled on her clothes, searching out the warmest underclothes and stockings, and fled downstairs to the warmth of the kitchen. Myfanwy was fussing around the range and Bethan was toasting bread on a long fork. They smiled at her, identical smiles.

'I hope it isn't too cold for the King,' Amy joked, and Myfanwy was almost shocked.

'Of course it won't be too cold for him. He'll come whatever the weather, the King will. He's promised, hasn't he?' They were proud of him, and proud that he was coming to Nantlas.

'Do you remember, he danced with Miss Isabel, the night she was presented at Court?' Bethan said. 'She looked so beautiful, in her long white train and her feathers in her hair. Tell Mam about when you went to Court, Amy.' It was one of Bethan's own favourite stories. Amy was about to launch herself into the fully embellished version of it when there was yet another knock on the back door.

The woman Myfanwy opened it to was small and thin, with brown hair neatly combed back from her face under the brim of her hat. She was holding the hand of a boy of about ten who stood quietly by her side, empty-faced.

Amy's cheerful story died on her lips as she looked at them.

'I'm sorry,' the woman said. 'I wouldn't have come if I'd known you had company.'

'Don't you worry,' Myfanwy answered warmly. 'Come in now

Dickon, you big boy. Do you want to go and see what I've got in my tin on the dresser?'

Amy watched him. She felt as cold as the frost on the window-panes. Dickon shambled quietly to the tin and lifted it down. His fingers fumbled at the lid, but he couldn't work out how to prise it off.

'Bring it to me, love,' Myfanwy said gently. She opened the tin and gave him a sweet biscuit. He took it away into the farthest corner of the room and hunched himself over it. He had black hair like Nick's, and the same well-shaped hands.

'This is Miss Amy Lovell, Bethan's friend, down for a visit from London.' The little note of pride in Myfanwy's voice was cruelly misplaced. Amy knew that she was nothing to be proud of. She was an intruder, and a spy.

'Amy, this is Mari Penry, and Dickon.'

Amy looked at her. She met Mari's level eyes, and she read in them that Mari knew just who she was. Nick's wife glanced at her face and hair, as if to confirm it for herself, and then her gaze travelled to Amy's warm clothes and down to her solid, smooth leather shoes.

And then she nodded at her, neither challenging nor defensive, but simply acknowledging. Mari would have been beautiful, Amy saw, living another life in anywhere but Nantlas. There were red, broken veins in her cheeks that gave the illusion of fresh colour.

Amy was ashamed. Hot shame at herself burned in her face, but still she was so cold that she was shivering.

It was the worst thing she had ever done to come to Nantlas. Vulgar, intrusive greed for Nick had brought her here to confront this composed, patient Mari. It was as if she had come to stare at Dickon, standing in the corner with his biscuit clutched in hands that were replicas of his father's.

'Excuse me, Miss Lovell,' Mari said softly. 'Hello, Bethan. A holiday, is it? I just came in to ask you, Myfanwy, if you were going up to the Welfare this afternoon before the King comes. Nick's speaking up there, and Dickon likes to hear his dad. I don't go myself, because it doesn't seem right. But if you've got company I'm sure you won't want to be bothered with Dickon. I'll take him just in the crowd to wave when the King goes by.'

'It's no bother,' Myfanwy interrupted her. 'Of course I'll take Dickon up. He should hear his dad, shouldn't he?'

'If you're sure it's no trouble.' Mari thanked her, and held out

489

her hand to Dickon. He came obediently and stood with his head hanging a little to one side, waiting for the next instruction.

Amy wanted to close her eyes over the burning behind them, but she made herself go on looking straight ahead, keeping her face very still.

'You should go to the meeting too, if you can.' Mari was talking to her. 'Nick's a fine public speaker. There's something about Nantlas that sets fire to him. You won't hear it anywhere else.' She was telling Amy that she knew, but there was no fight in it. She was just telling her.

Amy watched them through the door, and when it closed behind them, she stood looking at the coarse roller towel that hung on the back of it. Her tongue felt dry and swollen in her mouth.

'Nick Penry's her husband,' Myfanwy explained. 'Although he doesn't live up there any more. He's a big name in the Fed, and . . .'

'Hush, Mam,' Bethan cut in. 'Amy, what's wrong?'

She made herself turn and swallow back the heaving disgust. She made herself say something neutral out of her dry mouth. But all she could think of was Mari's quiet face, and Nick's son with his patient head hanging all on one side.

She was sick with the avid curiosity that had brought her here, and yet she felt the relief of a weight dropping away. It was the jealousy, fading away into nowhere. She wasn't jealous of Mari and Dickon any more. Of course Nick would stand by them. He wouldn't discard them, because he couldn't. He was a husband and father, and he couldn't change that. He couldn't give Amy any more than she had now, and she understood at last that he had told her the truth. She felt dizzy and light with the relief of it, even through her shame that she had needed to come here, and see them, to comprehend it.

Causes are more important than people, he had said. She remembered her futile anger. She had had to come to Nantlas, like a sightseer from her comfortable world, to recognize that they were one and the same. If the causes were won, they would be won for the men in their scarves and thin coats standing idle on cold street corners, and for Myfanwy and her friends unobtrusively helping one another, and for Mari and Dickon.

Amy's shame deepened because it had taken her so long to believe it.

She sat down in the kitchen and had breakfast with Bethan and her mother, listened to them talking and even managed to contribute a few words of her own. She washed up the breakfast dishes, and walked down the steep street to the Co-op with Bethan. By a strategy she succeeded in paying for Myfanwy's groceries herself. But all she could think of was Mari and Dickon, and Nick, and the jealous unhappiness that had eaten into her. She couldn't be jealous any longer, and to be unhappy because she couldn't marry Nick, and live with him in a pretty little house with a pink and blue nursery and a flowering cherry tree in the garden, was the same as being unhappy because the world was round.

The new perspectives left Amy numb.

She knew that she should leave Nantlas, now, at once, and go back to London where she belonged. But she felt physically powerless, as if the complicated manoeuvres the journey would call for were way beyond her.

In the early afternoon, Myfanwy took her old coat down from the peg in the scullery and tied a scarf around her head. 'I don't suppose the King will be looking at me,' she said. 'Come on then, the two of you. We'll be off up to the Welfare.'

Amy faced them as they waited for her, puzzled by her silence. The thought of Nick pulled at her like a taut line. If she could see him speak, see him amongst his people, then it would be enough. Then, she would go home.

They set off together in the grey, cold rain. Myfanwy went ahead of them because the steep pavement was too narrow for them to walk abreast. At one corner she ducked aside and went to knock at a brown-painted door.

'It's where that poor little Dickon lives,' Bethan explained.

The house was the same as all the others in the line, narrow-fronted and low enough for the bedroom sill to seem almost within easy reach. Amy lifted her head. The windows of the house looked back at her, sightless eyes. The brown door opened briefly and Dickon bobbed out. He came hand in hand with Myfanwy, looking unquestioningly up at her. The four of them went on two by two, with the rain driving into their faces. Amy became aware that there were more people in front and behind, walking in the same direction. They were the men that she had seen at the corners and in the knot outside the pub, some of them with children on their shoulders now, and their wives were with them, all trickling down from the terraces to the open doors of the red-brick Miners' Welfare.

The hall was bare and cheerless, with a dusty floor and long, smeared windows looking out into the rain. The SWMF posters decorating the walls were fading and curled at the edges. Rows of wooden chairs had been put out facing the low platform at one end, and the seats were filling up quickly. The hum of talk was muted except for the shouts of excited children. They stood on their seats or scrambled between the chairs, and the Union Jacks that they held ready for the King made incongruous patches of colour.

Myfanwy led Dickon firmly down to the front of the hall. Amy murmured to Bethan, 'I'd rather sit at the back,' and she slipped into a seat at the furthest end of the back row.

A moment later a handful of men walked down the aisle to the platform. Amy looked up for no more than a second, and then she fixed her eyes on the dusty floor again. But she saw Nick's height and his black head in the midst of them. Amy listened to the introductory words. They were partly in Welsh, but she had heard enough political speeches to follow the cadences in any language. Then, without ceremony, the speaker said, 'Nick Penry for you.'

She heard him stand up, and then the seconds of silence as he looked across the sea of faces. The room was suddenly still. Then he began to speak. The voice was Nick's voice, of course, but there was a note in it that Amy had never heard before. It made her shiver, and it made her want to lift her head so that she could see his face.

'I'm happy that the King is coming to Nantlas today,' Nick said. He spoke very simply, as if the packed hall was a single person, a close friend. Amy felt that he was speaking to her alone, even though he didn't know that she was there.

'I'm happy, because he will see us as we are. We haven't cleaned and polished for his benefit, although I know there are some of you who believe that we should have done. We haven't tried to sweep our poverty aside and decorate it with flags. The only flags in Nantlas today are carried by our children. We aren't ashamed, because we have nothing to be ashamed of. We have been asking for government assistance – you all know how long we have been asking for it, and we have been given nothing. Not the right to work, not the right to live decently.

'We're not asking the King for anything today. I don't believe it is in the King's power to give. We will simply let him see what it is like to be in Nantlas, to be anywhere in the Rhondda. Now, today, and all the years we have lived through since nineteen twenty-six.

'There are six hundred and thirty-one able men and boys of working age in Nantlas. Three hundred and eighty of those men, men born in the valleys, miners and sons of miners, have no work to go to. So our workforce will be down on the main road to see the King this afternoon. We won't have any welcoming committee at the pit gates with Lloyd Peris and his friends. Three hundred and eighty men will be the King's welcome to Nantlas. Three hundred and eighty men, carrying their unlit pit lamps. That is the real truth, and that is what the King will see for himself this afternoon.'

Amy could keep her head bent no longer. She looked up and saw Nick's face, and the light in his eyes struck her even at the back of the hall. This was Nick's lifeblood, the platform and the response of the packed room. Nick was a true politician, she realized, and he had it within him to be a brilliant one. He had said nothing exceptional, but he had held his audience rapt.

Nick finished what he was saying, words too intimate to be called a speech, and clapping and cheering broke out and rose to greet him. Amy saw him give a quick, almost dismissive nod of acknowledgement, and he jumped down from the platform. He went over to Dickon who was sitting with Myfanwy and the boy put his arms up around his father's neck. Nick hugged him, rumpling the black hair that was so like his own. Amy looked away again, hating to find herself a spy.

People began to stream out of the doors at the back of the hall. Amy slipped out with them and waited on one side for Bethan and Myfanwy. When they had caught up with her the three of them followed the streams of people down the hill to the route that the King would take.

Looking straight ahead of her at the bobbing sea of flat tweed caps and upturned collars, Amy said, 'I don't think I have ever heard anyone speak as impressively as that.'

Bethan glanced curiously at her, but Myfanwy said, 'Oh yes, Nick Penry's very good. He's done a lot since he's been back here. There are one or two who don't admire him, mind. They say he's a self-promoter, but I don't see that. He does well because people want to listen to him.'

Yes, Amy thought, that was true. People did want to listen to Nick.

They reached the valley road. Where it came into the village Amy saw that it was lined with men, a single file of them on either side. They were standing quite still, holding their lamps at their sides.

Myfanwy and Bethan and Amy found a place in the crowd just beyond them. It was still raining, and their hair and the shoulders of their coats were soon sodden. The wind was cold too and the crowd huddled close, turning their backs against the full force of it. Some people tried to sing, but their voices soon died raggedly away. The King was late. Half an hour and then three-quarters of an hour passed after the scheduled time for his visit. Amy was shivering and her feet had turned numb when she heard a ragged cheer in the distance. She craned her neck forward with everyone else and she saw three big black cars coming very fast up the valley. The royal standard flew from the middle one, a brave glow of colour.

The miners stood still in their long lines, but they lifted their dead lamps and held them up, a cold garland of them all down either side of the valley road. The King's motorcade came level with them. The cars slowed down, and purred to a halt. The doors of the middle one were opened and the King stepped out. He looked into Nantlas along the hundreds of silent men, and they held their lamps out to him.

Amy saw the lines deepen in the King's face. He looked small in the middle of the road in his black overcoat and bowler hat. There was a jaunty red carnation in his buttonhole, but he was tired and pale. He began to walk slowly with his retinue of equerries and dignitaries behind him. He stopped to speak and shake hands with almost every man, and his concern for the ill-clothed and badly fed ranks of them showed clearly in his face. It was a long time before he reached the last miner. There were a dozen jostling women and as many excited children waving their flags between Amy and the King, but she still heard clearly what he said. The last miner was chairman of the Unemployed Men's Committee, and the King said, 'Something will be done for you. I give you my word on that.'

'Thank you, Sir,' the man answered. His face was alight with pride.

The King moved on, coming closer to where Amy stood between Bethan and her mother. Amy heard Myfanwy's indrawn breath of awe as he stopped again. He was looking down at the children and their waving Union Jacks. Amy recognized the Minister of Health behind him, and the King's Private Secretary, Major Hardinge, who had been a friend of her father's.

Suddenly, in the cold rain and amidst the smell of wet clothes and hungry people, Amy remembered Ondine's like a brilliant tableau at the end of a tunnel. And as she remembered it she saw the King looking straight into her eyes. He recognized her, and his hand went up to tip the brim of his hat. An automatic, civilized little gesture of their own world that was stronger than his puzzlement at seeing her in the threadbare crowd. Amy began to dip into her curtsey, her own response bred into her in the same way, when she remembered something else. The King was going to abdicate to marry an American divorcee. He wasn't going to do anything for Nick's people, Bethan's people, with their lives as dark as their extinguished lamps. His walk up the valley between them was a sham.

Anger leapt up inside Amy and she went stiff, denying the curtsey. She was looking at the two warring halves of her life, facing her on the Nantlas road. Amy felt as proud and certain as she had done when she marched down to Trafalgar Square five years ago. But today, at last, her convictions took firm root in what she had seen and learned for herself. They were right to fight, these people around her. They were more than right, because that implied they had a choice. Amy knew now that they must fight because it was in order to survive. Nick was fighting for that survival too, and he was right to do it. Her love for him burned as hot as her anger.

Amy wouldn't curtsey here, or anywhere. Her face blazed with certainty, a vivid, strong certainty that was nothing to do with her own searching for happiness and peace. *It matters more than our own little loves,* Nick had said.

Amy smiled, a triumphant smile.

The King had already moved on, and she didn't even know whether he had really seen her or recognized her. It didn't matter. What mattered was what she had recognized herself.

Beside her Myfanwy whispered, 'He knew you. I saw him look at you.'

'Did he?' Amy said. 'I don't know.'

The crowds were eddying into the road now, following the King's party up towards the pit gates where a reception committee of owners and managers was waiting to conduct him around the pithead. There were children shouting, and miners and their wives waving and calling out to one another. In spite of their desperation they were awed and touched by the mystery of royalty. Amy was bitter that they should be deceived.

She was standing alone in the middle of the road watching the eager surge in the King's wake when she felt a touch on her shoulder. Nick was standing beside her with Dickon held against him, protected from the crowd.

They looked at one another, acknowledging, without accusation or surprise.

'I didn't come to spy on you,' Amy said. 'I felt like a spy, but I didn't come to do that.'

'I know why you wanted to come,' Nick said softly. 'Did you find out what you needed to know?'

'Yes. I found out what I needed to know. I'm glad I saw you. I'll go back to London now.'

A shadow crossed his face. 'Not yet, Amy. I want to talk to you. I want to tell you something. Are you staying with Bethan's mother? I saw you come into the meeting with them.'

'Did you? I didn't know.'

The shape of his mouth, the colour of his skin and eyes and hair were painfully familiar, and she loved him.

'I was talking to you at that meeting. Trying to tell you, to explain. I don't want to see you unhappy. I love you.'

'I know,' Amy whispered. 'I felt that you were talking to me. He won't do anything, you know. The King.'

Nick smiled crookedly. 'Of course not.'

'So it was just a gesture, lining those men up with their lamps?'

The crooked smile was suddenly tired. Amy wanted to put her arms around him and draw his head down against her. 'So many things we do are just gestures. Perhaps they all add up. I don't know. May I come and see you at Myfanwy's, before you go back to London?'

Amy nodded. She was afraid of what he had to say, but she pulled her new strength tighter inside her. Nick would have to be told that she had seen Mari, and that Mari knew who she was. Amy looked down at Dickon. His head was resting against Nick's chest, and his closed face was tranquil.

'Dickon looks like you,' she said softly. Nick's hand stroked the boy's crest of hair. Amy saw his protectiveness, and guessed at the bruised, impotent love that he felt for his son.

'I'll come at eight o'clock,' Nick told her.

They looked at one another for a moment longer. They didn't even reach out to touch their fingertips together, but the look was the same as a kiss. Amy felt her wet face warm with it. She lifted her hand briefly and Nick's arm tightened around Dickon's shoulders.

'Come on, son,' she heard him say. 'We've seen the King now. Let's take you back up the hill to your mam.'

'Ma-am,' Dickon echoed approvingly. 'Tea,' he added. 'Dickon tea.' Amy's heart twisted inside her.

Bethan was waiting for her further along the road. Amy knew that she had seen her with Nick, and she felt hot with her regret at not having told her from the beginning what was happening. They began to walk up the hill, slowly, in silence.

'I want to say I'm sorry, and to Myfanwy as well,' Amy began. 'Shall I talk to you now, or shall I wait till we can tell Myfanwy at the same time?'

'Tell me,' Bethan said. 'A version of it will suit Mam, if you would rather.'

That was so like Bethan, practical and sensible, that Amy felt almost easy again. They fell into step, walking shoulder to shoulder with their heads bent against the rain.

'I wanted to come and see Nantlas with you, and to meet your mother, just like you promised when Isabel and I were little. But I had to come because of Nick Penry.'

'Whatever for?' Bethan's dry scepticism almost made Amy laugh.

'I've known Nick for five years,' she began. 'I met him in Trafalgar Square. It was the day the hunger marchers came from here, from the valleys.'

'I remember the day,' Bethan said. 'It was not long after Miss Isabel was married. You weren't very happy in those days.'

Amy kept her eyes on the steep hill ahead of her and the terraces scribbled across it. She told Bethan about the evening in the old nursery at Bruton Street, and the cottage at the edge of the Chance woodland, in the summer of Gerald's death.

'We fell in love with each other then, Nick and I. I've loved

497

him ever since.' And then the years afterwards, with friendship growing out of passion, and the loneliness that grimly kept pace with it.

The rain chilled Amy's face and plastered her hair to her forehead. 'That's all,' she said at last. 'I've never told you. I don't know why. I'm sorry, Bethan.'

'I'm sorry as well,' Bethan said with her old quickness. 'I don't see him making you happy. How could he?'

Amy smiled sadly at Bethan's partisanship, as if her happiness were the only consideration. It had been her own preoccupation for too long, but Nantlas had somehow changed all that. Her expectation of happiness as a right had faded amongst the tiny houses and the idle machinery, and at the sight of Mari and Dickon.

'It isn't important,' she answered. 'Nick believes that causes are more important than people. I think I have to believe that too, now I've been here.'

They turned into Myfanwy's street. At the end of it Amy saw a huddle of sheds and then the bare mountain rising beyond them. The shoulder of it hunched against the sullen winter sky.

'I was jealous,' she said, finding the words with difficulty. 'I was jealous of here, because what he has to do here is more important than the two of us. I was even jealous of Mari and Dickon, because they hold more of him than I do. I came because I had to see for myself.'

'And have you seen?'

'Yes,' Amy said, thinking of the thin faces and the inadequate clothes and the King's empty promise. 'I know that what I have with Nick now is all I'll ever have. It makes it easier,' she lied. 'Knowing makes it easier.'

They reached the pitch-black entry that bisected the terrace and led to the back doors. Bethan's hand reached for hers and squeezed it. Their damp gloves stuck, palm to palm.

'If that's the truth,' Bethan said, 'I'm glad you came.'

Myfanwy's back door flew open and they blinked in the light.

'Wherever did you go? You're soaked through, the daft pair of you,' Myfanwy scolded. 'Get in here, now. I can't nurse you through pneumonia on top of everything else.'

They followed her sheepishly into the house and stripped off their wet clothes. Myfanwy rubbed their hair with coarse towels. Through the buffeting Amy murmured, 'I stopped behind to talk to Nick Penry and Bethan waited for me. I know Nick, in London . . .' She was driven by her need to be honest now.

'Nick Penry should have more sense,' Myfanwy silenced her.

Dry and warm again, they sat down to tea, poached eggs and bread toasted over the range.

Amy tried again. 'Nick Penry worked at Chance, on my father's estate. I met him there.'

'We knew he'd gone to get work, but he never said where,' Myfanwy told her. 'Most likely he thought it was his own business. Fancy it being at your place. Pass me your cup, Amy, and I'll fill it up for you.'

Myfanwy's shrewd glance told Amy that she knew, or guessed, and that that was enough because Myfanwy with her tactful good sense didn't want to hear any more.

'He may call to see me later this evening,' Amy said quietly.

'I don't think I'll be here to see him if he does.' Myfanwy's bag stood ready in the corner. 'They've sent up to tell me that Eirian Jones has started. I dare say Jim'll be up here for me before too long. She was quick with her first.'

After tea they drew their chairs up close to the fire. Myfanwy read the *Western Mail* with minute attention, her spectacles pushed down her nose. At ten to eight someone tapped on the back door. Amy's head jerked up, and she knew that Bethan was watching her as she stared at the place where Nick would appear. But the man who came in was an anxious stranger, twisting his cap round and round in his hands.

'Eirian said could you be quick, Mrs Jones? She thinks it won't be long. Her mam's with her, but . . .'

'There's nothing to worry about, Jim. She'll do well.' Myfanwy had her hat and coat on in seconds. At the back door she stopped and smiled at Amy.

'And you an SRN, and knowing all the latest hospital ways. You should go for me.'

The father's face stiffened with dismay. Amy saw how much Myfanwy was trusted and valued. She laughed back at her.

'I think I came third to last in midwifery. You could count the number of babies I've delivered on two hands.'

'I've lost count of mine.' Myfanwy was already out in the dark entry. 'It must be more than a thousand.' The door banged shut behind her. Bethan bent her head over her book again and Amy stared at the glowing coal making pictures in the high black grate.

At eight o'clock exactly there was another, firmer knock.

'You'd better let him in,' Bethan said sharply.

Nick seemed too tall for the little back kitchen. He stood with his head ducked under the beam, but there was a glitter in his eyes that brought back Amy's apprehensiveness.

'Hello, Bethan,' he said formally. 'I'm sorry to disturb your evening. Put on something warm,' he added to Amy.

Bethan nodded at him, but she didn't speak. She was all defensiveness for Amy, and her sad disapproval showed in her face. Amy and Nick went out into the entry and left her alone in the warm box of the kitchen.

It was bitterly cold out in the road, and Amy pulled her coat tighter around her.

'We'll walk to keep warm,' Nick said. They climbed in silence for a little way, past the blank windows of rows of empty front parlours. Lights showed in only one or two of them.

'Courting couples sitting on their own, that means,' Nick told her. The little streets were deserted and for a moment Amy felt the luxury of being alone with him, out in the wind under the black sky. She turned her face up to him and he kissed it. Their cheeks were cold, but their mouths were warm and hungry. He took her hand as they walked on, drawing it into the shelter of his pocket. But when they passed under the dim glow of a street-lamp he let her go again, and Amy knew that he was careful.

'This reminds me of courting,' he said, and she saw the white glimmer of his smile. 'Before I married Mari I used to take girls down the lane ends in the dark, and out on to the mountain.'

'Wasn't it cold?' Amy smiled too.

'We didn't do it in the real winter. Unless we were desperate. It seems hardly a year ago. They all wore the same face-powder that smelt of almonds, and it used to mix with the scent of the grass, and coal smoke from the last row of houses below us. When you opened your eyes after kissing the girl, you could see the lights in the backs all the way down to the valley, and the pithead. Half your mates would be down there and you'd think *They'd give a day's money to be where I am now.* It seemed very simple, then.'

There was something in his voice that made Amy catch her breath. It was valedictory, as if he was seeing and remembering for the last time.

'What was it you wanted to tell me?' she asked, with fear pulling insistently at her.

Nick stopped walking. The blind end of a terrace and a brick wall jutting beyond it made a little sheltered angle away from the nearest street-lamp. He turned and drew her into it, and then tilted her chin up so that he could look at her. He kissed her very gently, smoothing the tight lines at the corners of her mouth with his fingers.

'I wanted to tell you that I'm going to fight in Spain.'

She had known, of course. Of course he would want to go to Spain. The certainty that he would die there numbed her, and she stared past him at the bricks, counting them, eleven, twelve, thirteen.

'When?'

'Tomorrow.'

So soon, so soon that he was gone already. Bitterly she demanded, 'And your work here? Your work, that was so important?'

'Amy.' He pulled her against him and she clung to his arms, unable to help herself. 'It's a war. I'd be a coward if I didn't go.'

She nodded, suddenly unbearably weary. Of course he would go. Someone could be found to do his job for him, so long as it was war and not a woman he was giving it up for.

From somewhere inside herself she summoned a smile.

'Don't get killed, will you?'

'I don't think so.' His voice was soft, and so was his mouth, now, touching hers.

'Don't try to be a hero.'

'No. I'm a realist, not a hero.'

They clung to one another in silence. Amy was trying to think how it would be to let him go, not just on a station platform to come back to Nantlas, but across to Spain where the bombers ploughed across the sky and the Nationalist snipers crouched over their rifles in wrecked villages and in the trenches dug across wasted farmlands.

'What did Mari say?' she asked.

'Mari already knew that I would go.'

Amy looked over his shoulder down the hill towards Mari's house. She thought of Dickon's black crest of hair under the bed-sheet. If anything happened to Nick, she would make sure somehow tnat Dickon and Mari were looked after. If anything happened. Amy shivered and moved quickly out of the shelter he made for her in the angle of the wall. She needed to walk, pushing herself, to break down the fear for him. They began to walk up the slope again, passing the last line of houses. They came out on to the hillside past a straggle of allotments where the road petered out into a rutted track.

They climbed steadily upwards. There was a stitch tearing at Amy's side when they scrambled to the top of the ridge. The wind and the cold took their breath away, and Amy had to blink the rain out of her eyes before she could look down at Nantlas below her, huddled against the hill. Away down on the other side there were other villages, intricate chains of lights hung over the pitheads. The wind tore at them, stinging and straining to lift them. In the limitless, howling black space Amy felt dwarfed. She was dry and thin like a dead leaf, and the wind could whirl her away. It helped, to be made insignificant. By recognizing their smallness she could confront the fear. She wanted to open her mouth and shout into the wind, threats and childlike dares.

Take him. Take everything. Nothing will stop, will it? Not the wind and the rain.

Nick had to take her hand and pull her away from the bare ridge. She came stumbling after him, exhilarated. She was still afraid, but she knew that she was strong too. She had strength like Mari, and Myfanwy and Bethan, and Nick himself. Nantlas had given her that.

It was still and quiet by contrast in the lee of the hill.

'I don't know why I brought you up here,' Nick said. She felt the warmth of his breath on her face with faint surprise, as if she had already said goodbye to his physical nearness. 'You're cold, and wet through. There isn't anywhere else. I can't take you to my lodgings. There's just the bare mountain.'

Amy felt all the layers of their existence peeling away. All the accretions of place and time and circumstance dissolved to leave them with just one another and the bare land beneath them. They clung together and for the first time there was truly no divide between them.

They were equal in their frailty under the black Rhondda sky. The threat of death revealed their frailty to them, and they saw it, and they felt it drawing them close and sealing them indivisibly.

'I want to hold you,' Nick said.

They huddled against a rubble of rocks. Nick turned her face so that their wet cheeks touched. Their clothes were heavy, and their fingers were numb. They were too cold to make love, and they knew that they didn't need to. They already held one another closer than they had ever done before. Amy closed her eyes and felt his mouth move, and the rain dropped its cold points against her eyelids.

She didn't know how long they lay there, but she was stiff and beyond even cold when Nick lifted her to her feet again. They walked back down the streaming hillside and between the terraces in silence, as if they had already taken leave of each other. Only as they turned into Myfanwy's street did Amy ask,

'Have you already said goodbye to Mari?' She wasn't jealous any longer, there was no room for jealousy. The question came out of sympathy, almost closeness.

'Yes. I'm going very early tomorrow. I'll walk back down the valley to my lodgings now.'

This evening had been his goodbye to Nantlas, then, as well as to Mari and herself.

Amy looked up. Myfanwy's little house was in darkness. They were standing at the black mouth of the terrace entry when Amy reached out and touched Nick's sleeve.

'I saw Mari, this morning.' It seemed much longer ago, days rather than hours. 'She came here with Dickon, to see Myfanwy. She knew who I was. I don't know how. She didn't say anything, but we both knew.'

Nick bent his head, but not before she saw the pucker of pain in his face. 'I don't know how either.'

Amy looked at him, trying to imprint the lines of him on her memory. She thought of their separation with dread, and of the day when she would find herself unable to compose his features in her mind.

'You still love Mari, don't you?' The question was out before the words had fully formed themselves in her head. Nick looked up now, and she saw the grey, penetrating stare. She would remember that. She would remember the way that he could look at her.

'Yes,' Nick said. 'In a way.'

That was the plain truth. Nick wouldn't varnish it, not now, at this last moment. They stood facing one another with their arms hanging awkwardly at their sides, confronting the reality of having to leave one another. To leave and perhaps never to come together again. Nick saw the sudden tears on Amy's face and he felt rather than heard the low sound of pain in his own throat. He held her and kissed her, tasting the sweetness, and then they were apart again, almost pushing one another away. He turned and stumbled away down the silent street.

Amy's fingers came up to touch her mouth. She felt the heat and the hurt, and she knew how much Nick loved her too. She heard his footsteps walking away, each step taking him further, but she didn't look round. With her hand still at her mouth she went on up the entry and the brick terrace swallowed up the last sound of his going.

In the back kitchen by the red light of the fire Amy found some warm water in a jug that Bethan had left her. She splashed her face at the sink, and when she dabbed it with a towel she saw there was blood where his mouth had caught hers. Amy rinsed the tiny stain out of the towel before she went slowly up the stairs. She was so cold that her fingers could hardly undo her sodden shoelaces. She undressed and put her wet clothes in a neat pile in the corner. Then she lay down, shivering under the cold sheet that covered her.

Amy stayed with Myfanwy and Bethan for another two days. That was how they had planned it, and there was no reason to change now. On the third day she was due back at the Royal Lambeth to start a new shift in charge of a different ward. None of them spoke of Nick.

Amy thought about him constantly. She imagined him arriving at Dover, and then sitting on the deck of a ferry staring at the grey, heaped-up waves. Would he have reached Calais? she wondered. Was he in Paris, or heading straight for the Spanish border? She read the reports in the newspapers of the Nationalist forces ringing Madrid.

On Amy's last afternoon in Nantlas, Myfanwy went out to visit one of her babies in an isolated cottage up the valley. When she came back they would take Amy to the station for the train that would connect with the fast evening train to London. Amy would be travelling alone, because Bethan was staying on at home until Lord and Lady Jaspert were due to bring little Peter back from Switzerland. Amy's suitcase was packed and ready, but she had delayed her departure until the last possible minute. Bethan was knitting by the fire and Amy had restlessly dried the last of the dishes and hung the cloth on the rail over the grate when she admitted the reason to herself. As soon as it had crystallized she turned impulsively to Bethan.

'I want to go and see Mari Penry.'

Bethan frowned over the long grey knitted tube of sock.

'Why?'

Amy gathered up her coat and pulled on her gloves.

'I want to tell her I didn't come to spy on her. To say I'm sorry, if she'll let me. Nick's left her behind. He's gone to fight in Spain. She's all alone, Bethan.'

The back door opened and closed behind her. Bethan looked at it for a long moment and then turned back to her knitting with a sigh.

Amy almost ran down the hill. The rain had stopped, and there was a watery sun hanging low in the colourless sky. In its ironic light Nantlas looked even more hungry and hopeless. She reached the brown front door of Nick and Mari's house and knocked, keeping her back turned to the inquisitive stares from the street. After a long moment Mari opened the door. In her house apron and with her hair a little ruffled she looked younger, startled and then angry. Amy thought that she would close the door in her face, but Mari glanced past her at the curious neighbours. The door opened a fraction wider.

'You'd best come in,' she said.

Amy followed her down the bare passage. Mari didn't try to show her into the parlour. They went straight into the back kitchen. In the scullery beyond a copper was boiling with the washing, and there was a pile of soiled sheets heaped beside it.

'I'm sorry about the laundry,' Mari said coolly. 'I wasn't expecting a visitor. It has to be done every day, with Dickon. He can't manage himself.'

Dickon was sitting in his chair in the kitchen corner. He was bent over a plywood puzzle, cut into four simple pieces, with what had once been a picture of a blue kettle. The paint was almost completely rubbed away.

'I know,' Amy said. 'I know about the laundry. I'm a nurse.'

As she watched him, Dickon completed the puzzle and gave a row of pleasure. At once he broke it up and began again, staring

505

at the pieces and turning them to and fro as if he had never seen them before.

The work Mari must have to face was endless. In hospitals there were great steam laundries and porters to do the heavy carrying. There were night staff to take over at the end of even the hardest day. Mari had none of that.

'Are you?' She was looking at Amy, her cool stare taking her in from head to foot. Amy felt hot and awkward, wrong-footed in her impulsiveness. 'I wouldn't have imagined anything like that.'

'I came to say I'm sorry,' Amy said.

'Sorry for what? For taking my man, or whatever romantic way you see it? Don't be. Nick and I had come apart long before he can have known you. It isn't easy to hold a marriage together like this, in a place like this.' She meant Dickon, and the little house with the sheets that smelt, and Nantlas beyond it. Dickon dropped one of his puzzle pieces and gave a wordless cry. Mari picked it up and put it back, touching his hand reassuringly.

'I didn't mean that.' Amy was defending herself now. 'I wouldn't have taken him. He came, and I believed what he told me then, that he wasn't truly married any more. Although,' she added softly, 'I don't believe that now.'

Mari looked at her, and Amy thought that the hostility was beginning to break up and drift away. Mari had too much to do, and worry about, and too little energy to spare for hostility. Amy wished that everything was different, that they could have known and liked each other. Quickly she said, 'I came to say I'm sorry for having to come to Nantlas. I didn't come to . . . to stare at you and Dickon. I didn't want to spy, or intrude. I thought I was coming to make myself understand better.'

Mari half-smiled. 'Nick's easy to understand. He does what he wants.' She glanced at Dickon to make sure that he was happy and then went out into the steamy scullery. With a wooden dolly she lifted the sheets out of the copper and dropped them into a tin bath of rinsing water. The old mangle on its four-square iron frame stood ready beside it. Watching Mari's economical movements and her reddened hands, Amy felt the smothering weight of anger. It was hard for Nick, but it was infinitely harder for Mari.

'He shouldn't have gone,' she said fiercely. Dickon looked up blinking, and Mari came back into the kitchen.

506

'He had to go. Nick has to act on what he believes in. He couldn't live with himself otherwise. I've known that for twelve years. Ever since the day he gave me that.' She nodded up at a white china mug on the mantelpiece. It was too steamy in the room for Amy to be able to read the faded gilt lettering.

Yes, Amy thought. He's your husband. Of course you know him better than anyone. There was nothing else to say now. Her anger had gone and in its place was the faint, dry taste of defeat.

Mari was standing calmly beside Dickon, watching her, her hands folded over her apron front.

'I'm going back to London today,' Amy said. 'If Nick comes home from Spain he'll be coming here, to Nantlas. I do know that much.'

'It's Nantlas and his people he cares about, isn't it?' Mari rejoined. 'That was what you had to come down here to understand. That's how it's always been, with Nick.'

They stood for a moment longer, hesitating on the impossible brink of mutual comfort. It was another wordless cry from Dickon that reminded them of the distance separating them. Amy turned back towards the passage and the front door.

'I just came to say I was sorry,' she repeated in a low voice. She had almost reached the door when she looked round at Mari for the last time.

'Can I ask you, how did you know it was me, when you came to Myfanwy's yesterday?'

Mari did smile, now. It made her look young, and very pretty. 'How do you think? Nick came up here one afternoon to take Dickon out. It was a warm afternoon, and he left his coat on the peg. I saw that there was a button off it, and I took it down to sew one on. Your picture was in the pocket. Well creased, as if he took it everywhere with him.'

Amy remembered giving the picture to Nick. It was a little head-and-shoulders portrait that had been taken for her twenty-first birthday. She had been wearing an evening dress that made a gauzy ruffle around her bare shoulders, and a diamond necklace belonging to Adeline. Amy thought the photograph made her look haughty, but Nick had begged her for it and so she had taken it out of its silver frame and given it to him. There was no incarnation of herself that she would less rather Mari had seen and she looked away from Mari's smile, ashamed. 'And then Myfanwy introduced you as Miss Lovell, and I understood. All about the job, and everything. I suppose I should thank you, for getting work for Nick. It saved Dickon, you know.'

Don't, Amy wanted to beg her. *Don't make it worse.* Instead she whispered, 'I'm glad of that, at least.'

'Ma-am,' Dickon called from the kitchen. 'Ma-am?'

'In the passage,' Mari answered him. 'Come here, now.' He came out with his shuffling steps and peered up at them with his head on one side, his uncomprehending stare.

'While Nick's away, is there . . .' Amy hesitated, incapable of phrasing the question delicately enough not to chafe the discomfort between them.

'No, thank you,' Mari said. 'We do all right together, Dickon and me.'

The front door opened and Amy was almost out into the watchful street before Mari added, 'I was surprised, after that picture, to hear you're a nurse. But I can see it, now. You're lucky, having something valuable to do. As good as anything Nick can. I've only got Dickon, see. It's hard to believe that what I do for him is much good, in the end.'

Amy understood how hard it would be to live with the bitterness of that daily reminder. She bent her head. 'Yes. I'm lucky to have my work.'

Dickon was tugging at Mari's arm. Amy wanted to say *I hope it will change. I hope it will be right for you,* but even in her own head the words sounded vain. There was nothing she could say, or do. When she looked up again the brown door had closed, and Mari and Dickon had gone.

Bethan and Myfanwy had walked the little way down the valley to the station with her. The busy mountain train came in and Amy let down the window of her compartment so that she could lean out and wave to them. Their faces looked very alike, turned upwards.

'What will you do?' Bethan had asked.

'Now?' Now that Nick had gone to Spain, and now that she had seen Mari and Dickon and Nantlas. Amy had shaken her head. Mari's words echoed back at her. 'I'll go on with my work. I'm lucky to have that. People always need nursing.'

It wasn't the answer Bethan had hoped for. She looked sideways at Amy, unnoticed, and she sighed at what she saw.

Now the station platform was slipping back past the moving train. Amy lifted her arm to wave. 'Goodbye,' she called. 'Goodbye, Myfanwy. Thank you for everything.' Thank you for letting me see Nantlas. The train rounded a curve and carried her away. Amy sat back in her seat. The grey and black and surprising green of the valleys spread beyond the carriage windows, but Amy didn't look round. Instead she was looking straight ahead of her. She was trying to disentangle the knots of personal need and choice, trying to think with the dispassionate clarity she knew she would need to if she were really to go.

She began to count up her reasons, folding her fingers over in her lap as she went over them.

She was alone, and without responsibility. It would affect no one directly if she went. She would be valuable, because of what she knew she could do. And if it was freedom, justice and equality she had marched for so naïvely before, it was the grim denial of them that had held her rigid in front of the King, days ago in the Nantlas valley road. Staring ahead of her in the jolting train, Amy saw clearly that if her beliefs were the same as Nick's, and Jake Silverman's and Tony Hardy's, then the time had come for her to act on them too.

It was late, past ten o'clock, when the Cardiff train reached Paddington. Instead of going home, Amy went straight to Appleyard Street.

19

The train hissed grudgingly to a standstill and the high grey coaches jolted and clashed.

Nick stirred uneasily on the corridor floor, and then lifted his head from the rucksack that had served as his pillow overnight. He was cold and stiff, and he was very thirsty. Around him the little group of miners that he had shepherded out from Nantlas were waking up too, stretching and grumbling. Two of them stood up awkwardly in the confined space and peered out of the window.

'Where's this, then, Will?'

Will scowled. 'How the hell should I know? Some dirty Spanish town, just like all the rest.'

The other two, Ifor and Ieuan, didn't even bother to look. They sat with their knees drawn up to their chests, yawning, their faces dark with stubble. Nick's own spirits were no higher. The five of them had set off from Dover together, hungry for battle, but days of uncomfortable travel and unbroken boredom had blunted their appetites. They had travelled to Paris, where they had been met by Party workers and directed by train to Perpignan in the south of France. At Perpignan they had met up with several other small groups of men who were travelling to join the International Brigades. Amongst them was a gang of navvies from Liverpool, and it was their leader, Ken Coate, who bobbed up beside Nick now. He looked out into the grey light.

'Miles from anywhere. I wonder what chance there is of getting some bloody sodding breakfast.'

From Perpignan the recruits had been driven in lorries over the Pyrenees to Figueras on the Spanish side. Another long train journey had taken them to Barcelona, where they were billeted in a squalid training school. They had spent three interminable days in Barcelona, a polyglot crew united by no more than a vague common belief in democracy. The Communists had considered themselves the élite, and held frequent secret meetings that throbbed with the internal politics of the Party.

Nick had held his boredom in check by wandering aimlessly through the city. The churches were beautiful, and all desecrated in the waves of anti-religious Republican fervour. The sight of the smashed Madonnas and the marble columns smeared with black initials saddened him.

He had thought constantly of Amy, and on the last day he sat down at a pavement café table to write to her. The late November midday sun was almost hot on his head.

> I don't know what we are doing here. Everyone seems busy except us. There are long queues at all the food shops, especially for bread, and there are posters and slogans everywhere. Otherwise it might be any city. I can't believe that this waiting and travelling has anything to do with war. The rumour is that we are to be moved on tonight. I don't know where, I don't suppose I should say even if I did. Is this the right thing, being here? God knows. There is an element of Party manipulation in this that seems to have nothing to do with Spain. I hope I'm wrong. Oh, Amy, I love you.

Nick had scribbled his name and then sat looking at the crowded foreign street, thinking of the mountain above Nantlas.

That evening they were marched again to the railway station, and they had travelled all through yet another night.

Nick got up now, wincing with the cramp in his legs, and looked across the tracks overgrown with weeds to a group of shabby buildings. In the middle of one wall was a new poster, and he looked at it for a long moment. It showed a foot in one of the espadrilles that all the Spanish workers wore, poised in the air ready to crush a giant, bulging swastika underfoot. The simple conviction of the message helped to raise Nick's spirits and he straightened his back. He was here, in Spain, and he was ready for what would come.

After a few minutes some Republican troops came alongside the train. They wrenched open the carriage doors and gestured the recruits out into the misty air. Nick scrambled out gratefully. At the head of the line he saw an officer with flat, Slavic features dressed in a smart brown corduroy uniform.

'Where's this?' Nick asked him without much hope of a response. To his surprise the officer asked him in English for his papers. Nick handed them over, and the man nodded.

'Thank you, comrade. This is Albacete. The marshalling-point for the International Brigades.'

Behind Nick, the Welshmen and Ken Coate gave an ironic cheer. 'Thank bloody Christ. Now maybe we'll get something to do.'

In the cramped truck that took them onwards Nick found himself wedged against one of Ken's navvies.

'Why did you come to Spain?' Nick asked him.

Without hesitation, the man said, grinning, 'Boozing, looting and women. I've seen bugger all of any of them, so far. And you?'

Nick laughed. 'Less concrete reasons. Bugger all so far for me, too.'

The truck roared under an archway and out into a vast, square courtyard. As they scrambled stiffly out the men saw that it was enclosed on four sides by triple storeys of pinky brown stone, with slender arched galleries faced in marble. The flagstones beneath their feet were worn smooth by centuries of use, and over their heads soared a graceful bell tower. There were white doves settled in the recesses of it. The place might once have been a monastery; it was now a barracks. There was rubbish heaped in the corners, and a bonfire belched black, acrid smoke. A line of grey sheets bellied from one of the galleries and the air smelt of filth, vomit, and rotting food. As the new arrivals stood looking about them a column of men, marching four abreast, clattered in under the arch. They broke ranks at once and swarmed into the doorways and up flights of stone stairs. Nick saw a familiar head, taller than the rest, black-bearded. He gaped in disbelief, and then he shouted.

'Jake! Jake! Over here!'

The black head turned towards him. It was Jake Silverman, and he came running.

'Nick. Dear bloody hell, Nick Penry. Good to see you, comrade.' In the pleasure of the meeting they flung their arms around each other and hopped round in a clumsy, bear-like dance.

'What is this place?'

Jake grinned sardonically. 'Ahem. Welcome to the biggest

512

bloody shambles in Europe. Come on up to my bunkroom. I've got some bread and cheese. I'll tell you.'

'I'll get my blokes settled first. I take it we'll be stopping here.' Jake's grin broadened. 'Oh yes, you'll be stopping here.'

The new British arrivals were assigned a dark room at one corner of the barracks, the single unglassed window looking out over a descending jungle of rooftops and chimneys. The men seized an iron-framed bed each, arguing cheerfully. The sheets were filthy and the torn blankets even filthier.

'Not quite the Adelphi, but it's better than fuck-all,' said one of the Liverpudlians.

Nick watched his miners unstrapping their rucksacks and flopping down on their beds. Then he shouldered his way through the soldiers shouting in five languages who crowded in vaulted galleries choked with rubbish and broken furniture. It was relatively clean and quiet in Jake's bunkroom. Jake shut the door carefully.

'We're all Party members in this room,' he said, 'but you can't be too careful.'

Nick frowned. 'What?'

'There are Fascist spies everywhere. A French company captain, seemingly impeccable CP, turned out to be one. He was executed yesterday.'

Nick said nothing, but he felt a little bubble of disquiet rising within him all over again.

Jake went on casually, 'Got any cigarettes? They're the hardest thing to come by here.' Nick held out an unopened packet. 'Thanks. Everything else is rotten quality, but in reasonably decent supply. We get better food than the poor civilians. You should see the queues for bread, and baskets of it get thrown out here at every meal.'

'I saw the queues in Barcelona,' Nick said quietly. 'Tell me what's happening here.'

Jake shrugged, an expressive gesture, palms turned upwards and outwards. 'It's a mess. Twenty different factions lumped together, squabbling and stabbing each other. POUM versus CNT, Anarchists versus everyone else.' He gave a brief splutter of laughter. 'The Anarchists, you should see them. They don't believe in an officer class. Every decision, from when to take out rations to whether to attack a machine-gun post has to be taken by vote. I applaud the ideals, but you can't fight a war like that.

Some of them don't have guns, even though they've been to the front and back. One of them told me, "We play flamenco guitar at *los fascistos*. It scares the *shit* out of them." This place – ' Jake waved around – 'is supposed to be the Brigades' training centre. We've no kit, no weapons, nothing. They've had us drilling every day with sticks for rifles.' He dropped his voice and glanced round at the door. 'But there are DP machine-guns, new ones, rifles and T26 tanks en route from Moscow. Once we have those, we can drill properly.'

'And then?'

Jake leaned forward. 'All this is for Party ears only, remember.'

Nick's patience suddenly gave way. 'Why? Why shouldn't the Liverpool boys in my room, for example, be allowed to know whatever it is too? They're fighting the same war as us.'

Jake stared at him. 'You know why not. This is a Communist war. It is the beginning, Nick. The beginning of everything we've waited for, worked for. We must win it, and to win it we must control it. It's vital for the future, for all of us.'

'And for Spain's future?'

'*Of course*.' Looking into Jake's face, Nick suddenly thought of Cable Street. He gave up the attempt to soften the ideology.

'Okay. What will happen after we've trained?'

'We'll join the British Battalion. And after that, boy, the front. The Córdoba front.'

Jake reached into a box under his bed and brought out two glasses and a bottle. He poured them a measure each and they raised their glasses in a silent toast. The Córdoba front.

Amy had gone straight to Appleyard Street. There were no meetings held in the first-floor room now, but Kay Cooper was still living in the flat above. When she reached the street door Amy craned her head backwards and saw that there were lights in the top windows. She rang the bell, and waited. Kay stared a little when she saw who was standing on the step at such an odd hour, but she was friendly enough as she led Amy upstairs. Angel Mack was sitting in the splayed armchair beside the gas fire, drinking tea. She nodded at Amy over the rim of the cup, but said nothing.

'Angel moved in,' Kay said into the quiet. 'It's less . . . lonely.'

'Nick's gone, too,' Amy said. The two women were looking

warily at her. Amy knew why, but her concern was elsewhere. 'I'd like to go myself,' she added quietly. 'I'm a trained nurse, and they need nurses. Who should I go and see? Do you know?'

'You want to go out there?' Kay's black curls bobbed in disbelief.

'Yes. Why not? I know I can be useful.'

Kay smiled, but Angel went on looking at her through a veil of cigarette smoke and said nothing.

'God, you're lucky,' Kay said. 'I'd give anything to go myself. To be able to do anything out there. Of course you must go. I'll tell you who to see . . .' She jumped up and began shuffling through a pile of papers on a bureau.

Angel spoke at last. Her face looked hard. 'I don't think you should go. I don't think the Party should send you, anyway. You're not exactly one of us, are you, however you pretend?'

Amy faced her. 'Do you mean because of my family? I'm not ashamed of my family. My father was a good, honest man and my mother never knowingly hurt anyone. The world is full of people who are not automatically wicked because they don't believe the same things as we do.'

'We? If you haven't anything to hide, why did none of us know who you were until the papers let it out? Just a quiet nurse, Tony Hardy's friend, who then turns out to be Lady Amy Lovell, and related to Jaspert. Jaspert, who put Jake in prison, Kay.'

'I . . .' Kay pushed her hair back from her face, clearly uncomfortable, but Amy's chill voice cut her short.

'Yes. Peter Jaspert, who was entitled to his own views, just like Jake. But he was murdered for them.'

A cold stillness spread and held them, the three of them, facing one another. For a long time, nobody spoke. Then Amy shrugged. She said, 'I'm a nurse, and I want to go to Spain for the Republicans. I believe that to fight against Franco is to fight for democracy, and I'm proud of Jake, and Nick, and all the others who have gone to do it. I'll go and nurse the men who have been hurt in that fight. That's all.'

Amy didn't look at Angel. She was angry, quivering with it, but she was afraid too that she might let herself down by allowing the tears to show in her eyes.

'Well done,' Kay Cooper said softly. She held out a sheet of paper with an address written on it. 'Here. This is where you should go. They'll see you get to Spain.'

'Thank you.' Amy took it, and turned to the door.

From behind her back Angel asked, 'You really want to go out there after Nick Penry, don't you?'

Amy thought, *I understand now.* What was pricking Angel was neither suspicion nor idealism. It was jealousy, for Nick. Amy almost smiled at the thought of her jealousy, and that it should be so misplaced. And she had already confronted herself with Angel's question. She was certain of her answer.

'It's a big country,' she replied, without turning round. 'The war's being fought on several fronts. I wouldn't have thought that there was the remotest chance of seeing Nick out there.' She lifted her head and went on down the stairs. Kay came behind her, and unbolted the front door.

'Good luck,' she said. 'Amy, if you see Jake, will you tell him . . . tell him I love him?' Amy saw her white, strained face. I know, she thought.

'Yes. If I see Jake I'll tell him that.'

Kay held out her hand and Amy shook it. Then Amy folded up the slip of paper, put it into her pocket and walked quickly away.

The next morning she gave in her notice at the Royal Lambeth. She sealed the envelope containing it decisively, and without any particular sense of regret. She would always be grateful to the hospital for her training, but she had felt for a long time now that she lacked the qualities of patience, and submissiveness to authority, that the best nurses possessed.

At the same time she wrote to Spanish Medical Aid at the address that Kay had given her.

The days passed. The story of the King and Mrs Simpson had broken in the British press at last, and London boiled with speculation. Amy had dinner at Bruton Street one evening, and no one among Adeline's guests could speak of anything else. Amy felt oddly detached. If the King stayed or if he went, it wouldn't affect the people she cared about. She doubted whether the presence of the Duke and Duchess of York and the little Princesses in Buckingham Palace would make any difference in Nantlas.

On December 10th, as Amy made her way home from one of her last days' work at the Royal Lambeth, the newspaper placards proclaimed in tall black letters ABDICATION. The Pimlico flat was cold and bleak. Sitting in her armchair, in darkness except for the glow of the street-lamp outside reflected on the ceiling, she listened to the King's broadcast. Sir John Reith introduced him.

The familiar, clipped voice which followed wavered at first, but as he spoke the ex-King found courage.

'I have found it impossible to discharge my duties as King without the help and support of the woman I love.

'The Duke of York,' he said, 'has one matchless blessing, enjoyed by so many of you and not bestowed on me – a happy home with his wife and children.' Amy sat very still, listening with only part of herself. 'And now we have a new King. I wish him, and you, his people, happiness and prosperity with all my heart. God bless you all. God save the King.'

Stiffly, she stood up and turned the knob through the crackle of static into silence. Then she went back to her chair, drawing her knees up and wrapping her arms around them as if to contain her courage.

All through the December days that followed, Amy waited to be summoned by the Spanish Medical Aid Committee. Two letters came from Nick, one written in Barcelona and the other from a training centre that he was not allowed to name. He wrote just as he talked.

> Jake's here. It was such a pleasure to see him in the midst of all this, but there is a blinkered, Party fervour about him that makes him prickly company. The air is thick with rumours, dogma rules. I don't like it much.

Amy found it painful to read the strong, black handwriting because it brought him so close. She wrote back, news of the Abdication, descriptions of the consternation and hurried realignments in Adeline's circle that were intended to amuse him, but which sounded flat in her own head. She wouldn't mention Spanish Medical Aid until she was definitely on her way.

A week before Christmas she was summoned for an interview, in an anonymous office near Holborn. She presented her nursing credentials to a trio of doctors. They nodded their approval, then asked her what her political affiliations were. Carefully, Amy replied that she had been a Communist sympathizer. She had attended meetings at Appleyard Street for a number of years,

517

but she had never joined the Party. Nor did she believe that she ever would, she added firmly.

'I see,' the middle doctor said. They conferred briefly while she waited.

At last the spokesman nodded at her. 'That seems satisfactory, Miss Lovell.'

They explained to her that two three-and-a-half-ton Bedford lorries were in the process of being fitted out, one as a mobile operating theatre and the other as an X-ray unit. If she was indeed willing to go to Spain, it was possible that she could be drafted with the teams who would staff these units.

'Because of the urgent need for their services,' the doctor warned her, 'the personnel must be ready to leave as soon as the vehicles are. At twenty-four hours' notice if necessary. Can you do that?'

'Yes,' Amy answered. 'I can do that.'

She went back to Pimlico, and waited again.

The telephone call came on December 23rd.

'Miss Lovell, the teams will be leaving by tomorrow night's boat train. You will have Christmas Day in Paris, and travel onwards to meet the lorries at the Spanish border on the twenty-sixth. I'm sorry for the unseasonal timing.'

'That doesn't matter. I'll be there.'

At last, Amy thought. She made three telephone calls, to Isabel, to Tony Hardy, and to Richard in Paris.

Isabel replaced the receiver in its cradle and turned back to her drawing-room. The French windows looked down a slope of hillside towards Henstone village, but the light was already so dim that the cluster of houses was no more than an irregular black shape. Frowning a little, Isabel went over and pulled the curtains, but instead of going back to her seat beside the fire she stood holding one of the corded tassels, letting the silky threads slip between her fingers.

'Wh-who was it?' Bill Parfitt asked. 'Is anything wrong?'

He was sitting in the chair opposite hers, looking up at her from his book. The glow of the fire reddened one side of his face, and the length of his legs stretched out on the hearthrug. Isabel heard how the faintest anxiety brought the tremor back into his voice. She went to him at once and put her arms over his shoulders, leaning down so her head rested against his hair. Their closeness fed them with strength, as it always did.

'It was Amy. She's coming here to stay the night.'

'Here?' Bill asked comfortably. 'Surely she's spending Christmas at Chance?'

'No, she won't be doing that. Amy is going to Spain, as a nurse. She's leaving tomorrow night.'

Bill looked into the flames flickering against the black throat of the chimney. The pictures that he saw there must have disturbed him because he jerked his head round sharply, back to Isabel. She rubbed his hair comfortingly with her cheek.

'She wants me to go home with her, to see Adeline.'

'Amy shouldn't go to war,' Bill said. 'She can't know what it's like. You can't go back, once you have seen it. It lives with you for ever, all your days and into your dreams.'

'Bill,' she soothed him. 'She's going to nurse, not to fight. It may be that she wants to go because of Nick.'

Isabel and Bill Parfitt had only met Nick once or twice. Isabel was wary of him, but Bill had conceived a deep admiration for him.

'Nick's gone out there? Yes, of course he would want to go. He's a brave man. But if he comes through it he won't find anything the same again, either.'

'I hope he comes through it,' Isabel said softly. 'For Amy's sake.' She stood up, deliberately matter-of-fact. 'I'll go down to the station later, to meet her. Will you be all right for an hour?'

'Of course.' They smiled at each other, acknowledging and deprecating the minutes that they had to be apart.

Except for the crackle of the log fire it was quiet in the room, a silence that seemed to Isabel the most potent reminder of her new strength. She couldn't even remember, any more, the exact timbre of the screaming that had filled her head in the last terrible days at Ebury Street. But she could still remember the fear that it had created. And, with the fear, the way that she had lost hold of herself, the Isabel she had known, and had been forced to live within the wildness of a stranger.

Only in the long, empty days of solitude at Thorogood House had the noise begun to die down, and with its diminution the stranger's power had diminished too. She had met Bill then, and his need for quiet had answered her own. Even now she thought of the days when they had sat together, without speaking, as a kind of necessary balm. Bill had grown to need her then, because he had discovered that she could talk for him. As his dependence grew, so Isabel's strength returned.

She looked at him now, sitting in his accustomed place, his thin face calm and his attention absorbed in his book. They were a partnership, she thought, knitted together by the strength they gave one another and the weaknesses that they helped to defend. The contrast with the terrible failure of her marriage made her think of Peter Jaspert again, with sadness and with regret for the unhappiness that they had forced on one another. Yet when she thought of her husband now it led her inevitably on to her son, and little Peter was her greatest source of happiness.

Isabel smiled into the firelight. Peter was upstairs, with Bethan. Thanks to Amy's intercession with Lady Jaspert, he was here to stay for the Christmas holiday. As it always did, his presence made the little house at Henstone a haven for all of them.

Later, Isabel drove down to meet the train. Amy was the only passenger to climb out. Isabel called her name, and ran to meet her down the wooden platform. The sound of her feet and the smell of the station itself reminded her of meeting other visitors to Chance over all the years of her girlhood. The memory made her feel safe, properly placed. The sisters hugged and kissed each other.

'You shouldn't have come,' Amy said. 'I could have found my own way up.' But in her loneliness she was more than pleased that Isabel had done. With everything else breaking up and changing its alignment around her, it was doubly comforting to witness Isabel's tangible normality again. Isabel's car was in the station yard.

'How's Peter?' Amy asked. She had fought hard for his Christmas at Henstone. She glanced at Isabel's profile, faintly lit by the back-glow of the headlamps. Her sister's hair, grown long again, was drawn back from her face and the line of her cheek and throat was as lovely as ever. Amy thought that Isabel could have been a debutante, untouched by any of the years that had passed.

'He's well. In bed asleep now, but you'll see him in the morning.' Isabel said suddenly, 'I love him so much. I would do anything for him. Die, or kill for him. Is that how all mothers feel?'

Amy saw the movement in her sister's white throat. 'I don't

520

know,' she said softly. 'I'm glad you feel like that. I'm glad he's here with you.'

Isabel was looking straight ahead, intent on the dips and curves of the road.

'It's strange, isn't it? How everything unravels? Fanning out into a blur, so frightening that you can't breathe, and then defining itself again, as sharp as a needle. I didn't think I'd ever get myself back again, at Thorogood House, and in . . . in the times before that. And yet I did. I wake up every morning and think, *It's true. Here I am*. It's so beautiful, sharp and simple. Bill and I don't want anything except each other, and little Peter.' Isabel didn't turn her head, but Amy felt her stiffen with the importance of what she had to say. 'But I didn't want Peter to die, you know. I didn't want him to. I didn't will it.'

'You couldn't have willed his death, even if you had wanted to,' Amy answered.

They sat in silence, wrapped in their own thoughts, as the car headlamps cut white slices through the dark lanes up to Henstone.

The drawing-room was empty, although the fire had been banked up to a welcoming blaze and a silver tray with a decanter and polished glasses stood on a side table.

'Bill will be upstairs. He has a rest before changing for dinner.'

Isabel poured them both a drink, and watched Amy as she paced around the room nursing hers. Amy's face had changed, she thought. The lines of it were set firmer now, as if she had discarded her uncertainties at last. And there was a new maturity about her that consolidated her chameleon girlhood beauty with a kind of richness. Isabel glanced briefly down into her glass. She thought that Amy's sheen, like the glow on deep pile velvet, came from sexual confidence. Isabel knew equally that she would never develop that glow herself. Even with Bill, physical love was a matter of tenderness and intimacy rather than passion. Amy was different, Isabel thought. Amy was passionate in everything she did, and she was never afraid. Or if she was she confronted her fear, and by doing so she turned it into strength.

Amy had to go to Spain, as inevitably as Nick had done.

'What will you do out there?' Isabel asked. Amy finished her whisky with a shiver, and held up her glass to semaphore a request to fill it again. The lip of the decanter clinked against the rim of it.

'I don't know. Whatever they ask me to.'

521

'Are you going because of Nick?'

Amy smiled crookedly. 'I'm going because of Nick only in the sense that we believe in the same things. Isabel, did you mean it when you said you'd come over to Chance and face Mama with me?'

'Of course I did. We'll go after dinner, if you don't mind. Bill won't want to come, and I don't like to leave him to dine here alone.'

With a little flicker of envy, Amy saw the concern for him that shone steadily in Isabel's face.

There were only the three of them at dinner, eaten quietly in Isabel's small dining-room. Amy noticed how often Bill put his hand out to cover Isabel's as he spoke, and in turn she would touch his sleeve, looking for confirmation. They reflected each other, Amy thought, signal for signal, reassurance for reassurance. She envied them their peace, but she felt that the air was too close and still to fill her own lungs. She was restless, eager to move now that the time had come. She felt dizzy, and a little wild, as if she couldn't trust herself not to laugh too loudly at an inopportune moment or jump up and send her chair clattering backwards. It was the same combination of fear and elation that she had felt from the moment of being told that she would go to Spain.

Isabel drove her over to Chance after dinner. By contrast with Henstone, there were a dozen people staying in the house, and almost as many had come over to dine. The dining-room doors were closed when they passed, and the sisters knew that behind them the men would be sitting over their cigars and port.

The women were in the salon, a cross-section of the breed Amy had once thought of as cobras. They were talking about the new King and Queen. None of them, it now seemed, had ever been 'particularly fond of Wallis, even when one couldn't escape her anywhere'. The Duchess of York, on the other hand, had always been the dearest friend. Amy thought with her heightened perceptions that rats would be a better term than snakes, and felt briefly sorry for the Windsors.

Adeline was at the far end of the room, leaning over a sofa to murmur to a friend. She looked as slim and taut as a bow in her Schiaparelli. When she straightened up again the diamond collar around her neck blazed with light, a sparkling focus among the jewelled women.

'Darlings! Two of you.' She held out her hands, heavy with diamonds too. 'Amy, I didn't expect to see you until tomorrow. Why didn't you come in time for dinner?'

'I dined at Henstone. Can you spare me a moment to talk?'

Adeline began a pouting protest. 'In the middle of my party, darling?' Then she saw their faces. 'Look after yourselves for two minutes while I deal with my mysterious daughters,' she called to her guests. The nearest empty room, the Tapestry Room, was cold and forbidding.

'Ugh, how I hate this little hole,' Adeline said. 'If only I could rip down these gloomy old hangings.'

Amy took a deep breath. 'I've come to ask you . . . no, to tell you, that I'm going to Spain as a nurse. I've been given a job to do, at very short notice. I'm sorry that it means I'll have to leave on Christmas Eve. Tomorrow night,' Amy reminded herself.

It was worse, far worse, than she had imagined. Adeline went white and her mouth gaped in an ugly square. Amy stepped back as her mother's diamonds flashed on her fingers. Adeline was afraid, and the fear that she couldn't control made her wildly angry. 'You won't go. I forbid it. I forbid you to get yourself killed on a whim. You won't go, and you won't mention it again.'

'I have to go,' Amy said quietly, and she felt Isabel move closer to her, backing her up.

Adeline tried every tack, threatening to wheedling and back again, but Amy was firm.

'You won't go on my money,' Adeline hissed at last.

'I wouldn't use your money,' Amy told her. 'I've sold Jack Roper's diamonds.' She had taken the earrings down to a diamond dealer in Hatton Garden. He put them on a little square of velvet and screwed a black eyepiece into his eye-socket to scrutinize them. He had sucked his breath in in admiration of the flawless stones, and then he had offered her four hundred pounds for the pair. Amy knew that it was a fraction of their real value, but she didn't know where else to take them or have the time to find out. She took the money, and bought herself a sturdy money belt to keep it in.

Adeline shot her last bolt now. She opened her eyes very wide, and for an instant it was as if Amy was looking into her own imploring face.

'Please, Amy, don't go. You saw what Airlie's death did to your father. Do you want to do that to me?'

Amy knew that she meant it. Adeline believed that she would die, and worse, die for a mistaken cause. If Adeline had any sympathies they were for the Carlists. She put her hand out and tried to touch her mother's arm, but Adeline shook it off. The space between them was too wide, and it wouldn't be bridged now.

'I won't be killed. Soldiers will, but I won't. I'll just do what I can, and then I'll come home again. I promise. I'm sorry that I have to miss Christmas with you.'

'You can't promise.' Adeline turned sharply away. 'Go, then.' With her head up and her diamonds blazing, she went back to her party.

Isabel drove them home to Henstone, and Amy's face was wet with tears.

The morning was bright and frosty, with a pale blue-grey sky. Hunting weather, Gerald would have called it. The household was awake as early too as on any hunting morning because little Peter evaded Bethan and ran in and out of the bedrooms in search of Amy. His aunt was a particular favourite. When he opened her door Amy held out her arms and he launched himself across the room and burrowed under the eiderdown with her.

'Aunt Amy! Do you know who's coming tonight?'

She hugged the warmth of him for an instant, which was all he would submit to, feeling the simple force of her love for him. She pretended to consider. 'Tonight? Let me think. No, I don't know . . .'

Peter bounced up and stared at her, saucer-eyed. 'You don't? Santa Claus, of course. With presents. Only if you're good, you know.'

'Oh, Santa Claus.'

They smiled at each other. Peter had already wriggled out of her grasp. 'You did know. Are you going to get up now? Come and play with me, in my room.'

He darted away in his tartan dressing-gown and Amy followed him. They took down his toy farm and played for an hour with the little wagons and livestock. Amy watched the child's intent face eagerly, trying to fix it in her mind. There was this much, hours like this that she could share, even if there was not to be a child of her own.

She knew that Bethan understood her longing too, because

she left the two of them to play together until the last moment before breakfast.

After breakfast Amy ordered the local taxi to take her to the station. She didn't want any platform goodbyes. Tony Hardy would be the only person to see her off from Victoria tonight.

Isabel and Bill came and stood at the front door and Peter ran in swooping arcs across the lawn. The frosty grass glittered with points of light and Amy thought of her mother's diamonds again, and Jack's, sold in Hatton Garden. She knew that Jack would give her his blessing.

Bethan came out and put Amy's bag in the waiting car. She hugged Amy and then she whispered, 'Come home again, pet lamb. I'll worry every minute you're away, but I'm proud of you for going. All our people will be.'

Our people. The warmth of that buoyed Amy up through the wrench of parting. She hugged Bill and Isabel and then she swung Peter up into the air while he laughed with delighted fear and begged for more. There wasn't time for any more. Amy ruffled his silky fair hair and kissed the top of his head, then turned quickly away in case he should read her feelings too clearly in her face.

She climbed into the back of the car and turned to wave. Peter was standing in front of Isabel, suddenly quiet, his head against his mother's skirt. Amy's last glimpse of them before the taxi turned the corner of the lane was of Bill and Isabel side by side, waving, and little Peter sheltered in front of them. Almost a family.

Amy turned and faced forward. Isabel had found her place. She hadn't found her own, yet, but in a moment of sudden, exhilarated intuition, Amy knew that one day she would.

Her last preparations were simple. She packed a canvas bag of clothes and added some food for the journey. A package had arrived from Spanish Medical Aid. It contained, along with her travel tickets and papers proclaiming her a nurse with the Mission Sanitaria Britanica, two overalls and a mackintosh. She put the overalls in the bag with her clothes and kept the mackintosh out to travel in.

Amy was letting her flat in her absence to Moira O'Hara, but Moira had gone home to Ireland for Christmas. There was nothing to do when Tony came for her at eight o'clock but lock the door and walk away.

Tony eyed her beret and mackintosh. 'How practical,' he said drily. 'How very *Yes, Comrade!*'

As he always had done, Tony made her laugh. They had a cheerful dinner at a restaurant near the station, a dinner like the ones they had shared years ago. They talked mostly about the old days. Only when they had left the restaurant and ducked through the traffic towards the station did Tony put his arm around her shoulders.

'Keep safe,' he ordered her.

'I don't know what it will be like.'

'Hard. I'm sure you know that. But you're right to go, Amy.'

They passed the ticket barrier and began to walk down the dark blue, steam-hissing length of the boat train. Amy found the carriage with her booked seat, and paused with Tony on the platform outside it.

'I didn't know what to give you,' he murmured, 'so I just brought these.'

In the package were two books, *Barchester Towers* and Siegfried Sassoon's war poems. 'They might help, at different times,' he said. 'And these.' There was a bunch of violets, bought from the old flower-seller by the station steps. Amy took them and pinned them in her hat.

'Now you look like a flighty comrade,' he smiled at her.

The train was almost due to leave. Doors slammed, and heads poked out of windows for the last goodbyes. Amy became aware of a commotion at the barrier and turned around to see.

It was Adeline. Adeline, in her silvery fur coat and a huge hat, with her long legs and black kid high-heeled shoes, strolling regally down the platform as if the train would wait all night for her.

'Mummy.'

Adeline was carrying two baskets. She put them down and held out her arms, and Amy ran to her and buried her face in the soft fur. Adeline stood back and put her suede-gloved fingers to Amy's cheek.

'Don't cry,' she ordered. 'I'm sorry for last night, and I've come to see you off.' They hugged each other, clinging together under the flaring lights. There was no time for anything more. The doors were all closed except one, and the guard's flag was raised.

'I love you,' Adeline said. 'Here.' She picked up the baskets and Tony handed them into the train. 'Take this, as well.' Amy looked down. It was her mother's lace-edged handkerchief. Amy took it and scrambled up into the train, and a porter banged the door behind her. Adeline lifted her black-gloved hand in a salute as the train edged away.

'Don't let anyone hurt you,' she called.

'I won't,' Amy answered her, and she knew that she would come home safely. Adeline and Tony stood shoulder to shoulder and waved until the fluttering white lace handkerchief was no longer visible.

Amy stood in the jolting corridor and rubbed her face with the handkerchief. When she was satisfied that the tearstains couldn't show she picked up her luggage and Adeline's baskets and stumbled along to her compartment.

She slid the door open and seven faces looked up at her. Beyond the black window square the lights of Clapham slid past, faster and faster. Here were three men and four women, doctors and nurses, heading for Spain.

'Merry Christmas,' Amy said.

When one of the doctors had stowed her bag on the rack overhead, Amy peered inside Adeline's baskets. There were two bottles of champagne, with icy drops beading the green glass. There was a bottle of vodka, triangles of toast still warm wrapped in their Bruton Street napkins, lemons, and a big stone crock. Amy lifted the lid and saw that it was a pound of caviar. She bent her head to hide her face and felt the tightness in her throat. The present was so trenchantly Adeline that she might have been in the stuffy compartment next to her. Amy looked up again and glanced at the seven faces watching her. She stood up and took the covers off the baskets with a flourish.

'Will you drink a toast to Spain with me?'

The champagne sloshed and spilt with the swaying train and the black beads of caviar rolled under the silver knife, but at last they raised their glasses.

'To Spain.'

'To Spain.'

'And Merry Christmas.'

By Christmas Eve, Nick and Jake and their companions were ready to leave Madrigueras. They had been shunted on there from Albacete with its narrow, dirty streets that smelt of oil, and wine, and the unwashed soldiery that thronged them up until the curfew hour. At Madrigueras they had drilled again, and marched, and listened to lectures on fieldcraft delivered in hilariously broken English by Poles, Germans, and Frenchmen. They had been issued with uniforms of a kind, tin helmets, khaki coats and corduroy trousers, and kit that consisted of a plate and a mug, a knife and a spoon and a blanket. They even had rifles, and although they were twenty years old and there were no ammunition clips, Nick took his with relief because he had begun to be afraid there would be no arms at all.

In the Madrigueras days one hundred and forty-five men had been transformed, roughly enough, into the British No. 1 Company.

On Christmas Eve they received their orders, and they marched behind their company commander to the railway station. They swung along proudly like a proper army, and the streets filled up with cheering Spaniards. The people were shouting *'No pasarán! No pasarán!'* They shall not pass. The Fascists shall not pass. The memory of Cable Street came back to Nick, and he looked at Jake by his side. Jake's chin was jutting, and he was marching as proudly as a guardsman. Nick smiled a little at the irony of it.

Madrigueras station was a seething mass of soldiers, weapons and supplies.

'What's all this lot, then?' asked one of Nick's miners. They learned soon enough. A Polish soldier in the uniform of a general addressed them through a megaphone. They had joined the Marseillaise Battalion of the 14th International Brigade, and they were headed for Andújar on the Córdoba front.

Jake Silverman clapped his fist into the palm of his hand.

'We'll be in action by the day after tomorrow,' he exulted.

'No pasarán,' came the cry from the streets, *'No pasarán.'*

Amy and the medical team reached Paris at breakfast-time on Christmas morning. The Gare du Nord was practically deserted and out in the street the first thin flakes of snow were twirling in the wind.

Richard was waiting for her with his arms flung wide open.

'Amy!' he called, 'Amy!'

He was wearing an ankle-length wolfskin coat and a big blac

hat. Amy was vividly conscious of the little troop of travellers watching the two of them as she ran to him and hugged him.

The bottles of champagne, and the vodka and caviar had been the start of an odd picnic party that had lasted on to the boat and into the small hours of the morning when they fell asleep on the benches in one of the third-class bars. Talk, and drink, the disconnection of travel and the oddness of this shared Christmas had moulded them into a unit, even if they were not friends yet. The doctors were a surgeon and a solemn anaesthetist, and a middle-aged orthopaedic specialist who had left behind a wife and four children. There were three nurses besides Amy, one of them a highly experienced theatre sister from Guy's Hospital, and a ravishingly lovely radiographer who had been the target of endless attention from bleary Frenchmen on the half-empty boat. Amy sensed them stopping in a curious knot behind her now as Richard prepared to sweep her away.

'Breakfast and a hot bath, for you,' he carolled, 'and then some attention to Christmas celebration, don't you think?'

'Richard . . .'

But he was quick enough to sense what she was going to say, and to forestall her. 'Are these your colleagues?' Amy introduced them. 'What can you do in Paris on Christmas Day? Come home with me, won't you? It's a party. I can't promise how it will turn out, you know. Do come.'

Faintly bewildered, they came. Richard piled them into two taxis and they bowled away.

Richard's apartment was on the Ile de la Cité. It was up three flights of narrow stairs in a tall, thin, grey house. They came panting up to his door with their unwieldy baggage, and when the door opened they gasped in unison.

The long, uncurtained windows of the huge room looked over the rooftops to the towers of Notre Dame. Paris spread and rose on either side of the ribbon of the Seine, brown and grey and slate-blue. The view was so perfect that it eclipsed the pictures that covered the walls, abstract canvases in strong primary colours all clearly by the same artist, and outshone even the shimmering ten-foot Christmas tree surrounded by presents that stood in one corner.

'Do you love my tree?' Richard demanded. 'I had to fight for it at Les Halles. Come in, come in. There are only two bathrooms, so you will have to take turns.' There was a gallery at one end of the room, and a man came down the stairs to meet them. He was a little older than Richard, with a thin face and cropped black hair. 'This is Klaus,' Richard said. He turned to Amy and added quietly, 'I haven't explained about Klaus. He's a painter, and a Jew. He's left everything behind in Germany.'

Amy shook hands, smiling. Klaus's answering smile of relief unhooded his eyes and lit up his melancholy face.

'I am so glad to meet Richard's sister,' he said haltingly. 'I know that he thinks much of you. And now you go to Spain?'

'Yes,' Amy answered, 'we're all going to Spain.'

'Thank you,' Klaus said simply.

With his arms windmilling in his enthusiasm, Richard was marshalling the doctors and nurses, showing them where they could bath and change, flinging open doors into bedrooms and ordering them to go to sleep at once if they felt like it, otherwise they would miss the party.

Amy took a bath in one of the luxurious bathrooms, changed her crumpled clothes and put her hair up with a pair of combs. When she came down the gallery stairs again it was to a table laid with coffee, *pain au chocolat* and bottles of champagne. Her companions beamed up at her in a contented circle. The bells of Notre Dame were ringing, plangent, unmistakably Parisian.

'Better,' Richard confirmed, and hugged her again.

'I didn't imagine you lived in such style,' Amy teased him.

'If one has earned a little money through artistic toil and painful notoriety, one might as well use it to cushion oneself somewhat against the blows,' Richard said. But he added, with complete seriousness, 'It's worth it to be able to provide a comfortable home and studio for Klaus, who has more talent in his ear-lobe than in the whole of me.'

Richard's 1936 Christmas party was one of the oddest parties Amy had ever been to, but for the oddness of the day and the circumstances it seemed perfectly, hilariously appropriate. The guests surged in in a constant stream from midday onwards. Somehow there was a present for each of them from Richard's miniature mountain under the tree, and the champagne flowed like the Seine beyond the windows. It was taken for granted that Richard's sister should be there with a heterogeneous and bewildered British medical team. The guests themselves were heterogeneous enough for anything to be taken for granted. There were painters, eccentrically dressed and already ha drunk. There were writers and actors, and girls in furs and satin who might have been dancers in a chorus line. There were three French sailors in their red pompon bonnets who looked as if they had strayed in from a comic opera, and a beautiful transvestite with big hands and feet who reminded Amy of Madame Ondine. There was a very fat man who sat all day in a corner with a whisky bottle, and an ethereally thin girl who sobbed on the gallery stairs. There was a black jazz trumpeter and a clarinettist who snatched the swing records off the gramophone and played all afternoon. There was dancing and drinking and singing and laughing.

Looking around her in the hectic height of the afternoon, Amy saw the transvestite clinging like a leech to one of the sailors, and the anaesthetist with his spectacles knocked askew swaying blissfully in the arms of one of the chorus girls. Jennie, the lovely radiographer, was sitting on the sofa holding hands with a painter, and they were looking at one another as if there was no one else in the room. An impromptu, stumbling and uproarious chorus line was kicking to the trumpeter's rendition of *Gaité Parisienne*, and Richard was leaping in the midst of it like a mad conductor.

Amy was laughingly, light-headedly drunk, but the scene would have given her pleasure even if she had drunk nothing at all. Richard was happy here, with Klaus and his friends. Richard had found his place, too.

He was waving and beckoning at her to come and join the dance, but she shook her head at him and pushed through the crowd to the window. The sky over Paris was like a bruise and the shrouded city was still, dream-wrapped. The rooftops were finely powdered with snow. Amy found the surgeon standing beside her. They both looked up at the million black points, gentler and more random than rain, that came drifting down out of the purple sky.

'I was thinking about Spain,' the surgeon said. 'The contrast of it.'

Amy glanced back from Paris under its sparkling blanket to the hot, crowded room behind them.

Madrid was a siege city. The rebel Nationalists were drawn up on its outskirts and the Condor Legion of the Luftwaffe was trying to bomb it into submission. There would be few parties in Madrid this Christmas. Amy thought of the war, trying to fix an image of it in her swimming head, and wondered where Nick was. She had a sudden, vivid and terrifying picture of him huddled in a bullet-pocked ruin, waiting for the order to run to the attack across a bare and hostile plain.

'Yes,' she said, and terror made her voice sharp. 'I suppose it is thoughtless to be like this while men are killing one another in Spain.'

The surgeon peered at her, concerned, and then he smiled. 'I didn't mean that we shouldn't enjoy ourselves,' he said. His name was Victor, and from the moment when he had introduced himself Amy had wondered whether the name was a good omen. He had ridged black hair and a rather forbidding, saturnine manner, but his smile was warm. 'I think that this is the last innocent, harmless day we shall see for a long time. We should be grateful to your brother for letting us have it. Shall we dance, while the day lasts?'

He led her away from the window and into the room, and the chorus line snaked madly around them.

As darkness fell outside, they sat down to eat at long tables that Richard and Klaus had conjured up. A young man in a white chef's toque entwined with tinsel appeared from the kitchen. He clapped his hands commandingly. '*Mes amis!*' he called. '*A table!*'

Richard leaned over Amy's shoulder to whisper, 'He is from Maxim's, and he is doing this because he loves me. He isn't *chef de cuisine* yet but one day, mark my words, he will be the greatest chef of all.'

It was a wonderful, prolonged, gargantuan meal, part English Christmas dinner and part French fantasy. The young man carried out course after course on silver platters and at the end of the meal there was a plum pudding blazing in a nimbus of blue light. After the pudding came chocolate truffles, cognac, and gilt paper crackers with wickedly rude mottoes rolled up inside them.

It was nine p.m. when Victor the surgeon looked at his watch 'We should go now,' he said to Amy. Richard took charge a once. He wouldn't listen to their protests that he mustn't abando his party. In the end half of the party stayed put, preoccupie with its own momentum, and the other half streamed out int the empty snowy streets with them and whistled and shouted fo taxis. A line of them wound across Paris to the Gare St Lazare and discharged the revellers into the station. There was no time to spare. Amy and her companions gathered up their belongings and ran for the train. Richard took her hand as she swung herself up into the high doorway and kissed it. She looked down and saw his guests in a breathless cluster behind him, and the nurses and doctors leaned out of the windows around her to wave and call their thanks.

'Now,' Richard shouted, 'let's have "Good King Wenceslas" as a send-off.'

The last Amy heard of Paris was his tenor voice leading the sailors, the transvestite, the fat man and the dancers from the chorus line into a warbling rendition of 'When the snow lay round about, deep and crisp and e-ven.'

The British medical team sat in silence, smiling at the kaleidoscope of the day. The youngest, shy nurse was the first to speak. She sighed with pleasure, and turned to Amy. 'I didn't know that men like your brother were – well, like that.'

'They're like everyone else, really. A bit more so, perhaps.'

'Is he really a lord?'

'Yes, he is.'

'I didn't know lords were like that.'

The burst of laughter made her turn bright pink. 'I meant so nice. So friendly.'

Jennie the radiographer came to her rescue. 'I enjoyed my day too. I fell in love, and I didn't know love would be like that. Whatever happens in Spain, I'm coming back to Paris afterwards. Gérard will wait for me.'

They nodded their approval, and the conviction in her voice fortified them all. The train rattled south towards Perpignan and the border.

The morning light was dirty grey when they left the train again, and the party seemed years as well as hundreds of miles away. Above them the Pyrenees were sharp white teeth against the threatening sky, and the wind was as sharp as a knife. Amy huddled with her headache in her mackintosh and thought longingly of Adeline's silvery furs.

Drawn up waiting for the travellers were the two huge Bedford lorries that the drivers had brought down across France. They were painted in khaki and olive camouflage stripes. On the door of the nearer one were the words 'From the Battersea Aid Spain Committee to the Workers of Spain'.

A little ragged cheer went up from the nurses and doctors, and they picked their way through the snow to take possession of their hospital and home for the next months.

The engines chugged into life and the big, blunt noses swung round to face the mountains and the road into Spain.

20

Nick shifted painfully in the narrow trench. He tried to wrap himself in his blanket, and for the twentieth time he cursed the unknown man who had somehow stolen his greatcoat while he slept on the train to Andújar. The ground here was iron-hard with frost, and the air was so cold that it hurt him to breathe it. Then he thought that the pain in his chest might not be cold at all, but fear. He was waiting, and the men on either side of him all down the line were waiting too, for the first threatening light of dawn. At dawn they would attack.

It was so silent now, a black silence heavy with fear, that it was hard to believe that light and noise would ever return to the world. But Nick knew that they would come again, and they would send him and all the rest of No. 1 Company out of the makeshift trenches and running through the olive groves towards the enemy lines.

They had been briefed. Captain Berman had briefed them, and that's what they would do. Nick pulled at his blanket, and his fingers grasped the stock of his rifle. They had come up in this same darkness from Andújar, the infantry of the 14th International Brigade moving stealthily forward under its cover, without even a glimmer of starlight to expose them to enemy bombers. They had lifted their rifles and kitbags over the tailgates of the trucks, and the machine-gun sections had hauled up their unwieldy weapons beside the infantrymen. Away to the rear, the tanks that would support their attack rumbled up the skids on to the long tank transporters.

'It's a long way to bloody nowhere . . .' an English voice had sung softly in the dark.

When the trucks stopped again it was in the midst of mounds of rubble: bricks and stones and upended beams. As they came scrambling out it took the new reinforcements a long, gaping moment to realize that this wilderness had once been a village.

No. 1 Company's commander had marshalled them briskly. Captain Henry Berman was a British Guards officer and a War veteran. He had commanded immediate respect from his motley company in the chaotic days at Albacete. They stumbled behind him and came blinking into the lantern-light of what had once been a barn. Two walls were left standing, and a rough shelter of beams and tarpaulins had been lashed together against them. Captain Berman hoisted up a rough wooden oblong that had been a door. One corner of it was charred black. He pinned a blank sheet of paper to it, and turned to his men.

'I'm afraid there isn't a proper map for us to work with. There is a shortage of field equipment down here.' He smiled crookedly, acknowledging the inadequacy. It was the first of many inadequacies. 'You'll have to bear with my drawing. Can you all see? Our job is this.'

He drew quickly, with black chalk. The battalion had been brought up against the enemy lines. Berman drew in their position, a hard black zigzag that danced in front of Nick's eyes. They were separated only by the olive groves, and a low hill. Beyond the hill was a village, and the village was in enemy hands. Henry Berman had drawn it as a square behind his black zigzag lines, and beside it he wrote 'LOPERA'.

'Lopera is our objective,' he said. 'At dawn.'

There were rough wooden boxes stacked against the barn walls. After the briefing they were broken open under Captain Berman's orders and the ammunition was distributed, one hundred and fifty rounds for each man. There were still no ammunition clips. Incredulously Nick saw that there were piles of bandoliers instead. The men at the front picked them up and stuffed their cartridges into them, and then swung them experimentally over their shoulders. Nick pushed forward in the line, because he could see clearly that there were not even enough of those to go round.

After the distribution of ammunition the company cooks had brought round hot coffee, ladled into outstretched tin cups, bread and coarse ham. And after the hasty meal the men had moved forward to take up their positions in the shallow trenches. The silence in the annihilated village stretched on, and on. It was eerie, and awesome.

Nick leaned forward against the cold earth bank and thought of Amy, and of Dickon and Mari and Nantlas. When he looked up again he thought he saw a dirty smudge of grey under the blackness of the eastern sky. To the left and right of him there were creaks of webbing and faint clinks as buckles were done up and rifles hoisted. He felt the cold metal barrel of his own, and the weight of the cartridges in the bandolier at his shoulder. How much longer now? He wondered if his cramped legs and frozen feet would carry him out of the scooped hollow and into the trees. He could see the trees now, gnarled shapes like old men. The light was strengthening with every second. *Come on*, he begged under his breath, *come on, order us over*.

When the order came he felt the movement in the trench like a wave, rising and breaking over the lip of ground. It carried him with it and he was running, the pain in his chest all gone. Ahead Captain Berman was waving them on with great sweeps of his arm, Jake was away to the left with his bearded chin tucked into his chest as he ran, Ieuan and Dick from Nantlas were beside him, and Nick felt a surge of elation that stretched his face into a smile and carried him effortlessly forward over the pitted ground.

He was here, he was running into the battle.

Nick's rifle was loaded and he levelled it as he ran, ready to fire. They reached the olive groves before the fire opened up from the enemy machine-gun post on the crest of the hill ahead. As he wove in and out of the knotted trunks Nick heard the *ping, ping* around him with a moment's puzzlement. Then, almost running over it, he saw the little plume of dirt and stones raised by a bullet as it ploughed into the earth at his feet. He dodged to and fro more wildly as he ran, and peered forward to get a sight before firing back. He fired his first shot in retaliation, too wild, forgetting the kick of the old rifle that smashed back and jarred his shoulder. The lack of a clip meant that he had to stop, dig a cartridge out of his bandolier and reload, wiping the sudden sweat out of his eyes with his sleeve as he bent to the job.

Nick was dimly aware of a big man plunging along beside him, then stopping to aim and fire. An instant later there was a bang and a flash of vicious light.

'Christ,' the man said. 'Oh Christ.'

Nick half-turned and saw that the relic of a rifle had blown up on its first firing. The man was Ken Coate, and his hand was a red, pulpy mass. Nick had taken two steps towards him when there was a fresh splutter of bullets around them. When he looked at Ken again he had fallen down, with his mangled hand coated in dirt splayed out beside him. Nick ducked towards him, and saw that the front of his tunic was pocked with black-edged holes, and already sodden with dark blood. 'Jesus,' Ken Coate said. Nick knelt beside him and the boots and leggings of the rest of the company crashed past their heads.

Ken Coate closed his eyes. 'Go on,' he said to Nick. 'Go on up there and bugger them for me.' Then his mouth and his face seemed to lose their shape, flattening, shrinking inwards. Nick knew that Ken had sworn for the last time. In an instant's blind fury he kicked at the splintered remains of Ken's rifle, picked up his own, and ran onwards.

The bare land beyond the trees was churned into heavy mud that clogged his boots and tried to pull him down to lie beside other tumbled heaps of men. The moment of elation had evaporated completely. There was nothing now except the need to run through the mire, sometimes almost falling over, tripping and stumbling amongst those who had already fallen, stopping to load and fire a single pathetic shot and then scrambling on upwards in the shouting and the hum of bullets. Henry Berman was still ahead, and Nick thought he glimpsed Jake Silverman's hunched shoulders pushing forwards. He had no idea how he kept running himself, because he was badly winded and his breath came in irregular, tearing gasps. He wasn't afraid of what the bullets might do to him, but he was terribly afraid of being left behind amongst the dead and so he kept running, tripping and panting, and running for life.

Nick was halfway up the hill when he realized that the firing was all around him, rifle fire from his own company, and the efficiently deadly stream from the machine-gun post above had stopped completely. He covered the remaining few yards in an exhausted stagger, and came up with the survivors of No. 1 Company to the brow of the hill and the abandoned post.

It was in the shelter of a hollow, built up roughly with big stones that were almost the same colour and texture as the barren earth. The rebels had deserted it as the attacking battalion surged up the hill towards them. They had taken their ammunition belts with them, but they had left the machine-gun and a dead gunner doubled up beside it. The big gun was a German one, a new MG34, and the soldier was a boy of no more than eighteen. Nick glanced at his twisted face but the body was quickly heaved aside as his own company took the post and faced down the hill towards the village.

'Dinner down there tonight, then, lads,' somebody exulted, and Nick recognized Ieuan's Welsh voice. The sound of it brought the valleys back with sudden, utter incongruity, more vividly real than the machine-gun post in the midst of a Spanish battlefield, and Nick had to shake his head to dispel the lovely distraction of it.

Captain Berman reached them, scrambling sideways behind the shelter of the ridge. They were the forward line of the battalion now, holding it against the returned fire from the village. They were to hold the post, and the ridge, and go on holding it until they were ordered to advance.

Berman bent briefly over the captured gun. It mocked them with its muteness, oiled and gleaming and unusable.

'We'll get our own gunners up here with the Cauchot,' he promised them. 'Hold on till then.' The commander was off, then, moving on along the line with the new orders. Looking beyond the post on either side and seeing the sparse shelter for the brown and khaki figures crouched against the hillside, Nick was glad of the relative security of the gun post.

'Smoke?' someone asked in his ear, and Nick nodded. He cupped his hands around the flame and drew once, deeply, on his cigarette.

The first shell fell short. It sent up a big, threatening scud of earth into the air and a rain of stones fell around the gun post, rattling like hail. The second shell hit the edge of the hollow. Nick fell forward on his face and earth and debris clattered on his helmet. He had bitten the cigarette in two, and his mouth was full of dirt and shreds of tobacco. When he looked up again, cautiously lifting his face an inch or two, he saw another helmet. It had slipped forwards to cover the face underneath it, like Peter Jaspert's hat in Cable Street. Nick knew that he didn't want to see what was underneath the helmet, because of the angle it was dangling at. It hung away from the body: a piece of shrapnel had almost severed it at the neck.

The silence was smoky, stinking of burned earth and bodies that had been blown open and excrement. It seemed infinite, but a second later it was torn apart again. Bullets pinged over the scorched earth and sizzled in the air above their helmets.

'The bastards have brought up a machine-gun as well,' a voice said.

A third shell exploded on the ridge away to their right and Nick made himself look up, and look around the gun post. There had been fifteen men in it a moment ago. There were twelve living now, and one of those had fallen back against the earth bank with a face as grey as the stones and one hand held pressed against his chest. The fingers were squeezed tightly together, but the blood pumped through them. Another man had shrapnel splinters in his arm, and a third had a deep cut in his forehead.

Nine able-bodied men left to hold the post, and no officer or NCO amongst them. They were all novices like Nick himself, gaping at the hole that the shell had blown in their meagre defences.

Nick straightened himself up.

'You, and you,' he said abruptly to the two lightly injured men. 'Can you get him back down the hill to the trees? The stretcher-bearers should have come that far forward by now.'

They stared and then nodded. The man with the cut face heaved the wounded bundle on to his back and blundered out of the post, with the third man struggling to lift the trailing legs. They heard the first moan of pain back in the shelter, and then the three of them were off down the hill. 'Put the bodies in the corner,' Nick ordered the others. He saw that Welsh Ieuan was amongst the living, but nobody else he knew. 'And then let's start shifting the stones from that side and building them up on this.' They heaved the stones across the hollow and built them up with scattered earth to make a barrier.

When they had finished they crowded forward and peered through the crevices at the battle. Through the drifting smoke to the left it seemed that two or three of the French companies were advancing under covering fire from the trees, but the shelling from Lopera was still so heavy that nothing seemed to move anywhere in the distorted landscape.

The nine men left alive in the machine-gun post crouched in their positions and waited.

An hour ticked by, and then another, the longest that Nick had ever known. The shelling stopped briefly and then started again with fresh vigour. The morning dragged on into afternoon, and the shelling and machine-gun fire boomed on around them.

'Where's Berman gone?' one of the men muttered, 'and where's our sodding machine-gun, or a belt of ammo?'

The MG34 was a constant reminder as they waited, stiff and cold and increasingly afraid, that they could do nothing. Nick could see from their vantage point that the attack on Lopera had failed before it had got properly under way. The village was too well defended, and the Brigade was short of almost everything it needed to make a success of the undertaking.

The barrage of firing seemed to intensify, and Nick guessed it was a big burst before the Fascists counter-attacked. As if to confirm his worst fears the great grey shape of a tank rolled out of the village and then stopped with the long snout of its gun turned to the ridge.

Ieuan the miner came and sat against the barrier beside Nick.

'Attacking that tank with these, is it?' he asked, shaking his rifle. 'What do they want, martyrs?'

'I don't know,' Nick answered. It was three o'clock, and in less than two hours the winter dark would close round them again. If the attack didn't come before then, or if they could somehow hold it off, then perhaps reinforcements and artillery could be brought up overnight to plug the gaping holes in the thin line. But even as the faint hope flickered inside him, he saw the first wave of Fascist troops break cover from the village. They came running under the protection of covering fire, jumping and bounding over the shell craters towards them.

Nick swung his rifle up and trained it through the chink in the stone barricade. 'Fire,' he ordered. 'Keep firing.'

It took so long to reload between shots. There would be a little crackle of fire from the gun post and then nothing, and the grey tunics scrambled up the hill towards them. But with the next volley two or three of them pitched forward, and with the next the advance lost its momentum and the line wavered fitfully.

'That's it!' Nick shouted his encouragement. 'Come on, keep on!'

The check was short-lived. Another wave of troops followed the first, running past those who had fallen. They were firing back towards the hilltop, advancing steadily. One of Nick's men staggered back from the stone barricade, shot in the face.

'We can't hold out here.' Nick didn't know whether it was his own voice or someone else's, but he knew with simple certainty that the Fascists would sweep up the hill and shoot them where they crouched amongst the stones. Then he saw a man striding steadily along the ridge in all the deadly rain of bullets. He was waving a hand-gun, a little revolver, and the men looked up at him and then began to move. He reached the gun post and Nick saw that it was Captain Berman.

'Retreat by sections,' he called. His voice was calm and authoritative. 'Retreat, but keep firing.' They stumbled thankfully out of the shelter and began their retreat, leaving the useless machine-gun behind them. They ran at first, the wounded as well, but Berman's order came after them. 'Keep firing!'

They had reached level ground when they saw the first Fascist helmets outlined against the fading light. Nick dropped to his knees and fired his single shot, and then turned to run again.

He never knew how he crossed the open ground to the precious safety of the trees. The earth all around him kicked up under the bullets and so many men fell that it seemed he was the only one left running. 'Retreat by sections. Keep firing,' he shouted inside his head, but he couldn't have stopped to reload and fire again.

At last, gasping and almost sobbing, he was in amongst the trees. To his surprise he realized that there were other men still unhurt because they blundered in beside him and fell against the old grey tree-trunks.

The Fascist advance had stopped. They had re-taken the ridge, and that was enough for tonight. A soldier beside Nick took off his helmet and swung it despairingly. 'That's it, then,' he said quietly. 'They'll come down here first light tomorrow and finish us off.'

It was getting dark. The olive groves were a jumble of men searching for their sections, and of wounded limping or being carried back to the first-aid posts in the trenches. They were shocked by the rout, and exhausted; nobody spoke beyond asking one another hopelessly which way to go. Nick had no idea which way to move, so he stood still and waited. With the rapid darkness the cold returned, jabbing its icy fingers into his bones. His blanket was back in the trenches with the rest of his kit and he was shivering uncontrollably without his greatcoat. He began to walk to try to warm himself, without stopping to work out in which direction the remains of his company might be.

War, Nick thought as he walked through the army hastily reassembling itself. *Retreat by sections*. He felt breathless with anger that he knew was futile, but he was angry just the same with the random unfairness of it. He was angry for Ken Coate, and for the man who had had his head blown off in the gun post. He was angry at the lack of weapons and organization, and at the blithe, dogmatic assumption that courage was a match for machine-guns properly supplied with ammunition, tanks, and wave upon wave of enemy troops. He was angrier than he had ever been in his life before, and he knew after a single day, after the grimness and horror and death that he had seen, that war disgusted him. After a day's fighting and scores of violent, humiliating deaths, a single ridge had been gained and lost again. The futility and waste of it all was a sickening mockery.

In his blind anger Nick walked too far. The line petered out in a square trench manned by sentries who challenged him suspiciously at rifle-point. A French captain came up and directed him back along the lines to No. 1 Company. He found them at the same point in the trench system from where they had attacked this morning, a lifetime ago. Nick's blanket was there, and his mess kit. The cooks had prepared a sort of meal, and he took the mug of steaming mess back to his section. They greeted him, but their voices were subdued and their faces tense.

Jake Silverman was sitting smoking with his back against a tree.

He smiled a greeting at Nick. 'Good work,' he said, as if it was the end of a meeting at Appleyard Street. *Is it*? Nick wanted to say. *Is killing good work*? Beside them the machine-gunners attached to the section were morosely finishing their meal. Ieuan came up and flopped down on his blanket next to Nick. Leaning forward to the gunners he asked, 'Where were you lads, then? Berman said he was sending you up to our post. There was a gun up there, boy, you should have seen it. Beautiful as a woman, wasn't it, Nick?'

The gunners scowled. 'It was wonderful down here. A real picnic. Berman ordered us up, then a French major came and sent us round to follow the advance on the village. The advance failed and we were ordered to hold a hollow and cover the retreat. We got the gun set up and the old bitch jammed on the first belt. We had to pull her back here, getting our balls shot off from both sides, and strip her down again. Maybe she'll fire a few rounds tomorrow, if the Fascists give us time.'

At midnight, Captain Berman assembled the remains of No. 1

Company. Their orders were to take three hours' sleep, and then to move up to relieve the sentries at the edge of the olive groves. There would be a fresh attack, a new attempt on the ridge and Lopera lying beyond it, at dawn.

The men listened in low-spirited silence. Berman did everything he could to rally them, praising their performance of the day and promising them success tomorrow. The captain's clipped, upper-class voice reminded Nick of Richard Lovell's, and of Amy and her world, and his heart and body ached so that he hunched over in the blanket to contain the longing for her.

Under the grey smudge of dawn on December 29th the 14th International Brigade stood ready again.

It was a terrible day. The Fascists advanced to meet them, superior in numbers and firing power. The Brigade was driven back through the olive groves, beyond them to the hasty trenches, and back up against the ruined village itself. Ieuan was killed, and Ifor his lifelong friend from Nantlas. One of Ken Coate's Liverpudlian navvies had his leg blown off and was dragged back into the first-aid post screaming in agony. A shell landed squarely in the hollow occupied by the gunners of Nick's section and blew them and their recalcitrant Cauchot to fragments.

Nick and the others fought like machines amongst the twisted trees that they had learned to hate, and where the twisted bodies of friends and enemies lay piled on top of one another.

At last, like a curtain abruptly falling across a flickering screen to hide its horrible images, the darkness came.

The company marshalled itself in the sad remains of the village. Nick understood now how the rubble had come, and he wondered where the people had gone who had once lived here. It would have been a community a little like Nantlas, he thought, preoccupied with its own struggle for survival and uninterested in anything much beyond its narrow boundaries. And now it had become a battleground, and a graveyard for men who had never heard of it, nor known the names of any of the farmers and peasants who had lived there.

They waited a long time for orders, or even news, held captive in a heavy, despairing silence. Their depletion was painfully evident. Of the one hundred and forty-five men who had marched proudly out of Madrigueras, there were eighty-seven left waiting for Henry Berman when he came back from Brigade Headquarters.

The captain looked at the filthy, unshaven, exhausted faces drawn up in front of him. 'I'm sorry,' he said simply. 'The action has failed. The Fascists have taken Porcuna and the surrounding land, and the hydroelectric station at El Campo, and have driven our lines back east of here almost as far as Andújar. The support for another push forward from here will not be forthcoming from the Madrid front, because the command is expecting a further attack on the Madrid-Corunna road, which must be defended at all costs. I wish I could bring you better news after the last two days.'

Nick stared blankly ahead of him. He was too tired and defeated now even to feel angry, although he understood clearly enough what Henry Berman was telling them. The 14th Brigade would receive no reinforcements. They had lost their ground, the vital strongholds had fallen to the enemy in the mismanaged and undernourished battle, and the front was effectively being abandoned. Ieuan and Ifor, Ken and all the others had achieved less than nothing by their deaths.

Behind him, he heard someone murmur bitterly, *'No pasarán.'*

The International Brigades' base hospital for the Madrid front was at Colmenar Viejo, north of the city. Before July 1936 it had been a huge luxury hotel, and even now traces of the incongruous grandeur remained. There were wine-red velvet curtains, looped and tasselled with gold, in the cream and gilt-plaster dining-room where the international medical staffs ate in comradely confusion alongside Spanish porters, orderlies and ward maids. In her room, a basement cubicle near the hotel boiler-room shared with Jennie the radiographer, Amy found a stained towel, still thick and fluffy despite being used as a dressing, with the words 'Hotel Paradiso' embroidered in silk. The hospital was universally known amongst the foreign medical teams as Paradise Hotel, but in this paradise the ballroom and the banqueting hall had been turned into wards, the operating theatre occupied the grand first-floor suite, and the foyer was packed with a ragged, desperate, shifting population of Spanish people who came to the hospital in search of food, treatment, and news of friends and relatives.

Once they were united with their Bedford lorries, Amy and her group had driven non-stop through Spain to Colmenar. They had passed columns of troops, and streams of refugees, almost all of whom were women and children. When they stopped the lorries the children flocked around them and begged for bread, unshakable in their insistence until planes raked over the horizon and combed the grey-white sky overhead like black teeth. They were German planes, Junkers 52s, and the children and their mothers scattered with the speed born of practice. Amy stared upwards in a moment of frozen fear, but the bombers had passed harmlessly on towards their targets in Madrid.

When they reached the hospital the Austrian director came out to welcome them cordially. Within an hour, Amy and the other nurses were at work on the wards. The lorries were sent on to the forward medical posts with experienced personnel and heaps of supplies, and the newcomers were left to a period of acclimatization at Paradise Hotel.

Amy was sorry at first to be separated, even temporarily, from the big Bedfords and the immediate chance of helping in the front lines. The day changed her reaction into gratitude for a gentler initiation into war. A nurse took the newcomers through Paradise Hotel, and it was disturbing enough to see what was there, even in the clinically familiar surroundings of the improvised wards. Amy tried and failed to imagine the scenes that could have produced such wounds. They heard that the wounded poured in, sometimes more than a hundred a day, in ambulance shuttles that worked to and fro between the hospital trains. The men were filthy: if their wounds had been attended to at all it was with the roughest dressings, and even the dressings were alive with lice. They were all nationalities: French and German, Canadian and Polish and Belgian and British, but they were all the same. They were long-haired, bearded and exhausted, and they had often been fighting for weeks on end without a break.

Amy began her work in the reception ward with Victor and one of the other doctors. A seemingly endless line of shuffling and limping injured waited, and Spanish porters brought up the stretchers of those more seriously hurt.

Amy looked at the first stretcher. There was a big man lying on it. His head was swathed in bandages made from a torn sheet, his face was hidden but tufts of black hair showed through the dressing. She walked towards him as if she was struggling through quicksand. It was Nick lying there. She knew it was Nick. Her hands were shaking as she unpicked the blood-caked bandages and gently peeled them back. She looked down into the man's face. Part of his jaw had been blown away, leaving a black, pulpy mess spiked with shattered bone and teeth. The soldier's eyes were dark brown, staring unseeingly up at her. He was dead. He wasn't Nick.

Amy covered up the ruined face again. She was giddy, and choked with nausea. Victor looked curiously at her, and then he took her arm.

'Are you all right? Did seeing that upset you?'

Amy knew what he was thinking. She wasn't much of a nurse if she couldn't bear to look death in the face. 'It isn't that. I . . . thought he was someone I knew.'

'Would you like to sit down for a while?'

Amy looked at the rows of stretchers, the lines of men with their resigned faces and their dirty bandages. Any one of them could be Nick, waiting to be cared for. And if they weren't Nick, they were still waiting. She would do what she had come to do, somehow.

'No,' she told Victor, 'I don't want to sit down.' She walked away from him and knelt beside the next stretcher in the line. This soldier was a young boy, she saw, as she lifted back his blanket. His legs were badly damaged but he was conscious, watching her, and his smooth face was as pretty as a girl's.

'*Bonjour,*' the boy said, smiling at her.

'*Bonjour,*' Amy smiled back, and began to work.

At first, every time an ambulance truck arrived to discharge its load, Amy was afraid. She would watch the stretchers coming in, and for every broken body that wasn't Nick's she offered a silent prayer of thanks. Sometimes, amongst the walking wounded she would glimpse a man of Nick's height and colouring. Her heart would jump with mad relief, and she would think, Thank God. He's here, and he's not badly hurt. But it never was Nick, and the relief would ebb away and leave fear in its place again.

Then the days began to pass, Paradise Hotel and its concerns closed around her, and Amy stopped looking for his face amongst the exhausted, shadowed faces that passed through the reception ward. She began to believe that Nick would survive, and every day that came and went without him being brought in to her strengthened her conviction. It strengthened her endurance too. She found that she could work long hours, for as long as there

547

were still soldiers waiting to be taken in, washed and cleaned, dressed and stitched, and sent on to the theatres or on up to the recovery wards.

The work was urgent and endless in the first days of January 1937.

The Nationalists had mounted an attack on the road and rail links west of Madrid and the Republican forces and International Brigades were fighting desperately to hold their ground amongst the summer villas of the Madrid aristocracy. There was almost no news at Paradise Hotel, but wounded soldiers brought in their piecemeal stories of rebel gains. By the end of the first week of January it seemed certain that Franco's forces held the Corunna road from the last houses of Madrid to the little town of Las Rozas. From the terrible casualties Amy was sure that the battle must be lost, but as the men streamed in they insisted that enemy losses were just as bad.

It was on a night when Amy had worked for a continuous stretch of sixteen hours, when the reception ward looked like a battlefield itself and men lay waiting for attention in every corner, that the bombing started. She had heard the planes droning over day and night since she had crossed the border in the Bedford trucks, but they had always been high in the sky, little black darts in the daytime and invisible skeins of noise at night. They had always been heading elsewhere, but tonight, as she held up a morphia syringe to check the volume of its contents, they were much lower. The noise was so loud that it made her look up, as if she could see them through the roof of the Paradise Hotel. A second later there was a *thud, thud,* and the glass jars and metal instruments in the reception ward clinked, the walls shook and even the floor trembled like in an earthquake. The silence afterwards was terrible, as if just beyond it a whole community was screaming.

Victor had looked up too, and their eyes met.

The French doctor working with them didn't stop for a second, but he swore, just two or three words, not sparing the energy for anything more.

'We thought they had stopped trying for us, or the supply depot that is here too. Now we will have civilians, women and children, as well as soldiers. After the last bombing we gave our own beds, all the staff, and slept under the tables in the *salle à manger.*'

'Give that injection, Nurse, please,' Victor said brusquely. Amy bent to her work again, knowing that his harshness was an attempt to impose order in the chaos and bloodshed that frightened them both.

It happened that the bombs fell on the outskirts of Colmenar that night, and there were few casualties. But the planes came back the next night, and the French doctor was proved right.

Amy was preparing for bed in the basement cubicle when she heard them. The bombers were flying so low that the throb of their engines drummed around her even there. She stood for a frozen moment, looking at Jennie in her exhausted sleep in the other bed. Then the explosion came, a terrible, shuddering crash that almost knocked her sideways. For a moment Amy was sure that the hospital itself had been hit. But yet the ceiling over her head didn't fall in, and here was the silence that was worse than the noise that preceded it. Amy pulled on her overall again and ran to the door. Glancing back over her shoulder, she saw that Jennie hadn't even stirred. Amy left her where she was and ran up the stairs to the lobby. Doctors and nurses began to appear, some still in their overalls and others in night-clothes, grey-faced with sleep. The hospital director was already there, and he sent them to their places.

Amy went to the reception ward and waited. The bomb had hit a house crowded with refugees, many of them children. It was the worst night's work Amy had ever had to do.

They were brought in in ones and twos, their faces blank with terror. Their injuries seemed worse than those of the fighting men because the thin limbs were so small, the little bodies fragile and helpless.

The medical staff worked all night in silence. Amy tried to turn herself into an automaton that cleaned and dressed the wounds, held the small, bony hands, and thought of nothing. The hospital was fully equipped with supplies sent out from England, and everything was done that could be done. For those beyond help, they could at least relieve pain.

At six o'clock in the morning a little boy of five or six died in Amy's arms. She laid him down on a stretcher in the corner and covered him with a towel. Then she went out into the corridor and rested her forehead against the wall. Tears blurred her eyes and she pressed her face harder to the cool stone to force them back again. Beside her, a voice was saying, 'Señora? Señora?' A hand pulled at her sleeve.

Tears were suddenly a luxury that Amy longed for, a luxury that would soothe her and empty some of the pity and pain, and bring the oblivion of exhausted sleep. But she lifted her head, blinking them back so that they burned her eye-sockets, and looked to see who wanted her. It was a Spanish woman in a widow's black dress and black shawl. She had a brown, seamed face and could have been any age from forty to seventy.

'Señora,' she said imploringly, pulling harder at Amy's sleeve. 'Come. Si?'

Amy followed, steeling herself for what she might see, for what could conceivably be worse than the night that had just passed?

The widow led her to a bench in the corner of the teeming lobby. There was a young girl lying on it, a shapeless bundle under a coarse blanket. Her feet stuck out at one end, in the espadrilles that all the working people wore. Her face at the other end looked very young. Her eyes were wide with fear and drops of sweat shone on her forehead.

Amy knelt down beside her. 'What's the matter? Are you hurt?'

The widow delivered a torrent of excited Spanish, and Amy looked from the young face to the old one, and back again.

'Do you know any English?' she asked the girl. Amy didn't know if she even heard. Her head rolled from side to side and her eyes stared unseeingly. Suddenly she opened her mouth and screamed, and then just as suddenly the scream was bitten off. Her eyes closed and she went limp.

Amy glanced round desperately. She was afraid the girl was very ill. A little crowd of people gathered round to watch.

'Don't any of you speak any English?' Amy shouted. 'I have to know what's happened to her before we can help her.'

A boy of about fifteen stepped forward. 'Leetle,' he volunteered.

'Tell him,' Amy gestured at the widow.

There was another torrent of words and to Amy's amazement the boy smiled.

'What is it?' she demanded.

'Have baby,' the boy told her.

Amy dived forward and pulled the blanket back. The girl's

eyes opened again and she screamed. Her knees came up to the mound of her stomach. She was in labour. The last stage of it, Amy judged.

She almost laughed aloud. Birth, renewal of any sort, seemed so far away from this place of premature endings that the possibility of it had never crossed her mind. There was no time to dwell on her own obtuseness. Amy shouted for a porter and a stretcher and between them they hauled the girl through into the ward. She pulled a rough screen across the end of the stretcher to divide life from death, and knelt to reassure the girl.

The mother stopped screaming and bit deep into the back of her hand. Amy looked round to see if there was anything within reach that she could give to ease the pain, saw that Victor and the other doctors were all busy, and when she turned back to her patient the baby's head was born. Fear in the mother's face had turned into amazement.

'Rest,' Amy ordered, forgetting that her words meant nothing to the girl. 'When the next pain comes, you push.'

A moment later, there was the little, scarlet, folded body. It was a girl. Amy lifted her and her eyes opened, round and black as coal. The baby blinked and Amy heard the first suck of air into the tiny lungs, and then a thin, ragged cry. The baby was strong and healthy.

Any had seen enough births at the Royal Lambeth to be calm now. She clamped the cord and cut it, and wrapped the little creature in a clean towel. She stared around and saw an empty box that had held sterile dressings pushed away against the wall. She put the baby in it and turned to the mother. Her face had gone completely white. Amy looked down between her legs and saw that there was blood. Too much blood, and the pool was widening and spreading every second. It dripped through the canvas stretcher and on to the floor.

'Victor!' Amy shouted. 'Victor, come quickly.'

Victor left his patient and came round the end of the screen. The blood was trickling across the floor now, long predatory fingers of it reaching out to them. The doctor plunged past to the stretcher.

'Transfusion,' he ordered. Amy ran to get the things he needed, and two nurses went to help Victor. Amy opened the door of the cold store where the supplies of preserved blood were kept. She saw that the night's work had left it practically bare. Without wasting time she checked what there was and gave it to Victor's helpers. Then she flew across the corridor to the X-ray room. Jennie was sitting wearily on the high bed.

'We need some of your blood,' Amy demanded. 'There's a girl in there. She's haemorrhaging, post-partum, and there's nothing in the bank . . .'

'*Post-partum*?' Jennie shook her head, stupid with tiredness. 'How can there be a baby in this place?'

Amy brought the needles and the tubes and sterile bottles. Jennie had shaken herself fully awake and they helped one another, fumbling in their haste so blood sprang in dark spots under the needle prick. Amy thought of the other blood, spreading and seeping, and she shivered, hunching over her bottle and willing her own blood to pump faster into it.

'Is the baby alive?' Jennie asked.

'Yes.'

'Gérard wants a baby, a son. It was almost the first thing he told me. When this is all over and I go back to Paris, we're going to have a son together.'

'I'm glad,' Amy said automatically. In her heart she wondered if anyone should choose to have a baby in a world where it might be bombed, or maimed, or orphaned by war.

When the bottles were full she carried them back to the reception ward, cradling the warmth of them in the crook of her arm. She was reaching to push the door open when it swung open for her. Victor stood there. His white overall was soaked in blood, his trouser legs and his shoes were dark with it, and his arms almost to the shoulders.

'It's no good,' he said stiffly. 'She's gone.'

'No.' Amy shook her head, willing a single survival out of the terrible night. 'She can't have died.'

Victor stood aside, and she looked past him. There was blood everywhere. Towels soaked in it were kicked into a heap in the middle of the smeared floor. The mother lay motionless on her scarlet stretcher, covered by a hospital blanket.

Amy shook her head again. Victor gently took the bottles from her, more blood where there was already too much. Then he put his arms around her and they held on to each other, unable to speak.

The night's work was over.

Victor's saturnine face was creased, and he was too weary even

552

to move. He held on to Amy for support. Looking at him, she saw the beginning of defeat, and found her own strength to beat it back. She put her hands on his arms in the blood-wet overall.

'You should sleep now,' she told him. 'Eat some breakfast first, and then sleep.'

Victor looked vaguely around the room, and then his glance settled on the dressings box where the baby was asleep. To Amy's surprise he suddenly smiled.

'We should look after the baby. There's something we have to do before anything else. We have to go out and buy a feeding bottle.'

'All right.' She smiled soothingly back at him. 'We'll go out to buy a bottle and some milk powder, and some breakfast.'

But even before that, she would have to find the widow, mother or grandmother or whatever she was, and break the news to her. Victor went to change his clothes. Heavy-heartedly Amy fetched one of the Spanish student interpreters and set off in search. It wasn't difficult. The hotel lobby was almost deserted again, and the old woman was sitting alone in a corner. The student knelt down in front of her and spoke gently.

Amy had expected wails of grief, tears, imprecations. But the old woman simply nodded her black-shawled head. She answered the student's questions and then stood up, pulling her black clothes around her. Then she shuffled slowly away, her feet in the espadrilles that reminded Amy of the dead girl's.

The student explained. The old woman had never seen the girl before tonight. She had met her huddled in the street outside after the bombing, and had brought her in. She understood that the girl was a refugee, from Huesca in the north, and her husband had been taken by the rebels in July.

'She say sorry,' the interpreter told Amy, 'but she have many mouths in her own house and little bread.'

The baby was alone, then. If her father had been taken by the rebels he had almost certainly been shot long ago.

'Thank you,' Amy said mechanically to the interpreter.

She went quickly back to the reception ward. Greta, the senior sister from Guy's, had washed the tiny baby and dressed her in a child's vest that enveloped the downy, scarlet arms and legs. When Amy picked her up the heavy head lolled, and she cradled it in her cupped hand. Her hair was fine and very black, and the minute fists clenched as if to defend herself. While Amy held her two porters came in and stood awkwardly looking around the room in their shapeless overalls. Amy understood that they had come to take the baby's mother.

Wordlessly she pointed, and then turned away, sheltering the little thing in the hollow of her shoulder so that she should not see. The head close to Amy's mouth was warm and smelt of new-born life.

'I'm sorry,' she whispered. 'Somehow we'll take care of you. Somehow, we will.'

Victor was waiting for her, with Jennie beside him. Amy put the baby back in her box crib, and saw that she went to sleep at once. Leaving the baby in the care of Greta, the three of them went down the steps of Paradise Hotel and into the daylight. The cold, lemon sharpness of it made them blink. The narrow streets radiated away from the hospital and without looking at one another for confirmation they took the one that led in the opposite direction from the rubble of bombed houses. Amy felt raw, as if just for a little while she couldn't bear to see or hear any more suffering.

The streets were busy with people, shouting, queuing for bread, trundling piles of belongings and furniture on carts as the shaky houses were evacuated. A group of homeless were cooking in a sheltered corner, sending up smells of oil and garlic in the mist-damp air. A gang of children scuffled in front of them as soon as they turned the corner from the hospital.

'*Poco pan? Poco pan?*' they demanded, holding out their hands. Amy turned away, thinking of the little boy of the same age who had died in her arms this morning, and wondering if the bombers would come back tonight for these. She couldn't look into their vivid, hungry, living faces. They had no bread, but Victor gave them money and they ran away clutching the coins, hooting with pleasure.

Between the three of them they tried every shop in Colmenar. At last, in a dingy general store that smelt of rancid fish, they found what they were looking for. A curved glass feeding bottle and a sealed tin of powdered milk.

Jennie held them up, smiling triumphantly. 'There. She'll be all right now. Between us, we can take care of her.'

And in that moment, looking at Jennie's lovely face and smile, Amy did believe that the doctors and nurses of Paradise Hotel, working all the hours as they were amongst the wounded and dying, could be all the friends and family that the orphaned baby needed.

On their way back to the hospital they passed a café. Surprisingly it was open, and the proprietor was whistling as he swept the cobbles in front of his door. 'Let's stop for breakfast,' Victor said. They went in and sat down. In their tiredness, with the possession of the baby and the means of looking after her secure in Jennie's bag, they were suddenly hysterically cheerful.

'A drink,' Victor called. 'We must have a drink. And food for a feast.'

There was only vinegary red wine and fried eggs. They ate and drank, laughing at nothing, and then Victor raised his glass.

'To the little one.'

'To the little one,' they echoed, and drank the toast.

'She needs a name,' Jennie said. 'Let's call her Paloma.'

The dove, the white dove of peace.

'To Paloma,' said Amy. The wine had gone to her head and she felt warm, and confident without reason in the squalid café in the rubble-filled streets of Colmenar.

Paloma became a symbol of hope at Paradise Hotel. She thrived, growing round and rosy. One of the recuperating soldiers who had been a tailor padded her box with lint and muslin and stitched a petticoat into quilting for a lining. The nurses unravelled old woollens and knitted her clothes and blankets, and took it in turns to carry her crib into their rooms with them at night. Another soldier made a little wheeled cart and she was pushed out in it to lie in the fresh air of the hotel garden. She was welcome in any of the wards, and if the nurses were too busy the patients looked after her, the fathers of families joking amongst themselves about having gone to war to escape crying babies.

To Amy, she became the second source of strength. Nick never appeared amongst the files of wounded, and she went on believing that he was safe and well. Paloma grew, lying in the cocoon of covers in her box. And while Nick and the baby were still alive, the daily round of death and pain was within her capability to bear, even to see reason in.

Amy fell easily into the habit of going to find Paloma every evening in her hour's break from the reception ward. She would strip off her stained overalls and almost run through the wards.

Then, when she found her, she would hold her and talk to her, watching how the baby's eyes followed the movements of her head and hands, listening to the little contented sounds that followed her bottle. Amy began to believe that the baby recognized her, even looked for her, and greeted her when she came with the little, jerky movements of her arms and legs.

January passed, and the first week of February, without any word from Nick. Amy had no idea whether he had even received her last letter, posted at Victoria on Christmas Eve, telling him that she too was headed for Spain. She had made arrangements with Moira O'Hara to forward his letters at once with the rest of her mail, but nothing reached her in the efficient Spanish Medical Aid deliveries. Yet she believed that he was safe, and every day that passed and didn't bring him as a casualty into Paradise Hotel deepened her conviction.

Paloma started to smile. Amy was the only person who believed it, but she watched the solemnity of the tiny face dissolving into flickering animation, and she knew that it was the beginning.

On the same day, Jennie came down into their basement cubicle with news.

'I heard from the director. The teams who have been at the front with the Bedfords are coming in for rest and leave. We're going out to replace them.'

Amy sat still for a moment. Wartime security meant that they didn't even know for sure where the mobile hospitals were, or even which front they were working behind. They had seen the results of their work, standing out amongst the other almost untreated injured, after the battle for Las Rozas on the Corunna road. But the battle had ended in stalemate and there was only a trickle of men coming in from there now.

So they might be sent anywhere, Amy thought.

She leaned forward to look into Paloma's crib, suddenly fearful, turning back the covers so that they could see the puckered, sleeping face with its tiny curve of black eyelashes.

'Who will take care of her?'

Because of what had happened on the night of her birth, Victor and Jennie, with Amy herself, had been her closest guardians. Now they would all have to go and leave her behind.

Watching the baby's sleeping face Amy felt as if up until this minute she had been suppressing and almost denying the surge of her love for Paloma, just because she knew that she must leave her soon. Now that the time had really come the love swelled up to overwhelm her. Amy reached down and lifted the baby up, wrapping her arms around her and cradling the tiny black head against the warmth of her heart.

Jennie looked at her, her face full of concern and sympathy.

'We'll ask Elena,' Amy decided.

Elena had been the hotel housekeeper in the Paradiso days. She was a widow with grown-up children, a native of Colmenar, and the hotel had been her home. Now, in wartime, she ruled over the hospital supplies of linen and domestic materials, and organized an ill-assorted staff of cleaners from her little flat on the top floor. Like everyone else at Paradise Hotel she knew and enjoyed Paloma.

'All the nurses will help you,' Amy begged her. 'But I must leave her with one person who will be finally responsible. Please, Elena.'

Elena had been reluctant at first, but then she had held Paloma in her arms and her face had softened as she rocked her, and Amy knew that she was safe.

'For one month I will take charge, then. Until you come back from the front line.'

'Thank you,' Amy breathed. 'Thank you.'

After that, she vowed, she would find some way of making a proper provision for her baby.

Jennie and Amy took the baby back down to their basement room.

'Don't worry,' Jennie told her. 'Paloma will be safe with Elena until we come back. Everyone here knows her and loves her.'

Amy smoothed the covers over the little body. 'Please God,' she whispered.

Two days later the nurses and doctors were loaded into a bus and driven away from Paradise Hotel. They waved from the smeared window at a little group of patients and staff who had gathered to see them off. But it was Paloma to whom Amy was waving.

Silently, she promised her, 'I'll come back.'

557

21

━━━━━━━⌇━━━━━━━

The big Bedford lorries with their camouflage stripes loomed out of the mist, standing four-square in the centre of a jumble of tents and ruined houses. The ground around the front-line hospital had been churned into mud by the field ambulances, and then frozen into deep ruts. The bus bumped and lurched to a standstill and Amy and the others climbed out. The cold stung their cheeks, and their breath hung in the air in smoky clouds.

There was silence for a moment, and then they heard a dull, booming sound that the fog seemed to offer up and then swallow into its depths again. It stopped for a few seconds and then restarted, so loud and close now that the little group jerked round, looking instinctively for cover.

A bearded man wearing a khaki greatcoat with a beret pulled low over his forehead climbed down from one of the Bedfords and ran towards them over the rutted, iron-hard ground. He was smiling.

'Welcome to the Jarama,' he said.

Amy paused, looking at him, surprised. He was English, and his voice was the very sound of home. But there was something more in it too, something that stirred a memory from long ago. Then she looked at his face again and saw that it was completely unfamiliar. The memory slipped away again.

'Don't worry,' the Englishman said to her, and she knew that he was mistaking her hesitation for anxiety. 'Those are our batteries returning fire. The main front is about three kilometres from here now.' He glanced up at the grey sky that seemed to hang a foot or two over their heads. 'It's the bombers that trouble us mostly. But they don't perform in this fog.'

'There were bombs at Colmenar,' Amy said quietly.

The man was looking into her face now, and she saw his eyes

558

in his weatherbeaten face over the thick, fair beard.

The rest of the team was pushing forward over the rutted ground. The man held out his hand to them. 'And welcome to the field hospital. My name is Charles.'

Amy had heard of this Charles. He was the chief surgeon for the post, and a brilliant doctor. It was Charles who was pioneering the treatment of wounds in the field by bringing the surgical teams to the soldiers, instead of the other way round. It was difficult and dangerous work. Amy had understood that in theory, and now she heard the sound of the batteries thundering in the fog the reality was clear and frightening. But they had already seen the results of Charles's techniques back at Colmenar. His Englishness was a surprise, because the stories that circulated about him always gave his name the French pronunciation.

Victor took Charles's hand and shook it enthusiastically.

'Did you get breakfast in Madrid?' Charles asked. 'Not much, eh? Come over to the dining-room and we'll see what there is.' He led the way, striding over the ridges and talking cheerfully. They passed a canvas-covered area with rows of low folding beds. Two or three of the beds were occupied, and a couple of nurses were working there.

'Our *salle de triage*,' Charles explained. 'We shall have a quiet day here because of the fog, as well.' The *salle de triage* was the reception ward, where the drivers and stretcher-bearers unloaded the wounded. Past the *salle de triage* there was a house, no more than a shepherd's cottage, of which the upper storey had been blown away, leaving the roof beams pointing up into the blank sky like black fingers. The ground-floor room was warm, and smelt of cooking. Someone was working at a portable stove in the corner, and a group of men and women were sitting around a table.

'Relief detachment for you!' called Charles. One of the men at the table banged a tin plate, and there was a ragged cheer. Amy looked, and saw that the doctors and drivers were haggard beneath their beards, and the nurses were white-faced, with dark rings under their eyes.

'Did you bring insulin?' someone demanded, and Victor answered reassuringly, 'We brought a busload of supplies. Everything possible.'

There was another cheer, louder now. The hospital post staff looked at them with the beginnings of eagerness, as if the truth was at last sinking in, the truth that they were to be relieved.

One of the nurses moved her chair to make a space. 'Come and sit down. Have some food. This is the best place to be.' She gestured around the crumbling, damp cottage. 'There's even a sort of cellar for bombardments.'

The newcomers found places around the table. The Belgian cook brought them plates of food, fried pork and tomatoes and *udijas blancas*, the ubiquitous haricot beans. They ate, and listened to the matter-of-fact recounting of the forward post's daily work.

They learned that the Nationalists had launched the attack on February 6th. Their objective was to capture the highway that led from Madrid south-east to Valencia. They had pushed across the Jarama valley and forced the river itself. They were fighting for the heights now, and beyond the eastern heights lay the road to Valencia. The Republican battalions had been reorganized on the high ground, and were defending it to the last. Casualties on both sides had been high, Charles told them.

'But they won't take the road. Never.' Charles grinned cheerfully. 'All we have to do is sit here safe on the other side of it.'

Across the table, somebody laughed.

The post accepted all the casualties that were brought in, Republicans or wounded prisoners. Emergency treatment and operations were performed wherever possible, and those who were too seriously hurt or who needed more elaborate facilities were sent on down the line to Socorro Rojo hospitals.

'Simple,' said Charles. 'Now, the rest of you. I suppose the bus will take you out once it's unloaded. Are you ready to go?' They stood up, looking around the little room as if now the time had come at last they were reluctant to leave. They went stooping out into the raw mist again to collect up their belongings. One of the nurses ducked away into the canvas shelter of the *salle de triage* to say goodbye to a soldier.

'*Auf wiedersehn,*' she called past the canvas flap as she came out again. She rubbed her face crossly, as if she had been crying and was ashamed of the weakness. The old bus was revving its engine, ready to start the jolting journey back towards Madrid. The departing team went up the steps one by one. Amy stood on the crest of a frozen ridge of ground, and felt the cold striking up through the soles of her shoes. She lifted her hand in a wave that was also a salute of acknowledgement. The bus trundled away, and left them behind. Only Charles was staying. The surgeon had hardly left his forward post since December and the battles along the Corunna road.

Amy was aware of him standing at her shoulder watching the bus as it dwindled into the distance along the track. She tried again, fruitlessly, to catch at the vague recollection. Behind them the guns boomed, throwing their noise into the shifting air. Charles sighed.

'It's quiet,' he said. 'I think it's easier sometimes to be busy. That way there isn't time to think.'

Amy listened to the guns, feeling the echo of them pounding inside her head, mixing fear with determination. She was afraid, more afraid now than she had been since crossing into Spain, but she was more than ever determined to do what was asked of her. She thought with longing of Paloma, imagining her lying in her box in the corner of Elena's overcrowded room. Then she thought of Nick. Perhaps he was here, somewhere, in what had been the quiet river valley of the Jarama.

'Come on,' Charles said. 'Have a glass of brandy with me. If the fog lifts there won't be time at the cocktail hour.'

The word cocktail, with its pure incongruity, brought the image of Adeline, and the whiff of scent, and the soft brush of furs. Amy found herself laughing. 'All right,' she agreed, and she walked with Charles through the cold and the pounding noise to the warmth of the dining-room.

He poured Spanish brandy into two cups, and handed her one. They lifted them in a wordless toast, and drank. The brandy bit hearteningly in Amy's throat. She took off her nurse's dark cap and shook out her hair. The colour was like a flare in the dim room.

Looking at it, the surgeon said, 'You're Amy Lovell, aren't you?'

She stared at him for a second. And then she remembered. 'Charles Carew.'

She saw the blue sitting-room at Ebury Street, full of flowers, and Isabel and Peter Jaspert giving their first party. There had been a shy young doctor to partner her, seemingly so young that he had reminded her of her childhood dancing partners. She had felt at ease with him, and she had even imagined briefly that his company might, in a brotherly way, take the place of Richard's.

561

But Charles Carew had been too busy with his work, Amy remembered. Almost six years ago.

'I would have known you anywhere,' he told her. 'You haven't changed at all.'

'You have.' Amy looked at him across the table, still not quite believing it.

There was almost nothing to relate this big, quietly confident surgeon to the boy she remembered. Yet she had heard his voice and noticed his blue, direct gaze, and had made the connection at last.

Charles smiled faintly, acknowledging her surprise. 'A lot of things have happened since then.'

'Did you go back to India?' Amy was fitting the pieces together now. He had told her that he had grown up there, and was going back to practise surgery.

'Yes. As soon as I had my surgical qualification. I stayed for nearly five years. And then last summer, I came here. What about you?'

Amy told him briefly about the Royal Lambeth and her years of nursing, and Charles Carew in his turn described his work in a hospital for untouchables in Calcutta. She understood then that no one would look youthful once they had lived through the experiences that Charles had had. He seemed older than his thirty years now, and there was an edge of weariness that his brisk cheerfulness didn't quite disguise. They didn't talk about why either of them had come to Spain. Amy had already discovered that there were different shades of belief amongst the voluntary medical workers, and it was accepted that simply to be there and do the work was enough of a declaration.

Amy and Charles Carew were still talking when an orderly pushed aside the strip of sacking that hung over the doorway and peered inside.

'Charles! Ambulance come.'

Charles stood up at once, rubbing his beard with the back of his hand.

'To work,' he said, and Amy realized that the confidence of his manner came from knowing that he was in the right place. 'You too,' he commanded, and she scrambled after him. An ambulance truck was swaying through the mud and mist towards them, and Charles was already running towards the Bedford trucks.

Amy was touched by a cold finger of the old fear, the fear that had followed her from Colmenar, that it would be Nick in the ambulance. She shook it off and walked as resolutely as she could towards the canvas shelters.

Nick and his section were barely three kilometres away, crouching in a ditch while the shells from an enemy 155-millimetre battery whistled monotonously overhead. Nick was cold, and hungry, and dirty. Three days ago his entire company had been despatched for warm showers in a mobile shower-truck behind the lines. On the side of the cumbersome vehicle was the inscription 'In gratitude from the metal workers of Paris to the fighters for Spanish democracy'. Nick had stared at the words, harsh laughter that surprised him with its violence rising in his throat at the idea of *democracy*. What he had experienced and seen behind the lines in the weeks since December was a long way from democracy.

But he had taken the shower just the same, and it had been the first time in a month that the whole of him had been clean. Now, as he waited in the ditch, he felt the familiar itching under the waistband of his corduroy breeches that meant the lice were alive again. At first the fact of being lousy had revolted him. He had searched for the eggs in his clothing, and he had cracked the fat bodies viciously between his fingernails. But the battle was a hopeless one, living as they were without water for washing, sleeping in their clothes wherever they happened to stop at night, and the men had given up one by one. Now they were all crawling with vermin. Nick reached up and scratched his ragged black beard, and then his uncut hair. Looking bitterly at the other men squatting around him, he thought that they looked like gaunt, ragged scarecrows in their tattered uniforms. He knew that he looked just the same himself.

Nick was an NCO now, in charge of a group of ten men. Number 1 Company had been moved up with the rest of the Brigade from Andújar to the Madrid front, and there they had fought in the battle for Las Rozas. In one day, in the confusion of another fog when Russian tanks had swung malevolently to and fro crushing their own infantry under their tracks, they had lost eleven men. Of the five Nantlas miners who had travelled to Spain in December, three were dead. Nick and Will Goff were the survivors, with Jake Silverman and forty or so of the original company. Even Henry Berman was gone, not killed but promoted to leadership of a battalion. Now the remnants of the company, made up to strength with new recruits, had been moved on again to the Jarama.

They had been in action since the end of December, without a break, without food or shelter at night.

Nick scratched and shivered in his ditch, peering ahead into the fog until his eyes stung. He was waiting for a runner from company command, bringing him the order to lead his men up to relieve a sentry post at the head of the mountain pass above them. He knew that he would do what was expected of him when the time came, but he knew equally that he didn't care whether their mission was successful or not. Nick had seen too many men die in the battles for ground that brought no advantage even when it was won. But the pity for the loss and suffering was easier to bear than the bitterness he felt corroding his spirit. The bitterness was all at the Communists. Their ideals had driven him for almost the whole of his adult life, but now he believed that the ideals were being betrayed in the struggle for power. It was the struggle for control at any cost, oblivious of individual suffering or even of the destruction of Spain. The political commissars went stalking through the ranks of the Brigades, mouthing the Moscow directives, alert for spies, deserters, vacillation or denial of any sort. Nick watched them, and he hated them.

Jake Silverman belonged with them. Even when the company was pulled back a little way to rest in a village or a ruined church, and the cooks came round to distribute food to the men squatting in grateful groups, Nick and Jake never spoke now. Beyond the essentials of leading and caring for his little group, Nick spoke to hardly anyone except Will Goff. Too many people were already gone, a pitiful procession of them after Ken Coate. In his tiredness Nick believed that to establish a friendship was a guarantee of losing it by a bullet or a shell. He knew with perfect certainty too that his own bullet would come. He was too weary to be afraid, but he thought constantly of Mari and Dickon and Amy, and what his death would mean to them. At night he dreamed of Nantlas, vivid, detailed dreams that left him aching with longing for home.

The runner came. He materialized out of the noisy gloom, sliding in the mud down into the ditch. Nick took the instruction mechanically and motioned his troop around him. They were to use the fog cover to work their way upwards to the sentry post and find out why the occupants were failing to return enemy fire. They were to relieve the post and hold the pass against the expected Nationalist attack. It was narrow, and a dozen men should be an adequate strength.

Until the fog lifts and the planes come over, Nick thought, and the enemy can see our exposed rear.

'Right then,' he said aloud. 'Follow me up the track.'

In silence they left the shelter of the ditch and ran forward, bent almost double, rifles at their sides like a grotesque fifth limb. The ground rose steeply, thin grass and rocks shiny with moisture. The shepherds' track led over the heights to the river on the other side. Nick's hearing was blunted by the constant assault of the artillery but he heard the sharp panting of the other men as they scrabbled upwards, and his own breath began to come in painful, ragged gasps. Their heavy packs seemed to pull them backwards. Nick rubbed the sweat out of his eyes and started to swear under his breath, rhythmic imprecations to himself to keep moving, climbing, lifting one boot after the other in the shower of loose pebbles sliding away beneath them.

He had no idea how long it took, but he was almost sobbing for breath and a pain knotted agonisingly in his side when the sentry post suddenly loomed above them. It was no more than a heap of stones, loosely piled up like a cairn.

At the same moment Nick saw that there was a dead man sprawled face-up across the track in front of it. He lifted his arm in warning and the men bumped to a standstill behind him. They listened, straining desperately for the tiniest sound, but there was nothing. The wind was strong up here and it screamed across the rocks, silencing even the boom of the guns.

Nick waited a moment longer, then he led the way forward, picking his way through the loose stones to the foot of the cairn. Then he hauled himself up to peer over the top.

The men inside were all dead.

The sentries had been knifed, some in the back, and were slumped forward where they had stood. Those who had had time in the shock of the enemy attack to put up a fight had been overpowered, and their throats had been cut.

One by one Nick's men climbed up beside him.

'Christ Jesus,' somebody murmured as he looked down into the carnage.

'It's them Moors,' another man whispered. 'Those bastard Moroccans.'

The detachments of Moorish troops amongst the Nationalist forces were superstitiously feared as being half-mad, and wholly deadly.

Nick cocked his head, trying to listen for a clue through the shrilling wind, which unnerved him. At this height they were enveloped in low cloud, not fog at all, and the wind could clear it at any moment.

'Be quiet,' he ordered sharply. He was thinking, trying to make sense of what had happened. The Nationalists, Moroccans or otherwise, had somehow worked their way up to the post and overpowered it. They hadn't stopped to take any prisoners. It seemed impossible that they would have taken the post and then retreated again. They would surely have *advanced*. The Nationalists must have taken the whole ridge, unnoticed in the fog and thick cloud, and pushed on down the other side. By some miracle, Nick and his men coming upwards had slipped through the line. Perhaps they had taken the wrong path. It had seemed steep even for a sheep track.

'What does it mean?' one of the group asked. He was a slow-witted boy of nineteen, a new recruit from England. The other men teased him, calling him 'Brains'. Brains was staring down into the sentry post and his face was greenish and sweaty. Nick looked quickly around, expecting to see an enemy battalion stepping rank on rank out of the swirling greyness. They would be invisible, grey against grey rock and cloud, until they were on top of them. But there was nothing. Nothing, yet, except that they were cut off behind enemy lines, perched here in the pass with the dead men tumbled all around them.

'It means the line has moved forward overnight. It must be behind us now.'

Fear came back to Nick as he spoke, liquefying in his belly. And with the fear came renewed longing to survive. The desire for survival told him that there was nothing to be gained by staying in isolation at the post. They couldn't hold off a frontal attack for long without support from behind, and a dozen of them could hardly mount a noticeable rearguard attack except as a kind of suicide bid. Their only hope was to try and slip back the way they had come. Nick glanced around at the haggard faces watching him. He had led them into this, and he would lead them out again.

'Back the same way,' he ordered. 'Quick. And quiet.'

They slid and stumbled back to their path. Sure enough it led off a wider one, forming a lopsided, upside-down Y. Digging his heels in to stop himself falling, his head and neck stiff with the effort of listening, Nick guided them down. Downwards and downwards. The blessed cloud still clung around them, and suddenly the wind dropped. In the same instant there was a sound. It was quick footsteps, men moving fast in heavy boots. They all heard it and stopped like shadows. Through the mist ahead of them four soldiers crossed their path at right angles. It was an enemy messenger party, taking orders along the line. The greyness swallowed them up again, deadening the sound of their passage.

They were creeping through the enemy lines.

The enemy had moved forward and down, and must be digging themselves in now ready for the attack. Nick and his men began to move again, every clink of stone and metal freezing them.

They had lost their bearings, and had no idea how close or how far away they were from their own lines. The path led on downwards. They wanted to run, their legs quivered with the urge, but they dared not risk the noise it would make. Nick was watching the ground ahead of his toecaps, alert for any stone that might roll and betray them, when he saw that the light reflected back out of the wetness had changed. His head jerked up and he saw that the greyness overhead was thinning. Light shone through it, a pretty, ethereal green light. He felt warmth on his shoulders, too. The mid-morning sun was breaking up the mist. It was dispersing into wisps. The grass at their feet shone with colour again.

'Quickly,' he hissed. He stared back over his shoulder, pushing the men past him one by one. Then the dreaded thing happened. Someone shouted at them, unintelligible Spanish words, but clearly a challenge or a demand for a password. Nick glanced wildly around. None of them knew enough Spanish even to attempt the feeblest bluff.

'Run!' he shouted. The Nationalist forward line was now a little behind them and to their left, dug hastily into the shelter of a low stone wall. Nick remembered passing the wall on the way up. Their own advanced trenches were no more than three or four hundred yards away.

They were running, into the strengthening sunlight. At their backs there was a moment of stunned silence and then a shouted command, and a crackle of fire. Bullets pinged around them as they blundered on. The sun seemed blindingly bright now. Nick was staggering, winded, knowing that they were chasing him across the open land. He even looked round, wasting a precious second, and the bullets pinged faster. The ground behind him was empty. He lurched and almost shouted. Of course the enemy wouldn't chase them straight into the opposing trenches. They would stay under cover, and pick them off instead.

Crack. The bullet came so close that he thought for an instant it had hit him. But he was still running. Ahead of him he saw their own lines, even glimpsed the astonished face of a sentry.

'Hold your fire,' he was yelling. 'Don't fire.'

They heard him, but a second too late. There was a volley of shots.

Through the mist vanishing like steam the Republican sentries had seen the new enemy position because Nick and his men were drawing their fire. Now the little troop was strung out like competitors in some macabre race as they struggled for home. They were under fire from both sides.

'Hold your fire.' Nick's voice was hoarse with screaming.

Ahead of him, ten yards ahead, Will Goff seemed to be flung sideways into the air. His legs were still running as he fell. The rest of the group were almost home as Nick reached him. Will rolled, his hands to his thigh. Nick dropped to his side and Will looked up at him.

'My leg.'

Nick stared round desperately, knowing that he couldn't drag him alone. Then, miraculously, one of the sentries' heads bobbed up in the trench. A second later he was over the lip of it and weaving towards them. The firing from the home trenches had stopped, but the bullets crackled vigorously from behind. The sentry flung himself across the last few yards and flattened himself beside them. Nick saw that he was grinning fiercely under his tin helmet, thrilled by his own daring. Afterwards, Nick remembered thinking *you must be new to this war*.

Their rescuer was Polish and spoke no English. He gestured

568

to Nick to take one side of Will, and he would hoist the other. His clenched fists rotated in the air, signalling *run*.

Nick nodded, summoning his breath.

Will lay on his side between them, doubled over his injured leg. He rolled his head and peered up at them. 'I can hop,' he said.

They raised themselves to a crouching position and Will put his arms over their shoulders.

'Now,' Nick said.

They straightened up and ran for their lives, carrying Will Goff between them. The bullets sang after them. Fifty yards, twenty. Ten yards, and they were still running. Nick's heart pounded in his chest like a sledge-hammer.

They reached the rough parapet and hauled Will up it. Then they fell down the other side into the trench with Will on top of them.

They were safe. The soldiers on the Nationalist side must have been new recruits, or poorly trained in handling their weapons. They had been a simple enough target as they ran across the wet, steaming space.

Nick lay on his back for a few seconds, staring at the duck egg blue sky. The mist had vanished in the handful of interminable minutes since they had stumbled into the messenger party. The Poles of the sentry's section crowded around them now, grinning and gesticulating. They clapped their friend on the back and shook hands with Nick. They propped Will up against the trench wall and gave him a sip of lemonade, then put a lighted cigarette between his lips. Will was white with shock but he was grinning too. He didn't feel the pain of the bullet in his leg yet, and he was elated with the miracle of their escape.

Alone amongst the euphoria Nick stared silently at the mound of the parapet. He was shaking violently, and he felt sick in the pit of his stomach. They had come back, eleven of them, with only Will wounded. There wasn't any chance that luck like that would descend on them again.

The Poles had shouted for a stretcher, and the bearers came running down the communication trench now. Will lay back against the earthworks and smoked his cigarette while they cut his breeches away. Shock was an anaesthetic. He even looked interestedly at the burnt flesh and the blood oozing steadily out of the ragged pocket of flesh. They dabbed the hole with antiseptic and dressed it, and then lifted Will on to the stretcher to carry him back. Nick shook hands again with the voluble Poles and followed the bearers away.

The ambulance truck waited at the rear. Nick watched them load the stretcher into it. Will's face was beginning to turn grey with pain. Nick went up and touched his shoulder as the driver scrambled into his cab.

'You'll be all right now, Will. Perfect. Hospital, and then home to Nantlas.'

Will tried to smile. 'I'll be back with you in a month, when they've patched me up.'

Nick heard his exhausted relief at knowing he wouldn't have to fight today, or tomorrow, or the day after that. 'I don't think so, somehow.'

'Well then.' Will put his hand out to Nick's, and held it clasped for a moment. 'You'll just have to win the war on your own, Nick boy.'

The ambulance engine roared into life. Nick stepped out of the back.

'I'll try,' he said. The truck was moving away, and he shouted, 'When you get home, tell Mari . . .'

He saw Will nod his head, understanding what he would want Mari to know, and then close his eyes.

Nick turned and began to walk back down the trench to find the rest of his section. In the blue overhead a silver triangle of Fascist fighter planes, the first of the day, raked downwards. A second later the double-barrelled anti-aircraft guns opened up close at hand, and white puffs of smoke burst in the sky. He quickened his step instinctively, crouching a little, and then almost laughed. Nick knew that his luck was exhausted, along with his belief that this war was anything to do with democracy, and his will to go on fighting it. When the bullet came, as he knew it would, there would be no avoiding it. And then it would be over.

The quiet interval in the field hospital was short-lived. In the fog the enemy shelling had been blind, but the big German batteries were still devastatingly accurate. Then the fog lifted and the battle raged in the clear blue sky as well as down the hostile slopes of the Jarama mountains. Over the battlefield itself the

Russian Chatos supported the Republicans' increasingly grim defence of the ground, but the enemy pressed inexorably forward. Beyond the battlefield the sky was alive with streams of enemy bombers, protected by sharp new Messerschmitt fighters. The casualties poured into the canvas shelter of the *salle de triage*.

Charles with Victor as his lieutenant worked indefatigably. They performed dozens of operations in the Bedford theatre. The two theatre sisters had only time to scrub down after one operation before the next patient was wheeled in, on and on through the day and into the night.

Amy worked in the *salle de triage* with the orthopaedic doctor and a second nurse. They treated the minor injuries, giving anti-tetanus and anti-gangrene injections, stitching and dressing and sending the men on to hospital. They gave blood transfusions to the badly injured and left them to wait for the surgeons' decision on whether to operate at once, or send them on to the base hospitals at Colmenar or Tarragona. To those beyond help they could only offer comfort, and the relief of some of the pain.

When the bombers came they were almost always too busy to take cover. They helped the walking wounded down into the cellar of the house, and then went on with what they were doing amidst the explosions and the pounding of the anti-aircraft. Amy was too busy to think, or to be afraid.

The quieter times were almost worse, as Charles had said. Then, sometimes, she would go down with Jennie and the other nurses to the shelter. In the light of a lantern she would sit and read the copy of *Barchester Towers* that Tony Hardy had given her on Victoria Station. It was strange to recall the green and grey peace of an English cathedral close in this world of blood and smoke and thundering noise, but Tony had been right. It brought back the memory of safety.

But mostly the doctors and nurses were at work, and the stretchers came in to them in a seemingly endless line. The medical staff snatched their food and a few hours of rest when they could, lying down in turn in the bunks in the narrow space over the Bedford cabs.

At the beginning of this numbing series of days a prisoner was brought in to the canvas shelter. He was a Moor, dark-skinned and uncomprehending. A bullet was embedded in a grotesque welling in his neck. He stared wildly around, muttering the same words over and over again. One of his bearers explained that he was begging to be shot.

'Shot?'

'They think we stab all our prisoners to death. In his religion, he can't go to heaven unless he dies by a bullet.'

Amy bent over him. She saw that his lips were cracked and his mouth was crusted inside. She filled a cup of water and held it to his mouth. He stared longingly at it, but turned his head away.

From the next stretcher in the line, a voice said, 'He thinks you've poisoned it, see? Drink some yourself, to show him.'

The sound of the voice pulled at something inside Amy, so strongly that she almost turned. But the Moor's longing eyes held hers, and she sipped at the water in the cup, then held it out to him again. He tasted it unbelievingly, and then gulped at it. Amy did look round now. The voice, so familiar in its cadences, belonged to a little dark-haired man, a stranger.

'There you are, see?' he said to the prisoner. 'Not so terrible, are we? Not like you, with your knives in the dark.'

Amy was drawn to the stretcher. She looked down and saw that the hand on the edge of the blanket was calloused, and scarred blue-black.

'Where do you come from?'

The little man grinned, showing white teeth. 'South Wales, isn't it? The Rhondda. And now I'm going back there.'

Amy felt her cheeks burning. 'Whereabouts in the Rhondda?'

The Welshman was looking curiously at her now. 'Nantlas, the place calls itself.'

At the word, the memories swooped around her. The hollow-faced crowds waiting for the King. Mari's brown-painted door. The bare, cold mountain where Nick and she had clung together in the dark and talked about Spain.

'Know it, do you?'

'Yes, I know Nantlas.'

She went back to the Moor then, sponging his face and moistening his lips with a wet cloth. Only when he had been taken away to wait for Charles did she come back to the miner. He must be a miner: the scars on his hands were just the same as Nick's. Her voice was thick in her throat as she asked him the question.

'Do you know Nick Penry?'

The man stared harder now, and then his suspicious face broke into a wide smile. 'I know Nick Penry, right enough.'

The busy shelter seemed to go quiet for a long second. The man was still grinning. He wouldn't smile, would he, if Nick . . . She blocked the thought.

'He pulled me in, Nick did. Him and a Polish sentry who came out to us. Saved my life, between them.' Will Goff looked past the pretty nurse. 'Now I think of it, I never thanked him. I wish I'd done that.'

Amy came closer, bending down so that she could ask him in a low voice, 'Is he safe?'

Will looked at her again. 'As safe as either of us. Least, he was this morning when he came back with me to the ambulance.'

The happiness surged up and pounded in Amy like a tidal wave. Until this little man had put it to rest, she didn't know the dread had lurked in her subconscious like a dragon. Nick was alive, unhurt, and he was close. She wanted to run to the door flap and stare through the smoke towards him. She wanted to call out over the barrage, *Nick*. Instead she sank down until she was on a level with the miner. She was smiling foolishly, and there were tears in her eyes.

'Are you a friend of Nick's?' he asked her.

'Yes. That's what I am. A friend of his. I'm so glad, so glad he's alive.'

Then she put her arms around the man's neck and kissed him. Her tears made his face wet.

'*Duw*,' he said wonderingly. 'Perhaps it's my lucky day after all. Worth getting shot in the leg, this is.'

'Sir.'

Nick stood upright. He had been brought to the battalion commander himself to give an account of what had happened at the sentry post in the pass.

'Very well, Penry. Will you explain why you disobeyed your explicit orders?'

Nick stiffened. The commander was an English gentleman Communist, the kind that he had come to think of as the deadliest. He prickled with anger, but he made himself explain the débâcle and their miraculous escape.

The officer listened, poker-faced. At the end, he said, 'But your orders were to hold the post, were they not?'

'Yes.'

'Then why did you abandon it?'

Nick looked straight into the man's pale blue eyes. Very slowly, patiently, he explained, 'I saw no point in staying there, that's why, sir. What could we have achieved, eleven of us? At best we might have killed a dozen Fascists. We were cut off behind enemy lines. Without means of communication.'

'I congratulate you on your astute reading of the position. But you had your orders, Penry.' Outside the shack that served as battalion headquarters a motorcycle despatch rider slewed to a stop in the mud. A moment later the messenger stood in the doorway. The officer took the despatch and glanced at it, frowning. Nick stood stiffly, trying to isolate the knot of rage inside him. 'You will appreciate,' the officer continued, 'that discipline and the unquestioning execution of orders are of tantamount importance if this war is to be won. Deviation – *any* deviation – is a serious offence. As a Party member, comrade, you should be fully aware of that.'

And this was a volunteer army, Nick thought bitterly, brought together by fine ideals that were nothing more or less than a belief in democracy. That democracy was denied every day. They were all conscripts now, even Spain itself, pawns in a struggle for power that was controlled far away in Moscow.

Nick went on looking at the wintry commandant, and in that moment he knew as certainly as he knew that he was a pacifist that he was no longer a Party member.

Suddenly, instead of the officer's face he saw Amy's. Amy as she used to look when she argued with him, her eyes shining and her mouth slightly open. Amy had always believed in individuals before issues, and he had contradicted her. He wouldn't do that now. After Amy's, Nick saw the faces of the men he had led up to the pass, Will and the rest of them. They were alive now because he had brought them back. Nick was proud of that, whatever this man said. He noticed that his blue eyes were slightly prominent, as Peter Jaspert's had been. *I despise extremists*, Nick thought. The anger twisted like nausea inside him.

'Your dereliction calls for the severest disciplinary measures,' the officer was saying.

Nick waited.

Abruptly, the commandant said, 'Two men deserted their posts this morning. They will be executed at noon. You will make up the firing party, with five others.'

Nick turned sharply but two soldiers, guards, were already coming up behind him.

'You will wait with the rest of the firing party until noon. You are dismissed, comrade.'

The guards stepped up and locked Nick's arms behind him. As they took him away he twisted his head around and shouted. 'You're no more my comrade than bloody Franco is.'

The officer didn't move.

There was another shack twenty yards away, with a high, barred window. Another group of guards stood with their rifles at the ready outside the door. It was unlocked, and Nick was bundled inside.

Five men sat on the bare earth floor. They were prisoners, locked up for drunkenness or other disciplinary offences. And now they were sitting in silence, waiting to be marched out to shoot their fellows.

'Who are these deserters?' Nick demanded. 'Why are they to be shot?'

None of the other prisoners was British but one, a Dutchman, spoke a little broken English. No one knew whether they were truly deserters or not, he explained. They had left their posts and been caught by an enemy surprise attack. They had lain low, and then as soon as the attack was over they had been arrested by one of their own patrols. They were to be shot as an example, the Dutchman said. After that, they sat in silence again. Nick looked up at the single high window, but it was securely barred. The guards clustered on the other side of the door. He knew that if he tried to escape he would almost certainly be shot himself.

The minutes ticked by. He listened to the artillery ahead, trying to gauge whether they were still being forced back towards the Valencia road.

At fifteen minutes to noon the door was unbolted. The six prisoners were waved out at gunpoint and marched away into a belt of woodland. The groups of soldiers they passed, cooking, or cleaning their weapons, or lounging and smoking, stared at them as they passed, sympathy mingling with revulsion. Everyone knew what was to be done.

In a little clearing in the trees, the Political Commissar was waiting for them with a group of other Party officials and their orderlies. He faced the firing party and harangued them in French which was then translated roughly into English and German.

Nick heard that the deserters were Fascists and spies. The death penalty must be imposed to show that the Party would never tolerate betrayal. The firing party were to do their duty as comrades, and as fellow fighters for the cause.

So it had become his duty, Nick thought, to murder men who had been given no trial, nor even the opportunity to speak for themselves.

It was very quiet in the wood. The air smelt sweetly of resin and the smoke from the soldiers' fires. From somewhere in the branches overhead Nick heard a bird singing. The liquid curls of sound dropped down into the shivering, waiting quiet like honey into acid. One of the orderlies came round with the weapons. They were new Russian rifles, better than anything that Nick had seen in the front line. Each of the six men was given his loaded gun.

At noon exactly, feet came tramping over the crackling twigs. There were six guards in a tight phalanx around the two deserters. The prisoners' hands were tied behind their backs and they were hobbled together with a rope, like animals. Nick saw that one of them had white-blond hair. At the sight of the six men waiting for them with their rifles, the other man began screaming. '*Nein, nein.*'

The orderlies stepped forward and blindfolded them. The blond one stood patiently, his head tilted a little to one side, as if he was listening to something. Perhaps it was the birdsong, Nick thought. When the blindfold blotted out his light, the other went quiet too.

They stood against a tree, roped together, like sacrifices. Over their heads the bird went on singing, singing.

At a signal from the Commissar the firing party raised their rifles. Nick's felt heavy, a terrible weight. He took aim along the barrel. The blood pounded in his ears.

Fire!

Nick closed his eyes. As he squeezed the trigger he felt his shoulder muscles pulling the barrel wide.

After the volley he opened his eyes again. There was blood on the tree bark. One of the men lay still, but the blond one was moving. His arms and legs jerked convulsively. The Commissar's orderly strode over to him. He took out a Mauser pistol, held it to his head and pulled the trigger. The jerking movement stopped at once.

Nick lowered his rifle. For a moment he stood holding it b

the barrel, butt down. Then as if it might contaminate him he let it fall sideways into the bed of pine needles. Without looking backwards he walked away into the trees. When he was out of sight he stood behind a smooth, brown bole, leaned his forehead against the cold bark, and was sick.

The bird had stopped singing.

All Nick could hear now was the ceaseless cacophony of the guns.

Jennie peered round the flap that closed the *sulle de triage*. Amy was standing between two beds, washing her hands in the tin basin that stood on the corner of her dressings trolley.

'I need more plates,' Jennie called cheerfully to her. 'I'm going to walk down to the radio post and ask them to send a message through to Colmenar.'

Amy nodded, barely looking up. A soldier had just been brought in with a gaping stomach wound and he needed an immediate blood transfusion. Her attention was focused on that, and she didn't see Jennie go.

In the days since the new medical team had arrived in the Jarama the Nationalists had pressed farther and farther forwards. Now they were within firing distance of the Valencia road at Vaciamadrid, and they held a big bite of new ground that bulged in a threatening sweep south of Madrid itself.

The front line had come closer and closer, but the field hospital post had stayed put.

'It saves ambulance fuel and driving time, after all,' Charles had joked.

A radio communications post serving the rear of the 15th International Brigade was established a few hundred yards forward of them. The operators, mostly Americans, had developed the habit of coming back in their off-duty hours to visit the nurses in the field hospital. There had been two or three evenings of talk, singing and drinking in the shepherd's hut dining-room of the hospital.

The beautiful, lively Jennie was a particular favourite, although she was unswervingly faithful to her Gérard in Paris. Now Amy understood, without thinking about it, that Jennie had gone up to see their friends and to ask them to radio through for supplies of X-ray plates.

She was absorbed in what she was doing, and she had no idea how much time went by. She didn't even hear the planes, or if she did the sound was so familiar that she didn't register it. The first thing she was aware of was machine-gun fire.

Tacktacktack. Tacktacktacktack.

The planes were flying very low. The first one screamed over the hospital itself, followed two seconds later by another. The rattle of machine-gun fire came again. Amy heard confused shouting beyond the canvas walls, shouting and pounding feet. Two more planes, even lower by the sound of it, tore overhead. Amy stopped to reassure her patient who had flung up one arm to cover his face. Then she went to the door to see what was happening.

Six enemy fighter planes had broken through the aerial defences over the battlefield. They were machine-gunning the Republican support lines as they came over. Anti-aircraft fire boomed too late, sending white puffs of smoke into the air. Amy looked away as the planes banked steeply and swept victoriously away to the south-west.

Something had happened on the track that led from the hospital post forward to the communications trench. A huddle of white and khaki was lying on the rutted ground, and another flag of white showed in the ditch to one side.

As if in a nightmare, Amy's limbs wouldn't move. Charles was already running with Victor behind him. She started forward, stumbling, words caught in her throat. She saw Charles reach the bundle on the track, kneel down to it. Then Victor was at his side, kneeling too. They blocked whatever it was from Amy's sight. She began to run then, jarring her ankles on the uneven ground. Charles and Victor weren't moving. Why didn't they move? Why didn't they do something?

Jennie was already dead when they reached her. Her lovely face was white but unmarked except for a fleck of blood at the corner of her mouth. There was a line of bullet holes all down her back, black-edged pocks in the khaki coat that she had put on top of her overall. The gunner in the rebel plane had machine-gunned her in the back.

Amy looked up from her still face into the grey-white sky. Jennie wouldn't go back to Paris now. She wouldn't carry Gérard's son for him.

She had always worn pretty, impractical high-heeled shoe

One of them had come off and lay at an angle in the dirt. Amy picked it up and fitted it back on to her friend's warm foot.

Greta had gone with Jennie down to the radio post. She had liked one of the Americans, a big man who wore a leather and sheepskin flying coat. Greta wasn't dead. She had just managed to reach the ditch, and she was lying there hurt, bleeding and crying.

The stretcher-bearers who had come in with the latest ambulance ran forward, and then stopped. More than anyone else the bearers saw all the horrors of battle, and most of them had developed a protective, caustic shell. But even the tough Cockney whom Amy had never heard at a loss for an obscenity looked away from Jennie and Greta, wordless.

'Carry them in,' Charles ordered.

Greta was taken away for the doctors to attend to her. Jennie was carried into the little canvas enclosure that they used as a hospital mortuary. The bearers put her down beside the dead soldiers in their stiff, anonymous shrouds and turned silently away.

Amy knelt beside her for a moment. She closed the wide eyes and bent to kiss Jennie's forehead. Then she took the limp hand and held it. Amy was thinking of Helen Pearce, and Gerald, and Peter Jaspert, Paloma's mother and the little boy who had died on the night Paloma was born. She thought of the baby, and prayed that she was safe at Colmenar. She thought of the soldiers who were dying now in the valley of the Jarama, and then of Nick.

Amy didn't cry.

She heard a movement behind her and looked round. Charles was standing in the entrance waiting for her.

'We shall have to operate on Greta to remove a bullet,' he said. 'Will you scrub up ready to assist?'

She frowned, trying to disentangle the words. At last, she said helplessly, 'I can't. I don't know how. I'm not a theatre sister . . .'

Charles stepped forward and grasped her arm. 'You are now,' he said. And then, more warmly, 'Please. I need you to help me.'

Amy bent her head. 'I'm coming.'

They covered Jennie with a sheet and left her in the mortuary.

The day after the execution Nick and his section went with the rest of the Brigade into a counter-attack. It was the divisional commander's intention to force the Nationalist front back from the road. The attack was poorly prepared and there was no artillery support for the infantry. There were Russian tanks ploughing forward in uncoordinated waves, but the Chatos fighters had lost air control to Italian planes that flashed in white arcs across the sky. Nick glanced up from the mud once. The sky looked clean and clear, the only thing in the world that was. He was dirty like everything else. Filth was matted in his beard and hair and his clothes hung in tatters under his greatcoat. He felt the lice crawling over his skin, and the cold damp soaking through his boots. His fingers were stiff around the stock of his rifle, and pain gnawed at his chest and stomach. Nick didn't know if he was ill, or if the pain was the weight of sick disgust at yesterday. He did know that he would never forget what had happened amongst the trees of the little wood. He had eaten nothing since it had happened. Breakfast before the attack had been bread and an oily mess of cold fried vegetables. Nick hadn't touched it.

Their orders for the day were simple. They were to move up and reinforce the first wave of infantry that had taken a section of the enemy line. Their objective across the battlefield was marked by an oak tree, blackened down one side and with broken branches over the ruined ground.

The first wave had gone up. There had been no message or signal from them. There were no field glasses, and so no chance of seeing what had happened. Nick crouched with his men. They looked a desperate and dangerous company except for their hollow, vagrants' eyes. No one spoke because there was nothing to say.

'It's time to go,' he said at last. In the beginning – how long ago? – he would have added *Good luck,* but of course the luck was all used up now. They began to move, stiffly, out of the trench and across the whistling space towards the oak tree. The little group pressed forward together at first, then they were strung out in a wavering line. The distance was infinite. One step after another, up and down through the shell holes. There was a dead man here, another up ahead. Nick was only dimly conscious of the advance on either side of their section. There were too few of them, the line already stretched taut to breaking-point.

The noise was overpowering. The big Nationalist batteries up ahead. *We'll never take them,* Nick thought, but his feet went on, doggedly, one step after another. Yards ahead of him there was a yellow flash of light and an explosion that almost knocked him sideways. A plume of earth and stones shot into the air, and looking curiously up at it, Nick saw the remote glitter of planes dancing in the sky. He was faintly surprised to find that he was still walking on instead of lying with his face pressed in the mud. The shell's flash had burnt itself into his eyes. He shook his head from side to side to try and quench the blaze inside his head. He couldn't tell now whether the flames were real or his own optical bombardment.

On and on. He could see nothing through the flashes and drifting smoke but the black outline of the oak tree. Was it close now? Suddenly it was towering over him. There were bullets with their deadly, familiar hum, now, as well as the shelling.

The front trench, beyond the oak tree. How many yards? Without thought of what he would do when he reached it, Nick edged slowly forward. He held his rifle stiffly out in front of him like a bayonet. He felt that he was completely alone. A glance to either side revealed nothing, no one, through the smoke. Light still burned confusingly in the centre of wherever he looked.

Flatter ground, here. Another corpse. Then, suddenly, an enemy trench. Empty, so they must have retreated. Ha, that was good. Or no, not empty. The bodies of the first wave of infantry, toppled over on top of one another. Nothing else. The enemy had shot them as they attacked, then, and retreated with the rest as prisoners. Where to? How far? Nick turned his head a little, blinking through the glare of light, and saw Jake Silverman. He was sitting propped up, looking just as he did when he sat back against a tree behind the lines to smoke, or read, or lecture. Just the same, except that his stomach was torn out. Jake was dead. He had gone up to attack in the first wave.

Nick stood still, stupidly wagging his head from side to side. If he could make the light stop burning and the scream stop ringing in his ears, perhaps the vision of Jake would vanish too. He closed his eyes and held the palms of his hands up against his temples. But when he looked again Jake was still there. After a moment, Nick went to him. He sat down beside him, shoulder to shoulder, and tried to see the sky through the black, stinking smoke. It was difficult to believe that Jake wouldn't turn his head and grin at him again, jutting his bushy black beard. In a second

581

he would dip his hand into his pocket and give Nick a cigarette, and they would argue all over again.

Except for the red and greasy grey mess in his lap. He forced his eyes downwards to look at it. Nick understood that Jake *was* dead. He sat companionably beside him for a little while longer, and then he turned and touched his shoulder lightly as if he was a friend making ready to go somewhere, just for an hour. They hadn't been friends for a long time but just then, in the enemy trench under a pall of smoke, they were reconciled.

Then Nick stood up and looked around. He was lost. The only point of reference was the oak tree. He walked back to it and reached out to touch the black core with his fingertips.

A shell exploded in the branches.

Nick was blown backwards into the dark.

This is what it's like to die, then. Noise, and a howling wind.

It was February 27th, 1937. Nick had been fighting for Spain for exactly two months.

How many more? Amy asked herself hopelessly.

After Greta there had been four, five other operations. She scrubbed down after each one and made ready for the next. There was a big assault in progress. From the volume of casualties they guessed that it was almost certainly doomed to failure.

Charles and Victor and the anaesthetist worked doggedly, patient with Amy's fumbling with the unfamiliar instruments.

In the *salle de triage* the two other doctors worked through the chaos with just two nurses and some dressers pulled back from the ambulance shuttles.

They did as much as they could between them. The second theatre sister was ill and had been sent back to Colmenar. They had radioed for assistance and she would return with another radiographer as soon as possible. In the meantime the work went on. The cases that they couldn't handle were sent on down the line.

Greta would live. After her operation an ambulance took her away to the base hospital.

In a brief pause in the middle of the day Charles left the anaesthetist to prepare for the next operation. He led Amy away to the dining hut and sat her down in the chair nearest to the stove. He dipped a tin cup into a pan of hot coffee and handed it to her, then sat down across the table. Amy drank the coffee without tasting it. She could see Jennie's face against the damp stone wall. Except that Jennie's face was covered by a sheet in the makeshift mortuary.

Charles put his hand out and touched her fingers.

'You were a good friend,' he said gently. 'Jennie died, that's all.'

Amy nodded, understanding what he meant. The weight of irrational guilt pressed on her. If I had gone with her, she thought. Or if I had only said, *don't go* . . . But Charles was right. Guilt would gain nothing.

'I'm sorry,' she said. Sorry for needing attention in the midst of all this, for her weakness.

'Don't be,' Charles answered. They finished their coffee and then he said, 'Now. We must do some more work. Are you ready?'

They crossed the little open space between the hut and the Bedford. Another full ambulance was turning, ready to unload more suffering. It seemed that the guns would never stop firing.

At the little flight of steps up to the rear of the van Charles stopped and put his arm around Amy's shoulders. 'You are a fine nurse,' he told her. 'One of the best I have ever worked with. Tell me, Amy. When the war comes, the real war, have you thought what you will do?'

Amy looked up at him, stupid with grief and tiredness and shock. 'Do?' The idea of another war beyond this one was inconceivable. 'No, I haven't thought what I will do. It's hard to imagine beyond today, tomorrow, when . . . when people are dying.'

'You would be a good doctor,' Charles told her. 'Doctors will be important, when the time comes. Will you promise me that when you are home again, you will think about that?'

The bearers were bringing across the next stretcher. Charles would pick up his instruments, probe and cut and repair and stitch up again.

'Yes,' Amy said dully. 'I'll think about it.'

They didn't stop again until the winter darkness had laid an opaque blanket against the little slit windows of the truck. The sky overhead was empty at last, and one by one the guns fell silent.

Victor finished stitching the last patient. He pulled his mask down and stripped off his gloves to rub his fingers into the corners of his eyes. Amy picked up the used instruments from the gauze pad and put them in a bowl ready for sterilizing. She opened the big door at the back, intending to call across for some bearers to come and carry the last stretcher away to the recovery area. Charles came hurrying across from the canvas pavilion. She saw the white glimmer of his face turned up to her in the blackness.

'One more?' he begged. 'Just one. An amputation. I can do it if you will help me.'

Another. Amy nodded. She was still wearing her gown and gloves with the rubber theatre cap tight round her head. What was one more?

In the quiet she heard the busy hum of the generator and remembered that the big lights were sending a yellow splash through the dark. An easy target for a stray night-bombing patrol. Charles squeezed breathlessly in beside her and she shut the heavy door again. Victor and the anaesthetist were already giving their weary agreement to just one more. Amy turned to the sterilizing unit, trying to work out which instruments Charles would need without having to waste his time in asking. She heard the murmurs and bumps behind her as one loaded stretcher was removed and replaced with another.

'Radius and ulna completely shattered,' she heard Charles murmur. 'A high amputation, I'm afraid. And a strong chance of gangrene. I want to do it at once. Shrapnel fragments embedded here, and here. Burns on the upper torso, none on the face. Mmm, mmm. Strange-coloured scar, that. Coal dust, would you say?'

She turned round with a tray of instruments.

The man's long body was partly covered with a green sheet. There were livid burns across the chest. On what remained of his right arm, above the protrusion of bone splinters and shapeless flesh blackened with dirt and smoke, there was a deep, puckered scar. It was blue under the wrinkled skin, as if the old wound hadn't been properly cleaned before healing itself.

Amy looked at the scar.

She didn't feel shock, or fear, or even surprise. Instead there was tenderness. A strong, comforting well of it springing up inside her. That poor arm had held her, how many hundreds of times? She had kissed the scar and her hair had fallen over it as they lay down together.

Amy looked at the bare chest with its ribs ridged painfully under the burnt skin. It was rising and falling, shallow but steady.

She edged round behind Victor, moving delicately in the confined space. The anaesthetist's black mask and coiled tubes already covered most of the face. It was bearded, thinner, with hollows beneath the cheekbones and blue smudges in the closed eye-sockets. The long black hair fell back from his white forehead. Amy didn't need even that brief glance. She already knew it was Nick.

Quietly she went back to her place behind Charles' arm.

'Will he live?' she asked neutrally.

Charles glanced round at her. She saw the flicker in his dark eyes over the mask, but she met his look steadily. She wouldn't let them know, she thought with irrational guile. They might not let her stay, if they knew.

Charles turned back again. 'He's lost a good deal of blood. Been out in the open for some hours. But he's strong. Good heartbeat. A good chance, I'd say. Ready?'

The anaesthetist nodded.

Charles began work.

One after another Amy handed him the little, sharp, gleaming things he needed. Nick's ruined arm was cut away under her eyes. Amy watched Charles' blunt gloved fingers probe delicately in the mangled flesh. The scalpels flashed back the reflection of the big overhead lights, the surgical needles wove through the net of nerves and blood vessels. It took a long time. On the opposite side of the trolley Victor cleaned and dressed the burns and removed the shrapnel splinters. The anaesthetist sat impassively watching his dials. Amy's gaze kept flicking to his face from the raw stump under Charles' fingers. She dreaded a change of expression that would signal anxiety. But he was calm, intent. Nick's heart beat steadily and his shallow breaths came evenly.

He would survive. Her own tenderness and strength would make him survive.

Charles had left a loose flap of skin. At last he covered his creation of clean flesh and orderly sutures with the protective flap. The amputation was complete. Victor had finished his work too. The black, jagged shrapnel had gone and the burns were hidden under light strips of gauze.

'Good,' Charles said softly. It was the first word he had spoken all through the operation except for terse commands. He glanced round at Amy again and she saw from his bright eyes that he was pleased with his work.

Without warning, Amy was giddy. Relief and belated shock sent sickening waves all through her. She stepped back and put her hand out to the truck wall to steady herself, feeling the blood draining out of her face.

'Are you all right?' Charles asked.

'Yes. Of course.' She forced herself to turn and begin collecting up the dirty swabs and used instruments.

'You did well,' Charles said kindly.

Victor opened the truck door and called across for help with the stretcher. The anaesthetist edged out of his cramped corner, yawning and stretching.

Another operation.

Nick lay very still. Amy saw his thin face and the blue veins in his eyelids. The simple strength of her feeling for him steadied her again and she went on with her task of clearing up and laying out ready for the next day.

The bearers came whistling up the steps. 'Did all right, did 'e?' the Cockney one asked.

'Well enough,' Charles answered and Amy saw the movement of his wide smile under his mask. She wanted to reach out in gratitude and put her arms around him.

The bearers lifted Nick off the trolley and on to their stretcher. His head moved and he stirred a little as they shuffled awkwardly towards the door.

'I'm coming with him,' Amy said sharply. She had reached the steps in their wake when Charles caught her arm.

'Who is he?' he asked.

Amy was watching the stretcher's progress to the recovery tent. When she saw it was safely there she half-turned, impatient.

'My lover,' she said simply. Then she was away down the steps and across the muddy space to Nick.

The doctors looked at one another. Victor peeled off his surgical gloves and threw them down. 'Dear bloody hell,' he said.

Charles was watching her as she followed the stretcher. After a moment he said softly, 'She's lucky. So's he. You don't need two arms to make love.'

It was quiet in the shadowy recovery room. Dim lights hung from the canvas roof, swaying a little and sending the nurse's shadow flickering as she moved between the low beds. Most of the men were asleep. Nick was being settled in a corner at the far end as Amy ducked in through the entrance.

'Shall I stay here for a while?' Amy asked the other nurse. 'If you want to go and have a break?'

'It's pretty quiet,' the girl said. She went with alacrity.

Amy found a little folding canvas stool and took it to Nick's bedside. She sat down and reached for his hand, holding it in hers.

The time passed. Once or twice Amy stood up and went to take a cup of water to one man, gave a pain-killing injection to another. Then she came back to her place, fixing her eyes on Nick's profile against the grey-white canvas wall.

It was midnight when Nick's eyes flicked open. Fourteen hours since the shell had exploded in the oak tree. The first thing he saw was the glow of the lamp hanging from the tent ridge. He wondered if it was the flash of another shell, but it was too dim and steady for that.

'Nick.' The voice came from beside him. He turned his head and felt the pain of the burns across his chest. There was a girl in a white dress with her head tied up in a white muslin scarf. He frowned a little, trying to remember through the fog of pain and anaesthetic. He thought he remembered the dark, and the noise, and then the unbearable hurt of being lifted and carried when he wanted to be left to lie. He tried to lick his lips to moisten them, but his tongue felt cracked and swollen.

'Wait,' the voice said. He felt something move beside him and as they let him go he realized that other fingers had been twined in his. His hand felt empty and he wanted the other to come back. He moved it across the cover and winced at the pain. The white girl came back and bent over him. Her arm slid behind his neck and she lifted him just enough to touch his lips to the tin cup.

He looked up and saw that the face under the white scarf was Amy's. She was smiling.

'I'm here,' she said.

The simple words were like warmth, and peace, and comfort, wrapped round him all together. He moved his hand on the cover again and her fingers laced securely in his. Nick felt the wetness of tears at the corners of his eyes. They rolled down his face on to the pillow. Amy bent forward and kissed them away. She was still smiling but he thought that there were tears in her lovely eyes too. Nick drifted away into sleep again.

When he woke up the lamp at the end of his bed had gone out. There was light filtering in through the roof instead. He understood that he was under canvas, in a tent. Turning his head, he saw that it was laid out like a hospital ward. He had been injured and brought in, then. Today? Yesterday? The day before that? There was a nurse in a white dress standing with her back to him a few feet away.

'Amy,' he said. 'Amy.'

The nurse turned quickly. Her face wasn't Amy's. The realization struck him like a heavy, dull weight. It hadn't been Amy at all. He had conjured her up out of his fevered painful longing in the night.

The nurse came to the side of his bed. 'Amy's asleep,' she said. 'But she made me promise that I would fetch her as soon as you woke up.'

She rustled briskly away. Nick lay staring up at the canvas roof, not daring to believe or hope. A moment or two later he heard someone coming back. He didn't turn his head, but she stooped beside the bed.

'I'm here,' she said softly again, and then he looked. It was Amy, with her hair loose now and waving around her face. She was wearing an old khaki coat and trousers. For a long, quiet moment they looked at each other. She was beautiful, even though there were exhausted lines in her face and bruised shadows under her eyes. Nick wanted to reach out, to pull her down beside him and stroke her hair back from her cheeks, and touch her mouth and eyelids with his fingertips. The sight of her clean sweetness reminded him of his own filth and the itch of lice. He had hardly been able to move to her, but he dropped the little way back against the pillow, ashamed.

'Why are you here?' he asked.

'I've been in Spain for two months. Nursing, near Madrid and then here. I wrote on Christmas Eve to tell you I was on my way.'

'I never got the letter.'

Nick saw that the tent was busy behind her. Two men in berets and rough overcoats were carrying a stretcher out. Another man with a bandaged head was limping behind them. There were nurses moving to and fro, and some of the men in the other beds were propped up, talking. Then he looked at Amy again and forgot them.

'Why am I here?' he asked, childlike.

Amy took a breath. 'You were brought in yesterday evening. I don't know where from. You have some burns on your chest. There were shrapnel splinters. And . . . your right arm was crushed. It must have been by a shell blast.'

Nick remembered that he had reached out to touch the oak tree. That had been the last thing.

'It was too badly damaged for us to save it, Nick. I saw it, and the amputation. You had the best surgeon in the world.'

Nick shrugged. His arm was still there, because he could feel it. He was remembering other things now. The execution, and the blond-headed boy's limbs jerking under the trees. Jake. Jake, sitting staring ahead of him with the terrible thing in his lap.

He turned to Amy, looking at her warm face to blot out the images.

'It's finished,' he said wearily.

'What's finished?'

'All that. The Party.'

'Why?' Her voice was very gentle.

He heard the violent bitterness of his own as he answered her. 'Fuck the Party. Everyone's dead, aren't they?'

Amy brought a little metal bowl with a syringe in it. As she gave him the injection Nick noticed that there were tubes leading out of the crook of his arm, stretching up to a metal stand. There were two bottles, one clear and one half-full of blood. He fell asleep again.

With the change from light shining through the canvas to dark and the swinging lamp, and back again, Nick understood that he was in a surgical recovery ward. The occupants of the other beds were moved on, but he stayed.

Amy came when she could, hurrying from her work elsewhere.

She brought a bowl of warm water and towels, and washed him all over. He looked down and saw the stump of his arm in the white cradle of dressings. He understood, but he was oddly unmoved. He was alive, and he didn't have to fight any more. And Amy was here. She cut his ragged hair and shaved off his beard. Her fingers were light and gentle, and he caught them in his left hand and kissed them.

It grew quieter in the field hospital. Nick couldn't know it, but both sides had been reinforced after the failed Republican attack in which he had been injured. And which had killed Jake. They were strong on both sides now, and the battle for the Jarama had ended in stalemate. The Republicans still held the Valencia road.

Charles and Victor came in and out to see him, peeling the dressings off and nodding their approval. The flap of skin was knitting smoothly over the wound. And then the time came when Charles said gently, 'We can't nurse you here whatever Amy says. You need physiotherapy, if you are to have any use from those muscles in your upper arm. I'm sending you to the base hospital at Tarragona. Tomorrow.'

That evening Amy sat for a long time at Nick's bedside. The recovery ward was empty. She held his hand and they talked, long rambling talk about the things that they had done before Spain.

'Do you remember the night on the mountain above Nantlas?' he asked her.

'I remember.'

He didn't talk about Mari. She waited for him to, but he didn't.

They were quiet for a moment after that. Nick closed his eyes.

'I want to go home,' he said.

'I'll take you home,' Amy promised him. 'Somehow, I will.'

He opened his eyes and looked at her, seeing the red-brown springing of her hair and her smooth skin.

'You were the strong one, always,' he said. 'I'm not strong any more.'

She leaned close to him, resting her cheek against his. 'You will be, again.'

'I wish I could make love to you.'

590

'I wish you could, too,' she whispered. Amy tried to shut out the soft, certain sadness that was gathering around her.

In the morning, everyone came out to see Nick carried into the ambulance. The Cockney bearer hoisted the top end of the stretcher and joked, 'Better be careful with lover-boy, eh?'

Charles and Victor and the others waved and called their good wishes. Nick's stretcher was loaded into the ambulance and the driver folded up the steps and went round to his cab. Amy scrambled up into the rear. She kissed Nick's cheek.

'I'll come as soon as I can.'

'To Tarragona?'

'To Tarragona. And I'll take you home.'

The ambulance's ancient engine roared into life. Nick let go her hand and lifted his in an awkward wave. Amy jumped down.

I love you, she thought, as the dresser who was to travel with Nick climbed in in her place. Victor closed and secured the battered doors. The ambulance swung round and chugged away.

Charles put his arm round Amy's shoulders.

'Good girl,' he said.

'No,' Amy answered sadly. 'I'm not good. Not at all.'

22

Tarragona seemed to be full of maimed soldiers. On her way through the streets to the hospital Amy passed little groups of them, bandaged, or limping, or swinging awkwardly on crutches. It was a sad place. She ducked her head and hurried

Amy was on leave. She had worked her span of duty in the front line, twenty-eight days that had seemed as long as a lifetime. Now she had ten precious days' leave. When they were relieved by the incoming teams, only Charles had stayed on at the field hospital. Amy and Victor and the others had been taken back to Madrid by bus. The journey had made all of them think of Jennie and they had sat in silence for most of the way, exhausted now that necessity no longer kept them moving.

From Madrid, after hours of difficulty, Amy had managed to make a telephone call to Paradise Hotel.

Over the crackling line she spoke to a Spanish nurse she had never met.

'Sí, Paloma,' the girl laughed. 'Very good.'

'I want to speak to Elena. To Elena. Now, please.'

At the other end the girl was still laughing, and Amy could hear other people calling out in the background.

'Listen to me. The baby, is she well? Please, can't you fetch Elena?'

'Very well.'

She heard the receiver being put down and the girl's heels clicking away. Then, as she waited, the line went dead. Although she tried for another hour the operator couldn't make the connection again.

Amy was torn between going to Colmenar and Paloma, or straight to Tarragona as she had promised Nick. In the end she tried to satisfy herself with the nurse's words, *very good*, and *very well*.

592

As soon as she had seen Nick to safety, she promised herself, she would go on home to Paloma.

The base hospital at Tarragona was housed in a modern technical college. The gardens were to one side of it, with soldiers sitting quietly on benches in the March sunshine. She went into the wide hallway and enquired at the medical office for Nick. They directed her up to a long ward on the first floor.

Amy's shoes squeaked on the tiles as she walked down the corridor, in and out of the bright patches of sunlight slanting through tall windows. Her heart was thumping against her ribs. Nurses in starched dresses, with proper white caps on their heads, fluttered past her. She reached the doorway and stood looking down the ward. She saw Nick at once.

He was sitting on an upright chair beside his bed, reading. The book lay open on the bed, and as she watched he turned a page, awkwardly, with his left hand. He was wearing a khaki jersey and the empty right sleeve was pinned against his side. She went to him and put her hand on his shoulder. When he looked up she saw how pain had marked his face. But he was Nick, still Nick.

He stood up and made to put his arms round her. The lopsided movement almost unbalanced him. Amy steadied him against her.

'I forget, sometimes,' he said. His left arm circled her shoulders and she turned her face up and kissed him. They stood for a moment with their faces close together, in the midst of the busy ward.

'Let's walk outside,' Nick said softly. 'Out of this place. I'm glad you've come.'

They went out into the sun, warm at its midday height, and walked down the gravel paths between avenues of plane trees. The branches showed the first pale mist of green. Nick held her hand tightly in his.

'Are you discharged?' she asked.

'Honourably. Can't fire a rifle without an arm, can I? I'm free to go whenever I want. As soon as possible, I suppose. To leave my place here free for some other champion of democracy who's lost his arm, or his legs, or his balls.'

And how much else? How much had they both lost? Amy thought.

'Listen,' she said gently. 'This is what we'll do.'

Charles had given her the name of a friend of his in Tarragona.

Charles' friend was occupied in bringing important people into Spain, very quietly, over the mountains from Luz-St Sauveur on the French side down to Huesca. It was Charles' suggestion that Amy should take Nick out by the opposite route. It would be quick, and easy, far easier than waiting for the official channels through Figueras and Perpignan.

'I'll wire to Richard in Paris and ask him if he will come to meet us on the French side. I'm sure he will. Then he can take you back to Paris, or you can fly straight home from Toulouse, or anywhere.'

He didn't ask if she would come with him, nor did Amy volunteer any more than that. They stood side by side, still holding hands, looking down the avenue of trees. A fountain at the other end caught the light in rainbow glitters of spray.

'Home,' Nick echoed, so softly that she barely heard it.

'I'll go and see Charles' mysterious friend, then,' Amy said brightly. 'If he's as cloak-and-dagger as he sounds, we'll probably have to leave at a moment's notice. Be ready. Will you be strong enough for the journey?'

'Yes,' Nick said. 'I'll be strong enough.'

And so it was arranged.

Twenty-four hours later Amy and Nick left the hospital. Nick had nothing except the clothes he was wearing. Amy was carrying a blanket and the meagre supply of food that was all she had been able to find in the bare shops, bread and tomatoes and a piece of goat's cheese.

They walked through the knots of strolling soldiers with their lined faces and their crutches. Amy thought of Charles, working ceaselessly in the Bedford truck to save this stump of leg, those fingers, that life. To save them for what? Another war, perhaps. *You would make a good doctor,* he had told her. Seeing this parade, so many wounded men, Amy was sadder than she had ever been in the bloody mess of the *salle de triage* behind the Valencia road. Nick walked beside her, silent, his face set.

They found the café in the side street that they had been directed to, and sat waiting over cups of grey coffee. A little mud-coloured Citroën drew up on the cobbles and a man came in. He smiled at them, showing pointed white teeth, and Amy saw that he was a boy rather than a man. He bowed over her hand. *'Madame. Enchanté. Et M'sieu.'* They followed him out the little car, and between them Amy and the driver settled Nick as comfortably as they could. Then the driver leapt behind the wheel and they bumped out of Tarragona.

They drove all day. The roads were terrible, and they were clogged with traffic. Long lines of army trucks crawled in convoy, and big, dusty cars carrying staff officers howled past them. There were refugees everywhere, old men and women and tiny children plodding beside donkey carts piled with possessions. They were heading north, taking their lives to the refugee camps on the French side of the border. Once, the boy driver looked back over his shoulder at Amy huddled in the rear seat. 'Spain bleeds,' he said.

He wouldn't stop driving. He pointed at his watch as the day wore on and frowned. Amy gave him bread and cheese and he drove one-handed. Nick didn't eat anything. His face was grey and Amy watched him anxiously.

They came close to Huesca and then circled round the east of it. Beyond Huesca, to the west, was Nationalist-held territory. They had seen dozens of planes as they drove, but as the sun set they saw a tight V-formation over to their left. They were white planes, and as they banked their wings glittered. Nick looked up and saw it. It was the same glitter, tiny and clean and a long way off, that he had glimpsed through a shell impact on the battlefield. He shivered with a sudden remembrance of fear. Then he felt Amy's breath warm against his neck as she leaned forward and pointed ahead.

'Look, the Pyrenees.'

The mountains were black, jagged lines against the dark sky. The driver was frowning, throwing the little car up the winding road. 'They close the pass at dusk,' he told them.

When they reached the point where a pair of roadside huts guarded the steep road, it was already dark. Spanish guards stepped out in front of the car and waved them to a halt. The pass was closed for the night.

Under the suspicious glare of the guards Amy and Nick climbed stiffly out of the car and went into one of the huts. There were wooden benches, nothing else. Outside they could hear their driver arguing in ferocious Spanish. A moment later he came in, followed by a guard. The soldier looked hard at Nick's empty sleeve, and then admiringly at Amy. At last he nodded and smiled, and there was more unintelligible talk. In the end the driver shrugged and turned away.

'He salutes you both for your brave contribution to his country's battle. But he cannot disobey his orders. No one may cross now until dawn tomorrow.'

'My friend is injured . . .' Amy began, but Nick caught her wrist.

'It doesn't matter,' he said. 'What's one more night? This hut is luxury compared with a trench.'

There was nothing to do but make the best of it. Amy spread out their blanket in a corner and made Nick sit down on it. Working by the light of a lantern that threw a monstrous black shadow of herself against the wooden wall, she dressed his arm and chest. She was relieved that he had no fever, but she could see that he was exhausted. She tried to persuade him to eat what was left of their food but he couldn't manage it, and so the driver and Amy shared it between them. The guards brought in some coffee and a little red wine, and Nick drank that. Then the driver curled himself into an economical ball on the floor, with his head on his folded coat, and fell asleep.

Nick and Amy sat side by side in the lantern-light, quiet, thinking.

Amy was worried that Richard wouldn't meet them at the border. She had cabled him as soon as she had known their plans. *Nick injured. Bringing him out. Will you meet us Wednesday p.m. Luz-St Sauveur.* He would wait a day for them, surely? But perhaps he had never received the cable at all. Perhaps he was away . . .

Amy put her hand to her waist. In her money belt there was still enough of Jack Roper's diamond money to keep them in France until Nick was well enough to travel on.

And then?

You are the strong one now, Nick had said.

In the wooden hut, listening to the wind, Amy wondered if she had enough strength for what was to come. She turned her head, needing to see his face. Nick had fallen awkwardly asleep with his head tilted back against the wall. Supporting him with her arm, she wrapped the blanket closer around him and then drew his head down against her shoulder.

At first light the guards came and opened the hut door. Gratefully Amy and Nick and the driver climbed back into the little mud-coloured car and followed the mountain road on upwards. The sky to their left was lemon yellow, barred with grey and gold. They crossed the border into France without difficulty.

'Going the other way, is harder,' the driver said, grinning at them.

In the strengthening white light of morning they zigzagged down the hairpin bends and came to Luz-St Sauveur.

There was a square, marked out by plane trees, and a baker's shop where the wooden shutters were being taken down ready for the day's business. An old man with a basket shuffled under the bare branches of the trees and a woman standing on her scrubbed step called a greeting to him. It was very quiet, peaceful. None of the houses was damaged, and the old plaster walls were clean, bare of slogans and ripped propaganda posters. It was an ordinary village, waking up to an ordinary day. Nick and Amy blinked, looking at the mounds of fresh bread being piled up in the baker's window, and at the gleaming bottles of preserves, oil and wine revealed as the blue blind of the shop next door was hauled up. Amy realized that she was so used to bleakness that she had forgotten ordinary things, and the beauty of them. The humdrum square of the little French town glowed with the loveliness of colour and abundance.

She turned slowly in a circle, looking around her. Across the square she saw a car parked in the shadow of the only hotel. It had great mudguards that arched up like supercilious eyebrows, and a long, aristocratic, polished bonnet. The sun slanted across the bonnet and the silver radiator grille dazzled across the square at her.

It was Adeline's Bentley.

At the same moment a man came out of the hotel door. He was slightly built, but his long duster coat and wide-brimmed hat made him look bigger. He was pulling on a pair of pale yellow leather driving gauntlets.

'Richard,' Amy called out.

Richard looked, and ran with his arms open. A second later they were clinging together, tangled in exclamations, crying and laughing. Amy kissed her brother, and smelt expensive soap, cologne and the crisp freshness of laundered clothes. For the first time in weeks, she was aware of her own appearance.

Richard held her at arms' length, looking at her.

'Oh dear me,' Richard said.

597

'Is Mama here too?'

'No. Aren't you relieved? Can you just hear her? *Amy, your hair. And your hands. Are there no manicurists in field hospitals?* She gave me her car, you know. I drove down here in it the minute I got your cable. You've no idea the dash a Bentley cuts in Paris.' He was turning to Nick, holding out his hand to shake Nick's. 'I'm so glad you're safe, old man.' And when Nick's hand didn't grip his he looked warily, as if he was used to the snub but surprised to encounter it here. Then he saw Nick's empty sleeve. All the light faded out of his face. 'I'm sorry,' he said. 'Amy's cable just said that you were wounded.'

Awkwardly Nick held out his left hand and Richard held it for a moment, looking into his face. Then he turned abruptly to the driver who was opening the door of his Citroën.

'I'm Richard Lovell,' he said. 'Won't you at least come and have breakfast at the hotel with me?'

'Thank you, but no.' The boy smiled at all three of them. 'I'm very late, and someone is waiting for me.' He was already back in the driver's seat.

Amy called, 'Wait.' She turned her back modestly and reached inside the waistband of her skirt to the pouch of her money belt. She took out the folded wad of money, Spanish and French, and held it out to him.

'Will you take this, to help with what you are doing? Will you, please?'

The boy smiled again, showing his pointed teeth, and his brown fingers closed on the warm notes. 'Money is always helpful. My friends will be grateful. Thank you.'

'Thank you,' Amy said, and he drove quickly away.

'Not bad, for a ride over the mountains,' Richard murmured.

'It wasn't just for that,' Amy said sharply. 'It was for everything they're doing, for what we believe in.'

Neither Richard nor Nick said anything.

After a moment Richard put his arm lightly around her shoulder, the other around Nick's. 'Breakfast,' he said.

The hotel was very small and provincial, but to Amy the dining-room looked more luxurious than anything she had ever seen. There were starched tablecloths and thick, folded napkins, polished glasses and china and flowers and the smell of new bread.

They sat down at a table in the window overlooking the

peaceful square, and the waitress brought them their food. There was bread and fresh, moist ham, thick yellow butter and honey still in the comb, *pain au chocolat* and fragrant coffee. Amy had thought she was ravenous, but when she began to eat she found that she could only manage a fraction of what she had piled on to her plate. The food was too rich, too colourful, after what they had been used to eat in Spain. The *pain au chocolat* reminded her of Christmas morning in Richard's apartment on the Ile de la Cité. Jennie had sat opposite her at that breakfast, laughing and cupping her hands around her dish of coffee. Amy put her bread down and looked at Nick. He wasn't eating either. His hand lay curled on the tablecloth, not quite touching the knife that he could only manipulate with awkward effort.

Amy had the sense that they were both marked. Spain had marked them, and not only Spain but time itself. They couldn't go back now. In this quiet place war might have been on another planet instead of a few kilometres away across the mountains, but for Nick and herself it was all around them. Amy wondered if it would be like that for always.

Richard touched her hand. 'Shall we go, then? If you have both had enough to eat?'

He paid his bill and the bags were carried out and stowed in the Bentley. Carefully they settled Nick against the leather cushions of the back seat. Richard glanced at the blanket that Amy had brought, then gingerly put it down under one of the trees. He unfolded his own fur-lined rug and wrapped it around Nick himself. A few moments later they were spinning along wide, open roads lined only with trees. There were no army convoys here, no donkey carts piled with possessions, no children, hungry and staring. There was only the spring sunshine, the long nose of the car ahead, and the warm, moneyed smell of leather.

'Where are we going?' Amy asked.

Richard's profile tilted towards her. 'Going? Why, Biarritz, of course.'

She glanced back over her shoulder. Nick had already fallen asleep in his fur wrap.

'Biarritz?'

'Sea air. Recuperation and so on.' Richard was quiet for a moment and then he added, in a different voice that wasn't breezy any more, 'I thought perhaps you might both need some time. To be together, perhaps, before you decide what you have to do next. Mmm?'

Perceptive Richard, Amy thought. She seized on the promise of time, and of being together. Perhaps they needed that. But in her heart, Amy knew that Nick and herself were already decided. Nothing would change what was already decided.

The Hôtel du Palais, Biarritz, was exactly the same, from the ornate red and cream bulk of it looking out over the curve of the bay to the hushed marble and velvet and crystal-chandelier interior.

'I am so sorry that Lady Lovell's usual suite is not available,' the manager apologized.

'Yes. A pity,' Richard said. Behind his back Amy saw Nick staring up at the gilded ceilings high overhead, the wreaths and swags of plasterwork and the rainbow glitter of the crystal drops. She caught his eye and suddenly they were laughing, giggling like a pair of children caught out in their dirty clothes in the middle of a grand drawing-room.

Richard seemed to have brought enough luggage for all three of them. The manager himself, with a retinue of boys in little round caps and gold-frogged uniforms, escorted them up to their rooms. Amy had a second-floor suite facing the sea, and Richard and Nick had rooms a little further along on the south side, looking away over the bay towards Spain.

Amy saw that Nick turned away from the window and the sight of the sun's sparkling track across the choppy sea.

Richard pointed to one of the leather valises that the page had deposited for him. 'I brought some of Klaus's things for Nick, which was clever of me, please admit. For you, Amy darling, I can't provide a stitch of fresh clothing, although you do need it.'

'I'll go out and buy something,' she said faintly.

'Perfect. Now, I'm going to make telephone calls and unsocial arrangements of that sort. Shall we meet for cocktails before dinner?'

'For cocktails,' they agreed, stifling their laughter.

Amy and Nick wandered to and fro in Amy's suite. They fingered the cushions on the sofas and the linen sheets on the wide, soft bed. In the bathroom there were crystal glasses, polished tiles and jars of scented oil. Nick sat on the edge of the bath and turned on one of the brass taps.

'It reminds me of Jack Roper's house,' he said.

Amy stood close to him, putting her hand out to touch his shoulder. 'Do you remember Jack Roper's house? Let's have a bath together now.'

She helped him to take his clothes off, and pushed them into a heap in the corner. She ran water into the bath not deep enough to reach Nick's burned chest, and whisked drops of perfumed oil into a froth of bubbles. Then they lay back in the hot water.

'Are we really here?' Nick asked.

Here. Not under the guns. Not with Jake, and Jennie, and all the others who hadn't escaped.

'Yes,' Amy reassured him, closing her mind.

She washed him, keeping the sponge away from where the fresh pucker of new skin was beginning to show under the burns. Then she sat still in her turn while Nick washed her, steadying himself by leaning against the bath side.

Afterwards they dried each other with the thick towels and lay down under clean sheets. They were too raw yet, and too tired, to make love. Instead they fell asleep with Nick's left arm under Amy's shoulder, his knees crooked into the crook of hers. As she fell asleep she saw his hand unclench in front of her eyes and lie uncurled, defenceless.

Later, she left him still sleeping and slid away, dressing herself in her stiff, filthy clothes. She went down the duck-boarded promenade where she and Isabel had walked to Fendi's to buy ice-cream with Bethan thirteen years ago. In the smart little shops where the *vendeuses* stared curiously at her she bought new clothes and shoes, and silk underwear.

When she came back Nick was sitting up in bed, smiling. 'Would you like a drink?' she asked him.

'A drink is the thing I would like second best in all the world.'

Amy went and kissed him, and then danced out of his reach.

'There's only time for a drink. Richard will be here in a minute. Let's look and see what he has brought for you to wear.'

They peered into the leather valise. There were jerseys and trousers and, neatly folded in tissue, an evening suit and a boiled shirt.

'Again?' Nick said despairingly. 'Another attempt to dress me up in these ridiculous clothes?'

They laughed, and then looked soberly at each other. The evening in Bruton Street was so far away, so long ago now.

'You'll have to wear them if you're coming down to dinner here.'

'I'll have a tray sent up.'

'No, you won't. You'll come down and dine with Richard and me.'

Resignedly Nick let her help him into the clothes. She tied the butterfly bow for him and watered his hospital-cut hair so that it lay smooth to his head. The coat fitted neatly across his shoulders.

'Well?' he asked, standing upright for her approval.

'Perfectly acceptable,' Amy said lightly, turning away. She hoped that her voice didn't betray her. Nick was very thin and his face was hollow but she had never seen him so handsome as in that moment. She felt his dark height behind her, and his grey-green stare fixed on her back. She wanted to run to him, she wanted him, but she stood still. But they did have their fragile bubble of Biarritz time. It wasn't time to puncture it yet, was it? She hesitated, lost for a moment. Nick came and stood behind her and she felt the skin of her neck and spine prickle with his closeness. His fingers touched her shoulder, stroking, light as a feather. Then she turned and they looked at one another, acknowledging. Nick felt it, then, too. They had always wanted one another, like this. That wouldn't change, Amy told herself, just because everything else had.

His hand grew heavier on her shoulder and she felt the warm weight of it. Then, from downstairs they heard a burst of dance music and someone called out and laughed in the corridor outside. Amy reached and kissed the corner of his mouth.

'Let's ring for that drink,' she said softly. They still had their Biarritz time.

Nick watched her walk across the room to the bell.

'Amy,' he said, as if he was listening to the sound her name made, 'Amy.' Then, in a different voice, he asked, 'Who is Klaus?'

Amy grinned at him. 'Richard's lover.'

'Oh, dear God. Not only a penguin suit, but Richard's lover's penguin suit.'

They started laughing then, laughter that fuelled itself and grew louder, and they both knew that there was a touch of madness in it.

Richard came a moment later. He looked curiously at them,

but said nothing. In his wake came a waiter wheeling a trolley with a silver ice-bucket, clinking glasses and all the paraphernalia of cocktail time.

'Champagne cocktails,' Richard announced. 'I will mix them, thank you.'

He handed them their glasses with a flourish. 'What shall we drink to?'

'To Biarritz,' Amy said firmly, and they lifted their glasses to the sea, dark as oil now and threaded with glittering skeins of reflected light.

The champagne went to their heads. Amy felt herself beginning to glide, as if her new black silk shoes weren't quite touching the thick carpets. She pirouetted obligingly to show off her narrow black dinner dress to Richard, and felt Nick's eyes again on her bare back. They laughed together at Nick's scowl when Richard said admiringly, 'And Nick looks even more wonderful. Like a war hero in a film.'

Suddenly, everything was funny. All three of them were laughing. They had another cocktail apiece and then went down to dinner.

The great rococo dining-room was warm and scented and bathed in rosy light. They sat at a table in the wide, curved window overlooking the dark sea. The candles on their table reflected oval, wavering haloes of gold back out of the black glass, and when Amy stared beyond those she could still see the dancing reflections of lights in the sea. She looked back across the crowded dining-room, dreamily wondering if she might glimpse herself, and Richard and Isabel, as half-frightened, half-rebellious children at their parents' table. No, they weren't there. And if they had been, Amy thought, they had all come so far now that she might not recognize them.

Richard poured garnet-red claret into their glasses. The food came, laid in front of them on plates rimmed with gold and hand-painted with flowers. She tasted it, richness on her tongue, and sipped the violet-scented wine. Everything was hazy now, except for Nick's face. She saw the quickness of his smile, and the pull of the little muscles at the corner of his mouth. He was eating, one-handed, as if he was suddenly hungry again. Then he put down his fork to laugh at Richard. Richard was talking about the Coronation.

'You'll do it?' Amy asked, focusing her astonishment.

Richard's eyebrows went up into sharp peaks. 'But of course. I am the King's Defender, and I will defend him. Let anyone so much as breathe on my Sovereign and they will reckon with my sword, or mailed fist, or hereditary dagger, or whatever is the Lord Chamberlain's latest instruction.'

'I thought you went to Paris to escape all that.'

Richard beamed at her. 'Anyone would want to escape the Lord Chamberlain. And I don't relish the prospect of endless rehearsals in the freezing Abbey, with breaks for sandwiches and Thermos coffee amidst a horde of Papa's crusty old peers who will stare as if I am exhibit A. Not to speak of pallid maids-of-honour and wobbly prelates. But think of it.' Richard lifted his fork and stared raptly ahead. 'When the Day comes, I shall walk in that procession, behind the Archbishops in their copes and mitres and a step ahead of the King and Queen themselves. My right hand will be on the pommel of my sword, and I will look to left and right, fierce, ready to defend, to spring to answer any challenge.'

Amy snorted into her napkin and Nick leant back in his chair to laugh aloud.

'Why are you laughing? In my left hand will be the banner. An exquisite new banner that is being stitched even now by a little old lady in the rue Malebranche. Heavy black silk, with gold thread as bright as a princess's hair.'

'Richard, stop. I can't bear it.'

'And my regalia. I'm as proud of my calves as the next man, and rose-pink silk stockings with Tudor roses on the garters display them to perfection. Black knee breeches, of course, and a little coat, cut just so . . . Whatever is the matter with you both?' Richard put down his fork and glared sternly at them. 'To answer your question, Amy dear, of course I will do it. It is the finest piece of theatre in the world, and an enchanting cameo role in it is all mine. *Regis Defensor*. Wasted on generations of Lovells, up until this one. I know Papa took it all very seriously, but I'm sure for all the wrong reasons. He never cared much for pink stockings.'

Amy dried her eyes with her napkin. 'I'm very glad you're doing it,' she said weakly. And for all their laughter and Richard's studied mockery, she guessed that his ancient role was as important to him as it had been to his father before him. Everything changes, Amy thought, and yet it doesn't change at all. She was happy that there would be a Lovell in the Coronation procession again, even if Richard was to be the last one.

'Will you be there to see me?' he asked her.

'In May?' Amy looked through the glass at the sea, and saw the light catch the white ruffle of a breaking wave. She watched it fixedly, not wanting to see Nick's reflection caught beside her own. At last she said, 'No, I don't think I shall be in London in May.'

There was a moment's quiet before Richard answered, 'Well. Well then, I think we should have cognac now, don't you?' And he gathered up the threads of their evening's determined hilarity again, drawing Nick and Amy into the fragile weave of it.

After dinner, Amy remembered dancing with Richard in the hotel ballroom. There was a band playing insistent swing and the mass of dancers melted into a reckless blur in front of her eyes. Yet she was conscious of Nick watching her across the room, his face in perfect, sharp focus.

Later still the three of them went out on the huge, paved terrace that reared above the sea. The white chairs were tipped forward against the round tables and the white flagpoles stood out against the black sky. Their ropes tapped the staccato rhythm of the wind. Amy leant over the railings and looked into the swirling tide. The air was cold and the salt spray stung her face. Ahead were the pinprick lights of the fishing fleet. Away to the left, dark in the darkness, was Spain. Nick stood with his back to it and the wind blew the hair back from his face. They had stopped laughing now, and they stood together quiet in the wind.

Richard said in a low voice, 'I'm going to bed. If I were you, I'd do the same thing.' Then he turned abruptly and walked away, a slight, dark figure against the glittering blaze of the hotel.

Amy watched him go, feeling the touch of his sadness and the stirring of her own. They had anaesthetized the sadness tonight with champagne, and fine red wine and brandy, and with the determination of their laughter, but it would surely wake up again.

Then she felt Nick move beside her, and his mouth against her hair. 'Let's go to bed now.'

Just for a little longer, then. The sadness could lie still a little longer.

They rode the gilt cage of the lift up to Amy's suite. Nick tried to unlock the door, fumbling with the key in his left hand until he leant against the frame in a moment of blind frustration. Amy gently took the key and opened the door. It swung open to show the room's tall windows with the curtains drawn against the night, and through another doorway the bed with the covers turned back and shaded lamps lit on either side.

Nick pushed the door and it shut fast behind them.

They looked at one another for a moment and then his hand reached for hers. Their fingers knitted together and he drew her close to him. Nick's head bent slowly over hers until their mouths met.

Amy's eyes closed. Behind her eyelids the glow of the lamps swam and wove patterns. 'I think I must be very drunk,' she said. Nick lifted their locked hands and kissed her knuckles in answer.

'I am drunk too. I think we had to be drunk here, in this place.' He moved their hands in a wide gesture that took in the opulent room. They swayed together, and then balanced again. Amy knew that he meant here, in all this padded luxury after what they had both seen and learned.

Lie still. Lie still a little longer.

His mouth was harder over hers and Amy's opened to him. The blood began to move in her veins in a slow, tidal pulse and she heard the insistent wash of the waves beyond their windows.

'Love me?' she asked softly, and in answer Nick's body bent over hers like a taut bow. Their hands dropped and his mouth moved to kiss her throat, and then her shoulders left bare by the black dress. His fingers traced the long, vulnerable line of her spine and touched the tiny buttons at the back of her dress. He undid one and then another, frowning with the effort of it.

'Help me,' he begged her.

Amy undid the buttons and the dress slid to a heap at her feet. Nick knelt and took off her shoes and when she looked down at his bent head she saw that there were silver hairs thick among the black. Amy felt the heat of tears in her eyes, but she wouldn't let them fall. Nick looked up at her again and she saw how the longing in his face answered her own.

'Nick,' she whispered. 'Nick, it's all right. It will all be all right.'

He couldn't lift her now, but he took her hand and led her to the bed. She undid his bow tie and took the links out of his cuffs and folded Klaus's evening clothes neatly on a chair. She took off the rest of her own clothes and turned back to him. The dressings on his arm and chest showed stark white.

'You are very beautiful,' he told her. His left arm came across his chest and he touched the bandaged stump of his arm. 'If . . . Amy, am I . . .'

If this repels you. If I am less than whole.

'No,' she said swiftly. She moved and put her arms around his waist, her cheek against the bandage.

Nick touched her shoulder with the tips of his fingers, and then he helped her up and laid her on the bed. He knelt and kissed her breasts and then the soft inner skin of her thighs. He bent his head over her and his tongue moved, gentle. Amy's eyes opened once and she saw the high ceiling was still. She wasn't drunk any more. Every sense was alive, as clear as crystal, and crying out with her need for him.

'Please,' she whispered.

He knelt between her legs and then tried to lie down. She saw the blind contraction of pain in his face as his burned chest touched her. Amy turned, insistent, until Nick lay on his back. She fitted her hands over him, stroking. Nick's head turned on the pillow and his eyes stared sightlessly.

'Please,' he echoed her.

Amy smiled. Gently she lifted herself, poised for a second over him, and then slid down in a single smooth movement. The pleasure of his thrust within her drew out a long, shuddering breath. His arm came up to encircle her and drew her down so that their mouths and tongues could meet. Her hair fell forward over his face and they moved together, sweetly, the pain all forgotten. Amy heard the waves outside louder, gathering strength, and felt them within herself. Nick was whole, and they were one whole themselves, for a moment, just a moment. Then she heard herself cry out, and he answered her. The waves spilt over and ran away into the soft, shining sand.

They lay together, each breath drawn in unison, their ribs rising and falling together. Nick's arm held her tightly and when Amy opened her eyes she saw the fierce will in his face. It was quiet now. A moment later she felt him stir again inside her.

They didn't sleep until grey light shone through the curtains. Amy saw it as Nick drew her to him and touched his mouth to

607

her bruised lips. They had driven themselves through all the recesses of love, further, beyond the landscapes they had charted before, unwilling to stop and unwilling to lose the touch of one another. They had come up against the high, blank wall of exhaustion. Nick's face looked beaten in the dim light.

'It's daytime,' he said defeatedly. But they couldn't stop the day dawning. This day, or any of the others that would follow it. Amy put her fingers to his lips. 'Sleep now,' she ordered him, and as soon as she said it his eyelids dropped.

Before Amy slept she thought of the times and places of their other love-making. They had snatched their wild, defiant happiness in the little cottage by the woods at Chance. Amy remembered her defiance, and her own conviction that nothing mattered except the fierceness of their love. Her mouth twisted a little as she thought of it. Then Nick in the house in Chelsea and her fear of being parted from him. He had gone back to Nantlas, then. Afterwards there was the waiting at Pimlico, waiting day by day for him to come, and dreading his going again. And now, at the end, there was the Hôtel du Palais set on its curve of bay close to the edge of Spain. When Amy fell asleep it was with the thought of victory in Spain, and Paloma wrapped up in her box crib at Colmenar.

The bitterness faded out of her smile and she looked like a young girl as she slept, curled over her own folded arms and with her back turned to Nick.

They slept late into the afternoon, and when they woke up the sadness stirred and reared itself. Amy stood silently at the long window of her room and looked out at the grey-ridged restless sea, feeling a weight inside her that was as dull and blunt as sickness. She dressed Nick's arm and chest again, and they had been as gentle with each other as the touch of her fingers with the gauze and antiseptic. Once, twice, they had turned to each other ready to say something, but the words had failed to come. At last Nick went away down the corridor to his own room.

A little later Richard came and sat with Amy. He watched her concernedly, looking away as soon as she felt his eyes on her.

At last he asked, 'Did I do wrong to bring you both here?'

Amy turned her troubled face to his. 'No. You didn't do wrong.' She lifted her chin, apparently calm. 'We . . . I know what must happen. It's hard, that's all, when it comes.' She lifted her hand to shade her eyes and Richard's face was taut with his sympathy.

'Shall I stay, then?' he whispered.

After a moment Amy said, 'No. I think it would be best if you went.' Abruptly she stood up and went to him, putting her arms around him. 'Do you understand? Thank you for coming to that place, and for being here now.'

Richard reached for her hand and held it, wordlessly.

That evening the three of them sat down again to dinner in the glowing dining-room. The laughter had all evaporated and they were quiet now, talking in commonplaces in order not to be silent. Amy and Nick ate almost nothing, and the wine failed to raise their spirits.

Biarritz, Amy thought. She had seized on the little bubble of time that Richard had offered them. The bubble hadn't burst, but it was drifting away, out of reach, the iridescent colours fading as it grew smaller. They had had a day, and an evening of laughter, and a long night that had ended in grey dawn. Amy wouldn't forget the laughter, or the night.

After dinner Richard announced, 'I think I shall go back to Paris tomorrow morning. Klaus might run off with a sailor if I'm away too long.'

They smiled dutifully at him, making no protests.

It was early when they went up to their rooms, Nick and Amy a little ahead of Richard. At Amy's door they stopped for a moment and she turned to face him, looking clearly into his eyes. 'I think,' she said gently, 'it would be better tonight if . . .'

Nick had taken the key to open the door and now he held it out to her again, and the key swung from its heavy brass fob. He put his arm around her and held her, and then he said, 'Good night, my love.'

Amy watched him walk away. Weariness showed in his stooped shoulders. She would have called him back, but yet she didn't. She went into her bedroom and lay down on the bed, and listened for a long time to a different sea.

The Bentley had been brought round to the front of the hotel and now stood imposingly where the driveway curved to the porticoed doors. Richard's luggage was being brought out in relays by the porters.

Richard and Amy walked under the dipping branches of palm trees to the wrought-iron gates that were still ornamented with the Emperor Napoléon's arms. Beyond the gates the steep little streets of Biarritz climbed the cluster of hills.

Amy said, 'Thank you for coming to help us.'

As she spoke a big black Mercedes purred past them with an escort of two others. She glimpsed uniforms inside, peaked caps and gold stars. The Mercedes stopped at the portico and the driver sprang out to open the passenger door and then stood stiffly to salute. Big, grey-haired men climbed out and walked past the phalanxes of bowing porters. Richard frowned at the sight and then turned away. He took Amy's hand.

'I didn't help. I wish . . . I wish it was different for you.'

Amy smiled at him. 'I know. You warned me, remember? Long ago at Chance.'

'What will you do?'

'There are several things I have to do. After that, I'm not sure.'

His hand squeezed hers. 'Don't let anything happen to you.'

'Don't worry,' she promised him. 'Nothing will. And you?'

'Back to Klaus, and Paris, you know that. And my new book.'

'Are you happy, Richard?'

The German officers had disappeared into the hotel.

'As happy as anyone can be, now, at this time.' He paused and then added quietly, 'We all have to seize the chance of it while we can. I don't think that there will be much happiness in Europe in the next few years. Do you?'

The big black cars, empty now, rolled away from the hotel doors.

Amy had been oblivious of the bright spring sunshine and the salty sea breeze tossing the branches of the palms. It seemed now that a thicker grey cloud masked the sun and the wind struck penetrating cold into her bones. She thought of Spain and what she had seen there, and imagined that misery spreading across all the face of Europe.

'No,' she said. 'I don't think there will. I'm afraid, Richard.'

He put his arm through hers and turned her back along the driveway. Nick had come out of the hotel and was standing by the Bentley, waiting for them.

'Are you? That doesn't matter. You're strong, Amy.'

Nick had said that too. Was she, then? The sky seemed very dark, now.

They walked back to the car in silence. Richard took Nick's left hand and held it, then briefly hugged him. Amy saw their heads, black and brown, close together for an instant. Then Richard came and kissed her. He stepped back briskly and pulled on his leather driving gauntlets.

'Ho for the open road,' he grinned. He got into the driving seat and started the engine. Through the wound-down window he asked Amy, 'Do you have enough money?'

'Yes. All my allowance. Adeline wouldn't let me use it for Spain, but she couldn't object to new dinner dresses and the Hôtel du Palais, Biarritz, could she?'

He laughed. 'No, I don't think so.' He let in the clutch and the car began to roll forward. Amy saw his long-lidded eyes, wide open for once, as he looked up at her.

'If you need me,' Richard said, 'you know where to find me. I'll come at once.'

The big car slid away and crunched over the raked gravel. Amy and Nick stood side by side, watching it until it passed through the gates and swung around the corner out of sight.

Thank you, Amy said silently.

When she looked up at Nick she saw that he was awkward, hesitating, and there were lines of anxiety drawn deep in his face. Time was running out, then. She waited, but he didn't speak.

'What shall we do now?' she asked him.

Nick said quickly, 'I have to write a letter. To Kay Cooper. To tell her that Jake died usefully, and for a just cause. And other necessary lies.'

Amy remembered that Kay had said, *If you see Jake, tell him that I love him.* Yes. And so she and Nick would wait a little while longer.

'I'm going for a walk,' she told him. Amy went along the sea front, past the Casino where the steps were being swept and the shops with their windows of *patisserie* and cafés with the first tables of the season set up outside. Women in furs with little dogs on leads were sitting in the sunshine drinking hot chocolate and gossiping. She passed the corner of Fendi's and turned up into the old town. The crooked houses leant over until the top storeys almost touched, leaving only a slit of bright sky showing

611

overhead. There were lines of washing strung across the balconies and the urban smells of oil and cooking. Amy remembered how rich and foreign it had seemed to her as a girl. She climbed rapidly until she was panting with the effort. Then, at a corner, she came to the cave-like sweetshop where Luis the Spanish waiter had brought her. He had bought her sweets exactly like those ones, brilliantly coloured, in a twisted cone of paper. He had taken her home to meet his family. And then on the way back he had drawn her into an alleyway and kissed her. Her first kiss, and Amy remembered the exotic warmth of it as vividly as if Luis was still standing beside her. What had happened to Luis and his clever monkey-face?

Frowning with the effort of remembering the direction they had taken together all those years ago, Amy went on upwards. There, in front of her, was the steeply perched row of houses. Luis's family had lived in the end one. She crossed quickly to the door. It stood ajar, and when she reached it a girl peered out at her. She had black hair held up at the sides with combs, and black eyes. There was a baby in her arms, black-haired like Paloma. '*Sí?*' the girl asked coldly.

Amy took a breath. '*Soy amigo de Luis,*' she said.

There was a long pause and then the door inched open a little wider. Amy stepped into the tiny room. It was just the same, bare except for the holy pictures on the walls, and scrupulously clean. There was an old woman, another girl, children and babies. Round dark eyes stared blankly at her. The old woman said something sharp to the girl, calling her *Isabella*. The young mother was Luis's sister, whom Amy had last seen playing with stones on the step outside.

Isabella's answer carried the words *amigo* and *Luis*. The old woman looked distrustfully at Amy and then she beckoned forward a little boy, perhaps nine years old. She told him something in a low voice.

The child turned his lively face up to Amy. 'Luis fight. Since July. Not come home. Not hear. Nothing. *Nada.*'

The old woman held her knotted hand up to her face. Amy bent her head, ashamed of her intrusion.

Luis had gone to fight at the very beginning, then. And now he was either a Nationalist prisoner or, a thousand times more likely, he was dead. Isabella said, '*Mi marida, también.*' My husband, too. All the men must have gone.

Isabella hoisted her baby on to her shoulder. It was no bigger than Paloma, a few weeks old. One of the children sitting on the floor began to wail monotonously, and Isabella knelt to soothe her.

'*Perdone*,' Amy said helplessly. '*Mi perdone.*'

The old woman was crying silently but Isabella looked up as Amy reached the door. She nodded an acknowledgement that Amy had come in friendship, and had lost a friend.

'*Gracias*,' Isabella said. Thank you for coming.

Amy went out and on down the winding hills again. She felt suddenly that the weight of all the losses might pull her beneath the waves, submerge her. She walked for a long time on the deserted beach, looking out at the water. The wind grew strong and whipped the Atlantic waves into dull grey mountains. At full tide they crashed against the green piers of the hotel terrace. When she went up to her room she heard their dull thunder all around her, like the roar of the guns.

Nick came to her door before dinner. He had put on his evening clothes himself, but the ends of his bow tie hung loose around his neck. Amy tied it neatly for him. She had changed into the black dress again and Nick smiled crookedly at the sight of it.

They went down to the dining-room and sat at their table with the candlelight reflected back at them from the dark windows. They ordered food mechanically, and wine was brought and poured into their glasses. Amy lifted hers and tilted it, seeing the colours at the rim.

They were both waiting. It was a week since Amy had left Charles Carew's field hospital, and she knew that she should allow herself at least two days for the difficult journey back into Spain, to Colmenar. So this was the last day, the last night. The little bubble of time was drifting away, faster and faster. Which of them would reach up, blunt-fingered, and stab it?

Amy was sitting facing the room. There was a big table, fully laid but unoccupied, drawn into the secluded corner farthest away from them. As she watched, the heavy glass doors opened and a party of uniformed men came swinging in. They were army officers, high-ranking, their stiff tunic collars ablaze with insignia. Half of them were Spanish Nationalists. Amy's fingers tightened around the stem of her glass. The Spaniards stood back deferentially to let the others take their places. Amy saw black breeches and the clicking heels of highly polished boots. There were tunics with scarlet facings, and shining swastikas. They were Nazis. Nick saw her face and turned around to look. Then he laughed, a short, harsh sound. He sat back again facing Amy, picked up his glass and drained it.

Amy said, stiff-lipped, 'We can't sit here.'

'Why not?'

She stared incredulously at him. 'Those . . . those people are the enemy. Our enemies. We can't stay in a hotel with the men who killed Jennie, and Jake.'

Nick's bitter gasp of laughter came again. 'All kinds of people get killed in wars. I thought you knew that. I don't know why you should be so shocked to see a few enemy officers carousing together. This town is on the Nationalist side of Spain, in a neutral country. They have to go to have their parties somewhere, so why not here? And are you really so particular about who you sit down with? I killed a man, a helpless man who was tied up and blindfolded. I've killed other men too, Spaniards and Germans and Italians. But that was in fair combat. Does that make it better?'

Amy looked across the room at the Nazis. It suddenly occurred to her that she had assumed Luis would fight for the Republicans. She had no reason to do that. Perhaps he had been a Nationalist, thrown the grenade that had disembowelled Jake, trained the machine-gun on Jennie as she ran down the track from the radio post . . . Amy looked down at the tablecloth, then closed her eyes.

'You have a very clear idea of friends and enemies,' Nick said. 'I wish I did.'

Amy's head jerked up again. 'You are saying that the Fascists are friends? Hitler and the Nazis? Mussolini?'

'No, my love.' She saw that Nick's face was haggard, and her anger dissolved at once. She put out her hand to touch his. 'I just don't see the issues with the same burning clarity as I once did. After the things that happened there.' Nick looked through the solid hotel walls and across the bay to the spectre of Spain.

'Tell me,' she said gently.

Nick told her about the execution in the little wood. Through his cold, clear description she saw the blond soldier and his

614

twitching limbs. And he described, with a savageness that frightened her, the rigid Communist cadres that ruled behind the Republican lines. *Fuck the Party*, that's what he had said in the canvas shelter at the field hospital, Amy remembered.

'So, you see,' he said at last, 'I don't care very much whether I sit down with them or with our own generals. It doesn't seem to make very much difference. I do know that I hate war and I will never fight again. Or,' he laughed once more, 'even if I could, I wouldn't.'

The sleeve of Klaus's evening coat was tucked neatly into the right-hand pocket. Nick poured himself another glass of wine, and drank it at a gulp.

'Amy,' he said. They looked at one another, seeing the familiar lines and the movement of muscles underneath, the net of nerves and veins, and in an instant's perfect recognition all the little impulses of thought and feeling and sympathy. They knew each other completely, with pure intimacy.

'I know,' Amy said in a clear voice. 'You're going home to Mari. I've known it for a long time.'

Their hands clasped across the table. They had forgotten everything else. *There*, Amy thought. *Was that what I needed to be strong for, to say that*? She looked away, unable for a moment to bear the thought of losing him. 'I know,' she made herself say again. 'There isn't anywhere to go from here, for you and me. I think I always knew you still loved Mari. Oh yes, you did. Mari and Dickon and your own people. I wouldn't let myself admit it until I came to Nantlas and saw it. Saw you there, with them all. And,' she was close to crying now, but she fought against the tears and defiance hardened in her voice, 'if I can't have all of you I can't make do with just a piece any more. I don't want to go back to the half-life I lived in Pimlico. I don't. I don't.'

She wondered if the reiteration convinced either of them.

'Amy. I couldn't have all of you either, my darling.' She turned her hot eyes back to him, unbelieving. He looked so tired, defeated. 'Look around. Look at this place.' Their eyes held one another's but she felt the wide room with its opulence. 'Even these clothes. I'm a miner from Nantlas. I don't belong here. I don't even want to be here. Whereas you, you float through the place with everyone's eyes on you – no, listen to me – you don't see it because you are preoccupied with your work, your beliefs, causes – but it is your world. You can't just shake it off.'

615

'No. No,' Amy protested. Not the old divide. It wasn't that, was it, after everything that had happened?

'Yes. Listen. Even if I hadn't been married, didn't have Dickon for a son, you and I could never have been husband and wife to one another. Even though I love you, body and soul, with every fibre of myself. Even though I do now and always will.'

'I love you too,' she whispered. The tears were running down her face, unchecked. 'And I always will.'

'I'm sorry,' he said. The painful truth of it touched her.

'So am I.'

They were both sorry. A thousand other things, too, but sorry most of all. Amy felt the sadness around her, tangible, inescapable. There was nowhere for them to go from here. It was a blind end, the end of the road in the splendour of the Hôtel du Palais, Biarritz.

She thought of Spain, and all the sorrow of it. It had taken her own small part in it to teach her the detachment to face this moment, the recognition that the world would not end, neither the sorrow nor the happiness. She had constructed her painful edifice with Nick, sadly and blindly shoring it up, and now it had crumbled softly away. That was all.

Amy lifted her head and smiled at him.

'What will you do,' she asked him, 'when you get back to Nantlas?'

His hand still held hers. 'When we were in the Jarama, before I was wounded, a letter came through to me. It was from the chairman of the Rhondda Constituency Labour Party, a man I have known since I was a boy. He asked me, very unofficially, if I would consider standing for adoption as the next Parliamentary candidate. It's a safe seat, a mining seat. The present member is a Party patriarch. He's very ill. He may even be dead by this time.'

Amy stared at him, astonished. The shift was so complete.

'You are a Communist. You can't stand for Labour.'

'No,' he said carefully. 'I told you. I'm not a Communist any more.'

Sympathy pricked her. She knew what a vivid and important part of his life Nick's convictions had been. The loss of them would account for the defeat she sensed in him. Yet as she considered, she remembered Nick on the platform at Nantlas. He was a natural politician. And she guessed that the power of

616

the office would feed his own power, and he would grow. If it had to be through another party, he would say, so be it.

'What did you tell your old friend?'

'I wrote the letter yesterday, after I'd written to Kay. I said that I was coming home. And I said that if the selection committee was prepared to consider me, I would be proud.'

The words were there already, Amy thought. Yes, Nick would be a fine Labour MP.

'I can work for our people,' he said fiercely. 'The better, from inside the Commons.'

'Oh yes,' she said aloud. 'You will be very good. You'll probably become Prime Minister.'

Nick's face admitted a crooked smile. 'Well. I can't cut coal any more, can I?'

The bitter sadness that Amy briefly felt found its expression. 'It will be perfect, won't it? You will be able to go home and look after Dickon, and be happy with Mari. You won't be rich as an MP, but you'll have enough to live on. Perhaps you can give Mari another baby, and . . .'

'Amy.' His hand reached out and gripped her wrist, crushing it. 'Stop it. You will have a husband, and babies of your own. I love you, and I won't smother that chance any more. Don't you see it?'

'No,' she said sadly. 'I can't help being jealous. It's an ugly feeling, but I should be used to it by now. There won't be any babies. There never have been, not with Jack Roper or with you. I must be barren.'

She was crying openly now, and part of her shivered with shame at her own weakness. Nick moved his chair to shield her from the room. He leant very close, so that she felt the warmth of him.

'There will be a husband, then. Someone with a big brown horse to ride, and a long shiny car, like Jack Roper. Not a one-armed miner, my darling, my love. I can't tell you any more truth than that.'

'I know . . .' She breathed a long, shuddering sigh, 'I know what this costs you too. I'm sorry. I'd thought it all out. I was going to be brave and strong.'

'You are both those things,' Nick told her gently.

Amy took the handkerchief he held out to her and rubbed her eyes. She looked down at the white tablecloth. With a quiver of horror she saw that there was redness spilling over it, crimson red blotches that made her think of soldiers lying helpless on their stretchers, and the night Paloma was born. She jerked her head up to see where the blood was coming from. From the ceiling over their heads hung a huge glass globe, multicoloured facets of glass. From somewhere across the room the light inside the globe and the others like it had been turned on, and the coloured light spilt across the white cloths. It was nothing like blood at all. There was going to be a cabaret. The German officers called out their approval.

Amy said, 'Shall I tell you what I'm going to do? I'm going to go back to the hospital at Colmenar. I have to go back, but I want to as well. There's a baby there, a tiny girl called Paloma.'

The cabaret artists appeared. There was a pianist in a red coat and a vocalist, a buxom girl in a tight dress. The officers cheered.

As she talked, faster, Amy's conviction grew. 'If I can, I'm going to adopt Paloma and take her back home with me as my daughter. I can look after her. I want her so much. And when we get home again, I'm going to study to be a doctor.' She held her head rigid, not looking at the noisy soldiers. 'If . . . when the war comes, we'll need doctors. What do you think, Nick? Tell me what you think.'

Nick smiled. 'Do that. Your little girl will still be a Spanish baby . . .'

'I know. I wouldn't want her to be otherwise.'

'. . . but she will be very lucky to share some of the Lovell grace. And I think you will make a far, far better doctor, Amy, than I will ever make a politician.'

The pianist struck a noisy chord. 'Come on,' Nick said. 'Away from here.'

They stood up and walked across the room, past the covert stares, and past the high-ranking officers whose faces were red with food and wine, without a glance. They rode the gilt lift cage again, and stepped out into the silent, carpeted corridor.

They reached the door of Amy's suite. She looked down, suddenly awkward. 'Good night,' she said. 'Nick, I . . .'

His hand caught her chin, cupping it and almost wrenching it around.

'No,' Nick said. 'Not yet.'

He led her in and closed the door, and the wide bed beckoned them. They lay down together and gave themselves up, once more, for the last night.

They made love gently, with none of the earlier desperation. The tenderness was their farewell, and absolution. In the darkness, with the howl of the wind and waves outside the window, Amy felt Nick's face wet with tears as he moved inside her. Her own tears answered him.

But she said, 'Don't cry, my love.' She was strong, now.

The gentleness, hands and faces and bodies touching like a blessing, was their leave-taking. Although Amy went with Nick to the railway station in the calm early morning, they had already parted.

Amy bought him a ticket to Paris.

'No,' he said calmly. 'Not first class. A miner from Nantlas, remember.'

He took the third-class ticket and the money she gave him, the bare minimum he would need to get him back to the Rhondda.

'Will you be able to manage the journey?' Amy asked.

'I managed the journey here. And I brought four others with me.'

Three of those four men would never go home.

The train was waiting, and he climbed in and found a seat, a wooden bench crowded with travellers. Amy watched him through the dusty glass, a thin, war-marked man in borrowed clothes.

Nick.

He lifted his hand to sketch a wave, and her own wave answered it. Then she walked away past the long train, over the bridge and out into Biarritz. The storm had burnt itself out, and the sky was the pale, washed blue of a bird's egg.

'What do you mean, gone?'

The official in his little cubicle off the main hall at Paradise Hotel was a stranger to Amy. 'Gone where?'

He shrugged, a Spanish gesture. He kept his hand firmly on his pile of records, the fingers splayed out as if he was expecting her to try to snatch the information.

Patiently Amy tried again. 'She isn't two months old, yet. She can't have just gone. If someone has placed her elsewhere, there

619

will be a record of it, and her whereabouts. Most likely there.'
She pointed at his papers.

'Not posseeble. Ees regulations.'

Swallowing her fury, Amy went to find the hospital director.

She had been travelling for two days, and she had reached the hospital an hour ago. She had run up the stairs to Elena's apartment two at a time. She had found the door locked. It had never, ever been locked before, and she stood in the corridor helplessly rattling the handle and calling 'Elena?' When nobody came she ran back down to her basement cubicle, and found that it had become a linen store. She had gone, then, from one to another of the places where Paloma's box crib had used to stand. It wasn't in any of them.

Almost weeping with frustration and anxiety she had gone to the registrar. The man had explained that Elena had been taken ill, very ill with peritonitis. She had been operated on at once, and removed two days later to a civilian hospital. No, he told her, the baby had not been taken with her. Nor did he, Amy decided, really have any idea where Paloma had gone.

All she could establish was that she was no longer at Paradise Hotel.

Amy cursed her own complacency in imagining that Paloma would be safe at the hospital. She had been away for five weeks, a long time during a war. The nurses who had shared in the baby's care had been moved forward to field posts or transferred elsewhere. Even the soldiers who had hung over her crib had gone, to convalescent centres or back to their battalions.

Where had she gone? Who had taken her?

Amy was distraught when she reached the director's office.

He listened carefully to her gasped-out questions. 'Yes, of course I remember the baby.'

'Where is she?'

'I'm not sure. The Spanish authorities have a number of centres for war orphans. Little Paloma was registered as an orphan and in due course she was allocated a place and taken to it. Two Socorro Rojo officials collected her with a group of other children from here in Colmenar.'

Trying to think calmly, Amy looked at the things on the director's desk, a tray of pens and pencils and a pile of folders. 'Why?' she asked. 'Why did she have to go? She was well cared for here, with Elena.'

The director glanced up at her. 'I understand that you were attached to the baby. But this is a hospital, full of grievously injured men, and Elena herself was seriously ill. It was no place for an infant to live.'

'You don't understand. I want to . . .' Amy checked herself, breathing in slowly to steady her voice. 'Well. I would like to try and trace her, just the same. To make sure that she is safe and well.'

'Why should she not be?' The director was impatient with the fuss over one baby who was already being adequately cared for by the proper authorities. 'Probably Socorro Rojo will provide you with a list of their centres if you wish to go that far, Miss Lovell.'

'Probably,' she agreed. The interview was over, but Amy hadn't started yet. Paloma was somewhere in Republican Spain. The thought of the baby had drawn Amy back to Colmenar like a lodestone. The same thought had filled her head, mercifully, in all the hours since Nick had gone. She couldn't disappear now in the tidal wave of the war. Somehow, Amy would find her.

She left the director's office and began to search the hospital for anyone who could help. By a stroke of luck the student interpreter who had helped her on the night of Paloma's birth was still there. Amy explained, grasping the young man's hand in her insistence.

'Sí,' he said, 'Sí. I will help you.'

They went straight to the Red Aid centre in Colmenar. Amy stood defiantly in front of an official's desk with the interpreter at her side. She was determined not to leave until she had a list, a full list, of all the places Paloma might have been sent to. It took a long time. The documentation was chaotic, and Amy's heart sank at the sight of the muddled ledgers and wire baskets overflowing with dog-eared papers. To find one baby suddenly seemed an impossible task amongst so many in such confusion.

Her interpreter was stalwart. At length, after what seemed hours of shrugging and mumbling and gesticulation, the official produced a roughly scribbled list. There were fifteen addresses, in towns and cities strung out down the eastern side of Spain from Barcelona to Almeria. Through the interpreter the official told her, with a certain relish, that there was no guarantee Paloma would be in any of them. There were other centres not under his direct control, and some children who were not ill or hurt were cared for by families.

Amy held the list firmly. 'This will do to begin with,' she said. 'Thank you.' As soon as they were outside she asked the student, 'Will you help me telephone?'

'Yes, but the telephone . . .'

The student's pessimism was justified. It was impossible to get through to some centres, and those that they did reach gave inconclusive answers. Amy could cross only two places off her list at the end of the day, and that was because they housed no babies at all. At the others, there were baby girls who could just be Paloma. No one knew.

The student put down the receiver for the last time and rubbed his face. 'Not much good,' he said.

Amy looked up, still sitting in the hunched position from where she had listened to all the one-sided, inconclusive conversations. Her mouth was set in a straight line. 'Not yet. But I'll find her.'

It was dawning on her that she would have to go to each centre in turn, and look for herself.

At the end of March 1937 the Madrid front was quiet at last. The battle of Guadalajara had ended in what the Republicans claimed as a great victory over Mussolini's Italians. The flood of arrivals at Paradise Hotel slowed to a trickle, and Amy's job became the care of convalescents and post-operatives instead of the gory scramble of the reception ward. She was busy, like all the rest of the hospital staff, but there was time off too, sometimes more than a day at a time. Doggedly, without letting herself admit the possibility of failure, Amy began to visit the places on her Socorro Rojo list.

She started with the nearest ones, and drew a blank at all of them.

She began to travel farther afield, concentrating on the northern side of Colmenar, pinning her hopes on the possibility that the authorities would have known Paloma's family came from the north, and placed her accordingly. She saw baby girls amongst the little companies of children who had lost their homes and families, legs or arms or eyes, but none of them was Paloma.

She reached Barcelona after a bone-jarring ride in a lorry loaded with medical supplies. The address she was heading for was clearer than some of the others – a street name, and a number.

Amy found the place without difficulty. It was a tall grey house in a wide residential street, clean and almost prosperous-looking. Amy's heart began to beat a little faster, as it did every time. Perhaps this was the place. Perhaps Paloma's room was behind one of these blank windows . . .

The hallway was high and airy. A boy of twelve or so passed on crutches, swinging his injured leg vigorously. A woman came down the stairs and smiled at Amy. '*Si*?'

Amy's explanation was well practised now. 'I am an English nurse, from Colmenar. I am looking for a baby, a girl, born there in January of a refugee mother. We called her Paloma . . .' All the time, she would watch the other person's face, interpreting the blankness. Was it incomprehension, or readiness to say *No, there is no baby here like that* . . .

This woman was listening intently. When Amy had finished, she didn't say anything for a moment.

Please.

At last she said, 'I don't know. Will you come this way?'

She led the way upstairs. There were closed double doors ahead of them leading to what must once have been a formal drawing-room.

The doors opened. On the other side there were cots and little low beds, and the sound of running feet. Two very small children scuttled away in front of them, laughing and calling out. Amy's companion chased after them, mock-angry. Over her shoulder she called back, 'The baby girl in the end cot, there, she is named Paloma in her papers.'

Very slowly, Amy crossed the room. There were rough wooden toys discarded on the floor. There was a little crib, with a white blanket. She put her hand out to touch the bars, closing her eyes for a second.

Please, she prayed.

She opened her eyes and looked down into the cot.

Amy had even, amidst all her other fears, been afraid that if the time ever came she wouldn't be certain.

But the baby in the cot was Paloma. She knew it without a shadow of doubt. She was asleep, her hair so dark against the white sheet.

Amy stood still with her hands clenched on the cot bars, and the tears ran down her cheeks. The baby's clenched fist lay close to her face, her tiny, perfect fingers curved over as smooth as the ribs of a seashell.

Only now, now that she had found her, did Amy admit to herself the impossibility of her search. Belated cold fear possessed her and she shook with it. She could have hunted for ever, up and down the wreck of Spain, and never found the little, puckered face she longed for.

Amy knelt down, pressing her face to the wooden bars, with her hand forced between them so that she could touch the warm, curled fingers. With the tears still wet on her face she watched Paloma as if she would never take her eyes off her again.

'Paloma,' she whispered. 'Paloma, I'm here. I've come to take you home.'

She made the promise for both of them, and then she knelt for a long time, just looking at her.

At last, very slowly, Amy stood up. Still slowly, turning every few steps to look back at the sleeping baby, Amy went away down the long room to search for the orphanage director.

The adoption took months. She had had no idea, at the beginning, how difficult it would be. Official after official told her that it was impossible for an unmarried Englishwoman to adopt a Spanish national, in wartime, and take her out of the country. There were times when Amy was afraid that the waiting and the red tape would defeat them. Over and over again she made the difficult journey to Barcelona to visit Paloma, and almost as soon as she arrived she would have to wrench herself away again to go back to her nursing duties. During the weeks away from her Amy would dream repeatedly that she had disappeared again, and she would start up out of her sleep, sweating and shaking.

In her fight to adopt Paloma, Amy called on everyone she could think of who might have any influence with the Spanish authorities. She wrote to Charles Carew, care of Spanish Medical Aid because she had no idea where he was, and in the end it was Charles who sent her a name and address. Amy wrote one more imploring letter. Three weeks later the adoption papers arrived.

Amy completed her service with Spanish Medical Aid and she flew home with her baby in September 1937.

England, September 1938

There was a bowl of late-blooming roses on the low table, the big, creamy-white petals of the flowers streaked with pale gold. The haze of afternoon sunlight streaming through the window was exactly the same gold. Amy looked up from her scatter of letters and photographs when she heard voices, and went quickly to the window. Bethan was walking slowly across the curve of mown grass with Paloma at her side. Bethan held one finger of the child's outstretched hand, offering the last measure of security, and the reminder of restraint. Paloma's mouth was wide open, she was laughing and calling out at the same time. Her free hand made little clutching movements towards the dog racing in circles around them. It was Isabel's Yorkshire terrier, Amy saw. Bethan and Paloma must have been across the village to see Isabel.

Amy stood in the window watching until all three of them moved out of sight around the corner of the house. A moment later a door banged and the voices were much closer. 'Mamama . . . Mamamama . . .'

'In here! Come and see me!'

Paloma appeared in the drawing-room doorway, her face beaming under the shadow of her white cotton sunhat. She shook off Bethan's hand and ran to Amy, just reaching safety before she tripped. Amy caught her and swept her up.

'Be careful, lamb,' Bethan admonished. At twenty months Paloma was still not perfectly steady on her feet. Her curiosity and eagerness outstripped her abilities minute by minute, and she fell over a dozen times a day. Her fat knees and her broad, olive-skinned forehead under the black curls showed the bruises. Amy was terrified every time it happened, but Bethan just laughed.

'All children fall over. You were the worst one for it yourself.

A proper tomboy, and black and blue all over. Miss Isabel and Mr Richard were cautious little creatures beside you.'

Paloma climbed up on to Amy's knee. 'Dog,' she confided. 'See dog.'

'I know. I saw him on the lawn. It was old Tiger, wasn't it? Who else did you see?'

'Bel,' Paloma said, with clear satisfaction, and Amy and Bethan nodded proudly at each other.

'How is she?' Amy asked Bethan.

'Pink-cheeked and smiling. Resting, just as she should. I'm not worried about Mrs Parfitt.'

'Neither am I,' Amy said cheerfully. Bill Parfitt and Isabel had been married six months earlier, without telling anyone. They had simply gone to a London registry office and picked two witnesses off the street. It couldn't have been more different, Amy thought wryly, from the great fuss of the first wedding. And then they had come back as man and wife to live in the little stone house across Henstone village. Isabel was expecting their baby in the New Year.

'The first letter from Peter came in the afternoon post. Mrs Parfitt gave it to me to read.'

It was the first week of little Peter Jaspert's first term away at preparatory school. To Amy he still seemed hardly more than a baby, and she had asked Isabel, 'Must he go so soon?'

Isabel had answered tranquilly, with all the traditional convictions that Bill Parfitt shared, 'They all go at seven. You wouldn't want him to be different, would you?' And so he had gone, with his trunk and his tuck-box and his teddy-bear.

'What did the letter say?'

'It made me laugh, it was so like the ones Mr Richard used to write. Every line started *I need* . . . *I have left behind* . . . He'll be quite all right, you know.'

'Yes, I expect so.'

Paloma was bored with the adult talk. She scrambled down and headed for the inviting papers spread out on the table. A photograph crackled warningly in her blunt fingers. 'Paloma,' Bethan warned her. She glanced at the heap of memories, and then covertly at Amy. 'Shall I bring in some tea now?'

Amy stood up easily, stretching, and stifling a yawn. 'I'll go. I want to put on a stew for dinner at the same time. I'll come back and clear this stuff up later, when we've heard the news.'

She went across the hallway into the stone-flagged kitchen and took the cups and plates down from the dresser. She lit the gas under the kettle and in the oven, and put a stewpot in to cook, listening to Bethan and Paloma's footsteps in the playroom overhead. While she waited for the kettle to boil she stood looking out of the window over the slope of the garden. They grew a few vegetables on this side, and Amy thought absently that she must go out and pick runner beans for dinner. Beyond the garden Henstone church tower rose squarely out of a cluster of grey chimneys, with the sun blazing back from the old clock-face. Amy could almost hear the hum of bees over the lavender hedge.

The summer's end, a gold- and violet-shadowed English afternoon.

The kettle's shrill whistle made Amy whirl around, her hand to her mouth in sudden fear.

They had tea outside on the lawn in the last of the sunshine. Paloma had a boiled egg, and she crammed the bread fingers down into the yellow centre of it with gurgles of pleasure.

At five to six they carried the tea-things inside again, and Amy turned on the wireless. They sat side by side on the sofa, with Paloma squirming between them, to listen.

Chamberlain had flown to Germany again to meet Hitler at Godesberg. Hitler was no longer satisfied with the transfer of Czechoslovakian territory to German sovereignty. His demand was now immediate occupation of all Czechoslovakia by German troops.

At the end of the bulletin Amy turned the knob again. She looked out across the grass to the green-painted gate and the lane beyond it. Even Paloma was still for a moment, and they listened to the gentle quiet.

'What will happen,' Bethan asked at last, 'if Hitler does invade them?'

'If he does,' Amy said, 'France is bound to support the Czechs. And Britain will support France. We shall be at war.'

She reached out, still looking away into the green heart of the garden, and put her arms around Paloma. The child's head nestled comfortably under her chin. Amy could hear the Spanish guns again, the roar of them amplified all across Europe. Her arms tightened around the baby and she closed her eyes, her

627

cheek against the black hair.

'I talked to Mama on the telephone this morning. She had come home across Hyde Park, and there were platoons of soldiers everywhere digging air-raid trenches.'

Bethan said sharply, 'Her ladyship should come down to Chance where she'll be safe from the bombers.'

In spite of everything, Amy laughed. 'I said as much. And Mama said, "Oh no, darling, I couldn't possibly miss Diana's big party." There's no arguing with her.' Suddenly, closing her ears to the dull roar and turning away from the garden's overshadowed loveliness, Amy lifted Paloma and held her out to Bethan. 'Will you put her in the bath while I tidy my things away?'

When they had gone Amy began folding up the letters and slipping the photographs between the black leaves of her album. In the afternoon's gold glow she had felt that she wanted to arrange them, to draw neat lines under the old turbulence because her life was tranquil now, tranquil and ordered and without the pain of precarious happiness. But now, in the room's dimness, Amy realized that there were no lines to be drawn.

She put the album back in her desk drawer. There were no photographs of Nick. He had asked for just one of her. Did he still have it? she wondered. There were his few letters, tied in a neat bundle. The top one, the last, was written from Barcelona, when Nick was on his way to the International Brigades at Albacete. She didn't open it, because she knew it by heart. *Oh Amy*, he had written, *I love you*. Amy touched her fingertip to the envelope for an instant, as if to forge a tiny, tenuous link, and then lifted it again. She put the packet of letters away beside the album. A newspaper cutting and two books were the last things left on the table. Amy had clipped the report out of *The Times* six months ago. It was a brief news-item about a South Wales by-election. Nicholas John Penry, the Labour Party candidate, had been elected to the SWMF-sponsored seat with a majority of 16,218. Amy had thought of writing to him, a brief congratulatory note. But when she sat down at her desk she found that the words evaded her. She couldn't write a little, detached missive to Nick, but she couldn't write what she felt either. Sometimes she let herself believe that Nick had experienced the same impossibility. She had never heard from him.

There was a heavy, silver-cased cigarette lighter that had belonged to her father on the table in front of her. Amy flicked the cap to disclose the yellow flame and touched the corner of the cutting to it. It flared up briefly and then fell in a drift of black ash on to the hearthstone.

The books were stained and dog-eared. They were the copy of *Barchester Towers* and the Siegfried Sassoon poems that Tony Hardy had given her. She had immersed herself in the skirmishes of an English cathedral close at the hospital in the Jarama, with Jennie and Greta and Charles clustered around the light of the lantern. Amy ran her finger along the rippled fore-edge and then put the book away amongst the rows of others shelved in the fireside alcove.

The Sassoon was less battered and worn. She had found the war poems too raw in the midst of war. She picked the book up now and opened it at *Aftermath*.

> Do you remember the stretcher-cases lurching back
> with dying eyes and lolling heads – those ashen-grey
> masks of the lads who were once keen and kind and gay?
>
> *Have you forgotten yet?* . . .
> *Look up, and swear by the green of the spring that you'll
> never forget.*

There were so many of them, line upon line. Not just passed by, she knew that with the cold fear of conviction, but ranged ahead, shadowy, faceless, waiting. There was just one face. It was Nick's, looking steadily back into hers.

'I won't forget,' Amy said aloud. 'I won't forget, my love.'

She closed the book and put it away beside *Barchester Towers*. Paloma was calling out for her upstairs.

Amy went up to the nursery and found her in her white nightgown. Bethan had brushed her hair out into black, sparky waves. The curtains were drawn and the nightlight sent their shadows sliding hugely across the sloped ceiling.

Amy read Paloma a story and then lifted her into her cot. Paloma reached out to grasp her hand, as she always did, through the wooden struts. Amy held on to the small fingers and sang to her until she fell asleep.

Then Amy went down the stairs and out into the garden. It was dark under the trees with the sudden swoop of autumn evenings. She walked to and fro on the grass, breathing in the heady scent of the nicotiana in the flowerbed by the house wall.

There was a car coming up the lane.

To Amy's surprise it stopped in the recess beyond the gate instead of going on by. She heard the driver's door open and click shut, and footsteps scattering the grit on the road. A man stopped at her gate and fumbled for the latch, and Amy saw the glimmer of his face as he looked up at the house. It was Charles Carew.

She stepped out of the trees' shadow and he saw her.

They walked towards each other, moving silently across the grass.

The sight of Charles brought back the memory of the Jarama, the mud and the mist, and the roar of the guns. Amy remembered the huddle of canvas shelters and the big Bedford trucks, and Charles striding to and fro between them in his beret and khaki greatcoat. He was wearing a dark suit now, as if he had driven straight from town, and his thick beard was gone.

They stood in the soft quiet for a moment, linked by their memories.

Then Charles held out his hand and Amy shook it warmly.

'Welcome to Henstone,' she said, and then she added, 'I'm pleased you've come to see us, all the way up here.'

'I'm sorry to come without announcing myself first,' he said. 'I went to Chance, this afternoon. Your estates manager directed me up here.'

'My brother's manager,' Amy murmured. 'We live up here, Paloma and Bethan and me. Except in term-time, when I have to be in London, and they come with me. Would you like to come inside?'

Charles glanced through the twilight at the moon-white blur of anemones and nicotiana and breathed in the drifts of perfume.

'May we stay out here for a little while?'

'Of course.'

They turned and began to walk along the brick-paved path.

'It seems a long way away,' Charles said, and she knew that it was in his mind too. 'I'm finished there, you know. Packed off home in the first contingent. They're sending all the foreign aid home. Brigaders, everyone. Of course, you know that.'

Amy did know. The war in Spain smouldered on, but the Russians and Germans were withdrawing their support. To suit their own ends, just as they had originally provided it, Amy knew that too.

'So I came straight here to meet Paloma. How is she?'

'Very well,' Amy answered composedly. 'And more beautiful every day.'

It was Charles who had made it possible to bring the baby out of Spain. He had done other things besides, to help Amy herself.

'Thank you,' she said softly, but he made a little gesture to deflect her gratitude.

'It was luck, just knowing who to ask.' To change the subject he said, 'Chance is beautiful. You don't want to live there?'

'No. I don't want to live like that any more.' *After what we've seen. After all that has happened.* 'I'm not sure what my brother feels about it. He swears that as soon as the war comes they can have it for a convalescent home.'

They reached the gate into the lane and turned together, looking back to the house where Paloma's nightlight made a soft glow against her curtain.

'And your work, Amy? Is old Turner-Greville pleased with you?'

Turner-Greville was the Dean of Charles's old medical school. It was on Charles Carew's recommendation, endorsed by Victor, that he had interviewed Amy. But, Amy thought defiantly, it was on her own merits that he had offered her a place to read medicine. A long time ago. A year ago, when she had come back from Spain, exhausted and alone, with Paloma in her arms.

'I think he is. It's hard work, but not impossible. But I've got a long way to go yet,' Amy added soberly. 'I don't think from the sound of it that I shall be qualified in time.'

'The war won't come yet,' Charles said. 'Nobody's ready yet, not us or them. You might just make it.'

They left the gate and the path and walked diagonally, across the grass to where the deepest shadow lay, under the trees.

'And Nick?' he asked her. It was too dark here to see one another's faces. Amy saw the pale glimmer of a moth's wings float in the stillness. *And Nick.* She never spoke his name aloud, and it was awkward on her tongue.

'Nick is in Nantlas, with his family. He's a Labour MP now. I haven't seen him since he left Spain.'

That was all it took to sum it up, the little history. Amy thought of the love and the memories and the sadness that lay behind the words, and she felt the strength that went with them. *He's with me every day*, she thought. *Every day, all of the days*. She knew that Charles Carew was watching her, and the light was a little stronger as they came out from under the trees once again. She smiled at him.

'His arm healed wonderfully. You did a fine job.'

'Yes. I was proud of that one.'

They had made the circuit of the garden twice now. Amy stood on the path, looking towards her front door.

'Charles, would you like to stay to dinner? It's nothing elaborate . . .'

Charles lifted his shoulders, apologetic. 'I'm not dressed. It took me a little time to find my way here . . .'

In the Jarama they had eaten standing up, wolfing the cold food from dirty tin plates while the stretchers lay waiting for them in the *salle de triage*. Amy laughed, and she saw the answering glimmer of Charles's smile.

'We don't dress for dinner here. Mostly Bethan and I sit down in the kitchen together.'

'In that case, I would like it very much.'

They went on up the path and in through the front door. In the drawing-room Amy went to the drinks tray and picked up the decanter.

'Sherry?'

'Thank you.'

They held up their glasses.

'To?' Charles asked her.

'Oh, to Paloma, of course. To the white dove.'

'I'm sorry I haven't met her tonight,' Charles said. 'Can I call again tomorrow and see her then?'

'Yes,' Amy said. 'You can call again tomorrow.'

Their eyes met and they drank, still looking at one another.

A little while later Bethan came in. She stopped short in the doorway, seeing them.

'I'm sorry. I didn't know . . .'

They had been talking, a little sombrely, about their work and their fear that so little time was set between Spain and what was to come. At the sight of Bethan Amy's face brightened, and she stood up and crossed the room to stand by her side. 'Bethan, I would like you to meet Doctor Charles Carew. Charles, this is

632

my old friend Bethan Jones.'

Bethan looked from Amy to Charles. She saw a tall, fair-haired Englishman with fine lines fanning out in the tanned skin around his eyes. He held out his hand and she shook it.

'I'm pleased you've come, Dr Carew. Amy told me about what you did in Spain.'

Calmly, he said, 'I'm pleased to be here. I thought about coming here often – these last weeks in Spain.'

Bethan went slowly round the room and drew the curtains. The lamps on the side-tables threw warm pools of light on the polished wood.

If there had been thunder rumbling in the air at dusk, it was stilled now. From outside, where the bats were swooping low over the grass, they heard the church clock strike eight.

ABOUT THE AUTHOR

Rosie Thomas was born and raised in Wales and educated at Oxford University. She lives and works in London as a journalist, and has written widely on an assortment of topics for many major magazines. THE WHITE DOVE is her fourth novel.

SPECTACULAR ENTERTAINMENT ALL SUMMER LONG!
SUMMER SPECTACULAR FREQUENT READERS SWEEPSTAKES
WIN *A 1988 Cadillac Cimarron* Automobile or
12 other Fabulous Prizes

IT'S EASY TO ENTER. HERE'S HOW IT WORKS:

1. Enter *one* individual book sweepstakes, by completing and submitting the Official Entry form found in the back of that Summer Spectacular book, and you qualify for that book's prize drawing.

2. Enter *two* individual book sweepstakes, by completing and submitting two Official Entry Forms found in the back of those two Summer Spectacular books, and you qualify for the prize drawings for those two individual books.

3. Enter *three or more* individual book sweepstakes, by completing and submitting—in one envelope—three or more Official Entry forms found in the back of three or more individual Summer Spectacular books, and you qualify not only for those three or more individual books but also for THE BONUS PRIZE of a brand new Cadillac Cimarron Automobile!

Be sure to fill in the Bantam bookseller where you learned about this Sweepstakes . . . because if you win one of the twelve Sweepstakes prizes . . . your bookseller wins too!

SEE OFFICIAL RULES BELOW FOR DETAILS including alternate means of entry.

No Purchase Necessary.

Here are the Summer Spectacular Sweepstakes Books and Prizes!

BOOK TITLE	PRIZE
On Sale May 20, 1987	
ACT OF WILL	A luxurious weekend for two (3 days/2 nights) at first class hotel, MAP meals—(transportation not included) Approximate value: $750.00
MEN WHO HATE WOMEN & THE WOMEN WHO LOVE THEM	Gourmet food of the month for 6 months N.Y. Gourmet Co. Approximate value: $750.00
VENDETTA	Schrade Collector's Knife set Approximate value: $750.00
On Sale June 17, 1987	
LAST OF THE BREED	Sharp Video Camera and VCR Approximate value: $1,600.00

| WHITE DOVE (available in US only) THE MOTH (available in Canada only) | Lenox China white coffee service Approximate value: $750.00 |

WHITE DOVE (available
in US only)
THE MOTH (available
in Canada only)

Lenox China white coffee service
Approximate value: $750.00

THE BE (HAPPY)
ATTITUDES

Set of DP workout equipment
Approximate value: $1,000.00

On Sale July 15, 1987

THE UNWANTED

Bug Zapper and Samsonite Chairs—
Table—Umbrella—Outdoor Furniture
Approximate value: $1,300.00

A GRAND PASSION

Cake of the month plan
Approximate value: $800.00

110 SHANGHAI ROAD

$1,000 American Express Gift
Certificates
Value: $1,000.00

On Sale August 12, 1987

HIS WAY

Disc Player with library of
Sinatra discs
Approximate value: $1,000.00

SUSPECTS

Home Security System
Approximate value: $1,000.00

PORTRAIT OF A
MARRIED WOMAN

Minolta Auto-Focus Camera Kit
Approximate value: $750.00

OFFICIAL RULES

1. There are twelve individual sweepstakes, each with its own prize award. There will be twelve separate sweepstakes drawings. You will be entered into the drawing for the prize corresponding to the book(s) from which you have obtained your entry blank, any one or up to all twelve. Submit your completed entry on the Official Entry Form found in this book and any of the other participating books ... mail one or up to all twelve completed sweepstakes entries *in one envelope* to:

Frequent Readers Sweepstakes
PO Box 43 New York, New York 10046

. NO PURCHASE NECESSARY TO ENTER OR WIN A PRIZE: Residents of Ohio and those wishing to obtain an Official Entry Form (covering all 12 sweepstakes) and the Official Rules send a self-addressed stamped envelope to: Frequent Reader Sweepstakes, P.O. Box 549, Sayreville, NJ 08872. One Official Entry Form per request. Requests must be received by August 14, 1987. Residents of Washington and Vermont need not include return postage.

Winners for each of the 12 sweepstakes will be selected in a random drawing to be conducted on or about October 19, 1987, from all completed entries received, under the supervision of Marden-Kane, Inc. an independent judging organization. If any of the 12 consumer winners selected have included completed Official Entry Forms from three or more books, or have included completed Official Entry Forms from three or more books, or have entered 3 or more sweepstakes on the Alternate Mail-In Official Entry Form (See Rule #2) they are qualified to participate in a separate BONUS DRAWING to be conducted on or about Oct. 19, 1987 for a 1988 Cadillac Cimarron. In the event that none of the twelve individual sweepstake prize winners qualify for the BONUS PRIZE, the bonus prize will be selected from all completed sweepstakes entries received. No mechanically reproduced entries accepted. All entries must be received by September 30, 1987 to be eligible. Not responsible for late, lost or misdirected mail or printing errors.

THE WHITE DOVE
OFFICIAL ENTRY FORM

Please complete by entering all the information requested and
Mail to: Frequent Readers Sweepstakes
P.O. Box 43
New York, N.Y. 10046

NAME _____

ADDRESS _____

CITY _____ STATE _____ ZIP _____

BANTAM BOOK RETAILER WHERE YOU LEARNED ABOUT THIS SWEEPSTAKES

NAME _____

ADDRESS _____

CITY _____ STATE _____ ZIP _____

Completed entries must be received by September 30, 1987 in order to be eligible.

ISBN-0553-26457-5